THIS IS THE STORY OF MEN AT WAR AND
BETWEEN WARS . . . MEN OF THE 3RD
MARINE DIVISION, COMPANY H—KNOWN
AS THE "HORRIBLE HOG." IT IS A
MAGNIFICENT, STIRRING NOVEL THAT
SHOWS THE SIDE OF THE MARINE CORPS
EVERY BOOT AND VETERAN KNOWS BUT
WON'T TALK ABOUT, INTRODUCING
THE BLAZING NEW TALENT OF JERE
PEACOCK.

"*VALHALLA* joins James Jones' rough-tough
FROM HERE TO ETERNITY and Norman
Mailer's rough-tough *THE NAKED AND THE
DEAD*. . . . In fact, *VALHALLA* is . . . rougher
and tougher."

— WORCESTER TELEGRAM

"*The frankest and most earthy book I have ever
read. An enormously talented young writer.*"

— RICHARD POWELL (author of *The Soldier*)

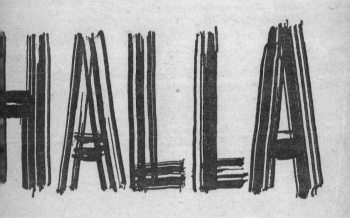

a novel by JERE PEACOCK

A DELL BOOK

Published by DELL PUBLISHING CO., INC.
750 Third Avenue, New York 17, N.Y.

© 1961 by Jere Peacock

Reprinted by arrangement with
G. P. Putnam's Sons
New York, N.Y.

Dedication: This novel is dedicated to
TIMOTHY N. THOMPSON who pulled me out
of the bucket, and believed.

First Dell printing—February, 1962
Second Dell printing—April, 1962
Third Dell printing—June, 1962

Printed in U.S.A.

VALHALLA

1.

While the first rumors of evening rose lazily in the vitiated air of the troop compartment, Giff Bohane left his bunk, waded through the squatting circles of men and mounted the steel stairs, going topside in his faded gray-green marine dungarees and yellow leggins.

Lean rather than slim, with an angular hungry-looking face, he swaggered a little on the stairs. Then he climbed upward, hearing the muffled cloud of conversation fade behind him: the flat snicker-snack of cards and the bony rattle of dice with the wild-fevered voices of the faders— "Little Joe from Yong-dong-po!"—bets faded and covered— "Baby needs a new pair of shoes!"

Late tomorrow morning they would be in Yokohama and by this time tomorrow evening they would be somewhere in Japan in a strange yet previously experienced life. Where in Japan, Giff wasn't sure. And he really didn't care.

Still lurking in his senses with its haunting refrain, like an acute hangover, was the barking castanet sound of machine guns and the bucket-swinging swoosh of mortars of Korea, the "cease fire" not two weeks cold. At times, like now, it seemed to him that it was only hours away, within his reach. At other times it was as long ago as a whore's dream.

Moving past two men whom he did not recognize, Giff felt his chest suddenly balloon with the carefree vitality of his emotions; immediately it was coupled with that inscrutably alien foreboding sense of transition. Even in a life that was inherently composed of perpetual change he had never quite gotten used to it. He shrugged and climbed onto the hatch that led to the deck outside and breathed the crisp salt air. It felt clean and good on his face after the mugginess below.

Around him, immersed in the deepening black of an

early August dusk, distorted knots of men stood in subdued talk, their features broken in livid irregular lines. As they spoke, the bright burning embers of their cigarettes jumped between their lips. Someone laughed explosively and the last hoarse timbre was carried away on the salty breeze.

Hands jammed deep in his hip pockets Giff listened to the fading laughter, a flicker of a grin creeping across his face at this humor he was not a part of; and watched a tall leaden figure break off from a knot and come walking over to him jauntily, his ass slung low, hardly swinging his arms at all. He recognized the confident walk of Cinamo Dallas.

The tall quarter Cherokee stopped in front of him. "You all packed?" he said in his slow calculating Oklahoma brogue. "And ready to leave this pig tomorrow?" his hands still hanging passively low, almost directly in front of his thighs.

"I been ready since we left Korea three days ago." Giff grinned. "There's no love lost between me and the Navy."

"That makes two of us," Dallas agreed. "Look," he said in that plotting methodical slyness that Giff had come to recognize in the three days he'd known him, "listen. How 'bout getting a game going down below? They's a couple guys back there"—he jerked his head toward the muffled tone behind him—"that's hot for a game, see? And they got shekels."

"If they play with you they won't have it for keeps," Giff said, remembering the $350 he'd lost to Cinamo Dallas their first day out of Korea. Damn near half his re-enlistment bonus! he thought, with the self-effacing ridicule of a man who's caught in bed with his wife's sister.

"Now I ain't that goddam lucky."

"No," Giff mocked. "You ain't lucky at all. You just got a four-way shuffle is all."

Dallas lit a cigarette and chuckled softly through the smoke, a little conceitedly Giff thought as he studied the quarter Cherokee: his eyebrows scowled in a truculent V above a dusky high-cheekboned face, giving him a sort of chilling killer's look. Behind that killer's face, belying it, was the deceptively cruel face of a man who lives his life walking on eggs, and knows it. Yet carrying on his shoulders the self-contained confidence that the eggs would not break.

Looking at him in the diminishing light, the only way Giff

could think of Dallas, to describe him to himself, was that he seemed ageless, timeless almost. As if he were some human form of petrified rock. And it always shocked him slightly. He was not really more than twenty-three or -four. Just a couple years older than himself. Looking at him though, this was hard to believe.

"So you don't want to play tonight, hunh?" Dallas' cigarette bobbed lazily with his words.

"Jesus Christ no! I don't wanna be broke when we get to Yokohama. With all them dollies runnin' round I'll need money." As an afterthought he said, "I wonder will we get any liberty in Yokohama before we go on up to camp?"

"Hell no." Dallas flipped his cigarette. "You ever hear of getting liberty like that? In this Crotch?"

"Sure. We got liberty in Kobe when I came over last year. During Korea."

"Yeah? Well so did I, cousin. But this ain't Kobe and it ain't durin' Korea. And they ain't going to let us run wild lopin' our mules in Yokohama. We'd tear that town down the seam."

Giff laughed suddenly, genuinely, seeing in his mind a picture of cynical hooting derisive marines "loping their mules" through the streets of Yokohama.

Dallas eyed him silently for a moment. "If you ain't going to play no poker, I'll see 'f I can get some other people." He started to walk away, then in one unbroken movement turned back. "You sure you don't want to play?"

"No." Giff shook his head. "I'm going below more skosh take a shower and hit the rack."

"This early?" Dallas asked, almost deprecatingly.

"There's nothing happening that I can see."

"There might be."

"I doubt that like hell." Giff stretched. "And goddamit don't step in my face when you climb into your bunk. Like you did last night."

"Was that *your* face I stepped in?" In the gathering darkness, Giff saw a faint tinge of devilish humor on the quarter Cherokee's face.

"It wasn't my granny's," he said.

"Okay I'll be careful," Dallas said, offhand. "I wouldn't want to disturb your love life none."

"This'll probably be the last full night's sleep I'll get for a long time," Giff said thoughtfully. "When we hit Japan

I'll be too damn busy hitting the bars and whorehouses for sleep."

"Are there whorehouses in Japan?" Dallas said in mock disbelief.

"Is the Pope Catholic?"

"All right. You get your sleep," Dallas temporized. "And you don't want me to wake you up at all? Even if I find Charley Escobar?"

"Well," Giff rubbed his chin, "if you find Charley Escobar all right. But I won't get up for anything else. And where the hell you going to find Charley Escobar on this ship?"

Cinamo Dallas did not answer. His lip curled into a sort of grin and he walked away. "I'll see you later," he called over his shoulder.

Giff nodded at his retreating back and moved on over to the rail and leaned against it. Far off to the west was the diminishing jaggedness of the Japanese coast, a long line of black mountains etched against the crimson aura of dying sun. He had seen a lot of sunsets on the ocean from a lot of different ships. And they were always the same. A sunset in the mountains was almost the complete opposite, he thought. In the mountains the sun would linger hesitantly, indecisive, as if maybe in some obscure way it was uncertain about how to place its bet. To set or to rise. It would always take its time, fooling you. You would see it dropping between two hillocks and later when you looked back it would still be there. Finally, after it did go down, its yellow tongues would kiss the tops of trees in the smoky haze. Here, on the ocean, it wasn't like that at all. You never quite saw the sun drop. Suddenly there it was, a red inflamed ball perched on the lapping waves. Then it was gone, yanked down as if by an unseen hand. And as he watched the rugged coastline sinking steadily under the now purple ocean the knowledge of his own rootless wavering existence bubbled up and flooded over him like a huge skunk bag, trapping him in its dusky lining. Back there, talking with Dallas, he hadn't even thought about it, lost in the conversation.

The cushioning sound of rubber heels on steel increased behind him as the knots of men began to break up. He looked down at the phosphorous sparkling in the water. It was really getting dark fast now and a chilling breeze was blowing up.

12

He stayed there for perhaps another hour while the moonless night cloaked around him. Even after the ship's whistle pierced the rhythmical sloughing of the surf in a challenging tattoo, he lingered.

Finally, when it was so black he couldn't distinguish between sky and water, he decided to go below. He wasn't going to freeze by God! he thought, and moved toward the inviting light of the troop compartment door.

There were still a few men lolling on deck, red coals of their cigarettes giving them identity.

When he got below, the acrid reek of close-packed men hit him heavily like a sweaty fist. He waded down the aisles through the murmur of voices and stale air to his bunk, suddenly deciding to hell with taking a shower. He would just start sweating again. There probably wasn't any *fresh* hot water anyway. Damned if he'd take a gummy shower in salt water. At least this would be his last night aboard ship.

Amid the cluttered confusion of seabags and dungarees and shoes and without bothering to untie his leggins and remove his old field shoes, he slipped onto the tight canvas of his bunk and lay on his back: dungaree cap set squarely over his face, thumbs hooked over his belt buckle, hands laying protectively over his balls, feet crossed and extended. Below him, on the first bunk of the tier of five, lay a nameless marine whom Giff had not spoken to once in three days. And he had never seen the man out of his bunk. It didn't appear that he left even for chow. Maybe he was seasick?

He lay there waiting for taps, darkness and sleep.

But when taps did come a heavier darkness pervaded his dungaree cap and the creakings of bunks mingled with the sonorous breathing as men scooted themselves out of their various daytime recluses and into their fear-filled nights of aloneness.

In the loud silence Giff lay in that no man's land of twilight existence: not asleep and not awake, but acutely cognizant; where everything was sublimated and sharp detailed pictures on a distant sound track roamed through his mind.

Through the thinness of his dungaree trousers he fingered the small bulky figure of the little man in his watch pocket: its image impaled itself in his mind. HoTi, the God of Good Fortune: hand-carved Japanee God, gift of an almost unremembered whore in Kobe, Japan.

She had given it to him that last day on R 'n R in May just before he went back to Korea. He had been drunk all the five days and the girl—whore—business woman had spent those five days with him in a sort of dreamy interlude between ambushes, raids and firefights, and even by the fourth day he was ready to go back: to combat and rest, because R 'n R was more devastating than combat, yet with a higher enjoyableness.

But the God HoTi.

In a nameless hotel on a nameless street on an unremembered day with a woman whose name he could not recall. Sometimes he was not sure if he even remembered her face. Or the way she smiled or any of those other things, like words she might have used.

Now the sharpness of it rose up on hind legs in his mind. She had given it to him while he sat cross-legged in his winter greens, like some alien Buddha. And in his half-numb, blank-faced, quite drunken stupor he had held it in his hand and by closing one eye and squinting hard he could make it out: HoTi was hand-carved from teakwood and stood about two and a half inches tall. Dark, smooth, hand-rubbed, HoTi stood with his arms stretched happily over his head, his round fat face cocked on one side grinning gleefully, almost leering. But the key, the power of HoTi, lay in his huge protruding belly: the salient dominating efficacy of HoTi; below that was an apronlike loincloth.

Squinting hard, Giff had grinned back at the leering rotund face with the shaved bald head. That was when the five-day girl told him that HoTi was the God of Good Fortune. In her clipped pidgin-American voice she explained how HoTi played the game. That what he had to do was to rub HoTi's belly until it shined and then he would have good fortune. Simply hold him and rub his thumb over HoTi's bulging belly.

"Rub his ol' belly, hunh?" he had said thickly. And then he had to have her explain it to him again so he would understand it completely.

Later on, he was never really sure if she had given it to him because he had picked *her* to spend the five days with *him* and given her a bonus, or if she truly meant for him to have it as a talisman for his own luck. Anyway, he had taken it back to Korea and always carried it with him. But he never did shine HoTi's belly very much.

14

Once, on Vegas it was, the first day of the battle, he did rub the grinning god's belly, and when he reflected on it he wondered all over again and was to remember it only in some obscure occult way as a deciding point in his life. Or maybe that was just his imagination.

Or maybe he did not really understand what good fortune was.

Maybe if he had rubbed HoTi's belly while playing poker with Dallas that first day he would not have lost that $350. Maybe he would have won? In *his* interpretation that was not exactly *good* fortune. Cinamo Dallas had good fortune though. A jackmine of it.

Could that ageless sonfabitch Dallas have rubbed HoTi's belly?

No, he didn't think so. He had carried it in his watch pocket. Dallas had never seen it. Maybe it was because he *hadn't* rubbed that solid little belly himself!

In the chainless no man's land of his mind Giff moved on. Jumping around like a flea on a dog's back, covering space and time and lives. And he was still in the suspended unearthliness when he heard the approaching footsteps, the soft smack of heel on steel breaking through his unguarded perimeter.

The footsteps stopped in front of him. There was a breathless moment of silence. Then his dungaree cap was snatched from his face and through the feral glow of the red night lights he was staring into the face of Cinamo Dallas.

For a hanging moment Giff was angry. "Goddamit what'd you want!"

In the red haze Dallas grinned down at him, his face a series of mauve shadows. "I found Charley Escobar," he said quietly.

"Well that's fine," Giff whispered hoarsely. "That's great. Now go take Charley Escobar off and leave me sleep."

"You silly bastard. You weren't sleepin' and I can't handle Charley myself."

"Oh Jesus Christ! I ain't going to play poker. And I don't give two farts in hell for no what's-his-name Charley Escobar," Giff's voice raised in a muffled choking irritation.

Lifting one finger to his lips Cinamo Dallas brought his other hand up triumphantly from behind him where it had been partially hidden. He held a thick square bottle throwing off glassy glints in the dim haze. "Charley Escobar," he said to the bottle affectionately.

Giff felt his anger subside, weaken, drain out of him, and finally it was no more. "Yeah?" he said interestedly. "Well whyn't you say so sooner?" He raised up and shook his head, grinning. "Charley Escobar."

"He's an old heathen friend of mine," Dallas explained. "Now come on. Get up."

"Where we going?"

"To the head. We start drinking it here they'll be more freeloaders around us than a horse got flies."

"I got to get some cigarettes," Giff said slipping out of his bunk. He pulled his seabag out away from the wall and worked the combination laboriously in the dark light.

"I got smokes," Dallas said from behind him.

"Ain't my brand." Giff at last opened the lock and snapped it off. He rummaged around blindly till he found the half-squashed carton and pulled out a fresh pack. And then, as he snapped the lock back on and shoved the seabag back against the wall and started to turn toward Dallas, he was staring into the open eyes of the nameless marine who slept on the bottom bunk. They were the coldest, most dead-looking eyes Giff had ever seen. More corpse-like even than on a Chinese or Korean, or American. And for a moment he thought the man had just died there. Then they were shut quickly and the man turned creakingly in his bunk.

"Well?" Dallas was impatient.

"Let's go." Giff turned to Dallas, feeling a coolness in the oppressive hot air of the troop compartment creep up his back. That man sure did look dead. Then he dismissed the thought quickly and walked up to Dallas, squinting at the bottle. "Have you got a *full* fifth?"

"It ain't a fifth," Dallas said disparagingly. "It's a quart."

"I didn't get a good look at it," Giff explained.

Two shadowy creatures, they moved through the gear-strewn maze of the troop compartment, surrounded by the snores and mixed hurried breaths of men tossing fitfully in their sleep under the feverish aura of red. They walked in silence to the open door of the head where a gleaming white light beckoned.

The head was off the compartment on the portside; nar-

16

row, long, stretching up in a curve with the hull of the ship to the bow.

Giff felt his eyes burn suddenly with the bright lights after the dimness. He blinked, rapidly following Dallas past the little washbasins littered with empty toothpaste tubes and rusty razor blades, to the far end of the head where salt water slewed through the open metal casings of the commodes.

When they reached the end, Dallas sat down on the long wooden planking that straddled the metal casings. Setting his ass firmly on one of the open holes he slapped the bottom of the quart with the heel of his hand.

Giff inspected the wood hole down from Dallas to see if anyone had missed. No one had. It was worn shiny from long use. He sat down and lit a cigarette. Up here, this close forward, he could feel the dip and rise of the ship's roll. It was more pronounced than in the troop compartment. The reverberating boom of sea on ship smacked loudly on the outside.

"You initiate it," Cinamo Dallas offered, passing the bottle.

Giff took a long unpausing pull and chased it with his burning cigarette. "It's good. Where'd you get it?"

Dallas took the bottle. "Bought it off a sailor. The cheap bastard," he said caustically, quietly.

Giff did not say anything. He wondered how much Dallas had paid for it. But he did not ask.

"Anyway," Dallas said leisurely, "I figure it was time to have a sort of celebration, see?"

"Celebration?"

"Yeah. Well, you know what I mean." Dallas shifted his eyes. "On leaving Korea and all that. And going to Japan."

"Oh. Yeah. Sure." Giff groped through his mind, suddenly feeling ill at ease, untalkative. "You ever been in Big J before?"

"Hellyea," the tall quarter Cherokee said. "On the way over at Sasebo. On R 'n R once. I like it."

"It's pretty good duty all right, I guess," Giff agreed.

Dallas paused before his drink. "Better than Korea, that's for sure."

"What draft were you?" Giff asked, wondering at their three-day friendship, thinking that neither of them had ever known the other existed. Never would have known in fact if it hadn't been for a series of heedless decisions. Actually it wasn't even a friendship, he thought: casual military acquaintances, that was all. Hell, he didn't even remember the names of the men in his old squad—still in Korea—any more.

"Twenty-fourth," Dallas told him. "I was with the Seventh Marines."

"You hit a good part of it then," Giff said.

"Yeah. All them hot ones. The Hook. T-Bone. Vegas. The whole shootin' match."

"I was with the Fifth Marines." Giff inspected his hands. "We were on Boulder City when it ended."

"Yeah; I know," Dallas said, handing him the bottle. "How come you to volunteer for Japan anyway?" he asked, turning suddenly to Giff.

"I shipped over." Giff paused in the middle of his drink. "Right after the cease fire. For six years. And I wanted Big J." He shrugged and finished his drink. "So they gave it to me."

"They give you the corporal's rating too," Dallas said, and Giff detected a note of sarcasm in it.

"Nope," he said, "I got that before. They give it to me when they gave me the Silver Star." Now why did he have to say that? What was he doing? Big-shitting because he had a medal? Well, he *was* vain about it. And why shouldn't he be? It gave him more of an identity, didn't it? Besides, he thought, a little ruffled, Dallas knew about it. Why was he asking questions about it?

Dallas lit a cigarette and took a drink in one sweeping dispassionate gesture. "Silver Star, hunh? Where'd you pick it up? Vegas? Reno?"

"Vegas. The first day." Giff stared back at Dallas, who was now studying him thoughtfully.

"You get hit, too?"

"Not a scratch." Shot at and missed; shit at and hit. Ought to have another drink. He reached for the bottle.

Dallas handed it to him. "I got shot in the ass."

"Oh yeah?" Giff kept his face blank. "On Vegas?"

Dallas nodded. "You could have got discharge, gone Stateside," he said suddenly. "If you hadn't shipped over. Right?"

"Sure."

"But you didn't want to?"

"What the hell for?" Giff demanded.

18

"So you got a corporal's rating and a Silver Star and shipped over," Dallas said softly.

"Yeah. That's right; for six years. What about it?"

"Nothing. How long you been in?"

"Three and a half, almost four years," he answered. There was a strange look masking Dallas' face. Giff decided it wasn't ridicule. It wasn't genuine interest either.

"I been in seven," Dallas said evenly.

Giff grinned, mocking. "And you're still a private."

"Pfc."

"Samey same," Giff said, goading, feeling more superior now.

Dallas took the bottle back and drank. "I like it. You don't hear me bitching."

A barefoot marine in skivvies came blinking into the head and they both stopped talking and watched him. He shuffled over to the piss trough, urinated, coughed wrackingly and shuffled out as if he were completely alone.

"Was that why you shipped over?" Giff asked, turning back to Dallas. "Because you like being a *peon?*"

"Among other things. I like the Crotch," Dallas scoffed. "And I'm a gungy bastard." He paused thoughtfully, took another drink then raised his head, quickly facing Giff. "Look," he said enthusiastically. "How long you think we'll be in Japan? Or how long you think it'll be before Korea starts again?"

"Not long," Giff said, startled at the sudden change. "Maybe a month. Maybe two."

"There you go." Dallas wagged his head. "And if it ain't Ko-rea it'll be somewhere else: Formosa; Indochina; someplace. But we might's well get in some good living while we're waiting." He shuttled the bottle back to Giff.

"And that's why you volunteered for Japan, hunh?" Giff could feel the whiskey's tentacles fingering out through him.

"That's why *I* picked it. Sure." Dallas looked at Giff, combatively again. "But I got almost three years left on this hitch. You coulda got out, discharged, gone back to the States."

"Gone Stateside and got discharged and done what? Get a job picking apples? Or collecting garbage? Pump gas in a service station? And wait for another war to start so I can be called back in? Not this old kid." Giff shifted the bottle back to Dallas. "There ain't a great demand on the Outside for a man who can kill a gook at one hundred yards with an M-1. Or toss a grenade twenty yards and spot it on a spider trap. And that's all I know, see? So what's all this talk about gettin' out, hunh? That's about as useless as pissin' up a rope."

Dallas grinned at him. "Well, I just wondered. Course your Silver Star wouldn't mean nothin' out there either."

"Jesus Christ, Dallas! Just cause I got a Silver Star—"

"Dammit whoa." Dallas waved him off. "I didn't mean nothing like that."

"Maybe not," Giff said, unmollified. "But you know what I mean. On the Outside it's nothing, see?" He snapped it away on his fingers. "It don't mean a goddam thing, you know what I mean. On the Outside it's worth sixty-eight cents."

"It don't mean anything in here either," Dallas said. "In the Crotch."

"And that's all you know. You ain't got one."

"And personally I'm glad I ain't," Dallas said. "You don't know it but you'll find out. It don't mean shit in here atall."

"Balls!" Giff said in disgust, and took the proffered bottle from Dallas. "Let's get off that. Okay?"

"Okay," Dallas said, suddenly cheerful. "Couple months from now we'll be in another war anyway."

"There you go," Giff agreed.

"But tomorrow we'll be in Japan."

Giff felt the tenseness of the Silver-Star talk leave him. Goddam that Dallas though. He was a strange bird. "Yeah," he said mellowly. "Big J. Land of sliding doors and slant-eyed whores."

"You know where we'll be stationed, don't you?" Dallas asked.

"With the Third Marines," Giff nodded, studying the whiskey level in the bottle. "At Camp Fuji. But I never been there. And the Third only been there for a couple weeks. Since the cease fire."

"Camp Fuji." Dallas rolled it around on his tongue. "They must be gettin' ready for something, bringing all them troops in like that."

Giff grinned at Dallas then, and the quarter Cherokee grinned back in the same bellicose humorousness. Giff was to remember it as a look of understanding; a grin, two grins actually, that carried a multitude of unspoken professional agreement. Upending the bottle he took a heady belly-knotting pull. "That's sure good booze," he said, appraising,

20

thinking this was a fitting climax, a righteous farewell to Korea: and an auspicious beginning—in Japan.

"Hell yes it's good," Dallas said fervently. "Not any of that cheap Korean shit."

Then they were talking Korea again, almost excitedly, with that tender regard for combat, lovingly as if it were a woman, that is only accorded those few things that men hold sacred: Frozen Chosen, the *Reservoir*—all that was before their time, Giff thought, but they knew of all of it; Seoul City Sue, who was spirited out of Seoul before the marines got there or she would have been raped and hung on the Capitol steps; Maggie Higgins, whom they all loved because she lived like one of them, unflinching, and shared their bitterness; Dave Duncan from *Life* who wrote their story in pictures; Luke the Gook and Link the Chink; Outpost Martini—Vegas—Reno—Carson City—East and West Berlin; wild crazy bottled memories of R 'n R and beer runs in Corps Reserve.

Giff sat there on the wooden planking with the salt water spraying up and wetting his ass through his dungaree trousers, talking listening telling the stories he knew well and mixing them at times with the stories other men had told him, losing himself in the wild whiskey-charged night air. And thinking too of this other thing, this going to Japan, to be ensconced again in an interlude between wars at some camp he did not know, waiting for the wars to move on with him.

And on they talked until finally, characteristically, Dallas led with his chin again. "Maybe in the next war you can get another Silver Star, you ol' Shanty-Irish sonfabitch you," he said thickly. "Or even a dingleberry cluster," he snickered.

"Dallas!" Giff bellowed. "Goddam you Dallas! You say that one more time I'll dust you off."

Dallas peered at him through his liquor-fogged eyes. "Don't let your alligator mouth overload your canary ass," he said tight-lipped. "Still crappin' yellow and think you're a man."

"Canary ass!" Giff bayed sharply, his face furious and congested with Charley Escobar. "Why you goddam Syngman Rhee-loving bastard!" He jumped unsteadily to his feet and stood, challenging, in front of Dallas.

"Syngman Rhee!" Dallas snarled, started to rise, still clutching the bottle. He looked at it in his hand indecisively as if he were debating whether to set it down or use it as a weapon.

While he debated, Giff stepped in and slammed his forehead back with the palm of his hand. Dallas' head snapped back and Giff hit him solidly, knocking him back down on the wood planking, and stepped in closer to hit him again. Taking careful aim he threw a right cross and connected with air as Dallas ducked quickly.

For a moment Giff was off balance, half spun around, and he could not see Dallas over his arm. Just as he was gathering his co-ordination to swing again Dallas, still sitting on the plank, lunged forward, the bottle still in the vise lock of his hand using it like a knife, the square heavy bottom on the bottle smacking Giff right above the hairline.

He grunted and fell back on his butt without bouncing on the steel deck and Dallas was on his feet, stepping in after him scowling triumphantly. Suddenly the ship lurched erratically and tossed him off balance. Still holding the bottle in his hand Dallas skidded across the steel deck and slammed against the shower stalls, yelling indignantly at being thwarted so close to the kill; his head kicked back and boomed off the stall, the bottle still clutched in his hand, unscathed.

Greedily sucking air into his lungs, Giff wobbled to his feet and very cautiously staggered to where the now peaceful Dallas lay: bottle in his hand, head on chest, quietly out.

Grinning with the sense of humor of a man who has carried the god HoTi with him, Giff bent down and snatched the bottle from Cinamo Dallas' imperious hand. There was only a little left in it. Some had sloshed out during the fracas.

Moving charily over this deck that threatened to rise up and hit him in the face, he walked out of the brightly lit head and into the slow bulky movement of the troop compartment.

Where the hell was his bunk? Couldn't see a goddam thing in this dark. Goddam that Dallas was a good old sonfabitch. Wonder did he steal the old bottle from an officer? Hah!

Where the hell *was* his bunk?

Groping, he tried several avenues of approach down the cluttered aisles. Finally, in desperation, he grabbed some life jackets and stacked them in the corner by the head and lay down on them.

22

Amid the sibilant snores of the troop compartment he felt a potent exaltation at being awake while all this sleep moved on around him undisturbed. A prideful smirk crept across his face thinking of Dallas lying against that shower stall his head on his chest lolling with the toss and pitch of the ship. Probably would want to fight all over again tomorrow.

Clumsily he propped himself up on the life jackets, scooting them around the way a dog walks around in a circle before it plops down, and nursed what was left in the bottle, savoring it, swilling its rawness around in his mouth before swallowing.

Poor old Corporal Gifford Bohane—Hero—can't even find his own bunk. Has to sleep on the floor on life jackets. He lapsed into a devilish chuckle, cautioning himself to be quiet.

Finally, the whiskey gone, he stuck the empty bottle under his head, propping a life jacket up like a pillow, and curled up feeling the heaviness of sleep cloud over him and thinking they would have to walk all the way to Fuji tomorrow with their seabags on their backs.

Giff woke with the heavy boom of artillery in his head and the taste of desert in his mouth. He lay sprawled on his nest of life jackets, sharp memories shuttling through his mind.

Marines passed by, looked at him curiously for a moment and walked on. Coming back from chow, Giff thought; he was hungry too. Not much though.

He was still sitting there contemplating his situation when Cinamo Dallas came grinning through the door of the troop compartment carrying a steaming canteen cup. The tall quarter Cherokee with the deceptively cruel face moved in his jaunty walk up to the pile of life jackets.

"Who shit in my mouth?" Giff said glumly.

"Charley Escobar," Dallas grinned. "Here. Take this coffee."

Giff reached out for the cup. "You been to chow; what'd they have?"

"Hard-boiled eggs and hash," Dallas said dispassionately.

Giff grimaced with the thought of it—reheated eggs and hash! "I feel lousy. Ain't felt this bad since I drank horsepiss and kerosene in Korea."

"You ain't got the market on hangovers."

Giff sipped the coffee, luxuriating in its warmth and efficacy. "How far out are we from Yokohama?" he asked through the steam.

"Be there in less than an hour. Couldn't you tell we're comin' into Tokyo Bay?" Dallas looked around at the troop compartment. "Christ, this the calmest we been all the way." Then he looked back down at Giff. "Ain't you going to shave or nothing?"

Giff rubbed his hand across the scratchiness of his lean jaw. "I guess I'll have to," he said, resigned. "Though I sure as hell don't feel like it. We'll be in Big J in a skosh, hunh?"

Reaching down, Dallas took the cup out of Giff's hand and sipped a short drink, then handed it back. "Well," he said suddenly. "I got to check my gear. See 'f I got all my contraband. When you finish shaving come on up topside. I'll be there."

Giff sat listening to the buzz of life, watching Dallas walk back out. Most of the troops were back from chow and they were talking excitedly in half-nervous voices.

Finishing his coffee he got off his life jackets and walked back to his bunk tier and set the cup on Dallas' bunk. He pulled his old shaving kit out of his seabag and walked resolutely to the head.

Shaving quickly he nicked himself several times and the Aqua Velva burned, stinging his face. He stood looking into the mirror and his black-fringed blue eyes (a curious tinge of red to them, eh?) and the thick black healthy hair above his rawboned face. The throwback coloring of some Connacht County Irishman who had shunned his homeland during the Potato Famine of 1846, he thought dramatically. (Even the redness around the whites was a throwback too.) And grinned sillily at himself, the song of his legacy running through his mind:

Have you ever been out to an Irishman's Shanty
  Where the water is scarce and the whiskey is plenty?
A three-legged table and chair to match
  And a hole in the floor for the chickens to scratch

Jesus God! he was still half shot down!

Zipping up his shaving kit he walked back to the familiarity of the metal casings and wood plankings, dropped

24

his trousers and sat firmly, enjoyably, on the wood plank.

Finished (feeling as if he had been reamed raw), he took his shaving kit back to the bunk tier and locked it up, wishing he had another cup of coffee but thinking how good a cold Japanese quart of beer would taste. Visions of frosted bottles danced in front of his eyes.

He squared his dungaree cap on his head and walked out of the troop compartment and up the steel stairs.

Topside, under the high blue of early-morning Japanee sky, the heat of dog days shimmered in the air. The sun glare hit him solidly with jackhammer force and his brain pounded behind his eyes. He cursed silently still wishing for a cold beer.

They were almost to the dock. The morning air sweltered with the belching groans of the tugboats and the *toot toot toot* of pilot boats. All along the ship was the contagion of approaching newness.

Looking at it, with that weird hungover feeling of apartness, Giff caught the scene in a blood-pounding gulp and felt it go plummeting to his scrotum. A scene laid out in the jerky spasmodic hand of a madman like an old Charlie Chaplin movie: broken groups of dungareed marines white faces brown faces black faces hooting scornfully, laughing neighingly, pointing cynically at the huge warehouses in echelon along the docks and the high naked-framed dockside cranes on railroad tracks shuttling with their morning's work, the packed-tight buildings of Yokohama stretching out in a frenzied welter of humanity. Rising above was the terraced lush green of rice paddies on the hills with stooped-back Japanee people moiling in the feces-smelling water. All along the hills were the black mouths of caves built during Big Two for shore guns, now yawning in the greenness, dejected silent and forgotten. And rising above all that, towering implacably, was Mount Fujiyama, Fuji-San, cutting a huge hunk out of the cerulean sky.

Giff looked at its blackness against the blue, remembering that the old Japanee believed the mountain was sacred, a god. He could not see anything to kowtow about. It looked as if it had suddenly popped up out of the ground and now stood embarrassed because there was no place to hide and simply sat there exposing itself.

Shouldering his way through the hordes of men on deck now milling around like freshly castrated sheep, he searched the maze of faces for Cinamo Dallas and found

25

him on down the rail under the partial shade of the criss-crossing cables, booms and lifeboats.

He was in a heated dispute with two other men whom Giff recognized immediately: Buck Sergeant Mook, meaty and red-faced with crows feet deep around his eyes. Private Gyp Castagno, heavy torso on spindly legs with a thin well-trimmed mustache. Castagno was an excellent poker player while Mook was mediocre and Giff had taken him for fifty bucks the same day Dallas had clipped them all and made his big haul. Wending his way through the crowd to them, Giff caught words like "Mongolians" and "Black Widow Division."

"You talk like a man with a paper ass hole," Dallas was saying disgustedly.

"Who is?" Giff asked. "The Wop?"

Gyp Castagno was shaking a huge hand at Dallas. "You think so," he said, excited. "How'd you know? You never seen them. And neither has Mook."

A grin spread up Mook's face touching his crows feet. "Hell no, I never seen them. You can't see nothing that don't exist for Chrissakes."

"They goddam do exist," Castagno argued hotly. "Cause I seen them with my own eyes. And they's seven feet tall, by God!"

"Oh Jesus H fucking Christ," Dallas wagged his head slowly, "Giff, will you tell this supersititous grape squasher that no Mongolians in Korea was seven feet tall."

"How the hell would he know?" Castagno demanded, turning on Giff.

"He was with the Fifth Marines, idiot," Dallas explained quietly. "And the Goonie Black Widow Division was always across from them. And they's the only ones had Mongolians with them."

Giff kept his face serious, and narrowed his eyes with heavy drama. "They had Mongolians all right," he said gloomily. "And they were big. I know. One of 'em came swooping down one night and carried me off in his pocket." He paused dramatically. "If I hadn't been carrying my knife and cut my way out they'd a had me for dinner."

Dallas and Mook whooped and guffawed, but Castagno merely opened his mouth a few times and eyed Giff. Then he grinned sheepishly. "Now that's a bunch of shit and you know it."

"No sir," Giff shook his head, "that's a fact. Why hell,

26

man, after that I wouldn't go out without a Thompson."

"Looks like me and Mook was wrong," Dallas grinned.

"Maybe we were just in the wrong place, Dallas," Mook offered.

Castagno turned on them fiercely. "It don't matter at all what you say. I saw them," and he clamped his jaws shut with finality.

Giff lit a cigarette and stared through the smoke at the Wop. "What outfit were you with?"

"First Marines," Castagno said laconically.

"First Marines, hunh?" Giff flipped the cigarette over the rail. It had been harsh and dry on his tongue. "You take a shot at this Mongolian you saw?"

"Hell no," Castagno said. "I just sat there and gaped at him."

"Shit, that wasn't no Mongolian," Giff said. "Either a Turk or a Greek. They were in your sector, you know? And they're pretty goddam big and clumsy."

"Then how come he was running the other way?"

"Probably chasing some Sexie," Dallas said thoughtfully.

Gyp Castagno clammed up tight. No one has proved me wrong, his face said.

"Hell no, Gyp," Giff said. "It wasn't no goddam Mongolian. They ain't no bigger than a gook or goonie. Maybe it was a deer?"

Dallas snorted in approval. "Maybe you're gettin' battle happy, Wop. You ought to take it easy; rest up a bit. I wouldn't want to fight a war with a guy like you."

"Breaks of the Korean conflict," Castagno said disconsolately. Then his eyes brightened up. "Hey, we're going to be on this ship for another hour yet. How about some cards? We can get a game going out here on deck." He looked at them questioningly.

"Not this kid," Giff said. "Just as I'd start getting hot we'd have to leave."

"Mook?" Castagno asked. "Dallas?"

"Three ain't a good game," Dallas temporized. " 'Sides, I got to take a check on my gear," he explained lamely.

"I'll play you some two-handed Casino," Mook gave in, his red face bored.

"Okay," Castagno said enthusiastically. "Half-buck a point."

"Jesus Christ!" Mook protested.

"Got to make it interesting."

"All right," Mook agreed. "But I get first deal?"

"We'll cut for it." Castagno pulled his old deck out of his dungaree pocket. "Let's go up the quarter-deck." He winked over his shoulder at Giff and Dallas. "We'll see you down below later."

Giff watched the two walk away. "I wonder what the sonfabitch wanted to lie for?" he said to Dallas.

"Maybe he wasn't," Dallas said.

"He was, all right," Giff said firmly. "There was a lot of crap going around about the Mongolians. The Black Widow Division put it out. I guess they were trying to scare us."

"I wouldn't know," Dallas said. "I wasn't in the Fifth Marines." Then he stretched lazily. "Guess I'll go below and cop some Zs till they holler for us."

"Won't be long now," Giff said anxiously. "Goddam! I wish I had a cold beer." He fingered the bridge of his nose and a cunningness moved into his eyes. "You got any yen?"

"Yeah; I got some from the last R 'n R that I couldn't ever get rid of."

"Well," Giff said happily, "that's good. Cause I ain't got any."

A man came crowding through and nudged Dallas on the shoulder. Truculently, Dallas glared after him. Then he turned back to Giff. "Yeah," he said contemplatively. "Maybe we will. I feel like it. But right now I'm going below. You coming?"

"More skosh," Giff evaded.

"Suit yourself," Dallas shrugged. He turned and walked back through the crowd.

Unleaning from the rail, Giff watched the weaving mass swallow him up; then he looked back toward the fantail. He felt lousy, sick, and he knew it wasn't just from the whiskey. The closeness of people suddenly infuriated him with a kind of slow-burning bullish rebelliousness. He walked back toward the fantail through the people.

The fantail was deserted and the din of people and harbor noises was slightly muffled. He leaned the trunk of his body over the rail and threw up three times, spewed chokingly, his eyes watered and burned; his face felt flushed but his belly thanked him gratefully with a heavy knotted emptiness.

Footsteps scuffed behind him and he turned to see two marine messmen sweating a huge GI can to the garbage chute. In silent unison they counted and heaved the can, spilling its rancid contents into the water, turned and carried the now empty can back.

Giff wiped his mouth with his handkerchief and blew his nose.

Lighting a cigarette (it tasted good now, clean, not bitter like before) he watched the rotten tomatoes and wilted lettuce and breakfast sloppings mingle with his own vomit on the greasy water as sea gulls filled the air suddenly, unexpectedly sweeping down from the ship and the dock pilings. The scavenging white birds circled methodically, their heads cocked on an angle to spot the choice bits of food, then dived plundering into the water.

Giff laughed out loud. It was all a matter of choice really. It all depended on what you preferred: rotten tomatoes wilted lettuce hash or vomit. And sea gulls made their choice and if it was wrong it was too late to spit it out.

Like the clan back home that he had forgotten so long ago now, that did not in fact exist in his mind or being any longer. It was almost as if no other life except this one of immediate urgency had ever existed, and in looking back now, the thought startling him, he wondered if it had ever really happened. Oh, he was sure it had, it must have, it had to start somewhere.

Back there in southwest Montana the clan had grubbed their lives away with the little shanties and railroad soot, railroad people—the goddam coal-smoke air when the trains shot by every minute, buildings trees streets all covered with the black harvest. Strange that he should even think of it at all. But right now, it was as if it had never happened, as if he had imagined it in some far-off time and space of his life and was only now looking back over the choices that led him to where he was now.

But the hanging phrase of a few words of *that* song that some mulishly stubborn Shanty Irishman had found one day looking at his life through the amber of a whiskey bottle:

And a hole in the floor for the chickens to scratch.

Oh Jesus Christ on a wobbly crutch! what difference did it make now that it was all gone and done with and why the hell should it suddenly now be in his mind?

Because he was probably not free of that either.

Then in his mind there loomed an image painted in solid deep-colored tones that was only there for a split second, just time enough to see it answering him: a picture of a small, dirty-faced boy in levis standing beside a chicken coop while the chickens scratched feverishly for food and the boy, watching them, reached into his levis pocket, pulled out a handful of shiny marbles and tossed them at the chickens. The chickens fluttered away, indignant, cackling, jerking their beady cannibalistic eyes around, then strutted back to the shiny marbles and in one swift motion grabbed single shiny ones in their beaks and swallowed while the grain and nourishment lay untouched on the ground. That was all: just that fleeting image, now gone.

Was a marble to a chicken any different than a Silver Star to Giff Bohane?

Behind him he heard the harsh grating of steel on steel. A sailor in rust and paint-spattered work fatigues was chipping paint in a desultory rebelliousness. Squatting on his hams he took a swipe at the old paint with his steel brush, then sloshed on some fresh undercoat. Giff turned back to the sea gulls which were now diminishing with the garbage.

It wasn't that the Silver Star meant so much, he reflected. It was the importance of what followed. A Silver Star wasn't really anything at all, he was forced to admit, a little reluctantly. There had been *clerks* in Korea who had gotten them—even higher medals. No one knew how, unless they were queering with the chaplains, which they probably were. And officers had written each other up, for no concrete reason at all. But it would look good on their record books. So what the hell did any of it prove? Nothing at all —or something: that it meant nothing.

Up until now there had only been himself and choice, his own right to choose what was best for him. Even if it had turned out worse, it had still been his choice. But the choice was no longer his. And maybe that was what Dallas meant about the Silver Star when he said it didn't mean anything. Maybe that there were no more choices for himself to make. That he had made his last choice. That from now on all the choices would be made for him. But it could not all of it be blamed on the Silver Star. Like the chickens and the marbles, he too had gone after that shiny glorious something, whatever it was, and his own clear choice had ended with the first man he had killed.

He turned from the rail and started to walk back to go below and wait. The sailor chipping paint looked up at him as he passed and grinned with the face of a man who has been slapped with a dead fish.

"At least you Jungle Bunnies don't have to chip paint," he despaired jokingly.

"You tell 'em, gearbox, you've been shifted," Giff said, without pausing or breaking his stride.

They did not have a chance to buy any beer. They had gone below and waited impatiently on their bunks till the officers lieutenants captains and staff NCO's came down with the mimeographed copies of the orders and passed them out. Giff sat leaning against the bulkhead by his bunk with the familiar thick sheaf of orders in his hand, his unquestioned passport that told him the Department of Pacific was still concerned enough over him to tell him where he was going; he would report, they told him, to Third Battalion Third Marines, South Camp Fuji, Honshu, Japan, at no later date than August 11 at 2400 with no delay en route, and they had even seen fit, he saw, to stamp a red arrow on the sheaf of papers down to his name which was only one of perhaps a hundred names. So he scanned through them, these orders that were made up by some vague people who were, without his knowledge, directing his life, and was not more than surprised to see Cinamo Dallas' name on the orders too. Dallas, who was lying on his bunk above him, had made no comment about it. Giff put the orders away in his pocket thinking it was one hell of a souvenir if he was a souvenir collector. And by that time, after the mass confusion of disgorging from the ship and riding the two-and-a-half-ton troop trucks to the railroad station, both Giff and Dallas felt beer was a necessity. But their plea went unanswered.

Walking behind Dallas past the two large warehouses, moving in a column to the troop trucks with the cumbrous unwieldly venerable seabag over his shoulder, Giff cursed savagely in a drumming steady stream. At the weather and at the Crotch and at Dallas, but mostly at himself.

They climbed up over the tailgate of the truck, holding their seabags between their knees as the trucks roared into gear and bounced and belched their way through Yokohama to the railroad station.

Giff and Dallas had captured seats next to the tailgate

and sat watching the town fade behind them from the canvas vignette of the crowded truck. Behind them, stretching out in a dirty green caravan were the trucks, playing follow the leader.

The pristine morning air was filled with varied sounds of activity: *clop clop* of wooden getas on stone, the horn-blasting little Japanee automobiles scurrying through the streets skillfully dodging pedestrians and bicyclists, the excited chatter of early-morning bartering over vegetables, the heavy slosh of water on stone.

To those who had been in Japan before, on R 'n R, it was a familiar picture. They could have been in Kobe or Kyoto or Osaka or even Hong Kong off China. There was the same intangible ambivalence of close relation and total alienation, something in the smiling looks of withered mama-sans with babies on their backs, and the hard-soft glares of mama-sans without babies on their backs.

And the troops reveled in this reflected offhanded glory, sitting in the bouncing jolting trucks grinning like a platoon of shit-eating cats as the mixture of people fell behind them.

"They don't look none too sad," Giff yelled to Dallas over the roar of exhaust.

"It's just a cover-up for pain," Dallas yelled back; and they both laughed as the truck lumbered on.

At the train station they were quickly shuttled off by a crotchety captain. "Let's move along now," he said wiping his forehead with his handkerchief, making a comparatively easy job into one of dramatic import. "Fill up those coaches. Don't forget your seabags, men."

"He uses shit paper just like the rest of us," Dallas commented.

On the train they grabbed window seats, wood benches back to back facing each other, and rolled their seabags under the small hard-bottomed seats. Dice and cards were brought out all through the car and feverish games started in the aisles, between the inverted seats and rest rooms, as the train started up moving swiftly out and away from Yokohama, then crossed the expansive mud flats of Tokyo Bay and cut to the southwest.

Dallas lay with his cap over his face and his legs propped up and crossed between Giff and two other marines who were playing Casino.

Rice stalks hung heavy, pregnant with their green seeds in the immaculate plotted rice paddies. Paddies on the flats and paddies on the terraced hills, while bandy-legged Japanese men and women paused from their toil to wave, grinning brassily as the train shot past picking up speed.

And on it rolled, winding up through the small succulent green hills and back down onto a long white strip of sandy beach. Far off in the blue-green of the ocean, sampans and junks scudded lazily in the small hot breeze. Veering inland to be trapped in the hills again, then out, onto a green and black low plateau, moving through tunnels, a series of black voids, and the poker players and crap shooters howled indignantly each time the darkness pervaded the coach. Yet on they moved inexorably west and the longer shadows of the afternoon moved with them. Between hills and cliffs, following a boiling river with only an occasional glimpse of a big chunk of sky. Once Giff could see Mount Fuji towering naked in the distance, and he felt a sweaty expectation form within him for this place he was going to.

At four o'clock in the afternoon, Giff raised himself from his hypnotic stare as the train slowed. They came out of the winding hills and onto a rolling flat, and the train bells were ding-donging, the shrill whistle blasting the air, steam puffing.

Gradually the train pulled groaning into the station beside the overhanging shed roof of the passenger platform under a huge sign that read GOTEMBA, lurched to a stop and Dallas straightened up and lit a cigarette. "We at Gotemba?"

"Yeah," Giff said, studying him. "How'd you know?"

"I think we get off here," Dallas said noncommittally.

Then the frantic captain who had driven them aboard that morning in Yokohama came steaming back through the coach. "All right, men," he said stoutly. "This is it. We disembark here. Outside are trucks that will take you to your various battalions. You have your orders. Good luck," he said heavily, and with great solemnity mingled with a tinge of dignity he walked out of the coach.

"I knew a captain like that in Ko-rea," Dallas observed cynically. "He had us sing *I am one of Jesus' lambs* just before Vegas. Great, ain't it?"

Laughing, Giff pulled his seabag out from under the seat and sat quietly while the troops shuffled around like accident victims and began moving off the train. When the coach had cleared somewhat, Giff and Dallas fell in line and headed toward the door silently.

33

Outside, they moved through the thick air of August afternoon, while the sporadic Japanee talk crackled in the air. Once again the solemn six-by trucks stood waiting, idling ponderously by the station. A fleet of bored drivers dozed in the cabs.

Another officer, a young-faced lieutenant, was directing the troops to their battalions. Giff listened to him as he hustled the troops along. He and Dallas, orders in hands, walked up to the trucks waiting to take them to the Third Battalion, Third Marines, sweating under the weight of their seabags balanced on their shoulders.

"I killed my first gook when he was a freshman in high school," Dallas said of the lieutenant as they passed.

With the trucks loaded they started off down the main street of Gotemba, where once again people smiled and glared at them. On out of town rumbled the truck column, picking up speed like a horse heading for the barn, and out onto a dirt road, the dust rising in heady waves, smothering the men in the trucks. Giff cursed and shut his mouth quickly as it filled with dust, wondering how long it would be now for Chrissakes.

Barreling up the dirt road Giff saw a large mountain range off to the east through the film of dust, and in the west, still in command of all situations, was Mount Fuji. Then finally the trucks slowed and braked and cut sharply to the north.

Now moving slow, the dust began to abate somewhat, and then Giff heard the yelling. It was not really yelling, but high furious talk—women's voices—fast and snappy and mellow and calm, a prominent tenderness overshadowing all of it. And hearing it, the female voices raising black shiny flecks within his eyes, a promise, an unsayable want for the people behind the voices rose up burstingly and he looked out, craning his neck, and saw the town.

Small clapboard bars with western false fronts painted cheerily in bright colors, and lining the street in front of the bars in the shadows of late afternoon were the women: hundreds of them it looked like to Giff; all dressed in American clothes, sweaters skirts blouses high heels flats, all Japanee (maybe some White Russian too? or Korean?) smiling invitingly happily and waving as the grumbling truck column moved down the dirt road.

Giff caught the flash of bar signs painted on the façades

as they passed: HONEY BAR, THE HIDEAWAY, THE BLACK CAT, THE SILVER STAR (that one pulled a smirk to his mouth) and the U.S. BAR. And hungrily, feeling his breath choke with the dust, he studied the stocky hips of the girls, full and supple, the small and large breasts—and! the panty lines under the skirts that covered the bee-stung lips of the swollen almost hairless triangles that were no more secret or denounced or unadmitted than the sun in the sky, and Giff Bohane, watching them, the naturalness of them, the never-would-be-defeatedness of them no matter how much any person tried to defeat them blot them out destroy the wom-enness of them. The women would always endure, he thought thankfully gratefully, and he felt suddenly as if he had just come home from a million light years away.

Mellowly, he savored the smooth creamy complexion of the women under the black gleaming hair and the dark slanting eyes.

Now the men were yelling back from the trucks entic-ingly, and had they been drunk, Giff suddenly thought, or had the trucks veered sharply, they would all have fallen out and probably gotten killed.

"Dollies on the hoof," Dallas grinned, observing.

Giff licked his lips and tried to catch snatches of faces of memory as they passed. "I wonder what the name of this town is?" he said distantly. "That's sure some welcome, ain't it?"

Dallas nodded. "Un hunh."

Giff looked at him. "You wouldn't have got nothin' like this in Korea."

"That's true," Dallas agreed.

The trucks slowed and then plowed unstopping through a wide gate, where the distinct unemotional lines of bar-racks hit Giff flush in the face, the town only seconds be-hind them—but barracks! sheets! real beds! showers! No more douche baths Korean-style! It was the first time he had seen barracks since the States, a long time ago it seemed, though it was only a little more than a year.

But it was barracks and their dilapidation was rescinded by their mere presence: low, long, rambling, green, single-storied, sparsely set out without a preconceived zoning. It hit him strongly; this that was his life. Suddenly, and simul-taneously with the emotion, he remembered that there was nothing more depressing than empty deserted barracks with the windows boarded up. A barracks deserted looked like a stray hungry dog with its ribs sticking out. But these barracks had life in them. Hell yes!

The trucks cut down three short streets and came to a screeching halt. Spontaneously, the men jumped out clutching their seabags, most of them talking about the "town" they had just come through: there were phrases of conversation in the air, hanging in the lengthening shadows of late afternoon: "Liberty tonight?" "You goddam betcha!" "I got lover's nuts." "VD or no, this ol' kid's gonna have some."

Giff and Dallas stood beside the truck, looking up a long expanse of purple cinder ash, the parade field where, at the end beside two cannons, stood two flags: an American flag and a United Nations flag; and lining the parade field were rows of long barracks.

Watching the deserted parade field, a sense of loss swept over Giff with a cloudburst force emotion: *Peace*time again; troop and stomp; rifle inspection; spit and polish. The loss of Korea with its prolonged existence in his life loomed in his mind.

"I ain't gonna like marchin' on that," Dallas said, as if reading Giff's mind. He spat onto the purple harsh cinder of the parade field.

Behind them rose the bored monotonous voice of a M/Sgt echoing in the long shadows. "All right," the voice said tiredly. "Fall in here. In some kind of formation. Any kind will do. A bunch is all right. Just fall in."

The M/Sgt, whom Giff quickly deducted as the Sergeant Major, called out names for each of the rifle companies, the one weapons company of the Third Battalion, and the Headquarters Company.

Listening intently, Giff heard his name called out for H Company, and wondered for a moment if Dallas would get the same company. Hell, he hadn't even thought about that. Well, what difference did it make? he asked himself. A friendship in the Crotch was only as long as a short burst of machine-gun fire.

But Dallas' name was called. The names for H Company ended with G. and Giff felt remotely at ease.

Then the Sergeant Major called Giff's name out again and he walked up to him, heaving his seabag on his shoulder.

"You Corporal Bohane?" the SgtMaj asked. He was a tall thin man, graying, with a broad nose, dressed in starched immaculate summer khakis, a pisscutter set low on his forehead.

"That's right, Sar'nt Major," Giff said.

"I don't know if they's any other senior corporals in this bunch," the SgtMaj nodded tiredly at the mob, "for H Company. But you march them on over anyway."

Giff looked at him questioningly.

"Well," the SgtMaj said, bored. "You don't have to march them over. Just move them. That's all."

"Right," Giff said, feeling military again. And when he turned back, Dallas was grinning at him like a gambler with a cinch hand.

Giff grinned back and summoning up the boom of authority, fell the bunch into a mob formation. Then he turned back to the SgtMaj. "Hey, Sar'nt Major," he called out. "Where the hell *is* H Company barracks?"

The SgtMaj waved his arm in the general direction of the dirt road going opposite from the parade field.

Shambling, Giff moved his flock down the road, looking at the little red and gold colored signs on double posts that designated each company in front of their barracks.

When they arrived at H Company's mustering area, the last barracks down the line, it was as if they all suddenly, if belatedly, realized they were *home:* simultaneously, talk broke out like sporadic rifle fire, crisp in the long shadows of early evening, and they walked onto the cinder ash of the mustering area where a M/Sgt and a commissioned warrant officer stood waiting, papers in hand, both looking a little disgruntled.

It took only four or five minutes of the most hectic activity to call off names, assigning them platoons.

While they straggled into the barracks, into their home, still alien yet recognized now, Giff had the feeling watching them waiting for *his* name to be called wondering where he'd be assigned, that it was no different than any of the other duty stations he'd been at . . . a hell of a lot of them, moving shuffling fighting . . . in four years.

Even the two men, the M/Sgt apparently H Company's First Sergeant and the marine gunner apparently H Company's Executive Officer (whose names he did not know, but whose faces always looked the same whenever he was checked into new barracks anywhere) seemed oblivious to it.

And when his name was called—for the second rifle pla-

37

toon—Giff picked up his seabag and moved off a little, still waiting. Then Dallas answered for the same platoon and moved off to meet him—they had both caught the same platoon. Giff had a hunch they would, their names being so close together in the alphabet. Silently, they walked across the black ash to the long low rambling old barracks and into the whitewashed double door on the end.

Inside they were immediately hit with that stony-faced speculation accorded to men who have suddenly infringed on the lives of others and are not yet accepted. Not hostile or unfriendly exactly, but a kind of blank-faced tight-lipped reserved study. And the air was tense with the descending weight of a hushed poker game.

Giff, moving in front of Dallas, was keenly aware of this professional digestion by his peers, but he looked neither right nor left. It was the same analyzing he had done in Korea when each new draft arrived: a chaffing down, weeding out the culls and winnowing down the bad seeds till there was only the unblemished crystal left. It had to be done quick—especially in Korea. There his *life* had depended on it. Now his senses reached out innate feelers, recording what was to be his home in the time it takes a man to wink, while consciously his eyes searched for an empty bunk.

Rolled field packs were set squarely on the tops of green wall lockers; blankets in an envelope fold over the pillows on bunks; bayonets hanging on the end of bunks. He walked on, testing his senses amid the snick of rifle bolts and cleaning of weapons.

Under the low-ceilinged squadbay of the second rifle platoon, a simple wooden plaque dangling from the ceiling designating it, he found an empty bunk and motioned Dallas with a jerk of his head, dropping his seabag on the stained yellow-gray mattress, surrounded by quiet scrutinizing stares.

"Well, here's where we all are," Dallas said, leaning his arms back on the top bunk.

Giff nodded. "I guess we ought to go check out some bedding," he said absently.

"You know where the supply shed is?" Dallas looked at him, his chilling killer's face blank under his deep V brow.

"We can find out." Giff was suddenly self-conscious of the metal corporal chevrons on his dungaree cap. "We can always ask somebody," he grinned tightly, and knew instinctively that the NCO's in this alien platoon were running around in their heads: How much time he got in? Is he up for Sergeant?

Just as he was examining faces to see whom he should ask, a buck sergeant laid down the rifle he had been cleaning and walked over to them; and Giff prepared himself with a mask of unreadability.

"I'm Sergeant Zorn," he spoke with a dull, dead-eyed inertia. "Right guide of the second platoon. You men been assigned to *my* platoon?"

"That's what they said." Giff was noncommittal, his face closed up solid looking at the round moon face with the tiny features and protruding ears wondering Jesus Christ!

Sergeant Zorn peered back at him uncomprehending. "Welcome aboard, Corporal," he said and Giff thought he could actually see the man's mind working over those tiny torpid eyes. Yet it really wasn't working, he decided, not functioning; more like thick mud trying hopelessly to sift through cement.

"Why, thank you, Sar'nt," Giff said pleasantly. Well well, he thought, throw the seal a fish.

"Where we get some bedding?" Dallas grinned his nothing-held-sacred grin.

"Yeah," Giff could not help but grin back at Dallas, "we been looking for the supply shed."

"Oh," Zorn said slowly, rolling his tongue around his mouth. Then he put his fists on his hips in a pose thoroughly unrelated to himself as if he had seen it done, did not fully understand it, but wanted to try it himself because other NCO's did it. "It's down behind the barracks on the other side of the road behind the bunkers," he said portentously. "There's a sign there and you'll be able to get sheets and blankets."

"Thanks, Sar'nt," Giff said, aware of Dallas still grinning beside him. "We won't have no trouble finding it."

Zorn nodded. "If you need any help at all," he offered dully, "just let me know, Corporal; I'll see you get it."

"Why thanks again," Giff said. "Come on, Dallas."

The two walked away past Zorn, leaving the moon-faced sergeant standing there heavy with weighty indecision, looking like a man on a dry dusty road watching the cars whiz by and letting the dust cake on him because he has forgotten which was his hitchhiking thumb.

Outside, Dallas laughed cacklingly as they walked down the road to the grass-covered bunkers where the tin roof of a shed was visible.

"What's so goddam funny?" Giff demanded. "We're stuck in that platoon."

"Oh Jesus," Dallas gasped, "Christ awmighty. My mother told me there'd be days like this. But she didn't say they'd come in bunches, like grapes."

Giff snorted weakly. "Breaks of the rice paddies," he said, shaking his head.

At the supply shed they stood in front of a half door while a blond curly-headed S/Sgt, disgruntled at the inconvenience, issued them pillows sheets and blankets and informed them they would draw web gear and rifles tomorrow. Then they each signed their names and arms loaded down trudged back up the road to the barracks.

Inside again, they tossed the bedding on their bunks, and Dallas sat down and lit a cigarette. Other men, who had come in with them, saw their bedding and without words began moving quietly out of the squadbay through the side door.

"I got to piss," Giff said.

"When you walk into a head you're holdin' your own," Dallas said cheerfully, sprawling out on his bedding.

Grinning, Giff walked back toward the head in the center of the long barracks, and looked around to see if Sergeant Zorn would maybe lumber out of some hidden place.

He walked into the steamy head, overcome by the shower-taking laughingness that is a precedent for liberty. Men lined the white washbasins, towels draped around their loins, shaving, sprucing up to go out and meet the women. No one looked up as he entered.

Through the steam he spotted the five urinals on the other side of the washbasins separated by a wall, and walked back to them. Several men sat complacently on the commodes in echelon by the urinals reading the Pacific *Stars & Stripes*. They regarded him somberly for a moment, then went passionately back to the adventures of *Winnie, the Breadwinner*.

Surrounded by the liberty preparations, Giff felt a sense of exclusion knowing he would have no liberty tonight, and how bad he now wanted it—needed it—after seeing the women in town, remembering all of them with exquisite detail. Well, he could make it tomorrow night! And thinking too that he had never transferred anywhere without a hangover or half shot down, and knowing how he would feel in the morning waking up in a strange place.

Why the hell did he ever re-enlist in the first place? But he knew the answer to that one before he asked himself.

Buttoning his fly, he left the head and walked back into the squadbay, the second platoon squadbay, wondering when and if chow would go and saw Cinamo Dallas talking, his face wreathed in his cynical smile, to two men, all three sitting on the bottom bunk—his bunk that was his home, and was to be held sacred, thinking of the legendary marine maxim that said a man's bunk, locker and rifle were his home and not to be violated. A man's home was not his castle at all; it was his bunker!

The man on Dallas' left was young, lanky and naked to the waist. The other was short and blocky with a bulbous nose, dressed in dungarees.

Now who the hell is that quarter Cherokee conning now? Giff wondered, walking up to them.

2.

"Well I'll be a kiss my ass," the lanky young man was saying in wonderment to Dallas as Giff approached. "I thought sure as hell you be buried in a poncho by now. Settin' up there on graveyard hill."

"Balls," Dallas snorted good-naturedly. "Take more'n some goddam slopeheads to kill this." He jabbed a thumb at his chest.

Giff leaned against the bunk nodding silently to the short blocky man with the bulbous nose, simultaneously aware of the unknown pairs of eyes studying them from the squadbay.

"Hey, Bohane," Dallas grinned. "This is Poke Turner." He bobbed his head at the lanky young man. "That's Giff Bohane."

"Hi," Poke Turner said, not rising from the bunk.

"Hi," Giff said, reserved, looking him over and aware of Turner's narrow sly eyes appraising the corporal chevrons on his cap.

"That's Stack Renshaw." Poke Turner nodded at the blocky, thick-set man, and Giff recognized a heavy hill-Georgian drawl in Turner's voice.

"Howdy," Stack Renshaw grinned.

Giff nodded at him again, and looked back down at Poke Turner as he talked to Dallas. On one hairy arm he had a tattoo that stood out sharply emblazoned in bright colors: a dagger piercing a heart with the words *Death before Dishonor* inscribed in the hilt of the dagger. On the other arm, tattooed in blocky letters were the words THIS MARINE IS GOING TO HEAVEN BECAUSE HE SERVED HIS TIME IN HELL—KOREA 1950-51. Nothing like advertising for yourself, Giff thought, and as if Poke Turner was aware of this he began picking imaginary things off his arm around his tattoo.

"You going to be in this platoon, hunh?" Stack Renshaw said amiably to Giff.

"I guess so."

Stack grinned. "You'll be glad to get some showers and sheets and real bunks after Korea, I'll bet."

"Won't I," Giff said, looking at the bright laughing eyes separated by the bulbous nose. "You in Korea, too?"

"Fifty-one and fifty-two."

"The both of you volunteer for Japan?" Poke Turner asked pointedly.

"Yeah; I did," Dallas said. "Bohane shipped over for it."

"No shit?"

Giff shrugged it away. "Sure." Why the hell didn't Dallas just tell them about the Silver Star, too?

"He got a Silver Star in Ko-rea," Dallas informed them. "On Vegas."

Here we go again, Giff thought, wanting to walk out of the squadbay and barracks and just keep walking till he was up to his neck in paddy water. Instead, he grinned a weak—but proud—grin back at Turner. "Were you with Dallas in Korea before?"

Poke Turner was still studying him intently. "With the Brigade," he said and stunned Giff for a moment. He had not known Dallas was a two-time loser in Korea. If he was there a second time that meant he had volunteered for it!

42

He thought fleetingly of Dallas' heckling on the ship last night. Well, well. He wondered why Dallas hadn't told him about it. Was he ashamed of it maybe?

"What ever happened to old Gordy Zimmerman?" Poke asked Dallas.

"He got hit with a mortar about a week after you went the hospital ship," Dallas said. "We didn't even have to bury him."

"Ohhh yeah?" Poke said. "Well how about that." He paused, reflecting. "He was always a shitbird anyway."

"I didn't expect him to last as long as he did," Dallas said mildly.

"You got liberty tonight?" Giff interrupted.

"Yeah," Stack Renshaw nodded. "We got it this week-end too."

"Sure," Poke said contemptuously. "We got libo; but we're broke and payday ain't till Friday."

"You want some shekels?" Dallas offered.

"You'll probably be needing it," Poke said, dropping his eyes. "I 'magine you'll get libo this weekend."

"Goddam we better," Giff said, recalling once again, for perhaps the seventy-eleventh time, the faces and bodies of the women he had seen through the dust in town. He felt the old belly-grinding urge accumulated over the three days aboard ship and that last week in Korea without any paddy runs.

"We might," Poke said tentatively, "go through the motherfucking fence tonight though. If you all want to, that is."

"They got double guards on the fence now," Stack piped up.

Poke Turner looked at him in disgust. "Yeah, that's right. Well, how about the slop chute then?"

"We ain't got any clean uniforms," Giff said, brightening a little at the thought of drinking beer. But he knew if he drank enough of it he would go through the fence anyway. Guard or no.

And suddenly he was thinking *peacetime* again—or rather, found himself *thinking* in *peacetime terms.* Dress uniforms for drinking and liberty; fences, high fences with barbed wire to keep him in: intimidation, threats, authority, all that he had not seen evidence of in Korea came rushing back now with incoming tide force.

"What time does chow go?" Giff asked, feeling more

43

foolish, still mulling over this rapid change . . . coming to Japan . . . leaving Korea. Quick like an underhanded deal.

"I ain't sure," Poke said. "I hocked my watch last week for a shack job. But I think our company eats last this week. Won't be good though. It's Monday and they always have leftovers on Monday."

"Was that the mess hall up by the parade field?" Giff asked.

"That's it," Poke nodded. "You got to use field mess gear, too. Like in Korea. We're too pore to have trays or silverware. The Army's got 'em though."

"How about it, Dallas?" Giff said. "You want to go to chow?"

"Not for leftovers I don't."

"Neither do I," Giff lied. He was suddenly hungry, in a nervous sort of way.

"You can eat at the snack bar over the PX," Stack proposed. "They got hot sandwiches; hamburgers and all like that."

"Yeah," Poke said. "You *could* do that. But you can't go in dungarees after 1630."

"All right," Dallas said wearily. "Why'nt you and Stack go get them? Get enough for the four of us and bring them on back."

"Sounds good." Poke shifted his narrow eyes to the cement floor of the squadbay. "Might be able to pick up some beer, too."

"How's that?" Giff was willing to do anything now to stave off the encroaching feeling of newness, being suddenly not a part of it and cursing himself silently for never taking off his pack and standing at ease. He halfway wished they'd bring up the Silver Star again.

"We do it all the time," Poke explained. "Couple of us go on over and pick up a case of beer, opened, and bring it on back."

"We'll have to wait till dark though," Stack said.

"That's true too," Poke agreed.

Giff looked out the window at the deepening shadows on the cinder ash, and the dark shadows of men going on liberty moving hurriedly out of view, knowing it was already cooling off but that it would not be cold tonight. Not during dog days. "Where'll we drink?" he said. "Outside?"

44

"Can't drink in the barracks," Poke said disgustedly. "That Right Guide Zorn may be dumb but he'd run his own mother up he caught her drinkin' in the barracks."

"Yeah," Dallas grinned. "We already met him."

"Then you know the score," Poke said. "That sonfabitch ain't got sense enough to pour piss out of a boot with the di-rections written on the heel."

"Sounds like you don't like him," Giff grinned.

Poke snorted. "The baby raper cost me two months at the brig in Pendleton."

"You make the brig again, Poke?" Dallas laughed, his lips pulled tight over his teeth.

"Yes I made it again," Poke sneered. "And goddam lucky Zorn didn't run me up here—yet. From what I hear this brig up at Middle Camp you don't come out of. Walking or any other way. It's tough."

"They's all tough." Dallas shrugged.

"But you can always walk out of them," Giff said, "if you want to. Ain't none of them so bad a man can't beat 'em."

"Okay then," Poke said. "Me and Stack get cleaned up and head for the slop chute, pick up some sandwiches and beer. Hell, it'll be dark in half an hour."

Dallas reached back for his wallet, but Giff brought his own out first. "Here," he said expansively. "I'll get it. Let me buy it."

"All right," Dallas grinned.

"Fightin' over who pays for the beer," Poke grinned flatly at Stack, "and we ain't got enough loot to bail our hock pieces out."

Giff handed a ten to Poke who stuffed it in his dungaree trouser pocket without looking at it.

"You might's well get settled," he advised. "Make your racks and all. If you need anything get it outa my wall locker. It's always open."

"You got your name on it?" Dallas asked. "On the bunk."

"Yep," Poke said. "It's down there by the head—the one that's all tore up."

As one, Dallas and Giff turned to look down the narrow aisle of the squadbay to the bunk in question. Indeed, it was torn up, looking as if some madman in a fit had grabbed blankets sheets mattress cover and all, wadded them into a ball in hopes of trapping some rare animal.

"Sar'nt Zorn," Poke Turner explained wryly. "He says my

rack ain't ever tight enough." He stood up. "We'll be back more skosh. Come on, Stack. Let's get some frosties."

Giff looked after them thinking, Strange, isn't it? The personalities a man just drifts into? And then just as casually drifts out of? There'd been that pfc in Korea (what was his name?) who had got it just eighteen hours before the "cease fire." On a patrol up Boulder City that Giff had volunteered his squad for. And the man slumped there, hit with a burst from a burp gun where the flak jacket did not protect, holding himself gingerly and peering through the darkness with that what-a-silly-goddam-thing-to-have-happen look on his face. Then he had gurgled slightly and heaved forward.

And Giff could not remember his name. Come off it now, he told himself. Forget Korea—you can't go back there. Not unless you ship over for it. Well, he couldn't do that for six more years anyway. By that time he'd have been in a dozen more wars. So forget Korea, old friend, that war is over with. Think of a new one—the one coming up. Besides, there was going to be beer drunk tonight. Think about Big J—and the women! No, don't think about that. The town was too close, too tempting, too easy to get to.

Strange though, how personalities just drifted in and out without navigation. Even his own.

"Which bunk you want?" Dallas asked behind him. "Top or bottom?" And Giff turned to face him, seeing the puzzlement on his high-cheekboned face, watching him strangely. "What the hell's the matter with you?"

"Nothing," Giff said. "Not a fuckin' thing. I'll take the bottom bunk. Maybe you'll step in my face again."

Trapped in the banging of wall lockers and the sardonic hoots of men going on liberty, and the clatter of mess gear as the broke, nothing-to-hock men filed out for leftovers chow, they made their bunks, exchanging wry comments at one another at the foreign feel of sheets after sleeping in Korean bunkers in musty sleeping bags for so long.

"It just hit me," Giff said. "They got flushing toilets in the head."

"Hellyea," Dallas fought a sheet, "this is a civilized country."

"Flushing toilets and showers," Giff said wonderingly. And the brunt of his emotions ripped up through him. It just all happened so fast any more with a frantic desperation

46

moving toward—what? Like a ring-tailed red-assed monkey searching furiously among the vine-hanging jungles for bananas.

Yes we have no bananas.

"What's the hell eating you?" Dallas was looking at him again, genuine puzzlement on his face.

"Nothing: No thing. Not a fucking thing," Giff dropped down on his newly made bunk. He lay awake staring at the sag in the bunk above him made by Dallas' body while the dark mauve shadows of evening permeated the squadbay and the Duty NCO came through, whistling, snapping lights on.

Through it all, Giff tried to collect his thoughts and gather himself together. Even when the troops returned from chow, their mess gear clattering emptily, he did not move. And then the barracks began thinning out with all those foreign—yet known—personalities skittering off to their various escapes: movies, slop chute, liberty; liberty, slop chute, movies. And he lay wondering at the myriads of choices in his life while the swiftness of his move began to creep into him and palliate some of the tenseness in his nerves.

A half hour later Poke Turner came walking quickly through the squadbay, taps on his dress shoes clacking and stood in front of their bunks, replete in pressed summer khakis, ribbons and all.

"You want some beer?" he said fatuously.

"I wants to thank you," Giff said, suddenly glad for these personalities to be swimming around him again.

"Your buddy asleep?"

Giff kicked his foot up at the sag in the mattress above him, jostling it several times. Dallas swung his legs over and jumped down to the cement, without remark.

"Outside." A wry conspiratorial grin crossed Poke's face. "We had a little trouble."

"Yeah?" Giff said. "What happened?"

"Wait'll we get outside."

They walked down the now quiet squadbay, Poke breaking his stride long enough to cast a withering glance at the single bunk of Sergeant Zorn (Zorn, he told them, always went to the camp movie whether he'd seen it or not; the sonfabitch spent most of his time eating licorice juju fruits in the back row ogling the goddam phony actors).

47

Outside, an undisturbed softness, a solacing warmth, seemed to emanate from the burnished black August sky. Giff caught a faint whiff in the air of the human excrement from the rice paddies.

"Over there," Poke said, turning toward a huge gnarled Japanee elm, its thick bark-encrusted limbs crowded with leaves protecting a blocky, shadowy figure sitting cross-legged leaning against its trunk. The three of them walked over to it.

"How's your head, Stack?" Poke grinned, squatting on his hams by the case of beer and greasy, delicious-smelling sack of sandwiches.

"How'd yours be if you just split the sonofabitch open?" Stack demanded angrily.

"Sure-foot Renshaw," Poke laughed. "It's a wonder you ain't been killed by a mine."

"What the hell happened?" Giff asked. Bending down he saw a black gash on Stack's forehead, the blood heavily clotted. Dallas pulled a sandwich out of the sack and began munching in contentment, washing it down with Budweiser.

Poke chuckled softly. "We were just comin' out the back of the slop chute when the three stooges—"

"The what?" Giff asked.

"The three stooges," Poke laughed. "You don't know them yet. They's three gooks that run the slop chute. Anyway, the three stooges come running out and tell us the OD is coming around back to check on uniforms—"

"What the hell's in back?" Giff interrupted.

"Oh, they got picnic tables and benches out there and that's where we sit most the time. You can see Fujioka from there," he said distantly, as if this was why there were tables back there—to see Fujioka.

"What's Fujioka?"

"The town," Poke explained. "So Stack there . . . Goddam," Poke howled, "but that was funny!"

"A regular riot," Stack said, unamused.

"They been diggin' a ditch over there, see?" Poke went on. "And Stack's carrying the beer—I got the sandwiches —and I holler for him to run.

"Well, he never saw the ditch atall and the next thing I know he's flying off through the air with this case of beer, still in his arms and he comes crashing down on all these rocks and dirt right on his goddam head."

48

"Can't keep my feet on the ground." Stack laughed a little sheepish.

"I grabbed him by the belt and hauled him up the other side of the ditch just as the OD rounded the slop chute. Hell, I thought he was all right, you know? So I started running again and old Stack wasn't with me."

"So what happened?" Dallas said without emotion. "These sandwiches are good."

"They're eggburgers," Stack told them. "Eggs fried on hamburgers."

"Old Stack," Poke finished up, "was walking around in circles with this damn case of beer in his arms, cold caulked nuttier than hell; he didn't know up from down. And I had to run back and lead him by his belt halfway back here before he came out of it."

Giff laughed up at the night, tossing his head back, a deep throaty laughter that threatened to tear him apart, an emotional letdown from the day, and he neighed right on, letting it all come out till his eyes watered. "You all right now, ain't you?" he asked Stack in a hollow voice.

"Sure," Stack said, the blood crusting on his forehead.

They sat there eating the food and watching the shadowy movements inside the barracks. Off to their left about thirty yards was the Bachelor Officers' Club and they could hear the occasional supercilious laughter and rising conversation of the officers. When they finished their sandwiches they started on the beer in earnest.

"So how long you been with the Third?" Dallas asked Poke.

"Since fifty-two," he said. "When they started it up. Been in Horrible Hog, our company," he grinned, "since then too. We thought we'd be going to Korea right after that. But we stayed there at Camp Pendleton till just a month ago."

"What about the troops that came to Korea to replace us?" Giff asked. "Were they volunteers too?"

"You kidding?" Poke said. "Volunteer for Korea? Now? With no war on? Nope; they's mostly all noncombatants. They put all the men hadn't had combat to Korea when you guys came over."

Giff jerked his head toward the barracks. "Most everyone in this outfit had combat experience, hunh?"

"Damn near all of them," Poke said.

"Well, that figures," Dallas said sardonically. "They must

be gettin' ready to send us somewhere; for something."

"Hellyea," Stack said. "We known that all along. But we figured it'd be Korea."

"Anyway," Poke said, "You can't beat the duty."

"If it's peacetime," Dallas observed, "no duty is good. All you do is stand around with your finger up your ass trooping and stomping."

"Sure, there's that," Poke agreed. "But I'm speaking of the liberty. It's damn near all jawbone, see? Hell, we got our own town out there, man. It's ours—ride now and pay later."

"We saw it coming in," Giff said, remembering and remembering.

"What about the company—Horrible Hog?" Dallas asked. "Are they all like Zorn?"

"Fuck no, man," Poke Turner retorted. "If they was we'd be all dead by now."

"What kinda skipper we got?" Giff felt the cool bubbling beer wear into him, thinking, So now Bohane drinks beer again: a totally ingrained process. It was hard for him to remember when, since he had enlisted, he hadn't drunk beer every night. Excluding Korea, of course. There he drank gook booze. Beer had been at a premium, reserved for the officers, who also got Stateside whiskey. Well, he couldn't have everything—but a Silver Star helped. Out of the corner of his eye he saw Poke talking to him. "What? What did you say?"

"The skipper. You'll see him soon enough."

Giff, watching the naked grin hook into Poke's eyes, tossed off his beer and sent the empty can clattering into the rapidly diminishing case. "Yeah? What's his name?"

"Kizer," Stack said. "Emil Kizer. Only no one calls him anything but *the Kizer*."

"Only you don't never want to call him that to his face," Poke warned.

"I heard of him," Dallas said quietly. "In Korea. But I thought he'd been retired. Or dead or something."

"Who the hell *is* he?" Giff suddenly felt as he was the thirteenth hound on a twelve-bore bitch. "The Marine Corps' answer to Heinrich Himmler?"

"Not quite; and he ain't even close to retirement either, Cinamo." It was the first time Giff had heard Poke use Dallas' first name and it startled him. In a life where first names were as meaningless as a burned-out barrel it always

50

seemed inarticulate to use a man's first name, or anything else connected with a past life. Sometimes, though not so much any more as at first, he repeated his own first name *Gifford* to himself, feeling its awkwardness roll around his mind. In fact, names weren't even used much at all in the Crotch: names nor faces nor bodies, all of them replaced by numbers rank and record books. Yet it was his life, his chosen craft, and all the rest of them too. There he was, back to choice again. And maybe he was imagining that about first names? He was imagining so fucking much any more, since (his beer can froze halfway to his mouth) the Silver Star.

"But to look at him," Poke was saying, "you'd think he should be retired."

"The Kizer started out with Lew Diamond," Stack informed them. "So goddam long ago it don't make sense."

"I'm not sure about that." Poke looked askance at Stack. "But he's plenty goddam old."

"And Lew Diamond's dead," Dallas said. "Died a lush. A juice-head. He was bum just like the rest of us."

Giff, Poke and Stack swiveled their heads as one to study Dallas. Lew Diamond, in the Marine Corps, was a venerated legend; more so than Blackjack Pershing of the Army or two-time medal of honor winner in the corps Dan Daly, who wound up as a guard in a bank. Lew Diamond, the marine who was two thousand years old, a powerfully built man with a gray goatee and mustache who lived on slop-chute beer and never drank without his dog Piss Pot Pete right beside him every night of every year, both of them so drunk they had to be carried back to the barracks when the slop chute closed. Lew Diamond, who was an even greater legend than Chesty Puller (whom most of them had served with in Korea, or somewhere—you were nothing, the slop-chute talk went, if you had never served with Chesty Puller, now a general). Greater than anyone before or since his death, Lew Diamond was the personification of all of them, and they all knew this, sitting there with their beer watching Dallas.

Master Gunnery Sergeant Lew Diamond—who, it was rumored, could drop a mortar shell down the smokestack of a ship at three hundred yards, and whose feats in drinking went unequaled, but who had died, after spending his life in the Crotch, of acute alcoholism—spent his life like they were now, twenty years along the road in a column of twos while the tanks rolled by showering them with dust and grime, and returning at night to drink in the slop chute and outquip one another to wake the next morning with heads the size of helmets.

And even now, facing it, the truth of it laid out by Dallas, they did not associate themselves with Lew Diamond's demise. It was better to think of it the other way, the glorious way, yet the truth was there, ever present, and they each of them knew it.

Dallas shrugged dispassionately, washing his hands of it by grabbing a fresh beer. "Anyway," he said, "from what I heard, his age don't slow him down none. The Kizer I'm talking about. I hear he's as good as he ever was. In combat."

"Nothing slows him down," Poke said.

"He's kinda odd though," Stack said thoughtfully.

"Was he with you in fifty-two when the divvy started up?" Giff asked.

"Un hunh." Poke nodded. "He joined up with us less than a month before we came over."

"What do you mean? Odd?"

"Well," Stack said slowly, "he does screwy things. You know what I mean. Like the day we were on Tank Infantry tactics in the field and ran into aggressor tanks. Hell, they was only a half-ass platoon of us."

"I hate Tank Infantry," Dallas snorted. "I hate tanks. And anything that goes with them."

"You'll see a lot of it around here," Poke said. "They's a company of Tankers right in this camp."

"In this camp?" Giff said, incredulous. "Jesus Christ! It ain't big enough."

"They got 'em all right," Stack said. "Anyway, we're out there facing this tank, see? And the Kizer, he's a sitting up on a finger watching us. I don't know where the rest of the company was. But he sees those tanks coming and he stands up waving his arms and hollering down at us *'Fix bayonets and charge that tank!'* How about that?"

"Oh Jesus," Giff mourned, while Dallas whooped enjoyably. He saw in his mind a picture of himself leading a raggedy-ass platoon of men against a tank with nothing but bayonets with some crazy wild man thinking they were *can openers!*

And that clutching rag-shaking-dog rootlessness, his heritage of impermanency, swept back over him with re-

52

gained vigor. Desperately, hoping to assuage the feeling of being a tethered ball on a long pole, he grabbed for a beer. And felt like Mother Hubbard. "We're all out of beer."

"Shit fire, we'll get some more." Poke said happily. "Me and the three stooges are thick as thieves." He took the bills from Dallas. "Hang loose till I get back. You want any more chow?"

They all declined and Poke moved lithely, sure-footed, through the darkness, his heels crunching on the road.

"How is the Kizer on Office Hours?" Giff asked. "Pretty rough?"

Stack shrugged. "He's odd," he said simply, as if this covered a multitude of vagaries. "Sometimes he'll hand out a court-martial for some petty shit offense. Then he'll give a warning to some shitbird who's been over the hill for three four days. You can't never tell."

"I don't think you'll have much trouble, Bohane," Dallas said. "When they find out you got the Silver Star you'll be in like Flynn."

"Why don't you stick to things you know about?" Giff snapped.

"I'm only tryin' to be helpful," Dallas said blithely.

"It'll probably help you some." Stack looked from one face to another, both of them scowling now in the dark. "But the Kizer's got guts. At the bayonet course one day he ran through the whole company, bayonet-fighting with each man—without scabbards." He paused and looked at the two again. They were still scowling.

"The Kizer won all of them," Stack went on. "Till he come to Poke. He'd knocked every man's rifle outa their hands till then. It was sort of a challenge, I guess. Poke sent his bayonet right through Kizer's arm just missing the muscle."

Giff turned from Dallas to Stack in disbelief, no longer scowling. "He put a bayonet in the Kizer's arm?"

"Right through it, clean as a schoolmarm's pussy," Stack said. "And know what the Kizer did?" he paused proudly, pulling in their attention. "The sonofabitch reached up and pulled the bayonet out himself. He didn't wince, or bat an eye. And Poke just stood grinning at him.

"Then the Kizer pulled out his old handkerchief, wrapped it around his arm and went back to sick bay. A half hour later he was back on taking the rest of the company through bayonet drill. Poke was the only one that beat him. But the sonofabitch never even flinched when it cut through his arm."

"Poke never was very good with a bayonet," Dallas said. "He shoulda had a belly cut."

Giff, his anger at the quarter Cherokee abated and moving away under the weight of Stack's story, could not help but feel an admiration for the Kizer—and resented Poke's left-handed glory for a little, thinking he could have done it himself. Poke had something to be proud of. Bayoneting an officer! Still, he was more impressed with the Kizer. Nuts or not, that took a lot of guts. Or no brains, one.

"But he goes for medals," Stack told Giff. "He'll respect that on you. Course, he don't have nothing to do with the platoons. And it depends on what platoon you're in around here."

"Yeah?" Giff said. "How's that?"

"What were you in in Korea?" Stack asked. "A rifle platoon?"

"Most of the time. I was with machine guns for a while; till Vegas."

"Well, you ought to take machine guns here," Stack said sagely. "It's a whole hell of a lot better than the second p'toon."

"I wouldn't want machine guns anywhere," Dallas said. "They's too much work involved in that."

"Maybe so," Stack admitted. "But they ain't got a platoon leader like us, like we got. Like Thorton. Gunny Thorton is almost like the Kizer."

"Jesus H. Christ on a stretcher!" Giff exploded. "What the hell is this? A company of psychos?"

Stack waved his thick hand at him. "Hell no, that ain't what I meant. Thorton's smart, see? And he ain't *odd* like the Kizer. I didn't mean that. But all them I know in the p'toon swears they're going to transfer out." Stack grinned in the darkness. "No one ever knows what Thorton's doing."

"But he knows his business." Poke Turner's voice leaped at them through the darkness, and the three of them turned as the lanky figure descended on them.

"Twenty-four cold dudes," he drawled, setting the case on top of the empty one. They all grabbed fresh cans.

"He's a Testical Serjint, hunh?" Giff swilled some beer.

Stack lit a cigarette with *savoir-faire* as if he were a mas-

54

ter of ceremonies. "He's the only other T/Sgt besides Gunny Finch. Finch the company Gunnery Sarjint."

"A damn poor one too," Poke added. "He's three-quarters shot down all the time."

"If Thorton's so smart," Dallas said, "how come he ain't got the job? Instead of Finch?"

"Like I said," Stack explained. "Ain't no one ever knows what Thorton's doing. But you can't top him."

"No one can," Poke said caustically with just a hint of respect. "That mustachioed sonfabitch."

"Don't sound like you got a great admiration for the man, Poke," Dallas grinned.

"Aw," Poke said. "Hell with it. Long's he don't fuck with me personally I don't mind him."

"Was he with you in the States?" Giff asked.

"Yeah. All the way since the divvy started," Poke said.

"I get a kick out of him," Stack grinned happily.

"Sure, he's a million laughs," Poke snorted. "But he is smart. Though I hate to admit it. And he *can* handle troops."

Dallas shifted around, leaning his back against the tree trunk. "How much time he got in?"

"He's got broken time is all I know," Poke answered. "I don't know when he started, but he's been out at some time and come back in. He was a prisoner of war during Big Two."

"Hellyea," Stack said excitedly. "I forgot to tell you that. And this is what's the twister, really."

"The whole fucking company is odd you ask me," Giff said.

"But he was a POW right here," Stack said. "That's what's odd."

"Here in Japan?" Dallas tossed his empty can into the case.

"Right here for Chrissakes!" Poke jabbed his finger at the ground.

"At Fuji?"

"Right here I mean!" Poke insisted. "Here goddamit! South Camp! These barracks! Right here!"

Peering through the darkness at the low rambling barracks and grass-covered bunkers and night shadows, moonless, Giff could not see Mount Fuji—its awesomeness—like he had that morning. And it stunned him slightly, thinking

55

of it, that it had been here, looking over a POW camp. That this place, which was now his home, had been a Prisoner of War camp. "This was a POW camp," he heard himself say, wondering at the vicissitudes while fogged images ran through his mind of what it might have looked like eight years ago when Big Two ended. Now it was an integral part of his immediate life.

"Goddam rights it was," Poke echoed. "Course they got it fixed up a bit for us now."

From outside where he sat Giff looked at the clapboard tin-roofed barracks thinking they were almost devoid of human content. Even for the Marine Corps they were lousy barracks. "Sure," he said. "I can see they're all fixed up."

"Anyway, it's better than Korea," Dallas said. "We done wore ol' Ko-rea pretty well out."

"Anything's better than that ass hole of the world," Poke said. "When there ain't no shootin' match on."

"And that's just about all anyone knows about Thorton," Stack said. "Unless it'd be Hobbs. Thorton don't really spend much time with the platoon. Hobbs actually handles it."

"And what kind of an idiot is Hobbs?" Giff belched.

"No idiot atall," Poke said somberly after the moment. "He's a staff sarjint—Jack Koko Hobbs—and he don't mess with no one. And *he* runs the platoon, like Stack said. Not Thorton. But Thorton sees to it that Hobbs runs it right enough."

"Right now," Dallas said, "I'm only interested in gettin' some liberty, that's all."

"Goddam right," Giff said anxiously. "How soon it be before they give us any? I ain't had a piece of ass since Korea. And that wasn't too hot."

"You got to be indoctrinated first," Stack grinned. "You know. How to conduct yourself in Japan. All that petty shit."

"That figures," Dallas said tonelessly.

"Well, how long does that take?" Giff demanded.

"No more'n two three days," Poke said. "And since we got liberty this weekend you'll probably have it by then. Be ready for libo on Friday."

"Well that's something anyway," Giff said. "And you say payday is Thursday?"

"Friday," Poke corrected. "Look," he said enthusiastically. "We'll get together Friday and me and Stack show you around. How about it?"

"Suits me." Giff shrugged. "Where you hang out in town?"

"Most of the platoon hangs out in the Blue Moon," Stack said. "That's down in Bamboo Alley."

"They got a lot of shitkickin' records there," Poke said, as if that was all there was important to say about it.

"What else is there," Dallas grunted.

"Bamboo Alley, hunh?" Giff rolled it around with the can in his hands. It had a nice sound to it, pleasing, inviting. But that was his imagination again, he amended. Beer always had a tendency to make him think romantically. Especially when there were women to be had. So damn close and yet so far.

"One place you don't want to go," Poke grinned. "That's the Condor Club. It's right at the beginning of Bamboo Alley and Skivvie Lane."

"Why not the Condor Club?" Dallas asked.

"It's a nigger joint," Poke said. "All the spear chuckers hang out there."

"They got their own bar then," Dallas said, satisfied.

"Sure," Poke said. "They don't fuck around in the white clubs or bars. They know better. And we don't fuck around in the black clubs either."

"But they fuck around in the company," Stack said.

"So that's what we'll do then." Poke ignored the comment. "We'll hit the slop chute in the evening and warm up on some beers and go out to town about seven or so."

"I ain't sure if I can wait that long," Giff grinned.

"It'll be worth it," Stack said with nostalgia.

"Are the dollies just like them at Kyoto?"

"Samey same," Poke said. "Only they don't cost as much. Fifteen hundred yen for all night here."

"Goddam!" Giff beamed. "That is cheap."

"You don't have to stay at the Blue Moon you don't want to," Poke said. "They's plenty others all through Bamboo Alley and up the main street right outside the gate. That's what you saw when you came through this aft'noon. Main street."

"How about Gotemba?" Dallas asked. "How's that for liberty?"

"Well," Poke said with the air of a man who has been

57

asked to lead legions to glorious victory. "Well, they's some suckahachi houses up there and of course you got your skivvy shows and baths and massages and all that but it ain't half the town Fujioka is."

"How long we going to be here?" Dallas asked, breaking it up. "How long before we pull out?"

"Not too damn long," Poke hinted. "They didn't bring us over here to skylark."

With that they all grinned at each other through the heavy darkness. Tight cocky rancorous grins, and Giff thought they must all be thinking the same thing: they would be here only long enough for something to break out somewhere, and they had best make the most of their lives before they went. Because they did not know how long this interlude would last—before another war. Or where the next interlude would find them.

They sat there, relaxed, under the umbrella protection of the Japanee elm, cigarettes glowing bright and dimming in their mouths while Poke and Stack answered questions and gave them the "straight scoop," and drinking the frosted cans of beer till finally, shortly before the lights snapped off in the barracks across the street from them, two empty cases sat at their feet like a dead campfire, a eulogy to the "cease fire," a toast for weapons yet to be fired.

Across from them, on their left, the officers from the BOQ Club slammed the door and staggered out one by one back to the BOQ for sleep, and the four men sat impervious, watching them with a baleful eye.

"I'm surprised they didn't sing no college songs tonight," Poke said. "Usually they come out singing something about Ivy or brick walls or something."

Dallas snorted approvingly. "College lieutenants. Leaders. The only thing they can lead is their nose up some general's ass." He stood up and wiped off his trousers. "Well, we may as well hit the rack. They's nothing left out here for us."

Disconsolately, the other three stood up and looked down at the two empty cases. Giff had thought of asking Dallas if he wouldn't maybe want to try a paddy run, hit the bars in town, thinking of the women again; but he discarded it along with the empty cans in the trash barrel outside the barracks.

They moved quietly into the sleeping squadbay, belching

a little, contented. Poke Turner stopped in front of Sergeant Zorn's bunk and glared down at it, where the snoring, mouth open wide Swede sucked in the night musty air. Then he turned back to his own rumpled bunk and plopped down tiredly.

Up at his still unfamiliar bunk and locker, Giff struggled with his seabag, unlocked it, and took out his old shaving kit towel and clean set of skivvies. "I guess I'll take a shower," he said absently, feeling the beer flow heavily through him.

Dallas leaped up to his bunk, snatched off his clothes and crawled between the crisp linen. "Ahhh," he sighed blissfully. "Sheets. And a mattress. To hell with Syngman Rhee and his motherfucking cornball peninsula."

Surrounded by the creaking springs and murmuring of sleep, Giff navigated his way to the soft shaft of light streaming from the head, moving silently between the bunks down the narrow aisle.

"Let me at 'em I'll kill the sons a bitches!" someone hollered chokingly in his sleep, and Giff instinctively dropped to one knee, adrenalin pounding up behind his eyes. Shamefaced, he rose, a redness spreading through his lean face.

In the head he startled a Pfc firewatch, a chunky young man wearing his cartridge belt and bayonet over his dungarees, who was trying to cop a smoke. The Pfc firewatch grinned guiltily, nodded and walked on out cupping the cigarette in his hand.

Giff stripped and turned on one of the showers in the long, paint-chipped shower stalls. He took the one at the end and stood under its stinging hotness relishing its taste on his leanness. In Korea he'd had only douche baths and an occasional flop in the cold waters of the Imjim River. (During the winter they had fixed up a shower tent by melting ice but the water was always piss warm and filled with kerosene from the immersion burners that melted the ice for the showers. They had only worked twice but it was mandatory that all troops take one and they were inspected to see that they had clean skivvies.)

Standing under this comparative luxury, he thought illuminatingly of all this sudden transition and the people involved in it: self-exiled *citizens* was the phrase that kept running through his mind; the only thing he could think of to describe himself and Dallas and people like Poke

Turner and Stack Renshaw. They were good people all right. Down home swingers.

Each of them moving with this quiet seemingly dormant desperation, shuttling from one war to another grasping this legacy that was theirs: men who did not have college diplomas, did not in fact have high school diplomas. No trade, no training, no roots of ownership coming from a country whose prime virtue was ownership: a house and a car on time and raise your family in a fast-growing modern America. But he, along with the rest of them in here, not a part of that Outside life, was the other element that had inherited by chance, necessity, and by choice too (chickens and sea gulls and people) they had all grabbed at the only logical opening left them, the only trade left them, the only one they were capable of holding. Maybe they wouldn't have if their government issued out slaves, land and horses and goats instead of the GI Bill of Rights (which they could not use anyway), giving these free gratis to their mercenaries who fought their wars for them. But they didn't. So they kept right on living these interludes and fighting their wars. (Oh they all knew it wasn't patriotism, they had found that out long ago—not fighting for the mother, God or country at all. Hell, no one was that foolish any more.) So that these other people on the Great Outside could buy their houses and cars and slaves and horses and goats all on time—credit and insurance—and raise their families in a rapidly growing America where the dark horse was deception to makes asses out of the masses.

Ought to get drunk a little more often, he told himself, lathering up with the soap thickly all over his body. See so many things about as loose as a goose drunk. No, not drunk, just feeling pleasantly tingled.

And here were the offspring of those other mercenaries who had fought in Big Two who were the offspring of the mercenaries who fought in Big One and right on back down the line, till it became wrapped in a nebulous haze.

So in the end it was nothing more than a multiplication of inheritances—or lives and experience—now living in the country their predecessors had beaten eight years ago. And not all of them predecessors either. Some of them were contemporaries: like that mustachioed sonfabitch Hugh Thorton. He grinned, remembering what Poke Turner had said. Here they were, to live it up in a country they had so badly whipped before, to be welcomed by its lower denizens. But the way the world was being carried to hell in a coal bucket a man had to get what he could while he could. Even if it was a meaningless thing like a Silver Star.

What a game, he thought, stepping back under the shower and luxuriating as the soap cascaded from his body.

And it wasn't any different in Germany or Italy than Japan. It was as if they were saying, "All right, you won this time, come on in and be friends with us now," so you fought them for a while and then you lived with them for a while waiting to fight again. So that existence was measured only by wars any more.

Hell, it was no different than in Korea. Except they hadn't won anything. But a lot of people had sure made some loot, all right. And like Dallas, who had been in China before that, training the Chinks that they were later to fight in Korea.

There is something to learn here, he told himself, but he wasn't sure what it was.

Thoroughly rinsed, he lathered up again, hearing the water splash around him and the steam billowing out into the head, lathering gratefully and thinking of the coming weekend. He would have his pick of women. Not any of that run and jump stuff like in Korea. And for that he was thankful. Take his time and pick the whore of his choice.

And lathering, he suddenly began to think of the States: Camp Pendleton, California, and Janie Dawson, Pfc. Janie Dawson, Woman Marine, BAM (broad-ass marine) of Twenty-Four Area in Camp Pendleton.

Strange that he should think of her; he did not think of her much at all, really. And that had been so long ago, almost two years. But when he did think of her it was always with a ruttish mood. He always saw her in the same place the same way: in the back seat of his '48 Packard convertible (that he had bought with his gambling money), her auburn hair framing that hot-eyed face while he moved over her.

Still lathering, he hoped the damned firewatch didn't come back in.

Janie had been a Pfc, and he at that time had been a private and they had had a hellish affair. She had told him, sorrowing, that her mother had made her tape her breasts down when she was just beginning to blossom. (They were large, firm.) Not that he believed this particularly but it made for better romance, a gimmick. So he, still bitter and incensed over not being shipped to Korea yet and just about on his last leg before getting booted out with an Undesirable Discharge for perpetually breaking regulations (a habitual offender of military law, they called him), had told her that he'd had malaria, that he had been tested and was sterile, sorrowing, and could never father a child. This provided for the necessary delusion of affection: lies plus more lies produce the tragic romances that the movies are always telling about.

What a relief this will be till the weekend, he told himself, lathering quicker.

And then, he remembered, in summer of '52, she had suddenly turned cold. And it was a crushing blow to his Irish ego. It was as if she hated, actually detested, to be touched by him. He was in a quandry and was beginning to think of himself as incapable. So naturally, quite characteristically, he made a larger fool of himself (he was always doing that, making a fool of himself).

The mistake was, he began hanging around her like a dog-pack leader over a bitch in heat, which only made her become more petulant and cantankerous. Once in a fit of despair, thinking he would never be sent to Korea and would spend the rest of his life on Skid Row in L.A. with the rest of the ex-marines, he had gotten bullishly drunk and, storming down Highway 101 in his '48 Packard, the rare time Janie was with him, asked her to marry him. When she refused adamantly, and he sobered up, he was horrified—and grateful she had refused. And he did not go off in a corner and sulk bitterly, sorrowfully.

Actually, it wasn't until he finally got his good-riddance-to-the-ten-per-cent orders for Korea that he discovered she had been having an affair with a S/Sgt from Tent Camp Two out in the boonies.

A roaring raid to Tijuana with one last drunk before being shipped out, a good laugh at himself, a fine Mexican lay, all restored his ego and his pride was quickly recovered and his '48 Packard convertible was left to rust and deteriorate outside the rear gate at Camp Pendleton.

Under the shower, he watched himself flow away from himself and down the greedy sucking drain, hand relieved. Christ! It was almost as bad as serving in the field!

Walking back through the sleeping squadbay in the late August night air, climbing wearily into his bunk, feeling the sheets and the nighttime wrap around him, he began to think sleepily about his new home.

And that it was just his goodam luck to get in that mustachioed sonfabitch Gunny Thorton's platoon. From what he'd heard it didn't sound like a picnic.

The last thought he had was that old Janie Dawson had surely been an exceptionally fine piece of ass, but that all good things must come to a shimmying stop.

3.

Gunnery Sergeant Hugh Thorton had not planned to go on liberty that night. But then he never really planned anything. Long ago, so far back now that he could not recall exactly when, he had discovered physical planning was as useless as tits on a boar. Moving intuitively, always impelled by an unseen force—the only inviolable contact he'd ever had with himself—he placed his bet on the red *or* black of the Dealer's Choice.

Either color, as far as Hugh Thorton was concerned, was a cinch bet.

At nine-thirty that night, a half hour before taps and an hour and a half before the bars in Fujioka closed, Hugh Thorton rose impulsively from his bunk in the staff quarters and began dressing in his blue cashmere Hong Kong tailored suit.

The staff quarters was separated by a partition at the end of H Company's rifle platoon barracks. And H Company's seven staff lived there in comparative comfort. Each of them occupied a single bunk in the spacious room; a large round poker table in the center under a dangling naked light, and a gratefully appreciated ice locker which they kept filled with cold beer from the payday kitty, completed the furniture.

Except for H Company's gunny sergeant, Leroy Finch, and Hugh Thorton, the second platoon leader, the staff quarters were now deserted. Leroy Finch sat dejectedly at the poker table smothering a fifth of whiskey. Gaunt, emaciated, with deep-sunk red eyes he stared at his hands in the circle of light and when Thorton got off his bunk the hollow eyes followed him.

Aware of the scrutiny, Thorton turned his back to Finch and tied a perfect Windsor knot in his white tie, startling over his pale blue shirt. Then he grinned at his reflection in the mirror, feeling the cockles of conceit rise in him, the sharp curled tips of his black handlebar mustache dipping upward with his grin. He twitched his mouth from side to side as the immaculate well-twisted tips moved forward and backward. Satisfied, he slipped into his blue suit coat, buttoned the single button and was ready to take his turn with the lance.

"Going on liberty, Hugh?" Finch asked soddenly from the table.

Hugh turned from his locker, his dark deep-set eyes under his beetling brow raking the cadaverous T/Sgt. "I'm not about to stay around here and get shot down."

"I got another bottle," Finch suggested.

"Then you better save it, Leroy," Hugh Thorton said. "You'll probably be needing it before the night's done."

"There won't be nothing happening out in Fujioka this close to payday." Finch's eyes went a little deeper red. "You must be pretty hard up to go out tonight."

"Hard up hard on," Hugh curled his mustache impishly, "I can't lay in here all night and listen to you groan and scream in your sleep."

"I'll bet," Finch said dully.

"If you could only hear yourself." Thorton shook his head in mockery. "A man would think you were breast fed till you were thirteen."

Finch snorted disgustedly, alcoholically, and gazed around the staff quarters. "You gonna shack up all night?"

"Maybe."

"*Maybe*, my ass!" Finch took a heady pull from the bottle he held in his hands. "What the hell you going out for if you ain't going to shack up?"

"Maybe I want some ham and eggs."

"Sure," Finch said. "And maybe I want a new set of teeth."

"The only thing you want, Finch," Hugh said unequivocally, "is a full jug in your locker box every day."

Finch went back to studying the label on the bottle.

Hugh, watching him, knew he would be going into one of his self-pitying monologues, rehearsed and acted out every day—or night. And he did not want to stand around and listen to it.

"That may be true," Finch admitted. "But don't think you're free of it." He turned his eyes balefully on Thorton. "I been in the Crotch seventeen years. I'm thirty-five and a washup. So take a good look at what you'll become," he demanded. "I'm layin' my cards on the table. Hiding nothing."

"No, you sure aren't," Thorton agreed, wanting to walk out but curious too, though he had seen it so many times before. Looking at this man who was only five years older than himself, but who looked like Methuselah, Hugh could not see how *he* could become *that*. Still, it was the first time Hugh had ever heard Finch make reference to him personally. No, he wasn't exempt. He grinned back, his mustache dipping.

"I'm no fool," Finch told him thickly. "I may be drunk, but I'm no fool. I know what you want, Hugh. Maybe the Kizer don't know; or maybe even Top Landrum don't know; but *I* do."

"Well that's dandy," Hugh said cheerfully. "Now how about telling *me* what I want." Since he didn't know himself, maybe this unbottled liquor could tell him. But that wasn't entirely true either, was it? He knew what he wanted vaguely. He just could never isolate it.

"No need to be coy about it," Finch accused him. "You know. Soon's I fuck up enough to get shitcanned you'll take over the company as gunnery sarjint."

"I think your cup finally runneth over, Finch," Hugh Thorton said levelly. Holy Jumping Jesus! he thought. Of all things *that* was the last he wanted: Finch to get shitcanned and him to take over. That was simply back asswards. But Finch didn't see it that way. Finch, in his perpetually foggy state, didn't know that he had been keeping him—alive?—lo these many months just so he wouldn't have to take over the company. Damn, but he sure had it twisted. "But thanks for letting me know anyway," he concluded. "I'll remember you for it."

"And maybe I ain't fit for the job." Finch's face showed great and monumental drunken dignity. "I was once though. I was like you once. Believe that or not."

Hugh Thorton, who had always loved Hugh Thorton for

65

some reason or another—usually tacit—could not conceive that this man in front of him was once like himself. He dismissed it entirely. "I'd prefer not to believe it," he said. "But if it makes you happy I'll pretend it's so."

"Your whole trouble," Finch philosophized, "is that you haven't been shot at enough. Not like I have. But there comes a time when you can feel it. And I feel it now. I won't ever make another one."

"Then for that, you should be grateful," Hugh philosophized back, although he didn't know if Finch was talking about war or bottles. "If you think getting retired is going to make things bright, you are wrong as four hundred hell. You should be damn glad if you stop one in this next war," he said, deciding to bet on war.

Finch looked up, pained. "A man's got to have something, Hugh," he said. "There's got to be more than this." Then his cadaverous, deeply lined face scrouged up and two large tears welled up in the red hollows of his eyes. "There has to be more than this," he said.

"You better go to bed, Leroy," Hugh told him, simultaneously feeling a disgust and pity for him, wondering what intangible unmentionable nuances had started the ball rolling in Finch so long ago, so that now it snowballed inside him with tremendous speed. And yet behind this he thought he could see where once there had burned a flame of dignity—or whatever it was they called it.

Finch snatched his bottle from the table and stumbled off in a sort of Shuffle-off-to-Buffalo dance to his bunk in the corner. There he plopped down and crying uncontrollably, began drinking again.

Hugh Thorton watched him for a moment, thinking that in the morning he would have to snap Finch out of it for muster and that he was not going to be doing this forever, even if it seemed like it. But he had to protect his interests, didn't he?

Turning, he walked out the door of the staff quarters and into the close air of the August night. He paused momentarily on the cement stoop and looked down the street. Toward the other end of the barracks across the street under the towering Japanee elm he saw the flash of cigarettes and the occasional glint of beer cans. He did not have to wonder who it was—the second rifle platoon, members thereof. Those bastards drank anywhere. Probably giving some of those new men just in from Korea the straight scoop. That was about the speed of *his* platoon. Well, he didn't care what the hell they did. As long as they were ready for the field in the morning.

That new bunch in from Korea, he thought, still looking at them. He had checked most of their record books almost a week ago; had even wangled the assignment of some of them. One of them—a something Bohane—he had picked out to replace that idiot Zorn who only got in the way. Bohane would not have to be much to be better than Zorn. The only thing to do was wait and find out.

If nothing else, that new bunch would fill some gaps in the equipmentless, miserably understrength company. Dear old Horrible Hog Company.

He moved down the three steps and began walking along the road toward the parade field, deciding he might as well try the U.S. Bar. Koko Hobbs was usually there after he got back from his black market exchange with HOCK AT HENRY'S (rain, nor snow, nor sleet, nor gloom of night could stay S/Sgt Jack Koko Hobbs from his black market runs). And tonight Hugh did not feel like drinking alone.

Moreover, there was this Jo-san, *business woman,* down there at the U.S. Bar whom Hobbs had told him about; maybe something special and he wanted to find out about it—being totally honest with himself, as much as he could without overstepping discretion—he had to admit that *she* was the reason for his sudden decision to go on liberty. According to Koko Hobbs, who knew his women well (knew all women well in fact), she was one rather standoffish woman. And this had made Hugh slightly suspicious and intensely interested. If she was standoffish . . . Well, Koko had never explicitly said he slept with her (Koko had a steady at the U.S. Bar and it wasn't like him to be butterflying), but Hugh was certain he had. Maybe Koko only said she was standoffish to protect her for himself in time of need. Anyway it was a challenge.

And Hugh, when Koko told him about her, described her to him, had remembered her, had seen her at the U.S. Bar. But he himself had never slept with her.

Well, he had never slept with a lot of them at the U.S. Bar. That was because he had taken to hanging out in Gotemba the past month until his permanent shack job there had gone back to her Army Major. Because of mental cruelty, Hugh guessed. Sooo . . . might as well hit the U.S. Bar, back to his old haunts again, start all over.

Even if it was with someone Koko Hobbs had picked for himself for a rainy day.

Between you and me and Mount Fuji, Hugh told himself, quickening his pace, he was the only insurance that stood between Koko Hobbs and a long-term berth in Leavenworth. It was a hell of a thing to hold over a man's head. But then it was necessary for the effectiveness of the company so that justified it. It wasn't his fault Koko had gotten in the black market. He had just been lucky enough to spot it. And a damn good thing Koko was his platoon sergeant! He really had it wired; the deck was his.

Hugh Thorton, you are a bastard of the first water, he complimented himself.

In the silence of the outside Hugh became aware of the warped personality this camp held for *him*. It was a far cry actually from what it had been in '42 when he was a POW. And it had even changed by '45 when he was released. As a hard-charging gungy Pfc on Wake Island he had been one of the first to be captured in the Big Two global game. But he, along with the rest of the island's inhabitants, had been treated considerably well. Above all things the Japanee respected courage. And Hugh Thorton had to admit that as reckless and malcontent as were the men on Wake Island (the *bait-for-the-crocodile battalion* he liked to think of it wryly) they did have courage. Or whatever it was; dumbness probably—but this the Japanee respected. So the internment had not been too excruciating. And in reflection, he knew it had all been worth it, the education of it, for he had learned a good many things. Things that some people in the higher echelons would dearly love to get their hands on. So they could put the quietus on it.

Reaching the parade field he turned right as the lights in the barracks began flicking off all around him. The layout of the camp, South Camp, was still the same. Except now most of them who had been there before were dead or gone off somewhere: killed in Korea, died of frustration, gone psycho . . . all of them somewhere in dispute with themselves. And he himself would never have come back at all, had no reason to, if he hadn't re-enlisted in '49 just before Korea after four years as a civilian.

And in all that time—before when he was a POW and even now, free—he had never gone up to the two other camps: Middle Camp and North Camp, replicas of South

Camp. For how many years had they been there? Twenty perhaps? Of course, the Army was at North Camp. The First Cavalry Division, horseless.

Frequently he wondered how he himself had ever happened to come back here—with so many other places in the world he could have gone. Well, a rolling marine never received any answer, did he?

As he passed the camp slop chute, last-minute drinkers grudgingly staggered out, wending their way back to their barracks, singing laughing insulting. He decided to stop at the Staff Club, pick up a bottle to take out with him.

There is only me and thee left, he told himself, and sometimes I doubt thee.

Still, it wasn't just Korea that had brought him back here. There was that precarious position—or rather, *positions*— of the four years that hid sneaking in between. Hastily, he shuffled the four years from his mind.

The Staff Club was a dimly lit reproduction of an American Legion or Elks' Club Stateside and sparsely packed now, this close to payday. Johnny-o, the Japanee bartender, solicitous and condescending, waited on him as he stood at the bar in the shaded light. He paid quickly and walked out the door without an additional word; he hadn't seen anyone in there from Horrible Hog Company. Probably all out in town.

Outside, Hugh moved past the guardhouse and the Japanee Security Police shed to the main gate. A lackadaisical sentry in summer khakis passed him through without checking his identification, bilingual or liberty cards—a privilege offered the staff. Then he was outside South Camp and in town.

Men, women, children and dogs wandered along the dusty rocky road, some toward Bamboo Alley and Skivvie Lane, others up the main street moving in and out of bars. A blues song, mixed with hillbilly, pervaded the summer night air. Lights gleamed seductively from the small clapboard bars laid out in disjointed echelon, splashed carelessly with paint.

The U.S. Bar was halfway up the main street. A stucco bar (the only one in Fujioka not made of wood), almost refined, and here most of the staff from the camp hung out— a sort of off-camp Staff Club. A beckoning light dripped through its door as he walked in under the extended eaves of the porch, holding his quart bottle leisurely, the thought of *the woman* playing in his mind. Life noises rushed out to greet him.

Walking in, Hugh was surprised at the unusual crowd this close to payday. Three couples were dancing on the sunken stone floor in the center of the bar. Half a dozen heavy-bellied staff sat hunched at the bar arguing over their beers. Three of the booths along the wall were packed and the whole of it was covered with a hazy blue cigarette smoke.

Hugh saw Koko Hobbs and Pappy Dreek, Hog Company's armorer, sitting at the middle booth with two Jo-sans. Koko and Pappy Dreek were both wearing summer tropical worsted uniforms, sharp immaculate, and to Hugh's eyes pleasantly getting stoned. Hugh waved his bottle at them casually, and they waved back just as casually.

With the controlled emotions of a man who is at ease wherever he goes, Hugh Thorton walked up to. Mama-san Tokudo who stood behind the bar in her ancient red-flowered kimono. When she saw him, she leaned across the bar and opened her mouth wide, her eyes glinting happily, and stuck her upper teeth out as far as she could. A pure gold tooth stood glitteringly and Hugh grasped it between his thumb and forefinger and tugged gently.

"Goddam, Mama-san," he said seriously. "Why don't you loosen that tooth a little? I'll never get it out."

Mama-san Tokudo pulled away, giggling. "Thoton-san, you all time makee joke, *ne?*"

"Sure as hell." He winked at her, aware of the eyes at the bar watching him. "I'm a happy sonofabitch. A real comedian."

"You come see Mama-san maybe, *ne?*" she said coyly.

"You know I do," Hugh said. Of all the Jo-sans in the U.S. Bar, Mama-san Tokudo was the only one he had ever joked with. And had never slept with. No one slept with the mama-sans. But she always appeared to be happy when she saw him. He leaned across the bar, closer, intimately, "Your old man ain't around is he?" he whispered cautiously.

Mama-san Tokudo laughed brassily, then straightened up. "You look *toxon* nice tonight," she admired.

Hugh curled his impeccable mustache, grinning seductively. "If Papa-san don't come around let me know. We'll get fixed up before the bar closes."

"Oh whatsa matta you?" Mama-san pouted. "You

70

catchee nice young Jo-san, *ne?*" But she was flattered.

"The young ones don't have the sense of humor that comes with age, Mama-san." Hugh tossed another wink at her with excessive charm, genuine though, knowing he was flattering her with his talk, his *charm*—and it *was* truly genuine! Mama-san Tokudo, though he had only known her a short while, talked with her triflingly, always aroused a sort of deep-rooted kinship within him that, had he ever taken her to bed, would probably not be there at all. And it always slightly and mildly surprised him. With any other woman it wouldn't be like that—with Mama-san Tokudo it would. And it had nothing at all to do with the fallacious folklore that a man could not respect a woman he'd slept with, which to Hugh was a total misconception, thoroughly antiquated. Sleeping with them had nothing to do with it at all. Sex was too natural. It was simply that Mama-san Tokudo, whom he oddly enough did *not* want to sleep with, could always keep emotions on a light basis.

Yet while talking to her, charming her, ribbing her, displaying his warmth and charm that was the real McCoy, he looked askance so slyly, so subtly—if you weren't watching closely you wouldn't have even noticed the glance—at the middle booth against the wall where Koko Hobbs and Pappy Dreek sat with the two Jo-sans, drinking and talking in low tones, apparently not truly enjoying themselves. Jack Koko Hobbs immaculate, military-looking in his tropicals, who was actually no sharper-looking than Hugh himself in uniform, but appearing so. And overshadowing it all was the cool handsomeness of him that was not conceit or even vanity but simply there for the female's benefit and for his own unviolated easiness. That more than anything else made him look so impeccably sharp, a deception Hugh knew. Pappy Dreek wore clean pressed tropicals also, but remained sloppy-looking because of his chipped face manifesting a caricature hewn from white pine and left to wither and darken in the sun, as if he had spent his life facing a west Texas wind.

But the two men did not capture and hold his attention. With that furtive shift of his deep-set almost black eyes Hugh caught the women, bringing them into sharp focus. Koko Hobbs' girl, his steady, Judy-san, tall thin with long arms and full lengthy legs, always and immediately reminded him of Olive Oyl in *Popeye*.

It was the other one, the other Jo-san, who caught him

71

magnetically: short, shorter even than most Japanee women, sitting next to Dreek, unaware of his underhanded study. Or was she? Hugh quickly recognized her as the one Koko Hobbs had mentioned. She was delicate yet firm, fine boned, full-rounded: petite, he thought. Her hair was cut short around her oval face and, incongruously for her size, she had large high breasts. And hiding playfully and perhaps cunningly behind her eyes was a sort of secretiveness, a sort of I've-got-a-cinch-on-this-hand-look, positivity. It set her apart—quite a way from his ex-shack job in Gotemba who had retreated back to the Army —emanating a true warmth and charm that made Hugh feel like a bungling counterfeiter. He had seen her before, in here, but he did not know her name.

In a few split seconds he had caught all of it, while Mama-san Tokudo and he talked, Hugh only subconsciously with his second mind grinning and answering, joking. Then he straightened up from the bar.

"You be sure and let me know if your old man don't show," he grinned, turned toward the booth, feeling the short stiff bob of necks of the heavy-bellied staff that sat at the bar, paying them no attention, stepped around the dance floor and walked over to the booth, still carrying his bottle.

"Hello, Dreek," he said, not looking at the women. "How's my favorite geek? Been snapping off any chicken heads lately?"

"Welcome to the club, Hugh," Hobbs said. "Sit down." He nodded across the booth.

Grudgingly, Pappy Dreek moved over, crowding the short, capable-looking Jo-san against the wall. "What's all this 'geek' stuff anyway?" he demanded sourly. "What the hell is a geek anyway?"

"Wipe those feathers off your mouth and I'll tell you." Hugh ignored the open spot next to Dreek and pulled a chair up from the vacant table behind him, straddled it and leaned his arms over the back rest. Then he set the full quart of whiskey on the table, catching the eagerness in Dreek's eyes.

The Jo-san who had been pushed against the wall smiled professionally at him. She was wearing a satiny white Hong Kong slit dress. Hugh glanced fleetingly at her, wondering what she looked like from the waist down.

72

"What's happening at the barracks?" Koko Hobbs asked coolly over his tall quart of Nippon Beer. Koko Hobbs said and did everything coolly. He was a cool stud. He had to be, and the coolness always tickled Hugh because on himself it would have been an affectation. "That new bunch all fixed up with bunks?"

"If they ain't by now they're shit out of luck," Hugh said, looking at Koko's pale green eyes and that calculating mind behind them. Whenever he was in a moment of decision his cheeks would twitch as if he were flexing his jaw muscles and his green eyes would give way to hidden lights behind them. None of it detracted from his handsomeness.

"When new men catch liberty?" Judy-san said interestedly. She was wearing a gray cotton suit.

"Maybe Fliday," the short Jo-san said in a deep resonant whiskey voice.

"I wouldn't be a bit surprised," Hugh said. "You want some whiskey?"

"Me no drink whiskey," the girl said in her whiskey voice.

"Yeah?" Hugh questioned. My my, a whiskey-voiced girl who doesn't drink whiskey, my my. "What the hell you drinking that gin for!" he exploded suddenly at Dreek. "When there's good whiskey on the table?"

"I was waitin' for you to offer it to me," Dreek drawled in his thick Texas voice. Horrible Hog Company's armorer, a buck sergeant, was the most efficient man with weapons Hugh had ever known.

"Help yourself, Pappy," he grinned. "It's community property."

"Did you see the new men?" Koko asked as Judy-san lit a cigarette for him. "The ones in the platoon?"

"Nope," Hugh said lazily. "But I seen their record books." He grinned at Koko. "You been thinking about Zorn?"

"Yeah, that's right," Koko said. "Anyone be better than Zorn. It ain't good for the platoon, him being in it. You know that."

"It ain't good him being in the company," Hugh said, conscious of himself being the center of attraction.

"Then whyn't you get him out?"

"Hell, Koko," Hugh said elaborately, "I'm not the gunny sarjint. Have to see Finch about that; or Top Landrum."

"Top *Condrum*, you mean." Koko snorted. "The only way he gets rid of people is sending them to jail." He paused. "But you could fix it. You and Gunner Haley can get the Kizer to fix it. Anyway, you'll be *the* gunny before long."

"That seems to be common knowledge," Hugh countered. "Everybody knows it but me. But it'll never happen, buddy. What would happen to you and the platoon if I became company gunny?"

Koko's eyes faded slightly, and Hugh Thorton read in them that he would say no more about it, at the same time wondering what Koko was working toward. Well, maybe he was pissed off because Hugh held the black market over his head. But to hell with that! Think of the woman there, he told himself, studying her from the corner of his eye.

"Well," Koko said, "I want Zorn out of there, that's all. Maybe as police sarjint or something," he hinted.

"Goddam no!" Pappy Dreek protested. "Not as po-lice sarjint. I'd have that sonfabitch around my armory alla time."

"Are you a beak or a comb man, Pappy?" Hugh said seriously. Buck Sergeant Pappy Dreek's face froze adamantly in Texas belligerence, his wrinkles deeply eroded. "I hear Zorn's a comb man," Hugh chided. "You two ought to get along fine."

"*Toxon baka.*" Dreek circled his finger around his forehead and the two girls laughed. Thorton listened attentively to the whiskey laugh of the short Jo-san with the fathomless eyes.

"How was business tonight, Koko?" he asked suddenly.

"The usual."

"Staying all night?"

"I guess so," Koko answered. "I sure as hell don't want to go back to the barracks."

"How about you, Pappy?" Hugh glanced at the girl again.

Dreek took a long satisfying drink of Hugh's whiskey. "Sure. I had to borrow from the five-for-tenners, but I gotta stay out. Away from the barracks." He looked warmly at the bottle. "This all you got?"

"Yeah," Hugh said. "Go ahead and drink it though. I don't feel much like drinking tonight anyway."

"Well thanks." Dreek took another drink.

"Judy-san," Koko said. "How about getting me another beer?"

74

"Dai jobie," she said dutifully. Koko stood up and Judy-san got out of the booth and walked over to the bar.

"What's your name?" Hugh asked Dreek's girl abruptly, turning his face full on her.

"Mitchiko."

"Do you dance, Mitchiko?"

"Hai."

"Hey goddamit!" Dreek roused himself. "She's my girl, Hugh."

"I ain't going to run off with her," Hugh reassured him. "I'm just going to dance. Finish your drink."

"Oh," Dreek said meekly, but not unwarily, and went back to the bottle.

They walked out to the stone dance floor and began dancing to a slow rhythmical—and glamorous, Hugh thought—number. He remembered it had been popular a year before he left the States. He thought he remembered it from as far back as '51.

"Mitchiko," Hugh said. "You sure are small." She came to about four inches below his chin. "How come they don't call you Chebe-san?" he asked. *Chebe* was the Japanee word for squirt, the little one.

She smiled up at him. "Because my name is Mitchiko."

"You know what my name is?" Hugh said, feeling idiotic.

"Thoton-san?"

"No," he said. "Thorton-san."

"Me *say* Thoton-san," she said doggedly in her low voice.

"You leave out the 'R,' Chebe-san."

"My name is Mitchiko. No Chebe."

"Not even a little bit Chebe?" He grinned. Oh! he was a romantic bastard he was. "Not even a skosh Chebe?"

She laughed then, a deep whiskey-voiced laugh. "Long time you no come around."

Hugh did not remember. In fact he was certain he had never spoken with her before, never had anything to do with her, and it startled him that she had noticed him, flattered him. But she was obviously lying, he thought. She had to play her role, and she was convincing enough for some jerk. He would have done the same thing if he'd been a whore—*business woman*. And suddenly he liked her, more so than before, weightily attracted to her. There was some-

75

thing about her that made him think of himself. Some nice constructive virtues of his that he admired.

"Are you catching Dreek?" he asked.

"He ask me," she said carefully. "He pay."

"Fifteen hundred yen?"

"Hai."

"What if I'd pay more?" He eased with the music, facing himself toward the booth and Pappy Dreek.

She grinned at him. "Me no butterfly. No changee-changee."

"What would you do if he got too drunk to be any good?"

"He have to have place to sleep anyway, *ne?*"

Unable to find an answer to that (he himself would not put a fellow comrade in arms out in the cold), he remained silent through the remainder of the dance. When the music stopped he complimented her suavely on her dancing, and they walked back to the table where Dreek consoled himself with Hugh's bottle.

"Your girl's a good dancer, Pappy," Hugh said.

"She sure is," Dreek stated laconically. Dreek couldn't dance for beans and Hugh knew he seldom danced at all unless he was loop-legged.

Hugh looked at his watch casually. It was almost ten-thirty. The bars would close in half an hour.

"Jesus Christ!" he exploded sharply. "Is that all the whiskey you drink for Chrissakes? If I'd known that I would have kept it for myself."

Obscure guilt and Texas pride spread slowly into Dreek's wrinkled face. "Well," he said, embarrassed. "I didn't want to make a pig outa myself." He took a long drink this time.

"You ain't drinking much at all tonight, are you?" Koko asked.

"I drank too much back at the barracks," Hugh lied. "With Finch."

Koko nodded, dubiously. "Want a beer?"

"Yeah, I'll take a beer."

"Get a couple more beers, Judy-san," Koko said.

While Hugh watched Judy-san walk up to the bar again, a middle-aged Japanese man came in solicitously through the U.S. Bar door, dressed in a flowery kimono and holding a large black rectangular box. Beside him, and slightly behind, was a little Japanee girl no more than seven or eight years old, dressed in an identical kimono with a bright child's face, eager and emotional, almost esthetic. Hugh watched them, curious.

The girl, carrying a record, walked over to the bar and handed it to Mama-san Tokudo. When the music started, Hugh recognized it as an old myth tune and the little girl began dancing in the center of the bar, obviously in an interpretation of the myth.

While this was going on, the older man, ostensibly her father, walked around with the black box accosting the marines.

When he got to Hugh he repeated the spiel he had used at the bar. In the box was an odd assortment of pornography: books, booklets, pictures, stories, eight-pagers. In one corner of the box were some French Ticklers and other clever devices and costumes. The other four at the booth were hypnotically engrossed watching the little girl spin her tale.

Taking advantage of their preoccupation, Hugh bought a French Tickler from the old man and quickly folded it in his hand. The man bowed in thanks and backed away, completing his rounds as the girl danced.

With the dance and business transactions terminated, the old man and the little girl left just as suddenly as they had appeared.

"I never could figure those dances out," Dreek said, summing up eleven years' service. He was drinking faster now and Hugh watched his eyes focus swimmingly.

"You don't understand art, is all," Hugh told him, leaned forward and slipped the French Tickler into Dreek's trouser pocket.

"Maybe not. But that little girl sure is cute though, ain't she?"

Koko Hobbs, on Hugh's left, sat silently appraising him. Nothing ever got by him, Hugh thought. But he knew Koko would not say anything.

With nothing to do now but wait, Hugh nursed his beer, watching the hands on his watch sweep around to five till eleven, not joining in the conversation except for an unconscious "yeah" and a few mind-a-thousand-miles-away nods, becoming increasingly happy over Dreek's sluggishness.

"Better drink up," Hugh prompted. "Bars close in five minutes."

"I can drink in back," Dreek said with finality, but he had a rough time getting the words out.

"You *toxon* stinko." Mitchiko shook her head at Dreek. She had been as silent and noncommittal as Hugh.

"I'm all right, I say," Dreek mumbled.

"Maybe you shouldn't drink any more," Hugh essayed.

"Let's go on back, Mitchiko." Dreek ran his tongue over his lips.

"No go back till bars close." And Hugh thought he saw a faint glimmer of humor in her eyes.

"You going to stay?" Koko asked Hugh. "If you are you better get a dolly before they're all taken."

"I don't feel like that tonight. I think I'll get a room just for sleep." Hugh cast a quick glance at Chebe—*Mitchiko-san*, and curled his mustache.

At eleven o'clock the MP's came in, twins in size and uniform, and fatuously reminded Mama-san Tokudo it was time to close up. Mama-san bowed courteously and followed them to the door and closed it behind them. She snapped off the porch light and shuffled back behind the bar and began putting the empty bottles away.

One by one, Hugh Thorton watched the pairs from the bar move heavy-lidded to the corridor leading to the back rooms as Mama-san snapped off the lights in the front.

"Well," he said, "I guess I'll see about a room."

Koko Hobbs stood up with Judy-san. "Pappy, you ready to go back?"

"You goddam betcha." Pappy Dreek staggered up and waited for Mitchiko. For a moment Hugh thought he might fall. And he didn't want that. Not yet.

"I'll wake you up in the morning," Hugh said to both of them.

"All right," Koko said. "Come on, Judy-san."

Sitting in the semidarkness, Hugh watched them walk off down the corridor, all four of them: Koko and Judy-san sober, Pappy Dreek wavering, using Mitchiko (Chebe-san was a much better name really; he liked it)—using Chebe-san as a support. When they disappeared he got up from the table and walked over to the bar.

"Hey, Mama-san," he said quietly.

The old Japanee woman smiled encouragingly and came out from behind the bar.

"You still got those two fifths I left here about a week ago? When I was with Koko?"

78

"*Hai, hai,*" she said, stooping down behind the bar and proudly raising the full bottles. "No one touchee."

"You're a good old gal," Hugh said affectionately, but he wondered how the hell she had kept them from Papa-san Tokudo? "I want that single room way in the back. By myself. How much?"

"Oh Thoton-san," she said with great sorrow. "Me see maybe me can get Jo-san for you, *ne?*"

"No," Hugh shook his head. "Look, Mama-san. I just want that room for myself, see? I'll pay two thousand yen for it if you do me a favor."

"What you want Mama-san to do?"

"If there's any trouble," Hugh explained carefully, "and that skosh girl, Mitchiko, ain't got a place to sleep, send her down there to my room."

Mama-san looked at him curiously for a moment, then a wide toothy grin spread across her face. "Ah so," she said slowly, wisely. "Me fixee up." She laid her hand on the bar. Hugh lay two one-thousand-yen bills in it.

Quietly, walking on the balls of his feet, clutching the two bottles, he walked back into the corridor. At the end, where it broke off to the separate rooms, he removed his shoes and moved softly down the hall to the last small room in the rear.

Inside, he set the two bottles on the floor, rolled out the straw *tatami* mat, and threw the heavy quilt on top of that. He moved with familiarity in the small room with the single sliding window, smiling to himself.

Meticulously, he took off his cashmere suit, shirt tie skivvies and socks and hung them neatly in the small closet that already was full with another huge quilt. He would not need that one till later. Maybe he wouldn't need it at all? Maybe it wouldn't work, he thought. No, it would work all right. And in the morning Dreek would have forgotten all about it. That was what made life interesting. Mingling with people's lives.

He switched off the single light and, naked, lay down on the first quilt over the *tatami,* the midnight summer heat thick in the room. Leisurely, he uncorked one of the bottles, lit a cigarette, and lay there to wait, lazily.

Pappy Dreek would not be worth a damn anyway, he decided. After all the whiskey he'd consumed out there, he'd be about as useless as a wet rag doll. But if that didn't work, the French Tickler would be the clincher.

Hugh liked old Pappy Dreek. Pappy reminded him a lot of the fools he had dealt to in Vegas for a while—a very short while—between the wars. At that time, in '48, he had been the best blackjack dealer in the house. Pappy Dreek should have learned what he had: you can't beat the dealer.

After two cigarettes and three good slugs under his belt, Hugh was beginning to doubt his own sagacity. Either that or he had misjudged the girl, Chebe-san. She sure had large breasts for such a small girl. He did not think he had misjudged her though. He seldom, he reminded himself, ever misjudged anyone. He prided himself on that. So, the only thing to do was wait!

He lay there not thinking, drowsy, not wanting to think about the Camp or the Company—Horrible Hog Company —or Finch or the new bunch in from Korea. He had divorced that completely when he came out tonight. They would still be there in the morning. No matter where a man slept he always took those things to bed with him, and they were always there when he woke up, enhanced.

When he'd snuffed out his third cigarette, a shriek pierced the paper-thin laminated walls of the bar, followed by two loud clumps, the sliding open of a door and the angry closing of it. Hugh snuggled back under the covers, his back to the door, congratulating himself.

A minute later he heard the padded footsteps of *tabis* on wood coming down the hall, approaching his room. Then his door slid open and he turned abruptly and started blinking, feigning sleep, at the open door.

Chebe-san, still wearing her Hong Kong slit dress, stood there with a furious smoldering indignation on her face, holding an expensive kimono over her arm.

"What's the matter?" Hugh asked innocently.

Glaring hotly, Chebe-san raised her hand and dangled the French Tickler in front of his eyes. "Him no good son-bitch!" she said scathingly, and went on a fitful cursing in Japanee, punctuating each phrase with a hot nod of her head, Hugh catching all the language and interpreting it in his mind, thinking not even he would call old Pappy names like that!

"He tried to use that on *you?*"

"Him no sleep with me no more!" she said fervently in her whiskey voice.

"That *is* a pretty foul thing to do."

"You Hog Comp'ny samey same!" She glared defiantly down at him.

"Now that's not true at all. Why don't you throw that thing away?"

Chebe-san looked at it in her hand as if she had just now discovered it was there, held it up as if it were some poisonous snake and angrily threw it back in the corner of the room. Then she stepped all the way in and slid the door closed behind her.

"You going to sleep here?" Hugh leaned up on his elbows.

"Only room left," Chebe-san said, still a little furious. The hot smoldering look in her eyes remained, and Hugh did not know if it was sincere anger or just plain heat.

"I can't pay you," he said, matter-of-factly.

"No pay," she said, and tossed her kimono down on the *tatami*. "No push push, too. No *mocko*." Then she reached behind her and snapped the light off.

Thinking quick, feeling somehow that Mama-san had played a dastardly cruel trick on him, he sat up crosslegged in the dark. "What'd you turn the light off for? You embarrassed to undress in the light?"

The light snapped back on and Chebe-san glared at him. "Me no embarrass no! goddam you!" She unzipped the white satin slit dress, letting it fall carelessly to the floor. She was wearing no slip, not even a half slip. She reached behind her, still staring into Hugh's eyes, openly, defiantly, unsnapped the brassière, and the foam rubber, two twin cones, fell out on the floor.

Well I'll be go to hell, Hugh thought wonderingly, following the rubber mounds to the floor and watching them bounce and roll. Then he looked back up as Chebe-san shucked out of the tiny silk panties.

She was small and firm (without the stocky hips that most Japanee women have or the country-hardened, work-in-the-rice-paddies-all-day thick legs), letting the panties fall imperviously, exposing the pulsing V, almost hairless, thoroughly Oriental, and the smooth creamy hairless thighs.

Hugh felt his throat constrict. Japanee had the most beautiful complexions of all. Goddamned if they didn't!

"You embarrass!" she taunted.

"Me?"

Impishly, a faint smile on her lips, the first sign of friendliness since she'd come in the room, Chebe-san reached down and snatched the quilt off Thorton. Instinctively, more out of recoil than anything else, he dropped his hands down, catching himself midway, and placed them sheepishly on his thighs.

"You going to stand there all night?" he grinned, congratulating himself on his subtle scoring, thinking Koko Hobbs might be saving her for a rainy day but tonight it was cloudless.

For the first time, Chebe-san grinned back sincerely, widely, but there were still the hot smoldering coals in her black eyes. In one agile movement, she reached behind her and snapped the light off and moved down beside him.

Then she was all over him playfully, giggling at times, cooing at others, whimpering some. At first it startled Hugh momentarily, and then the start quickly vanished. Of all the whores he'd had (and he prided himself on the fact that he could not even make a conservative estimate), this one now was the strangest of all, and he had to admire her professional skill.

With her lying under his weight, nipping at his ear until he thought his head would explode, he wondered how so small a Jo-san could hold up his one hundred and ninety pounds, and then he was lost in the rapture of his own throes.

It was the wildest, most satisfying, singing, insane sex he'd ever had: rolling over and over until the quilts lay forgotten off somewhere in that belly-slapping belly loin pounding loin forgetfulness, while the convulsive tremors shot through his body.

"*Etai! etai! etai!*" she breathed jerkily, biting and clawing. "No come yet! No come yet!"

"Oh Christ!" Hugh was aware somewhere far off of his mustache tickling him. "I got to go! Now!"

Then he was floating out of himself in a long, whimpering, hand-groping thickness, convulsively lost—and immediately shot back into reality as she trembled heavily, her breath caught and choking, and then yelled in a soft and loud, harsh and mellow voice, and for a moment, a timeless second Hugh thought she was dying, had died, the last wincing gasp before the death rattle. Then she was silent again, undulating like a sea of wheat in the breeze, and he felt his own heart clamor with this, a red deepness glinting in his dark eyes.

82

She ran her hands along his back, all the way from his shoulders to his butt, for quite some time. "You've got nice buttocks," she said finally, dreamily.

Hugh chuckled softly.

"Well, you do."

"You're not so bad yourself," he said, one hundred and ninety pounds of dead weight.

"No," she said. "No move yet."

So he lay there for a while savoring it, feeling himself go limp, his own swelling beginning to abate, the heady blood quit pounding so demandingly in him.

Finally, he eased off her as she wiped him off with skivvie paper, and he rolled over on his side, still facing her.

Silent, Chebe-san slipped into her kimono, the lazy blurred lights from outside casting smooth glints on her, and walked quietly out of the room to the familiar water closet where the syringes and tubes and rubber hoses hung heavy with the smell of disinfectant.

Hugh was smoking thoughtfully, reflectively, gathering his strength when she came back and lay down beside him, slipping out of her kimono.

"Tobacco *jodi?*" she asked.

He gave her his cigarette and lit a fresh one. Then he laughed explosively, confused, a belated reaction, almost hysterical.

"Whatsa matta you, *dio?*"

"Where you come from, Chebe-san?"

"Everywhere," she said, girlishly noncommittal. "Where in *Baykoko* you come from?"

"Everywhere."

"You like Mitchiko, *ne?*"

"Sure," Hugh said, thinking: *Chebe-san.* "*Number one.*"

"You come back stay again?"

"With no *okane?*" he said. "No money?"

Chebe-san hesitated, puffing on her cigarette. "Maybe skosh bit," she decided.

Once again, as he had earlier, Hugh felt that thing about her—that certain strong quality—that he admired inside himself. A strange something that made him see more of himself in her. And he wondered if she might possibly see something of herself in him. Those things she liked about herself. For that was what it was, wasn't it? A man could only love what he saw of himself in other people. Reflections, sort of. He had known that all his life. But he had never seen a part of himself in a whore.

"How come you to be a business woman?" he asked, thinking that probably every goddam cunthound in South Camp, or the world for that matter, always asked a whore this—because no one ever asked him why he was what he was. It wouldn't have made any difference; he couldn't have told them.

"How come?" She paused, and he expected to hear a typical run-of-the-mill Old Ma Perkins story. "I like it," she said simply.

"Hunh?"

"I like it," she reiterated. "It's fun. You meet so many new people. It's a good job."

Hugh was caught short by the sudden drop of pidgin into almost perfect American. He hadn't caught it before, had missed it entirely when he was all caught up with himself, but now it was there in front of him pronounced, unmistakable. What the hell is this? A whore who likes being a whore and who speaks damn near faultless American?

Well, why shouldn't she like being a whore? He liked being a whoremonger.

"Where the hell did you learn to speak American like that?"

"Me no speakee Amelican," she said in her whiskey voice.

Hugh laughed softly, a to-hell-with-it-all laugh, and then they were immersed again, with the same identical intensity of the first time, but a more close feeling, and Hugh sketchily contemplated shaving his womb broom off but decided against it. If it tickled it tickled and that was that. He hoped she wouldn't yell again, like the first. He didn't mind admitting that it scared the be-Jesus out of him.

Three more times that night and instead of being worn out as he thought he would, Hugh felt exhilarated, lifted. Whatever it was, there was no swollen hanging feeling between his legs any more.

The third time, the last time, Chebe-san did not douche and she did not wipe Hugh off. Either she was too tired or just didn't give a damn, Hugh thought, and they neither one, through tacit agreement, spoke about anything else. It was weird almost, unearthly—to Hugh at least—and oddly enough he did not really want to talk, found that he couldn't. After the third time she pulled the thick warm quilt over them and they both went immediately to sleep.

In the morning Hugh woke late, too late, and he leaped out of bed and began dressing hurriedly. Chebe-san jumped up and excitedly began jabbering in Japanee to him, and her face spread in astonishment when he answered her in Japanee.

"Where did you learn to speak Japanee?" she said.

"Hell," he said, struggling with his trousers, "I can't speak Japanee."

They both laughed crazily, goofily. To hell with being a little late, he decided, starting to yank his trousers off.

"No no, Thoton-san," Chebe-san warned. "You catchee trouble back at Sous Campo."

"All right goddamit," he said. "Go see if Koko's awake. Get him and Dreek both up."

She eyed him distantly for a moment, nodded okay, and walked out, wrapping her kimono around her.

The life he had left last night now came rushing back in full force on him. The night was over; the playing was done. It was time to start work again, wiring the deck, placing the bets. He'd undoubtedly have to hold muster for Finch. Then he'd have to get those new men all squared away with Gunner Haley's help—that was the problem: getting rid of Zorn and putting in that new man, a something Bohane, as right guide. Get it all set up before they all went on liberty and killed themselves.

4.

Friday, August the fourteenth, Giff Bohane received his first liberty from Horrible Hog Company.

Under the auspices of the payday weekend he felt a quickening of his thighs, a thick scrotum-filled anticipation. The shekels he had brought from Korea plus the $133 payday money (he drew every last penny from the books) gave him a neat wad to explore the hidden subtleties of

Fujioka. And more important, a chance to lower his emotions, scatter them around a bit.

The keyed-up tension of those first three days of getting acclimated had left him wide-eyed and sleepless at night. And the swiftness of the military machine being geared for war, setting up its combinations like a die-in-harness fighter, found him thrown once again into the tight conflicts of "peacetime" preparedness.

During that time he felt much like a man who sees himself in a movie, but one that has no beginning or end. It reminded him acutely of the old now-passé combat films he had seen in boot camp back in '50. Especially the one on Okinawa where the cameraman, through some macabre sense of humor or a reflection of himself, had filmed the Okinawan natives committing suicide leaping from a cliff, then had reversed the camera so that the natives came flailing wildly back up through the air to the top of the cliff, mostly women with babies in their arms, embracing death instead of the liberating marines.

In his own mind Giff saw himself falling through space, kicking and spinning, then being jerked back up from the void, swearing and fighting, never consummating the journey—which in a way was good. Because if he had completed a journey somewhere, he thought, he wouldn't know what to do when he arrived. Still, he felt like the man who invented the Yoyo.

It had taken three days of furious shuffling to get themselves integrated within the ranks of the company and assigned positions in the various platoons.

Giff, as he thought was befitting his talents, was delegated as the right guide of the second rifle platoon. He had no qualms over ousting Buck Sergeant Oscar Zorn from the job (Zorn had been relegated to the Hog Company Police Sergeant). And it was enjoyably clear that the platoon, and in fact, the company, appreciated the shift. No one, it seemed, wanted Zorn anywhere close to the rifle platoons. Even Zorn, who did not fully understand the meaning of the change, took his freshly appointed position in the way the Aga Khan receives his weight in gold, though it did not assuage any of the Swede's blundering uncontrolled noisiness. He could be seen walking around the company area till darkness closed in heavily on his dull uncomprehending face, ferreting out bits of work—picking up cigarette butts, paper, checking the heads to see that each commode was plenteous with toilet paper—as if fanatically possessed with one single-minded drive: *Keep my Horrible Hog Company clean!*

As far as Giff was concerned he felt it was only just that the job should have gone to him, even over the other NCO's of the second platoon who had time and grade in rank and in the company. There was actually only one man who was, Giff felt, a contemporary—or competition. Corporal Jesus Queecho, a deadly little Guamanian (who, it was said, carried a Black Belt in judo and no one disputed this), did have time in grade on Giff. Silent, almost taciturn, with deadly black beady eyes, Jesus Queecho made no comment when Giff got the position over him. Jesus Queecho was good, Giff felt, efficient, a sharp handler of men. But Jesus Queecho did not carry a Silver Star.

He reflected a good deal on his Silver Star in those three days while he waited for his first liberty. The knowledge of his having it, sole possessor of a 68-cent citation, spread through the barracks that first night and by morning everyone knew of it.

When he had gotten up that first morning, shaking his head dumbly like a fish who has deep-swallowed a hook, belly deep, the men had watched him curiously with professional reserve and—to Giff's mind—expectation. He felt as if he should perform some miracle or at least say something profound or soul stirring.

On that first morning, after a rib-sticking breakfast of shit-on-the-shingle, he sat on his bunk smoking silently, watching the platoon scramble around for drill, not knowing what to do, when a S/Sgt walked into the squadbay: impeccable, clean, confident, assuredly handsome. The S/Sgt walked charily around the squadbay, nodding to several of the men, his eyes flicking around until he caught Giff sitting on his bunk and walked over to him. Giff watched him, unsmiling, smoking lazily, thinking about what Poke Turner had said about Staff Sergeant Jack Koko Hobbs.

"Your name Bohane?" Koko Hobbs asked, his jaws twitching thoughtfully.

Giff snuffed his cigarette out in the Planter's Peanuts can by his bunk. "Yeah; that's right."

"I'm Sar'nt Hobbs," Koko said flatly. "The platoon sergeant of this platoon. T/Sgt Thorton is the platoon leader. But I guess someone already told you all that," he grinned, looking around at the suddenly vacant faces in the platoon. Then he turned back to Giff. "You're the new right guide," he said laconically. "But your duties won't start till you been indoctrinated."

Giff nodded, knowing the platoon had heard Hobbs, aware that none of them so much as batted a bloodshot eye over it, and he was partially grateful for this. But he felt a little ill at ease. Maybe they had all known he would step right into a choice spot in the platoon. Giff Bohane, Leader, he thought wryly—and in self-congratulation. "Okay," he said, trying to sound unimpressed and as unconcerned as Koko Hobbs. "I'll get the feel of things in a couple days."

"Sure," Koko Hobbs said. "No rush. We ain't got a war to fight—yet. You take charge of the new men," he said authoritatively, "when you go on indoctrination. It'll start this morning." He turned back toward the bulk of the squadbay, started to walk away, stopped, and looked back over his shoulder. "Almost forgot. The skipper wants to see you. Now."

"Who?"

"Captain Kizer," Koko said, and walked on.

It was only then, after Hobbs had left the squadbay, that Giff remembered how Poke Turner had so aptly put it the night before, *"Hobbs is no idiot atall, and he runs the platoon, not Thorton,"* and Giff could see it now. It was almost as if Koko Hobbs had never even talked to him! As if the conversation hadn't taken place! And yet he knew it had. Hell, he had been right here! But that was what old Poke must have meant. Koko Hobbs was slick all right, so slick he could move around you without even being sensed or noticed; and simultaneously Giff remembered what Poke had said of Thorton, *"But Thorton sees to it that Hobbs runs the platoon the way he wants it."*

Apparently, no one seemed to know who ran the platoon. Especially himself. But he was the right guide—it hit him belatedly, like a bullet, the pain of it coming several seconds after the hit—right guide! Well, it was nothing new. Just a glorified squad leader. But he could not help but wonder how he fit in if no one knew who actually ran the platoon.

Still wearing his Korea-wrinkled dungarees, Giff rose from his bunk, left the barracks, feeling strangely familiar

88

in the early-morning hot sun rays, and walked over to the company office to see Captain Kizer.

Horrible Hog Company's office was a half barracks located between the rifle platoon barracks and the machine-gun mortar platoon barracks. It was the same as last night when he'd come in, and yet it looked different in the morning, a part of him now—or maybe he was a part of it.

A short flight of wooden steps led up to a sliding window that was the door, large enough to walk through stoop-backed. Feeling like a man walking to the scaffold after tying the thirteen knots in the rope himself, Giff climbed up the steps, slid the window-door open, and stepped down into the office.

"I'm supposed to see Cap'n Kizer," Giff said unobtrusively, thinking *they* had found out about *them* drinking outside the barracks, and that they were not going to waste any time in court-martialing him. Visions of brigs danced worriedly through his mind, the old ingrained intimidation of military authority looming within him. "Is he in?" he asked, amid the clack of typewriters and early-morning furor, a tall slim brown-wavy-haired Pfc with a hungover look. The nameplate on the Pfc's desk read: QUILLER CARPENTER USMC.

"The Kizer?" Quiller Carpenter looked up vaguely. "Oh, sure. What's your name, Corporal?"

"Bohane. Giff Bohane—1444004."

"From Korea?"

"Yeah." Giff looked around at the small office. The M/Sgt who had called off the names when they'd come in was nowhere around. Another clerk, a corporal, stood detachedly over a file cabinet across the office.

Quiller Carpenter looked hard at the confused pile of record books and papers on his desk. Hand shaking visibly, he reached for the steaming cup of coffee on his desk. "I can't find your record book," he said without effort. Then he grinned up at Giff. "I can't find anything this early in the morning. You see that corporal over there?" He jerked a dispassionate thumb across the narrow office at the prissy-looking corporal in starched dungarees still leafing through the file cabinet.

"See him?" Giff asked.

"Yeah," Quiller Carpenter said with unconcealed humor. "Maybe he can fix you up."

Giff walked over and got a better view of the corporal: smooth-faced, skinny, with feminine features. He looked down at the nameplate on the corporal's desk. It read: SOLOMON KING USMC. Inverted, Giff thought, in the military sense, it would read KING SOLOMON. Jesus! what an outfit. He looked back at Carpenter. The slim Pfc was grinning like a shit-eating cat. Automatically, Giff grinned back.

"You got a record book for me?" he asked, turning back to the corporal at the filing cabinet.

The corporal looked up, as if he was just then aware of Giff's presence. "I don't know," he said prissily. "Just what is your name?"

Oh Jesus Christ, Giff thought glumly. "Bohane," he said. "Corporal Gifford Cael Bohane—1444004."

"Yes," King Solomon said, businesslike. "But I don't have it sorted on file yet. After all," he said, "you just arrived last night."

Looking at him, Giff felt his anger rising steadily, that old innate half-Irish rebellion, and took a deep breath. "Corporal, just let me know if I can see Cap'n Kizer. That's what I'm here for," he bored. "If I don't need a record book just show me the hell in, hunh? But quit givin' me this goddam fucking around."

"You don't have to get nasty about it," King Solomon said stiffly, a hurt no-one-understands-me look on his face. "Come with me. I'll see if Captain Kizer is ready for you."

"Thanks."

King Solomon rapped lightly on the private door of the company office, opened it and stepped in one pace. "Corporal Bohane to see you, sir."

"Send him in!" a voice boomed out of a bottomless well and Giff recalled Stack Renshaw's story: 'Charge that tank!' with fixed bayonets. The shit-on-the-shingle turned queasily in his stomach.

Corporal Solomon stepped aside as Giff snatched off his dungaree cap and walked in, holding the worn cap at his side. "Corporal Bohane reporting as ordered, Sir." His eyes fixed over the figure sitting at the desk.

"At ease, Corporal! At ease!" the voice boomed again as Giff heard the door shut behind him. He spread his feet eighteen inches, clasped his hands behind his back, more at Parade Rest than At Ease, and looked down, not expecting what he saw, not after Stack Renshaw. Captain Emil Kizer sat hugely at his desk, large boned and large featured with a cropped bullet head, graying, and combat-hardened eyes. There was a certain Prussian stubbornness about him; he looked every inch the military and Giff thought he did not look half as old as Stack had made him out to be, until he looked closer and saw the tired yellow in the two war-ravaged eyes.

"Pull up a chair there, Corporal!"

A shade ill at ease, Giff sat down, sitting almost at attention.

"How do you like H Company by now?" Emil Kizer demanded, holding a shiny black swagger stick with a gold .50 shell casing on the thick end and the sleek slug on the other, clutching it tightly like salvation.

Giff cleared his throat. Might as well lie. "What I've seen I've liked, sir," he said. "Of course it's still a little unfamiliar yet." He tried desperately to sound intelligent, but only succeeded in sounding foolish to himself.

"It's a good company," Kizer exploded proudly. "I've never had a company yet that wasn't the best. That's my belief. If you don't have the best you might as well not have one at all, right?"

"Why, yes, sir," Giff agreed.

Emil Kizer leaned back in his swivel chair and locked his hands behind his bullet head. "I've molded a perfect line company here," he said, and his battle-ravaged eyes lit up. "When and if we go back to combat—and I don't think it'll be too long, eh?—this company, *my* company, will make the others look sick. That's because I take pride in it, eh? I owe the Marine Corps that." He looked at Giff demandingly.

"Oh yes, sir," Giff said, unable to move his eyes, wanting to badly. We each of us in our own small way owe the Marine Corps a great deal, he thought, thinking of his unrequited Undesirable Discharge they had tried to give him in the States—how long ago? He wondered did the Kizer know about that too? Probably not. It was taken from his record book when he shipped over. But they still had it in Washington, D.C., didn't they, as their ace in the hole? They sure as hell did.

"I've been informed that you received the Silver Star in Korea," Kizer snapped. Giff silently cursed and adulated the military grapevine. Maybe the old bastard went through all the record books. No, he didn't think so. It would be someone else. How about King Solomon?

"Yes, sir," Giff answered. "On Vegas."

"Ah yes," Kizer said nostalgically. "Vegas. After my time of course. *I* was with the Brigade."

"That was rough, sir."

"That it was, Corporal, that it was. I daresay a bit rougher than Vegas or anything after '51." Kizer's eyes seemed to throw out glints of shrapnel. "But I suppose you men had some dandies yourself."

"Yes, sir." Dandies, that's for sure. Real dandies all right.

"I haven't had a chance to read your citation at all yet," Emil Kizer exploded apologetically. "How about some coffee?"

"Say what . . . Oh! Yes, sir! Coffee. Fine, sir."

Emil Kizer rose massively to his feet and in two heavy strides was across his office standing in front of a small table where a mess hall aluminum pitcher steamed with hot coffee on a pre-World War I hot plate.

Giff followed the powerful man over, thinking it wouldn't be right if the Kizer brought his coffee back to him. He took his black, then went back and sat down.

The Kizer stood at the coffee mess holding a can of evaporated milk, its drippings congealed on the edges of the twin punctured holes. Giff wanted suddenly to go on liberty bad.

"What was it you did?" Kizer demanded. "To get the medal?"

Giff took a thoughtful, reflective sip of his coffee. "I killed seventeen gooks the first day on Vegas," he said, not without pride. "Personally accounted for. Then I—uh—helped pull some wounded off the hill and—uh—took over my platoon after our lootenant got it with a mortar and uh—I encouraged the men to hold their perimeter and kept their morale up. But it was mostly for killing the seventeen gooks," he repeated doggedly.

"You don't say!" Kizer erupted. "I myself got the Navy Cross on Guadalcanal. I was with the first Raider Battalion. Got a Purple Heart there, too. Got my first Heart on Nicaragua."

Nicaragua? Giff thought, searching his mind. That was long before he was even born! Long before he was even an opaque gleam in his old man's eye. Fascinated, he looked at the ancient man in front of him who—it hit him forcibly—was his contemporary! "I guess I was lucky, sir. I never got a Heart. Never got a wound. Not one."

"You don't say!" Kizer roared. "A bit lucky I'd say."

"Yes, sir."

When the old man had poured his coffee, he had taken a stained teaspoon heaped with sugar apparently to add to his coffee. Now he stood holding it as if he was unaware it was in his hand.

"Well, maybe you'll get one in this next war." Kizer looked down at his spoon then. With Prussian fastidiousness he poured three-quarters of the sugar back into the bowl, dropped the remaining dab into his coffee and stirred it up.

Giff thought he should have said "I hope so, sir." The Kizer would probably have liked that. "I wouldn't be a bit surprised, sir," he said instead, still watching the Kizer curiously. The beefy man looked at his now-empty spoon, then suddenly stuck it back in the sugar bowl bringing it scooping full again, studied it for a moment, poured half of it back in the bowl and the rest in his coffee.

"Have you been informed of your position in my company?" Kizer demanded.

"Well, yes I have, sir," Giff said, unsure. "If you mean in Sar'nt Thorton's platoon?"

"Exactly! Ordinarily I wouldn't want to place a lesser rank in as Right Guide. But I believe I'll get better results from you. Zorn was all right. A good sergeant. But he didn't have the combat experience. And he's an ex-Army man," the Kizer said in loud disgust.

"Oh really, sir?" Giff wondered how the Kizer had known about him being right guide so fast? Who had told him? Hobbs? And Giff watched him pour a third spoonful of sugar in his coffee, this time not bothering to put any back in the bowl. Then with the can of milk in his other hand, he poured in an excessive amount of cream. And quite suddenly turned from the coffee mess and in two steps was back in his chair behind his desk, the creamy sugar-laden cup sitting on the small coffee mess, completely forgotten.

"No," Kizer blasted. "Zorn is a noncombatant. You may have already guessed that the Third Marines has sent most of its noncombatants to Korea. And brought all you men over here. I can proudly say that my company is ninety per cent combatant!"

"Well, that's good!" Giff said excitedly, feeling the electricity-charged air the Kizer exuded keying him up.

"And like I said: Zorn is an ex-soldier. If you know what I mean," Kizer winked one of his eyes, slyly. "But there's nothing we can do about that."

"No, sir!"

"Now, Corporal Bohane, I don't think you'll have any trouble in the second platoon. If you do, just let me or Sarjint Hobbs or Thorton know about it. Hobbs is an excellent Staff NCO—trustworthy and gets his job done well. You shouldn't have any trouble with him!"

"No, sir!"

"You may have already heard this camp is not the best in the world!" Kizer thundered. "But by God it's fine enough for the Fleet Marine Force! We have excellent training grounds. And by this time next week when we're all set up we'll have some damn rough training. I mean to see that my company is sharp—the sharpest of the sharp, right?"

"Yes, sir!"

"You'll have liberty explained to you during your course in indoctrination. Fine liberty area this." Kizer's battle-trained eyes narrowed. "As good as anything you had in Kyoto on R 'n R!"

"Yes, sir!" Giff said exuberantly. "I've already heard about it!"

"Even for me!" Kizer roared. Then he chuckled foxily. "I may not be as good as I once was but I'm as good *once* as I ever was, eh?"

Giff felt groggy, pounded. "Yes, sir!" He put his empty cup back on the little mess table.

"Well, that's all for now!" Kizer pummeled. "I'm a good judge of character and I know you won't cause any trouble in my company. If you have any problems at all don't hesitate to see me. In person!"

Giff rose to his feet and snapped to attention. He felt his heels should have clicked and he should have bowed or something. Emil Kizer picked up his personalized swagger stick and began tapping his beefy hand thoughtfully, looking out the window, almost in a daze. "That's all, Corporal!"

Executing a perfectly military yet natural about face, Giff walked out of the office and closed the door behind him. He felt as if he'd been in an automatic washing machine, or some mangy powerful dog had clamped his jaws

94

on the scruff of his neck and shaken him senseless. It was a sensation of swimming hard under water.

Shaking his head, he gradually came back into himself, aware of the industrious sounds of the office, his senses back to normal operating procedure, and saw a tall, slim, heavy-shouldered T/Sgt with a black handlebar mustache, dressed in tailored dungarees and spit-shined boondockers under leggins bleached white, sitting half on Quiller Carpenter's desk. Giff did not need a second look to know who it was.

Hugh Thorton swung his dark deep-set eyes on him.

Giff set his cap firmly on his head and walked over to the inside stairs leading up to the window door by Quiller Carpenter's desk.

"How's the Kizer this mornin'?" Carpenter grinned.

"I'm not sure," he said absently. "All right; I guess."

"How you like being platoon guide?" Hugh Thorton said over the smoke of his cigarette.

Giff studied the faultless tips of the mustache. "I ain't had a chance to find out yet, Gunny," he said, still wondering who ran what around Hog Company—*Horrible* Hog Company?

"You might have to change diapers for some of the troops, but you'll get along all right," Hugh Thorton said. "You won't have any trouble at all with that *medal* of yours." He grinned in such a way that his mustache swept upward in mocking contempt, like two sharp spears.

"That's what everyone tells me," Giff grinned back, but there was no validity in the emotion and he knew they both saw this. King Solomon sitting across the company office neither looked up at the conversation nor appeared to be listening. Giff looked out the window at the troops lining up in formation for indoctrination.

"You better make that formation, Corporal," Thorton said to him, "if you want to be indoctrinated. Or you won't get any liberty."

"I guess so, Gunny," Giff said, acting impervious to Thorton, feeling like an ass but still trying to smile genuinely! Sometimes it got so goddam hard . . . He started up the stairs.

"You almost got put in D'Agastino's platoon," Thorton stopped him.

"Yeah?" Giff said. "What platoon is that?"

"Machine guns."

"No thanks, Gunny," Giff grinned wryly. "I had enough of those in Korea."

"I know it. I know all about it. I figure you be better off in a rifle platoon. I like to be fair," he said, mocking. "Did the Kizer tell you to see him if you had any troubles?"

"Yeah; that's right." Giff wondered what kind of deal he was getting.

"I'll give you some good advice," Thorton said evenly. "You got any bitches at all, see Hobbs; don't see Gunny Finch or the Kizer. You'll get along a lot better."

"Well thanks, Gunny," Giff said. "If I have any tough shit bitches I think I'll take 'em to the chaplain. Ain't that what he's here for? I wouldn't want to ace him outa job."

Quiller Carpenter chuckled delightedly as Thorton's mustache dipped, his eyes going black under his beetling brow. "I'm telling you for your own good, *Hero*." He curled his mustache skillfully with both hands. "Let your conscience be your guide."

Giff looked back at him feeling a dingy pall in the air, a hint of some intangible foreboding in clean starched dungarees curling a sharp handlebar mustache. "It always has been," he lied, and walked on out.

The three days' indoctrination were—to Giff at least—unbearably painful, but it kept all of them away from the rigors of the company, the field, the inspections, the troop and stomp that they all so combatively hated, tried to hold off; but they knew eventually they would be inflicted with the peacetime monotony. Even though they all knew—had been told repeatedly by their superiors—that there was no such thing as a peacetime marine corps. It was becoming damn hard to swallow. Especially since they saw it around them all day. It was only the sweet honey-tasting thought of liberty, the town and the *women*, whom, he knew, were his salvation, that kept Giff plodding along over the three days. Anything, he decided, was worth a chance to see up close, to touch and feel the shaded hollows and swelling triangles of the women he had seen lining the streets—in Fujioka.

It was that single goading fact, the prospect of the women (always the women that motivated him) over and above anything else that made the indoctrination physically bearable. And with that in front of him he resigned himself to survive the three-day crucifixion.

So he listened, along with the rest of them, to the soporific lectures by the chaplain, who expounded heartily on the importance of maintaining virtue. It was not like Korea, the chaplain informed them. In Korea, it seemed, the prostitution of virtue was pardonable because they were defending (here the chaplain paused) . . . well, they were defending—well, Democracy! That was it, Democracy. So it was pardonable and God-forgivable if they, in a tight moment, ran off to the boonies with a Sheba between fire fights, because it was for the righteousness of Democracy. The end, the chaplain said, justified the means, and catching that in a sort of acute drowsiness Giff wondered—simultaneously thinking of the women—just what the end had been?

It was all too obvious, Giff could see by the faces of the other men, especially on Cinamo Dallas' killer's face which during the lecture was smirking disdainfully, that the chaplain did not believe what he said and the men never had believed it—and never would! You could no more tell a dying man he wasn't dying, Giff thought, than you could tell a living man he was not invulnerable. Neither of them believed you, and in fact Giff had to admit that he himself, though he'd been shot at a good many times, still firmly believed in his own immortality.

Nevertheless, he listened to the lectures, all of them, the whole three days—about the only thing he could do with a lecture: Listen. And he knew that the other men, the whole kit-and-kaboodle of them, found it distasteful too.

And with that he devised a sort of playday iron-clad defense. Mounting his 68-cent soapbox with his God HoTi, he found warmth in his own observing self, his own imperiousness, and looked down on the indoctrination lectures with a wry condescending bullishess and total revolt within himself. He thought of it as a sort of non-aggression pact between himself and the things he could not alter—or even fight against, really. Inertia, it seemed, and his own thoughts were his absolute weapons. So all along with the lectures he sat smugly and bitterly, listening, playing his own game with it all, thinking ruttishly about the women.

The chaplain repeatedly informed them of the shame, degradation, and punishment if they picked up a fat juicy case of venereal disease. The Kingdom of God would not accept unregenerates. Besides, the chaplain pointed out, what would their families, their mothers, think of them if

97

they got VD and took it home with them—which drew an unheard laugh from all of them who thought only of the barracks as home and could not conceive of their buddies turning against them because they happened to have VD. But for force the chaplain tossed in the fact that any man with three VD charges against him was in position to receive an Undesirable Discharge.

No matter what, Giff thought playing the game, listening to the Navy Commander chaplain, there was always intimidation, but he was getting pretty damn sick of that. It was time they brought something else in. Something other than the threat of being run up with the morning colors; perhaps, instead of death or prison or hellfire, they could instead lose their little pinky? or a small toe? In his mind, Giff rewrote the UCMJ covering the various punishments, replacing them with minor, if austere, short-lived sentences. Like for a dose of clap, perhaps the victim would receive a loss of one square inch of skin off his ass. He thought that was a just punishment, and besides, who would ever miss any skin off his ass?

Along with the lectures, they sat through three films on VD, which most of them enjoyed vicariously, watching the women proposition an unsuspecting marine, snickering at most of it with the knowing nudges of who-they-trying-to-kid winks. There was always Salvation Penicillin, the Queen of the Orient.

One Japanee film was horribly grotesque; obviously, the Japanee did not have a Hollywood Censorship Board because the film had been taken in VD Wards with real people, not actors! For ten minutes after the movie Giff thought he would become an ascetic, not wanting his dingus to rot off, or else rely on his hand.

"Hell," Cinamo Dallas told him during the smoking break following the movie outside the camp chapel. "I've had all that before. Skinning off the root, I call it. It ain't such a much."

They had other classes on the Penalty of Black Market. Listening, Giff felt suddenly that everything everywhere was being run by intimidation—not just the Crotch. Maybe the Crotch had picked it up from the Russians? or the churches? or the schools? And it was a weapon. For every "sin" there was a punishment, and it seemed that living to them, whoever they were, was a "sin." In fact, as he listened to the young-faced college graduate CID Officer, he realized be-latedly that they were always threatened with the punish-ment first before they were told what they should not do, before they were told they should not live. It was a star-tling revelation, one he had been aware of all his life but had never truly seen, and he half wondered why he had never seen it till now. That came from living in a police state, he guessed.

But on with the black market! Now take a man, an aver-age marine, who deals in the black market. And he is caught—by the CID? Well, instead of life imprisonment or whatever it was they handed out, suppose the culprit re-ceived instead . . . a black mark branded on his fore-head! Only painful for a few minutes, make it in the form of a cross, and he would still be able to serve in the ranks! No jail! Or, if it called for it, they could lop off a number of fingers according to the size of his black market and then teach him to shoot a rifle left-handed, a sort of left-handed gun. That way, Giff suggested to Dallas, the marine would still be able to fight.

"He might do that," Dallas half agreed. "But how would he fight if he was a ha-bitch-ual fuckup? Sooner or later he'd lose both hands."

"Well," Giff said seriously, "then he could mount a rocket launcher on his back, be a sort of portable cannon."

"I'll write Washington in the morning," was Dallas' re-ply.

Following the CID Officer came a film made in Holly-wood starring Don Taylor, whom Giff remembered along with several other actors and actresses, all of them promi-nent. Fittingly, the movie was a tell-all version of the old venerated marine phrase: *"You can't buck City Hall,"* but Giff felt he could always shit on their doorstep.

Don Taylor, after being kicked out of the Navy, served two years in Leavenworth, became an alcoholic, a pick-pocket, a sneak thief, a pimp, and finally naturally a rapist, and sent back to Prison. Giff found himself pulling for old Don all the way through.

"I'd of had him become a admiral or something," Giff told Dallas. "Naw," he decided, "not that. Maybe the best pickpocket in America. That'd be something to be proud of."

"Yeah," Dallas said. "He wouldn't like being a admiral. I was him I'd a stayed a pimp."

"Maybe," Giff laughed. "But he sure had a ball before they finally got him."

"To hell with him," Dallas said. "Let's get on over to the PX and pick up a can of Vy-enna sausages. All these lectures makin' me hungry."

"You don't know the half of it," Giff said, thinking of the women again.

They received lectures from just about everybody in any way connected with "Sins": black market, VD, not writing to their mothers; a corps that prays together stays together (Giff improvised his own little ditty: a man who plays with himself stays with himself); a short lecture on God and the Christian fulfillment of life—the good life and the good living, don't mingle with the prostitutes or ye shall inherit eternal damnation roasting in Hell. The vengeance of the Lord is not penicillin, the chaplain pointed out, and he rounded that one out by leading them with a rousing "Onward Christian Soldiers."

The final lecture, conducted on Thursday afternoon, the last lap they had all been waiting for, concerned getting along with the Indigenous Personnel of Japan.

Listening to this one Giff could only wonder what the hell? Here they were being told they were guests of this country here on good will and should conduct themselves accordingly, without malice, and without any trouble, angelic. It was almost howlingly funny, Giff thought. Here was a hand-picked (a leprous hand perhaps, but nevertheless a hand) mass of men, ostensibly the finest in their country, the world's finest fighting organization, the recruiting posters said, sitting in a foreign country waiting to fight a war sometime, someplace, for someone (the soap manufacturers, hunh? The ones who relied on coconuts?), spending their money freely each payday to bolster the Japanee economy and probably eventually having to fight right alongside the Japanee against China or some other so-called Heathen Race. And now they were being told to conduct themselves accordingly, like junior G-men, so the people would get a good impression of the American way of life. Democracy builders, Good Will ambassadors, with rifles, bayonets and bandoliers, and a killer's instinct. About the only good will he could think of, listening to this one, was good will to the "business women" and instead of peace on earth, which threatened his profession—piece on a *tatami!*

So what the hell was all this good will crap anyway,

hunh? Giff wondered, summing it all up on his 68-cent soapbox. Did the sonsbitches giving the lectures actually believe all of that themselves? Had they convinced themselves it was true? He doubted that, and anyway he wasn't about to be convinced. Nor were any of the others by the looks on their faces.

"Well," Dallas said philosophically, "they get paid by the same people you and me do."

"That don't mean they got to try and brainwash us!"

"They couldn't do that in a million years," Dallas said. "They got to have somethin' to work with first."

A month later, when he found out from the Jo-sans in town that the chaplain had a special shackjob on the sly, Giff happily marked up a score for his side.

Also, during those three days, they had a chance to get acquainted with South Camp, snare the feel of their environment. And they were not surprised at the smallness of it, firmly and unshakably squatting in an octagonal shape, enclosed with high barbed wire, that had been cut unbelievable times for rice paddy liberty. Only the Third Battalion, Third Marines and one company of tanks, Charley Tanks (Chicken-shit Charley it was called) were located at South Camp.

Giff had already heard about Charley Tanks and the Tankers from Straight Scoop Turner, who let it be known that he "knew every hog path for five square miles," and the Tankers in his estimation would do well to clear the hell out! For some unannounced reason, Poke Turner hated the Tankers implacably. Giff thought it must have something to do with Korea, when he and Dallas were with the Brigade.

And Poke Turner, not to miss out on anything, made up a song about them when he had first arrived. (Poke was a singer of the first wine, and wasted no time extolling his throaty merits. In his high Georgian drawl he spent most of his spare time singing: ballads, folk tunes, and little sham bits he had made up.) The song, Poke said eloquently to Giff and Dallas the second night when they had pressed sets of khakis and had gone to the slop chute, was an especial song that he Poke firmly believed would someday be taken up by the Crotch as the Marines Hymn:

> *I didn't know she had a chancre,*
> *She musta caught it from a Tanker*
> *And they called our love a South Camp affair . . .*

That was just one of Poke Turner's repertoire, and when he finished he sat proudly over his beer can, his eyes glinting.

When Horrible Hog Company had been paid that Friday morning following the indoctrination course, they all of them broke up into groups of twos and threes and sixes and sevens for gambling. Of course, they had to wait in line moving slowly but inexorably into the staff quarters where Lt. Van Preter, whom everyone called Van Prick, a Yale graduate, was the pay officer and with his customary "Don't thank me, men; you've earned it," Yale dramatics, gave them their pay.

It drew a laugh out of Giff when he got outside and pocketed his money. Lt. Van Preter acted as if he was everyone's father. Lt. Van Preter was only twenty-two, and he was wont to refer to men like Pappy Dreek, who was ten years his senior, as "boy." In fact, comparatively, Lt. Van Preter and all the other college ROTC inductee officers were the youngest men in the camp. It always pissed Giff off when he heard them calling the combatants "boy."

Giff did not do any gambling that day although he hungered to feel the cards and dice in his hands. He was too busy getting his own gear straightened up for liberty; and with the imminent hazy unreal forms of women in his mind —only a few hours away now!—it was enough to satiate the craving for gambling.

Wistfully, he watched the cards being dealt on the bunk blankets around the squadbay and listened to the dice rattle faintly against the sideboards in the head with watery voices playing a losing background music, the stony silence of the winners who would not harpoon their luck by talking about it. (Dallas, Giff had seen when he went to take a piss before turning to cleaning his rifle, was winning a big hunk; as usual, he thought sweatily.)

So he sat cleaning his filthy rifle amid the bluster of talk and the payday holiday atmosphere, waiting for liberty call. He wanted to be all set when they went to the field Monday, have nothing to worry about over the weekend.

At four-thirty in the afternoon when liberty call went, Giff showered, shaved and donned a fresh set of tropical worsteds, sat back down on his bunk again to wait for Dallas' final toss of the dice.

Poke Turner and Stack Renshaw, both of them not winning so much as a satisfied mind, had gone nervously over to the slop chute to ease the pain of defeat with cold beer.

Giff sat on his bunk, replete with ribbons and medals all new and shiny, the brass on his belt buckle gleaming with the magic of a Blitz Cloth—clean, rawboned and sharp, watching the rapidly dispersing troops walk laughing cursing loud silent out of the squadbay, and wondering why now after so long a wait he was no longer in a hurry to go on liberty? Maybe it was because it was now immediately in front of him, three days of it!—and he wanted to wait, savoring the tangible feel of it, able to relax now because he felt he was finally being returned to his eternal place of existence.

Cinamo Dallas came walking lazily out of the head, grinning, coldly vain, military script thick in his hands.

"You ever lose?" Giff grinned.

"I don't know what the word means." Dallas tossed his dungarees on his bunk. "But they's a couple sharpers in there from Gruesome George Company won't ever forget what it means." Snickering slyly, he began dressing in his uniform, pressed and clean, and spit-shined shoes. Giff wondered how much Dallas had paid to some jarhead to be his valet. He had never seen the tall quarter Cherokee work on his gear.

The mid-August heat hung stale in the air of late afternoon when they checked out their liberty cards. An occasional whiff of the honey-bucket man drifted in from the rice paddies. Far off, along the jagged black peaks of the Fossa Magna Range, black-bellied clouds scudded slowly to the east, a pregnant hint of rain promising to bring a freshness to the camp.

They had both started sweating before they reached the slop chute and had taken off their ties, sticking them neatly under their belts, and turned back the cuffs of their shirt sleeves, both casting a wary eye for any officer who might happen along and reproach them for their flagrant disregard for regulations.

When they passed the PX, Giff felt his pace quicken involuntarily, increasing as they neared the slop chute and heard the packed din of voices over the blaring jukebox and the tinny rattle of empty beer cans.

Dallas opened the screen door and Giff followed him in feeling at once and obscurely a heavy sense of giddy superiority, like an errant husband pulled to the bosom of his all-forgiving wife. He let the screen door slam shut behind him and stood just inside the door, adjusting his eyes to the comparative dimness of the slop chute. Two large fans whirled softly on the high ceiling, swirling the thick beery talk-filled cigarette smoky air around the tables and booths where khaki-dressed troops sat, pugnacious and flushed faced, arms laid heavily on tables, pisscutters pushed back on their foreheads, swapping lives and lies, each throwing a clenched fist out at the threatening arm of Monday.

The three Japanee men, whom Poke referred to as the Three Stooges, were sweating laboriously behind the small counter, opening cans for the long khaki queue of perpetually thirsty men. Stacked behind them on wooden shelves were brightly colored cans of soda pop, dust covered, forgotten, rows of tin bastards at the family reunion.

It had all of it, Giff thought in those few fleeting seconds, changed from that first time he had been in the slop chute two nights before. It had not been busy then, when everyone was broke. Now it was payday, the twice a month date that each man timed his life by, the rudimentary germ of the Wesak Festival: the forces of all infinity showering foamily through the slit tops of cans, where walls crumbled with the combative thought of destruction; and edifices rose from the burned-up seas in the spiraling creativity following the devastation, and in all the hard bitter cynical smiling faces of the elbow benders, the kings and servants, the killers and the killed, the raped and the rapists, the living legends, and the dead never remembered, unrecognized, those who had never made the trek to the tree to scratch their mark just one notch higher than the last, and those whose marks were always imbedded higher up the tree, insatiable—in all of it Giff saw himself, in every dead and every living, in every raper and every raped, his mark high on the tree, and his decaying body ten million light years from the tree. Then all the noises and laughter boomed back, awakening him, and he was aware of the fans overhead sweeping a breeze across his face.

"You see Poke or Stack anywhere?" he had to yell behind Dallas, who was passively scanning the slop chute.

"I think they's probably out back; on the tables," Dallas yelled back without turning.

They walked through the thick air to the screen door going out to the picnic tables in back, Giff feeling the adrenaline pounding in him hard, playing a drum solo *cash in your chips as a time expired man* boom boom boom behind his glinting eyes. And he was able to forget momentarily that Monday he would be back as right guide of the second platoon.

Proud, but not exceptionally conceited, he was aware of the lean florid faces turning to scan the Silver Star on his shirt above his Korean ribbons. He swaggered a little.

Out back, sitting on a rickety rain-worn and sun-dried picnic table, staring off across the rice paddies through the high barbed-wire fence that encompassed the camp, Stack Renshaw and Poke Turner were working their way through a case of beer. There was another man sitting with them whom Giff had seen around the company but he did not know his name. Several other men drank at other tables, leaning sitting standing.

"Hey!" Poke called. "Come on over chere and set your asses down!"

"How much beer you got left in there?" Giff asked.

Stack Renshaw peered in the case. "We got to get some more, by God. We're sure drinkin' fast!"

"I'll get the motherfuckers," Dallas offered. Giff turned around to give him some script but he was already going through the screen door.

"Take this." Poke held up a frosty can of Budweiser, and grinning happily Giff took the can and drank in one unbroken motion and sat firmly down on the old table.

"Hi!" the man whom Giff did not know said exuberantly.

"How are you," Giff nodded, feeling suddenly dwarfed beside the man, who towered over him. He was six ax handles across, no neck, just a square head set on wide thick shoulders. He was not, Giff thought, over six feet tall, but he was so enormously solid he looked taller; and out of his square face loomed a huge ax-blade nose that stuck out like a rock, like a piece of red coal in a snowman's face.

"This Willy Woechowski," Poke introduced him. "He's in machine guns."

"Ohh, yeah?" Giff said. D'Agastino's platoon. Did he have all men that big? Willy Woechowski would have been an asset to any platoon—or anyone! Hell, he could probably carry a Fifty and two light Thirties. Jesus, he'd hate for that sonfabitch to get a hold of him!

Willy was concentrating on Giff's ribbons. "What's that there?" he asked, with just a trace of abashment.

"This?" Giff looked down at his ribbons. "This top one is a Silver Star."

Willy looked at it admiringly, started to say something and stopped, as if he could not formulate his thoughts into words. "That's all right," he said finally.

"What time you wanna cut a choge?" Poke asked with the air of a man who is throwing a party.

"Hell, I dunno," Giff said and tossed off his beer, beginning to cool off. "Might's well wait till it gets darker. And cooler."

"That's what I was thinking," Poke agreed.

"It ain't what I was thinking," Stack said. "I ain't had a piece of ass in almost a week!"

"Well Jesus Christ!" Poke said good-naturedly. "You'll have three days to make up for it; the whole weekend."

"You going out too, Willy?" Giff said, grinning at Poke.

"Yeah; you damn rights!" Willy laughed boisterously. "At's my town out there."

"You might's well come along with us," Giff offered.

"I'd like that all right," Willy said happily.

With debonair flourish, Poke Turner tossed an empty can into the case. "Willy has a hard time with the women," he grinned. "Evertime he goes to town they see him and whoop 'Too beeg! Too beeg.'" Poke bugged his eyes in mock amazement.

Giff laughed. "Too beeg, hunh Willy?"

"Ahhhh," Willy grumbled, shifting his weight, the table rocking slightly.

"That's one hell of a long line in there." Cinamo Dallas came up behind them quietly and set the full case of opened cans on the table.

"I thought you got lost in there," Poke said reaching for a fresh beer.

Leaning his elbows on his thighs, holding his beer in both hands, drinking quietly, Giff stared out through the fence as the faint lingering of red sunset moved through the valley on the other side of the wire. The crickets and insects began to chirp harshly, competing with the bubbling shallow rapids of the creek that twisted through the valley. From up the creek, the first promising sound of evening laughter mingled with the unrecognizable music carried

106

down from the bars of Fujioka. Lights began to burn in the town, the first call of liberty hung pleasurably in the air with the delicious smell of wood and charcoal smoke and the delicate whispers of ten-cent perfume.

Through the screen door of the slop chute behind him he could hear the caterwauling music from the jukebox, mourning under the hubbub of raised voices. He looked back out through the dying sun shadows across the valley where the Hakone Range jutted up sharply and mesa-less in the middle of the thick green, and halfway up were the burning lights of the Leper Colony. Another race, another civilization, separated from the rest of the world. Giff felt a deep well of security sitting there looking at it, glad he was not up there, never would be up there. He wondered if the Leper Colony had whores too?

Finishing his can, he set it on his thigh and brought his arm down in a judo chop, the heel of his hand bending the can sharply, then tossed it into the rapidly filling GI can and got a fresh one.

Willy Woechowski, sitting next to him, watched intently. Then he studied the can in his own enormous hands and looked back at Giff. He cleared the phlegm from his throat with a slightly bullish growl. "Want to see a trick?" he asked bluntly.

"A trick?" Giff said. "Sure."

Furrowing his heavy brow, Willy smothered his empty can in his thick hand, holding it in front of him. Looking ponderously out through the fence, he raised the can and smashed it across the bridge of his ax-blade nose and dropped it disdainfully on the cinder ash. The rolling can showed a deep V, bent deftly, as if it had been hit with a meat cleaver.

It had happened so quickly and had taken Giff so unaware that he simply sat, staring dumfounded at Willy Woechowski, wondering what to say, surprised by the nose that did not even smart, but which, Giff thought, should be crushed, with the cartilages and bones sticking out through the skin. Belatedly, he felt he should congratulate him.

"Well, that's a pretty good trick, Willy," he said in a stunned voice.

"It's not too bad, is it?" Willy reached proudly for another beer. "Never seen anyone else could do it."

"Willy!" Poke Turner exploded humorously, turning from

Dallas and Stack. "Goddam you, Willy! Are you showing off again?"

"Just my trick." Willy belched, grinning widely.

Confounded, Giff turned his head at Poke, who had been arguing with Stack and Dallas. Apparently, Dallas had not seen Willy's "trick." If he had, his face belied it. "You mean he does that all the time?" Giff asked.

"Goddam rights." Poke nodded. "Old Willy's the only sonfabitch you ever seen could do it, too. I seen a guy once bend cans over his head, but they's a trick to that. Never seen a man bend one across his nose. That's somethin', ain't it?"

"Yeah," Stack said. "Ain't that a slick trick?"

"Willy's about a slick sonfabitch," Poke said. "I'm gonna sign old Willy up when he gets out; we'll make a mint tourin' the country," he said expansively. "In lights: Willy Woechowski—the man with the steel-jacket nose. How about that?"

Giff laughed, and watched Willy grin with a broad slyness. "You're pretty slick with that trick all right," he said.

"But I ain't gettin' out, Poke," Willy said suddenly, as if he'd just then heard Poke's remark. "You know that. I'm a twenty-year man."

"Well," Poke shrugged defeat, "there goes all my ritzy ideas."

"Slick, hunh?" Willy said to Giff, obviously pleased by his attention.

"Maybe not all the way slick," Giff joked. "Maybe just about half slick."

"That's it!" Poke snapped his fingers. "Half-Slick Willy Woechowski, the marine with the number-ten-can nose. We could still make a fortune on USO tours. You and me and Gunny Thorton; he'd carry the empty cans," he said enterprisingly. "What'd you think of them onions, champs?"

Looking at the massive Half-Slick Willy, Giff envisioned a man his size trapped in those huge powerful arms, could actually hear the bones and sinews and tendons popping and splitting, tearing into thin strips. He would not want ever to fight Willy unless he had a large club—or a hand grenade. Yet Half-Slick Willy showed neither anger nor bitterness over the razzing. It was hard to believe that a man of his size and strength would not take advantage of it. But then maybe he did. Maybe he was so aware of his strength he could look down on all the rest of them with condescension, because none of them would be worth the exertion of his effort to fight them.

"Yeah," Stack Renshaw was saying heatedly. "Dillinger was shot in the back of the head. I know."

"Sure you do," Poke challenged. "Hell, you weren't even born when he died."

"But I know it just the goddam same," Stack insisted. "I heard about it enough."

"Stack's right," Dallas said boredly. "Johnny Dillinger did get it in the back of the head. That crap about him fighting a running gun battle was shit for the birds."

"There, you see?" Stack persisted. "What'd I say."

"Mel Purvis shot Dillinger right behind his ear," Dallas sneered. "He didn't have a chance."

"Yeah, sir," Stack said. "My old man told me all about that."

"I suppose your old man was there," Poke said disgustedly.

"No, he wasn't," Stack grinned in his unobtrusive way, "but Dillinger lived right around where he did in Indiana. All the people down there still can tell you the straight of it today."

"Shot in the back of the head," Giff mused. "I always thought he made a fight. That's what I used to read in the comic books."

"It ain't the truth though," Dallas said hotly, his deep V brow wrinkling. "They put out just as many lies about him as they did about Charley Floyd."

"Pretty Boy Floyd?" Giff said. "I seen a movie about him once. He was from Oklahoma wasn't he?"

"Right up there around Cookson in the hills," Dallas qualified. "I know some Indian who hid him out up there when the FBI was after his ass. They give me the straight scoop."

"Floyd wasn't like Dillinger," Poke said. "Floyd was a killer; Dillinger was a bank robber."

"Horseshit!" Dallas snorted, turning on the four of them. "They both did their share of killing. But you ask me they had a damn good reason. The best I can think of. They weren't like the Barker Brothers who killed just for the hell of it. And they resented Floyd."

"Oh, those Barker Brothers were some mean bastards," Poke agreed. "And that dolly what's-her-name?"

"Bonnie Parker," Dallas said. "Yea; an' I'll tell you

'nother thing; Floyd couldn't hit his ass with both hands in broad daylight. He was a lousy shot. Dillinger was pretty good."

"Well, what the hell were their good reasons?" Giff said, watching Dallas closely. It was the first time he had ever seen him get upset, or even excited, over anything; it was almost like an obsession with Dallas, and hard casings of hate wrapped over his face. "They just wanted money was all."

"Not true." Dallas shook his head slowly. "The goddam insurance companies screwed them to begin with, took their land and everything they owned. Just like they's doing to-day," he spat. "And they never committed half the crimes they were accused of. But Old J. Edgar Hoover took ad-vantage of this, see? It was a good gimmick to get his start and build a name. After that," he said with contempt, "after they got a few of the big ones like Gillis, Floyd, and Dillinger, you couldn't stop the glory boys."

"There's your goddam robber barons," Poke agreed. "The FBI."

Dallas shot a withering glance at Poke. "I don't know if they're robbers or not," he said thoughtfully, as if the idea had just occurred to him. "But if I had to cast my lot it'd be with people like Floyd and Dillinger." He started to say something else, paused, and his face unlaxed its wooden-ness, a deep toothy grin glinting tight over his lips. "Naw, I wouldn't cast my lot with anyone—not one damn person."

"I bet those bastards had some fun," Poke chuckled. "Before they got killed."

"About as much fun as we have," Dallas said in a cold voice. Then he lit a cigarette and blew the smoke out with a song:

> *"Way down yonder in the Indian Nation,*
> *Ride my pony on the reservation,*
> *In the Oklahoma hills where I was born.*

"Shit fire and save matches," he mocked. "You bastards sure do get some shitty talks goin'."

"Just don't let anybody tell you Dillinger had a chance to fight," Stack told Poke.

"All right for Chrissakes," Poke said. "I'm convinced."

Through it all, Giff sat silent with a detached, consciously hearing, unconsciously listening, mind. The mention of Dillinger and Floyd plus what Dallas had said—"about as much fun as we have"—made him aware of a definite blood relationship. Like all these men sitting around drinking, preparing to go whoring, ready to fight at the drop of a hat (except for Half-Slick Willy), moving in shadowy skirmishes through the welter unknown, unmapped, all the way to a preconceived goal, that was not a goal at all. Yet he was suddenly quite sure that each of them knew what the goal was but refused to voice it. Were times any different than say when, like Dallas said, the insurance companies fucked Dillinger and Floyd and they went on a bank-robbing spree? Were they any different at all? Insurance companies and the GI Bill? With sudden illumination he pictured all of them suddenly forced to the *Outside,* seeing Poke Turner crouching under a hayloft firing at the law with a service .45 he had been trained to kill with; Stack Renshaw being strapped into an electric chair to ride old Smoky; and Cinamo Dallas—? Well, there was Cinamo Dallas. Where? Why, Cinamo Dallas, that heathen quarter Cherokee, was out of his time, that was all. Besides Dallas, like he said, never tossed his lot in with anyone. Then there was himself—this was the juicy one—himself locked in the deep dark of his mulish stubborn rebellion, forced away from living forever—an undesirable citizen, an incorrigible. And going all the way, there was Half-Slick Willy, who would not bend beer cans over his nose on the Outside.

From the corner of his eye, Giff caught Poke Turner talking to him. "What? I didn't hear you."

"Who had the best generals?" Poke demanded furiously. "The North or the South? I want your opinion."

Giff looked at the seriousness on Poke's face and laughed. "Hell, I don't know. You ask me, neither of them were worth a shit. Look at it this way: who has better officers, us or Idiot Item Company?"

Dallas laughed happily and stretched. "There's your answer, Poke. Now maybe we can get some liberty."

"What the hell time is it?" Stack said.

"Almost eight," Poke said, rising. "Dammit whoa! Three hours till the bars close."

"We ain't accomplishing anything here," Giff said, feeling his beer, feeling no pain at all now. God! But it had gotten dark fast—and the deepening visions of woman—any woman, all women—came tap-tap-tapping back inside his head, sinking to his scrotum, and rising back sweatily. All the old loving female hunger was back within him, unsatisfied.

They all stood up as one and downed their beers greedily, then chucked them into the GI can.

"Come on, Half-Slick Willy," Giff said, rolling down his cuffs and adjusting his tie, "let's cut a choge to town. Maybe you can try your nose on some fucking bottles."

5.

They moved boisterously through the main gate in a khaki body, Poke Turner in charge talking with the proud air of a host showing his guests his own personalized woman-filled bachelor apartment.

All along the street the music from the bars spilled out into the night, rivaling in a provocative fugue against the sometimes loud belligerent, sometimes soft mellow voices from within. Determined groups of twos and threes and fours moved unsteadily through the streets over the dusty rocky ground in the moistly warm air.

Behind them, inside the fence across the camp road from the main gate, was the South Camp guardhouse. Off-duty guards leaned against the back door next to the fence looking hungrily at the town, wistfully at the men on liberty walking by. Occasionally a Jo-san would stop and talk with the guards, only to be run off by the Officer of the Day, and the men who could look but not touch followed her with their eyes as she walked on.

The rack of charcoal-feverish clouds that had come plowing down on the Fossa Magna range earlier now began to blot out the stars, and a heavy sultry thickness muted the air. The first tasty smell of rain bottled the rancid land, the land of no flushing toilets, and the earthy smell of raw vegetables in the single open-faced grocery market of Fuji-oka. A casual whiff of fried rice and noodles retreated under the heavier wet smell.

Walking steadily toward the gap between the Condor

112

Club and the Hart Bar, scuffing their shoes on the rocks and clods of the street, Poke Turner chattered excitely, waving his arms at the various bars, allowing they could try *them* if they wanted, but that the Bar New Blue Moon in Bamboo Alley was the best—"more like home"—as far as he was concerned. Besides, he told them, he had jawbone credit there.

Giff felt a party-driving buoyancy swelling in him as they passed the hot smoky blues and jazz of the Negro Condor Club. His senses, keenly attuned to the sounds of night, grabbed quick flashes of laughing women, their hips hanging pendulously, leaning against the doorjambs of the bars.

A special night, all of it said: a special occasion because there were new faces in the camp now, and hot-eyed women waiting for them in town. Then they were swallowed up in the frothy blackness of Bamboo Alley.

Along both sides of the narrow path bars were jammed close together. Soft lights threw caressing shadows on the ground from the windows, a magnitude of unpolished brilliance that said life moved on and around. "You take long time, *ne?*" a twittering voice called out. "I'll show you *toxon* good time, pussy good!" answered by the thick chuckle of a marine who held a copious handful of round Japanee bottom.

DREAM BAR . . . QUEEN BAR . . . RED BIRD BAR . . . WHITE KITTEN . . . NEW TOKYO . . . bars, bars, bars: the honky-tonk gathering of camp followers, all of them re-enlisted for a second, third, and fourth hitch, twenty-year women carrying their reverential time-honored douche bags and VD check cards, following and waiting, while the twenty-year men descended heavily on them with their ribbons, medals, unhealed wounds and liberty cards.

A scream in the darkness the crash of splintering glass the combative cry of a belligerent drunk.

"MP! MP! MP!" Whistles blowing shrilly a heavy tread of boots the dull thud of hickory on head.

> *Take down that Silver Star, Mother,*
> *Replace it with one made of gold.*
> *Your son was a hard-charging Barman,*
> *But he died in a whorehouse in Seoul—*
> *Tough shit! tough shit!*
> *He died in a whorehouse in Seoul.*

Laughter, tight bitter loving cynical tender, the ghost of Korea brought back hauntingly with the sardonic derisive songs written in frenzy by an anonymous artist firing short bursts from his machine guns—songs that would wither and die and lie down with the wind at night when new artists moved killing through infested jungle swamps or snow-cold Chinee hills, writing new songs in a sanguine fit of expression.

Bamboo Alley, where mirth and death stroll hand in hand, covering lost bets and dead deals, where no Phoenix bird arises from the ashes, but where all of them raise their beer high and hold their women close, each a self-locked, self-sealed entity, with the always present never-able-to-stave-off autobiography:

> *Aye lads, it's cold outside;*
> *Colder'n the edge of an ice-bound pool;*
> *Colder'n the head of an Eskimo's tool.*
> *Aye lads, it's a wee bit chilly;*
> *But it's not as cold as my boy Willy.*
> *He's dead . . .* FUCK HIM!

Bamboo Alley widened past the New Tokyo Bar for an island in the middle of destiny—a public *benjo* (crapper)—and opened out into a cul-de-sac of five bars evenly spaced. The Bar New Blue Moon was the first on the left followed around in the circle by Walles Glee Bar, the Copacabana Bar, the Cabaret Lilly and finally, directly across from the Bar New Blue Moon, disdaining all the rest, the Arizona Restaurant: hot evening smells of cooking letting them know that people still ate.

The Bar New Blue Moon, as Poke Turner had told them, was where most of the company hung out (most of the platoon at any rate) and they could now hear the strained groan of a worn phonograph blatting out a hillbilly record.

Giff felt the personal warmth of long associations with honky-tonks flow through him as he followed, third in line, up the path to the swinging saloon doors of the Bar New Blue Moon: honky-tonks of the railroad people, Shanty Irish, Bohunk, Roundheads, no pure strains allowed, the frenzied never-satisfied searching people who crowded in them. And he was a part of it. Had been for a long time.

It was like meeting an old friend, stolid unwavering loyal, the only one he could count on.

Poke Turner hit the swinging doors with his hands and they boomed back as the five men walked in. Delightful squeals of Jo-sans hit the life-riddled air; grenades of excitement exploded in the clapboard bar showering fragments of *happy-days-are-here-again* anticipation all over them.

All the chickens, Giff thought, had come home to roost.

He watched Poke saunter over to the crowded bar, nodding to some men, winking at their women, following him with his eyes and nodding distantly to those men he knew by sight, and caught the friendly smiles and inviting faces of the Jo-sans, manless, who politely waited to be called. It was odd, he thought, that they called to you from the doorways and then when you got inside changed to just the opposite. Well, they knew their trade better than he did.

A row of low-set tables lined the windows facing Bamboo Alley extending to the back of the bar and coming up to the beaded curtain hung over the door leading down the corridor to the back rooms. The bar, with a dozen or so stools, mostly occupied, was being run by a single Jo-san. She wore her blue-black hair in an American pony tail, but the salient feature, the thing that caught Giff, was her natural pouting mouth, not quite a Hapsburg lip, dominant in her heart-shaped face. Busily she was opening quarts of beer and keeping the single-shot phonograph working. Giff studied the small high breasts under her blue blouse. They rose and fell steadily.

"Let's put two of these here tables together," Stack suggested. "Poke's goin' back to pay Papa-san. For us," he added glumly.

"All right with me," Giff grinned, turning away from the girl bartender, surveying the bar again, and watched Cinamo Dallas walk unconcernedly past him over to the back of the bar where the empty tables were, looking neither right nor left. Behind him, he could hear Half-Slick Willy breathing heavily.

"Let's go sit down, Willy." Giff walked on back to the table.

They pushed two of the small tables together, grabbing some unoccupied chairs, Giff feeling the acute naturalness of it relax him, and sat down. Before he could take off his pisscutter, three Jo-sans, "business women," came walking over with three quarts of beer and set them down on the table.

"What the fuck's this for?" Giff looked at the round-faced laughing one who set a thick quart in front of him.

"Poke-san buy," she said cheerfully. "Presento."

"Hi, Peanuts!" Stack grinned. "Sit down. All of you sit down," he said and pushed some chairs back.

"You new boy-sans, *ne?*" Peanuts sat down beside Giff.

Boy-san! he thought indignantly. "Yeah, we come in from Korea," he said. Shifting his head a little he saw Dallas talking softly with a thin blank-eyed girl. The girl was smiling with her mouth but her eyes were dead.

"Me Peanuts," Peanuts said in a small-girl voice. "what's your name, *dio?*"

"Giff," he said. It always embarrassed him to say it like that—like a goddam idiot! "Giff-san," and wondered now, why he was being bastardly. Apparently no one else was pissed off. Maybe he was different? Hah! He was different all right. He was probably half nuts. He shouldn't have drunk so much beer back at the slop chute.

"You like Bar New Blue Moon," Peanuts solicited happily. She pulled out a card and handed it to him.

WELCOME

Any time is drinking time—but drink at the

AMERICAN SPOKEN BAR NEW BLUE MOON

There are: Refreshing drinks, cheerful music, prompt and courteous service by American spoken Charming girls!

---

*Once you come, you'll always come—
So you will find it out yourself.*

*   *   *   *   *

BAR NEW BLUE MOON

"You shacked up for tonight?" Giff asked suddenly when he'd read it, the depression gone.

"You like Peanuts, *ne?*" She grinned.

"Sure, I like you lots," he said. A little plump, but that

116

was all right, he liked them meaty. "Where the hell you get a name like Peanuts?"

She laughed genuinely, not quite raucously, and Giff looked around the table. Stack was in the midst of an intense conversation with a sullen-faced Jo-san with long hair. Dallas was still talking softly to the thin dead-eyed girl. The eyes bothered Giff somehow but he could not quite isolate it. Half-Slick Willy, womanless, sat powerfully over his quart of beer.

"Pick up name long time now." Peanuts stopped laughing. "See Jo-san at bar?"

Giff looked up. "Yeah. I seen her when I came in."

"Her name Popcorn," Peanuts said, grinning.

"Hunh?"

"Popcorn!" Peanuts burst out laughing again. "Me Peanuts, her Popcorn."

"Yeah?" Giff grinned easily for the first time. Peanuts and Popcorn. Salted Peanuts and hot buttered Popcorn. A rare treat, he thought, thinking he would like to have them both—tonight.

Poke Turner came bustling through the beaded curtain hanging over the door to the corridor, holding a small Japanee boy, possibly four or five, in his arms. The boy was scowling blackly.

"What the hell?" Giff started.

"How you like my boy?" Poke said.

"The kid belongs to Mama-san and Papa-san Yoshido," Stack took time out from his heated argument with the sullen-faced girl to tell Giff. "They own this place."

"What'd you think his name is?" Poke asked.

"Hell," Giff shrugged, "how should I know?"

"8 Ball," Poke said admiringly. "Ain't that a rich one? 8 Ball."

"8 Ball?"

"Sure enough," Poke averred. "This kid is sharp. Ain't you, 8 Ball?"

8 Ball, lowering darkly, with his young child's face inquisitively studying the faces in the bar, hooked his thumbs through the straps of his American overalls. "Marine *joto-ni*," he said.

"Hey! You hear that?" Poke said. "Marine *joto-ni*. Marine no good. And after all I done for him too."

8 Ball shook his head. "No hucking good. Number hucking ten."

117

Peanuts sitting next to Giff, rattled off a barrage of Japanee and 8 Ball scowled deeper, but he shut up, his slopehead scissor-cut under a bowl shaggily.

"Want to ride a horse, 8 Ball?" Poke asked, pulling a chair and bouncing his knee.

8 Ball frowned at the knee, picked a chair for himself and turned it over on the floor, mounting it like an experienced horseman. Giff grinned at him wondering how the hell the kid found out about cowboys. Jesus Christ, a Japanee cowboy! Shades of Jesse James.

"Me an' 8 Ball are thick as thieves," Poke said. "Hello, Yoko," he said suddenly to Stack's sullen-faced girl.

"Usssh," was all Yoko had to say.

"She really likes me," Poke said airily across the table to Giff. "Really she does. Say! Look's like Dallas really makin' out."

Once again Giff looked over at the vague-eyed girl, and this time he caught it. He had seen that look on old Koreans smoking their long pipes. He had seen it veiled in the eyes of the marines who hung out in the rear echelons of Yongdongpo, and oddly enough, it was the look of himself even, and all the rest of them, the heavy look of carrying a fifty-pound monkey on their backs, each monkey with a different name.

"What's she use?" Giff said.

"Kayo-san?" Poke said. "Cocaine mostly, I guess. She's higher than a kite tonight. Highest I ever seen her. How come old Dallas mixing with her?"

"If you find out let me know," Giff grinned.

"That'll never happen," Poke snuffled. "Hey, Yoko," he said to Stack's girl, "what you pissed off about?"

"How long I been comin' down here, Poke?" Stack demanded hotly.

"Oh, lessee now"—Poke paused as if he did not know whether to lie or tell the truth—"since we been here in Big J." He looked at Yoko again. "Why?"

"And ain't I spent all my shekels in the Blue Moon?" Stack prompted. "And mostly on Yoko?"

"I guess so," Poke said cautiously.

"Well," Stack said, holding his hands in front of him, "well, alls I ask is that she shave under her arms and she gets pissed off."

Yoko sputtered out some sneering Japanee, and Peanuts sitting beside Giff, burst out laughing. She was the laugh-ingest woman he had ever seen. But the humor made for good *tatami* times, he thought.

"Honest to God!" Stack complained. "It ain't that I think you're cruddy, Yoko. But I wake up in the middle of the night with my face buried and it scares the hell out of me."

Yoko folded her arms implacably.

"Maybe we'll have to start hanging out somewhere else," Poke teased and caught a stabbing look from Yoko.

8 Ball, who had been rocking on his improvised chair horse with utter disregard for the bar, suddenly fell over with a loud plop, landing square on his bottom. Glaring, he got up. "Piss on you, horse." He stared at the chair for a moment, indecisive, and then with great dignity walked back through the beaded curtain.

"That's the least you could do for me," Stack said, "goddam you, Yoko."

"You want to sleep with me, all right," Yoko said adamantly. "You no have to you no want to."

Giff watched her, thinking what his granddaddy had said about his grandma a long time ago, whom he had never seen since she died before he was born. Grandaddy Bohane would say, profoundly drunk: *"She was a good old gal all right. But she had a long hair growing outa her nose and every time she sneezed it cracked like a whip."* Then he would laugh happily and wipe the whiskey off his chin. Remembering now, Giff laughed out loud rendingly. God, what a life! Sitting there embroiled in the burning question of whether a whore should shave her armpits because it scared Stack Renshaw. What was that about have you ever seen a grinning bear?

"Whatsa matta you, *dio?*" Peanuts inquired. Poke was looking at him oddly too, while Dallas talked in hushed tones to a junkie and Peanuts and Popcorn and Cracker Jacks and 8 Ball— Oh Jesus Christ on a BAR!

"Peanuts," he said, gasping, his eyes still watering. "You want to stay with me tonight?"

"Hai," Peanuts said.

"Good," Giff said breathing deeply, the hysteria subsiding. "How about Willy here?" he said, jerking his head at the brooding massive man. "How about getting Half-Slick Willy fixed up?"

"Nani O?" Peanuts said.

"Willy," Giff said. "How about fixing him up with Popcorn maybe?"

"Willy him too beeg fella," Peanuts said. *"Toxon* beeg." She measured off about two feet with her hands.

"Me?" Willy stirred vaguely. "Oh no," he said slowly. "No, I'm gonna leave in a bit. Right now in fact."

"Hell, Willy," Giff said. "Stick around and enjoy the festivities."

"Naw," Willy said lugubriously. "No, I got to leave. I don't ever stay at the Blue Moon."

"Okay." Giff turned back to Willy detachedly. "You got another bar you want to hit, hunh?"

Half-Slick Willy nodded heavily, finished his beer and stood up, a lumbering bear flanked by possums. "I'll see you all," he said, his square face blank.

"Come on back around you get tired of roamin' the streets," Giff offered. "I'll buy you another beer."

"By God I jist might do that." Willy hitched his trousers up with two shank hands, lumbered past the bar and the front tables, moving like a battleship through a sea of fishing boats and out the swinging doors. No one looked up.

"You know where he's going?" Poke said, a sly grin playing with his mouth.

"Willy?" Giff said. "No. How the hell should I know where he's going? I ain't his keeper."

"And neither am I, champ," Poke said. "They's an old White Russian got a place down in Skivvie Lane: Rotten Crotch Mary. She runs the bar. Old Willy alla time goes down there to shack up. I think maybe he an' Rotten Crotch Mary got a romance going." Poke grinned. "Hell, maybe I can get her in with my USO show, too. Thorton, Willy, and Rotten Crotch Mary."

"Rotten Crotch Mary." Giff grinned, hearing the words strange and remote. Well, wouldn't you know it? Rotten Crotch Mary. Over the hills and through the woods out to old Rotten Crotch Mary's. If what he'd heard about White Russians was true, he might even give it a try himself someday. He looked back up at the bar, at Popcorn with the dangling pony tail and pouting mouth.

"You want some more beer?" he asked suddenly. "Poke? Stack? Dallas?"

"Sure as hell," Poke said. "Always want beer."

Peanuts started to get up, straightening her flower-print dress over her stocky hips.

"No," Giff stopped her, "I'll get it. There's a guy at the bar I wanna see."

120

Smiling in compliance, Peanuts sat back down as Giff rose and started to walk around the table.

"Hey!" Poke called after him. "Pick up a couple quarts of gin, too."

Giff nodded, turned and walked to the bar where Popcorn sat perched on a high stool, her legs hidden by the bar, dutifully operating the single-shot phonograph. He passed several marines sitting at the bar, most of whom he did not recognize, and took the last stool next to the window, his back to the swinging saloon doors. The window was open to the motionless night and the air smelled of the sweaty evaporation before rain. He put a handful of yen on the bar as Popcorn swiveled around on her stool and smiled, a distant ungenuine smile.

"Beer-O," he ordered, thinking it sounded dramatic, and watched Popcorn's pony tail bob as she bent down to the cooler and drew the quart out.

He watched while she uncapped it, poured the beer into his glass, and placed a box of Bar New Blue Moon matches in front of him. "You got 'Honky-Tonk Blues' in that stack?" He nodded his head at the stack of records and kept his eyes on her. "Hank Williams?"

"I no know," Popcorn said distantly with the demeanor of a person who has abruptly been snapped back into a world she is unfamiliar with. "Me sink so maybe." She started going through the stack.

"I'll look through it, Popcorn," Giff said, watching her eyes carefully. "It'll be easier for me to find."

Pausing, she set the records on the bar next to the matches. "How you know Popcorn's name?"

"Hell, I know everybody's name," Giff grinned. "Your friend Peanuts told me."

"Ah so." She nodded her head. "Popcorn—how you call it?—nickname. Watashi Hanoki Shiro."

"What?" Giff moved recklessly through the records.

"Hanoki Shiro." She pointed at herself, then refilled his glass. "You no come Blue Moon before, *ne?*"

"Here it is, Popcorn." He raised the record triumphantly. "No, I never been in here before."

"You new boy-san come from Korea?" She took the record and placed it on the phonograph.

"With that new bunch, yeah," Giff said wryly—boy-san, hunh! Well, maybe that was the *way* of the town and its citizens. Still, it punctured him. When he looked up from his beer he saw her flick her eyes over his corporal chevrons and ribbons.

"Are you Eye-talian?" she asked quickly.

"Christ no!" Giff took another drink of his beer, emptying the glass. "I'm Irish, mostly. A nip of this and a nip of that, too. But no Eye-talian." Popcorn refilled his glass.

Moving her lips, she tried to say the word. She could not pronounce the "r" correctly and when she breathed it out it sounded like "Ilsh." "No?" She shook her head, the pony tail swinging like a hanged man.

Giff grinned at her, mustering up all the suavity and charm that was in him (enough to fill a beer cap, he thought dourly). "No, but that's close enough. Listen," he said softly. "Can you say Shanty?"

"Shan-tee," she repeated.

"Then that's good enough," he agreed. "It's one and the same for me."

"*Ne?*"

"Nothing." He looked at the supple line of her neck sloping into her shoulders, wishing he had not made the business deal with Peanuts already. Popcorn looked much more interesting. He cursed himself for his inveterate abandon.

"So," she grinned. "You like shitkicking music, *ne?*"

"Hellyea, I like shitkicking. I like Hank Williams. You know who Hank Williams was?"

Popcorn shook her head no.

"Well," Giff explained, "he was an American shitkicker. But he's dead now."

"Your name is Shan-tee-san," Popcorn said, puzzled.

Off to his right at the back of the bar, Giff heard Poke raise his voice in heated dispute; then more voices joined in arguing.

"No," he said turning back to Popcorn. "That's not my name but you can call me that."

He pulled a fresh pack of cigarettes out of his sock and lit one without offering one to her. She had reached for the box of matches to light it for him but he was too fast. She looked hurt, as if her profession had been infringed upon, sitting on her stool with a sullen pout.

A cannonade of thunder broke through the thick night air. Rain slanted down heavily, not coming slowly and increasing, just flooding down, pelting steadily on the tin roof of the Bar New Blue Moon, and there was an expectant lull in the beer-filled talk of the bar. Drops converged on drops on the window next to Giff, forming a rivulet running dirtily down the pane. Water began to splash in on him. He closed the window. Hank Williams sang on, unperturbed.

"How long will it last?" Giff asked Popcorn as the conversation filled the bar again, renewed and reheated.

She looked past him out the window. "Maybe tonight. Maybe three four days. Maybe week."

Giff remembered it was the rainy season in Korea. The trenches would crumble under the pouring beat and have to be dug back out, and there would be a swift influx of sniffles and yellow-phlegmed colds, while bones ached freezingly—unless there was some banana oil and kerosene or Aqua Velva to drink. He envisioned staying in the Bar New Blue Moon all weekend while the rain washed on around him.

"You go to field next week, *ne?*" Popcorn said, eying his pack of cigarettes on the bar.

"Yeah," Giff said bleakly. "All week. The whole shootin' match." Then he caught it. "Go ahead; help yourself."

He watched her take one of the white tubes and light it, very delicately, as if she had seen it done in some American movies, holding it in her hand while she lit it, blowing smoke straight up into the air and lowering it quickly, not quite distastefully. She was a real hot one, he thought, seeing in her a reservoir of unlocked emotions, and wondered why no one had made a stab at her before, before now, tonight. Evidently these marines at the bar were not planning to stay the night—maybe no room at the Inn? He looked at the clock on the wall behind her. Almost nine o'clock. Two hours before the bars closed. Well, if he was going to set it up he had better do it now, just to put the cinch on it. He could think of something to tell Peanuts later.

"Listen, Popcorn," he said, calmly hot, "you ain't fixed up with anyone tonight, are you?"

She looked through the thin smoke of her cigarette, curiously. *"Nani O?"*

"You ain't got someone for a long time, all night, have you?" he said, trying to sound nonchalant, and knowing his heat was showing through like a red flag.

A cool, inscrutable protectiveness sparked in her eyes, just a flickering, but Giff saw it; then it vanished, replaced by a thin smile. "Popcorn no business woman."

Giff sat silently, staring at her. He did not think he had heard right. He felt a deep rumbling in his scrotum bellowing up his spine. Not a business woman? Well, what the hell! He looked around sharply, at the faces the bottles the people; it was still the same bar: a business establishment. There were still women. Then he turned back, aware that the rain had ceased as suddenly as it had started. The night returned to its dense listlessness.

"What'd you mean?" Giff said, harshly infuriated with himself. "You ain't a business woman? You're workin' in the bar, ain't you?"

"No business woman," Popcorn said aloofly. "No have both legs. No can be business woman with one leg."

Giff's first reaction was one of apathy. He sat on the stool and merely looked directly at her, into her charcoal-colored eyes. Then instinctively, like a man who has been wounded and knows it, yet looks at the gaping hole when someone mentions it as if it had gotten there by mistake, he leaned over the bar and looked down. (He had wanted to do that all night, see how she looked from the waist down; it bothered him when he could only see half a woman.) Her right leg was manifestly intact, dangling casually from the pale blue skirt, but the left leg—or rather where it should have been—extended from her hips to slightly above the knee—or where the knee should have been. In his mind he could see the cauterized stump and wondered professionally if it had been a clean or jagged wound and just how old it was.

To a man who has seen other men (women, civilians, all people) lose legs, arms, balls, eyes, and lives it was not disconcerting. After so long a time he was inculcated with the sense of awareness that casualties, termed superficial or grave, are a necessary part of the trade and consequently no trauma or shock or emotion is solid and enduring. Seeing it, Giff only felt that it was as natural as taking a crap, as customary as a payday melee, as monotonous as a short-arm inspection.

He straightened up, not wanting to say anything or become entangled in a personal argument because he could already hear in his mind: *It came from the bomb at Hiroshima or Nagasaki,* with a pointed allusion to the Americans, a certain sly instinct hoping to arouse in him a guilt —but no thanks kid he had been that route before and to hell with it.

124

So he did not speak, only looked at her directly, and was startled to find a mask of amused indifference on her face. He grinned back at it, good-naturedly. "Well, one leg shouldn't stop you from being a business woman. I know one who's only got one eye. She wears a patch. Gets more business than if she had two."

If he had intended it for a joke it went over like stale beer at a battalion field day. "You want hear record again, *ne?*" she said demurely.

A real hot-eyed creature, he thought. "Yeah, play it again. And you can play all them other Hank Williams you got in there too." He tapped the stack of records he'd set aside, looking up at her as she started the phonograph again, abruptly forming a picture in his mind of moving into one of the back rooms where she was lying naked on a *tatami* waiting for him—but what played uppermost in his mind, the tantalizing stud-driving thought, was that she was not a business woman! Not like Peanuts, or Yoko. Which only meant that she had never slept with a jar-head! Had not been touched by one! How many had slept with Peanuts? Dozens perhaps. Thousands maybe. Maybe even that sonfabitch dumb Swede Zorn. He looked quickly over at the table where Peanuts was laughing at something Poke had said.

"You stay all night with Peanuts?" Popcorn grinned at him.

He finished off his last glass of beer. "I guess so. But I haven't asked her yet," he lied.

"She *toxon* good Jo-san," Popcorn said loyally. "Me and Peanuts *tamadachis.*"

"That's her," Giff grinned. Buddies. Old-home week at the Bar New Blue Moon. National fuck-your-buddy week, or better yet, national fuck-your-girl's-best-friend week. "You work up here all the time?"

"Hai," she said. "Me number-one bartender." She made a motion of uncapping beer with serious humor.

"That all you do?" he asked, the nonchalance and dramatic romanticism he had dredged up previously now evaporated and gone with the rain. "Don't do nothing but tend bar?"

Popcorn waved her arm around the bar. "Clean up; makee chow."

"Hey, Giff!" Poke Turner yelled behind him over the raucous voices of the bar. "What you doing? They's some thirsty people back here."

Giff grinned back at the shadows around the table. "Give me a couple bottles of gin," he told Popcorn.

Popcorn reached behind her and set two square bottles of Ginko Gin on the bar. Giff paid her. He got off his stool, pocketed his cigarettes and started to walk away, then turned lightly on the balls of his feet and winked at her. "If you change your mind about being a business woman, let me know before eleven," he grinned, "or I probably lash up with someone else."

"Me no changee mind, Shan-tee-san." She grinned back at him.

Clutching the two square bottles he walked back to the two tables and Peanuts sitting alone. It had started to rain again, drizzling, a choking smell of water on dust and parched earth, and Giff, seeing Popcorn in his mind, watched her hobble around on a crutch throwing the water on the wood floor of the bar to keep the dust down, one inert thigh hanging unobtrusively.

"I was beginning to think maybe you forgotten all of us," Poke Turner said, taking one of the bottles.

"I sorted out some Hank Williams records." Giff sat down beside Peanuts.

"You catchee *toxon* big medal," she said, studying Giff's Silver Star ribbon, top one on his shirt.

"Well so what for Chrissakes!" he said angrily, casting a furious glance at Cinamo Dallas, who was above and beyond all of them with his junkie girl. That bastard and his big mouth, Giff thought. All the time bringing *that* up. But looking back at Peanuts, seeing her examining the medal, he felt a wave of pride, conceit mostly, bubble over him.

"You like Popcorn, *ne?*" Peanuts looked from the ribbon to his face.

"Your friend?" Giff said, the anger gone, replaced by momentary supremacy. "Sure; she's nice."

"How about some cider with this gin?" Stack suggested. Yoko had apparently been pacified. The sullenness had left her face. Giff wondered if Stack had convinced her she should shave under her arms.

"Cider!" Poke said, indignant. "With this? What'd you want to do? Get sick?"

126

"I got to have something with it," Stack said. "Need something to lose that taste of hair oil."

"If you're gonna build a fire, don't pour water on it," Dallas spoke up for the first time, then was lost with his girl again.

Giff turned to Peanuts. "Get a couple bottles of cold cider," he said. "And some glasses." He took a short nip of the hair-oil-tasting gin. "And a bowl of ice, too."

When Peanuts returned and sat down, she pinched the inside of Giff's side.

"Hey!" he cautioned. "Careful of those family jewels."

Laughing, Peanuts played a hillbilly beat on the inside of Giff's thigh to the music from the phonograph. "You dance, *ne?*" she asked.

"Me?" Giff said. "Dance?"

Peanuts looked crestfallen. "No dance?"

"Not at all. None." Giff looked at Poke and Stack. They shook their heads.

"Come on, Yoko," Peanuts said. "We dance."

Yoko, looking slightly bored, stood up with Peanuts, grudgingly refilled Stack's gin glass, and walked out to the center of the bar.

Giff surveyed himself with a full glass of gin and ice in his hand, firmly and warmly encased in the payday-night darkness. It was all of it so characteristic. He wouldn't have traded anything for it, not even the next five paydays, for having it taken away. It was a part of him, a bigger part than he had ever seen before: the bar, the women, the atmosphere, a divorced settlement within himself, a something which he could always have every night (broke or rich—broke, he had Poke's jawbone; rich, he didn't sweat at all, no strain no pain). It was the something he should have had in Korea. If, under his command, they had had the bars— No, this town!—just a few miles rearward of the MLR to come to every night after patrols through no man's land, he could see how much better it would be. How much more natural it would make it: simply to have this town, these women, always behind, just a few miles within truck distance, where they could go each night, battered and shot up, and receive through them, the women, the shots of adrenaline that reinvigorated them for the next day. If he had his way, that would be just how he'd handle it.

Well, why couldn't it work like that in the next war? he

asked himself. Of course, in the next war, it would be like that. That was all there was to it. Then, if it was that way, his way, everyone in the whole world would be satisfied and happy.

"If I was God," he said suddenly, "I'd allow war."

"Okay," Poke said. "I'll vote for you."

"So will the chaplains," Stack echoed.

Quietly, they all returned to their gin.

Peanuts and Yoko came back from their dance and sat down and Giff turned to Peanuts, suddenly interested in her since Popcorn was out of the race, and he needed a woman any woman now. She smiled at him widely, and he ran his fingers over the scar on her forehead, the dim lights from the bar catching it, a half-moon scar above her eye. "Where'd you get that?"

"Hiroshima," she said cheerfully, putting her hands up in a large circle and going "whoooo-boom!"

"Yeah," Giff said seriously, rubbing his fingers on the bridge of his nose along the scar that ran down one side. "You know where I got that?"

"Pearl Harbor." Peanuts clapped her hands and giggled.

Giff grinned shyly, still rubbing his nose remembering the fight he'd had in Oceanside with another marine who had sliced him with a beer-can opener. "How'd you know that?" he said.

"Peanuts get straight scoop," she beamed.

"If I wake up screaming tonight," Stack said glumly, "you'll know I been trapped under Yoko's arm."

Poke guffawed with delight. "You really ought to shave, Yoko," he said, and received a murderous glare from her for his agreeing.

They worked their way hurriedly through the two quarts of gin and ice, the cider hardly touched, chasing most of it with cigarettes. At eleven o'clock they had finished the two quarts and Giff, feeling magnanimous as hell, still excited with the way he would run things, bought four more quarts so they would each have one in the night. One apiece, he thought, would last them till morning.

"We go now," Peanuts said. "Me show you pussy good time, ne?"

"Soon's I finish my drink," Giff said, watching Popcorn at the bar lock the phonograph up.

"Come on, Yoko," Stack resigned, "let's go wrassel."

128

"She won't wrassel," Poke qualified, "cause she thinks she's a sacred vessel."

Yoko ignored him.

"You won't wrassel either," Stack said, "unless you got a woman."

"Goddam that's right!" Poke said. He jerked around in his chair scanning the bar. A Jo-san in a green sweater and gray skirt was talking with a marine at the first table by the door. The marine was earnestly, if drunkenly, trying to explain something. "A Tanker," Poke said slowly.

"I'll be back directly, hear?" Poke walked over to the first table. Giff watched him move casually up to the girl's side. The Tanker shot a perfunctory glance at Poke. Poke said something to the Tanker. The Tanker leaned back in his chair. Poke spoke again and the Tanker swiveled around to look at all of them; Giff thought he sort of grinned back pugnaciously; then the Tanker got up, smirking unconvincingly, defeated, and walked out the swinging saloon doors into the rain. The Jo-san said something in bitter Japanee to Poke and he laughed. Then she got up and followed him back to the table.

"Who was that?" Giff asked.

"A motherfucking Tanker," Poke said. "The sonofabitch. Couldn't you tell?"

"You luin business all time," the Jo-san said to Poke.

"Ahh, Nancy," Poke said lazily. "You don't want to shack up with a goddam Tanker."

Nancy looked at him enterprisingly. "You got *okane?*"

"Jawbone," Poke said.

"Tanker got *toxon okane,*" Nancy pointed out.

"Tanker got a chancre," Poke grinned. He grabbed Nancy around the waist. "I'll see you all in the mornin'."

"Sure," Giff said, watching them weave through the beaded curtain. Stack and Yoko followed, Stack shaking his head wearily, dumbly, like a steer hit between the eyes with a hammer. Cinamo Dallas still slumped in his chair, his hand caressing Kayo-san's neck.

Giff sipped his gin while Peanuts played a dit-dash-dot on his thigh. Up at the bar Popcorn snapped a wall switch and darkness struck the room. In the dark silence of breaths, he watched her move from the stool gingerly, reach under the bar and bring out a crutch. Through the small opening of the door in the wall behind her, glints of light shot in as she put the crutch under her arm and hobbled out from behind to the swinging saloon doors. There was the skinny wooden crutch clacking on the wood floor and a smooth clean right leg touching lightly. She closed the inside doors and locked them, the rain increasing in a strumming tempo suddenly deafening in the dark room.

Watching Popcorn, Giff felt his throat constrict thickly. He tossed off his drink as she hobbled back from the door silently and moved through the beaded curtain.

Dallas scraped his chair on the floor and stood up, helping Kayo-san up beside him. "Welcome to Japan," he said woodenly in the darkness. "I'll see you in the morning, buddy."

"You should live so long," Giff said as they disappeared through the beads. Then he and Peanuts were all alone in the bar under the pelting of rain on the tin roof. He turned and kissed her almost knocking his bottle of gin over.

"Come on," Peanuts said. "We go back now."

"Why?" Giff asked. "What's wrong with right here? How about the table? Or the chair? Or the fucking floor?"

"Whatsa matta you, *dio?*" Peanuts said, her teeth glinting white in the dark.

"How about in the rain or on the steps only you might get some slivers in your ass," he said. "All right. Let's go. You love me, Peanuts?"

"Hai," she said cheerfully. "Me love you."

"Well, that's fine," Giff said. "I love you, too." See? Falling in love is easy! I am a hero come home from the wars, he told himself. And the women are lying at my feet. Hell yes! Look Mommy, no leg! He stared at the ice glinting in his glass. There were certain fallacies in that ice. It destroyed the gin around it.

"Let's go," Peanuts prodded. "You drink more you no good."

"That's what you think!" he bellowed.

"Shhhh." She put a finger to her lips. "You makee *toxon* noise wake up all people."

Giff chuckled. "They ain't nobody sleepin' in there. If there are they're all damn fools. Fools, do you hear!" he exploded. "What'd I say?" He grabbed her and pulled her down on his lap. "You know something? When I look at you from the side I can see both your eyes. That's cause you ain't got no bridge in your nose."

Peanuts studied him through the darkness, quietly. She

130

rubbed her hand along the bridge of her nose, then she rubbed Giff's nose and laughed softly twitteringly. "You and me go rub noses," she said.

"All right," Giff grinned. "I'm an old nose-rubber from way back. Actually, I'm just an old rubber, dammit." He stood up and grabbed the bottle, almost knocking Peanuts to the floor. "Oh, pardon me, lady," he apologized, reaching down to help her get her balance. Together again, they walked through the beaded curtain, Giff watching their two pairs of legs moving.

Peanuts' room was two rooms down from the curtain, a small thin-walled square with a *tatami* and a closet and a sliding window where rain threatened to pour in. It was such a nice room, Giff thought, homey, and he slapped her on the butt for thanks. "You didn't have to do all this for me," he said.

"Takee clothes off." She smiled, handing him a kimono. She took her own from the closet and snapped the lights off.

Giff shucked his uniform, congratulating himself when he folded the shirt and trousers neatly and set them on the floor, laid the ribbons up so they would not sully. Where the hell was his pisscutter? Must be out on the table. Hell with it. Pisscutters are a dime a dozen. He dropped his skivvy shorts and jumped onto the *tatami* but Peanuts was not there. She was still undressing. Well, he would get the bed warm for her, by God!

He snuggled under the quilts easing into the soft hardness of the *tatami* while rain cascaded down the eaves of the roof outside. He reached up and opened the window, the dampness feeling good on his face, then lay back down and stared up at the window.

Noiselessly, Peanuts drew back the quilt and slipped in beside him.

"Hey!" Giff said. "Take that kimono off."

Peanuts giggled and grabbed him.

"Ouch! Dammit. Peanuts, you're a good little gal." He kissed her to prove it. "You ever work in Kyoto?"

"No," she giggled again and brought her knee up between his legs.

Giff reached around and unstrapped her kimono. "You remind me of a girl I met in Kyoto. Hey!" he said suddenly and leaped from the *tatami*.

Peanuts said something tiredly in Japanee.

Giff fumbled around through his clothes till he found the little idol. He pulled the light string and stood naked in the center of the room proudly holding the leering fat red idol.

"Ah so," Peanuts laughed. "HoTi."

"Old HoTi," Giff said affectionately, rubbing HoTi's belly. Satisfied, he snatched the light off and leaped back onto the *tatami,* setting HoTi on the floor beside him.

"You catchee HoTi in Kyoto?" Peanuts asked.

"Yep." Giff pulled the kimono from her. "Come here," he said.

Giggling, she snuggled up to him, and grabbed him again tenderly hard. "That's my HoTi."

"Be careful," he said. "I only got one of those."

"Mine," she said.

"Yeah, that's right, yours—all yours." All the waiting, the fervor of the past week, the goading of the gin, steamed up in him now and bubbled over and he felt that he would burst if not relieved, because now he was so close to this woman, almost inside her and what little control he'd had over himself fell apart.

"Oh," she said in a stifled cry. "What you do, *dio?* Oh."

Giff felt her helpless beneath him, helpless but wild and powerful, her legs clutching him tight as he pummeled with staccato force as if he were a pivot on the endless cycle of life; and he, tossing and rolling her over the *tatami,* holding her so tight that she winced and moaned but did not desist; lunging forward to that single unwavering heat that was the only salvation for his barbaric feeling.

"Oh God, I'll fuck you to death!"

Then, sinking his teeth deep into her flesh just above the dark paps of her breasts, her legs no longer around him now but almost up on his shoulders in the air, her breath coming in terrified gasps, his throat opened up into a growl of relief and power as he shuddered in a spasm that was like the convulsion just before death, and the hush of night mourned over him.

Peanuts dropped her legs down slowly, wrapping them back around his buttocks and lay there stroking the back of his neck, her breasts red with teeth marks. "Pussy good, *ne?*" she gasped.

"Pussy good."

"You like huck Peanuts?"

"Yeah." He raised his head and looked down to where they were still coupled, feeling that great satisfaction that

132

he got whenever he saw it, and, looking at it in the dark like that, a reinforced power swept over him. He started to move her.

"*Nani O?*"

"Over here," he said. "This way. No. Yeah. That's it. Like that." He was able to move without breaking the action, his pulse still way down in his scrotum, still unrelieved, still begging.

Peanuts muttered something in Japanee, her hips undulating rhythmically, meeting him in challenge.

In the violent storm-heaving, body-in-body, exploring, searching probing, he felt a strange thing form within him this time, a feeling of not becoming a part of another person at all but instead moving yet further away from himself, losing identity and at the same time becoming a larger greater part of himself.

And suddenly he was thinking of Popcorn, Hanoki Shiro, with one and a half legs, while enclosed with the two legs of Peanuts. Eyes closed, visions swirling in front of his mind, he saw Popcorn's pony tail bobbing on the pillow, her almond eyes closed, with that one leg flailing wildly in the air while the other one held him tight. Then he was overflowing, feeling shaky and weakly split in two.

Peanuts grabbed some skivvie paper and eased him out of her, wrapping the skivvie paper around him. He rolled over on his back as she wiped him off. Silently, she inserted some skivvie paper in herself and slipped back into the kimono.

Giff lay on his back watching her shuffle out of the room and tippy-toe up the hall to the water closet. The rain thrummed steadily on the roof and windowpane.

He took a drink of gin and lit a cigarette. Where did Popcorn sleep? What obscure room in this maze did she live in? Did she have a fur-lined *tatami*? No, he didn't think she did. Probably just an ordinary *tatami*—half a *tatami*, he corrected. Looking down at his two legs, he suppressed a weird desire to get up and go searching through the bar for her. But he lay on his back, wearily keyed up.

Was it only Friday? Had he only been in Japan since Monday? Where was Korea? Who is Gifford Cael Bohane? Bohane?—why he's a fellow I know: a good boy, but a poor boy, a corporal who carries a Silver Star and is right guide of the second rifle platoon of Hog Company, Horrible Hog Company, who will have his first day in the field

133

with Hog Company on Monday. That is who Bohane is, see? Well yes, partly, but *who* is he? It is unfair to ask leading questions. Confine all questions to simple answers like what color is red. Okay?

He turned on the bed and snuffed out his cigarette. Did a one-legged bartender, *female type one each,* know what a Silver Star was? Did a one-legged bartender get tired of serving beer to a two-legged Silver Star carrier? Did two legs and one leg make three legs? A three-legged chair, okay, but who ever heard of a three-legged right guide?

Peanuts slid the door open and crept back into the room softly, the silvery lights of rainy darkness catching a smile on her face. When she slipped into bed she explained to Giff that Stack was snoring uncomfortably in the room with Yoko.

He was only good for two more times. After the fourth time, which left him feeling excessively better, fulfilled, he finished off the gin and quietly passed out while rain spattered through the window on his rawboned face.

They all of them spent the entire weekend in the Bar New Blue Moon, and Giff kept Peanuts the whole three days. He did not accost Popcorn Shiro or make a play for her even when he was at his peak in drunkenness, although he perceived a decided change in her from the first night. There was none of the distant standoffish dog-in-the-manger attitude that Saturday and Sunday when he saw her. He wasn't sure, but her refusal of Friday night seemed to subside. She didn't come right out (like he had wanted her to) and say, "Damn betcha I'll sleep with you." But there were certain leanings toward that, and Giff knew he had only to wait. Also, to all appearances, she hadn't known about the Silver Star Friday night, but she learned fast enough, thanks to Cinamo Dallas (whatever game he was playing) and that more than anything was going to be the clincher.

He did not know really why he wanted her so bad. If she was a virgin (which he was sure she was not: he had never met one), that could have something to do with it—with one leg? Well, maybe it was pity, of a sort. He wasn't sure on that either. She was actually no better-looking than Peanuts or even the hairy Yoko; at least to the others, Dallas and them, she was no more beautiful. Yet all women were beautiful to him, he thought drunkenly, in a way. But really, truthfully, he could not isolate a bona fide reason for wanting to sleep with her as bad as he did. If he had the reason, he thought, if he knew it, he would probably *not* want to sleep with her. Sometimes it got very confusing. Adding Korea, Japan, Popcorn, Peanuts and himself, and all his recallable experiences, it all totaled up to—well, simply to a large overfed nothing.

The rain that had come swooping down Friday night petered out foggily, and by Saturday morning it was gone, a bright sun in a soft blue sky chasing it away, and it was stifling hot again all the rest of the weekend. The only existing wetness that Giff was cognizant of was in his belly, and it was a mellowly burning wetness. He thought it had all been an enjoyable weekend, promising, with the seeds planted for next liberty's harvest. (He could wait, hold off till the right time, let Popcorn get used to his being around, let his *legend* work itself up some, and then—by God!—he would advance under full force!)

And Monday morning, when Hog Company was scheduled to go to the field, he was ready to take over his first command as right guide in the second platoon. Hungover but efficient, sweating it out in the heat of early morning, he along with the unholy three (Half-Slick Willy had never come back) returned to the barracks and donned their dungarees and combat gear. He thought it was about time he found out how it was to work under Gunny Hugh Thorton.

6.

Hugh Thorton did not go to the field that Monday. As usual he had taken early-morning muster for Gunny Finch. The cadaverous hollow-cheeked T/Sgt had been too drunk to take it himself. In the line of duty, Hugh had made certain Finch would be enough gathered together to take the company to the field, having forced three cups of black coffee slightly diluted with some of his own V.O. down him, strangling but efficacious.

135

A warm pulse of satisfaction flowed through him at the knowledge that he could make his intermittent inventory of the company that day. With the company (except for Top Condrum) and Finch out of his hair Hugh could find out just how fucked up everything was. Then he could stack his cards and prepare to unfuck it. Carrying Finch the way he did, Hugh sometimes had the feeling he was keeping the man from drowning, as if he held him by the scruff of the neck while Finch doggedly persisted in bobbing his head under.

At seven-thirty that Monday morning, Hugh stood at the window in the staff quarters watching the barracks disgorge its uniformed contents: a long short tall mass of men in dungarees and shiny black boondockers under scrubbed leggins, looking unwieldy with the appendages of weapons and web gear, hooting and chiding as they formed ranks on the cinder mustering area.

Feeding time at the zoo, Hugh thought, feeling the August sun warm and clean through the dust-streaked window, its oblique rays raising dark glints in his black handlebar mustache. All the animals of the circus: the scooping off of the bad beer in a huge vat and shitcanning it into the Marine Corps so that in America the good tasty patriotic beer could flourish uncontaminated.

He reached down and raised the window a few inches. In the heat of the day, if the wind was right, the stench of human feces from the rice paddies would pall over South Camp. His mustache twitched in reminiscence. He closed the window.

Behind him, he heard the soft industrious polishing of shoes being shined by Itchie, the thirteen-year-old Japanee houseboy whom the staff had hired to handle the menial tasks: washing of web gear, shining of shoes, pressing of the uniforms, and being number-one major-domo for the whims and desires of his employers.

Itchie was a good houseboy, Hugh thought, watching the company move out in a column of twos. Even if he was a little on the larcenous side, playing a mediocre black market to bolster his ten-thousand yen monthly wage from the staff. But he couldn't begrudge a kid making an extra yen. Hell, he'd do it himself. Fundamentally, Hugh decided, fundamentally Itchie was a fundamentalist.

He watched the tail end of the company disappear around the company office with Finch weaving ever so slightly

136

bringing up the rear. In his mind Hugh could see Emil Kizer strutting at the front of the company with tenacious Prussian bullishness. Even though he didn't know where he was going.

When the company was gone, the last echoes of rifles slapping on canteens settling with the dust, he turned from the window. Eyes deep set under a black heavy brow, beetling and inquisitive, he regarded Itchie squatting gook-style shining shoes. His young Oriental face seriously multiplying yen. One of these days, Hugh thought, old Itchie would probably own Fujioka. Or be the mayor.

"Where's my *Stars & Stripes*, Itchie?" He walked over to the poker table and sat down.

Itchie responded quickly, dropping the shoe he had been laboring on. "Me catchee light now, sah-jint." He opened his own little locker box, which he kept filled with so many unrelated odds and ends it looked like a treasure chest, and brought out the paper. "Itchie number-one houseboy, *ne?*" he grinned, handing the paper to Hugh. "Got a smoke, sah-jint?"

"Itchie number-one rice paddy daddy," Hugh said. "What the hell happened to those two cartons I gave you three days ago?" He tossed his pack on the table.

Itchie took one, lit up, and puffed suavely. "*Toxon* sad story," he said mournfully. "Papa-san in hospital, him bad sick. No can smoke Nippon tobacco. I give to him." Itchie rubbed his belly in mock pain.

"How much you sell them for?" Hugh asked.

"Fifteen hundred yen," Itchie grinned. "*Toxon* shekel but no have smokes."

Hugh watched him thoughtfully, wondering how much the little shit made in a year. "You got a big family, ain't you, Itchie?"

"*Toxon* big," Itchie savored the smoke. "Four sisters, one baby-san brother."

"Your sisters all country girls?"

"*Hai!*" Itchie raised his feet high and set them down. "All time do *toxon* work in rice paddy."

Hugh ran his hand in a large curve over his chest. "*Toxon* big?"

"Skosh. No like Stateside." Itchie shook his head ruefully. "Like in book with pictures."

"You like Stateside dollies?" Hugh curled his mustache, an immaculate gleaming scimitar.

"*Toxon*," Itchie said fervently. "No like Nippon dollies."

"You better stick with Japanee dollies, Itchie," Hugh advised him. "You could never satisfy *baykoko* women. None of you could. You're all hung about as well as field mice."

"Ah, sah-jint," Itchie grinned. "It no matter how much you got. Matter what you do with it."

"Yeah?" Hugh said innocently. "Well, hell, Itchie, you can't plant rice shoots and have *toxon* tits too. Personally, I think I'd rather plant rice shoots. More of a future." He paused, looked at his paper, then looked back up at Itchie suddenly. "When you going to invite me over for dinner?"

"Ah, sah-jint, you no want eat Itchie's house. Old Nippon custom no good. Him *toxon* bad. Number hucking ten."

"I thought maybe I'd help your sisters plant rice shoots," Hugh said. "Maybe they'd give me an interest. I always wanted to own a rice paddy. Besides," he added, "I've always had a tender regard for country girls."

"You maybe want chatchee sister, *ne?*"

"Hell no," Hugh said. "I just want a cottage small by a waterfall with a rice paddy."

"You want seliously come house for dinner," Itchie proposed, "me fixee you up with sister, you damn betcha."

"I can't afford it, Itchie." Hugh shook his head. "I'm only a destitute testical sergeant. Don't make *okane* like a houseboy."

"All light," Itchie said. "Fix you up presento. You no pay."

I will in the long run, Hugh thought. "Okay, Itchie, you fix it up; I'll come."

"Me do," Itchie said elaborately.

"Now get your little motherfucking ass back to work you want to get paid this month!" Hugh chided in dismissal, watching the little Japanese shuffle away in his hand-me-down khakis.

The *Stars & Stripes* carried the usual assortment of lies. Hugh turned back to the comic section. There was nothing funny in them. He read the nobody's all-American *Steve Canyon*, but did not feel any more patriotic. Then he worked his way through the word puzzle game quickly and tossed the paper in the GI can next to the table.

Shinny up a dog's hind leg, cat turd tea, the girls won't let my tallywagger be, he thought lazily. Ought to go down to the armory for a look see. Never get anywhere as a poet.

138

He stood up and stretched in his Itchie-pressed dunga-rees, a little vain over the military creases. "When you get done with the shoes, press up Gunny Finch's uniforms, Itchie," he said peremptorily.

"*Hai*, sah-jint!" Itchie said. "You got another smoke?"

Hugh tossed him his pack, turned and walked out of the door of the staff quarters that opened on the company of-fice side next to the boiler room.

Pausing for a moment, he adjusted his cap against the strong sunlight. Black smoke billowed up from the hot fur-nace in the boiler room. One of his men from the second rifle platoon, Pfc. Yabarra, was on boiler room duty. Hugh walked up to the open door and stuck his head in. Pfc. Ya-barra lay sleeping on the cement coalbin, a chunky Mexi-can from Arizona.

"Teeen-hut!" Hugh bellowed.

Yabarra almost fell off the coalbin, his cap dropped to the floor, as he scrambled to his feet wide-eyed, then grinned sheepishly. Yabarra had a ? tattooed on his fore-head between his eyes; on both brown hands were the cross marks of the Pachuko.

Hugh looked at the sooty dungarees, lifted his leg and farted insolently. "Carry on," he said.

Hugh walked across the street into the sun to the grass-grown high bunkers that shielded the supply-armory shed. He had helped build the bunkers in 1944, but no one had ever come up this far to do any bombing. At the time he had been slightly disappointed. Even now he could not see how they did much good for protection.

Walking between one bunker and the side of the shed toward the rear where the armory door stood open, he stepped up the single step and stood just inside leaning on the oil- and cosmoline-stained counter.

Sergeant Pappy Dreek sat on a .30 caliber ammo crate surrounded by .45s, sweatily engaged in cleaning them. Cursing lovingly, he rammed a bore brush through the large ugly barrel. "What's you want?" he said without look-ing up. Two naked lights burned in the shed, one over the small armory and one over the precise stacks of equip-ment in the supply section. Up front, S/Sgt. Carlisle, a curly blond young man, sat over a game of solitaire.

Hugh leaped up on the counter, spun around on his ass and dropped his legs on the other side. "I want a cigarette, Pappy," he answered blithely.

Pappy Dreek looked up, pained, his gnarled face shadowy in the dim light. "I thought you were in the field," he said. "Why ain't you in the field?"

"I got more important things to do than run off to the field and supervise the digging of crappers," Hugh said, curling his mustache like the villain forcing the rent from the orphaned maiden. "What if I was an officer and you sat there like that when I came in? Your military courtesy is lax, Pappy, real sloppy."

"I can sense officers coming," Pappy informed him. "They walk different. I was supposed to have a working party this morning," he bitched. "All these weapons here"—he waved his hand at the stacks of M-1's and machine guns and BARs—"got to be cleaned by tomorrow morning. Gunner Haley's gonna inspect 'em. But I didn't get a workin' party, and I don't think I'll get the bitch wolf done."

"You're the armorer," Hugh said, catching the pack of cigarettes Pappy tossed grudgingly. "A good armorer don't need other men to clean his weapons."

"Your ass!" Pappy howled. "With all these weapons I do. Why'nt you give me a hand since you got nothing to do?"

Hugh cleared his throat aloofly. "I need some more cosmoline," he said.

Fuming, Pappy stood up among the piles of pistols. "More cosmoline for your goddam cookie duster." He shook his head wearily. "Why the hell didn't you use mustache wax?"

"Mustache wax!" Hugh said. "For this?" He fingered his mustache tenderly. "I like the smell of cosmoline under my nose. It reminds me of this armory which is very dear to my heart."

"Balls," Pappy said.

"You need help," Hugh suggested, "get Carlisle to help you. That's what he's here for."

"It ain't my job," Carlisle said from the front of the supply shed. "I got enough to do." His blond curly head bobbed back to the cards.

"Sure you do," Hugh said. "You sandbaggin' bastard. I can see you're busy as hell."

Carlisle did not say anything.

"Aw to hell with it," Pappy said. "I guess I can get this done." He looked at the weapons disconsolately. "I wonder why Gunner Haley wants to check this now?"

140

"Ham Haley," Hugh said, "is the only sonofabitch in the company with enough sense to check them. Other than me," he added.

"All right," Pappy nodded, "but he don't usually do it till October. Hell, he just checked them last month."

"Maybe someone put him up to it?" Hugh grinned.

Pappy rubbed his jaw, a tentative motion, puzzled. "You're a big help."

"Pretty Boy Carlisle," Hugh jumped in. "Can you get away from old Sol long enough to tell me how many flak jackets you got on hand?"

"Flak jackets?" Carlisle laid his cards down.

"Yes, flak jackets," Hugh said. "And flak girdles, too."

Carlisle looked around at the shelves filled with packs, shelter halves, ponchos, web gear. "I don't know," he scratched his head, "I ain't never had to count them."

"Well, you can count them now," Hugh said. "I want to know if we got enough for every man in the company. Also the goddam leggins."

Lazily, Carlisle got to his feet. "When you want it? Today?"

"This afternoon." Hugh turned back to Pappy, who was still looking at him in puzzlement, with a far-out look as if someone had called his name. "How many machine guns you got on hand?"

"Not enough," Pappy said distantly.

"How many is that?"

Pappy looked at the light thirties stacked along the wall. "Nine countin' all of them. With not enough spare parts for three."

"Make out a requisition for them parts," Hugh said. "And check to see which of those guns need surveying."

"A requisition!" Pappy choked. "Jesus Christ, Hugh! I've tried to requisition parts for them before. And get new guns too. It just can't be done."

"The hell it can't," Hugh grinned. "Maybe we can't get them on requisition, but we can get them."

"I'd like to know how." Pappy shook his head. "The fucking Army's the only one with the gear."

Hugh nodded. "And they got too damn much of it. That's where I plan on getting it."

"You think they'll give it to you?" Pappy frowned. "I've tried that."

"They'll give it to me," Hugh said. "Because I'm going to

141

take it. Don't worry about that. Just make out a list of what you need. You'll get the parts."

"I got to see that to believe it," Pappy snorted. "Say," he said thoughtfully, "you ever seen the gear the Japanee Army got?"

"Sure," Hugh said. "It's all brand spanking new. Most of their weapons haven't had their cherries busted."

"You goddam rights!" Pappy said furiously. "Look at this crap." He waved a disgusted hand at his weapons. "Whores. World War One gear. And we can't even get it surveyed. What they want us to do? Fight with clubs?"

"We'll get the weapons, Pappy, don't worry about that," Hugh said, knowing he wouldn't, knowing there were no weapons to be given. Christ, they couldn't even buy them! But it didn't hurt to say they would get some.

"How about the supply?" Carlisle called out from his part of the shed where he was stacking flak jackets, bullet-proof vests that were no more bullet proof than negligées, and Hugh wondered why he had asked Carlisle to count them?

"What about it?" he said.

"You want a list of bad supply gear, too?" Carlisle asked.

"I don't need one," Hugh said. "You haven't issued out anything since you been supply sarjint. You ain't had anything to issue out.'

"That's the truth," Carlisle said glumly. "I can tell you right now I ain't got enough flak jackets for the company. Hell, I ain't even got enough for a full platoon."

"How many carbines you got, Pappy?" Hugh said.

Pappy Dreek grinned cunningly. "Carbines? We ain't supposed to have carbines. That's Army gear."

"Sure."

Pappy opened a huge trunk next to the stacked machine guns as Hugh, sitting on the counter, peered in at carbines, Thompson guns, and outmoded totally rejected Reising guns, and half a dozen miscellaneous pistols.

"Twelve Carbines," Pappy said proudly. "My dried cunt collection. And four Thompsons. And three Reising guns. And your pistol," he added.

"My old Parabellum," Hugh said fondly. "Let me see it, with my hands."

Pappy handed the large weapon to Hugh: a 1908 Navy Luger, ten-inch barrel, carbine-type holster stock, and a thirty-two round drum magazine—a work of precision art that did not have the muzzle heaviness of the .45 or the

142

lumbering balance, but fit his hand like a kidskin glove. Hugh had owned it since the Reservoir in Korea when he'd taken it off a dead M/Sgt who obviously had no more use for it, and he had carried it with him ever since. Now he held it up and hefted its perfect balance. "I think I'll take it with me," he said. "Keep it in my foot locker."

"It's your pistol," Pappy said. "I only wish that bunch that came in from Korea last week woulda brought some Russian weapons with them."

"That's against Geneva, Pappy," Hugh said. "They can't take any weapons out of Korea."

"Maybe no," Pappy said, "but they got a million of 'em stacked away in their bunkers over there."

"Saving them for a rainy day," Hugh said, "when Luke jumps off again."

"And when he does," Pappy sorrowed, "this company won't have beanshooters. This battalion won't for that matter."

"The whole division," Carlisle called from up front.

"Don't tell me," Hugh said. "Tell the Kizer, or Gunny Finch, or Top Condrum."

"Top Condrum," Pappy said with disdain. "He's too busy sending people to the brig. I never seen a man wanted to put people in jail as bad as Condrum."

"He's been in too long," Hugh said, "him and Gunny Finch both. The Crotch fucked 'em both up. Better be careful it don't happen to you, Pappy."

"No way in hell," Pappy avowed. "I ain't never had the syph," he tapped his knuckles on the wood counter top, "like Top Condrum."

"You can't blame it on the syph," Hugh grinned. "Blame it on the USMCVD."

Pappy laughed raucously. "You're a great one to talk. You been in since before Big Two. I don't see you gettin' out."

"You don't see me shipping over, either," Hugh said casually. "By the way, Pappy," he taunted, "how was that dolly you slept with last week?"

"Oh, yeah." Pappy flushed slightly. "At the U.S. Bar? Yeah. Mitchiko?"

"The little one." Hugh bobbed his head.

"Oh, she was pretty good, all right." Pappy looked at his machine guns. "Yeah, she was really fine. A choice piece of ass."

Hugh's mustache rose sharply with his grin. "I might have to give her a try someday," he said. "When you ain't got her."

"Well, you can have her," Pappy offered. "I ain't been back to see her since then. Hell, she ain't my girl." He picked up his .45 again and started cleaning it.

"That's damn noble of you." Hugh slid off the counter with his Navy Luger. "I just might do that," he said, turned and walked out into the bright morning sunlight.

"He's really high today, ain't he?" Hugh heard Pappy say in an odd voice to Carlisle.

Leisurely walking back to the staff quarters to have a beer from the ice locker before noon chow, Hugh thought of Chebe-san Ito, whom he had only thought of fleetingly since the last time he'd slept with her which was—lessee, Saturday night? Yep, Saturday night it was and a balling good time. A sharp little dolly all right. Must have made five thousand yen that night. He had to admire efficiency like that, and he seriously doubted that she was lying when she said she liked it: liked her work, although it *did* hurt her back occasionally. Still, if she was acting, it was a damn good act. Yet he was sure she liked the money a hell of a lot more—he sure bet she did, he thought, moving past the bunkers out to the street.

Really ought to go see her again one of these nights, just on a hunch if for nothing else. Just to see if he could still see a reflection of himself in her. Something about himself that he liked excessively. He did not see it in many people. Certainly not in Gunny Finch, or Pappy Dreek, or especially Top Condrum! A trace of it in Koko Hobbs; some in Ham Haley and Quiller Carpenter. Perhaps there was even a skosh bit in his new right guide, Bohane. If there was it wasn't because Bohane had a medal. Maybe it was because Bohane led with his chin, something that he himself had not done for a long time now.

He thought about it sketchily for three days, not going back to the U.S. Bar to see Chebe-san for proof but merely thinking, feeling there was something there to be gleaned and learned.

He spent the next two days in the field with his platoon, congratulating himself on placing Bohane in as right guide. The lean corporal knew his work, knew his trade extremely well. It appeared that he had served an observant appren-

144

ticeship in Korea, and Hugh was pleased with the way things were working out. He had even outdone his previous deck wiring, he thought, and now he held *all* the cards, the winning hand. *No more Zorn.* That was the happiest thought. Getting him out of the platoon had been the best gimmick yet. Maybe in a couple months he would have Koko Hobbs recommend Bohane for Sergeant.

On Thursday, the twenty-seventh of August, Horrible Hog company did not go to the field. They were scheduled for class on battalion weapons—the water-cooled .30s, the heavy chugging .50s and the 81 MM mortars—at the bleacher classrooms on the other side of the parade field.

Hugh Thorton, who had left Gunny Finch sleeping in the staff quarters (no reason to waken the dead when the company did not have to go to the field), did not prefer to attend the classes on weapons everyone knew about. With Top Condrum over at the battalion office making plans with his comrade in courts-martial, SgtMaj Halloran, for the expedient disposal of one marine who had defiled law and order, Hugh lolled complacently in the company office with Gunner Ham Haley over the early morning's lazy cup of coffee.

He and Ham Haley, a mustang with a muscled bloated belly from twenty-five years' accumulation of beer and a bulldog phiz, who acted more like a rear-rank private than a marine warrant officer, were languidly discussing the pros and cons of the Fujioka "business women" using alum to tighten their vaginas, when a jeep pulled up in the cinder mustering area outside and two men got out, one carrying a camera, and walked up to the window-door of the company office.

Hugh looked up quickly when the window-door slid open and the two men came in, photographing in his mind the unfamiliar faces, thinking rapidly what did these two want?

The two marines in dungarees looked like the faces displayed on the recruiting posters outside the post offices. They stopped at Quiller Carpenter's desk; obviously the man not carrying the camera was in charge.

Quiller Carpenter, still immersed in his previous night's escapade, was staring glumly at his coffee on the littered desk.

"Hi there," the man in charge said. "My name is Sergeant Morgan from PIO. You have a corporal around here named Bohane?"

"PIO?" Quiller questioned distastefully. "Yair, we got a Bohane, only one I know of; you want him you can have him. Less work for me. I'll tell him to pack."

"Oh no," Sergeant Morgan said. "We just want to talk to him; get some pictures."

"Everyone's against me," Quiller said. He jerked his head at Hugh and Ham Haley. "Over there. See them? The man with the bush is his p'toon sargint."

Sergeant Morgan and his tail with the camera walked over. "Good morning, sir," he said militarily to Ham Haley.

"What're you sellin'?" Ham Haley hooked his thumbs in his belt, both ham hands disappearing under his belly. "Passports to Heaven?"

"We're down here to do an article on one of your men, sir." Morgan smiled. His shadow followed with the cue.

"What's the man's name?" Hugh asked over his coffee.

"Corporal Bohane, Gunny," Morgan said. "The clerk said he was in your platoon."

"He still is," Hugh said, the steam from his coffee drooping his mustache.

"What you want to do an article on him for?" Ham Haley asked gruffly.

"Well, sir," Morgan began. "Regiment found out he had a Silver Star and re-enlisted in Korea. They want an article on him. It might even make *Leatherneck*."

"If it does," Ham Haley sneered, "we'll have one man from this company in outer space." He picked up his coffee. "You take care of it, Hugh." He walked over to Quiller Carpenter's desk, punched him huskily, almost knocking him over, sat down across from him and grinned, deviling him.

"So that's what you want to do?" Hugh said. "Take some pictures and a little write-up?"

"That's right, Gunny," Sergeant Morgan said.

Hugh studied him for a moment, then set his cup down and carefully lit a cigarette. "You want to see his record book? Or just him?"

"No; just him." Morgan smiled, his camera-carrying replica nodding.

"That's what I thought," Hugh said. "Well, come on. We'll get him."

146

Hugh, leading the way, walked over to the inside stairs leading up to the window-door. Ham Haley was busily chastising Quiller Carpenter about his liberty fiascoes. Haley would never get rid of Carpenter, Hugh thought. Although he didn't warm up till the afternoon, he was the best company clerk. Better for sure than King Solomon. Probably because Quiller had been an infantryman, a field marine, before. How the hell did he ever become a clerk?

When they got outside, Sergeant Morgan said, "I'd like to get a picture with Mount Fuji in the background."

Looking at the both of them, standing under the hammering of the August sun, the ideas that had been sloshing around in Hugh's mind solidified. "Say," he said, "you know anything about Bohane?"

"Only that he got a Silver Star and shipped over," Morgan said.

"Well, he's quite a guy," Hugh said leisurely. "Make damn good news."

"Is that right?" Morgan exchanged glances with his double.

"Sure," Hugh said, curling his mustache. "You know what the sonofabitch did in Korea?" He waited until the twin got his notebook out and balanced it on the camera. "He'd go out on night patrol, see? Through no man's land and stay maybe two three days, making maps and studying enemy positions. All alone, and he wouldn't eat a damn thing for three days. Just drink water and not much of that."

"No shit?" Morgan said. "You getting this down?" he asked his twin.

"Hell," Hugh said, "that ain't the half of it. Once he carried his platoon leader piggyback all the way down Vegas when he was shot up—the platoon leader that is—Bohane never got a scratch."

"Never got a hit," Morgan said incredulously. "All the time he was in Korea?"

"No siree," Hugh said. "And that's a funny thing, too. He told me about this once. Seems he went to see a Korean fortuneteller in Seoul before Vegas. Well, this fortuneteller told him he'd never get hurt, not even a scratch." Hugh looked at the two mystically.

"You get that?" Morgan asked the other. "That's what they want," he said to Hugh. "Human interest like that. Helps get recruits."

"Well, Bohane's really got the news," Hugh nodded, "if you can get him to tell you. Fact is he was up for the Medal of Honor in Korea. You know that?"

They both shook their heads.

"They had him written up for it," Hugh said. "But they couldn't get it past channels because this light colonel had written himself up for one too. They couldn't send two of them in."

"Oh," Morgan said charily, "I don't think we can use that."

"Probably not," Hugh agreed. "Anyway they relegated him to a Silver Star. But that kid should have got a lot more."

"How's that?" Morgan checked his double to see if he was getting it all down.

"For what he did!" Hugh said. "Man, that kid's got guts! Carried twenty men, all of them wounded, down Vegas while Luke was shooting at him all the way. Then he went back up and took over the platoon, what was left of it, and personally accounted for killing thirty gooks."

"Where is he?" Morgan asked. "We want some pictures of him."

"The company's having classes on battalion weapons up to the parade field," Hugh explained. "I'll get one of the clerks to go after him."

They walked back to the office, Hugh hearing them chattering behind him; he clenched his jaws to dampen an explosion of healthy guffaws. Well, it wouldn't hurt Bohane any.

He opened the window-door and stuck his head in. "Hey, Solomon! Run over to the parade field and get Corpril Bohane."

King Solomon looked up from his desk, sniffed once, looked at Quiller Carpenter who was still being gouged by Ham Haley's deviling spurs. "I have these unit diary forms to fill out, Sergeant Thorton," he said succinctly.

"Get your ass over there and get Bohane!" Hugh bellowed.

"Yes, sir!" Solomon jumped quickly to his feet, snatched his cap off his desk and breezed out prissily.

Hugh walked back to the two PIO men, smiling encouragingly. In the next ten minutes he expounded on Bohane's uncanny abilities with weapons, his propensities for lead-

148

ership and his devout religious undertones. He also explained that Bohane felt so badly about killing so many gooks he had given half his re-enlistment bonus to the Yamanaka Orphanage.

If they expected to see a six-foot broad-shouldered fire-breathing, yet modestly boyish defender of their country, the PIO met instead a lean five-foot-ten 155 pounds of raw half-Irish rebel, skin taut over his sharp rawboned face. Wrung out from a scrotum-roaring never-to-be-satisfied raid on Bamboo Alley the night before and wearing a frayed dungaree cap, mud from the field adorning the knees of his dungaree trousers he swaggered belligerently up to them, leaving King Solomon walking girlishly behind.

"What the fuck's this about an interview?" Giff Bohane said, irascible.

"These men here to do an article on you," Hugh grinned, catching a red light in Bohane's eyes.

"We've heard a lot about you, Corporal," Morgan said. "All about how you killed those gooks and gave your money to the orphanage. I myself was never in Korea," he said solemnly, "but I know exactly how you feel."

Giff grimaced at Hugh. "What the hell is this about an Or-fucking-age?"

"He's modest," Hugh explained. "Now what kind of pictures you want? With any weapons? Helmet? Any of that?"

"Hey wait a minute," Giff said. "Goddamit! Why you doin' this article on me?"

"You got a Silver Star and shipped over in Korea, didn't you?" Morgan asked pleasantly.

"Yeah; that's right," Giff said. "What kind of a article is this now?" he asked, giving a suspicious half-glance at Thorton.

"The PIO wants it," Sergeant Morgan soothed. "They'll probably send dispatches of them out to all the recruiting offices in the States. That's what they usually do. It's good propaganda for the Corps."

"Was all this *your* motherfuckin' idea?" Giff said, turning full face on Hugh, a sort of wild look, addled.

"My idea!" Hugh feigned surprise. "Hell, I'm not a PIO man."

"Then you're in the wrong racket," Giff said, with just a hint of mockery.

"That's what the dollies tell me." Hugh grinned dashingly at the barracks. If he'd looked at the two PIO men he would have doubled up helplessly.

"I guess you've got my life story," Giff said to Sergeant Morgan, still carrying that wild wondering look.

"We need some pictures now," Morgan smiled. "Stand off a ways from the barracks. We don't want that in."

"Well, how about the gunny?" Giff suggested. "To add some color. You know what I mean?" He nodded toward Thorton. "Put the *old* man up with some young blood. He's got quite a story too. Quite a life—"

"Naw," Hugh said quickly. "Not me. I've never done anything great. Nothing interesting about me." Where does that punk Bohane get that "young old" stuff? he thought indignantly. You could never tell about them Irish bastards, he thought.

"We'll just take the corporal," Morgan apologized. "He's the one we came to do the story on."

Hugh backed away, smiling at Bohane.

For the next five minutes they took an assortment of pictures. Hugh beamed as if he had just pulled off the greatest tour de force in history, while Bohane posed for each shot. It was amusingly obvious, to Hugh at any rate, that Bohane was enjoying it in a sort of left-handed way, simply from the way he conjured up his face in combative histrionics, as if saying *"Not everyone can become a marine,"* like the porgy-bait generals giving a farewell speech to a bunch of boots.

When they finished with the pictures the two PIO men thanked Bohane effusively, tossed their notes in the jeep and climbed in after them.

"Thanks a lot, Gunny," Morgan said pleasantly to Hugh as the jeep shot off, showering fragments of rock and ash behind it.

"You're entirely welcome," Hugh said, turned back to where Giff was standing and smoking reflectively. "See?" he said. "It was painless."

"Like bullheaded clap!" Giff grinned tightly. "I guess I should thank you too, *Gunny*. If they's ever anything I can do for you, just let me know. I'll go out of my way to do it. I really will." Cigarette dangling from his mouth, hands in his hip pockets, he walked back up toward the parade field.

What you had to do with a man like Bohane, Hugh analyzed, watching him swagger off, was play on his vanity—on his pride of being a man in his own definition of a man. Bohane's definition was obviously to become a living legend, he considered. That was it: a living legend. And as long as he Hugh played it that way he would have no trouble. Not from Bohane.

Priding himself on his own perception of people, his thorough knowledge of them, feeling the sun's enervating warmth spreading around him, he suddenly knew he was going to leave, going to take off right now for the weekend. There was no reason for him to stay around, Koko Hobbs could take care of anything, no one would miss him, and he hadn't had a long liberty weekend in a long time anyway—and he knew, really quite sure of himself now, that he would see Chebe-san.

More than anything else just to satisfy his curiosity about her though, he reminded himself, and when he'd done that . . . Well, Hugh who hesitates is lost!

He wouldn't even have to stay in Fujioka either. To hell with that. He would get out of the town for a while: Gotemba or Numazu. No, not Gotemba—he might run into his old shack job and her Army Major. Better stay away from there. Numazu, then. That was the slick deal. Get in some swimming and living, a weekend away from the Crotch.

Itchie was pressing Finch's uniforms when Hugh walked into the staff quarters to get dressed and ready to go to town. The wise small Japanee boy did not look up this time at all, but kept right on working. Hugh laid his civvies out on his bunk, feeling relaxed and happy now, everything was going so damn good.

When he finished dressing, he walked over to Koko Hobbs' bunk, jotted down a quick note from his ubiquitous NCO's notebook: *Koko, gone to town for the weekend. Be back Monday or Tuesday. Don't wait up for me.* And signed it, *Your Great and Glorious Mentor, Hugh.* He laid it on the pillow and walked back out of the staff quarters, Itchie still impervious to the life that moved around him, complimenting himself on how well he had this one wired, and thinking if Chebe-san did not want to go along with him (Nay, only a fool would not want to go along with him), *could not* go along, then he would find someone else.

Naturally, he would ask her first.

7.

Chebe-san Ito was more than delighted to go and said so with a bright-eyed girlish enthusiasm.

Of course, she explained to Hugh in her smoky-whiskey hoarse voice when he came to the U.S. Bar that afternoon after leaving the camp early, she would have to be paid for it: more or less rented out from Mama-san Tokudo for the weekend. Mama-san Tokudo speakee ten thousand yen for a deal like that, Chebe-san told him.

"Hell, she'll get paid," Hugh said over his beer, one buttock propped up on a stool at the bar. He was wearing his white Hong Kong tailored suit with a black and white Aloha sport shirt. "Everyone'll get paid," he said extravagantly. "Especially you. You'll get paid. I'll even pay the cab driver who takes us down to Numazu."

"Why you want to go Numazu?" Chebe-san grinned.

Hugh looked at the smallness of her in the blue jeans and white shirt knotted around her round-flat copper-colored belly. "I want to join the communists," he said facetiously. "Go to a rally, see? Swimming, nice hotels. We'll go sightseeing like all them tourista sports."

"Hokay," Chebe-san laughed deeply. "You pay *okane* now, *ne?* Me go catchee clothes get ready."

Hugh pulled his wallet out, counted ten thousand yen (Jack Koko Hobbs' money) and paid her, the fee as it were like renting a goddam house, and watched her walk swivel-hipped, pendulously, to the corridor leading to the back rooms.

"Take your toothbrush," he called after her. "I don't share mine."

She laughed throatily and disappeared around the corner.

Hugh leaned back against the bar feeling the laziness of afternoon generate silence around him. This early in the

152

day there was no one in the bar—except the girls, naturally, he thought with a sly grin. And most of them were in the back curling their hair. Nighttime and roses he'd do a little curling of the hair himself.

Outside, through the open door of the bar, bright sunlight glared down on the dusty street, rousing flies from their shady garbage-filled recluses, stifling the parched paint of the bars.

Hugh shrugged in the silence of the bar and killed his beer, set the empty bottle on the stool beside him, and looked out the open door, contemplating the deserted street.

Breaking his line of vision, a figure would move down the street casting a long shadow on the powdery dust hiding behind rocks, feet ploofing on loud flaps, move on and the sun would be back where his shadow had been, a yellow alley into the door of the U.S. Bar pressing the dust motes back onto the floor.

It was while he was looking, lazily impatient, staring across the street at the A. J. Hideaway, that the old Japanee man, Tex, and his loyal waddling nameless goose moved in front of his vision. Tex, a Fujioka institution—perhaps a legend, Hugh thought, a social enigma—dressed in the same clothes every day of the year: cowboy hat, vest, cheap imitation leather holster and gun belt carrying his fiddle lovingly, the fiddle and the fat sassy hissing and protective goose flanking Tex everywhere.

Hugh could see clearly the single glazed white eye in Tex's face: dead bloodless unseeing, not glass or fake, but merely a dead eye. Contrastingly, the other eye was so narrowed it appeared closed.

Watching from the concealed dimness of the U.S. Bar, Hugh wondered with professional curiosity about old Tex every time he saw him. It was common knowledge that Tex had been a soldier in the Imperial Army during Big Two, and Hugh watched fixedly, thinking the Japanee man looked like a papier-mâché statue into which some amateur artist had breathed life—a veteran of a nonexistent army. And what had he been? An officer? An enlisted man? Perhaps a T/Sgt like himself? A platoon leader? Maybe even a POW, somewhere. Now inarticulate, incapable of expression through a nonmusical fiddle: the end of a twenty year hitch.

After a moment of detached indecision Tex moved on, his goose walking evenly beside him, hissing and craning its white neck.

The inarticulate voices, energies swimming in the air, had left Hugh cold, with an impaled picture of himself in his mind, still staring into the hot afternoon and wondering who it was in Horrible Hog Company that reminded him of Tex.

"Darn your pictures anyway," he said to the empty street.

"Nani O?" Chebe-san Ito questioned, walking out of the corridor carrying a night traveling bag, wearing a cool-looking pale green suntan dress, short poised and ebullient.

Hugh turned to look at her, noticing she was wearing her falsies again but looking exceptionally sharp. "How about taking a couple bottles with us?" he said, nodding behind the bar. "Some of that black market Stateside stuff?"

"Hokay, Thoton-san," she said cheerfully, setting her bag on the bar, and she walked behind it, bent down, reappeared with two quarts of V.O., smiling warmly, and set the bottles on the bar. "Now you pay five thousand yen for drink, *ne?*" she said in her bubbling throaty voice.

"Oh, always." Hugh grinned sardonically, pulled his wallet out and paid her (Jack Koko Hobbs' money). "Now let's get to hell out of here."

"We go havo us *toxon stekki*-nice time." Chebe-san walked back around the bar, picked up her bag, and slipped her free arm through his.

"You don't know the half of it, doll," he said.

They caught a cab at the taxi house across from HOCK AT HENRY'S by the main gate, both silent after the dusty hot walk down from the bar, and Hugh had to awaken the cab driver, who had a fly crawling hungrily over his nose in the small box office.

It was a Mitsubishi cab, manufactured by the same people who made the Jap Zero during Big Two, small boxy whinnying.

Hugh had one hell of a time sitting in it, crouched over bending forward, his back cramped. Chebe-san sat beside him very comfortably as if she was riding in a Cadillac limousine, and Hugh made a mental note if he ever did this again he would for goddam sure take a train.

The sleepy-eyed cab driver sped off jerkily, bouncing

over the rocky Fujioka main street, raising a rooster tail of dust. They left the dirt road and sped up the cement highway toward Numazu.

Moving south, Chebe-san watched the thick green of the Japanee countryside, a happy smile on her oval face, and Hugh watched her out of the corner of his eye, figuring.

"You no know how happy Chebe-san is now?" She smiled up at him crouched over. "No like stay bar all time."

"No?" Hugh said, craning his head down to her, sharply surprised at her calling herself *Chebe-san*. "I thought you liked it at the bar. You told me you did once."

"Me no know *you* then," she said softly hoarsely. "You come stay one night with me. It is the business."

"Well," Hugh feigned surprise, "I guess I was wrong."

"All time," Chebe-san said with historic oldest-profession dramatics, "all time I work in U.S. Bar catchee marines no like. They drunk and no good. You different, Thoton-san. You kind." She leaned over and kissed him on his cheek. "You Chebe-san's number-one skivvie *honcho*."

Was *this* a part of him he saw in her? For Chrissakes surely he was more subtle than that, feeling badly that she didn't give him any credit. As was expected of him though, he rubbed the spot on his cheek that she had kissed, running his fingers over it tenderly, probing. Might as well play the role, Thoton-san. Goddam but his back was beginning to hurt! "We'll have a swell time," he said happily. "We'll go swimming and dancing. You brought your swim suit, didn't you?"

"*Hai,*" she smiled.

"You sure you don't drink whiskey?" Hugh looked at the two quarts between his legs.

Chebe-san laughed. "Agggu," she made a wry face. "All time make me sick sick."

"How much farther we got to go, anyway?"

"Seven eight miles maybe," Chebe-san said.

As if the cab driver had caught the impatient inflection in Hugh's voice he opened up, the little engine singing, straining. He must have been a Zero pilot during Big Two, Hugh thought.

It took fifteen minutes to get to Numazu. They passed trucks and cars and pedestrians on the outskirts of the city. Through the open spaces between buildings, hunching down lower painfully, Hugh saw the dazzling blue of Suruga Bay that grabbed all the tourists from miles around. Japanee

155

and American both. It was also the Japanee Communist headquarters.

Hugh had once spent a weekend at the Hotel-No. 1, a grade-"A" hotel that extolled cozy rooms with Stateside beds and a pleasing atmosphere with cuisine, music and liquor—but no women, unless you brought your own. It was also, the manager had told Hugh before, highly recommended by servicemen of the U.S. Army, which meant it was a low-grade hotel. But it was on the beach, only one hundred yards from the water, and today Hugh meant to stay there. Chebe-san was thrilled, or acted it; it didn't matter to her where they stayed at all, she told him, squeezing his arm with the ancient promise of things to come.

They got out of the cab in front of the Hotel-No. 1, where a young Japanee boy in an Australian digger hat served as doorman, and Hugh unwound, gratefully sympathizing with all the tall people in the world.

Flocks of people scurried along the streets and sidewalks in the Numazu afternoon; rickshaws, loaded and empty, were pulled steadily along the street by determined-faced coolies, a bustling of quiet afternoon before the weekend tumult.

One arm around Chebe-san's waist, the other clutching the two bottles, Hugh walked her up to the glass door. Inside, he registered at the desk while Chebe-san waited demurely in the lobby amid the usual early mingling of tourists. Some, ostensibly Americans, cast withering moralistic glances at them: shameful shameful.

"Come on, Chebe-san," Hugh said, unnecessarily loud. "Let's go testo testo that bed." He walked over to her, picked up her traveling bag and his two quarts, and started for the stairs.

Chebe-san clutched his arm fondly all the way to the room which was on the third floor overlooking the bay, waited smiling while Hugh unlocked the door.

Inside, she turned and kissed him, pulling him down to her, then snuggled her head on his chest. "Oh, Thoton-san," she said softly, whiskily. "Chebe-san think *toxon* much of you. You Chebe-san's wonderful wonderful man."

Over the top of her head, Hugh looked speculatively at the bed, the Stateside bed with the innerspring mattress. Through the window over the bed he saw the two blues of the sky and ocean conflict on the horizon.

156

Silently, he led her over to the bed and sat down, pulling her down on his lap; he opened one of his bottles and drank heavily.

"You want makee love now, Thoton-san?"

"Right now," Hugh said.

"You pay two thousand yen, *ne?*" she said with a sorrowing face. "Mama-san takee all money. Chebe-san poor girl. Need money to pay for family, very poor."

"Ah so," Hugh said with a grin. "Everybody's so very poor. It is a destitute country and the only one making any money at all is little poor Chebe-san."

"Nani O?" She leaned back from him.

"I said," Hugh grinned widely, "the only one making any money is Chebe-san Ito."

She got off his lap quickly and stared down at him hard. Tears formed in her eyes and she began speaking softly in Japanee, sounding as if she were making a plea for understanding, but Hugh understood every word explicitly, interpreting with a wide grin on his face. In short, standing there almost weeping looking lovingly down at him, she was calling him a mealymouthed prize sonofabitch.

"Now I ain't all those, doll," he said, but thinking he was *almost* all of them. "You are a bad actor," he spoke in Japanee.

Immediately the tears stopped. "Hokay, Thoton-san," she said defiantly. "Me need money. You pay or me go back. Acting is the only way I can make money," she explained in her fluent American. "Shit," she said. "You no fucking better than all the rest."

Hugh pulled up her night traveling bag and opened it before Chebe-san could move, reached inside and brought out the ten thousand yen he'd paid her, plus the five thousand for the whiskey. "You think Mama-san Tokudo will starve?"

"Goddam you," Chebe-san said.

"Now, Chebe-san," Hugh soothed, "that's no way to talk to your number-one skivvie *honcho* is it?"

"Don't call me Chebe-san," she said flatly. "Where the hell did you get that anyway? *Chebe-san.* How goddam corny can you get?"

"About as corny as skivvie *honcho,*" Hugh countered. "Where'd you learn to speak American, anyway?"

"None of your damn business."

Hugh curled his mustache.

"And why the hell don't you shave that thing off?" she said. "It tickles the hell out of me."

"Speaking of tickling," Hugh grinned, "that reminds me of something. You remember the first night at the U.S. Bar?"

"Hell, yes," Chebe-san said adamantly.

"It wasn't Pappy Dreek bought the French Tickler," Hugh explained. "It was me. But you wouldn't know that, would you? You didn't even suspect it at all. Not much you didn't." He paused, taking another drink. "You even saw me slip it in his pocket. But you didn't waste any time coming into my room after Mama-san paid you that money."

Chebe-san's anger faded into a grin, both sly and genuine. "You knew all the time, didn't you?"

"Sure did." Hugh nodded. "And if I'm going to make love to some dolly I want to know at least what or who she is. I'm a curious bastard."

"You sure are." Chebe-san walked over to the bed and sat down beside him. "I don't know why it's important though." Then she laughed genuinely. "If you knew that all the time why didn't you tell me?"

"Hell, I was enjoying myself," Hugh grinned. "I haven't had it that good for a long time."

"You really liked it?"

"Sure. Really."

"Well, I like it too," Chebe-san said appraisingly. "I usually like it. I guess that's why I'm a business woman."

"You like *it?*" he asked. "Or the money?"

"Both. I wouldn't be in it if I didn't."

Hugh actually had not expected that, and it surprised him. That a whore would tell the truth was almost unbelievable. At least in the States. No whore in the States would say that—an average woman, yes. An ordinary affair-type woman, of course—it was only natural for them to like it and admit it. But a whore: usually there was the you-made-me-what-I-am story. Either they had been raped when they were real young or some slick sly sonofabitch had seduced them under false pretenses. This now was honesty, like the first time: it opened a chink, a narrow tube to start the knife gouging around to find that part of himself that he had met in her, in her mind—rapport or whatever it was.

"Say," he said suddenly, aware of Chebe-san's warm presence. "Do you believe in love?"

158

She shook her head. "No," she said whiskily. "Not at all. Maybe you think I was dishonest. Probably I was. But I am at least too honest to fall in love. Anyone who is honest with himself is not going to fall in love."

"No, not that kind," Hugh qualified. "I don't mean the romantic to-have-and-to-hold, contagious puppy-dog love. I mean the love of rapport. Mental communion. A seeing of yourself in a woman, where sex and love are split. Where," he groped through his mind, seeing it, what he wanted said, afraid if he did not say it right it would never be. "Where a man and a woman attain the highest degree of sex without any physical contact," he said excitedly.

"But of course," Chebe-san agreed. "That is all there is. That is love. Yes, I believe in that. It is something I have known for a long time."

Hugh was caught short by the perception, the bare convincing honesty in her face, her knowing of something that had taken him a long time to see, to understand the way he wanted to understand it—yet he had known and lived by that all his life (hadn't he?). Or at least the past ten years. But now there was this: a rare quality of honesty in this woman which he had seen in himself. Like seeing his own soul in the face of her, a contact without physical touch. But how could he thoroughly enjoy himself physical with his soul? Or was he meant to? Was anyone meant to? Was that why the Sphinx was half spirit and half matter? Was there soul love? Did souls make love? Yes they did! He had always thought it might have existed: but it was hard to remember. There was *Seoul* love and then there was *Soul* love.

"Well, I believe it too," Hugh averred, back into himself. "But I don't think we're ready for it yet. Not in this life or perhaps this solar system. But it will come," he said assuredly, and took another drink. "And you're right about that being honest. But I'll tell you something, Chebe-san—"

"Mitchiko."

"Mitchiko," Hugh conceded. "You ain't going to make a wad of dough or anything else being honest in this life. If you don't play it like you did first with me all the time you'll get nothing," he said futilely, repudiating himself, thinking it had been so very very close.

"Hell, Thoton-san," she smiled. "I know that."

"Hugh," he said, watching his belief fly away on the

159

matter wings of the Sphinx. "You can call me Hugh. All my friends call me Hugh."

"You're an odd man," she said.

"Oh I sure am." He looked over at her. "There's nothing odd about you at all."

She scooted up on the bed and leaned her back against the wall, folding her arms around her knees. "Why did you bring me to Numazu if you knew all that?"

"I wanted to have some fun," he explained simply. "But I wanted it without any goddam false pretenses."

"And so do I," Chebe-san said. "But I have to make money too. I'll have it made if the Americans stay around here long enough."

"They won't though," Hugh said with a suave twist at his mustache. "And you know it. You'll be lucky if we stay here another year."

She nodded. "I know. You'll all go back to war again," she said matter-of-factly. "Might as well make hay while the sun shines." She smiled.

"That's probably the shortest philosophy anyone ever had."

"All right goddamit," she snapped, slipping back into the anger again. "Maybe it is. But I'm not going to grow old and lose my teeth and wind up in a VD hospital."

"Nobody says you have to," Hugh said airily.

"No and I'm not going to either," Chebe-san said. Then she grinned again, the anger evaporating quickly like rain on a hot summer day under a ballooning two o'clock sun. "You know what the good little girl said?" she asked.

"No," Hugh said. "What?"

"The good little girl said, 'It's hard to be good.'" Chebe-san widened her eyes. "Know what the bad little girl said?"

"No."

"The bad little girl said, 'It's got to be hard to be good.'" She tucked her chin down on her knees and peered at him intently. "That is the way of my life. It is much like yours."

When she said that about the good little girl and the bad little girl, the old fatalistic predestination belief that was here rose up again, and he remembered how they all thought of their lives as merely an illusion, and lived it accordingly, rolling where they were kicked. Yet before, when they talked about "love," she had superseded all that other, the old stuff. He had unmistakably seen that, even felt it. It was almost mystical—occult, in a way. She was still staring at him, studying him.

"Since you're sure you got my life all picked out," he said finally after a pausing drink, "I'll let you in on one of Hugh Thorton's personal secrets: a rare philosophy, though I don't know what the hell for. Except it's the closest thing to a truth I ever found that fit me, made me see a little of myself. And I don't even remember where I got it."

Chebe-san looked at him questioningly, her oval face framed by the shiny black short-cut hair looking girlishly interested, lively, life giving, and for a moment Hugh felt he would just shuck it all and take her to bed, forget himself with her who was to him so vital and vibrantly alive.

"I call it 'The man who wouldn't eat his wife,'" he said easily, staring back at her. "The time don't make any difference. Any time. Time present if you prefer.

"Well, there was this band of cannibals, see," Hugh explained. "They were making a journey to a new land, a strange land, leaving their homes because they had run out of people to eat. Sort of like Ma Hubbard and her old dog.

"There was this one cannibal, Slim he was called, who was not exactly one of their number. Oh, he was a cannibal all right," Hugh pointed out. "But something bugged him. Maybe he was slow. Anyway, he couldn't understand why if they were all moving why the hell they didn't change their life too, as long as they were changing their environment. Old Slim wanted to progress."

Hugh lit a cigarette carefully, pausing. "On the trek to this new land Slim's mother, who had been a high-ranking member of the tribe, died. Just simply died and since they were hard up for chow they decided to barbecue her up for dinner. Slim did not enjoy his supper too well. He even had a little indigestion. Somehow, he didn't feel he was changing, reaching something new. Nevertheless, he feasted; he didn't want to starve, and they moved on.

"Finally they arrived at their promised land." He waved his arm around the small hotel room with the Stateside bed. "It was beautiful. Almost tropical. Something like Numazu, a resort. Slim was happy as hell living in a completely changed environment, and hoped for a change in their lives. But that night," Hugh said softly, "Slim's wife died. And in honor of the tribe reaching the promised land the

161

honchos decided to celebrate by feasting on her; a victory celebration." Hugh paused and studied Chebe-san's eyes, the curiosity in them.

"Of course Slim was grieved, but he had no appetite. He wouldn't take his part of the meal. So the tribesmen banished him, calling him unfit, accusing him of treason. So he walked away from the table where his wife was dripping with A-1 sauce and sat alone on a rock looking out at the sea: a pariah, an outcast, a criminal among his own people, but he still felt he was right, and his thinking differently convinced him he was right.

"The thinking brought back his appetite," Hugh said blithely. "While he was sitting there a grasshopper jumped up on the rock beside him. He snatched the grasshopper up and ate it. It was delicious. Slim loved it.

"From that day on Slim has been searching the world for people who will eat insects but he never finds them, because everyone he meets is a cannibal."

Chebe-san sat looking at him in the silence, unwavering, arms still folded across her legs, knees tucked up under her chin. A pale sweet breeze blew in from the window.

"That's my story," Hugh said. "It's the only story I know that makes any sense."

"I got my streetcar fare in my shoe." Chebe-san shrugged.

Hugh laughed. "I'm not kicking you out." He stood up and capped the bottle and left the other one on the floor.

"Aren't you staying?" Chebe-san asked, leaning forward on the bed.

"I got to go look for some grasshopper people," Hugh grinned. "Look; why don't you use this room to work out of? You can make a few thousand yen on the side this weekend."

"All right," she said simply. "If you don't care if I use the room."

Hugh looked around, suddenly feeling he was in a strange unfamiliar room. "Sure; go ahead. I'll be back Sunday night to pick you up," he offered, wiring his deck for a fresh deal. When the hell was he going to quit forcing people to plop in lakes like rocks?

"You're not pissed off, are you?" Chebe-san asked.

"Pissed off?" Hugh said, puzzled. "Pissed off about what?"

Chebe-san pushed a lock of hair back from her forehead. "Nothing, I guess. Hokay," she smiled, "you come pick me up Sunday, *ne?*"

Grinning, Hugh opened the door and stepped out into the uncarpeted hall. "Sunday night," he called back and shut the door.

He jammed the half-full bottle into the pocket of his white Hong Kong tailored suit and walked back downstairs. Tourists still mingled in the lobby as if they were afraid to stay there and dreaded to go out on the streets where people moved wildly.

Outside, he paused under the marquee amid the horn-blasting tire-squealing afternoon where people moved all along the streets, strange unrecognized alien, searching for one another in chattering nuances.

Standing there under the protective shade of the marquee, he seemed to go a little way off from himself, looking back at himself as if he were some kind of sun-stroked signpost, each sign pointing a different way at right angles to one another; three roads, three paths, and the barracks were always in the distance, the longest road leading to them, irrevocably.

With a belated shock, while the afternoon diminished around him, he wondered what had made him hold forth so back at the hotel room. What was it that had unlocked him, made him articulate, helped him to say what he wanted to say? Up there he had forgotten himself completely: his own reason for living, for being alive, for calculating lives—for shuffling people like a deck of cards just to see what silly pissyass thing would happen next.

Like what a silly pissyass Testical Sergeant in the Marine Corps would do?

8.

Up the street Hugh saw the sign—SHANGHAI LIL's—flashing on and off in green and red neon. He stepped off impulsively and walked through the late afternoon sunlight to-

163

ward it, the bottle thudding against his hip through his jacket pocket.

After the glare of outside, Hugh was almost blinded in the smoky noise-riddled dark air of Shanghai Lil's. He gradually discerned people packed along the bar and in the tables across from the dancing floor in several stages of drunkenness. Behind the curtain of powdered light, music drifted in a taunting laziness.

He walked over to the bar, squeezed in between two soldiers and sat down. A rather stocky (but not too) Jo-san with high breasts and a wide mouth scurried up to wait on him.

"Bring me a glass and a bowl of ice," he said with sudden alacrity and watched the Jo-san move away. She was, in a way, quite attractive, just the womanness of her was attractive, and it would be fine, just dandy, he thought, if he could only think of Chebe-san that way, as just a plain ordinary everyday woman. But it went farther than that this time, it went a long way beyond that. And the farther it went the more puzzling it became, because he suddenly wanted to be the innocent again, the kid with the best-looking girl in school, but it had not quite worked out that way this time.

When the Jo-san came back with the ice and glass he leaned forward on the bar, his mustache dipping waggishly. "You got a date when the bars close; if you haven't got one already."

"Dai jobie." The Jo-san shrugged. "You no forget; I be here."

He sat drinking all the rest of the afternoon and evening, drinking slowly, not wanting to get drunk, just wanting to get mellow, trouble-free. Yet Chebe-san kept popping back into his mind and remained there when he took the Jo-san up the stairs to her room, and did not really leave him when he fucked her, and he was quite sure she knew this, could sense it, that if his tallywagger was in it, his heart sure as hell was not, and shamefaced he was good for only one time. He felt as if he were in a cave with no escape and simply had to lie there, helpless.

In the morning, hungover but happily undismayed, he had a choice ham and eggs breakfast at the restaurant across from Shanghai Lil's. Over his coffee he pondered his situation and made his plans for the day. What he should have done, possibly, was stay with Chebe-san in the hotel

164

room, but then where would that have left him?

Well, he would walk around a bit that morning and swim in the afternoon, loll on the beach. He did not want to go back to the Hotel-No. 1 too early. He had to time it right.

In the afternoon he swam on the beach and lazed in the sun. There would probably be only a few more days of hot sunshine before the autumn monsoon swooped down from the Gobi Desert and the rain would hang in the sky like gray beads. So he enjoyed lying there in the relaxing sun watching the young couples. Japanee, coo over one another. He wondered how many of them were just married and on their honeymoons.

At seven o'clock that night, Friday night, after an enjoyable dinner of fried rice and sweet and sour pork in the same restaurant he'd eaten at that morning, he walked along the streets of Numazu studying the faces of people walking by, and the flashing on and off of neon signs. He would give it another hour.

When he returned to the Hotel-No. 1, it was just half past eight. The lobby was quiet with very few lingerers.

Climbing the stairs he mentally placed five bucks on his hunch: his other bottle would be untouched. Whenever he placed money on himself he never lost. It was becoming exquisitely clear that Hugh was the only one he could gamble with any more—without being cheated.

Chebe-san Ito was sitting up on the bed in a blue kimono when he walked in. A soldier, a corporal, rather pale-looking, towheaded, sat on a *tatami* mat across from the bed. They both looked up as he shut the door behind him: Chebe-san totally unsurprised, cool and inscrutable, the soldier blank-eyed and goggling.

"Business him pretty good, fella?" Hugh grinned.

"Hey, what is this?" the soldier demanded like a man who had been sniped at.

Chebe-san modestly pulled her kimono over her breasts, obviously not wearing falsies under it. "It no Sunday yet."

Hugh turned on the soldier, curling his mustache rakishly. "You're a long way from home, aren't you?"

"Who the hell is he?" The soldier looked from Chebe-san to Hugh.

"Suffice it to say that I'm a grasshopper eater." Hugh studied the First Cavalry Division patch on the soldier's sleeve. "From North Camp Fuji?"

The soldier rose slowly to his feet. "That's right." He

165

looked like a man who has just run out of toilet paper with a severe case of GI's. "Who in the hell *are* you, fella? I got a date with this girl."

Chebe-san remained solidly silent.

"That horse on your patch"—Hugh wagged a finger at it—"you got horses up there at North Camp?"

"No."

"You don't ride horses?"

"No." The soldier's face froze belligerently.

"And that line there." Hugh pointed again. "Did you ever hold a line? Anywhere? In Korea?"

"Now listen here, buddy," the soldier said hotly.

"Mind telling me about that large *yellow* background on the patch? What does that mean?"

The soldier started to step forward, almost involuntarily, checked himself and turned back on Chebe-san. "Hey, goddamit; what the hell's goin' on here?"

"Oh," Chebe-san spoke in a voice from behind a wall, "he Mitchiko's papa-san."

Cautiously, the soldier kicked into his scuffed shoes. "I don't know what game you two are playing, but I'm gettin' to hell out," he said in disgust. And his face registered surprise when Hugh opened the door, stepped aside, bowing courteously like the Hotel-No. 1 doorboy, and ushered him out. Then he turned back to Chebe-san and chuckled softly.

Chebe-san got off the bed and walked quietly to the closet. She pulled out Hugh's other bottle of whiskey, still full, and tossed it to him. He caught it and mentally collected his five bucks.

"Have a good time last night?" he asked. "Or did you do anything?"

For the first time Chebe-san smiled, distantly. "I always have a good time. Did you?"

"Excellent," Hugh said. "How much did you charge the doggie?" He jerked his head at the door.

"He no pay yet." She pouted. "You come in too damn soon."

"Well, hell." Hugh walked over and sat down on the bed and looked up at Chebe-san. "You didn't want to stay with him anyway."

"How come you come back so early?" she said.

"Ran out of things to do," Hugh said with a slight shrug. "I thought maybe you'd want to go dancing or something."

166

"You want to have a party?"

"Sure." Hugh nodded. "Celebrate the victory over the Army." He uncapped the bottle and took the first drink of the day. "The first one today with both hands. Well, if you want to make hay while the sun shines," he said with a grin, "you better get ready."

"I'll get dressed," she said cheerfully.

Hugh, sitting on the bed, watched her peel off the kimono and hang it up in the closet. She was really small, all right, but compactly firmly softly built—and not stocky. He studied the lines of her back, butt and legs, took the second drink of the day with both hands again, feeling very satisfied.

A crisp night breeze blew salt air in from the window.

Contented, he thought of her total unabashment, so unaffected. Honesty, he thought; there was an inscrutable intelligence—perception—about her that puzzled him. Tonight he would find out. Or tomorrow. Or the next day.

Chebe-san opened her night traveling bag and placed a fresh set of clothes on the bed beside Hugh, slipped into her panties, brassière without falsies (which surprised him), pulled her nylons on delicately watching for runs, and covered it all with a pale blue off the shoulder chic-looking dress. Then she draped a silk shawl over her shoulders and picked up her purse—that was not red.

"You all ready?" Hugh heard himself say like a cannon echo. "Where you want to go?"

Chebe-san smiled mysteriously. "Let me show you."

"Okay." Hugh set the bottle on the floor beside the bed and stood up. "Let's go, baby-san."

"Aren't you the romantic?" Chebe-san slipped her arm through his. "Skivvie *honcho*," she giggled.

They stood outside the hotel on the sidewalk listening to the music of the juke joints muted but audible in the night.

Hugh turned his back on the flashing sign of Shanghai Lil's bar, on up the street. "Will we need a cab?" he asked.

"We can walk; it's not far." She pulled him around, the other way from Shanghai Lil's.

Moving around hurrying people, down narrow alleys and out on lighted streets, always parallel to the sloughing beach, Chebe-san told him of her previous night: she had picked up an Army lieutenant and made him for seven thousand yen.

"I'm real proud of you," Hugh said as if she had just been elected chairwoman of the WCTU, thinking sketchily of his ex-dolly in Gotemba and her Army major.

"Well," she countered, laughing, "I had to have some money for us tonight."

"You knew I'd be back?"

"I knew you would be back," she nodded; "you left your other bottle there. I didn't think you had enough money to last until Sunday night."

Hugh listened to the click of her spiked shoes on the stone alleyway and thought of the single yen piece in his pocket. "I didn't bring too much with me," he admitted, remembering what he had brought was Koko Hobbs' money anyway, and now he was about to spend Chebe-san's money, and he tried to recall at what time in his life he had ever spent any of his own damn money?

"I was quite sure you didn't," Chebe-san grinned up at him, way up.

They came out of the alleyway onto a wide paved street adorned with juke joints and pachinko parlors and restaurants, explained by a huge sign, arched pagoda-style, over the beginning of the street: *TOA ROAD* in bright red neon. Hugh figured they could not be more than eight blocks from the hotel, tossing a distant glance at the boat lights in the harbor and hearing the rolling surf murmur on the sand behind the bars.

"This it?" Hugh paused, looking up at the sign, and lit a cigarette.

"*Hai,*" Chebe-san said. "We havo number-one time now, you betcha."

"Why not?" Hugh felt an overwhelming fascination for the road, which went up no more than two blocks; for the bars, clustered together like hot dogs on a string; for the night people, loiterers, servicemen, women, shoeshine boys, the movement of lives within lives. A feeling of his own inconsistency swept over him, a wonderment at himself that he knew had been coming for a long time now like the first sudden chills of the return of malaria, as if he had suddenly been tossed into a pit with a pack of drooling wolves.

"Why not?" he said again, grinning tightly. "It's your dough, doll."

Chebe-san laughed, her face speculative, watching him.

"We'll just work up one side and down the other," Hugh essayed. "You want a party? So do I." He grabbed her by the arm and pulled her into the first bar on the left side of the street, moving swiftly, heedlessly.

Burning, the hot embers of his inconsistency lying like a bed of coals in his mind, Hugh drank furiously silent from one bar to the next, pulling Chebe-san with him, she remaining just as cautiously silent, paying for his drinks, traces of apprehension playing on her face like reflections from a wood fire.

All the bars are the same, Hugh thought moodily, drinking shuttling from one to the other, drinking *sake*, whiskey, beer, wine, pouring the liquid on the fire, feeding it. All the same goddam same. All the faces the same, identical: like . . . like charcoal reproductions of the same label on every bottle.

Yet there was the inconsistency! He could never run from that, the inconsistency of being the same. The great Inconsistency that he could never lose, would never give up, because he could always recognize it and acknowledge its existence within himself. Did the other same identical faces acknowledge it?

Did Chebe-san, who stared at him appeasingly shy and wary as he downed his drinks, did she recognize the inconsistency? Or the bartenders (how many?) who filled his orders fast recognize it? Or did the women in the bar, the business women (how many of them?) who ran one step ahead of their breasts ever recognize it?

Remember the one somewhere sometime lying under the spawning trees in the apple orchard, her coat back covered with rotten apples? The one he never told anyone when they got back to town that he'd made. But he didn't tell her about the apples on her coat either. Remember that one? Sure. A true inconsistency, that one.

Or the one whom he told it was good for her complexion? But whose pimples never went away? Or the one whom he told it was the way to God? Hugh Thorton the preacher.

Remember them all, all the lives, and the inconsistency of it, and remember too, while you're remembering, he told himself detachedly, that they had to see the inconsistency too; they knew too, saw through him.

And the inconsistency of being a POW, that was the

169

cinch bet of all time, that inconsistency. Or the coming back in after four years a civilian—for what? Where the hell was he going?

"Come on, Hugh," Chebe-san prompted as he was working his way down the other side of the street. "Let's dance, ne?"

"Shut up," Hugh said curtly, drinking faster now, pugnacious belligerent happily wild.

Down the right side of the Toa Road, not missing a bar, only missing himself, he thought, fending off the night, the time when all the bars would be closed, the phonographs shut down and snapped, the bottles all empty tossed out, the streets womanless— Hold off that time, don't let any of it catch up with you, he warned himself. Talk about it, recognize it, think about it, but don't let it catch up with you.

But he could no more keep the harsh wind of inconsistency from blowing through him, irrevocably catching up with him, than he could keep his mustache from becoming sodden with the drinks. Ought to have a mustache cup.

And suddenly, when it did catch up, it all left him, like the eye of a hurricane, or the moving back in of the sun after a storm, quietly peaceful in its pure crystallized touch. He saw through it clearly, the long never-ending inconsistency that moved delicately before him. Moving like the graceful arched back of a woman beneath him, the gleam of a saber in salute, the crisscrossed patterns of laces in leggins, quivering now like the second-short long life span of night in darkened barracks.

While his naked soul, that he had so hotly desired, unclothed in the calm after the storm now lay cuddled in the corner ashamed—ashamed in front of the inconsistency. Shorn of glory now in its own unviolated reality; and he moving on and living and changing, aware of the luck that had brought him here so far when it had not died, would not die, even when he prayed for it to die.

And then, that which had been coming for so long now moved on with the tail end of the inconsistent wind as the lights in the last bar snapped off, the last procurement of the evening walked swayingly to the back rooms, the bottles tossed out clattering. Hugh recognized its leaving again, for how long he didn't know; anger and love at the nakedness of himself that he had seen tore vitally into him.

"Let's go," he said thickly, grabbing Chebe-san by the

170

arm as the bartender sighed relief, and pulled her to the door.

They hit the outside on a run, the salty crisp air smacking them darkly.

"Oh Jesus," Hugh moaned, the night kicking him in the ass with all fours.

"Are you sick?" Chebe-san asked, awed.

To Hugh, peering waveringly through the darkness across the street, she sounded like a little girl pleading for a gift he'd never had to give. "Fuck it," he mumbled, rubbing his hands vigorously over his face. "I got to piss; where hell the hotel; goddam slopehead gooks."

"We'll get a cab," Chebe-san suggested anxiously. "Come on."

"Get to hell away from me, you little shithead," Hugh said savagely, trying to orient himself. "You wanna go back to hotel go on. I don't give a large rat's ass."

Chebe-san tugged gently on his arm. "Come on, Hugh," she pleaded, "let's take a cab."

"Go on back to hotel!" he bellowed furiously, shoving her away. That goddam beach was around here somewhere. Got to find that beach get in the water. Across the street he made out a shallow flight of wood stairs leading off to the beach. "Chebe-san!" he yelled.

"I'm right here!" she said exasperated.

"You ain't supposed to be!" He lurched away from her weaving across the street. "Get your money-making ass back to the hotel. Nothing but the hairy end of a wet gut!" he yelled dramatically at the night. "A hole with a body around it and I'm the stopper!"

Clutching the rickety bannister for support he moved in blind swiftness down the stairs. Who the hell she think she was any fucking way? Who the hell he think he was? A popcorn popper? A douche-bag stopper? Goddam but it's dark. Black as a cat's ass at midnight.

The stairs went out from under him and he had a silly sensation of walking rapidly through the air knees driving high before he took a nose dive plowing into the sand. Spitting sand out of his mouth he lunged forward again, peeling off his jacket kicking off his shoes. Who needs shoes anyway? Go native! On with the dance!

By the time his feet hit the wet chilling sand of the surf he was naked in the night and he kept right on running bounding into the waves then diving out in a shallow belly-slamming splat! The icy water cut burningly through him like a ribbon of machine-gun fire, but he did not turn back. Long strokes moved him farther away from the beach. He bobbed his head under the water blowing out the air from his lungs, the breakers tossing him around. He came back up and swam on. So what if there was an outgoing tide? Where would it take him? He envisioned himself being court-martialed for desertion: *But I was swept away on the tide, sir!*

Or sharks! Hah! Let 'em come, by God! They'll die of food poisoning they clamp onto this old carcass. Jeee-sus Christ but his balls were cold! But keep swimming, clear the old head, fight the booze and the thin line of resistance.

"Roll on, Cimarron!" he bellowed, caught a thick plop of water, choked, and kept his mouth shut.

Finally he stopped swimming, turned back and saw the faint lights burning tearfully on the shore. He had sure as hell come a long way. A hell of a lot of kelp out here. But he felt better. His mind was decidedly clear and his eyes could focus.

Undismayed, he started back, hoping he hadn't lost that ten-yen piece he'd had in his pocket, and calculating how he was going to get back to South Camp. As far as the weekend, his vacation, was concerned it was over. Finished. Hung up to dry with the wash. He had been one colossal ass to come down to Numazu in the first place.

When he made the shallow water he walked steadily through the surf up to the dry sand. It was colder than a schoolmarm's pussy standing in the breeze off the sea.

Up the beach in the loose sand, he fell to his knees and began scooping out dry sand. In five minutes he had burrowed down to the warmth left by the sun. Feeling excessively proud over his presence of mind he lay down in it. Might as well get warm while he could. And dry.

The testing breeze kissed over the top of his grave and he relaxed contentedly in the warmth. Breathing deeply, a slumbering weariness crept over him, the rumbling exhalation and the soft inhalation of the ocean unceasing in his ears.

He woke quickly, unblinking, like a dog. He did not know how long he had slept but it was still abysmally dark. The surface breeze had stopped and the air was thick and heavy, evaporated. Leaning forward he listened to the breathing of the surf.

172

Glows of heat lightning crackled in the sky out at sea, looking like an artillery barrage firing white and red salvos. The belated roar of thunder rolled through the muggy darkness and he caught himself straining to hear the familiar *whoosh* as projectiles fell through the air.

Watching the lightning illumine the night, he saw black rain-swollen clouds moiling in across the water, though still a long way out. The dog days were over. The monsoon season had finally arrived. There would be continual rain now for eight months. Not spitting casually like the sudden break in the dog days of a couple weeks ago.

Hypnotized, he watched the weather, the fulminating night, the black and white surf, the end of dog days. His mustache drooped shaggily; specks of sand festooned it. He tried curling it to retrieve those immaculate sharp tips. It was useless; the salt water had done its damage.

Suddenly he laughed out loud feverishly, exhilarated by his own voice competing with the thunder. Any man who says history doesn't repeat itself rates a Maggie's Drawers: one shot in the butts and a red flag waved. A man's personal history that is, his experiences. The last time he'd gone swimming at night like this he did not have a mustache. Also he had been quite sober. The only similarity was that he had been broke then, too. Personally, it seemed he had always been broke. And that was where the paradox came in: he was never without money. Of course it was never *his* money.

It was a strange thing about money, he had found out (half of him had always suspected this and wanted to prove it to himself, while the other half reared its ugly head in dispute). Money, in quintessence, did not even exist, did not belong to those who had it. It was actually never anyone's money, for money was an accumulated energy that only a fool hoarded or thought was his, and he Hugh Thorton did not think of himself as a boob.

He had always been a rather cheerful, sufficient-unto-the-day-is-the-evil-thereof sort of man, even before his first enlistment in 1940. But it had taken the nurturing of those five years during the war to culminate it into a rather ingrained belief, and the four years where he was trapped (trapped! like a ten-o'clock spider in a five-o'clock shadow) to divorce himself imminently of that too. The more he lost the better he felt, which was very strange for an ex-blackjack dealer who consistently won.

173

Potently, and with a closer insight of himself than he'd ever had at any time, feeling suddenly as if he were on the verge of finding the key to unlock a lead sealed casket containing still another dead past glamour, Hugh ran his mind back probingly with shrewd detail, tying it all together.

The beach that time had been at La Jolla, California. It hadn't been a night like this. More tropical, he decided. Yeah; a lot more warm and there was no monsoon season coming in. 1948 and he was twenty-five and already picking up the strength and bunched muscles he'd developed as a CCC worker and harvest follower during the Depression, filling out to his 190 pounds that he'd lost as a POW during the war—that other one—

He'd gone for an early-evening swim under one of those rare clear sunsets of Southern California, feeling good that night, refreshed from his swim and wondering what dear Donna had planned for the evening. She always had something planned, Donna did.

When he'd finished swimming he walked up the beach to the little beach cottage (which was not really little at all but Donna referred to it as little as she did everything, including herself, which was a lie but nonetheless injured his ego) and walked on in, still damp in his swimming trunks, to find Donna sitting by the radio with a drink in her hand, half lit, feeling no pain at all. She was wearing black Capri pants (the movie stars had brought them in) and a red blouse.

"We ain't going anywhere tonight?" he'd asked her, sitting down wetly on an expensive chair and lighting a cigarette.

She shook her long blond hair. "No, we are not going anywhere tonight. I thought we'd stay home."

Looking at her thin spare face that masked her forty years, he was aware too of her scrutiny on his dark beetled brow, deep-set almost black eyes and determined lantern jaw.

"All right," he'd said. "Fine. We'll just stay home tonight."

She stood up and walked with great dignity over to the liquor cabinet and sloshed a drink in her glass. "Why do you stay with me, Hugh?" she demanded quietly.

"Because you've got money," he said truthfully. "You support me in the manner to which I'm growing accustomed."

174

"At least you're honest, painfully so," she said. "That's more than I can say for the rest."

"That why you picked me?" he asked, thinking: A day in the life of Donna and Hugh. Make a good soap opera.

"I'm not sure," she answered. "Certainly not because you're an ex-blackjack dealer. Even though you did let me win."

"I didn't figure you did," he told her. "But if I'm some woman's stud on allowance I'm at least curious to know why."

She turned on him viciously. "You already know why."

"Then why tell all your friends I'm thirty-five and you're only thirty? Or why take me to meet your political big shots and introduce me to your bankers?"

Carefully she walked back to the chair by the radio and sat down. "You know everything, don't you?" She looked at him bitterly. "How would you have liked to live with a man sixty-five years old when you were only twenty-one?"

"Hell," he said. "I wouldn't like living with a man any time."

"Old and foul and stinky," she said softly, "and painfully boring." She looked down toward his feet, two tears squeezing through her lashes. "I put up with it for five years."

"You didn't do too badly. Both dough and the prestige."

"You don't love me, do you, Hugh?"

"Now that you've mentioned it," he allowed, "I am fond of you. Even though you are fifteen years older than me."

She studied her amber glass. "We should have had more fun, Hugh."

"Maybe if you'd taken me off an allowance it would have been."

"Was that all you wanted? The money?" she said crisply. "You never quite got over being a marine, did you? Or a prisoner of war?"

"I never lost anything in the Marine Corps!" he exploded. "Or being a POW either. Maybe that's what's bothering you," he added.

Donna stood up again and picked up the bottle. "Let's go for a walk on the beach."

He eyed the bottle, nodded, and they left the house. They walked down the wide expanse of beach, Hugh listening to her tale of woe silently; all the while she was drinking the whiskey straight from the bottle. "You don't know what it's like," she accused him. "Living with that old son-ofabitch Elton Olson, just waiting for him to die."

Finally she stopped and glared resentfully at him, cursing him obscenely, hating him for something she did not have, could never have, something he himself was ignorant of because it had always been in him.

"I don't want you around any more," she said, stately, a little out of breath. "You can leave in the morning." And with sudden fury she tore her large, glittering emerald ring from her finger and flung it at the surf. "I hate him! I hate him!"

He moved forward to stop her, then thought better of it, and watched Elton Olson's last earthly gift plop into the surf. He carefully dug a furrow with his toe to mark the spot from where she'd thrown it. "Come on, Donna, let's go back to the house," he urged hastily, noticing that it was almost high tide, the surf pulling everything out.

He got her back to the house, half carrying her, soothed her into having another drink and going to bed. Then he left her and ran back down the beach and searched for over two hours in a wild frenzy, looking for that large stone that would have been a nice graduation present for himself, ten grand worth. But the ring was gone, carried off to the bottom of the ocean, and he sat there on the sand wondering if it would come up again, and when, and where?

When he got back to the house, Donna was sitting in her chair by the radio again, with a fresh drink.

"I thought you went to bed," he said carelessly, walked over to the liquor cabinet and took a fresh bottle out. "Might's well drink a toast to my departure."

She did not answer, just looked as if she were listening to some faraway concert. He shrugged, and took the bottle to *their* room and began packing silently: a pair of socks—a drink; a set of skivvies—a drink; no ties—but a drink anyway!

"And what are you doing?" she asked, eyebrows raised, from the door behind him.

He turned around. "I'm packing. I have to be out of here in the morning. I got evicted." He took another drink of *her* whiskey.

"You can put those things back," she said coolly, sloshing the ice around in her drink. "You don't have to leave."

"That's just it," he said. "I *don't* have to. Suddenly I want to."

Tears crawled down her face. She turned and went back into the living room. He continued packing: belts—a drink, his back to the door. Then something exploded over his head, ringing like a grenade concussion, and he fell forward in his suitcase. And at two o'clock in the morning he left Donna carrying one suitcase between his handcuffed arms, escorted by two slack-faced North San Diego policemen.

"You ought to know you can't beat up women in this town, bud," one of the cops said.

"Or throw milk bottles at them," the other added.

Hugh took one last look at her, his head pounding under the nasty gash she'd put in it with her whiskey bottle. "I should have known." He essayed a grin, while she looked triumphantly back at him.

He spent thirty days in the San Diego city jail. It seemed to him, then, a very propitious culmination of his life since he'd been released from the Japanee in '45. He could write a book on it: *From Prison to Prison*, or: *The Private Life of an Immature, Maladjusted Veteran*. That was what the trend was those days. Headshrinking in an educated America would undoubtedly classify him as *emotionally immature* and *maladjusted*, a medal for the muddled, worn bravely with all the distinction of an inferior intellectual mind.

Yet the thirty days had given him his decision, his slightly belated but irrevocable choice of life. (And who was to say he chose it?) In one way of looking at it, it was the end of an era—for him. The last ride on the civilian merry-go-round. And he'd sure had a fistful of tickets.

He knew, of course, through sources and contacts with Donna, that there would be another war shortly. All the bankers and industrialists and scrap metal dealers, whom Donna knew, were getting ready for it. There would be that one, then another one after that, and so on, the story-without-end right on down the line. Another locust moving in and carrying out another grain of corn—Shades of Scheherazade!

The surprising thing was that he knew it, and still decided on re-enlisting, for ultimately it meant for him the loss of predestined existence. He could see how it would all fall

177

out in front of him, day to day, and no more. If the war-myth makers wanted to start wars, well he would fight them. It was simple. No glory involved, for that was a myth too, a brainwashing that went hand in hand with the Marine Corps.

And the lives he crossed (or those which crossed his own), reached out for, and made contact with, sometimes even destroying, did not matter. He felt he was learning something. Important facets of himself. Maintaining a cool detached dispassionate objectivity, he could look at all of it, from the mount as it were, and call the shots even before they were fired. He felt he had come a long way, and the turbulent initiations he'd gone through were merely the beginning.

With the experience and knowledge he had there was no trouble getting back in. Where rank had been frozen in the thirties it was then hot. He moved right on up, still wiring the deck, still playing it close to the belt, relishing it. His only surprise was that he had not been captured in Korea.

If his luck held, which he was sure it would, he wouldn't be captured in the next one either.

Not with what he knew about it.

And there was not one man in the rest of the company that could be sure of that, he thought, feeling a tiredness again in his pocket of sand. Not even that egotistical Bohane with his fucking medal and cockiness. That sonofabitch would be one of the first to be captured, he thought with a twitch of rancor, singling out one man of the old bunch who he suddenly felt were all definitely against him, just before he dozed off again. You goddam rights, Bohane would be the first one to get captured!

9.

The only thing Giff Bohane had been captured by was Horrible Hog Company's barracks. He prowled nervously around the squadbay that Friday afternoon, the eleventh

178

of September, while the clouds kicked up a black rain outside. With Gunny Thorton on special liberty and the field training secured there was nothing to do but wait. And there was no liberty to wait for.

So he waited. He and all the rest of the barracks in a disgruntled tight-lipped combativeness, waiting for the slop chute to open and the word to come down saying they could go in dungarees.

At four-thirty that Friday afternoon when duty was secured and the slop chute doors were flung open for a long queue of shining wet marines, Giff roused his coterie in Hog Company's barracks and the four of them prepared to go to the slop chute. They had five hours to drink, and had best by God take advantage of it.

The slop chute was not particularly crowded. Only those men who had won a nifty wad gambling, or had judiciously tucked some money away, or had reluctantly borrowed from the five-for-teners could afford beer. The rest of the men in the camp, the ones in the companies who rated liberty, would dig deep in their lockers for hockable items: wedding bands, watches, even their best buddies' shoes.

Giff opened the screen door of the slop chute and stepped out of the rain, the heavy life-invigorating smell of beer and cigarette smoke smacking him fully. The other three followed him.

"You go on back and get a booth," he said. "I'll go pick up the first case."

"I'll go with you, old friend," Poke Turner suggested. "I wouldn't want you to get lost with all them cold dudes." His narrow eyes shining cunningly, he started whistling the spiritual, "I Saw The Light."

"We'll take this one close to the door," Dallas said with the bored air of a man who is too familiar with making decisions.

Stack Renshaw feigned shock. "What you want us to do? Freeze our ass?"

Gently, but forcibly, Dallas pushed him into the booth. "I like to see who all comes in."

Giff bought the case, exchanging quips with the three Japanee men who ran the bar. They all three of them looked as if they came from the same family: father, number-two son, and number-one son. He hefted the case

over to Poke. "You carry it for being such a rotten motherfucker."

They walked on back to the booth where Dallas and
Stack were sprawled out lazily. Poke slid the case onto the
center of the table and they both sat down, as all four
hands reached for a can.

"It's a fine night for some cool ones," Giff grinned, un-
buttoning his raincoat and easing his dungaree cap back.

"If the OD don't come in," Stack said. "The bastard's always comin' around cussing me out cause I'm outa uniform."

"Motherfuck the OD," Dallas said wryly, his deceptively
cruel face mocking. "You're only suffering from what they
call a battle shock. Since the night you fell on your head."

"A trauma," Poke corrected. "I read it somewhere.
Maybe in *Stars & Stripes;* they call it a trauma. It's the
thing to have these days. A sort of fucking fad, you know
what I mean?"

Giff laughed tightly. "Well, if that's the current thing to
have you can count me out. I ain't never had that in my
life, don't intend to neither."

"That why you been making eyes at ol' One-Leg in the
Blue Moon?" Dallas jeered.

"I wouldn't talk any I was you," Giff said carefully. "Not
since you been spending your shekels on a junkie."

"It ain't the junkie part," Poke broke in. "Ain't that atall.
She's just too skinny. I don't like skinny women. For me I'll
take 'em hefty."

Dallas finished his beer. "The closer the bone the
sweeter the meat."

"Ain't none of you as bad off as me," Stack complained.
"If I ever get Yoko to shave under her arms I would be one
happy fucker."

They all laughed and Stack looked at them seriously.
"No, goddamit," he said. "I mean it. I woke up with my
nose down there one night and woulda sworn to God I was
staring that old grinnin' bear right in the face."

"You don't know what you're missing," Giff grinned. "A
fine experience, that's what."

"I wouldn't say that," Poke interjected. "I always main-
tain that he who eats the hole will eat the pole." He
paused, grinning. "But I wouldn't take my word for nothing."

"What a shitty weekend," Stack observed funereally. "No liberty and nothing but rain."

"You're drinkin', ain't you?" Dallas said. "What the fuck more do you want?"

"I wanna quit this goddam screwing around in the field," Stack said. "I get so goddam sick of marchin' out the field like a goddam boot and running at high port I could throw up."

"A trauma," Dallas sneered.

"You fucking A," Poke agreed solemnly. "This peacetime is for the goonie birds. I'll take Ko-rea any day."

"You lose somethin' in Korea," Giff asked, "that you can't find somewhere else?"

"My cherry," Poke said.

Giff grinned over his shoulder at him. "Don't worry about it, Poke. We'll be outa here before long."

"Suppose we ain't," Poke challenged. "Suppose we don't go anywhere?"

With that prospect staring the four of them in the face, they desperately reached for fresh beers.

Thoughtfully, Giff drank his beer wishing Poke would not say any more about it, embarrassed for him in an odd way, and wondering why—even with the open friendship—he felt like a black chicken in with the white ones—or vice versa. Perhaps it was something in Poke's and Dallas' and Stack's faces that made him feel like that—a something that excluded him while at the same time tolerating him. He suddenly felt uneasy. Then he was aware of Poke's singing.

He had broken into a parody of "Old Soldiers Never Die":

There is a mess hall not far away,
Where they serve shit on the shingle three times a day;
Ham and eggs we never see,
Not ee-ven on EPD,
There you see us slowww-ly . . . fading away.

"I'll get some more beers." Dallas slipped a five-dollar script note, funny money, to Stack who dutifully left the booth and headed toward the Three Stooges.

Giff watched him walk away, looking too at the other anonymous faces in the slop chute, sparse and unusually quiet. Hard-bitten men, hunched over their towering

181

cans of beer, their raincoats shiny black from the rain. All young faces from eighteen to forty-two, except Dallas who was ageless. A strange breed of men who were savagely cursed one day by the pompous American public and religiously erroneously eulogized the next for saving them their pomposity. But Giff knew he was with his own kind. It was the only niche he had been able to carve out of the welter of his life. And now, he felt, in a few short weeks he was beginning to lose that. Then he remembered it had started in Korea on Vegas.

Someone walked listlessly over to the jukebox and played "We're in the Jailhouse Now."

"I better go piss; make room for some more suds," Giff said absently, turning back to Dallas and Poke who were arguing over, of all things, the rehabilitation of the Chinese soldier in civilian life. They did not stop to answer him.

He stood up and walked on out without deigning to square his dungaree cap or button his raincoat.

The rain hit him, washing down his face and trickling behind his ears as he jumped across the little wash-off ditch and moved through rain-bewhiskered dusk to the small head by the PX.

He stood alone over the urinal wondering just when they would leave. Suppose Poke was right? Suppose they never did leave? Fright and panic and the indefinable uneasiness crawled over him. Quickly, he shut it off from his mind, lit a cigarette and stepped back out into the rain. The large fast falling drops splattered on the cement stoop in front of the door, sounding like hail on a tin pan. It was really dark, almost black, and the fog would roll in later. It was the only country where Giff had ever seen fog and rain at the same time. Well, he thought, familiarity breeds contempt. He walked on in.

"But the Chinee soldier don't have no trouble rehabilitatin'," Poke was making his plea at the booth. "Hey!" he said, turning to Giff, "I was beginning to think maybe you got lost."

"So what's this about the Chinee soldier?" Giff said, slipping in beside Poke, grateful now to be back among the people again. His people. And reached for a fresh beer.

"They's both nuts," Stack gave his opinion. "Who the hell cares about Chinee soldiers? They's all twenty-year men."

"No they ain't neither," Poke said emphatically. "I was

182

readin' somewhere that they got a VA just like us, and they help you get jobs of work."

"That's a crock of shit," Dallas said disgustedly. "And you know it. You didn't read that anywhere. You never got farther than *True Confessions*."

Giff looked over his shoulder at Poke. "Personally," he said, "I don't think the Chinee soldier ever gets out. He's a fool if he does."

"How's that?" Stack said with a demanding belch.

"Cause he eats three times a day," Giff qualified. "He gets his three squares and that's all she wrote. Nobody but a fool would leave a set-up like that to work on a rice paddy."

"I get three squares a day," Poke said. "And that ain't the reason I'm in."

"You ain't a Chinee," Giff said, and that seemed to pretty well cover it. Who the hell cared about the Chinee soldier! In his mind he saw a picture of four Chinee soldiers sitting over a bottle of Chinee hemlock juice excitedly discussing the problems of the returning American marine. If it wasn't so impotent, it would almost be funny. A real howl.

Just then the screen door boomed open and three marines in civvies, and civvy raincoats, came bouncing in with three Jo-sans wrapped around their arms. Giff thought he recognized one who worked in the White Kitty in Bamboo Alley but he wasn't sure. All the eyes in the slop chute followed the three couples to a back booth.

"I fucked the one on the left," Poke said.

"You've fucked just about all of them, ain't you?" Dallas mocked.

"I'm a cocksman from the word go," Poke said. "Me and Stack here"—he reached over and tousled Stack's hair—"we are truly a couple of cunt-hounds."

"I know one you never fucked," Giff said uncontrollably. "You never fucked Popcorn down the Blue Moon."

Poke shrugged. "She don't count. Nobody's ever fucked her. She ain't a business woman."

"She could be had though," Giff said anxiously, burning, trying to convince himself. "I mean if you played it right."

"Who would want to?" Poke said. "Hell, she only got one leg." He reached for a fresh beer. "Me, I'm a two-leg man."

Giff had to laugh, but his mind was not with it. Instead,

183

it traveled down to the end of the slop chute, past the dispersed customers (hardly anyone at all tonight) to the last booth where the three couples sat drinking. Now, if I had a steady girl, he told himself, I wouldn't bring her in here. No sir. The thing to do was to get a little place outside the camp. But maybe the girls wanted to come in here. Wanted to get away from the town just like he suddenly right now wanted to get away from the camp. And wouldn't that be nice? Him going out, the girls coming in. And never the twain would meet. "She can be had though, I'm sure," he said hastily. "I'll bet you shekels she can be had."

"How much?" Dallas regarded him. "I got fifty bucks says you can't."

Giff, without forethought, purely on the spur of the moment, slapped his wallet on the booth top. "Put your money where your mouth is."

"I'll hold the stakes," Poke offered.

"I'll hold my own," Stack said.

Dallas complied and Poke counted out fifty bucks from each and pocketed it, a rich man's smile playing on his cunning mouth. "I'll pay the winner. But I can't promise I'll be able to keep it too long," he warned cautiously. "One of you better win more skosh."

"It won't take long," Giff said, staring at Dallas. "Buddy, you just lost fifty bucks." But he had a sneaking hunch it was false bravado.

Dallas shrugged the fifty bucks away carelessly. "We'll see."

"The way Giff's been hanging around ol' Popcorn like a dog in heat," Poke said slyly, "he just might do it, by God."

"You'll have to wait till next weekend to try it," Stack said over his can. "It'll probably take a weekend. It's a pretty big chore. Needs a lot of work."

Before Giff could answer, the screen door opened again and Half-Slick Willy Woechowski lumbered in, an enormous creature in a too-small raincoat, way too small for him (as was everything; he was just too big for regulation issue uniforms), followed by private Guppy Talagua, a short, heavily muscled Hawaiian with a broad happy face.

"The wind blew the shit flew and in walked Half-Slick

184

Willy," Poke said exuberantly. All four of them were grinning up at the large man.

Half-Slick Willy stepped over to the booth, smothered an empty can in his huge wall-smashing hand and bent it deftly across his nose. "Haaaa!" he laughed ponderously. "Who's buyin' the beer tonight? Haaaa!" he yelled. The three couples in back suddenly grew quiet.

"Sidown, Willy." Giff slid over toward Poke and Willy plopped into the booth.

"How you doin', Corporal?" Willy said to Bohane. Willy always called him "Corporal" even when everyone else called him either Giff or Bohane or shithead or something like that; and Giff interpreted it to be a mark of respect—for the Silver Star.

"Fine, Willy, just fine," Giff said, grinning crookedly. "How you doing, Guppy?" he said to the meaty little Hawaiian.

"Wet," Guppy laughed. "And thirsty."

Giff had seen him cold-caulk a man in the platoon with a short left, knocking him ten feet back against the GI can. His shortness was no hindrance to his fighting prowess. Guppy Talagua, Giff thought suddenly, was a good man to have on your side, and wondered too with the instinctive combative truculence how he would fight Guppy if he ever had to.

"Get some beer, goddamit," Guppy said. "Me and Willy got tired waiting in the line for the movies."

"What the hell you want to see the movies for?" Dallas said. "They's worse than Poke's romance books."

Guppy laughed, pulled out three soiled singles in script. "I'll buy if you go get it, Willy."

Willy snatched the three bills, catapulted off the booth and walked hugely over to the Three Stooges.

Giff looked back again over his shoulder at the three couples in the back booth. One of the marines was mellowly stroking his Jo-san's breasts. Face it; admit it. He wanted to go to town badly. And there was no liberty. If he had to spend two more—hell!—three more days aboard the camp he would run headlong through a window. He cursed himself for making the bet with Dallas.

"Corporal Bohane," Poke was saying, "has got a bet on with Dallas that he can make ol' Popcorn in the Blue Moon."

"Hunh?" Guppy said. "Her? With one leg? Nah, ain't no-body can make her, man. She ain't no business woman."

"So everybody tells me," Giff jeered.

Half-Slick Willy steamed back, set the case down on the booth top and bounced into the booth jarring the men slightly. With one enormous hand he swilled down a can of beer. "Hey!" he urged. "You see the three girls in the back booth?"

"Hell, yes," Stack said. "We been watching them for the past hour."

"Well . . ." Half-Slick Willy said.

"By the way, Willy," Stack said. "How you and Rotten Crotch Mary getting along?"

"Haa!" Half-Slick Willy guffawed. "Rotten Crotch Mary. Haa!" Then he looked pained, hurt. "Now you shouldn't call her that," he admonished Stack.

"That's right, Stack," Giff agreed. "You shouldn't cast no insults at Mary."

"Bohane's a business woman's philanthropist," Dallas said from the corner of the booth. "He's snappin' in to take Hock at Henry's place."

"You fucking A," Giff said suddenly savage. "I'm gonna run for mayor of Fujioka; or didn't you know?"

"That's what we need," Guppy Talagua laughed de-lightedly. "A mayor of Fujioka."

"What time is it?" Giff asked.

"What difference it make?" Poke stared glassily at the dwindling case. "We ain't goin' anywhere."

"I am," Giff said, and the eyes in the booth converged on him curiously. He felt an abrupt change of mood. Maybe it was the beer that groped its way thickly through him; he was not angry any more; or irritable. He had just suddenly decided, or rather found the decision already made up staring him in the face, to go over the hill. If he didn't, he rationalized, he'd be in the psycho ward by morning. "I'm going to town," he said simply.

"Oh hell; you can't do that." Half-Slick Willy shook his head. "We don't have liberty this weekend. You'll have to wait till Monday."

"I ain't waitin'," Giff said. "I'm going tonight."

"Going through the fence?" Dallas said lazily, looking askance at Giff with a rippling expression of a man who has just placed a large bet on three aces only to be beaten

186

by four kings, and Giff caught it—a fleeting look that said nothing yet said many things.

"No, you can't do that," Half-Slick Willy tried to explain. "I'm telling you it's not our liberty weekend."

"Why not!" Poke Turner demanded. "Let's all go. We can have us a ball. There won't be nobody checkin' on us. Nobody comes around on the weekend in the barracks; no muster; nothing like that." He looked rather forlornly at the case of cans.

"It ain't our liberty weekend!" Half-Slick Willy said.

Giff stopped looking at Dallas and turned to the battering ram of a man. "We are going over the hill, Willy," he said. "We are going to go through the fence."

"Not me," Willy said apprehensively. "I'm not going."

"You don't have to," Poke explained. "Stack? You're going, ain't you?"

Stack Renshaw jerked his head up from his can. "I'm broke."

"I got to go clean my rifle," Half-Slick Willy said suddenly.

"Okay," Giff said, "listen. I'm going. That's a fact as sure as we going to be in 'nother war in 'nother month," he said, pushing it all the way. "But I ain't asking anyone to go with me. If you wanna go then you're welcome. But I don't want no one saying I took them with me." He looked mordantly at them.

"I'll go," Poke agreed. "You goddam rights I'll go. But I'm broke too."

"You got a hundred bucks," Dallas said. "Our betting money."

"That don't count," Poke said quickly.

"Whoever comes," Giff temporized, "I'll pay their way."

Guppy Talagua, who all through the conversation had been watching each of them judiciously, pulled out his wallet and counted through his money. "I'll go," he threw in with them. "And I got money."

"Don't any of you go cause I'm a corporal," Giff said. "My rank ain't any insurance at all."

"Me and Stack are going," Poke said for the both of them. There was a vague nod of the head from Stack Renshaw.

"Then that's four of us," Giff said. "You ain't going, hunh Dallas?" He turned to the quarter Cherokee who seemed to be outside all of them.

"No thanks," Dallas' face spread in a wide grin. "If I go it'll be all by my lonesome."

"Suit yourself." Giff shrugged. "How about it, Willy?"

"You ain't got liberty," was all Half-Slick Willy said.

The four of them put their heads together over the case of beer and hashed it around. Poke Turner, as was characteristic, had a pair of TL wire cutters they could use on the fence. The best place, he told them from experience, was to cut through behind the water purifier in back of the company armory shed. If they ran into a guard they could simply bribe him.

"What would be the best time to go?" Giff asked.

"Well," Poke said extravagantly. "This being a non-payday weekend they won't be many men in town; the bars'll be pretty empty. I would say that the best time to go would be right after eleven o'clock. That's when the MP's leave."

"But goddamit!" Giff protested. "That's three hours away."

Poke turned hands up on it. "That's the best time. That's all I can say."

"Okay," Giff said, resigned. "Eleven o'clock then. We can stay here till nine-thirty."

They talked over the prospect of an enjoyable weekend till nine-thirty when the OD and the Sergeant of the Guard came around and swept everybody out with the cigarette butts and burnt matches. Giff watched the three couples walk out arm-in-arm. Odd as hell. Go out and pick up the girls bring them to camp then go back out to shack up with them.

During this time Dallas had quietly remained drinking with Half-Slick Willy, listening to them talk excitedly, and Giff noticed he neither agreed nor disagreed with them. To hell with Dallas! he thought. He could sit around all weekend but Giff Bohane wasn't going to.

Half-Slick Willy appeared impervious to all of it, and only bent three cans over his nose during the course of the evening's drinking.

The six of them trudged on back through the rain to the barracks and got there just as the lights were beginning to snap off. Half-Slick Willy left them on the mustering area without speaking and tromped across to the machine-gun barracks.

Inside the rifle platoon barracks, in the second platoon

squadbay, Dallas fumbled in his wall locker and produced a fifth of Canadian Club which they took to the boiler room and stood in the dark warmth drinking casually till eleven o'clock.

"You sure you don't want to go with us?" Giff said thickly.

"Nah," Dallas said. "I'm afraid I'd fall in a rice paddy and drown."

"Okay," Giff said. "Let's get this old show on the road."

Carrying the contagious excitement with them, they walked silently out of the boiler room, crossed the street and on through the bunkers guarding the armory and came out in back of the water purifier: four figures moving furtively through the downpour of night; and Giff still carried the shadowy image of Cinamo Dallas standing in the boiler room, a bright coal of a cigarette dangling from his mouth. Well, he could stay in barracks if he wanted to, but it was a damn fool thing to do, especially when they were this close to town. And if their platoon leader could up and take off whenever he wanted, there was no reason why the ruck couldn't.

10.

An indolent breeze whispered across privileged Hugh Thorton and the beach, chased by a barrage of thunder fired hot in the night. Lightning fingering the sky showed clouds moving in closer, there was the heavy smell of rain in the air.

Hugh stood up and turned back to the dim sparse night lights on the street above the beach. Well, he had better get started back. He didn't want to get caught in the rain. He found his shirt and trousers ten yards apart, wadded up, his jacket off to the side between them, but no skivvies. No skivvies anywhere. He was positive he'd dropped them next to the suit; but it might have been closer to the stairs.

Slipping into his clothes, skivvieless, he felt for the ten-yen piece in his pocket and smiled, satisfied. Walking up the beach, searching, he did not find his shoes either. Could some Japanee beachcomber have sneaked down here and run off with them?—and his skivvies too!

Okay, he shrugged, skivvies were only an affectation.

Barefoot, hair matted, mustache drooping, he trudged on up across the sand. The rickety wood lines of the stairs gloomily illuminated by a single street light flickered, helping him out of the darkness.

When he reached them he stopped short, immobile, a wave of tenderness rolling over him as he looked up the flight of stairs where the pool of light had collected around her. She was sitting on the top step, her knees tucked under her chin, arms locked around her legs, his shoes and socks set carefully beside her.

Hugh climbed up to her slowly. "I'm sorry about calling you a shithead, Chebe-san," he said, shifty-eyed. "I didn't mean it."

She looked at him cautiously for a moment, then laughed pealingly, convulsively and clapped her hands to her face.

"What the hell's so funny?" he said, grinning. "What's so goddam funny, huh?"

She continued laughing, holding her face in her hands and shaking her head. "You," she gasped finally. "Your mustache. It looks like a bush. No more tips."

"Yeah?" Hugh reached his hand up and stroked his crestfallen mustache. "Well, you try swimming in salt water. Won't do your hair any good either," he said foolishly and sat down beside her.

"You feel better now, *ne?*" she asked, still smiling with a warm light in her eyes.

Hugh pulled his socks on. "Whole hell of a lot better," he nodded. "I guess we'll have to walk back to the hotel. Can't get a cab this time of night. Not even a rickshaw."

"It will start raining pretty soon." She looked at the lightning glimmering naked in the sky. "Monsoon."

"And for a long time," Hugh agreed. He shouldered into his jacket and slipped his hands into his pockets. "Goddamit, I lost my watch," he muttered.

Smiling, Chebe-san pulled his watch off her wrist and handed it to him. "It doesn't keep very good time."

"Never did," he grunted. "Postwar watch. Say, you didn't find my skivvies down there anywhere, did you?"

"Skivvies? Did you lose your skivvies?" She laughed again. "Oh, Hugh-san."

"Yeah," he said. "Some heathen sonofabitch ran off with my skivvies." Then he turned to her, studying her intently. "Why did you wait? You didn't have to."

"You didn't have to come back to the hotel tonight either," she said.

"No. And I'm still wondering about that."

"You promised me a party tonight." She smiled. "I wouldn't want you to go back on your word."

"*My* word!" Hugh questioned. "Yeah; all right, you want a party you'll get one. Now let's get to hell out of here before it rains." He pulled her up gently, wrapped his arm around her waist and they began walking back down the deserted street.

The rain started before they reached the hotel. There were no few drops of advance warning. It came gushing down quick slamming against the buildings and bars bouncing high off the street, wetting them thoroughly in the smothering darkness.

Chebe-san giggling happily, ran in front of Hugh pulling him who was almost a foot taller than she, and weighing almost twice as much, while he speculated on her pale blue summer dress clinging wildly wet to her slim body, wondering at the duplicity in people, and thinking how strange this harmony through conflict was.

The lobby was deserted and they moved quickly, soddenly, up the stairs to their room. When they got to the door Hugh opened it, picked her up and tossed her on the Stateside bed.

Bouncing happily, she doubled up with laughter. "You'll get the bed all wet."

"Hell"—he grinned at her—"it'll get wet anyway." He walked over and picked up the quart bottle and took a healthy invigorating drink, shuddering slightly. "Chebe-san, you sure you don't want a drink?"

"Never hotchie GI," she said coyly. "Business woman no drinko."

"Not even if you ain't doing any business?" Hugh said.

Chebe-san opened the closet. "Take your clothes off or you'll catch cold," she admonished. "I'll get a towel."

Setting the bottle on the little night stand by the bed, he stripped the soaked suit, shoes and socks, still wondering who ran off with his skivvies, looking disdainfully at his white Hong Kong tailored suit lying crumpled on the floor, then took another drink of the V.O. and watched Chebe-san unzip her dress with female meticulousness, step out of it, and hang it on a hanger on the closet door handle. Delicately she slipped out of her blue panties, unsnapped her brassière—and Hugh studied her firm round cheeks, small back, shaded half tones of smooth creamy skin, want-ing suddenly to walk over and hold her, just hold her, touching, yet sat dumbly transfixed seeing something in her nakedness he'd never seen before.

She grabbed two kimonos and a large beach towel and walked over to him. "You *toxon* wet." She shook her head.

"I suppose you're not," Hugh said softly, as if for the first time in his life he had seen a naked woman and was sud-denly fascinated by the smooth hairless legs and the three-dimensional softness, as she moved lithely over to him and lay a sparkling new man's kimono beside him. "Hey," he said coming back into it, "you bring that for me?"

"I bought it yesterday," she said, smiling at the awed gratitude on his face, and she began drying him off.

"No," he said, "don't do that. Come here." He pulled her down beside him, but she kept running the towel vigor-ously over him. Gradually he submitted, knowing this was what she wanted, and lay there luxuriating as the towel moved beneath her tender fingers, soothing him.

"You're awful wet," she said quietly.

"So are you."

"Your mustache is shaggy."

"So is your hair," he said stroking his hand over it, feel-ing its texture and the shape of her head, feeling dreamy and far off, completely relaxed.

Then she stopped, stood up and dried herself off. Fin-ished, she walked over to the closet and hung the towel back up. "Oh hell," she said suddenly. "The window is open. The rain is coming in."

"Do you care?" Hugh said from the bed.

She snapped the light off in answer and in the rain-scented darkness he watched her walk over to him, a doll-like figure that nuzzled down beside him. "No," she said in her whiskey voice. It sounds good outside."

"Do you feel good now?" he asked. "In here out of the rain."

She bit his ear lobe tenderly and he felt his thighs

192

tighten. Odd that she knew exactly the spot that s[ ]
into a sweet hotness. Maybe not so odd, he though[ ]
gily, she's had experience. She snuggled down beside[ ]
so that they were lying side by side, and he bent his h[ ]d
down and kissed her small pointed breasts.

"Why do you wear falsies?" he nuzzled.

"For a joke," she whispered into his ear tugging gently
on the lobe.

"A joke?"

"*Hai*. Americans all think of big-breasted women in
States." She ran her thumb along his spine and he quivered. "But they're not. I don't think American women have
big breasts," she whispered huskily. "I think they wear falsies like Chebe-san." She strained against him. "Do you
care?"

He ran his large hand over her hip, almost covering it,
feeling its mold under him.

"There," she said. "Right there."

He moved his hand back closer to her waist.

"Yes, right there." She bit his ear a little harder.

"You like that." He probed his fingers delicately over
her hip.

"*Toxon*," she said quietly, and eased her slim but firmly
rounded leg over his thigh, pulling him up to her with tender lightly touching hands, guiding him, and he entered
softly and felt something constrict within her and he lay
there, motionless.

Her tongue flicked at his ear. "You one big fella."

"You one soft dolly," he said, muffled between her
breasts, her small delicate breasts, peering down through
the darkness at their loins coupled, motionless. It was a
familiarly new experience to him, not strange or foreign,
yet it was: a slow not quite rhythmical probing that just
when he was trembling through he wasn't, surprising him
with hidden nuances in silent separateness as she con-
stricted gently and he could feel her muscles and joints in
her hips under his hands twitch hungrily. Then he raised
his head and kissed her, breathing hard in her mouth and
throbbing below.

She ran the firm round calf of her leg over the back of
his thigh, speaking in Japanee. "Your mustache does not
tickle, Hugh," she whispered. "Really it doesn't."

"Does anything else tickle?"

"*Hai;* but a good tickle; a *manzuko* tickle."

"And your *mune?*" he uttered. "Does it throb?"

"*Hai,*" she quivered. "Your *karada,* it is mine, *ne?*"

"And yours mine?"

"*Hai.*"

"And what of *moko?*" He bit her lip. "Does it *odori?*"

She ran her fingers across his chest tentatively. "It is *kawaii* like *Chimpo.*"

Hugh felt fumes in his head that were not from the whiskey. "Yours is a beautiful *hadaka.*"

"And yours also." She threw her arms over him grabbing the small of his back, pulling him in farther, slowly. "It is *futoi, ne?*"

"It is like heat," he said. "It is like a bad cut. A pain and the medicine will burn the cut hotly; at first tormentedly. Then it will die."

"It is that with you?"

"*Hai,*" he said. "And with you? Is it a *kaji?*"

"It is a *kaji.* It too burns. There is a wonder to the burn. It wishes to burn more but it is afraid."

"There should not be any fear," Hugh temporized.

"No."

"With me is there fear?"

"With you there is *kaji.*"

Time measured by inconsistency, he felt himself go tight and Chebe-san quivered beside him, and ran her calf up and down rapidly from back to thigh.

"*Okosu,*" she trembled.

"*Okosu okosu.*" He grabbed her head in his hands, her short hair soft under his touch, then moved his hand down and grasped her swollen thigh, "*Okosu okosu!*" and held her tight in one last trembling instant as hot 'kaji, dammed, held back, building up, searching timidly for contact, was released in a single life throe while the smothering heat of a flame thrower flowed over him and a death rattle echoed deep in his scrotum.

He lay with his eyes open staring at the black of the open window where spattering rain strummed in, one hand behind Chebe-san's head, stroking.

"It is good when it happens together, *ne?*" she said after a moment, softly.

"Has the *kaji* been quenched?" he grinned at the window.

"Skosh," she said happily.

"Me, just a skosh too," he said, feeling himself go soft.

194

"No," she said, "not yet."

So he lay there contentedly then, silent, thinking he still had two more days of his "vacation" and wishing it would rain all the time so they could stay in the room and challenging implacably whoever it was that said "after sex there is only sadness"—because it wasn't true, not any of it, not at all, not even on a short spree like this with Chebe-san. Or for that matter any other woman, not if the woman was like Chebe-san of course. Unless by sadness, it meant the consternation he'd felt with Jo-san in the Shanghai Lil bar (only last night?), but the Jo-san was not saddened at all! He let the thought fall quickly with the rain.

"What are you thinking of, Hugh-san?" Chebe-san asked, as she rovingly nibbled his neck, cheek and ear lobe.

"I am wondering if"—he paused—"I am thinking how I have never felt such beautiful smooth skin before in my life. You have hardly no hair."

"You like?"

"*Toxon*." Hugh felt her round dusky plateau rising up from the conmingled honeycomb. "How's my hairy old body feel?" he asked.

She laughed tinklingly. "It feels like a hairy old body."

"What do you want me to do?" he joked. "Shave my legs?"

Chebe-san jabbed him playfully in the ribs. "I don't want you to shave anything. Not even your mustache," she said tenderly. "I have some face cream you can use to curl it with. The curls, the sharp tips, are cute."

"It's merely an affectation," he said. "Like your falsies. Anything I'm affected by is a ham act."

"I love you, Hugh-san," she said.

"And I love you too."

"What is love?"

"I don't know."

"Then how can you love me and I you?" she asked, and he thought he saw a faint glimmer of a smile on her face that time, an impish twist.

"Well," he said inconclusively. "Well, the reason we love each other is because we don't believe in love."

"That is what I said before." She grinned in the darkness. "If you are honest you will not fall in love."

"There is honesty and then there is honesty," Hugh mulled. "I'll tell you something: any person who ever says

195

there is love is a liar. Because nobody knows what the hell it is but they sure as hell like to think they do; preach it and write songs about it."

"If there is no love," Chebe-san said in a voice from an echo chamber, "then what is it?"

"Ah," Hugh said submissively. "That is where the chink in the armor is. Love, because I can't think of a better name for it, is an ambivalence of emotion," he propounded, feeling like a man of the world, unlike a Testical Sarjint in the Crotch. "Let's say you hated me."

"But I don't!" Chebe-san protested.

Hugh kissed each of her eyes. "Let's just say you do. If you hate me there must be a reason. And if there is a reason for hate, then also there must be a reason for love. Simply because you could not hate something, or someone, you didn't care about. And before you can love someone you must hate them first," he said, getting confused, needing a drink.

Chebe-san edged away from him and propped her head up on her elbow. "You mean you have to hate them personally, for themselves?"

"No," he said carefully, running the back of his hand over her breasts. "Not for themselves. It's something within you that you hate. Like say, when I see a dirty old man who don't have good sense any more I hate him. Why? Because I see myself as that dirty old man."

"For the same reason I love something that is attractive to me," he reasoned. "The something of course, or someone, has those qualities I love in myself. But you are also attracted to someone you hate; if the hate is valid and strong enough and you can really feel it, then you actually love the hate."

"*Hai.* I see that. It is like the Japanee people hating the Americans, because they love them—"

"Their way of life," Hugh corrected.

"Yes, their way of life," she said excitedly. "Because they hate them their admiration is stronger. It is like two people, isn't it?" She looked over his arm at the window. "You want to know why I waited for you tonight?"

Desperately, Hugh reached behind him and heisted the bottle off the floor. Wash it away, that was the only thing to do. Hugh Thorton, paragon of success, a thirty-year-old philosopher who is a quacking shitbird in the Marine Corps. "Why did you wait for me?" he said around the bottle.

"For that same thing that you were talking about," she qualified. "Only it wasn't hate."

"So what does that leave us now?" He swilled the whiskey down. "Two goofballs who don't believe in love talking about it. Okay," he conceded. "I-love-you. Happy?"

He thought he could see her grinning that time. "I love you too."

"So we are right back where we started." He shrugged. "We're both of us too honest to fall in love. And we tell each other we love each other. 'Me too,'" he mimicked, chuckled softly, and waved the bottle in front of him to catch the fleeting glints of light from the rainy early morning, still black.

"You can't hold your liquor worth a damn," Chebe-san said good-naturedly.

With heavy dramatic sorrow, still holding the bottle in front of him as if he were about to shed a tear into his beer, Hugh turned to face her, forcing the lines around his mouth to go very deep, the mustache shaggily drooping. "Walk the floor, ginger blue, get over double trouble," he lamented, happily sad.

She giggled and buried her face in his neck. He put the bottle up on the night stand and pulled her down on top of him.

Then they were tossing fitfully, not like the first time at all, totally different, surprising Hugh. Exploring one another, the cool hot hidden subtleties rising powerfully to the surface. Then he was down by her thighs touching the faint copper-colored skin and the soft pliant place and simultaneously aware of her own searching and probing and heated quiverings.

Relenting, she moved up on top of him, burying her face on his chest, almost sobbing, moving slowly on him like a rolling ship, and he held her close to him trying to sum it all up as the pale hint of dawn, sallow and gray like a dying man's face, touched a watery sky outside the window.

They lay like that for perhaps an hour, him holding her on his chest, belly and thighs unconsciously running his hand along her back, in a sleepless uncognizant suspension.

Vaguely, as it lightened, he picked the bottle back up.

"You one big fella," she murmured finally.

"Hell yes," he said. Galvanized, he held her face up in front of him. "How did you learn to speak so damn good American anyway?"

197

She laughed throatily and ran her fingers across his disheveled mustache. "I'm a college girl."

"A college girl?" Hugh said incredulously.

"*Hai*. I went to the University of Tokyo," she explained. "But I learned American before the war."

"Which one?"

"The Nipponese war," she said stolidly. "My father was educated in America. He worked for the government when the war in China started."

Hugh looked at her curiously. "You come from a wealthy family?"

"Oh," she said, "there were *toxon* wealthy families before the war. My father had saved a little *okane*, enough for me to go to school. So I went to college right after the war."

"And you came out of college and started being a who—business woman."

"Whore," she grinned at him playfully. "No, I take a job in Tokyo with your Standard Oil Company. Make *toxon okane* and save it."

"For a rainy day," he said facetiously. "Like today."

She put her face back on his chest. "Just to have it. I had very good pay and lots of prestige."

"And you quit it; because you could make more money as a business woman?"

"No," she said irrefragably. "No more money. But no more cheating either. At Standard Oil everyone false face."

"And you're not as a business woman?" Hugh felt her stiffen a little.

"Some think so," she said. "But it's not true. Is a business woman any more false-faced than the client she does business with?"

Hugh mulled that over. "I could take that as an insult. But then I'm not a client. I never pay."

"That's no lie," Chebe-san said with a giggle. "No," she said seriously. "You no false face."

"I might hedge a little."

"Hedge a lot. You Chebe-san's number-one skivvie honcho."

Hugh laughed, pleased. A slight chill dripped into the room. "Are you cold?"

"No."

"Good." He pulled a blanket up over them.

"Were you?"

"A skosh."

"Chebe-san make you nice and warm."

"You already have, doll." Hugh snuggled down under the thick quilt. "See?"

Chebe-san looked down. "Ah so," she said with a grin.

"How long you planning on being a business woman anyway?"

"How long you plan on stayin' in Marine Corps?"

Hugh snuffled, looked at the bottle, wondering what in the hell he was still holding it in his hand for, and set it behind him. "Those are two very interminable questions, I guess."

"How long have you been in, Hugh-san?"

"Nine years; off and on." He stretched extravagantly, then pulled her close to him. "Off my ass and on my feet. Yeah; I was in five years the first time and four this time. With two to go, so far."

"You were a civilian?"

"Four years."

"Say, Hugh-san," Chebe-san said running her thumb along his back teasingly, "where did you learn to speak Japanee?"

"You really want to know?"

"*Hai.*"

He told her of his enlisting in 1940 when he was seventeen and being sent to Wake Island and the subsequent internment at Camp Fuji, all the while watching her reactions in the darkness—slowly at first, then fast, talking with a heat that carried him away from reality and imagination until there were only facts.

"Being a POW wasn't really too bad," he said. "Not here. Other places were worse, I guess. Sure, we lost weight and all that. But we got some special privileges too. And the guards weren't regular Army; they were old men, or 4F's. The being a POW didn't piss me off too much—it was the circumstances behind it."

These circumstances, he explained, were what actually led him to a carefree life. It gave him a knowledge that all facts, everything read in newspapers, propaganda, hid the true meaning of why and what everything went on. It was a standard joke in the South Pacific how all the marines were guarding coconuts for Proctor and Gamble—and look at Spain and its olive oil, samey same. But the upshot was in the POW Camp: that was where, strangely enough, all the information leaked in. Oh sure, he was working for the Japanee Government, mining copper building roads, things like that. But they all knew that the copper was being sold on the side to the Americans and other Allied forces and after a while it got confused and no one was ever sure who was fighting whom. The only thing they were sure of was that a great deal of money was involved. Very strange. Then too, there was the Red Cross—they got packages and goodies from everywhere but couldn't give them to us so they sold them to the Japanee—oh, a very strange situation, and it was then that he began to understand a little something about war.

When he was released in '45, he left with the conviction that no one man could change the world, especially him, and the only way to exist without going completely crazy was to be on the inside, to find out when everything was going to happen and to make sure he would be there for the fun. It became a game with him: Hugh Thorton against the world. How to keep the world from destroying Hugh Thorton in ignorance. Or better yet, by letting them destroy him when he knew how they had wrangled it all around. It was not much of a lot to cast, but it was his and he was happy with it—and if it wasn't for his theory on the Forty Years' War . . . "Anyway, Chebe-san, it doesn't make much sense to me even when I figure the last details. So I'm sure it won't make any sense to you. But it's something to think about."

For a long time after he'd finished, Chebe-san lay looking at him silently. He saw a series of expressions cross her small face as she started to speak several times. "And you are sure now that there will be another war?" she asked.

"Sure," he said. "Not for a few months yet, though. I'll tell you about it sometime," he evaded.

"And you will spend that time with Chebe-san?"

"Sure, why not. Hell, maybe I'll take you with me. Hell, the whole company will take you. Got to have our camp followers, by God," he said fervently. "If you can play a bugle or beat a drum you're in like Flynn."

"You're crazy." She shook her head.

"That's what the talking doctors in the Vet's Administration told me," he said. "And all the while he was telling me I shouldn't lie to him because he was Jesus V. Christ."

They did not go anywhere that day, Saturday, but sat in their room in their kimonos (Hugh in the one Chebe-san had bought for him which he loved exceedingly), talking—sometimes in Japanee and sometimes in American and that night she took him to the public bath in the hotel and washed him thoroughly and they both sat in the hot tub, luxuriating.

But Chebe-san had to be back at the U.S. Bar in Fujioka that night, she said. Hugh told her he did not have to be back till Tuesday morning and if Mama-san Tokudo put up a bitch about it, he would see that she was reimbursed, which drew a healthy laugh from Chebe-san, puzzling Hugh, and playfully she decided to stay.

The rain did not abate all weekend, nor did it stop Monday, carrying right on through in its howling deafening slant. Midnight Monday they took a cab back to Fujioka. (Hugh had applied Chebe-san's face cream to his mustache —it was not as good as cosmoline—and had resurrected his tips.) He was to remember it later, the weekend, as one of the finest periods of his life.

When they arrived at Fujioka, the cab coming to a jerking muddy stop in front of the dark-faced U.S. Bar, Chebe-san paid the fare. As was the order of the day, Hugh thought, stepping in under the flat marquee out of the rain. The cab pulled off in a skidding frenzied drive, straightened up and headed back to Numazu, its taillights winking good-by in the murky night.

"Well, thanks for the weekend," Hugh said cheerfully, peering through the darkness at Chebe-san's face.

"You're not going to spend the night here?" she said, surprised. "I'll get you up in the morning."

"Don't coax me," he grinned. "If I stayed I wouldn't be worth a popcorn fart in the field tomorrow. And tomorrow I got to go to the field," he said as an afterthought.

"Oh," Chebe-san said in mock sympathy. "Did Chebe-san wear you out?"

"Chebe-san did more than wear me out," he laughed in the darkness. "Anyway, thanks again for the weekend. I'll be seeing you."

"Hokay." She reached up on tiptoes and kissed him on the mouth lightly. *"Synada."*

"Synada," he said, turned and walked down the street through the hammering rain to the bleary light of the main gate of South Camp, his wet suit coat collar turned up around his neck, thinking how strange it was that in those three days of being together neither he nor Chebe-san

knew each other. They didn't know anything about each other at all. It was that simple. But did any two people know each other at all? No, they never did. And that, he thought conclusively, was the way it should be.

But he would have liked it to be different.

At least he didn't have to worry about the platoon, his platoon. With two men like Koko Hobbs and Bohane running interference for him he felt smug, a trifle complacent. He could distribute his energies around the company, solidifying it, doing Finch's job for him. He did not expect any war action till next year, actually. In 1954—forty years after—that was his year. Still, someone could precipitate it. It could come earlier. And it never hurt to be prepared: have that ace in the hole.

Hugh carried this feeling of opiate elation all the way to the staff quarters in the rear of the rifle platoon barracks of Horrible Hog Company. Then, the old ingrained military intangibility that worked from the inside out enfolded him again.

When he entered the dark snore-filled room, S/Sgt Jack Koko Hobbs was sitting in his skivvies on Hugh's bunk, lazily holding a fifth of whiskey in his hand and thoroughly awake.

"What's the matter, Koko?" Hugh grinned. "Someone kick you out of your bunk? Or you snapping in for Gunny Finch's role?" He took his wet coat off and tossed it on his pillow.

"Let's go outside," Koko said furtively, his green-eyed handsome lady-seducing face emotionless, except for the twitching jaws.

Hugh studied him in the darkness. "You nuts? It's raining outside. Ain't you heard the monsoon season's here?"

"This is important." Koko stood up.

"All right," Hugh said disgustedly, and picked up his wet coat. "Ain't you got anything to wear?"

"We'll go to the boiler room," Koko said.

"Here." Hugh tore his envelope fold blanket off his bunk. "Drape this over you. If anyone asks, you can tell 'em you're a monk lost from your monastery."

"You're real high, ain't you?" Koko said, wrapping the blanket around him protectively, clutching the neck of the bottle in front of him.

"You look just like Chief Crazy Horse," Hugh taunted.

"Come on, don't be stingy with your liquor, Chief. I wouldn't want you to go on the warpath."

"Wait'll we get to the boiler room," Koko said quietly. "You're making enough noise to wake Chief Crazy Horse from his grave."

They walked the short distance in the rain to the darkened dry boiler room and stood just inside by the warmth of the furnace.

"Okay," Hugh said, taking the bottle from Koko, "who killed who?"

"You should be so lucky," Koko snorted, wrapped in the blanket. "Boy, you can really pick 'em." He shook his head wonderingly. "You really can pick them, all right."

"Pick what?" Hugh said around the bottle. "This is good on a cold, cold night. Take that blanket off your head. You give me the feeling you're trying to convert me."

"Good on a hot night, too," Koko agreed, shaking his head again, coming out from under the blanket like a turtle's head from its shell. His jaw muscles twitched in calculation. "Pick leaders in your platoon, that's what."

Hugh stopped the bottle halfway to his mouth. "Let's have it." Rain pelted down on the tin roof.

"Our right guide, Corporal Bohane, went over the hill this weekend and is now a Pfc," Koko said bluntly. "Yes sir, you can really pick 'em."

"Went over the hill?" Hugh grimaced.

"Oh, but that ain't the good part; Bohane took three men with him." Koko took the bottle back. "Jesus Christ!" he appraised. "What're you tryin' to do? Live on the stuff?"

"Shithouse mouse." Hugh stared across the wet ash at the staff quarters. "Did he take Sergeant Leroy Finch with him?"

Koko laughed genuinely in a short snuffle, his handsome face lighted. "No, you're still safe on that one. He's in there sawing them off. Drunk."

"Goddamit!" Hugh exploded. "Dirty son of a fucking bitch!" Filled with silent imprecations at the fates howling in the wet night he grabbed the bottle from Koko's hand. "Did you know anything about this?" He took a long belly-punishing pull.

"How the hell could I?" Koko demanded. "I was on liberty all weekend myself. Hell, I didn't find out about it till this morning when Top Landrum told me to run them over for office hours."

"Ah yes," Hugh said distastefully. "My old buddy, Top Condrum. Did he threaten to send them all to jail?— And who the hell else did Bohane, goddam him! take over the hill with him?"

Koko took the bottle back. "Did a beautiful job. He took Renshaw, Turner and Talagua."

Hugh leaned wearily against the bare wall. "Great. That's just dandy. I take off for a couple days and four of my men go over the hill." He paused thoughtfully. "Did you put Queecho in as right guide?"

"Sure," Koko nodded. "Jesus Queecho's the best in the platoon, 'cept for Bohane."

"Oh yeah; sure," Hugh said. "Bohane's great. A born leader. One of the best men I've got. Shit," he snorted. "Bohane got bust, huh? What'd the other men get?"

"Two weeks company punishment, EPD, which they were damn lucky to get," Koko qualified. "I hadn't talked with Gunner Haley, Old Top Condrum woulda had all four up the Middle Camp brig."

Koko draped his blanket around him modestly. "Condrum was dropping hints about your inefficiency all over hell's half acre. But he didn't do no harm." He watched Thorton's face fill with anger. "Ain't nobody'd listen to him but King Solomon and the Kizer. But they don't count." Koko shrugged, the blanket sliding off his shoulders. "So he can't fuck you up."

"No; and he better not try," Hugh said. "The syphilitic queer old bastard."

"Well," Koko said, "I just thought I'd wait up and tell you the good news. Thought you'd be interested."

"Yeah, sure," Hugh said. "Did you talk to Bohane? Did he tell you why he done it?"

Koko nodded. "I talked with him, but he didn't tell me nothing. Just grinned kinda cockily and took his bust."

"He and I are going round and round in the morning," Hugh said murderously. "Just cause the sonofabitch has a Silver Star don't mean he's God."

"Funny thing about that," Koko reflected. "He didn't bring that into it at all. I did."

"Very magnanimous of him," Hugh snorted.

Koko laughed. "I'll say this for him: he's the only bastard I know can take men and lead them like that. Hell, he'd get them all killed he had his way."

Standing there, a murderous indomitable fury rising in him, quite suddenly Hugh felt an icy clear thought worm its way out from the recesses of his mind. "I'll see Bohane in the morning." he said. "Thanks for telling me, Koko."

"It's my job," Koko said.

"It's a wonder Finch didn't drown and the CID didn't get you too," Hugh said.

Grinning tightly, Koko took the bottle back. "They'll never catch me, Hugh," he said evenly, his handsome face bland. "I've been around as long as you have, remember?"

"If you hadn't been," Hugh grinned back, "I wouldn't have been able to know what you were up to, would I?"

In the silent rain-beating darkness, Hugh watched Koko's face unchangeable, assured, unflinching. A face that would never give away anything, he thought, neither hate nor disgust nor admiration. Even when he had a good reason for hating him. And yet Hugh was not worried that Koko would ever deep six him. Since Koko had been in the black market (and how long was that?) there had been that mutual tacit agreement between them. But he would never want Koko to turn on him.

Hugh unwound from the wall. "There ain't nothing left to do now but go to bed."

They walked on back to the staff quarters, Koko slouched under his blanket, Thorton impervious to the rain.

Inside, Hugh dropped his wet clothes (no skivvies) on the floor by his bunk. Itchy could pick them up in the morning, the little crook he thought, as Koko coughed lightly across the room, putting his bottle away.

Gracefully, he slipped between the sheets, not feeling any more the way he had previously out in the boiler room; out there he had felt like storming up through the squadbay, pulling Bohane out of his bunk and beating the living shit out of him—if he could. Now he lay there and fumed at it wonderingly.

Bohane could lead. That was a fact. But where the hell would he lead *himself?* With a guy like that no telling. Funny he hadn't seen it before. He should have noticed. Dammit! Maybe Bohane should have been killed in Korea. Except that lean sonofabitch probably had nine lives.

Not tired, not capable of sleep, his mind racing unanswered, he threw the sheets and blankets back and jumped out of bed. He found his old boondockers and slipped into

205

them, then walked out the door of the staff quarters into the rain in his skivvies and trod over to the company office where the light burned over the Duty NCO's desk.

He climbed up the stairs and down inside, soaked, and glared for a moment at the Duty NCO, Corporal Wessington. "Well?" he said. "Well?"

"Nothing," Corporal Wessington said. "I didn't say anything, Gunny."

"All right." Hugh walked over to the Service Record Book file cabinet, yanked the drawer open, leafed through the B's and pulled Bohane's record book out. Then he walked over to King Solomon's desk, sat down and began studying it. Corporal Wessington watched him warily from Quiller Carpenter's desk.

Hugh could see from the record book that there was really nothing new to learn about Bohane. When he had shipped over, all his other previous records were rescinded. It told about the Silver Star, about his promotion to Corporal, about his re-enlisting. That was all. Hugh went back to the front page and scanned his picture and personal data. Then he saw the Serial Number: 1444004. Well, well, well. 1444004, he thought relaxedly.

Using the Pythagorean system of numbers, he added the serial number together, number by number; the figure totaled 17: One and seven made eight. Aha! Bohane was behind the eight ball. Hell, that solved it.

He snapped the record book shut, put it back in the file cabinet and walked over to the window-door.

"Many are called but very damn few re-enlist," he grinned at Corporal Wessington.

"Sure, Gunny," he said. "I guess so."

Hugh walked back out into the rain and headed toward the staff quarters, this time to sleep; his mind was calmed and he didn't mind the rain at all.

11.

Chebe-san Ito had remained standing under the extended eaves of the U.S. Bar after Hugh Thorton was swallowed up by South Camp.

Exceptionally short, slim, capable, she stood there pensively listening to the drumming rain on the eaves and the smack on the mud in the street with a sort of pensive Oriental wistfulness.

All along the street the bars were dark, except for a few narrow yellow beams shining out from back windows. The bars of Fujioka, she thought with a faint smile; they were always dark this time of night. In the monsoon though they seemed darker. More silent and alone—*toxon* alone!

But that was the way of the bars.

She had not been alone this weekend. If anything, she had been childishly happy, a rather cast-your-life-to-the-wind-and-wish-it-luck carelessness. And Thoton-san Hugh had been the same way too, she decided. He was a strange . . . whatever it was the Americans called them.

Chebe-san mused at the rainy night.

Rain seemed to pour down more heavily, killing the fetid miasma of the rice paddies behind the bars. There was no laughter in the night, no mingling of music from the bar phonographs to hold off at skirt length the perpetual, eternal, three-o'clock-in-the-morning feeling that lay heavy within her like a never-to-be-born pregnancy.

Juke joints the Americans called them, she remembered. Juke joints and honky-tonks. They had names for everything always. It would have been an insult, a personal affront, if a Japanee would have called her *Chebe-san*. Chebe-san! Squirt; shorty. *Hai!* Hugh-san could call her that, and there was no derogation to it at all. She giggled, shivering. Hugh-san number-one skivvie *honcho*.

But for how long would Hugh-san be around? Did

207

it really matter? He was a rare one, all right. He didn't lie on your *tatami* and make believe love.

A tender concern for him swam hotly through her and she looked down the street at the watery light of the main gate.

It was odd that he had been a prisoner of war here and then returned to the same place again. Grasping reality, she decided it wasn't odd at all. She had seen war from the time she was born, lived with it; no, it was not odd.

Also, it was not any different than Hugh-san. It was the same with him. But he did not believe Shinto any more than she did.

She had been raised in the Shinto religion and it had taught her that life was merely an illusion, did not exist, was not permanent. It had taught her that there was only the drifting through this dream and then the next life and all the other lives, working everything out step by step. That there was no permanency, only impermanency. So she had rebuked Shintoism, eschewed it entirely because she wanted permanency. Wanted desperately to have the feeling of *being*.

Out of this she had formed a simple easy-to-understand philosophy. A day-to-day existence. A living in the *Now*. She did not agree with the other Jo-sans who lived their lives like a seed of bamboo, shooting up wherever they were planted. No, she refused to believe that. Each day brought a new decision and as each decision was made there would be other ones. True, she had never actually had the feeling of being, a feeling she had wanted for so long.

There had been some of it this weekend. Hugh-san had made her feel it. But Hugh-san would not be around forever. Even if he was, they would still never truly understand their connection. It was useless to think back to the weekend. Or look eagerly forward to tomorrow. The weekend was gone and tomorrow had not come. Perhaps it might, but only a fool would count on it until it was there.

Perhaps that was why Hugh-san had gone so wild that second night. No map of tomorrow. There had been a terrible fear in him that she had recognized, a terror of something that she could partially understand. If he had not been a POW so long ago and then returned to the same place, she might not have been able to understand it: but she felt that was it. Many times she had felt that name-

208

less gnawing in her viscera and had tried to fight it, use-lessly, herself. When you reach a point where there is nothing ahead for you, she thought analytically, that is when the cataclysm comes. That is when it is three o'clock in the morning.

Standing there under the dripping eaves, she felt quite suddenly hungry. They had eaten at eight o'clock but she had always had a large appetite for so small a woman. Chebe-san, she thought funnily. Me Chebe-san, squirt, with big appetite and small breasts.

She shrugged, small, slim, with delicate hips, and turned to the door of the U.S. Bar, her short thick shiny black hair embracing her oval-shaped face.

Taking the key from her night traveling bag she opened the door and stepped into the darkness as a shuffle of cotton *tabis* approached in the corridor where a single light burned, and a young-old face appeared with a single shining gold tooth. Mama-san Tokudo, clad in her perpetual kimono, short-stepped up to her.

"*Kombawa.*" Mama-san Tokudo bowed graciously. "Mama-san worry over Mitchiko. No come back yesterday."

"*Kombawa,*" Chebe-san exchanged good evenings. "Do not call me Mitchiko," she said. "My name is Chebe-san."

Mama-san Tokudo grinned, uncomprehending. "Ah so, Chebe-san."

"Is there any food?" Chebe-san set her night traveling bag on the bar. "I am very hungry. The monsoon always bring a heavy appetite on me."

"*Hai,*" Mama-san said. "The monsoon brings in the cold that warps the bones. There is food. And the money Koko Hobbs brought."

"Ah, that is *toxon* good," Chebe-san smiled. "Did Koko Hobbs bring too the cigarettes and soap and toothpaste?"

"*Hai,*" Mama-san said. Then her wrinkled face pulled into a frown. "We have skosh trouble this weekend."

"There is trouble every weekend," Chebe-san said indifferently. "There is trouble every day. Mama-san should not worry about it. Chebe-san pays the bills," she declared. "Come; we will eat and you can tell me about it."

Mama-san nodded. "Did Chebe-san have a fine weekend?"

"*Hai,* a lovely weekend!" She took Mama-san by the arm and they walked back to the corridor, and Chebe-san

209

could smell the delicious odors of fried rice and cooked vegetables and fish coming from the large kitchen far in the back.

When she had bought the U.S. Bar (actually she had had it built to specifications) two months before the marines arrived in Japan, she had sternly separated this last room from the others. It was more of a council room, a board of strategy could meet there, and on nights such as this when the marines were broke and there was little business, all the Jo-sans would sit around the large round table eating and talking. Although they all knew that Chebe-san owned the U.S. Bar (along with the Pachinko Parlor in Bamboo Alley), she was treated as an ordinary business woman when the bar was open, for that was the way she wanted it. Back in the kitchen, away from the tentacles of night, she was treated with deference. No one had ever asked her why she wanted it that way and she had never offered any explanation.

Coming into the room, the mouth-watering smells of food exciting her olfactory senses, Chebe-san lost the three-o'clock-in-the-morning feeling and smiled down at the three Jo-sans sitting around the round table, a quilt over their legs trapping the heat from the habachi pot in the center of the floor under the table.

"You see!" Judy-ko said to the other girls. "Mitchiko comes back."

Mama-san Tokudo shambled over to the girls. "No more Mitchiko," she admonished them. "Chebe-san now."

"Ah so," Judy-ko said. "Chebe-san now Sah-jint Thoton-san's baby-san."

"Never hoppen," Chebe-san said, sitting down across from Judy-ko and pulling the blanket up over her legs. "And what did Koko Hobbs bring you?"

"He brought everything we needed," Lucky said. She was a stocky girl with long hair and a heart-shaped face with very narrow eyes. "Even some shampoo."

"And who are you?" Chebe-san said to the new girl whom she had never seen around Fujioka. She was a thin girl, skinny, with a bony face and apparently wearing a new permanent. "I have not seen you before," she said clearly to the thin girl.

"Her name is Cherry-san," Judy-ko said helpfully. "She has come up from Tokyo."

"Cherry-san will speak for herself," Chebe-san said, and

the table fell into a hush. There was only the noise of Mama-san Tokudo filling Chebe-san's plate behind them. "How long have you worked in Tokyo?" Chebe-san asked.

"I have worked for almost two years," Cherry-san said, almost insultingly but with a great pride.

"And why did you not stay in Tokyo? Isn't there *toxon okane* there?" Chebe-san took the plate of rice and vegetables from Mama-san. "You will learn to fry ham and eggs, Mama-san," she informed her.

"Hai." Mama-san nodded dutifully and repaired back to the small kitchen.

"Tokyo is too much Navy town," Cherry-san said, lighting a Japanee cigarette. "Too much of the sickness is brought into Tokyo."

"So," Chebe-san said. "Did you catch the sickness?"

"Who has not?" Cherry-san countered, contained.

Unable to answer that one, Chebe-san smiled at her. Cherry-san's brazenness was a good thing, it showed a stubbornness that she liked in Jo-sans.

"And why did you come to me?" Chebe-san nibbled at her rice and vegetables, suddenly having lost her appetite. She wished Mama-san would get the ham and eggs fried. She set her chopsticks down.

"I stopped first at Gotemba," Cherry-san said. "But it is not a good working town. Not profitable enough for business woman."

"Have you ever been a streetwalker?" Chebe-san asked, thinking *Hai!* this is the end of the line. Eventually they will all come to Fujioka when they have had the sickness and lost their prestige in the cities.

"Who has not?" Cherry-san said again. "I must eat."

Chebe-san speculated on her skinniness for a minute; her bony face was not really pretty, but interesting, and there was an attraction about her that would certainly catch some marine. But Cherry-san was just a little too ambitious. "Do you have a VD card now?" she asked tonelessly.

Cherry-san stubbed her cigarette out, reached behind her to her purse and brought forth the little VD card, the calling card of the initiated few, and handed it to Chebe-san.

Studying it, she saw that Cherry-san had had no sickness for five months. That was good, but she could have arranged that herself, punched her own cards.

"You will not work in Fujioka until you have a VD check next Monday," she told her. "But you can stay here till then. If you pass your check you will find work."

Cherry-san lit another of her cigarettes slowly. "But you do not have room for me to work here at the U.S. Bar."

"No." Chebe-san shook her head. "I can fix you up in Bamboo Alley," she said. "At the Bar New Blue Moon. In the morning I will go down there with you. Mama-san Yoshido will take you I am sure."

Cherry-san still did not look ruffled.

"I have seven Jo-sans working here," Chebe-san explained. "Room for no more. Bar New Blue Moon has room."

"It is all right with me." Cherry-san shrugged. "One place of working is as good as another."

"Are the other Jo-sans in bed?" Chebe-san asked, wiping her hands clean of the business deal, casting a glance at the kitchen nook where Mama-san Tokudo was industriously frying ham and eggs. "Or were there clients?"

Lucky, the stocky girl with the heart-shaped face, laughed in a gravel voice. "Two." She raised two fingers. "Big-belly Tanker-san and Mess Sahjint," she ran her hand over her belly. "Belly go slap slap!"

"Why did not Koko Hobbs stay with you?" Chebe-san asked Judy-ko.

"He is *toxon* upset," Judy-ko said, pained. "There is trouble in Hog Company and he is very angry."

"There is always trouble in Hog Company," Lucky laughed. "Hog Company number hucking ten."

"Hog Company number hucking one," Chebe-san corrected. "*Toxon* good company."

"You only say that because you spend the weekend with Thoton-san," Lucky said, and Chebe-san gave her a withering look and Lucky looked blandly at the table.

"What is the trouble in Hog Company?" Chebe-san stared at Lucky, unappeased. "Mama-san! The ham and eggs!"

"*Hai!*" Mama-san yelled. "More skosh."

"*Baka*-boy go on rice paddy liberty," Judy-ko said. "Koko Hobbs say *baka*-boy take other marine-sans with him."

"It is of no consequence," Chebe-san said. "*Baka*-boy is of no importance. All marines skosh *baka*."

"But Koko stay all weekend," Judy-ko said.

212

"Judy-ko hot for Koko Hobbs," Lucky said. It was a known fact that Lucky had at first been Koko's steady Jo-san, but Chebe-san had always believed Koko was a butterfly—changee changee. But he was *toxon* good-looking!

"Hai," Judy-ko said. "Koko number fucking one." She put her hand to her forehead mimicking a daze. "He is so handsome."

"But he no good on *tatami,*" insatiable Lucky said. "He only do one way. Have no fun."

Judy-ko transfixed her with a murderous glare. "You are a liar, Lucky," she said curtly. "It is only because you do not know how to handle Koko."

"There is only one way to handle it," Cherry-san grinned.

Chebe-san laughed, recalling what Hugh-san had done to Pappy Dreek that first night, then looked up as Mama-san Tokudo came shuffling back with ham and eggs (the ham was burnt and the eggs hard) and a glass of real milk. *"Arigato,"* Chebe-san said. "In the morning you will go to the Arizona Restaurant in Bamboo Alley and watch them prepare ham and eggs." Belatedly, she caught the look of consternation on Mama-san's face. "But this is very good now for the second time."

Breaking into smiles, Mama-san Tokudo bowed out of the room.

"Where is Papa-san?" Chebe-san asked when the young-old woman had left.

"As always," Lucky said. "He is lying drunk in his room after losing at the Pachinko Parlor all day."

That was not good, Chebe-san thought. Although she owned the Pachinko Parlor and the money Papa-san lost was her money to begin with, it made for bad relations. Mama-san was too kind a woman for Papa-san Tokudo, she decided suddenly. But then, it was their life.

She cut into her ham and eggs and ate voraciously. "So Hog Company have *toxon* trouble?"

"It is not news." Lucky shrugged it off. "They are excited because of the war."

"They are always talking of the war," Judy-ko said, "as if it were here right now."

"But it will not come yet," Chebe-san said. "It will not come for maybe a year or two."

"It will come sooner," Cherry-san said suddenly. "I know of that. It will come sooner."

"And how do you know this?" Chebe-san snapped. "Have you been making love with a general from the Daii-chii in Tokyo?"

Cherry-san did not reveal her source. "I only know the one thing. It will come sooner."

"You do not know what you speak," Chebe-san admonished.

Cherry-san did not answer.

"It will not come for at least a month," Judy-ko grinned.

"You should not live so far in the future," Chebe-san said. "It is bad to live that far ahead. If it comes tomorrow, okay; if it comes next year, okay too."

"But it will not come for a month," Lucky said with a grin, "the sickness that is."

Chebe-san stood up then, her belly filled and empty, feeling very tired. "Do you have a room, Cherry-san?"

"Judy-ko is sharing me her room," Cherry-san said, her thin bony face taut. "I will be out in the morning. And you don't have to get me work at that bar you were talking about. I can find my own bar to work at. In Bamboo Alley or somewhere else," she fended, the smile still lingering un-rancorously honest on her, a skinny but juicy drifting business woman who carried that I'll-go-as-far-as-any-marine-will look: bunker material.

Chebe-san, who thought she had never in her life seen such a bitterly strong Jo-san, found herself respecting the skinny girl for something none of the others in the U.S. Bar had. But she did not betray herself.

"Suit yourself," she said, still standing. Then she walked to the door without saying good night, left the council room and walked down the hall. Harsh tense breathing filtered through the thin walls of the two rooms in use, but there was not the sound of belly slapping belly.

In her room, her private unadulterated room far back past the corridor where no marine had ever been, a night light burned above her Stateside bed in dull acknowledgment of her entrance.

She flopped on the sofa chair in the corner as great waves of enervation washed over her like floodwaters over sandbagged barricades. Stretching her slim well-rounded legs out in front of her she gazed down at her pale blue dress where the lines of her thighs formed a deep V between her legs.

Hai, she thought wearily, this was the last stop on the

circle, and if the Jo-sans did not make it in Fujioka they would marry a farmer and plant rice shoots for the rest of their lives, getting stooped-shouldered and thick-legged and rotten teeth.

She sat there for ten minutes staring down at her dress. Once she looked up at the Stateside bed and thought fleetingly of bringing Hugh-san back there someday—if she ever saw him again. No one had ever been in the room but herself. She'd had it fixed up specially with blue curtains on the window, a deep fluffy rose scatter rug, and a wood bath off the closet. The Stateside bed had real sheets and a large, laboriously acquired wardrobe hung in her closet.

It was the nicest room in Fujioka. Even nicer than many of the hotel rooms in the larger cities. Better even than the Hakone Hotel where the rich Japanese spent their holidays, she told herself hotly. You damn betcha. Business him pretty good fella—or him pretty bad fella.

Chebe-san Ito, Mitchiko Ito, third daughter of an ex-wealthy ex-government man, holder of a diploma from the University of Tokyo, one-time fiancée of a Japanee newspaperman, stood up and unzipped her dress, in the Stateside room with the Stateside bed and the Stateside atmosphere that a myriad of Jo-sans had squirmed on a *tatami* to pay for.

She stepped out of her dress and tossed it in the corner, too lazy to put it in the laundry bag in her closet, and walked over to her bed, lay down on it and flipped on the black leatherette Zenith portable (that Koko Hobbs had given her), tuning in on the late Japanese one-string guitar special, thinking pleasantly of Hugh-san.

"Wake me early in the morning, Mother dear," she said with an amused grin, relaxed, "for tomorrow I'm to be Queen of the May."

12.

If Pfc. Giff Bohane had any way of knowing that the business women of Fujioka referred to him as *baka* he would have been as unmoved as his bowels as he sat meditating on the last commode in the barracks head. Because he had finally, after two weeks' preparation, seduced Hanoki *Popcorn* Shiro, bartender of the Bar New Blue Moon: one leg and all.

Sitting there hunched forward, elbows set firmly on his thighs, amid the clean smell of creosote and Bon Ami, he stared thoughtfully at the bleak gray wall in front of him the Tuesday morning after the calamitous weekend, listening to the rain fall heavily outside, streaming past the window.

With the field five-week training schedule shot for the day and the staff in the company office arguing over just what to do—give lectures, show combat films, have a good time-venerated field day with sand soap and rocks, there was nothing else to do that morning except catch up on lost time. And that was exactly what he was doing: because his bowels had not moved for three days now, something which was, for him, a rarity.

Somehow, since he'd been in Japan, Giff had felt squeamishly and ferociously guilty: over the Silver Star which he knew was a farce really, merely a happenstance, and which was connected oddly with Popcorn, or the seduction of her. She wasn't just a lay—hell, he could get a lay anywhere two bits a throw. Inscrutably, he felt if he could have her when none of the others had had her, he would have accomplished something that linked the Silver Star and his re-enlistment with the awkward fierce guilt: which was not even a guilt exactly but more like self-hate or a drive inside him for a repudiation, a disavowal, of that which had been given him in the name of Sanctity God Country and Service. Because he knew it was merely a lot of shit for the birds. And he was the bird, the shitbird, for becoming their dupe.

What he should have done, he realized, was not accepted it when he was put up for it in Korea. That would have solved it. The way he looked at it, the taking of it had made him vulnerable to an obscure onslaught by the powers behind the giving.

It would always leave him shook up when he thought of it like that and although it still wasn't clear, still obscurely focused, he could see it partially and he had answered it by going over the hill because he knew he had to, even before he was certain what it was—before he could reach out and touch it and understand it.

He simply had nothing more now, since the Silver Star, than what the generals and colonels and on down the line to the clerks and brownnosers had. By taking it he had placed himself in their same class. By letting them get away with it, the giving of the Star and his acceptance, he had become one of those whom he implacably and unrelentingly hated. He had fooled himself into believing that the Silver Star set him above the rest of the ruckers, when what he had actually done was let himself be placed with those sniveling cowardly leaders whom, even with his four years' service, he had never before seen clearly.

And they were right at the point of taking him in all the way; and he had been at the point of letting them get away with it.

If you let them get away with it, he told himself, you are just as guilty as they are.

Maybe that was one of the reasons for his wanting Popcorn so bad?

Unclear, but moving closer, he was sure it all tied in somewhere, and in going back over it in his mind, he tried to tie the ends together, pinpoint his own motives for doing it—the motives that he knew lay hidden behind the crude camouflage of illusion that had taken him over the hill that night . . .

. . . With surgical movements, Poke Turner had cut the most beautiful hole in the fence, big enough for even as large a man as Half-Slick Willy to walk through standing up.

"You didn't have to cut such a fucking big one," Stack said. "They's sure to find it in the morning."

"Hah!" Poke snorted.

Following a paddy dyke down to the creek that was high now from the rains, they moved single file Indian-style while the night closed in around them like a heavy wet shroud. Giff immediately recalled the unforgettable sensation of moving out on a night patrol through no man's land while all around him lurked ubiquitous mines and a prone Goonie with a full magazine in his burp gun.

From far up the creek, where the bridge spanned it on Fujioka's main street, came a silent sparsely lit deserted call. They crossed the huge stones in the creek coming up the other side stealthily on a narrow paddy dyke.

Giff was bringing up the rear, his eyes peering foggily through the rainy darkness at the town, thinking progressively of Popcorn Shiro and how to handle her. He would have to play it cool which was, and always had been, highly impossible for him. Nevertheless he would have to try. Wondering why it was so important to make a one-legged girl whom he would never see again when they left; hell, what was all that talk about staying here forever!

Musing this over and looking ahead, he saw Stack Renshaw's head slip and disappear, followed by a resounding splash and a feeble indignant cry. Giff edged carefully up the path where Stack had vanished.

"Goddamit, Poke," he whispered harshly. "Hold it up." He crawled on his hands and knees, thinking his raincoat would have to go to the cleaners goddamit, to where Stack Renshaw was sputtering and coughing lying belly down in the rice paddy.

"Out!" he gasped. "Get me to hell out of here. I'm covered with shit. Oh balls!"

Giff rumbled in healthy laughter seeing in the darkness Stack's woebegotten face, stuck out his hand and pulled him up on the dyke.

"What the hell happened?" Poke said, coming back with Guppy Talagua.

"Jesus Christ but you stink, Stack," Guppy sneered.

"Fuck you," Stack mumbled.

"You all right?" Giff asked. "Ready to go?"

"How'll I get in a bar like this?" Stack demanded, throwing his hands in front of him. "Covered with shit," he lamented.

218

"You can undress outside," Poke suggested. "Let's go, man. It's getting late."

They moved on up the dyke, Stack being more cautious now, and Giff grinning behind him, till the dyke petered out to a path that came up between the A. J. Hideaway and the Silver Star Bar on Fujioka's main street.

Gingerly, they peered down the street to the main gate where a lone sentry was industriously practicing fast draws with his .45 in the sentry booth.

"The MP's already gone," Poke whispered. "See?"

"Let's get on down to Bamboo Alley," Giff said.

"We can't cut down Main Street."

"We go down and cut across the creek at Skivvie Lane," Guppy offered.

"Oh shit," Stack moaned, catching some light from the U.S. Bar across the street. "Look at me. Oh shit."

Laughing, Giff nudged him forward. "We'll do what Guppy says. Cut down behind the Florida Bar, cross the creek again, come up Skivvie Lane and be right at the Blue Moon."

"It'd be easier to hit one these other bars," Poke said, jerking his thumb around Main Street.

"I wants to hit the Blue Moon," Giff said.

"Okay," Poke said. "I hope you win your bet."

"Just get me outa these clothes," Stack wailed.

They ran quickly across Main Street, slipped into the small alleyway beside the U.S. Bar, ran on behind the Florida Bar, crossed the railroad tracks and came down to the creek. But there were no rocks and at this part of the creek the water was almost waist high and swifter.

"Jesus Christ on a Crutch!" Poke snorted. "You sure you want to go the Blue Moon?"

"You three don't have to go," Giff said. "I am." He stepped warily into the cold water, killing what little shine he had left on his boondockers, feeling the current fight his stability. "You'll get some of that shit washed off you, Stack," he said over his shoulder through chattering teeth, "if you come on in."

"That's right, by God!" Stack said, inspired, and jumped in, stumbling and falling and moving downstream about ten yards before he regained his balance.

Giff waited to see that Stack's head came up, thankfully hearing Stack sputter.

"Ahhhhhh!" Poke hollered behind him. "My balls are froze!"

Half fighting the current, half keeping himself from laughing, Giff pushed through the rough waters to the other side, climbed up and waited. Across the creek under the trees he could see Guppy Talagua, a short bunched figure under the darkness that hung like wet gunpowder. Twice Guppy started to leap and stopped. On the third try, he took a run at the creek, plunged in and fought desperately, swimming to the other side, passing both Poke and Stack.

Poke came half running through the water in slow motion, his arms raised high with Stack a little way down from him standing up now and inspecting himself carefully. When both of them joined Talagua and got up to Giff they started off on another paddy dyke, teeth chattering, toward Skivvie Lane where it cut up to Bamboo Alley.

They came out of Skivvie Lane between the Arizona Restaurant and the White Kitty in front of the Blue Moon now dark inside, a pale light burning from the back lighting the heavy slant of rain that fell incessantly.

"Let's hit the back door," Poke chattered. "If they don't let us in I'm goin' back down and jump in that creek and let it take me out to sea."

Giff led the way this time. Bulling his head to the rain so as not to get wet—pointless because he was already thoroughly saturated both inside and out—he moved stealthily behind the Bar New Blue Moon. Poke Turner was cursing fitfully behind him, his teeth chattering in loud clacks. Stack Renshaw was furiously silent, and the happy chuckling of Guppy Talagua brought up the rear.

The light flickered through the fogged panes of glass in the rear door promising warmth and shelter. Giff stopped and checked over his shoulder. They were all here. Where the hell else would they be? He rapped loudly on one of the panes.

Feet shuffled somewhere within, mixing with several muted voices, all apprehensive. Giff rapped again, impatiently.

"What if they won't let us in?" Poke wailed. "We'll have to cross the goddam creek again."

"They'll let us in," Giff assured him. "Long's we got *okane* they'll let us in."

220

"For Chrissakes don't talk so loud," Stack reprimanded furiously. "They might still be some MP's around."

Squeaking, the door slid open just far enough to reveal Mama-san Yoshido who looked out at them through thick glasses. "Whatsa matta you, *dio?*" she said charily, shaking her head. "Bar him close. No doee business." She looked up and down at their sodden dungarees. "Ahh, *baka* boys, come out through fence."

Giff bowed graciously, his dungaree cap falling to the ground in the mud. "We are four lost orphans left on your doorstep, Mama-san," he said. Then he grinned sillily. "But we got *okane.*"

"You want stay all night, *ne?*" Mama-san Yoshido's face brightened.

Giff waved his arm at the unholy three behind him. "Maybe all weekend, Mama-san. *Toxon* money."

"Mama-san, for shit's sake," Poke said wearily, "let us to hell in. I'm freezing out here."

Mama-san Yoshido grinned at the recognition of Poke's voice, but she did not open the door farther or invite them in, and Giff was beginning to wonder what the hell?

"Let 'em in, Mama-san!" Cinamo Dallas' voice boomed from the back room, followed by a chorus of girlish laughter.

Giff looked through the pummeling rain at the three faces staring dumbly at the door, rain running down their faces like tiny rivers. He wiped his hand across his face and looked back at Mama-san who was grinning as if she had just pulled the greatest *coup d'état* in the history of Fujioka. It was Dallas' voice, he thought numbly. Or course it was. "Was that Dallas?" he heard himself say.

"It wasn't your mother's," Poke said miserably.

Grinning, Mama-san Yoshido opened the door all the way; Giff's legs moved him into the small hall not bothering, or having the slightest notion, to retrieve his cap which lay in the mud. The sudden warmth and the quick lifting of rain left him groggy. He shook his head vaguely, thinking somewhere far off there still should be something pounding on his head. Then it was gone and he started to walk up the single step into the back room.

"No no!" Mama-san Yoshido raised her arms in protest. "Takee off shoes."

"Oh yeah; I forgotten." Giff knelt down carefully to keep

221

from falling and began untying his leggins. Goddam! but the heat put dizziness like another flow of blood all through him.

"How about some kimonos?" Poke said, standing naked and wet after a furious stripping.

"Me catchee." Mama-san bustled off to the back room, and Giff heard the Jo-sans laugh gleefully again. Dallas said something he couldn't catch; the heathen sonofabitch, he thought furiously; how'd he get out here?

"I feel better already," Poke said, leaning against the wall. "All's I need now's a woman and a bottle. Hot damn! How about you, Stack?"

"Ain't even got a dry cigarette!" Stack lamented, squatting.

"I still don't know why I cross that creek. I'm afraid of water at night," Guppy, the beefy Hawaiian, confessed.

When Mama-san got back with the armful of kimonos they were all four standing naked in the foyer with a sort of drunken mock-pathetic look on their faces. She smiled sympathetically and issued out the warm dry kimonos. "You pay Mama-san now, *ne?*"

Giff cinched his belt tight. *"Okane?* Hell, I ain't sure what's happenin'," he said. He bent back down to his clothes and pulled his wallet out. Everything in it was soaked. He handed her five watery ten-dollar bills in script.

"No havo yen?" Mama-san looked surprised.

"No," Giff shook his head. "You'll have to exchange it on the black market."

"Let's get the hell on in there," Poke said. "Lemme at that habachi pot."

Mama-san took the money and the four of them followed her on into the back room. Cinamo Dallas was sitting at a low round table, a blanket draped over his kimonoed legs with Kayo-san the junkie, Peanuts, and Yoko—who would not shave under her arms.

"You all about the most miserable-lookin' crew I ever seen," he grinned.

"I thought you said you weren't coming out." Giff walked over and sat down at the table wondering where Popcorn was. "Hello, Peanuts!" he said enthusiastically. There was always Peanuts, he told himself. Besides what was fifty bucks? On a bet?

"Didn't say that at all." Dallas looked at them, as one

222

by dejected one they sat down around the table. "Said I wasn't going through the fence."

"It don't matter," Stack said. "Hello, Yoko. You got any business tonight?"

Sullenly, Yoko shook her head.

"You have now," Stack said.

Dallas produced a quart of Canadian Club three-quarters full and passed it around. Giff took a healthy pull, feeling very secure with the rain and night outside. "So how'd you get out?"

"Went through the main gate," Dallas said laconically. "Buddy, when I go over the hill I go in style."

"You come stay with Peanuts?" the stocky firm-bosomed Peanuts said to Giff. "Me wait up for you."

Giff smiled at her, then turned back to Dallas. "So you came through the main gate. On what? A horse?" he passed the bottle to Poke.

"On a liberty card," Dallas said tonelessly. "On an old Item Company liberty card. Hell, the sentry don't care. He's a field marine like you'n me. He ain't no MP."

"Where the hell's all the girls?" Poke demanded. "They ain't all shacked up, are they?"

"They're running around here somewhere," Dallas said. "You got to look 'em up. Try their rooms." Kayo-san, the junkie was staring glassy-eyed at the table, sitting by Dallas, an ineffable grin on her mouth.

"Come on, Yoko," Stack said unhappily. "Let's wrassel." He reached down and pulled her to her feet. "I'm goin' to charge a bottle of Akadama to you, Giff," he said and half pulled Yoko out of the room.

Five minutes later, much to her chagrin, Guppy Talagua escorted Peanuts out of the back room and on down the hall.

"This is great," Poke complained. "I ain't too hot for sleeping with you, Giff. Where's 'at old Nancy at?" he demanded Kayo-san, who was off in another land.

"She's in her room," Dallas said. "I don't think she feels too good tonight.

Poke got to his feet. "I'll fix that, I will. This old rebel going to make her see the light, by God." Giff watched him navigate out, grinning after him. "So that leaves me," he turned to Dallas. "Where's Popcorn?"

"Where she always is," Dallas said. "Goin' back to see her?"

"How about another drink?" Giff said, like an obvious bluff in a poker game.

Dallas handed him the bottle. "Look's like I'm going to be fifty bucks richer, don't it?"

"Personally, I don't think so. You don't know me very well. I have hidden wealths of romance."

Dallas grunted. "If you don't score tonight, friendo, you lose."

"Tonight!" Giff grimaced. "Right now?"

"You didn't think I bet for any other time, for Chrissakes!" Dallas said. "The bet was for tonight."

Somehow, Giff felt he had been outwitted. "I got to have support," he said profoundly. "I'll take your bottle with me."

"What the hell am I going to drink?"

"Drink gin," Giff said heavily. "I'll even pay for it."

"Okay," Dallas acquiesced. "I'll give you all the support you need. 'Cept I won't hold it for you."

"I didn't intend for you to."

"I guess you know where she sleeps." Dallas winked at Kayo-san, who giggled for no reason.

"I have known lo these many nights," Giff said profoundly. "And I am on my way." Clutching the bottle he stood up and looked down at Dallas with total indifference. "We shall know within the night how I make out," he said dramatically.

"Good luck, buddy," Dallas called after him.

Weaving down the darkened hall past the small rooms, Giff began laying out his plan of attack; his avenue of approach. Ought to have a drink on that he decided, stopping by the water closet. The smell of disinfectant wafted out into the hall. That Dallas was a sly sonfabitch. A-good-old-sly-son-of-a-bitch. He was one old friend you could count on—the sonfabitch. But he ain't about to win this bet. The best way to handle it, he thought craftily, was to be romantic as hell.

Capping the bottle, he walked quietly down to the first room of the corridor just inside the beaded curtain. A flat sheet of light loomed at the bottom of the door. Aha! she wasn't asleep. Now what to do? Well, she had always made eyes at you before, hadn't she? That she had. And she was highly impressed with the Silver Star; as was everybody, just about everybody, except himself, he thought glumly. He slid the door open.

224

Popcorn was sitting with her legs crossed—one leg, he had noticed reluctantly but enticingly—on the *tatami* in her kimono reading a Japanee-American movie magazine, her full pouting mouth moving with the words. Her hair was done up in her customary pony tail; cute, he thought, as she suddenly looked up at him, and never been touched by a marine. A virgin maybe, he thought. And then, seeing her, with that one leg gone, a great passion rose in him, stimulated some by the weather and the booze he'd consumed, and he wanted suddenly to love her as was her right to be loved, really show her what love was, just for an instant, and make her understand; he thought with his part-Irish drama that tomorrow they might be at war. "Hello, Popcorn."

"Shan-tee-san!" she said, eying him cautiously. "Oh," she said, understanding. "You *toxon* stinko."

"Just a skosh," Giff said, sliding the door open a little farther and stepping in. "I"—he paused, and looked dramatically down at the bottle in his hand—"I want to see you," he said.

Quickly, but with reserve, Popcorn laid her movie magazine down and motioned with great flourish for him to sit beside her on the *tatami*.

"Why, thank you," Giff said courteously and squatted, crossing both his legs, and uncapped the bottle. "Want a drink?"

"*Hai*," she grinned, took a dainty sip, made a wry face and swallowed. "You come spend weekend at Blue Moon?"

"I'm over the hill," Giff admitted. "I came out through the fence."

"Whatsa matta you, Shan-tee-san?" Popcorn said worriedly. "You catchee *toxon* trouble? Go Monkey House?"

"It doesn't matter." Giff shook his head. "I had to see you, Popcorn. I had to come out and see you."

Popcorn looked at him, her mouth pouting. "You want to see Popcorn?"

Giff nodded, avoiding her eyes. "I'm in love with you," he said, raising his eyes and staring intently at her. "I guess I've been since the first time I was in here."

For a moment Popcorn almost smiled, then she shook her head, the pony tail dancing like a man who has just been hanged; her lips pouting a little fuller. "You are in love with Popcorn?" She shook her head again. "Shan-tee-san, you *toxon* stinko. You no mean what you say."

"The hell I don't!" Giff blurted. "I'm in love with you." Through his hazily chosen words, he could see the fifty bucks fly away with his vanity.

"Popcorn is not even a business woman," she declared. "Only a how you say—bartender. No can dance. You maybe go see Nancy or Peanuts, *ne?*"

"Now listen," Giff said fervently. "I ain't stringin' you along, see? I'm serious," he said, seeing *everything* lying in the mud with his dungaree cap. "Popcorn, I really love you."

"You are serious, *ne?*" Popcorn looked down at the *tatami.* "I am not sure; sometimes me too feel that way. I like you *stekki* nice first time; but Popcorn no good; only have one leg."

Taking advantage of this, Giff moved over to her and lovingly held her face in his hands. "There, you see?" he said quietly, aware of her nose twitching when she caught the alcohol on his breath, wishing for shit's sake he knew what to say next.

Popcorn looked up at him, waiting.

"I don't care about the one leg," he half lied, convincing himself he didn't actually, telling himself she *was* beautiful really, wondering if he was going bamboo obviously! "I love you for you and you alone," he said, remembering he'd heard that line in a movie somewhere. He bent down and kissed her lightly on her pouting mouth, then looked into the darkness of her limpid eyes.

She began trembling, shaking a little, and grasped him desperately with her hands, her dusky fingers turning white. "Shan-tee-san," she said.

"I'll get the light," he offered, wanting to shout and run down the hall and collect his bet, and his cap.

Before she could say anything to that, he spun around knocking the bottle over, scooped it up hurriedly, and snapped the light off. Then he was back by her side, the good one.

Feeling her tremble beneath his hands, he wondered now how to go about it? Suppose she was a virgin?

But he didn't get any farther. With a desperate, frenzied new savagery, she flung her arms around him pulling him down to her, kissing him hotly all over the face. Belatedly, taken by surprise, he was aware that she was stripping the kimono from him, running her hands all along his torso, whimpering a little, muttering in Japanee.

226

Popcorn was not a virgin. She was tight, yes; but not a virgin at all, he found out. Gradually, he caught up with her ferocity in a rolling loin-bruising-loin mouth-searching hungriness: a cataclysmic contagion and the stump of a left leg did not hinder her at all.

In the last quivering throe that sent a charge stiffening his spine as his thighs tightened, he reached down and ran his hands along her legs, the full one and the short one, feeling strange things move within him. It was almost as if she hungered for him, actually physically hungered for him alone. Or hungered for something he had. And he became just as violently hungered as she, and then she began swearing, profanity that seemed to charge the room with barbaric excitement. In a way, he thought, it was almost like combat: the same identical adrenaline pounding killing instinct when a rifle bucked against your shoulder and you saw a man fall dead.

"Etai! Etai! Etai!" she whimpered, shaking her head, her pouting mouth hot and wet, hands clutched around his buttocks pulling him in; then she began crying.

"Don't cry," he gasped, kissing her. "Don't cry; please don't."

Whimpering like a small sleek cat in a monsoon, she would not release her hold on him. "Oh, Shan-tee-san," she cried. "You are the first one; the first; the first."

"It's all right. It's all right, Popcorn." He lay his head down beside hers, listening to the convulsive sobs and thinking if it was her first time with a marine it was the first time in a long time. No wonder she was so savage.

Then she was on him again, he having risen himself sufficiently, with the same animal hunger, but this time he met her.

For the first time in his life Giff felt his own dormant, unrepressed, untrained, never having been checked, always there within him begging for release, expressions of emotion that had never been stimulated enough to bring to the fore all those things that kept him locked up tight, now flowing over in a torrent of force.

And after the second time, she lay sobbing again beside him. If he was going to go again he would definitely need a drink—gratefully pleased because this, Popcorn with the one leg, in some unfathomable way had alleviated the pain of stagnation that had welled up in him since he'd

227

been in Japan. And he didn't even care about the fifty bucks any more.

Yet he was still not certain what to say. He reached for the bottle and took a drink. "I love you," he said, and even to him the words sounded phony.

Popcorn, still weeping, pulled away from him.

"What is it?" he said. "What's the matter?"

"You, Shan-tee-san," she gasped. "You have become a part of Popcorn."

Giff mulled this over, feeling close kinship to a trapped muskrat. "Tell me about yourself, Popcorn," he said evasively. "Where do you come from?"

"No." She shook her head angrily. "No tell about *watashi*. It no good."

"It can't be that bad," Giff reasoned.

She moved back over to him, snuggling, and he thought he saw her smile in the darkness as shiny tears wet her cheeks.

"Go ahead; tell me about it," he prompted, playing the game.

"You true want to learn about Popcorn?" she asked.

"What? oh, yeah; sure." He set the bottle down, capped, and moved up to her seeing the curved outline of her firm breasts and the rounded hips, and the short stump. Well, Sara Bernhardt only had one leg too.

There was not much to tell about Popcorn, Giff soon found out. If there was, she did not tell it. The only thing she enlightened him on at all was how she lost her leg— not by the *bomb*—Fukui, Japan, in the earthquake of 1948 when she was twelve years old, she said. Mathematically, straining hard, Giff deducted that that would make Popcorn seventeen—counting, as they did in Japan, the year spent in the womb. In reality, it would make her sixteen. Peanuts was eighteen.

She did not speak of her family and he didn't find out if she even had one. In fact, all of it boiled down to the earthquake in Fukui. There was a legend, she told him, that Japan lay on the back of a huge catfish and every time there was an earthquake the Nippon people say, *"The Catfish has turned on its back,"* and that summed it up. She was more interested in his life; he got out of that one by saying it would take too long to explain all of it right now. Some other time. He was more interested in getting acquainted physically with her, remembering all the white-hot shell fragments of the first two times.

So they did. All weekend, and Dallas grinned like an exceptionally fine loser and didn't say a word about the bet, simply let Poke pay off. Apparently, the Jo-sans in the Blue Moon were not surprised. Poke and Stack and Guppy Talagua did not care one way or the other. They told him they thought his winning the bet was *dai jobi* when he met them for breakfast in the back room the next morning. And that was all. All of them stayed in their respective little rooms over the weekend because of the MP's nosing around out front from time to time, and planned to head back late Sunday night, go through the fence and slip into the barracks without any trouble.

And they probably would have made it back clean, without a hitch, Giff felt, if it hadn't been for Kayo-san, Dallas' junkie girl friend, who, either through an overdose of her happy dust or a bad fix or maybe not enough of a fix at all, none of them were ever sure what caused it, Kayo-san sang out with a banshee scream bolting out of her and Dallas' room, naked, to the front of the bar, tossed a chair through the window, no small feat for a woman her size, and jabbering in crazy Japanee began a ritual of animal craving, bringing Giff and the rest of them out of their rooms all with a sort of blank-faced gaping awe.

"The shit hit the fan," Poke said.

"Jesus!" Stack cried, "I was just about to come."

"Who the hell is it?" Giff demanded, taking a leap through the beaded curtain with Poke and Stack right behind him to confront Kayo-san lying on the floor with a bottle of Akadama in a vise lock between her legs.

While the chair, which had nothing against anyone, had gone through the window and come to rest at the feet of two MP's, and Giff could see their shiny white helmets through the broken window turn to look into the bar.

"Oh shit!" he said, as the whistles broke the night.

Papa-san and Mama-san came running out with Peanuts from the rear, scooped up a reluctant Kayo-san and hustled her back through the curtain. Giff and Poke and Stack, with Guppy coming dumb-struck up to them past the limp figure of Kayo-san, all stood there naked in the front of the bar as one MP came running in the front door, another in the back.

They were a sorry kettle of four men standing in front of the Officer of the Day in the guard shack right inside the main gate. Cinamo Dallas, who had his Idiot Item Company liberty card, had been passed right on through by the MP's at the Blue Moon and none of them acknowledged knowing Dallas. There was no mention of Kayo-san, on the other hand, because the MP's were convinced that they, the four marines, had caused all the trouble, and again they remained silent about Kayo-san. Honor forbade them to shoot one of their own down.

The Officer of the Day, a second lieutenant with a confused face, was in favor of sending them all to the provost marshal at Middle Camp but the Commander of the Guard, a S/Sgt from George Company and a personal friend of Koko Hobbs, saw to it that they were escorted back to their barracks. But you silly bastards, the S/Sgt told them, when you goin' to learn you cain't get caught?

When they arrived at the barracks, under the protective wings of two privates of the guard who both thought it was a howl and said so, the four of them climbed wearily into their bunks. Before he fell asleep, Stack Renshaw found time to swear savagely at Poke, who snickered and they all slept with heated imprecations.

Giff, who did not see fit to swear at anyone (mainly because it was his fault in a way), closed his ears to it feeling a sense of triumph and chagrin that he could not express.

In the morning they were all four marched dutifully over to the company officer by a thoughtfully silent Koko Hobbs to meet an anticipant Top Condrum who already had court-martial papers made out.

The first sergeant sat smugly at his desk, his eyes cold and dead under the reddish-white feathery brows.

"I'm here to help you," he said in his flat voice and went into the Kizer's office with Poke and Stack and Guppy, Koko Hobbs behind them as a neutral referee. Giff was the last to go in, and he went alone.

Waiting his turn, he sat in his immaculate starched dungarees and spit-shined boondockers under clean leggins talking with Quiller Carpenter. Quiller gave his professional opinion, without reserve, that what they all should have done was beat the hell outa the MP's that arrested them too, then they wouldn't be up for office hours. Yes sir, he told Giff, that's what they should have done. And personally, Top Condrum was out to get some more scalps for his belt.

"He ain't gettin' this brave's hair," Giff grinned, a little nervous.

"I don't think he'll get your companios' either," Quiller said. "But him and old fuddy-duddy Solomon over there"— he pointed his thumb—"sure tryin' their best." King Solomon, head bowed over his desk, did not look up.

The three came out of the Kizer's office, grinning sheepishly, relieved. Top Condrum labored behind them with the look of a man who had been robbed of a sure-fire seduction.

"Two weeks' extra police duty," Poke said in his Georgian drawl. "Not bad, huh?"

"All three of you?" Giff asked, standing up and straightening his dungaree shirt.

"Sign the punishment sheet, you three," Top Condrum said. "And report back to your platoons. The punishment starts tonight." He glared at Giff. "Okay, Corporal, let's go on in."

Without answer Giff walked past Landrum into the Kizer's office, stopped one pace in front of his desk smartly at attention beside Koko Hobbs.

"Sir, Corporal Bohane reporting as ordered, sir." The Kizer did not offer him any coffee.

"You're a damn poor example of an NCO!" he boomed right off, sitting massively behind his desk, his Prussian countenance and bullet head red with rage. "It is an NCO's job to help men; not by God send them over the hill!"

"Yes, sir."

"I knew I'd have trouble with you," Kizer stormed. "I can always tell what men plan to fuck up *my* company!"

"Yes, sir," Giff swallowed.

"You're a disgrace to the uniform you wear," Emil Kizer said scathingly. "You deserve a court-martial. At least that!"

"Yes, sir." Giff heard the door open behind him and Top Landrum moved up softly as though he had heard a sign of agreement with his plans.

"This man is your right guide, is he not?" Kizer demanded of Koko.

"Yes sir, he is," Koko said.

"Well!" Kizer boomed. "Well! I'm going to authorize him battalion office hours and I hope he gets a special court-martial."

"Beg your pardon, sir," Koko said. "It might be a bad thing to send a man with Bohane's combat record up like that. Bad for the morale."

"What's this?" Kizer ranged his war-ravaged eyes at them both. "Combat record?"

"Corporal Bohane's a carrier of the Silver Star, sir," Koko said.

"But of course!" Kizer snapped. "Certainly. Yes. I've taken that into consideration, Sarjint Hobbs. It's been a hectic morning. Actually"—he leaned back in his chair, cocked his arms behind his head and smiled disarmingly—"actually I was merely throwing a scare into the boy. You may leave, Sarjint Hobbs!"

"Aye aye, sir," Hobbs executed an about face and marched out of the office.

"You too, Top," Kizer added.

Indignantly, Top Landrum left.

"Well!" Kizer boomed, throwing Giff off balance. "Sit down, Corporal. Sit down."

"Yes, sir." Giff sat down, at attention.

"Now what you've done," Kizer said stolidly, "is something that is actually not too serious. Hell," he grinned, "I've even taken a few trips over the hill myself, in my time: Nicaragua, China . . ." He ran over his thirty years' service, telling Giff his life history as he had before, and Giff felt the same electricity-charged air move within the office.

"You'll have these problems from time to time," Kizer said. "It's only natural and when you do you should come to me. I can help you. Now—why did you go?"

"Well, sir," Giff said, "I was bored."

"Bored!"

"Yes, sir! Bored! Too damn much sitting around, nothin' happening."

"Of course!" Kizer conceded. "But we'll start pouring on the training harder the rest of the month. Lots of field training coming up, lad. Lots of it! We'll be able to utilize it before long, eh? Heh heh. Maybe in China, by God; haven't been to China since the thirties."

Giff moved groggily in the head-battering air until finally Kizer summed it up with a temporary bust—so as to pacify everyone, eh?—and with the promise that Corporal Bohane would get his rank back in a month—on probation—if he did not fuck up again. And that was that. . . .

Back in the head, ensconced with the Bon Ami smell and the leaking of toilets, sitting there still unrelieved, he mused over his weekend tour de force: the unanswerable why of it. Now thinking back, he belatedly realized that he had actually expected to get caught! But he hadn't expected to get the rest of them pulled down with him. Although neither Stack nor Poke (Guppy Talagua regarded the whole thing with a fatalistic occupational hazard) held this against him, Giff could not help but feel they were slightly pissed off. Not personally at him, more at Top Condrum and the EPD. The EPD knocked hell out of their liberty. The Top had seen to that with his customary deadpan *"I'm here to he'p you,"* can't-wait-to-get-you-men-locked-up speech.

Stack and Poke had to pull their EPD from eight o'clock at night till ten. Since liberty cards could not be drawn after ten they were as Poke put it, "screwed, blued, and tattooed." They would come trudging back from the battalion mess hall (this was where they pulled almost all their EPD as it turned out) with the smell of rotten eggs and defiled chickens clinging to their dungarees. And the platoon: those men who were not on liberty would be subjected to vicious cursing until finally just from exhaustion and lack of fresh imprecations for one another Stack and Poke would fall disgruntledly to sleep.

Last night, Giff reminded himself, his bowels growling a little uneasily— Last night he had gone out on liberty the right way. He and Dallas, who never failed to interject his aloof asides, had gone right on down to the Blue Moon. Dallas had taken Kayo-san, as usual, and why he picked a junkie Giff could not understand at all. There just wasn't any reason for it. So he had waited around at the bar pleasurably drinking beer and talking to Popcorn till the bar closed, then gone back to her little room just inside the beaded curtains.

It had been just as satisfying if not more so than the weekend. They had gotten to know one another better in all ways and she had commiserated with his temporary bust while the other Jo-sans looked askance at him for losing them two of their best customers. Even Yoko, who would not shave under her arms, appeared displeased. He had promised Popcorn to bring her out some soap and toothpaste and some new panties.

233

All of it—the seduction of Popcorn, the going over the hill, the re-enlisting and the Silver Star—had somehow tied in together. But the awkward guilt remained, still unchecked. He had thought perhaps the office hours would have changed some of it. But it hadn't. The Silver Star had reared its head in there too, thanks to Koko Hobbs. And he had not repudiated it as he wanted to—as he could have. Yet all of it, he reasoned, had given him an inkling to changing it, provided a springboard onto something else which would destroy it within him.

Because as long as it remained, he was still the *duped*. The shitbird. If he conned himself into believing his own legend he knew he was done; he would have irrevocably crossed all the way to the other side. And he felt he was very, very close to it.

Dallas, he knew, would not have the Silver Star shoved up his ass. And said so. But that did not help him himself. Sometimes it got so close to him, he felt like running his feet through the window lights.

He was still staring bleakly at the wall in front of him, running it all through his mind, praying for a war, when the mustachioed T/Sgt walked blandly into the head, advanced to the end and sat firmly on the commode next to Giff without dropping his pants.

"Hello, Gunny," he said pleasantly. "How'd your weekend go?"

Hugh Thorton grinned at him, curling the sharp spears of his handlebar mustache. "How was your weekend?" he said just as pleasantly. "Did you patch up the fence when you came back through?" He reached over and pulled Giff's cigarettes from his dungaree shirt pocket, and lit one.

"Help yourself."

"How you like being a fire team leader?" Thorton said.

"Not bad at all, Gunny." Giff strained a little. "I been one before. They didn't get no cherry. It's only a temporary condition," he said "I'll get the rank back in a month."

"A month might be too late," Thorton warned. "In a month you might be dead." He paused, studying his cigarette with distaste. "But I suppose it could always be arranged to have corporals' chevrons put on your marker."

Giff looked at his hands, at the wall, down at the floor, then he grinned up at Thorton cockily. "Ain't you heard? Heroes don't die. Heroes just live on forever, and gradually fade away." He waved his arm out slowly.

234

"What heroes?" Thorton dropped his cigarette on the floor and squashed it out with his toe. "I don't see any heroes or a hero. I see a man who helped fuck up my platoon and get three buddies on Company Punishment. You striking for president of national fuck-your-buddy week?"

"Funny," Giff said, "accordin' to what you told them two idiots from PIO I'm quite a guy. Did you know I donated half my re-enlistment bonus to the Yamanaka Orphanage?"

Thorton did not answer.

"I wouldn't take it so personal," Giff went on. "After all, you didn't lose anything, did you?"

Thorton grinned. "Nope; I didn't lose anything. In fact, I gained. Believe that or not. Where'd you go?"

"Over the weekend?" Giff questioned. "Fujioka."

"That was smart."

"I thought it was."

"You know something?" Thorton said levelly. "If I was to go over the hill I'd hit out for some small town where they weren't any MP's around. That way I wouldn't get caught."

"That's the difference between me and you, Gunny," Giff grinned. "I'd rather take my chances in a town where they's law."

"Real gutty, ain't you?" Thorton grinned back, his mustache dipping upward. "For a corporal with a Silver Star who just shipped over you don't show me much."

"I ain't in show business."

Thorton, sitting on the next commode staring at the wall, did not seem to have a rejoinder to that one, and Giff congratulated himself.

"Anyway," he said, "it's all over with now. Done. Hell, I'll be a sar'nt in couple months."

"You collect your fifty bucks from Dallas?" Thorton ask the wall.

"Hunh?" Giff grunted. "Oh that; yeah, as a matter of fact I did." Now how the hell did Thorton know about that? he wondered suspiciously.

"How is that one-legged stuff? Pretty good?"

Giff looked at him sharply, glad there was no one else in here now. "Yeah; sure," he said with slow heat. "Not bad atall."

"I wouldn't know," Thorton said to the wall. "I ain't never been too interested in cripples."

"It was the best I ever had," Giff said.

235

"You ought to know," Thorton said. "I imagine along with everything else you've been a real lover in your day."

"They usta call me the snatcherini kid. Since when you so interested in my love life?"

"Interested!" Thorton curled his mustache deftly. "I ain't interested in anyone's love life. Just curious about why people go for cripples. Maybe I'm missing something." Suddenly he made a horrendous face. "Jesus Christ!" he bawled. "What crawled out of you and died?"

"It's that cheap slop chute beer." Giff furrowed his brow.

Thorton got up and walked down to the other end of the head, stopped and leaned against the wall. "Well, you better take advantage of it while you can," he said flatly, turned on his heel and walked out, leaving Giff wondering whether he meant the beer, Popcorn, or what? Did Thorton know something he was keeping quiet about?

Finished he stood up, the inveterate irritability moving back in on him heavily, like booms of artillery, and the bowel movement had not helped. He was still full of shit.

Had he only been in Japan six weeks? Forty-two days? It seemed like six years. Here, in the barracks, it seemed as if it would never end, never stop. Nowhere to go, nothing to do. With Popcorn he could forget some of it for a while. Then it was right back clawing at his chest like a huge predatory cat. At least in Korea after the cease fire there had been the occasional line crosser to take a shot at.

He walked on out of the head and into the squadbay where the platoon existed in a listless quick-tempered stagnation. And no liberty tonight, he reminded himself. No liberty till tomorrow night. Yet he could always borrow Poke's TL's and . . . No! He could wait one night, couldn't he?

Glumly, looking at the water cascade off the eaves of the barracks onto the cinder ash, hearing the time-lapsing sound of shoes being shined, rifles being cleaned, locker doors being banged shut amid soft sibilant harsh talk, he walked up to his bunk by the space heater where Cinamo Dallas, his squad leader, was showing some pictures to Poke and Stack.

"Hey Giff," Dallas called out. "Come on an' take a look at these pictures," he grinned. "They's some I got in Ko-rea."

"Oh go fuck a duck!" Giff said angrily.

236

"And the feathers flew," Stack said poetically.

"With all that squawking goin' on!" Poke guffawed.

Giff flipped his foot locker top open savagely, amid the chortles and whoops of the men who had nothing else to do; and turned to on shining his shoes as the barrack walls closed in on him.

13.

Captain Emil Kizer, while Bohane was desecrating ducks, killed the haranguing party and thrust of the staff over what to do now that the monsoon had quelled the field schedule, and locked himself in his office.

A ponderous, bulletheaded Prussian hulk, he pulled his fifth of anisette out of the top drawer of his desk, set it in front of him, untouched, leaned back in his swivel chair and sat looking out the window at his company's barracks, brooding.

It all followed an old pattern, he thought, watching the blurred lights of the barracks where occasionally a distorted figure moved across the windows. Everything repeated itself eventually. When the peacetime training schedule went berserk no one knew what to do. And the truth was, there was really nothing to do at all—no constructive routine.

What he had done (the only thing left to do) was give each of the staff platoon sergeant's time. Then, it was up to them to keep the men pacified.

Peacetime and pacification, he thought wryly, reaching for his bottle of anisette. He uncorked it, took a long licorice-thick drink and set it back on the desk in front of him.

A huddled figure moved soddenly across the cinder ash mustering area outside.

But he had known it was coming, all right. The handwriting was on the wall. Only yesterday, when Corporal (now temporarily busted, he amended) Bohane had told him explosively that he was *"bored,"* had he known for sure it was about to break. The boredom was the thing no one could combat, Kizer mused, the anisette coating his stomach, relaxing him. It wasn't just Bohane either; it was all of them, himself included.

But he would have to keep himself intact, not giving himself away, play the bluff, pretend not to be bored, act happy.

Sure, they all might call him crazy and—and, he thought a little affectionately, "The Kizer"—yet it did not affect him. Being crazy or being called crazy did not upset him at all.

Actually, it was his only defense.

If he could say, or express exactly, what it was that was wrong, he would be either relieved of his command or court-martialed—or both—for dereliction of duty and defamation of service.

After almost thirty years' service that was an extremely unpleasant thought. He took another drink of the anisette, rolling it on his tongue.

Yet what he would like to do—love to initiate—would be to stand right out there on that damn miserably wet mustering area and tell them, his company: "Men, no one hates this peacetime horseshit more than me. At least the way it's being run.

"You know and I know that training in the field does not compensate for combat. It never will.

"Peacetime must be equally as stimulating as combat if there are to be satisfactory results . . ." Here he would pause, for effect naturally so as not to lose the bluff. "You have to all be in a position where you don't give a shit whether you live or die. Then, and only then, will any rifle company be sharp enough to defeat any enemy. With God willing," he would have to add if there were any of the indoctrinated officers around like Lt. Van Prick—Van Preter, that is!

That was what he would have liked to do, would have given a great deal to do. But he wouldn't. Or couldn't.

Possibly, he didn't have the guts.

Savoring the anisette with the gleaming idea of calling a muster and telling his troops just that, Emil Kizer muddled it over with relish. It was a fine idea. But . . . he couldn't do it.

He had seen it tried though!

Remember? Remember Chesty Puller? Of course you remember, he told himself. How could you forget? Chesty had tried that very same thing, had the right idea, but Chesty did not become Commandant. He wasn't enough of a politician, a kowtower to the civilian puppeteers; so they jumped someone else in over him. Passed him over because he told the truth.

But at least he told the truth.

You haven't the guts, he accused himself.

The sparse office, quiet under the din of rain, seemed to emanate with repugnance. The coffee had turned cold, the floor was dirty, the desk was littered. Carefully, he reached for the anisette again, his swivel chair squeaking, warning. To hell with it.

The order of the day had changed noticeably, he mulled, for officers— Keep your mouths shut. Express nothing but what is watered down and told you to express.

When he had first become an officer (when was it? sometime in the thirties?) they had not had those silly indoctrination courses. Now it was different. All the ROTC lieutenants, unbaptized, came in with the tacit agreement of the closed-mouth policy: seen and heard but not related. Hear no evil, see no evil, speak no evil of the great White Father in Washington or what all of it stood for—evil, of course, being any abuse of the Corps, verbal or physical.

A sort of conspiracy was the way he thought of it.

A police state within a police state.

Or perhaps it was because he had been an enlisted man before. That wasn't it either. Chesty Puller had been an enlisted man, too. And Lew Diamond!

Old Lew, Kizer reminisced, the goateed rumpot. Dead now; died the death of boredom. But at least he was dead. He had served his time and died. And it wasn't important how he died. They hadn't got him.

Funny, he could just barely remember old Lew. There were few things he could remember any more, to the detail.

Edging away from that horrifying thought he had another drink.

From the other side of the locked door there came the sporadic bursts of typewriters and the cursing that accompanied mistakes.

But he could not arise, as it were, and deliver a message of truth without of course giving up his own position, relinquishing it for the nut ward or a court-martial.

239

So, the only thing he could do, and had done, was act a trifle nuts: Gung Ho nuts! That way, it was overlooked. No marine had ever been court-martialed for being over-enthusiastic about the Crotch.

Sluggishly, he looked at his bottle of anisette, then back out the window at his barracks, where his troops were doing God knows what. *His* troops. Men of various ages, none as old as himself, doing what? The same as he?

It was weird almost, he thought, placing himself in the same category as the ruck. Here he was, more than three generations away from most of them. Though to himself he didn't think so at all.

Was he a contemporary? Or had he passed that? Had he repudiated that chance when he continued to play his bluff so long that it was no more a bluff? The prickly re-appearance of the knowledge of his own failing memory moved up on his back, reinforced.

The office groaned quietly, rain hammering on the roof, torrents of wind dropping around the barracks like pecker-tracked sheets.

It wasn't an act any more, he decided finally, honestly. It had ceased being an act when he first discovered he could no longer express himself, was incapable of expres-sion—or had he always been that way? Had he been im-paled by the Officer's Saber too? Had they thrown so much shit at him that some of it stuck?

Look down the barrel of the rifle of your life, he ordered himself, and what do you see at the other end? Oblivion, came the answer. You, who have fooled yourself all along and not fooled them, can see nothing ahead—nothing but the bleakness of the uncleaned carbon-coated barrel.

Or could he? Was there something there to be seen: a glimmer of thin, slim-chanced way out?

Yes, there was, if . . . there was a war, which he was certain there would be—Korea was too late; he'd had his chance there and fluffed it: why? Because he hadn't seen it then like he could now, so crystal clear—the war would have to come fast. There wouldn't be another chance.

Time was against him. Time had been against him in Korea, but he'd failed to notice it. Or perhaps luck had slipped in somewhere. But now was the time! One more war was all; they wouldn't keep him around for another one. They would (speak of it in hushed tones) retire him.

Schemingly, thinking about the coming war, Kizer knew

240

definitely what he would do. The answer lay before him at the end of the gleaming black, dull-gray barrel. It was simple: he would get killed.

Think they could retire him! Muster *him* out to some shacky cottage to rot! No, sir! The sons of bitches would never do that. He'd outwit them in the end!

And maybe by doing that he could rescind the act and finally, at the long end of the barrel, express himself. He would outwit them at last, and leave them to sing their damn foolish songs about him.

Smiling to himself at that last thought, he drank a toast of anisette to it, with the rain rolling heavily down the window, obscuring the view of his barracks.

14.

The monsoon did not break for two weeks. Howling winds brought the rain swooping down from the brilly Fossa Magna Range, pummeling across South Camp, beating on the shanty bars of Fujioka. Typhoon warnings were up and all liberty was canceled. There was the tacit understanding in the barracks—silent, unspoken, but always present—that if the rain did not cease there would be an explosion of men, showering heated fragments right through the walls. Men moved bullishly through the barracks with tight-lipped belligerence. If anyone laughed, or even chuckled, he was looked upon with disdain. Even though the laugh was always acidly bitter and the misguided humor directed at the laughter.

Horrible Hog Company, as well as the other companies in the battalion, did not fall out for rifle and personal inspection in the morning. Platoon sergeants ambled into their platoon squadbays and held perfunctory rifle inspections under the dim low-ceilinged lights. In their frame of mind the weapons were always dirty, and the men unshaven and boots and boondockers unshined. And soon even the troops began to believe it. They would look at their boondockers so glassy clear they could count their wrinkles and mutter savagely that some heathen bastard had put sand in their shoe polish. The rifles, which were sparkling now, not having been fired or exposed to weather, suddenly had dust and grime all over them and carbon caked in the barrels.

Naturally, there was still the slop chute. It kept its regular hours and did a land-office business. Troops with money waited around the barracks all day watching the gray wet sky turn black smothering into night, then desperately threw on their raincoats and plowed to the slop chute, looking for all the world like Nazi Storm Troopers, where they would sit soaked in the beery air and down unbelievable amounts of beer, with Indochina *the* topic of heated controversy.

This had its drawbacks too. With no liberty there were no women and the beer simply augmented those sharp clear memories of women lying on *tatamis*. Three men in the battalion were court-martialed for going over the hill. Deserting their duty as it was called, because it turned out that these three men were on a typhoon warning team and if a typhoon had come up, who would be around to secure all the movable objects?

Privates Poke Turner and Guppy Talagua were two of the men court-martialed. They each drew thirty days hard labor at the Middle Camp Brig following a swift informal dungaree-clad summary court-martial. The third man, a private from Whoring Weapons Company, received forty-five days' restriction. He did not have the record of the two brig rats from Hog Company.

It was rumored, although no one knew if it was true, that Poke Turner had said: *"Give me liberty or give me death!"* at this court-martial. The leanings were for the plausibility of it because everyone knew Poke had been drunk when he was court-martialed. Guppy Talagua, on the other hand, who was also drunk, remained silent.

To the men of Hog Company, excluding Giff Bohane, Cinamo Dallas and Stack Renshaw who were openly recognized as loyal friends to the two archcriminals, it was a minor incident, merely a dry spot in eternal wetness. The three sympathizers of their comrades' distress quickly held a drunken wake after the court-martial and then they too forgot about it.

Other men knew better than to make paddy runs while the camp was on restriction. They would send word out to Fujioka for a special girl to come in on a movie pass. The bunkers around the supply sheds of the various companies suddenly disclosed the imprints of bodies and huge toe marks deep in the wet ground. This too became boring after a while, too slippery, so the men just waited.

Lectures were given on all conceivable subjects. Lt. Van Preter of Horrible Hog Company, the first platoon leader and one of the ten youngest men in the company, gave a lecture on the Uniform Code of Military Justice—or the Uniform Code of Miscarried Justice, as it was called by the troops. They sat on their locker boxes in the dreary squadbay listening to Van Prick extol its merits. So they listened and waited. There was just simply not anything else to do.

Rumors ran amuck in the barracks. And once a private from the machine-gun platoon of Hog Company, who was powerfully drunk, came charging through the barracks announcing in a vociferous voice that the Korean War had started again!

Immediately the men responded to the call to arms, jumped from their bunks and were half packed ready to go; wisecracks and sly digs ricocheted in the dimly lit squadbays under the torrent of rain. When the falsehood was discovered the men moved with narrowed eyes back to bed. The private from machine guns suffered a broken arm, apparently, it was reported, from a fall in the shower.

A buck sergeant from Weapons Company was found one morning passed out on the parade field. If the parade field had not been volcanic ash, the slop chute philosophers agreed, he would probably have drowned. As it was he only died of pneumonia and everybody went to his funeral because it gave them something to do.

So they waited in miserable stony silence.

The typhoon never did come and the bets that were placed on it were happily collected by winners although they scratched their heads wonderingly because they had no place to spend it. Except the slop chute. No one was ever really sober in the two weeks and no one was envied who was.

Payday stakes gambling prevailed in the barracks and men lost heavily, gambling with reckless abandon until they had their next six paydays owed out.

243

Finally, the consensus of the Regimental Staff was that something desperate would have to be done to fight the monsoon's tolling effect on the men. But the officers, from the Regimental CO, whose name was Colonel Calvin Klepteris, on down to the last junior college-lieutenant like Van Preter, had their liberty and could go out. They did not come to any decision. They could only shake their heads wearily when explaining their problems to the higher-class girls in Gotemba: there just wasn't anything to be done, God made the weather, the Devil sent the typhoon, and they were forced to hand out court-martials—and insist that the various chaplains pray harder for the rain to stop.

If there was one exception in this, it was Hog Company's commanding officer, Captain Emil Kizer. He was seen hunched over his desk in the company office, his cropped bullet head glistening under a dangling light, plodding over his collection of war maps. He never went on liberty, not once. Ham Haley, though, the company Executive Officer, let it be known that one of the Japanese maids in the BOQ was found in the Kizer's room one morning.

Eventually, however, the monsoon blew itself out on the twenty-eighth of September and the plans for an Ark were put away. With a belated and totally ignored training schedule two weeks behind.

The sky cleared just as swiftly as it started. The men had gone to bed drunk on Sunday night and woke Monday morning to a dazzling blue sky and bright sunlight with a misty clean smell in the air. Mount Fuji had a fresh cone of snow and the clean warm weather was met with great whoops and cheers as the troops began figuring out their liberty expenses once again.

Still, they did not get liberty.

There was, at first, the contagious furor of a break in the weather that stimulated and excited their senses while at the same time depressing them. As the first sun in over three weeks was kissing the wet roofs of the barracks, a deep despondency descended.

Special orders signed by Colonel Klepteris at Regiment (made out by a never-seen faceless unknown breed of men) volleyed through the rifle companies in the battalion. Field training would be stepped up—and hardened because the men had become rusty during the monsoon. In special memorandums, Colonel Klepteris went on to say that the Marine Corps was always combat ready, prided itself on

244

that, and in this year it was patently obvious that they would see combat.

The troops of Horrible Hog Company walking briskly back from a breakfast of shit on the shingle stopped at the bulletin board outside the company office and read the appalling news. Most of them had *not* gone over the hill during the monsoon (though they had all had women brought in: if you couldn't lead the horse to water you could lead the water to the horse, was the way they thought of it) but had waited for liberty. When they discovered that they were going to the field, to spend a non-liberty week in the field, an embryonic mutiny arose. Deftly smashed by the rope-swinging law of intimidation.

Grumbling, kicking uselessly, shaking their heads, they staggered crestfallen into their barracks and prepared to go to the field: all of them bitterly disappointed and touchy as pregnant bitch wolves. Especially Pfc Gifford Cael Bohane, who had lost his lean and hungry look and now appeared absolutely underfed.

"Two fuckin' weeks!" he railed bitterly at his squad leader Cinamo Dallas as they cinched up each other's pack straps in the clangor of the squadbay. "Two fucking weeks I've waited for liberty; and now this!" Giff felt it was just too much. He had though, he thought foxily, been satisfied by a rather skinny Jo-san whom Half-Slick Willy had brought aboard camp for him on a movie pass. Cherry-san, her name was, he remembered; and she had been a wild, give-it-to-me kind of dolly whom he was more than interested in—but there was still Popcorn and after all he was loyal. But not to have any goddam liberty! "For two mother-fuckin' weeks!" he fumed.

"You always got this weekend," Dallas grunted, cinching up the strap. "You got liberty this weekend. What the hell you do with this pack, for Chrissakes?"

"Hell with this weekend!" Giff yelled, flashing his eyes nervously around the squadbay at the men struggling into their antiquated harnesses holding up packs loaded down with sleeping bags, ponchos and shelter halves. "I want liberty now, by God. Tonight!"

"Who don't? Look at Stack. He just come off EPD and he don't get liberty. It hadn't been for you an' me, he wouldn't even had any beer while he was on it."

"We're generous," Giff said, quieted down somewhat. Standing there while Dallas worked on his pack, Giff knew it wasn't the liberty really. Not at all. It was the bare cold naked realization staring him in the face that perhaps they would be here longer than he anticipated.

Perhaps there wouldn't be any war for a long time. Jeesus Kee-rist! So he would just sit here in the ass hole of the world while it rained all the goddam time and rifle inspections and lectures and combat films. Balls! He felt himself trembling a little with frustration and anger. If they didn't go soon he was afraid he would never have the chance to refute what they had given him.

Well, he thought miserably, maybe the field would change some of that.

Dallas popped him on the helmet. "You're loaded for bear, killer."

Giff turned around and began cinching up Dallas' straps wondering what the goddam quarter Cherokee was so happy about. Apparently the two weeks without liberty had not affected him. Well, he had always known Dallas was half goofy.

"Fall out! Fall out!" Koko Hobbs' voice ran authoritatively over the din of scuffling in the squadbay. Handsome, jaws twitching, immaculate in his military creased dungarees, he moved from bunk to bunk prodding the men on. "Let's get this circus hitched up. The company's already outside. Why does *this* platoon always have to be the last?"

"Bohane!" Koko hollered.

"What!" Giff jerked Dallas' pack strap, bending the tall man's back.

"Your fire team all ready?" Koko stopped in front of the two.

"Been ready for a month," Giff said.

"Yes goddamit, I know," Koko said. "Where's Ramirez?"

"Poncho?" Giff said, tugging and cinching. "I don't know. He ain't in my fire team, for shit's sake."

"He is now; as of this morning," Koko said, moving his handsome face under his helmet around the squadbay. "I said fall out!" he barked. "You men deef?"

Grumbling, the troops began falling out, shuffling down the narrow aisle to the double doors in front of the barracks, their weapons and web gear clattering wildly.

"How come I get four men?" Giff asked. "Ain't no other TO fire teams in the p'toon?"

"Thorton wanted it that way," Koko explained with a grin. "He says you're a good leader so you get four men."

Giff released Dallas' pack and picked up his rifle. "Okay, I got four men. That means Dallas has an extra man in his squad."

"More mouths to feed," Dallas said wryly.

"So that leaves you with Renshaw, Gorsuch, and Ramirez," Koko said. "Quite a fire team, I'd say."

"Best one in the company," Giff boasted with a tight grin, lips taut over his teeth.

"Okay," Koko said shortly. "Get out there in formation. You're late."

Giff and Dallas walked slowly behind Koko Hobbs, the last men to leave the barracks, and a heavy stillness pervaded the room. Giff had never liked empty barracks; deserted barracks. A cold wind blew up and touched him deeply.

Outside, they sauntered over to their platoon already formed under the morning's bright sunlight that they had not seen for so long now. It was like being awakened with a bright flashlight in their eyes.

T/Sgt Hugh Thorton looked at them in disgust as they fell in. "There's a pair to draw to," he said to no one in particular.

Giff moved on back to his fire team lugging the sixty pounds of gear and fell in beside Renshaw.

"You get the word, Poncho?" Giff looked past Stack at his BARman. "You're in my fire team, you know."

"I got it," Poncho Ramirez said, shifting the weight of his unwieldly BAR. He was a big-bellied Mexican from El Paso, Texas, with a round solid face and perennial good humor, who was always carrying some man from the company back from Fujioka who was too drunk to walk. Poncho, although his bloated belly contained astronomical amounts of beer, never did get drunk. He had never been anything but a BARman either.

"Hell, fire team leader," Stack Renshaw teased. "We going out and play marine today?"

"Yeah," Flin Gorsuch, a private, the last man in the fire team, said. "We're gonna go bang bang."

"Knock off the bullshit in ranks," Thorton commanded.

Tight-lipped, Giff stood at attention as the Kizer strode out to receive his report from Gunny Leroy Finch, whose legs looked a little wobbly like a three-day-old calf's.

So here we go again, Giff thought glumly. Out to charge those tanks with fixed bayonets! A while before, he had felt that maybe going to the field would alleviate some of the tension in him. Now, the black listless fury moved and grew and the thought of spending the week in the field left him heated and raw.

They moved out in a column of twos, Kizer stepping off the pace at 180 steps per minute with full field gear. Like a long green and camouflaged snake moving up the road past the tank park to the rear gate, the men five paces apart ("So one grenade won't get you all!") passing a smug-faced sentry in his little protective booth.

Behind the rear gate a gentle sloping hill rose upward for a quarter of a mile before it leveled off to become a flat rolling plain, green and weedy from the rains; off in the distance on the road to Middle Camp was the small pine forest, a clump of tall green spires growing in formation like a company on line for a general's inspection.

Marching on the soft muddy road, still slushy from the rain with the midmorning sun arousing alcohol sweat from their bodies, putting one foot in front of the other in endless repetition, they trudged up the long sloping hill. A silence fell over the column as they climbed with only the steady swish of full canteens on their hips, the sloppy slap of boondockers in mud, and the sweaty grunts of toil as a chaperon.

When the tail end of the company (which was the second rifle platoon) crested the hill, stragglers hurrying to catch up, talk broke out all along the line. There was the bitching mixed with curious observations of the field that they had not seen for so long and the incredible clearness of Mount Fuji etched against the sky like a geological bastard.

As the second platoon rejoined the company on the level roll of the road, Cinamo Dallas broke out with Horrible Hog Company's unchallenged ditty, never sung for the Inspector General, but always perpetually within the confines of the troops as much a part of them as packs and rifles, a lone quivering ballad expressed in the quarter Cherokee's rococo, plaintive sorrowing, belligerent voice:

> *"My right guide's a satchel ass bastard,*
> *My squad leader drinks all my gin,*
> *My second lieutenant's a fairy,*
> *What a hell of an outfit I'm in."*

And from the head of the column someone in the first

rifle platoon broke into the Hank Snow favorite when Dallas had finished, a liveliness in the air with all the company joining in, their voices deafening in the chippering morning:

"*Doggie and Marine were on the line,*
Doggie said; Marine! you're doin' fine!
But I'm movin' on, I'll soon be gone,
They's a shootin' too fast for my little ol' ass
And I'm movin' on . . ."

Followed by a hoary repeat, voices dropping in a raucous, gravelly boom:

"*Luke the Gook comin' down the pass,*
Playin' the Burp Gun Boogie on that doggie's ass,
He's movin' on, he'll soon be gone,
They's a shootin' too fast for his little ol' ass,
And he's Pusan bound . . ."

Falling off on the last note, giving way to the stutter of falling feet and the sudden ashamed snickers of the troops as they recognized their own kind in their untrained voices.

The field, like an old friend, gripped its fingers around them tightly. And too, like an old friend, no one knew quite how to react to it.

They bivouacked on the other side of the pine forest on a ridge ten miles from South Camp. Shelter halves were put together for two-men tents and water runoff ditches dug around them, each platoon encamped in straight lines overlooking the pine forest.

Giff was shacking with Stack Renshaw, the rifleman in his fire team, Poncho Ramirez with Flin Gorsuch, his assistant Barman. Dallas, as was his right according to platoon protocol, was shacking with Jesus Queecho the right guide, the little Guamanian who was Giff's predecessor until he got his corporal's rating back.

They ran platoon problems all afternoon: skirmishes, echelons, V's, working their way under imaginary fire to an imaginary enemy, and all of them knowing they would never use any of it in combat actually, wondering what Pentagon genius had thought it up, because in combat they all knew there was nothing but improvisation.

T/Sgt Hugh Thorton, it was obvious, did not give two hoots in hell for any of it and administered his wrath by having the second platoon repeat each drill ten times, which was not only disconcerting to the men but also to Thorton; only none of the men knew this.

"Sufficient unto the day is the training thereof," he told them.

C-rations for dinner: spaghetti, meat and noddles, beans and meat, beans and franks—and beans; with the complimentary packages of cigarettes old enough to carry the V for Victory sign and a suspicious *"I shall return"* ad gimmick; topped off with the small packets of toilet paper gratefully appreciated because the weeds produced an irritable rash.

That first day there had been no firing, no blank rounds that someone somewhere had decided long ago would helpfully simulate combat condition. If the men had known who that someone was they would gleefully have strung him up by his family jewels because the blanks only succeeded in gumming up the bores of the weapons, urging the rust on, and it was no closer to combat conditions than the kid game of Jacks.

Consequently there were no "brass bandits." Brass bandits was a name some obscure rear rank private had thought up for the withered stoop-backed Japanee people, old and young, who dutifully clamored on the heels of the marines, scooping up the expended cartridges as fast as they were fired. And they never missed one. Brass bandits were as keen-nosed as blue-ribbon pointers. Ferreting out the glinting brass was their subsistence; they could get 2 cents a pound for them in Numazu selling them to the Communists. A weird new occupation brought over from the West to open the slanted eyes of the East to progress and civilization. And if there were any occupational hazards, they did not mind. Once, up at the live firing range in North Camp, a marine had picked one off at close to five hundred yards, catching the brass bandit just off center from the center of his chest. The brass bandit died immediately. The marine was arrested immediately by the Japanee police. He explained that it had just been too tempting a shot not to take, just to see if he could do it. There was no mention of the marine after that.

Although the troops hated the blank cartridges with indignant outrage they were nevertheless pleased when the brass bandits came around. The brass bandits always had

Tory's Whiskey or Ginko Gin tucked neatly in the bands and the more enterprising men of the saved their brass and traded with them. The slow men either had to save portions of their C-ration and coffee and goodies were excellent bartering it trade them or buy outright. Sometimes too if they were very hard up and had been in the field a good while and grown bored with waking up in the middle of the night to help a wet dream along, they would convince the brass bandits, the females of course, that they loved them, then quietly disappear over the side of a hill, one hand around the baggy-assed drawers of the woman, the other clutching an envelope of instant coffee.

This enterprise was short lived when a Pfc Brown, a tall thin sallow-faced Texan from the third platoon, contracted what Dallas called *psoriasis of the lizard*. Brown, placed on restriction for two weeks (the natural VD restriction time, although the doctors in sick bay did not know what it was but since it was a malady of the loins it was stamped with approval: VD), was seen sitting on his bunk in the barracks bitterly soaking his dingledangle in a beer can which contained a beautiful purple liquid. Eventually, Brown's dingledangle recuperated and he made a bull snorting raid down Bamboo Alley only to return four days later with a bonafide dose of bullheaded clap.

No one went blind from the Tory's Whiskey or Ginko Gin as the chaplains and corpsmen said they would, so they continued trading, buying and finagling the booze. Everyone knew where the brass was going of course, but no one cared. A sort of professional reciprocity. There wasn't much difference between their giving it to the brass bandits and the brass bandits passing it along to the Communists, than there was between the businessmen who ran the United Nations selling it outright. Some of the older breed, who had served with the Seventh Marines in China in '47 and had helped train MaoTsetung's army so they could fight them later in Korea, merely shrugged their shoulders at this professional hazard. It was all in the performance of their duties, they said wryly.

But there were no brass bandits that day. So there was no White Lightning. And everyone went dry to bed, disappointedly sober to their tents at sunset.

There were the usual half-assed sentry posts and the

251

ght moved in quickly with the silent suddenness of snapping a light on and off, leaving the troops in a quiet retrospection of their lives.

In the morning it started all over again with one modification: they had blanks! And too, naturally, with the joy came the pall; they had to sit through a lecture on Company Tactics and Efficiency in Combat by Lt. Van Preter.

Giff sat on his pack, dangling his helmet between his legs, along with the rest of the company on a sloping knoll that served as a classroom, listening without hearing Van Prick's Yale-cultured voice as it droned on. Of course, Van Prick always tossed in some of his pat Yale jokes, fraternity classics at which Giff snuffled automatically with the other men simply because it was the thing to do.

Van Prick was in the furious midst of "the company on line at night!" when Giff, in final rebellion, clamped his ears shut on it all, and masked his face perfectly with that strained I-am-here-to-learn-sir intent phiz, simultaneously aware of the other men not listening either. None of them were listening, none at all. Hugh Thorton had gone back to South Camp with the water jeep right after morning muster as he wont to do whenever anything bugged him, leaving the company in the hands of Gunny Leroy Finch, who had also bugged out—probably to the crapper for a tiptoe drink.

The only staff that Giff could see was sticking it out was Jack Koko Hobbs, standing off in the background, jaws twitching in his handsome face, smoking coolly and deceptively.

It was this more than anything, the thinking of the company and the platoon and its vagaries, sitting there scholarly listening without hearing, that gave Giff the idea for the *game*. A mental visual entertainment far superior to a combat lecture of dead words that evoked no emotion given by a man who blanched at the clack of a rifle bolt going home.

Staring intently at Van Prick, Giff's mind caught up with the rapport of the game, roving dispassionately over every man in the company, examining each one in actual combat.

Since it was *his* game and he was omniscient in it, it was his sacred choice of where they would go, how they would react and what would happen to each individual man.

252

Now Van Prick there, to start with, would not even last one day, one morning.

For clarity's sake he would make it an amphibious assault on, say . . . Indochina; after close observation, he decided, Van Prick would be one of the first ones to get it. He would do something inane like standing up on the beach and hollering for "more C-rations—Yale rah rah rah!" and catch a sewing-machine stitch of machine-gun fire right across his chest diagonally, in and out like a dog pissing on snow.

Giff crawled up to him silently happily cradling his rifle in his arms as Van Prick erupted in a loud choking spasm, convulsed and died.

That took care of Van Prick! Officers first as was the custom and tradition. Second Lieutenant Fischer, a post-graduate of Stanford who was majoring in Majors, a ferret-headed, sleepy-eyed slightly buck-toothed young man, platoon leader of Rocket & Mortars, would naturally be the next to go. Lessee, now how . . .

A mortar!

Lt. Fischer, Giff calculated, would be checking his maps and co-ordinates for TARABLES (target areas) while his men would already be in position dropping the fat shells down the smooth bore. Fischer, in a typical thumbs-in-suspender-straps-pose, would gaze sternly out at enemy land lacking only a corncob pipe and major-domo carrying a pair of dry boots and quite naturally would not hear the mortars coming in, picking him up and tossing him heavily to the ground. Fischer bounced like a beer can off Half-Slick Willy's nose, dead and bisected.

Giff moved over the blackened macerated corpse of Lt. Fischer, looking more ferret-headed and sleepy-eyed than before.

Two Gold Star Mothers in five minutes! Not bad. Now, the Kizer; well, the Kizer. Yes, the Kizer. Humn, the Kizer.

And then Leroy Finch, of course! Giff thought happily, Gunnery Sergeant Leroy Finch.

Realistically, Finch would be kneeling far up the beach and, having completely forgotten his role as company gunnery sergeant, would be digging a hole furiously to hide his bottle. Carefully Finch would want to dig the hole deep enough so no artillery round would scathe it.

But a raggedy Chinee guerrilla, higher than Dallas' girl Kayo-san on *sake*, now trotted up to the gaunt T/Sgt, jabbed a bayonet, one of those triangle pronged jobs, right through Finch's throat, making a sound like a toilet being flushed.

Giff fired from the hip hitting the Chinee in the mouth; the Chinee fell crazily on Finch. Then crawling up carefully he picked up the bottle, stuck it in his belt and moved on.

Then there was Thorton. Ahhhh yes, the mustachioed sonfabitch. He would be doing his job to his best ability, Giff thought, moving in where Finch had fallen. But they had moved farther in and by this time, with the beach secured, moved quietly and cautious through the thick jungle and *he* was on Thorton's flank.

"Hey, Gunny," Giff called out, raising his rifle as the dark handlebar mustache hove into view under the camouflaged helmet. Then the face was no longer recognizable. Giff crawled forward and inspected his marksmanship accurately. Hell, no one could miss at that range.

And so Hugh Thorton had curled his mustache for the last time.

That left the platoon without a platoon leader so quite naturally Koko Hobbs would take over as they moved inexorably inland under heavy fire. And that was when he ran into Cinamo Dallas who was point for the platoon. Alas, poor Cinamo, I knew him well. Dallas, while ignoring personal safety with utter disregard for personal life (which he had never thought was sacred anyway and was a stolid atheist in the foxhole and out), had a neat clean black hole in his forehead. That goonie was quite a shot!

Giff brought what was left of his squad up to the point to cop Dallas' personal gear and C-rations, but the chaplain had beat him. The chaplain was pasting a gold star in his little black book and mumbling something about three more souls to save and my book will be full and I can send in a quarter with it and get a passport to heaven from the Pope, by God! So Giff flipped a ten-yen piece with Poke and Stack to see who would take care of this heathen who had defiled their buddy and grinning happily, Giff won.

Breaking out in a slight sweat as the day's sun gathered force, Giff studied Van Prick. Laughing automatically at jokes he did not hear, nodding solemnly at planned precautions that no one would ever take, he went right on down the line slaughtering Horrible Hog Company on the beaches of Indochina until finally, he was the only one left.

254

Hog Company had been butchered, quartered, dressed out, and hung in the smokehouse: a fine side of pork.

And then there was one!

Giff stood over the fallen company, rifle in hand, helmet pushed back exposing his thick black hair, a glint in his black-fringed blue eyes, smoking a cigarette in leisure. . . .

And when the shooting was done, Giff's call was a gun,
He had fleeced the saps on the brine;
But the Goonies on the ridge had Seven Lady Lou's,
And a bullet shattered his spine. . . .

And then there were none? . . .

Hell no! Got to change that. Didn't even see those goddam goonies on that ridge. It wasn't fair; unconstitutional —where was the Bill of Rights?

In a sort of sweaty ecstasy, listening to the somnambulant Van Prick, Giff looked, in his mind, at himself lying face down. He turned himself around to various positions, making it more dramatic. But he could not get his body to rise and move around again. And he did not like this feeling of being alive looking at himself and the company all dead.

"Ohhh, what a mean way to go," he mumbled indignantly.

"You have a question, Bohane?" Van Preter interrupted.

"Uh, yes sir"—Giff came out of it—"why do—the—uh communications help the company more at night?"

"I'm glad you asked that," Lt. Van Preter said, and moved into a heavy treatise on communications, and Giff felt sheepish under the baleful glances of the men around him.

The lecture broke up at noon and the men walked to their tents for a dinner of C-rations and Tory's Whiskey that they'd bartered for that morning when the first brass bandits appeared.

Giff sat, legs crossed, with his fire team in the searing noonday sun that was unusually hot for late September, wolfing his meat and beans.

"Beans are the best," Flin Gorsuch assured them in the voice of a food connoisseur. He was a hard-faced blond man from Tennessee with deliberately slow movements that refuted a catlike quickness with his fists. "Lima beans,

255

big and green," he grinned, nibbling on one bean delicately.

"They grow those in Ohio?" Poncho Ramirez asked in his thick Mexican voice, scooping up meat and noddles. "That why they call them Limas?"

Giff set his can down. "Nah; they grow 'em in Peru."

"Bullshit," Stack said. "That's one a them eastern Fancy Dan colleges like Van Prick went to."

"Goddam, Stack," Gorsuch said in wonder. "Where ya'll been all your life? That's Perlew; a college. Ain't Peru. Peru's a country in Pan America."

"Where the hell you learn so much?" Stack said.

"I read a lot. I'm a scholar."

Giff laughed and finished off his meat and beans. "Hey, did that mustachioed sonofabitch Thorton come back yet?"

"Nope, and he won't," Gorsuch said. "Hobbs says he's goin' to stay back to barracks the rest the week. That ol' boy leads a golden life."

"How the hell's that motherfucker rate?" Giff demanded. "He ain't no better than the rest of us."

Gorsuch drew imaginary chevrons on his naked sleeve. "Rank has its privileges. Anyway, Thorton does. He don't ever come out the field much."

"I think I'll get sick," Poncho said, "and go back with the water jeep tonight. This field killing me." He shook his round sweating head wearily.

"That's a pussy good idea!" Stack said. "You better get sick fast or I'll move in and take over, Poncho. Get sick myself."

"It's only good for one man," Giff said, lighting his after-dinner cigarette. "Any more'n that and they'd get suspicious."

"It was just a thought," Stack yielded. "Just a fucking idea. Guess I'll spend the rest of my life in the field."

"Count your blessings, boys," Gorsuch said. "For tomorrow we die."

"You die," Poncho said. "But leave me your beer ration card."

"I'll leave it to my old bitch of a mother," Gorsuch said piously. "So she can weep over her itty-bitty baby."

"Yeah," Giff said. "Wouldn't leave it to mine though, she'd drink it all up."

"Your mother wears combat boots," Stack grinned.

"Which reminds me," Giff said. "I seen your mother in

256

Seoul one weekend. She's takin' in washing for the Army."

Poncho Ramirez crossed himself with his mess fork.

"Both them old ladies," Gorsuch said, "are bad lays. I know; they don't charge nothing."

"I hear your mother made Mastrubation Sergeant," Giff said to him. "Gonna take Top Condrum's place."

"Naw," Gorsuch shook his head. "She got aced out by Mrs. Renshaw."

"Mrs. Renshaw," Giff said, "drives tanks."

"How is Mrs. Bohane?" Stack asked. "She still got spring in her ass—or still winter?"

They drifted into the dirty dozens with a sort of concealed bitter humor directed at the field, smugly hidden by unrepressed emotions because they had never been trained, not any of them, Giff thought playing right along, to repress any emotions. Until of course they enlisted and were taught: *This is my rifle, this is my gun, one is for war, the other for fun.*

Yet even with the gleeful imprecations there was still the field. And at one o'clock they were back at it again. And this time it proved to be almost unbearable for Giff.

This thing of field training for a field marine was inconceivable to Giff Bohane, especially since the field training of a field marine was basically composed and developed from the kid game of "guns." It was such an extravagant waste of energy. Here they were, he thought, grown men running through problems with blank cartridges until they were expended, then going "bang-bang" as was the order from Van Prick who was convinced that it stimulated combat conditions.

During the first hour of the afternoon Van Prick was in charge, more or less on orders from the Kizer, who believed in giving his junior officers a chance to run a company. The first hour of training was directed at "how to keep your command from withdrawing" under any circumstances but mostly in combat. The way to keep the company from withdrawing, Van Prick explained in his theory, was to keep them moving ahead. Not altogether an original idea. The way to do this, Van Prick explained, was to keep the leaders behind the company and always in contact with one another. This would probably have turned out all right but there were no Prick Six Radios and much of the terrain prohibited sending arm-and-hand signals.

They, the company, started out about a half-mile from

257

the pine forest and their bivouac. Giff's platoon was to be the point of a company V flanked by the first and third platoons in the rear. Giff's squad, or rather Dallas' squad, was the point of the platoon. The company was spread out across the line for about seven hundred yards when they started on Van Prick's signal. They had gone forward about two hundred yards when the second platoon disappeared and lost contact with the rest of the company. Up ahead in the pine forest were the aggressors, the enemy, the machine-gun and mortar platoons, whom they were to try to defeat.

When Giff descended the slope with his platoon, losing sight of the rest of the company, his first thought was one of just sitting down, taking a smoke, and saying to hell with it. Sweating, bitter, he kept right on moving with the rest of the squad and platoon under Koko Hobbs who expressed no comment at all, still heading for the pine forest but moving a little faster now. Some laughed and hollered, "Hey, Sar'nt Hobbs! Hadn't we oughta wait for Van Prick!" But Koko was not buying. He pointed to the pine forest and they kept going.

The scheme behind all this, Giff knew, was that they were to be opened up on by simulated fire from the enemy in the pine forest and they were just now within good killing range, no cover no concealment, and from the pines any one of the men in there had a great field of fire. Koko Hobbs did not issue any other orders. He did not say get down, hide or anything. He just pointed to the pine forest. Then finally he gave the signal for double time and they took off on a hard run, Giff cursing.

They got all the way up to the pine forest, up to the long shadows of the trees, none of them firing or going "bang-bang," then were swallowed up in its green thickness. That was when Koko stopped them.

"Crap out for a while and take a smoke," he said. "The company won't be up here for quite some time."

The troops plopped down on their packs and lit up, none of them registering surprise, just boredom.

Koko, Giff watched, leaned up against a tree, lit a cigarette and stood looking out from where they had come across the gullies and dips and flats, impervious to any semblance of a training problem. Giff wondered where the enemy was.

They were all about finished with their smoke when

S/Sgt D'Agastino, the platoon sergeant of machine guns, came stomping through the brush of the forest up to Koko.

"What the hell you doing in here?" he asked.

"Fighting," Koko said.

"Yeah? Who you s'posed to be fighting?"

"You."

"Oh; well, my platoon ain't finished lunch yet," D'Agastino said.

"I didn't figure they had," Koko said. "But don't worry about that. We won't withdraw. We're waiting for the company."

"What we gonna do this aft'noon?"

"The same thing we do every afternoon," Koko said.

Ten minutes later the company hove into view just outside the pine forest and Koko ordered all smokes out, off your asses on your feet, spread out in a skirmishers' left, and wait. Jesus, Giff thought, Jesus Christ.

When Van Prick arrived, Koko met him at the edge of the forest, informed him that this side of the forest had been secured and the enemy had been routed; and, sir, not once was there a danger of withdrawal.

Van Prick held a happy critique right there in the forest, congratulating the company on its obedience, took a proud thanks from the Kizer, who had not seen any of it but was sure his junior officers were capable of handling any situation. Gunny Leroy Finch, who had walked up with the Kizer, stood looking at Mount Fuji.

The second hour of the afternoon was reserved for camouflage, personal and in groups, and the Kizer informed the company that the man who was best camouflaged of all and who could not be seen would get a special liberty weekend. Giff Bohane was the first one to get caught. The man who received the liberty weekend was a corporal from Mortars and with proud tears in his eyes he thanked the Kizer in gratitude.

Then they split up into platoon problems and platoon tactics, which involved nothing more than a lot of running. Koko Hobbs would pick out a target, a knoll or something, tell the men how he wanted it taken, then send them after it, running. After they had taken it he would walk up to the target. It was an endless cycle.

Running, throwing one heavy foot in front of the other, sweat burning down into his eyes, Giff silently savagely cursed all of it, everything: the field for being so stinking

259

hot, Van Prick for being such an ass hole, Thorton for being back at the barracks, himself for being there in the first place!—and Cinamo Dallas who had scorned rank and authority when he'd first met him on the ship out of Korea but who now held the position of leadership over him: a motherfucking squad leader, *his* squad leader, who would probably become the goddam commandant!

And thinking of all that, the field which he could take no more of but which was not the prime reason for his hatred, hating himself, while he sweated his lean ass off running through the field he suddenly decided to go back: to Fujioka: by himself: that night.

And so the plan formulated itself in his mind. It would be simple. He would go straight across country, not taking the road, and thereby knock off about two miles, spend a few hours in town and come back. He figured two hours, maybe three for the round trip, and he'd be back in the morning for muster.

And all the rest of them could take the field and shove it.

15.

Throughout the afternoon the thought goaded him, like a sore tooth that was enjoyable to gnash down on.

At eight o'clock that night under a downpour of full moonlight, Giff crawled gingerly out of his small tent, leaving a snoring Stack Renshaw huddled in his sleeping bag, and stood up breathing the crisp night air greedily.

Encompassing the bivouac area was a tense silence while pregnant emotion seemed to rise from the immaculate rows of small tents, reaching out and touching him, awakening a red tracer-bullets-in-the-snow dream behind his eyes. For a moment, one split second, he debated over taking his rifle and bayonet. But he wouldn't need it. No enemy out there.

Cautiously, he shouldered into his field jacket, flipped the collar up, took a quick glance around him to see if the sentries were in their proper places. They were, he grinned; not a soul in sight, all of them asleep in their tents. A good raiding party could come slipping down here and annihilate the whole shooting match, he thought professionally.

There was a brushy finger leading off from the bivouac that he followed down to the shadowy shelter of the pine forest, and he moved quickly silently, not looking back. Light-footed, he scurried past the tall star-reaching pines to the gravelly dirt road.

In the safety of the small ditch off the side of the road he lit a cigarette. The road would be easier to follow, but it was longer and there might be some surprise traffic on it. He would save at least an hour moving cross-country.

Determined, he crossed the road, cupping his cigarette in the palm of his hand, and stepped out quickly, moving sure-footed through the weeds in a faint breeze weaving.

He thanked nature for the full moon. In a way it was almost like a cloudy day. All bushes, rocks, ravine, ridges and fingers stood out blackly in sharp detail. It was the full moonlight that always played tricks on your senses, he remembered, made you see things that didn't exist: a rock that suddenly looked like a dead man, a bush embraced by the wind like a kneeling man holding a burp gun, and myriad figures that crawled along the ground, feet cushioned by sneakers. Sometimes the figures never moved, and you would strain your eyes in the darkness wanting furiously to send a burst of fire smashing into a bobbing shadow because you swore it was a man, an alien man, the enemy, a man like yourself—hear the bullets whack against flesh and the surprised shriek of a man hit, congratulating yourself because you were right after all.

Yet in the morning, when the horizon was touched with the first strained gray of dawn, you would look out with dismay at the bushes and rock that were only, as a part of you knew, bushes and rocks.

At night like this in Korea, sometimes they did move he remembered, and came in their choppy Carolina Cakewalk and you were certain and fired at them. But never till you were sure and when *they* moved you *knew* it wasn't rocks or bushes, he remembered with a weird unearthly melancholy, for when they moved like that they were people. Three people, three little North Koreans . . .

. . . Leaning on the sandbagged parapet of the listening post, Giff watched them come chugging up out of the rice paddy, humped over under a Korean full moon, walking quickly, not knowing they were going anywhere other than south.

He eased his BAR up on the parapet, his face chilled by a cold dry wind shooting down from the north with the unbearable cold that starts in the bone marrow and works its way out numbing everything; watching them come up the shallow rise of the hill moving quickly as the bushes and weeds undulated, the three quilted-uniformed creatures who even in the dark were recognizable, coming right on toward the listening post.

Bringing the BAR to his shoulder, barrel aiming, feeling his head go light under his cold helmet and a touch of moisture entering his hands as he followed them with the awkward front sight of the barrel, coming closer in jerky short steps, as closely bunched together as they were, Giff knew it would only take two long bursts, three at the most.

Under the full moon he saw that their hands were empty, weaponless, unarmed, and it made him uneasy; perhaps they were carrying booby traps like they used to do dressed like women with enough TNT to knock out a bunker with a sleeping squad in it. Feeling a flooding of power surge wildly over him as they drew closer, silently praying they would not step off into a mine field, or attract fire from on down the line and no one from the Outpost behind him would try to contact him through Sound Power, and maybe these three were a decoy for a Chinee raid? While they drew closer in the eerie light he could see their faces, almost discernible over the barrel of his BAR, a cautious apprehension in their slanted eyes. And waited. Let them get closer, let them get close enough so he could see their faces when they fell, one chance in a million like this; never this close without being fired at before. Catch that last human expression—squint carefully, fast bursts, all twenty rounds.

Three series of fist-slamming jolts pummeled his shoulder, the BAR kicking up and out. The first gook's hands leaped instinctively to his throat as the burst caught him, and he spun crazily and fell rolling. The second toppled backward as if he had been football blocked, lit on his rump sitting there momentarily, then fell backward all the way supine. The third man dropped quick to his knees, leaning forward slightly as if he were praying, head bowed, arms hanging at his sides.

Firing broke out on down the MLR, red tracers in hiccuping bursts ricocheting in crazy, straight and looped patterns, a drunk man's view of the neon signs on Tokyo's Ginza. The firing stopped like electricity gone off all over the world and voices broke out in the night.

When the BAR that had been bucking his shoulder finally stopped, Giff was aware of the code word crackling through the Sound Power.

He waited a few minutes while the talk abated along the line carried in haunting echoes: a mortar flare burst high up in false daylight, and he peered intently, wondering at the kneeling gook who did not fall, whose limited breath was fogging in the light, and he saw the steam rising from the other two where they were hit—and, fascinated, studied the one gook who refused to fall.

The Sound Power broke behind him again: *"Marilyn Monroe One; this is Marilyn Monroe Two."* The code word smacked the cold air, then Outpost came through with their own personal code: *"Foreskin, Foreskin; this is Peter. How's the loose skin?"*

Forcibly, Giff tore himself away from the praying gook, picked up the Sound Power phone—it was cold on his already cold ear under his helmet—and flicked on the butterfly switch. "Skin her back and milk it down—Out," he acknowledged, then set it back in its sheath and crawled over the parapet on the frozen ground. The flare died and he waited a moment adjusting his eyes, then crawled carefully forward to the kowtowing gook.

Carrying only his K-Bar trench knife, he moved stealthily forward till he was close enough to reach out and touch him, thinking it was a foolish thing to do, crawling out like this, but could not help himself, and looked up into the gook's face that was now settling fast like a quick-drying cement job, settling faultlessly with the first quick gasps before the death rattle. Then the gook made a sound like a baby blowing spit and toppled forward on his head, silently.

With reckless abandon Giff edged up closer to the man, wondering why they hadn't been carrying weapons. Almost fearing to touch them because they could be booby trapped. Without further thought, he rolled the man over and tore furiously through his pockets.

Under the quilted coat he found a neatly folded paper, pulled it out, and in the moonlight stared in wonder at it. Then he went through the other two gooks the same way, pulling the same papers out of their pockets. All identically the same: one side written in American, one side in Korean and Chinee. Surrender pamphlets.

He let them drop to the ground, dirt-stained and smudged, smelling of kimchee and old rice as a wind blew them off into the sparse brush, and surveyed his work professionally. It had been a clean job, except for the one who didn't die right off, but they'd all been hit with the first three bursts.

Still feeling the heavy deadly weight of his K-Bar knife in his hand, he moved over each one, and in three deft strokes cut their balls off neatly. Grinning happily, he tucked the three pairs in his belt, jammed the knife back into his boot sheath and walked stealthily back to the listening post. It would be a fine joke, in the morning, to toss them in front of his squad while they were eating breakfast . . .

. . . It was strange, he thought walking under the Japanee full moon as the weeds brushed against his leggins, that he should remember that now; remember it with that old divorced feeling of security that warmed its way over him. A security that was not really security at all to him. A hazardous elbow-bending knees-raised-high-in-free-flight security.

And maybe those three gooks that he'd cut down had that same security too? he questioned, moving swiftly across the rolling plain, coming up to the last rise, starting to sweat a little under his field jacket. Maybe those three had it too, but were in danger of losing it. Maybe that was why they had tried such a foolish thing as coming through enemy positions so brazenly. Probably they did. They probably had the same feeling he carried with him, had always carried, but only recently was beginning to understand.

It was the feeling he woke to every morning at reveille, raised on an elbow and looking around the squadbay at the men in white skivvies emerging from a fit-tossed sleep, in all the squadbays in all the camps everywhere, the same; façades broken down, the wild thoughts that the sleep brought down flashing in their faces for just one brief instant.

In places unexplained, unmentioned, never shown on geography maps in school classrooms, where no brush flourished on naked brown hilltops, all life shot and blown away, buildings and shops and streets reduced to rubble,

264

and they, these silently determined resolute men, had all unknowingly turned their backs on the people and flocks who had eschewed them, had moved on clutching their weapons tightly, the thoughts of protecting virtues and possessions lost like the intestines of a man gut-shot. Until there was only a single edifying unwavering belief in each of their naked souls, because after so long being repressed, denounced, humiliated, they could walk narrow-eyed, jaws set with weapons firing, untouchables, artists.

Breathing hard, he topped the rise and stood looking down at the camp and the town below him. The camp and the town, he thought, two partners immersed in intercourse with neither of them ever experiencing an orgasm.

He started down the hill through the weeds to the tired winking lights of Fujioka. He remembered a rice paddy running up to the Blue Moon from behind with well-fortified dykes. That would give him cover and concealment. He didn't want to run into any MP's.

Trees swayed in a small breeze on the north side of the camp outside the fence. Music from the bars awoke a hidden compassion in his eyes as he looked down the road past the Condor Club where the Negroes hung out. Not many people in town tonight. Not many people at all. That was good.

Feeling buoyantly free he half ran across the paddy dyke, coming out on a brushless knoll behind the Wagon Wheel Bar, cut behind it, moved through the powdery hanging night and came out behind the Blue Moon.

He paused for a moment attuning his senses for the night. Laughter, small and girlish, floated out from the bar. There were no heavy treads of MP's boots along Bamboo Alley. Then he moved around the side and rapped on the back door, standing in the shadows. Through the dirty windowpanes he watched Mama-san Yoshido shuffle across the foyer and unlatch the door.

"Hello, Mama-san"—he eased his dungaree cap back on his head—"how's business?"

"Whatsa matta you, *dio?*" Mama-san Yoshido gaped. "You in field, *ne?*"

"I was," Giff admitted. "Got tired of it." He bent down and untied his leggins and worked the string loose in his boondockers.

"MP come catchee you, you go Monkey House," Mama-san warned.

"No MP comin' here, Mama-san. They do, you just tell 'em to get to hell out. How about getting someone to take Popcorn's place at the bar?"

"Ah so," Mama-san grinned, her brassy teeth shining. "You like Popcorn *toxon* much, *ne?*"

Holding his boondockers and leggins, Giff stepped in. "I'll be in her room. Tell her to come on back and bring a bottle of gin. Oh yeah." He turned back. "I'll pay you extra for being so kind."

Mama-san waved it off. "You good boy-san," she said. "Mama-san no huck up good customer."

"Okay," Giff laughed. "I'll buy you a pie at the PX." He walked quietly, hugging the wall down the corridor to the first room behind the beaded curtain, slid the door open and walked in with a quick glance through the beads. There were only two marines in the bar. Probably both Tankers, he thought.

The room was bathed in moonlight and he did not bother to snap the light on. He walked over to the *tatami* and sat down with a contented sigh and leaned against the wall. Then he heard the rubber-tipped single crutch bounce along the corridor mingling with the pat of a good foot. A deep belly-tightening decisiveness stirred in him, and dark black lights glinted in his eyes.

The door slid open and he saw her etched against the outside light, the crutch under her left arm, her mouth pouting sensuously, the pony tail swinging with each breathing movement of her head.

"Why you come down?" she said softly, and slid the door closed behind her.

"Don't turn the light on," he said.

Popcorn hobbled over to him, set the crutch against the wall and sat down beside him. "You are over the hill, *ne?*"

"Just for a short time." Giff grinned in the moonlight streaming through the window. "Just for a while."

"Popcorn no want you go Monkey House. You all time huck up in trouble."

"Why didn't you bring the gin with you?"

"Me forget. Go catchee right now."

When she left the room Giff lay back with his hands hooked behind his head. It was really odd how it had all started to become clear, as if he had looked ahead of himself, the answers laid out before him like an open-faced hand of solitaire.

266

Popcorn came hobbling back with the bottle of gin, the room still hushed in the moonlit darkness, handed him the bottle, and began undressing.

Giff watched her thoughtfully without taking a drink, then began undressing himself, slowly and deliberately. Naked, still leaning against the wall, he watched her ease down on the *tatami,* then moved over to her.

It was, as he knelt down to her, like a dark force, a black angelic premonition swimming in front of his eyes as he touched the soft pliant skin. The crack of rifle fire echoed hotly behind him and bullets bit their way into his flesh tearing him apart, and blood flowed richly as he descended, sinking in, while it seemed as if it had all occurred so many thousands of lives before, and he knew definitely, just then, at that instant of touch, that this entire life had been chosen long ago, because he now moved weaponless in no man's land.

Afterwards, he stood up and looked down at her, his breath coming in choppy gusts, and leaned against the wall as Popcorn, unflinching, lay looking up at him silently.

They stayed that way for perhaps five minutes, he standing over her looking down, she lying there looking up, staring into each other's eyes in the pale darkness. That pouting mouth and the hair combed back in a pony tail, with the large red paps high and dark against the creamy smooth skin, all of it a sea of soft flesh and curving lines; and he, lean and hungry-looking, with an angular chipped face and a tumid hot distention that was like a weighted brain where no thought existed.

Gradually, as if she understood it all without his having spoken a word, she got up and dressed. Then hobbled out of the room leaving him leaning naked against the wall.

He remained indecisive in the wan moonwash of the little room for a breath-gathering time. Then he sat back down on the *tatami* easefully, smacked the bottom of the bottle with the heel of his hand, uncapped it, and began drinking.

The gin was hair-oilish slick on his tongue and he lit a cigarette to offset it, taking it straight with each drag on his smoke, all the while looking out the window up at the sky and its sparkling illumination.

By the time he'd finished the quart of gin the last worn record had spun its last cycle on the single-shot phonograph out in the bar, dying out in one long fiddling guitar wail reincarnating into silence.

267

His body drunk but his head amazingly clear, he stood up and slid the door open. Through the beaded curtains the bar creaked dark and empty, dejected. Footsteps slapped on Bamboo Alley outside, coming in muffled through the thin walls. All the footsteps were going to the Arizona Restaurant. Everybody went there to eat after the bars closed. If they didn't have the money or the mood for an all-night shack-job they went out to eat when the bars closed and the drinking was done. There weren't many places to go after the bars closed, he thought. Except places they'd already been.

The moonlight streamed through the frosted windows of the bar casting up high lights of tables chairs bottles and bar. It was almost as if he could see life images in the walls: laughter and happiness and fatigue and futility and puzzlement. Bars always did that to him. Not bars especially, but honky-tonks, juke joints; he suddenly felt that all the times he, and all of them from Hog Company, had been in there their thoughts were ingrained in the wood and glass and bottles and now echoed alive to him. Before, when they'd all been in there, there was the atmosphere of recklessness and beery talk and spontaneous emotion. Now, dark except for the moonlight, there was something lurking there he did not want to see. Something that had he asked himself in front of a crowd he would have vigorously denied.

He brushed through the beaded curtain, walked over to the bar and picked up two bottles of gin, then retreated back to the room. Popcorn was not there and his cigarette was still smoldering in the ashtray.

Unconcerned, he began working his way through the two bottles. Once he heard laughter from the back of the bar in one of the small rooms. No one came trodding down the corridor. No one came into his room and bothered him.

Time seemed neither to move forward nor backward in the room. He sat under the moonlight all night, drinking, and finally passed out.

When he woke Tuesday morning, the bright September sunlight was piercing his eyes. He turned his head away from it, smiled contentedly and lay there dozing. It must be about nine o'clock.

Nine o'clock!

He was over the hill!

Scrambling to his feet, eyes wide open now, he stood silently frenzied on the *tatami*. The company was in the field. He was here. Too late to get back to the company. Shit!

Nervously he lit a cigarette and looked around the room. There was still half a bottle of gin left on the floor beside him. He picked it up and took a drink, and sat back down. Uneasily, all the futility began to work itself out.

The best thing to do was take it step by step, look at it objectively, he told himself. He was over the hill, that was fact 1; it was too late to get back to the company, that was fact 2; even if he got back he would still get run up for being over the hill, that was fact 3; the only thing to do was stay over the hill till the company got back, that was fact 4; might's well get drunk again, that was fact 5.

Wouldn't that frost their balls, he thought, when he didn't show up till they got back? The rest of them could sweat it out in the field, he wasn't going to.

The idiots!

And Dallas! That rank-happy bastard could ass-kiss all he wanted to; could even make Sergeant—so what?

He pulled himself around, still naked, and finished off what was left in the third bottle of gin. Then he got up and walked out of the room and into the morning emptiness of the bar, picked up two bottles from under the counter and walked back to the room.

On the floor beside the *tatami* was a heaping bowl of steaming fried rice, an American spoon jammed in the center of it. He paused, looking at it, suddenly hungry and thinking Popcorn must have heard him get up, brought it in, and left again, not wanting to disturb him. That was the way it should be, by God! If he didn't want to be disturbed she wouldn't disturb him.

Still, it would cost him extra on his bar tab. But he had dough, enough to buy and sell the whole lot of Fujioka—even a goddam bowl of fried rice. He ate it voraciously, washing it down with little nips of his gin, set the bowl aside and started drinking in all seriousness.

He sat drinking in the sunlight all that morning; vaguely numbed, divorced, insensate and still no one came into the room (though he was never sure of this because at times he thought Popcorn stuck her head in or said something to him but when he looked around she was gone).

Sometime in the afternoon—he knew it was afternoon because there was no sunlight left in the room—the bottles empty, he staggered out into the bar unabashedly naked to get refueled. Peanuts and Nancy, whom Poke had shacked with, were splashing water on the floor cleaning it and they grinned at him oddly. He grinned oddly back, picked up his bottles and returned to his room.

That night he ate again, only this time he was partially sober having drunk himself into that state, and Popcorn brought in a plate of ham and eggs from the Arizona Restaurant. He ate hungrily and talked with her as best he could. After he ate he started drinking again, and the gin moved back over him in drowning waves. He thought he had tried to make Popcorn or something like that, but he wasn't at all sure. It seemed as if he'd slept with her, could remember it, but couldn't either. It was almost like a wet dream except he was sure he had . . . he was pretty sure . . .

All of Thursday, or what he figured was Thursday, he didn't even leave the room. Popcorn brought him food from time to time which he ate sometimes and sometimes let grow cold, but he continued drinking, getting blindly and unhumanly drunk and passing out.

That night, Thursday night, it started raining and the moon was no longer full. Water gurgled past the open window of the room, splashing loudly on the ground outside and pelting furiously on the tin roof. With the darkened wet sky black as reblued gun metal blanketing soddenly around him, he began to come out of it, a little shaky.

Wearily, with the ponderous weight of a storm heavy on his back, unmoving, a full bottle of gin and a cold bowl of noodles by his side. A filmy gown of washed night seemed to pull up over him like a robe and he could hear his own breathing very loud, but he could not feel his chest expand or sink.

From out front came the jabbering inconsistency of two customers, sounding like they were bickering for a hock job for all night. The jibberish ceased, footsteps stalked out indignantly and music replaced them.

They must not of had any money, Giff thought, and nothing of value to hock. Well, that was how they fell. No money no mocko. No wrist watch no havo piece of ass. He wondered how much money he had left?

The rain increased, spattering outside, and he thought of the company out in the field under it. If it kept up they'd come back in the morning instead of the afternoon like was on the training schedule. In the morning, he decided, he would go back. He wanted to beat the company and be in the barracks waiting for them. He thought it would be a fine joke.

He reached for the bottle again, warding the morning off, and started drinking.

That night, his last, he remembered that Popcorn did come in and sleep with him and he remembered also that he had to pay her first that time, 1500 yen, and wondered over how she had suddenly become a bona fide business woman. It was not as especially enjoyable as the first few times, he thought reflectively, but a lot of that was due to the gin he'd consumed, and the sudden inbred fear of retaliation from military law when he got back; and had nothing at all to do with Popcorn because she was merely doing her job, wasn't she? Doing her enlistment the same as he was and he wouldn't have done his work without pay either. But through the fogginess of the gin he felt that something had gone wrong somewhere, something was amiss.

Friday morning, about eight o'clock, he sufficiently roused himself, almost sober, and dressed to go back. The rain was still hammering furiously outside in wind-driven waves. Dressed in the old field dungarees, he left the room to find Popcorn and tell her he was going back.

"I figure the rain brought the company in," he said testily, standing in the foyer. Popcorn was leaning against the wall for support instead of using her crutch. "They'll probably be in the barracks already, so I better get on my horse."

"You catchee *toxon* trouble." Popcorn shook her head seriously.

"No, nothing'll happen to me," he said in a quavering voice. His hands were shaking slightly too, he noticed. Shouldn't have drunk all that gin. He wasn't very pretty either with his three-day beard and red-rimmed eyes, but he'd have time to clean up before the company got back. "I'll be out to see you this weekend. It's our liberty weekend."

She watched him while he put on his boondockers and leggins, squared away his dungaree cap and buttoned up his field jacket. The rain waterfalled off the eaves, making a squishy din outside.

"I'll be seein' you then," he said and lit a cigarette.

"This weekend," she affirmed.

He patted her pleasantly on her firm butt, slid the door

open and stepped out. "I'll get those panties for you, too," he said through the rain.

"Dai jobie." Popcorn smiled with a curious distant look in her eyes.

Giff nodded, slid the door shut, rounded the bar and walked up Bamboo Alley bulling his head against the slant downpour. The best way to work it, he decided, was to go right up to the guard shack, tell the OD and let him handle it. If he went through the fence it would only add to the other of being over the hill. It wasn't much of a tossup.

Swaggering cockily, he came out of Bamboo Alley shouldering the monsoon and walked up the deserted road between the fence and the town to the main gate.

The sentry at the main gate, a Pfc, huddling against the little portable heater dropped his mouth and gaped as Giff trudged up to him, unshaven, thoroughly soaked, looking like he'd just come off three months on line.

"Well," he said to the sentry hunching his neck against the rain, "what're you lookin' at, banjo eyes?"

"You over the hill?" the sentry said foolishly, too startled to notice the insult.

"I ain't lopin' my mule," Giff grinned.

The Pfc, a chalky-faced young man whom Giff did not know, checked his post orders carefully.

"I don't think I can let you in." The sentry shook his head. "There ain't nothin' in my orders covers that."

"Jesus Christ!" Giff grumbled and stepped into the booth with him out of the rain. "What're you gonna do? Leave me out in the rain?"

The sentry studied the little metal corporal chevrons on Giff's cap. "I guess I have to let you in," he said. "You outrank me."

Giff, who still thought with the mind of a temporarily busted man, grinned genuinely. "Yeah; I can order you to let me in. Hell, I live here!"

"I guess so," the sentry laughed. "Man, I don't give a shit. But I think I'm supposed to report you to the OD."

"I'll save you the trouble," Giff said. "I'll go over myself."

"He's in the guard shack," the sentry explained. "He asks you, tell him I sent you over. By the way," he said sardonically, "he's a prick; best thing to do would be to con him."

272

Giff laughed. "Con him? Buddy, he takes one look at me I couldn't con his granny."

"You do look pretty rough," the sentry grinned, with the humor of a man who enjoys being secure while watching another man in trouble. "Careful or they'll lock you up."

"Be good," Giff said, and walked over to the guard shack.

Inside, the Officer of the Day, Lieutenant Clyde from Gruesome George Company, stood talking with the Sergeant of the Guard and did not know any more what to do than the sentry at the main gate. He looked authoritatively at Giff who was grinning at the Sergeant of the Guard, a friend of his from Charley Tanks whom he'd drunk beer with at the slop chute, slapped his hand on his pistol holster a few times, shook his head stolidly, looked at Giff's noncommittal sergeant friend, and at last washed his hands of the whole matter by assigning a supernumerary to escort Giff back to the barracks while he, as the Officer of the Day, rode off in his jeep to check posts.

"I'm sorry you got to walk in the rain," Giff told the supernumerary, a private with a hash mark, as they left the guard shack. Up at the main gate Giff saw the sentry whom he'd talked to speaking unconvincingly to the OD, who was waving his arms in an I-don't-care-what-the-orders-are impotent rage.

"I don't mind," the career private said. "I didn't have nothing to do anyway, 'ceptin' play a little cahds maybe."

Giff nodded. "Did the battalion come in from the field yet?" he asked, trying to smoke a cigarette before the water fizzled it out.

"Hellyeah," the private drawled. "They come in yestiday aft'noon when it started raining."

"You mean last night?" Giff said.

"Thay's what I said," the private sniffed. "Yestiday aft'noon."

They walked the rest of the way in silence, past the slop chute and PX, the battalion office and down the road from the parade field to the mustering area of Horrible Hog Company.

"Okay," the private said. "You're headed for the barn. Good luck."

"See you," Giff said, walking around the end of the barracks to the side door. Damn! He wished the company hadn't got back. No telling what now. Damn!

All the platoon were sweatily involved in a field day. Bunks were jammed against lockers; the troops were on their hands and knees scrubbing the cement floor. No one looked up when he came in.

S/Sgt Jack Koko Hobbs was leaning against the wall just outside the second platoon squadbay watching the work, his jaws twitching.

"Just in time for going to work." Giff tried a joke, walking up beside him.

Koko turned his handsome face around slowly. "The AWOL Kid," he said. "The night rider of South Camp."

Giff rubbed his three-day beard, a little sheepish. "Who they got building the scaffold?"

"Already built," Koko grinned back. "Pappy Dreek's getting the rope tied now, all thirteen knots. They're going to run you up with the morning colors."

"That's nice." Giff looked around at the men working. "They look tired."

"They been in the field," Koko said. "They're field marines."

"Where's Dallas?"

"Over the PX gettin' some doughnuts," Koko said, "for when the platoon takes a break."

"Thorton ever go back to the field?" Giff asked casually.

Koko looked back down at the men making strident cries with their blocks of sandstone on the floor. "Nope; never did. He's a busy man though. He's got to keep the company going."

"I'll bet," Giff said. "He's got to keep Fujioka going, you mean."

"No, that's your job."

"Okay," Giff said, deflated. "When you want to take me up for Office Hours?"

"For what?" Koko said.

"For being over the hill," Giff said heatedly. "What else, goddamit?"

"Did you go over the hill?"

"Quit playin' games," Giff said. "You know damn well I did."

Koko shook his handsome head. "I'll say this, boy—"

"Don't call me *boy*," Giff snapped.

"I'll say this," Koko went on, unruffled. "You got some good friends in this platoon. Too bad you can't keep 'em."

"All right," Giff sighed. "Who reported me?"

274

"Dallas."

Giff was staring at the men on the floor and when Koko told him the name seemed to drift in and out with each sweaty movement of the sandstones. "Dallas?" he heard his voice say— *Dallas* put him on report? That wasn't like Dallas. Hell, Dallas was his . . . But look how he'd fucked up. He hadn't told anyone he was going, hadn't asked anyone to cover up for him. What else was there for Dallas to do? He belatedly realized that he had done no better to Dallas than that what-was-his-name in Korea so long ago who'd gone to sleep on Outpost and had died for it. A chill climbed up his back at the thought of what Dallas would have done to him if it had been in Korea. It was a sort of heated anger at Dallas for doing it and at the same time a grudging respect. "The motherfucker," he said.

"So you best get ready for office hours," Koko said. "Goddam but I'm getting awful tar'd of taking you up to see the Kizer."

"Maybe this'll be the last time. Maybe I'll join the march of dimes too."

Giff unbuttoned his wet field jacket and moved on into the squadbay, feeling the security of the barracks wrap itself around him. He spoke soberly to several men. Stack Renshaw goaded him cheerfully and Flin Gorsuch wanted to know why the hell he hadn't asked him to go too for Chrissakes? No one, it seemed, was disappointed to see him, if only because their curiosity needed fulfillment. They wanted to know how was the town? Any new girls?

Giff answered them cockily, stripped off his old field dungarees, shaved, showered and began dressing in a fresh set of winter greens. He wished Dallas was there. Maybe he'd get back from the PX before he went to office. He just wanted that goddam Cherokee to know he didn't give a shit if he put him on report or not. Simply wanted to let him know that it hadn't bothered him, the miserable motherfucking bastard.

Stack Renshaw ambled over and leaned on his swab looking at him.

"What'd you think you'll get, Giff?" he asked in his Hoosier twang.

Giff grinned at the bulbous nose and the blocky head. "Probably another medal." He winked. He tied his field scarf meticulously, adjusted his ribbons on his battle jacket, dusted off his dress shoes and he was ready.

Stack ran his swab around on the floor, making a mess. "I got your rifle in my locker," he said. "I brung it down with me from the field."

"I wondered what happened to it," Giff said. "I guess they got that one on me too. Desertin' my rifle."

"Get your ass to work," Koko said to Stack, moving down from his position of overseer. "I want this squadbay cleaned up before noon chow." He looked around the squadbay. "This fuckin' platoon is last at everything," he said wonderingly, "except for court-martials, slop chute and liberty. You ready, Bohane?"

"Let's go," Giff said, snapping a seagoing dip in his pisscutter.

The two walked up the barracks through the first platoon squadbay where they were met by a horde of wisecracks and catcalls, Giff grinning cockily at them, and stopping just outside on the flat dry porch hemmed in by the curtain of rain.

"Look," Koko said, "what you going to tell the Kizer?"

Giff lit a final cigarette, tossed his match at the falling rain and watched it snuff out. "Tell him the truth. That I went over the hill."

"I mean, *why* you went?" Koko said. "What you going to tell him your reason was?"

"Hell," Giff shrugged, "I just wanted to go to town. Got tired of the field. That's all she wrote."

"Dear John," Koko snuffled. "Okay, it's your ass. You do what you want. I wouldn't interfere."

Giff flipped his cigarette out into the rain, where it turned ugly and gray. Then he turned back to Koko. The suave S/Sgt ran his tongue over his lips—taller than Giff, handsome, unreadable, foxy, slim but compactly built, that face that Giff guessed attracted women like a fight attracts cowards.

Koko hitched up his dungaree trousers with a dispassionate gesture and turned his head back to Giff with an undecipherable grin on his mouth. He reached into his tight front trouser pocket and pulled out a stubby hand-carved idol, handing it to Giff with *savoir-faire*. "You better rub HoTi's belly for luck, kid."

Startled, not aware that he had ever been without HoTi, he slapped his hand against his pocket, then stood there grinning sheepishly. "What'd you do? Go through my locker?"

276

"You lost it on the way in from the field the night you left," Koko said. "Just outside your tent."

Giff reached out slowly and took the god, rubbed his belly once for luck and slipped it into his pocket. "The best friend I got," he said.

"You ain't telling me anything," Koko said. "If I was you I'd be a little more careful about my charms. A man's lucky if he's got one; one he can count on. It don't do any good to shit on it."

"Thanks for the advice," Giff said, looking at Koko thoughtfully, wondering if that handsome bastard had in some cunning way watched him leave the field that night? But he couldn't have done that; he'd have stopped you, wouldn't he?

"You want a blindfold before you face the firing squad?" Koko said, nodding toward the company office. "If you don't, let's get it over with. I got more important things to do than play patty-cake with Top Condrum."

Giff nodded and they stepped off through the rain toward the company office, where naked lights burned drearily behind fogged windows. They walked up the steps to the window-door, slid it open and climbed down inside.

Top Landrum sat at his desk laboring slowly and painfully over charge sheets, his feathery eyebrows concealing the dead eyes, and the large red-veined nose seemed to twitch unwelcomingly as they entered. King Solomon as usual was filing through his filing cabinet while Quiller Carpenter brooded over his morning's tenth cup of coffee.

"Welcome back," Top Landrum snarled. "Ready to go to jail?"

Giff stared back at him, his face unbetrayingly blank.

"I got the charge sheets made up," Landrum said balefully. "Recommended him for a Special Court," he said to Koko.

"Who recommended him?" Koko asked.

"I did," Top Landrum said, rising from his desk.

Quiller Carpenter looked up from his coffee and grinned at Giff. "How they hangin', stud?"

"Empty," Giff grinned back, keeping his eyes on Koko and Top Landrum.

"Now I ain't tellin' you your job, Top," Koko said, "but you got no right to recommend Bohane for anything."

"Then don't tell me my job," Top Landrum said in his flat voice. "As first sarjint I can recommend anything I want."

277

He bobbed his head over at Giff. "I'm here to he'p him, Hobbs, you know that."

"Everybody wants to he'p everybody," Koko said.

Top Landrum ignored Koko. "It'll only take five minutes to send you to jail," he said to Giff.

"This kid ain't going to jail, Top," Giff said audaciously. "Now or any other time." He could feel the old hackles of resistance at being shuffled like a deck of cards.

Top Landrum's nose flared hotly as a rainy silence permeated the office. "Don't get wise with me, boy."

Giff snatched off his pisscutter and tucked it neatly under his battle jacket. "Don't ever call me *boy,* Top," he said icily. "Don't ever call me *boy* again."

"All right," Koko slipped in deftly. "I got a fucking platoon to run. Let's get in there and get it over with."

Top Landrum's impotent fury seemed to abate and Giff remembered what Poke Turner had said about his having the syphilis. How he had to go to sick bay every week for a shot, a gnarled spasmodic old man of thirty-eight.

"I'll get you in jail yet, Bohane," Top Landrum said, "I'll get you in jail." He turned around and rapped on the Kizer's door.

"Come in!" Emil Kizer's voice roared.

Top Landrum went in, Giff following and Koko bringing up the rear. Giff stopped in front of Kizer's desk, snapping his heels together.

"This man has been over the hill for four days, sir," Landrum said, laying the charge sheets on his desk. "I've checked his record book and recommended him for a Special Court-Martial."

"Over the hill for four days!" Kizer leaned forward on his desk, his massive hands folded together. "Yes, of course. The young man who deserted from the field." His eyes fell on Giff's Silver Star.

"Obviously," he boomed, "you think that medal is some kind of privilege!"

"No, sir," Giff said.

"Don't interrupt me," Kizer growled. "Top Landrum, you may leave. Sarjint Hobbs, at ease."

Top Landrum walked jerkily out and shut the door quietly behind him.

"Now I'll tell you something, boy," Kizer said tightly, and Giff sensed Koko stiffening beside him, but in front of the

278

Kizer it was not so bad, he rationalized. "You might think it's a privilege but it sure as hell is not!"

"No, sir!" Giff said.

"Privileges are given to those who earn it," Kizer said furiously. "You haven't earned anything. From the day you came into *my* company I've had two courts-martial and nothing but trouble. And now, because we've started field training, which we sorely needed, you have to go over the hill," he fumed, his bullet head bristling red.

"Yes sir."

"Now just why," Kizer demanded, "did you have to go over the hill? Too rough for you? Somebody picking on you, boy?—Have a cup of coffee, Sarn't Hobbs— You don't feel you're being treated fair? Answer me!" Kizer smacked his swagger stick on his desk.

"No, sir," Giff said levelly, feeling for the first time in Kizer's office a strange unruffled calm. "I went over the hill because I wanted to, sir. I think the field is just plain horse-shit, sir."

Koko Hobbs dropped his coffee spoon.

"Horseshit?" Kizer furrowed his massive brow. He looked at Giff, then over at Hobbs. "Sarjint Hobbs! What about this? Have you talked with this man at all? Has he been giving you trouble in your platoon?"

Koko recovered his spoon. "No, sir. In fact, Corpril Bohane is the best NCO I've got. He's a leader, sir. The men look up to him."

"A leader!" Kizer said hotly. "Yes—I'd say a leader. A leader of rabble. A rabblerouser. A mutineer, by God!"

"No sir," Koko said, stirring his coffee. "If the Kizer—I mean Cap'n Kizer—would let me handle this I think I can work it out all right by myself."

"I don't think he can, sir," Giff said. "Ain't none of his fault what I do, sir." He stared over Kizer's head at the bare wall behind him.

"There. You see?" Kizer shrugged. "Open, flagrant insubordination. Bites the hand that feeds him."

Koko remained stirring his coffee. But Giff felt his murderous anger flowing out on him because he had stuck his neck out only to have it shot off.

"The last time you were in front of me," Kizer said, "I gave you a temporary bust. Obviously that wasn't strict enough. Consider that waived. I'm busting you all the way

279

this time; to private. And if you ever"—Kizer slapped the palm of his hand with his swagger stick in a sharp drummer's roll, his hard-bitten leathery cheeks flushing with combativeness—"if you ever come in front of me again I'll run you up with the morning's colors." He jabbed his swagger stick at Giff's ribbons. "Silver Star or not. No man, regardless of who he is, is going to pull shit like that in *my* company and get away with it."

"Yes, sir!" Giff said. "Thank you, sir."

"Get him outa here!" Kizer exploded. "Put him on boiler room duty; do anything you want, Sarjint Hobbs. If he fucks up again, if he so much as breathes wrong, I'll hold you and Sarjint Thorton personally responsible."

"Yes, sir," Koko said.

"This is still a marine rifle company," Kizer went on, his voice modulated sternly. "It has to be run as such. That's all."

Giff forced himself to break protocol and look down at the Kizer, seeing the red glimmer of pissed-offness in the scraped cheeks, and suddenly felt the guilt of having lost something more than the rank: a man he should have recognized as an equal. Any way he looked at it now, he was an outsider.

He did a sharp about face and walked through the door that Koko held open for him and stood waiting in the company office, his face impervious, flat, and uncontrollably exposed.

Top Landrum's eyes probed under his feathered brows. "You didn't get a court, did you?"

"Just a bust," Giff said. "All the way."

"You got no more stripes to lose," Top Landrum said.

Koko jabbed Giff lightly in the kidneys. "Come on, Bohane," he said, urging him toward the window-door. As they passed Quiller Carpenter's desk, the haggard clerk gave a Romanesque thumbs down, grinning at Giff.

Leaving the office they moved through the sheet of rain silently to the front porch of the barracks and tacitly stopped under the eaves looking at each other—two faces masked, belying all emotion.

"You silly sonofabitch," Koko said finally, "You're a hot one." He turned and opened the door and stepped inside.

The barracks was moving grudgingly to life for noon chow. Amid the clatter of tinny mess gear Giff exchanged jibes with the men, who were all anxious to hear how he'd made out, what he'd got. He pealed his chevrons from his sleeves in mute cocky answer to their questions and walked leisurely down into the second platoon squadbay watching Koko Hobbs disappear around the head.

Cinamo Dallas and Stack Renshaw were leaning against the space heater in the center of the squadbay, bundled up in field jackets, swinging their mess gear, prepared for the hour of contrition before they advanced on the field day again.

Giff, eying the tall quarter Cherokee, unflinching, with that odd ambivalence of respect and contempt, walked slowly up to them and lit a cigarette, wondering now what motive Dallas had had, if any.

"How you like being a private?" Dallas grinned, studying Giff with a sly inquisitiveness.

"Like it fine," Giff said, "great. You outrank me now. In another week you'll be ready for Officer Candidate School," he said with the air of a man who is on a hot streak of luck but has run out of chips.

"In a month I'll run the Divvy," Dallas grinned. "If I keep my nose clean."

"You making chow?" Stack asked, fumbling with the buttons on his field jacket. "That old field day made me hungrier than hell."

"Naw," Giff said. "I ain't got much of an appetite."

"You should eat," Dallas prompted. "A man's got to eat to stay alive. I guess you didn't eat much when you were over the hill?"

"Enough," Giff said.

Stack turned his collar up and started walking away as if he had tacitly understood to make himself absent. "I'll see you in formation," he said to Dallas.

Giff watched him walk up the aisle, joining the rest of the company as they tread wearily out for noon chow to wait in the rain in front of the mess hall. Then he turned back to Dallas who was inspecting his mess gear.

"I ain't pissed off cause you put me on report," Giff said.

"You don't have a right to be," Dallas said.

"Well, I just wanted you to know I wasn't," Giff bored, a little angry. "You were just doing your job."

"That's all." Dallas scraped some dried egg off his mess fork.

"It was something you had to do," Giff said.

"Doing my job," Dallas said.

"All right goddamit!" Giff said angrily. "I shoulda told you I was going. But I didn't. I didn't feel like telling anybody. I just felt like leaving. That was all. Don't you ever feel like gettin' up and taking the fuck off? On your own?"

"Quite a few times," Dallas nodded, his mess gear dropped to his side and he looked up, his brow in a deep killer's V. "I could have covered for you if you'd a told me. You wouldn't a had any trouble."

"Maybe I wanted trouble," Giff said, smoking bitterly. "Maybe I'm begging to get hung."

"You've got enough rope," Dallas said. "What you want to do with it is your business. And like I told you before, I . . ." He paused, shrugged, as if suddenly embarrassed and ill at ease, inexpressible. "Hell, a bust ain't bad. You still got liberty and all. Going out tonight?"

"Sure," Giff said lamely. "It's our liberty weekend. I wouldn't stay around the barracks."

Dallas grinned, a jitterish wanting-to-move-on grin. "How's everything down the Blue Moon?"

"*Itchiban,*" Giff said. "Number fucking one. They's all waiting for us to come down and tear it up." He looked out the window at the company falling in for chow. "You better get out there; you won't make chow."

"I always make chow," Dallas said, his voice ringing of the old confidence again, and started to walk away. "You better rest up," he said, walking down the aisle. "With those last few days at the Blue Moon and the weekend coming up, you'll need it. We'll cut out about five o'clock, after hitting the slop chute a few licks." He turned his back all the way and moved quickly up the aisle as the formation outside was called to attention by the Duty NCO.

In the silence of the deserted barracks with the continual staccato of rain on the tin roof that he had gotten so used to, that had it stopped it would suddenly have made him deaf, Giff felt a strange calm move over him as he leaned against the warmth of the space heater: unvanquished, with an entirely new perspective of himself, and he wondered just what things or events or actions or culmination of so many forgotten nuances had caused all of it.

To himself he had changed. And he knew definitely that he would keep changing, following the course—an irrevocable chain, each link filed half in two, neither having beginning nor end, and with each step wondering what the hell it was that shackled him?

Sometimes, he thought moving away from the space heater to his locker, it got very confusing and it was damned hard to isolate Bohane's Virus.

He took his winter greens off and hung them neatly in his locker. Then he donned an old pair of field dungarees so he would not get his good dungarees soiled when he worked on the field day that afternoon. It was essential to him that he have clean uniforms, tailored and neat. Just as essential as it was to know the nomenclature of his M-1 Rifle, or any of those other things that went head to toe with being a field marine.

16.

S/Sgt Jack Koko Hobbs, when he left Bohane behind him in the second platoon squadbay, was feeling tolerably amused over the morning's hassel in the company office.

Walking through the third platoon squadbay to the staff quarters, Koko thought it was odd that a man like Bohane who had all the breaks with a cushiony position in the Crotch—or could have if he wanted it—seemed hell-bent on destroying it. He simply could not understand why a man who had any brains at all would prostitute his chances for the gravy.

While it actually amused him in a left-handed sort of way, it filled him at the same time with an acquisitiveness for all those things, talents perhaps, that a few of the men carried with them—and wasted. For Jack Koko Hobbs had always moved through the Marine Corps with a boxer's feint, throwing his adversary off balance, bobbing and weaving, changing style, gearing eternally for that one Sunday punch that would give him security.

Running his thumbs along the inside of his waistband in a sort of dispassionate trouser-straightening gesture, handsomely cool, he opened the door of the staff quarters and walked on in, glad that today was Friday and he had the entire weekend for his enterprises.

The five other staff, excluding Top Landrum, sat tensely

around the poker table in the center of the room under a cigarette-smoke gray aura of light from the dangling bulb, like a misty protective halo over the payday money that was changing hands as fast as the Disciples had changed their minds.

They were playing stud poker, joker on aces, straights and flushes, last man under the gun bets: the face-up game of cards where each man tosses in his chips hopefully praying his pair of deuces will fluke the rising pot.

"I'll call and raise half buck," S/Sgt D'Agastino, the platoon leader from Machine Guns, said confidently.

Koko watched each man, watched Thorton especially, whom he knew was not going to be pleased when he found out he'd have to inspect the field day himself that afternoon because he, Koko, was going to cut a choge to town early. He had already assigned Corporal Jesus Queecho, the right guide, to supervise the field day. And if Thorton was going to be displeased, well, he would just have to be displeased.

Lighting a cigarette, he walked on past the table to his bunk and wall locker. Off in the corner Itchie, the houseboy, sat cross-legged shining shoes, his black eyes calculating.

"Open game," Hugh Thorton said, calling D'Agastino's bet and raise. "How about sitting in, Koko?"

Koko unbuttoned his dungaree jacket and slipped it off. "Noop; I got more important things to do," he grinned at Thorton. "Our pride and joy got bust, all the way," he said.

"I tole you he would." Thorton shuffled his hole card around.

"Pay attention to the game," Gunny Leroy Finch said, his red eyes beady on his cards. "It's your bet; high man."

"It was an easy call," Koko agreed, opened his wall locker and sat down on his bunk watching the game.

"One-eyed jack bets a buck." Thorton tossed in a dollar in script. "Going up the U.S. Bar?" he asked Koko.

"It ain't worth it," D'Agastino said in disgust, turning his cards over, a large solidly built Italian with a round nose, several times broken, who spat out words just like the machine guns he commanded.

"For a while," Koko answered. "Maybe I'll catch a train and head for Tokyo."

"You stayin', Finch?" Thorton said. "Cost you two bucks."

"Cost me nothing," Finch grunted. "You sharpie." He

284

reached down beside his chair for his ubiquitous bottle, took a drink without offering any to the rest of them, and washed his hand of the deal with a swipe across his mouth.

Staff Sergeants Gross and Wasluski both stayed with Thorton, tossing their money in with that slow thoughtful obvious bluff. Like a whore playing she had a heart of gold, Koko thought, sitting lazily on his bunk.

"I recommended Dallas for Meritorious Corporal. He'll be Actin' Corporal Monday, and next month he'll get his rank with full honors," Thorton said to his two up cards. "Well, well! Two tens, twenty miles of railroad track—a buck."

"Twenty miles is a short haul," S/Sgt Wasluski grumbled, tossing in his buck. He was a short beer-barreled belly, red-faced Mortarman.

"I should ought to get to hell out," S/Sgt Gross said cautiously, peeking at his hole card. "But I'll stay."

"Dallas'll make a good corporal," Koko nodded. "He'll take the place of Bohane anyway."

"Deal the goddam cards." Gross took another sly look at his hole card, the washed-out eyes in his horse face blinking.

"We need some new leaders," Thorton said, dealing each card with a thumb-snapping click. "A whore for Ski, a deuce for Gross, and a hook for me— Now, how about that, people? Twin tens and a jack bet a buck and a half; get out while you still got enough for a can of beer."

"Anyone else besides Dallas?" Koko said, wondering if Thorton had actually put Dallas up for it already or if he was going to? If he had put him up for it, why hadn't he told him? After all, he was the platoon sergeant.

"Queecho up for buck sarjint," Thorton said. "That ought to cover it. Well," he prodded, "you two campfire girls going to stay for that buck and a half? With tenners staring you in the face?"

"A pair don't beat trips," Wasluski said, calling the bet.

"Make it a buck better," Gross probed.

"Yas," Ski said. "Always a shitbird got to raise; never satisfied with the bet." But he called.

"Maybe Bohane'll get his rank back, he straightens up," Koko said.

Thorton laughed. "Maybe I'll lose this hand, too."

"Are you going to call the raise," Gross gloated, "or ain't you?"

"Bohane'll shape up," Koko said. "He's just havin' a weak moment."

"Ha!" Thorton hawked. "Anyone here want to trade one man for a late corporal. I got a man—Bohane—you might be able to use, Gross. Be an asset to the first platoon."

"Calling or not?" Gross demanded.

"Oh, excuse me." Thorton called the raise. "And I bump you back another buck; cost you two long greens, Ski."

"I'm getting sucked in," Ski said to his pair of eights. "Payday only comes twice a fucking month you know— Two bucks you say? Okay." He laid two bills down on the GI blanket.

S/Sgt Gross fiddled around with his hole card, looked at it three times as if perhaps it might change number or suit, glanced around at the faces and finally, grudgingly, called the raise without raising back.

"At least Bohane'll make a good private," Koko jeered.

"Bohane," Thorton observed, "would make a good A-frame for a North Korean."

"How about leaving the fucking company out of the game?" D'Agastino, who had folded and was no longer playing, spat quickly. "Poker is the topic. Not the comp'ny. Deal 'em."

"Last card coming up." Thorton flicked the cards, skimming them off the top of the deck adroitly so that they fell on the other face-up cards. "I'm hotter'n a two-dollar pistol shooting downhill."

"Just deal and wheel," Wasluski said, licking his lips.

From his point of observation Koko watched the cards fall evenly, thinking back to the time when he had approached Thorton, back at Camp Pendleton it was, about going into a poker duet with him. The way he had it figured they could made a haul every payday and by playing it safe no one would get suspicious; simply the goldbrick system where they back each other and keep the other players in. Koko had worked it before in China with amazing results. But when he'd asked Thorton, the mustachioed sonofabitch had only grinned slyly, he remembered, and said it wouldn't be fair.

Now, or rather since he'd come into the staff quarters, Thorton was doing just exactly that. By talking offhandedly to him, he had distracted the other players until they couldn't concentrate wholly on the game. In short, Thorton was using him for a left hand doesn't know what the right hand is doing! Koko suddenly decided Thorton was a neat-handed inveterate freeloader—and a moralistic one at that! Jesus, but he hated moralists.

And he hadn't by God taken Thorton to raise either; he was getting pretty tired of supporting him. It was a good thing Thorton was the only one who knew anything about his black market or he'd be broke paying off the company's extortionists.

"Trip eights for Ski." Thorton dealt the hand out. "Nothing for you, Gross, terribly sorry— And up jumped Jesus!" Thorton laid the other one-eyed jack, showing two big pair.

"Two pair don't beat trips," Wasluski said.

"A full house does," Thorton grinned. "You couldn't beat a full house, Ski, not with that hand."

"Sure, a full house," Wasluski sneered. "Who you tryin' to shit, Thorton?"

"You're under the gun," Thorton grinned. "You bettin' into me, Ski?"

S/Sgt Gross folded his cards slowly in disgust, and a heavy silence hushed over the table and room. The soft rubbing of rag on leather came from Itchie, who dutifully did not cease his duties.

"I don't think you got it," Wasluski said.

Thorton shrugged. "It's your bet."

"If you ain't got it," Wasluski stared at his hand, "I got you beat."

"Only one way to find out," Thorton grinned.

"Gonna call or ain't you, Ski?" D'Agastino snapped.

"You're bettin' into a full house, Ski." Thorton lit a cigarette and leaned back in his chair. "You'll lose sure as Billy be damned."

"I don't see no full house," Ski said, studying his hole card. "You're trying to bluff me, that's all."

"Goddamit, call 'em, Ski!" D'Agastino shot out in a short burst.

"It's my bet!" Wasluski said, flustered. "He's got to call me!"

"Then bet!" D'Agastino yelled.

"A buck!"

"Raise you two bucks, Ski," Thorton said.

"There; you see!" Wasluski jumped up from his chair and pointed accusingly at his cards. "He trapped me," he railed.

287

"What'd you want me to bet for, you goddam wop?"

"He's still bluffing!" D'Agastino said, casting a dark glance around at Thorton. "Raise him back!"

"You're awful free with my money," Wasluski said indignantly. Carefully he sat back down and resumed looking at his hole card.

Koko watched from his bunk, knowing who would win. It was obvious. Thorton had the full house. Because Thorton was an honest gambler, he would tell you exactly what he had and you would walk right into it. It wasn't at all fair, Koko considered, to be an honest gambler.

He stood up, stripped his dungarees and pulled a tan and black sport jacket and gray slacks out of his locker and started dressing for town as the momentary hush wafted from the poker table.

"Okay," Wasluski conceded, "I call; no raise, just call. But I bet you ain't got it."

Grinning, Thorton flipped his hole card over: the ten of clubs, tens over jacks, a full house. "You can't win for losing, Ski. You locked horns with the wrong bull. I told you what I had.".

Wasluski's round moon face reddened. "Dirty sonofabitch!" he cried, "dirty sonofabitch. Goddam you wop! What you tell me to bet for?"

"I didn't say nothing." D'Agastino raised his hands innocently. "I don't play no one else's cards but my own. No right to be pissed off at me. Come on, come on, new deal." He rubbed his hands together.

Gunny Leroy Finch smirked and prepared himself for the new hand. S/Sgt Gross, grumbling about the rottenness of cards, straightened in his chair. All around the table descended again the hushed passionate expectancy as the sweating Wasluski picked up the deck and began shuffling.

Dressed, Koko locked his wall locker, amused at Thorton's detestable honesty, slipped his raincoat over his civvies. His handsome clean features unreadable, dapper, unexcitable and cunning, he worked out his method of business for the weekend as he knelt to his foot locker.

Usually he averaged around five hundred dollars every payday weekend which was swiftly amassing into a good hunk of dough in the Gotemba bank—all in yen. And that was only from his money exchange black market.

He unlocked his worn locker box, pulled out a thick envelope and stuck it in his raincoat pocket, then walked unobtrusively over to the poker table and watched the new hand fall.

"You really ought to get in for couple hands, Koko," Thorton offered.

"I can make more money off the pachinko parlor," Koko evaded, half wanting to stay for this hand just to see if that honest sonofabitch Thorton would be honest and win again; but he had things to do, places to go, and people to see.

"I'll see you boys later." He walked over to the door.

Outside the staff quarters, Koko paused under the eaves, slapped the thick envelope in his pocket happily and stood enjoying the plummeting rain. There was almost one hundred and fifty bucks in the envelope in greenbacks—State-side money: that would make almost four hundred bucks when he sold it for yen. Yes sir, his old bank roll was really increasing.

And hell! that wasn't even counting the goods he sold on the black market: watches, rings, all the luxuries—and coffee. Don't forget the coffee, that was the profitable item.

Once a month he would stroll over to the mess hall at night, take the key from his pocket (the one he'd had specially made to fit the lock there), unlock the storeroom and take out two five-gallon cans of coffee and forge the mess sergeant's name on the inventory log and carry them back behind Hog Company's armory. Then the next day he would check out a jeep from the motor pool (he had a real good buddy there, too) and stack the two cans in the back of the jeep and drive right out through the main gate big as life and twice as healthy. He got one hundred bucks apiece for the cans. And it was all so obvious.

That was what he congratulated himself on really, he thought watching the rain fall around him, the obviousness of it. He had learned long ago, way back in East St. Louis, Illinois, that the way to fool the people was to make every-thing obvious. Hide nothing, leave everything exposed. A man couldn't go under the counter with anything; over the counter was the only way.

It was almost like a doctor who was in cahoots with the medicine people, he reflected, and just a few words, a scare headline or article, and the people would be desperate. Something simple, like say liver—the foul-tasting meat that was served once a week in the mess hall—liver then; no one liked it, but as soon as the doctors came out with the certified fact that liver was good for anemia people bought it up like hotcakes.

Or cigarettes: the ones they were beginning to manufacture that didn't cause lung cancer they always sold the best. Except the cigarette manufacturers never told the consumers that the doctor who'd said they didn't cause lung cancer worked in their research laboratories.

And him, Koko Hobbs, he appraised himself staring through the rain slashing across the barracks and streets and cinder ash—him, was he any different? He had a product: luxuries and money. Yet he hadn't caused the scare or the need or the desperation to possess any of it.

He had simply walked in on a good thing, that was all.

The war had done it, Big Two. The inflation of yen on the market and the desperation for coffee and food and cigarettes and luxuries that none of the Japanee people had. There had been a lot of men before him who had worked it, and a lot would come working after he was gone.

But most of them would get caught. They just weren't smart enough.

He breathed deeply of the refreshed wet air, not feeling cold at all watching the rain pour down. With all the money he had in the bank and the way it was mounting each week he would have enough salted away by the time they went to war again to . . . The thought brought a smile to his mouth, and he chuckled at the rain.

Well, he wasn't getting anywhere with his plans standing there under the eaves.

With that female-devastating countenance, he walked on through the rain up Pearl Harbor Street, carefully avoiding the puddles, his hands jammed in his raincoat pocket.

The sentry at the main gate nodded him through with a quick glance at his ID card because he was not in uniform and recognizable as a Staff NCO, and Koko belatedly remembered that starting Monday, Horrible Hog Company went on guard and he hadn't made up a guard roster. It was a cinch Thorton would never make it up and no one had informed Jesus Queecho about it. So, he thought distastefully, he would have to cut his weekend short and come in early Sunday to make it up.

Fujioka appeared dead, the fronts of the shops and bars closed up tight with only the lighted windows showing it was not a ghost town.

Koko shoved his wallet back in his pocket and walked the thirty muddy yards to Hock at Henry's.

Henry was a sly one, he thought, and suspicious and even back-stabbing. That was why he had made a fortune off the troops who were eternally broke and wound up hocking everything from watches to raincoats. Of course they were never ahead enough to get them out and Henry took advantage of this. He sold them on the black market in turn, making two quick profits. Sometimes Koko had a sneaking hunch that Henry was related. Sometimes he even felt obscurely that they were *all* related, like one big family of thieves. And he was right out there in front: the Patriarch —with the Matriarch.

The announcing bell jangled as he opened the door and stepped in out of the rain, pulling his collar down from his neck and wiping the rain from his face with his handkerchief.

Hock at Henry's display counter was filled with knives, souvenirs, trinkets, flags, scarves. On top of the counter lay the venerated record book of items hocked and unhocked and hocked again, and those that were hocked and left.

Koko leaned forward studying the display case as the footsteps, cotton *tabis* muted on wood, came louder from the back room and Henry of Hock at Henry's shuffled out, bowing graciously.

"Aft'noon, Henry," Koko said amiably. Henry was the only name he had ever known him by: a long-eared, almost chinless, baggy-eyed Japanee man, his withered mushy face displaying fourteen years of fighting fruitlessly for the Emperor and the Southeast Asia Co-prosperity Sphere. "Been takin' any wooden yen?" Koko grinned.

"No takee wooden yen," Henry grinned back, bowing again, appearing incongruous with his American white shirt and cheap slacks. "Long time no see, Koko-san. You no havo *okane* before, *ne?*"

"Got it now," Koko said calmly and slapped his pocket. "Going to be some meat on the table tonight."

"Ah so, very good," Henry beamed. "You come havo cup of hot *sake* with Henry maybe?"

"Yeah, I'll have some hot *sake*. Is Mama-san Henry home?"

"She go town today," Henry said. "All time last month she go Gotemba. Sister there *toxon* sick."

"Well, that's too bad, Henry." Koko moved around the

291

counter following Henry into the living quarters of the shop. It was good that Henry was tight-lipped. Old Henry never spill the rice. No *sir*. Anyway, if he did, there were always more Henrys—a whole world of them.

The living quarters were small but comfortably sufficient with one old-fashioned electric heater (now who the hell would ever have hocked an electric heater?) a radio, ironing board and iron and a hot plate, while incongruously, right in the center of the floor, was the ancient habachi pot and the low-set table with the cushions beside it. It always bewildered Koko—the duality in the Japanee since the war. Half Western and half Oriental, and the twain never did quite meet in them. One day, or one minute, they were American, the next they were Japanee, and it was even more pronounced in the women, the business women.

He took his raincoat off, handed it to the bowing Henry in American clothes, and sat down on the cushion by the low Japanee table beside the American iron and ironing board.

Henry hung up the coat, produced a silver urn with ornate engraving on it and steaming with hot *sake,* still grinning politely, and set two cups down on the table, poured first in Koko's cup, then his own, set the urn down and then himself.

The man with the brass yingyang, Koko thought.

"Ah, is very good." Henry savored the hot bitter liquid. "You catchee *toxon* rain no can work, *ne?*"

"Which is a damn good thing," Koko said. "I needed the break." He shrugged. "But—you got to train if you're going to fight."

"That is true." Henry nodded sagely. "An army must train well."

"That's what they keep tellin' us. But you know all right. You were in the army quite a while yourself, weren't you?"

"So," Henry qualified. "Fourteen years, long time. Long time to fight and no win."

"You can't win 'em all."

Henry stared at his cup of *sake* with melancholy beagle's eyes. "We would have won, it is true, if we did not have to fight the Americans or the British," he said good-naturedly.

"The British!" Koko snorted over his *sake.* "Hell, Henry, you had them on the run. They've always been on the run.

292

But you should have known you'd have to fight us sooner or later."

"So," Henry nodded. "The Chinee we beat; the Philippine also—but no could beat Americans. I know this when they start helping us before Pearl Harbor. *Baykoko* send all raw material to Nippon for war. I know then we will not win."

"We had manpower."

"The Nippon State also havo manpower," Henry said.

"But no *okane*, eh?" Koko grinned. "It takes money to run a war."

"But even the Americans are running out of money for war," Henry said glibly, his eyes twinkling.

"So they'll start a war to make money." Koko shrugged. "Someone will. They always do."

"No," Henry raised his hand in dispute, "it is not for the money, Koko. It is for the labor."

"What labor?" Koko questioned.

"For cheap labor," Henry explained. "All war is fought for cheap labor so the victors may invest money in the vanquished countries. Look at Nippon." Henry waved his arms around the room. "Hotels, factories, everything foreign with Nipponese as cheap labor and yet we come up, move ahead. No," he shook his head, "it is for the cheap labor."

"Sounds like slavery to me," Koko laughed. "But I don't see anyone in ball and chain."

Henry sipped at his *sake*, replenished both cups and crossed his legs under him. "You are the ones being fooled," he said stolidly. "You fight but you not know why; I tell you."

"It ain't important," Koko said, "to me. I only fight because, well, hell, I'm in the Crotch," he finished lamely, telling himself cautious, Koko old buddy, play it dumb like a hick.

"You will find out," Henry said. "You will find out that the one war you should have lost was your first, the rebellion."

"I don't know too much about that one," Koko said. "I quit school as a small boy."

"Someday you will learn, someday it will all become clear."

Koko grinned. "I'm not much of a politician, Henry," he said calmly. "That ain't my job." He pulled out his envelope and handed it to Henry across the table. "I got to be shoving off. I'm planning on going to Tokyo."

"Ah so," Henry said curtly, pulling the military script from the envelope and thumbing through it, eyes greedy. His back still ramrod straight from the fourteen years in the army, feet shuffling jerkily, he moved back out to the front of the hockshop and returned quickly with the yen.

Koko, as he knew Henry wanted him to do, counted the yen slowly, then nodded in approval. "I'll see you in a couple weeks, Henry," he said getting up. "Thanks for the *sake* and tell your wife I said hello."

"Come back soon any time," Henry grinned. "Come back see us. No need *okane*. We glad to see you."

"I'll do that," Koko lied over his shoulder, opening the door, the announcing bell jingling, and walked on out back into the rain.

The four hundred bucks in yen secure in his pocket, he trudged on up the street to the U.S. Bar. He would, as usual, leave two hundred there. That was part of his deal too. Insurance. Something that even Henry who so obviously thought of himself as sly had never figured out. No one else had either, he thought with a grin, thinking of Thorton.

When he left the U.S. Bar, he turned off on the railroad tracks and started walking toward the South Fujioka train station.

It would take two hours to get to Tokyo, then another hour rounding up the "boys" who paid off for the watches and cameras that he would buy at the Fleet PX, but he figured he could pick up an extra two hundred bucks, which would make it, all in all, a tidy weekend.

The long expanse of wetly gleaming railroad tracks leading up to the South Fujioka train station seemed to Koko like a long illuminated tunnel when he turned and started up them, carefully stepping on each tie. A tunnel that was dry and protective, and individual.

He fervently wished, as he neared the end of the long dry tunnel with his face so wet from the rain, that people would stay out of his way for just a skosh while: just long enough to fill that cache in the Gotemba bank. Then he would leave them all alone, altogether, and they could remember S/Sgt Jack Koko Hobbs with a sweet nostalgia.

He walked in under the awning of the train station, grinning broadly as two Japanee looked up at him, shaking their heads at the *baka* no-good malines, and stepped up to the ticket window thinking after he transacted his business in Tokyo he would go on a classy drunk and maybe even try one of those high-class Jap broads on the Ginza.

Then he remembered that he would have to be back early Sunday evening to make up the guard roster for Monday, and he unbelievingly hoped that no one would fuck up over the weekend and get sent to jail. That was all he needed.

It would be just like someone in the platoon, Bohane especially, to knife someone over the galling question of whether or not duck-billed platypuses laid eggs. Then he and Thorton would have to stand Camp Guard all by themselves.

And that would tie the pink ribbon on it quite neatly.

17.

By a throw of the dice Giff Bohane eased through the weekend without even a minor altercation. He was contented to remain in Popcorn Shiro's small room just behind the beaded curtain in the Bar New Blue Moon.

It seemed to him, when he was shaken awake by Popcorn at four-thirty Monday morning, that it had been the most solemn and uneventful weekend he had ever known. Dallas and Stack had both come back to his room on occasions and spoken to him, joked a little and then drifted back out to the bar. There was no mention of a fight, no one getting cut up, and no one from the company was arrested by the MP's. It was all very weird, he thought sleepily when he got up and started dressing to go back to South Camp and start the week of guard duty. The only thing that was customary to the old way, the weekends before, was the occupational hangover which, he felt, he would never ever be free of.

He was still struggling with his trousers feeling the liquor-logged fatigue weighing him down, Popcorn lying on the *tatami* under the quilt watching him silently, when Cinamo

Dallas slid the door open and stuck his face in, grinning, the dark V of his brow prominent in the still-dusky early morning.

"Stack up too?" Giff mumbled groggily. "Man, I hate guard. Four on, eight off. Four on, eight off. In the miserable fucking rain." He stood up and cinched his belt, shivering.

"It ain't rainin', cousin," Dallas grinned, looking down at Popcorn with a curious glint in his eyes. "It stopped last night. About midnight."

"Yeah?" Giff turned toward the window, listening attentively, not hearing the rain, not even a dripping, and he was startled. "Been raining so long thought it never stop," he yawned.

"We got about ten minutes," Dallas said. "Stack's waitin' out front for us." He slid the door closed, then abruptly opened it again as Giff was bending down to Popcorn.

"What, goddamit?" Giff demanded crossly, looking back up at him.

"Hear about what happened last night?"

"Heard nothing happened," Giff said. "Quiet weekend far as I'm concerned."

"Ha!" Dallas grinned. "That's all you know. Get your ass ready or we'll be late. I'll tell you about it when you get outside." He closed the door again and Giff waited till he heard his footsteps retreating down the corridor to the back door.

Curious, but not excited, he wondered what had happened as he bent down and kissed Popcorn, telling her he'd be back when they got off guard next week. She smiled in assent and he turned his back and left the room.

Dallas and Stack were standing by the back door blowing on their hands, rubbing them together, their breath coming in foggy spurts.

"Colder'n my boy Willy," Stack said, repeating the last line of the parody. "If it ain't rain it's freezing. Goddamest place I ever seen."

"So what happened?" Giff kicked into his shoes, tied them loosely and slid open the door. *"Man, it is cold, ain't it!"* Outside, covering the ground and the roofs of the bars and the sparsely leaved trees, a clinging frost sparkled. "Somebody die over the weekend we didn't know about?"

"Better'n that," Dallas grinned.

"Ten minutes," Stack said. "We got ten minutes to make

296

it back or Top Condrum'll have himself a field day. Tell you about it on the way."

They slid the door behind them and walked around the bar and started up Bamboo Alley in the chilly darkness, embraced by the eerie morning silence of the bars where not even the life stirrings of sleep could be heard.

"Tell him, Dallas," Stack said.

"You tell him," Dallas said. "You know more about it than I do."

"Yeah," Giff said suddenly alert. "What the hell happened anyway?"

"Well," Stack said, clearing his voice, "they had a race war up to Middle Camp last night. All of yestiday in fact."

"A race war?" Giff said, surprised. "The gooks and the 'Mericans?"

"No," Stack shook his head, "the niggers and the whites up there. Couple staff sar'nts tossed a bomb into the nigger club up there, the Blue Bird, I think they call it."

"Jesus Christ!" Giff lit a cigarette hoping to warm himself up. "A bomb, hunh?"

Stack Renshaw, his bulbous nose redder than usual from the sudden cold, blowing fog with each chattered word as they moved up Bamboo Alley, related the incident. He had found out about it, he told Giff, when he'd gone out to eat at the Arizona Restaurant Sunday afternoon, and he'd got it firsthand from the MP's, one of whom he knew personally from Middle Camp.

No one, Stack said levelly, knew for sure what had prompted all of it. But early Sunday afternoon these two staff sergeants had tossed a bomb into the Blue Bird Club, damn near destroying the bar (couple of Japanese business women were cut, but not bad) and there were only three or four niggers in the place at the time. They didn't get hurt at all. Well, Stack said, before the MP's could put a halt to anything, all the marine niggers had banded together and all the white marines had banded together and went a-courting, so to speak, with knives, belt buckles and fists, and the casualty list was higher than his old company in Korea, so Stack had heard.

Anyway, the two staff sergeants, both battalion clerks at Second Battalion, were found first and hauled off by the Japanee Security Police, a civil crime, they claimed, and they doubled up the MP force in Skosh Town, for that was what the town's name was outside Middle Camp, and still it didn't do much good. There was all kinds of fighting going on, Stack said wistfully, and about ten or fifteen men, both black and white, were locked up, going to get court-martial sure as hell.

They had to double up the MP's in Fujioka too, Stack said, because they figured it would start a chain reaction in the whole regiment and after the black and white marines would kill themselves off, there wouldn't be anybody left to fight the wars.

But they was all hell going on up to Middle Camp, Stack said, and one old boy got hisself killed. Seems a white boy had been pretty bad cut up with a razor and had gone back to camp, busted into his company's armory, stolen a .45 and a pocketful of rounds, then come charging back out into the street, that .45 hanging in his hand and he meant to kill some people. Well, the MP's seen him coming and got their own .45's out and shot him down before he could do anything.

"Six times they shot him was the way I heard it," Stack said. "How about that?"

"I wonder was he going to kill anyone in particular or just a bunch?" Giff said.

"Don't guess anyone'll ever know that," Stack said. But that wasn't all by a long shot, either. A half a dozen whites had caught some nigger by his lonesome and beat him good, put their boots to him, Stack said. They had to haul him off to Charlie Med to get patched up. And they was even a guy sitting in a bar, didn't know nothing about the race war, just sitting there minding his own business having a beer, when couple niggers come in, couple guys he knew. He nodded to them, went back to his beer; next thing he knew he was going through a window, glass and all.

"Oh Jesus," Stack said, "what them two MP's didn't tell me. Everyone up there was using knives and belts and hibachi pots and rocks, just about everything they could get their hands on to fight with. Sometimes the MP's would get it quieted down a little, get to thinking they had it all in hand, then it would bust out again in another part of town."

"It started when they tossed the bomb, hunh?" Giff said. They came out of Bamboo Alley between the Heart Bar and the Condor Club, Fujioka's Negro bar, and he looked over at it thoughtfully. "Wonder what made them two do it?"

"I don't know," Dallas grinned. "But you ask me, they didn't throw a big enough bomb."

298

Giff laughed, seeing the light of the main gate on up the road, thinking Goddam! they must have been some hell up there, wondering about it, and why it hadn't come swooping down to South Camp.

"It busted the monotony up there," Stack allowed. "But I bet those two Staff's are a couple sorry-lookin' sacks of shit this morning."

"The Japanee," Dallas said, "will put them away for a long time. The Crotch won't be able to interfere none, either. On a deal like that the Crotch can't do nothing, less its among their own people."

When they got back to the barracks, three minutes before muster in just enough time to don their dungarees and fall out in the darkness, there was a contagious rumbling through the barracks, a direct current of animosity in the air, and everyone was talking excitedly about it. The Negroes in the company huddled together with anxious whispers, flashing their large eyes around cautiously, while the white men of the company huddled together in larger groups. And it carried all the way through morning chow and back into the barracks as they dressed for guard, a distinct line of separation between the two factions. Each interpreted its own version, carefully avoiding contact with the other color, and when a white man had to ask a black man something or vice versa it was done with a shame-faced belligerent sober reserve.

Giff, immaculate in his tailored green with the sleeves dark where the corporal chevrons had been, did not see anything really exciting in the whole business. Over what he was going through—his belated decision—it took a secondary position of importance. Even when he checked the guard roster and discovered that Dallas had been promoted to Meritorious Corporal, it did not surprise him any more than the rest of it. The platoon however, except for the colored faction, who knew Dallas was from Oklahoma, all complimented him on the promotion.

As the sun peeked up on the crisp morning, the race-war talk seemed to abate a little, as if in some foreign way the light of day had put a loud hush on it. But it still remained in all of their faces, a distance, a bridge that could not be crossed, and they all knew it as they avoided one another's eyes.

When they fell out for guard mount at seven-thirty, it was to a surprisingly clear cold sunny morning. The heavy rain, having expended itself, now lurked somewhere far off gathering strength. Hoarfrost glistened on the purple cinder ash of Hog Company's mustering area, the first probing jabs of winter moving out of its autumn corner.

And to Giff, as he fell out rankless carrying his rifle, it was a deceptive day, the beginning for the week of guard that he looked forward to the way a man looks forward to dying before he's through.

The only way he could describe his feeling was that someone had pulled the pin on a hand grenade, forgotten to throw it, and everyone just stood around and stared at it waiting for it to explode. No one yelled "Mine!" and chortling happily belly-flopped on it in hopes of getting the Medal of Honor for saving his buddies' lives, because actually the grenade did not exist. Except for Giff.

That was the way he looked at it, thought of it—a sputtering grenade, fuse burning quickly, then exploding, disrupting the radius of his life once again. So he was prepared, he thought; for when the white-hot fragments seared him ripping his flesh, he would not hate it at all. But he saw all of it instead as something inevitable. And he never did find out who it was had pulled the pin.

Hungover, he fell out for guard thinking at least it was a break from field training. It was clearly written on the faces of the other men too, as they stood disgruntled in the ranks, that guard was a loathsome part of their inveterate duty. It was etched in their cheeks that were red from the nipping cold and the weekends' winebibbing, each of them knowing it would rain when they went on post, adding to the misery of guarding something utterly worthless like the camp— which, they knew, no one would want to steal.

Still, the guard, plus the freakish sunshine, helped to alleviate a fraction of the tension mounting from the race war.

The single devastating hatred was not so much directed at the guard as it was at the non-liberty that was the offspring of guard. A week without liberty.

If there was one consolation it was the knowledge that they would not have any interference from the company staff. On their moments off they could work on personal gear. Or ferret out an island of security for gambling far from the abodes of keen-eyed staff members who scooped up the money on an improvised table saying that gambling was illegal didn't they know that?

So falling out for guard (before S/Sgt Hobbs appeared from the staff quarters of course) they broke into their old mutinous song, Giff taking the chorus and feeling the spine-tingling emotion of camaraderie:

> *"When this bloody cruise is over*
> *Oh how happy I will be*
> *They will find my pack and rifle,*
> *But I'll be damned if they'll find me."*

And the platoon followed discordantly along:

> *"No more falling out for roll call,*
> *No more First Lieutenant's sass;*
> *You can tell the Gunny Sarjint . . .*
> *To stick his details up his ass."*

Then hooted emphatically as Koko Hobbs walked across the cinders toward them.

"Knock off that shit," he shouted. "And fall in. This a platoon or a men's glee club for Chrissakes?"

Finally the platoon marched at right shoulder arms up the street and onto the parade field, feet crunching in the ash and hoarfrost.

At the other end of the parade field by the Tankers' mess hall the two flagpoles stood naked in the slanting cold early-morning sunrays. The color detail from Idiot Item Company, which Horrible Hog Company was relieving on guard, stood holding the two flags: one American and the other United Nations. Flanked by the twin Russian Big One cannons, they waited for the Corporal of the Guard to blow his whistle at eight o'clock for colors.

Koko Hobbs stopped the platoon halfway up the parade field, facing them toward the flagpoles.

"Stand by for colors," he said with a glance at his watch.

"How you like that?" Stack spoke in a low voice to Giff. "Not even a goddam bugler. How come the Crotch don't have no buglers?"

"They're too poor," Giff said. "It ain't on their budget. Hey!" he called out. "Sarjint Hobbs!"

Koko Hobbs swiveled around irritably. "What now?"

"How about writing Washington, see'f they can get us a bugler. We can't go into combat without a bugler," Giff said seriously, leaning on the muzzle of his rifle. "How'd we know when to charge without a bugler?" he questioned, and was pleased with himself as the platoon chuckled in approval, some of his tension easing off.

"I'd have my bayonet up your ass," Koko grinned. "You'd charge." He shook his head. "Ain't nothing in my platoon but skylarkers and instigators."

The Corporal of the Guard's whistle shattered the air.

"P'toon!" Koko commanded in a well-trained-coming-from-the-belly-NCO's voice: "tee-en . . . hut!" executed an about face and saluted smartly as the color detail struggled with the two flags.

All praying silently, Giff thought, because they don't want the flags to hit the ground. Which was natural by God, there wasn't any glory in getting shot by a firing squad for dropping flags on the ground.

When colors were over they marched on up the parade field, passed by the Tankers' mess hall, did a column right, and headed for the square guardhouse just inside the main gate, Giff thinking that if he was still a corporal he would be able to sit in the guardhouse all night drinking coffee, but now, because he was a rear rank private, he would get a miserable post—But maybe he would get supernumerary?

He did not get supernumerary. Nor did he get slop chute watch, which was keenly prized by all the men—a post where they would spend three hours in the slop chute at night to keep order and drink beer on the sly. Nor did he get movie watch, but got, just as he knew he would (the rest had been wishful thinking)—a walking post!

He found out, when he got inside and had stacked his rifle in the corner, that he had caught the twelve-to-four fence post: the twelve-to-four was the graveyard watch where nothing ever happened except the dragging of time. Even though it was the fence along the side of the camp that skirted the town toward Bamboo Alley there would be nothing to watch, not from midnight to four o'clock in the morning.

Settling down in the guardhouse with an almost resigned complacency, men hooting and yelling loudly in the small almost unlivable space, he decided to catch up on his sleep so he would not be tired that night.

He slept for about an hour, then awoke quickly to the sound of guardhouse philosophers analyzing the race war. Off in the corner away from him sat several of the platoon's Negroes, their backs to the rest of the men, and all around the close bunk space of the guardhouse, whether the men were playing cards or reading comic books, the race war still reigned supreme. But it was losing a lot of its force, he thought, not nearly as important as it had been earlier in the morning. He could not understand how the race war could affect him personally, or any of them, when it was up at Middle Camp. If it had started down here at South Camp it would have affected him. He simply did not see anything to get in a stew about. Nothing at all that affected the hand grenade that was still sputtering within him.

Sleepily, he wondered why none of the staff or officers had mentioned it? Hobbs had said nothing at all about it. Maybe they had decided on a mute ignorance of the whole thing. He went back to sleep.

He got up for noon chow, a greasy meager portion of meat loaf from the Tankers' mess hall where the company on guard ate, and immediately went back to bed, only to wake for evening chow and back to bed again, but feeling better now after halfway replenishing the reservoir of strength that only sleep would bring back.

At eleven o'clock that night when Cinamo Dallas moved through the darkened guardhouse rousing the men on his watch, shaking them vigorously, Giff was awake, having awakened automatically as if from instinct when it came time to go on post. He lay on his bunk watching the tall quarter Cherokee peer through the darkness at the sleeping faces, occasionally waking the wrong man and receiving a stream of curses. Dallas could do nothing about it because he was in the wrong and it was a damn good thing he was, Giff thought, or the sonfabitch who cursed him would be picking his ass off the floor.

Watching this, Giff wondered at the change that had come over Dallas, too. He was not the same irresponsible to-hell-with-rank-and-authority man he'd been two months ago at all. He was still the same man, and yet he wasn't. It was strange.

"I'm awake," Giff said, watching him walk through the darkness to his bunk.

"Then you're the only one who is. I have to make the rounds waking these bastards once more, they'll be on the deck."

"You're a real bad ass." Giff slipped his legs off the bunk

and rubbed his face. "A real bad ass for a guy who don't like rank."

Dallas offered him a cigarette. "Me," he said, "I like rank. I'm a leader."

"We're all leaders." Giff lit up the smoke, tasting it, relaxed.

"Sure, why not?" Dallas shifted his head around at the men he'd roused, who had raised up on an elbow then collapsed again. "Goddam them. Yeah, I got to start makin' some rank. That's how she lays."

"What's so important about rank to you?" Giff asked. "All of a sudden?"

"Ain't you heard?" Dallas said seriously. "They're giving the country back to the Indians and I want to be Chief." He walked away, waking his men again, more roughly this time, and Giff chuckled softly as he had to raise some of them by the neck and sit them up.

Finishing his cigarette, he stood up and walked back to the little single commode head in the rear of the guardhouse, pissed, came back out, grabbed his rifle and helmet-liner and walked on into the guard office for coffee and sandwiches.

Jesus Queecho, the deadly little Guamanian, Acting Sergeant of the Guard, sat at his desk fanning his .45 pistol cowboy-style.

"The Polynesian Wyatt Earp," Giff grinned, setting his rifle and helmet-liner down. "How many Indians you kill?"

"No Indians. Can't do that with Dallas on Corp'rol a guard. Had to kill niggers," Jesus grinned. "Got fourteen. Hey, good sandwiches with the coffee tonight." He was really very small, smaller even than Guppy Talagua, Giff thought, but very efficient with those judo-chopping hands.

"Sure; good sandwiches," Giff mocked. "Horsecock?"

"Horsecock," Queecho nodded, grinning, still fanning his .45 at some imaginary bad man.

" 'At's what I figured. I hate that shit," Giff said in disgust, but he got one out of the grease-stained cardboard box by the mess hall pitcher of coffee and ate, relishing, washing it down with the black liquid.

Jesus Queecho flipped his .45 around once and holstered it neatly. "I'm hot tonight," he grinned. "Don't fuck with me, I'm too fast."

"Not's fast I am," Giff said.

Queecho made a slap at his holster, brought his pointed

finger up and said, "Bang!" at Giff who held his hand in front of his fly and said, "I'm pissin' on your grave."

Queecho laughed and poured a cup of coffee for himself.

One by one, eyes puffed with sleep, grinning unhappily, the men of the graveyard watch stumbled out to the guard office and began eating the sandwiches, drinking the coffee.

"Take them guard raincoats with you," Dallas said, coming out of the guardhouse prodding the last man. "It's been spittin' a little. Probably rain hard before the night's over."

"Always a pissyass rain," Pfc Mattox, a thin-faced cold-mouthed Mississippian said. "I catch the twelve-to-four every goddam time there's guard. An' it always rains."

"You can see the chaplain in the morning," Dallas offered.

"Yair," Mattox said. "I get my tough shit card punched."

"Everybody hates us," Giff mocked. "I feel sorry for us motherfuckers."

When they finished the guard rations with one last protesting bitch, they grabbed the raincoats from under the gear locker and fell outside in the chilling damp night under a fine spray of rain.

The fence guard on the eight-to-twelve, Poncho Ramirez, was waiting around the side of the guardhouse, apparently having stood there from the time Dallas began waking the watch up till now, waiting shivering for Giff.

He and Dallas walked over. Giff, his rifle slung on his arm, felt suddenly very alone, staring the next four hours in the face.

"Didn't think I'd make it," Poncho said, handing the clip of ammo to Giff. "Colder'n a witch's ass on Halloween."

"You're relieved," Dallas said dispassionately to Ramirez, and the porcine Mexican gratefully disappeared around the corner of the guardhouse. "And don't eat none of them sandwiches!" Dallas shot after him. "They's for the four-to-eight."

"All right," Poncho's voice echoed weakly. "Goddamit."

"And you're posted," Dallas said to Giff. "Know your orders?"

"Shoot to kill," Giff grinned, "and holler halt three times."

"Only don't shoot at the guardhouse," Dallas cautioned. "You might hit me."

Giff slung his rifle barrel down so the rain would not fall

in the bore and draped the raincoat over him like a cape. "The OD got a piss-call in?"

"Huh-uh," Dallas shook his head, "but he might get up for the hell of it. He does, I'll send someone around to tell you about it; probably have to wake you up."

"In this weather?" Giff grimaced. "You think I'm a duck?"

"I got to post the rest the watch," Dallas said. "I'll see you about three-thirty."

"Okay." Giff watched him walk away and turned around toward the fence and the tiny cowpath beside it, and began walking slowly, looking out at the town, dark now, musicless, no sounds in the night.

In how many places in how many climates had he walked the twelve-to-four, he wondered, feeling a yawning instability opening below him. The lonely midnight hours when there is no one around and there are all the thoughts running through the mind, and no one there but yourself to answer them, plead with them, agree and disagree, but always losing the debate.

Or the four-to-eight—don't forget that. Was the four-to-eight any better than the twelve-to-four? No, not really. Except with the four-to-eight you could see the sun come up in the morning, and it was always strange how untired you'd be as soon as it got light. But that was a deception, he told himself, you're actually just as tired anyway, only if you let yourself feel tired you'd feel awkward because everyone else was just getting up. Anyway it was a stimulus.

Never did see the breaking of day on the twelve-to-four though. Not even a midnight sun. Not even a light from the bars.

Hunched under his raincoat, walking slowly, he counted his steps. The drizzle of rain increased and began pouring down, saturating him. That was SOP, he thought bitterly. Four hours in the rain.

He remembered a shed down by the motor pool right next to the fence where he could get some cover, smoke a cigarette. He headed for it quickly. By the time he got there, he had counted 514 footsteps. He wondered how many more it would be before the night was over.

It was an old shed, used for storing oil drums, with grease and gasoline packed hard on the dirt floor, and he stood shaking himself off under the door arch pulling out his cigarettes and matches.

306

From his dry corner of observation he could see the dim outlines of the bars on the other side of the fence—and on up the sweeping curve of the fence the single burning light of the guardhouse.

He smoked hungrily, watching it all, thinking of his orders. What was a fence guard anyway? Was it his duty to see that no one came into the camp? Who would want to come in? No one. There was nothing here for them to come in for. And look at the way the fence was built. Hell! It wasn't made to keep people out, but to keep people in! Anyone could climb over it from the outside but no one could climb over from the inside.

Now suppose a man was trying to climb the fence there and he saw him—would he shoot? He visualized putting his rifle to his shoulder, taking careful aim and squeezing one off, and the man half falling half hung on the barbs of the fence.

Naw, he wouldn't shoot. More than likely he'd just let the man come on in.

Four hours of it. And nothing to do. No one to talk to. Well, five hours from now he'd be back in the guardhouse asleep. Two hours from now he'd be two hours closer to getting relieved. Twenty-four hours from now he'd . . . It'd be a different day, that was all.

It wasn't right, he told himself with a yawn, to build a fence to keep people in. It should have been built to keep people out. There was something to think about for four hours, he thought, watching the rain fall swirling with the light fog. Fog and rain. Very strange.

It was at times like this that he ran back over his life. That helped to pass the time. Except there was really not much to his life, he thought, not much at all. Because he didn't count anything before he enlisted; there was simply no life before he enlisted. Nothing existing before that made any sense, could hardly be recalled, let alone deline- ated. It seemed that his life history had begun when he enlisted, in '49, and since all the days were the same since then there was not really much to tell about himself, he told himself. Besides, he got very tired of himself telling himself about himself when himself could not understand himself and answer himself.

It helped pass the time though. He wondered if it was 514 steps back to the guardhouse. He'd try that and see.

He flipped his cigarette out into the rain and followed it,

shifting under the weight of his rifle, walking carefully back up the path counting his steps.

When he got up to 200 steps he was just opposite Bamboo Alley, still a long way from the guardhouse, and he looked over at the black hole that looked like a fish's mouth and led down to the Blue Moon.

Once he thought he heard something, a night sound that was like an animal shriek or a strange wailing laugh, coming from the other side of the fence. He turned around but saw nothing. He walked on.

The unearthly moaning, laughing, crying, screaming sound started again. Giff stopped counting, fixing the number in his mind, and turned all the way around staring hard through the rain.

Out of the black mouth of Bamboo Alley emerged a running weaving figure, still indistinct, looking naked, moving along the street, sometimes falling in the mud and groaning, staggering up again and moving on.

Giff rubbed his eyes and squinted as the figure moved closer, about twenty yards away from him on the other side of the fence. Then he could discern through the fog that clung like black powder smoke to the rain that it was a woman, clad only in panties and brassière and covered with mud. Gawking, as she moved past him, he recognized the skinny body of Kayo-san, Dallas' junkie girl friend, from the Bar New Blue Moon.

The number he had been so careful to affix in his mind suddenly left him. He moved up touching the fence, watching fascinated as Kayo-san tore down the street, the loud-soft ineffable animal sound gushing from her throat in a long quivering bellow, moving quickly away from him now, nearing the main gate. He saw the sentry come charging surprised out of his booth, pistol in hand. Then two Japanee men, security police from the shack across from the guardhouse, ran past the gate sentry up to Kayo-san, clubbed her deftly over the head with their finely polished hickory sticks and dragged her back through the gate out of Giff's sight, as the last echo of her screams washed out of the night behind the rain.

Bewildered, Giff stood staring at the main gate sentry booth as the sentry walked back in and shut the door behind him. A quiet mingled with the rain and the night silence returned. It was as if nothing had happened. Up at the guardhouse nothing seemed disturbed.

Cursing himself for having forgotten the number of steps he had taken, he decided to start all over again. He bet Dallas hadn't seen it at all. So impressed with his new rank he probably just went back to bed when he got the sentries all posted. Man! but wouldn't that be something, to tell Dallas about his girl friend when he got off post! He wondered what Dallas would think about it when he told him, and the curiosity filled him, overpowering even the rain.

He started walking again, counting carefully.

18.

When Corporal Cinamo Dallas finished posting the sentries, and the relieved watch had stumbled wearily into the guardhouse and gone hungry to bed, he woke his supernumerary, told him to get his ass up, then walked out to the guard office and sat down at his desk to sign the Corporal of the Guard log.

It was regulation that the Corporal of the Guard write down everything that happened on his watch and initial it. The Corporal of the Guard was a big responsibility, just as big as the Officer of the Day or the Sergeant of the Guard. And just as abso-fucking-lutely ridiculous, he thought.

He was just completing the log book, half hearing his supernumerary's footsteps coming out of the sleeping guardhouse, when the scream blasted through the night.

Dallas looked up from his logbook quickly, slapped his hand down to his holster feeling the comfort of his pistol. He listened again, straining. The mournful lament raised an octave, chilling, and he knew it was not coming from the guardhouse. It was coming from outside.

He stood up. Without taking his pistol out of his holster he jacked a round into the chamber in one swift sliding action, walked over to the door and on outside and stood under the small portico.

Across the street beside the main gate sentry booth, two

Japanee police in their blue uniforms and white helmet-liners ran from the security police shack toward the main gate. Pfc. Jennings, the main gate sentry, pushed out of his booth, pistol in hand, and stood facing the street, the startled look on his face illuminated by the booth light. Dallas could not see down the street past the guardhouse. He watched the hurried running, then belatedly remembering that he was in the beam of the portico light, he stepped off into the shadow of the rain, his hand waiting on the butt of his pistol. None of the three of them had seen him, and he stood flat against the wall of the guardhouse, wondering if Pfc. Jennings was going to shoot at whatever was out there.

The two Japanee police disappeared. A minute later the yelping stopped, replaced by the excited jabbering of the two Japanee. Dallas watched the security police drag a body back through the main gate, an almost nude body pulled over the muddy rocks. Once her body twisted in the narrow beam of light from the sentry booth and he saw her face, blank, withdrawn; higher than last year's war, he thought, and watched them drag Kayo-san into the security shack.

His face expressionless, except for that cold dark V of a brow, he pulled his pistol out of the holster, ejected the round, let the slide go home on an empty chamber and slammed the pistol back into the holster. She was still sexy, he thought, even with all that goddam mud on her. He wondered if she'd be just as sexy in prison, when they took her off the junk.

He walked through the rain to the sentry booth, glancing once at the security shack that was now silent and forgotten, opened the door and stepped in.

"Hot damn!" Jennings said. "You see that Jo-san? Man, I thought sure's hell a wildcat was roaming around out there."

"She made a lot of noise all right," Dallas said tonelessly. "I thought for a while you were going to shoot her," he grinned.

Jennings looked surprised, his full face flushing. "Aw hell no," he said. "I just pulled my pistol out. I didn't know what it was." He looked back out at the empty Fujioka street. "Who you think she was?"

"I ain't got the slightest fucking idea," Dallas said. "You log it in your book there, Jennings?"

"No, am I supposed to? The orders don't say nothing about it."

"Then don't log it in," Dallas said. "I'll take care of it." He turned to go out, saw the burning cigarette on the floor, and turned back to Jennings. "If you're going to smoke for Chrissakes, smoke; but don't burn up the goddam sentry booth. They's a premium on 'em."

"Oh, sure." Jennings laughed sheepishly. "I forgot it in the excitement."

"Unh-huh." Dallas nodded, left the booth and walked back over to the guardhouse.

Inside, Private Smiley Burnett, a bony red-haired young man with a hawk's beak, was stirring a generous supply of cream in his coffee as Dallas walked in.

"What's all the yellin' about?" Smiley said. "Like to scare the shit outa me."

"Well, you can't be a good supernumerary if you're full of shit." Dallas walked over to his desk and sat down.

"Well, what was it?" Smiley demanded. He pulled one of the horsecock sandwiches out of the cardboard box and began eating voraciously.

"Some Jo-san," Dallas said, picking up his logbook and pencil, "some dolly flipped her wig out in town. The gook police pulled her in."

"Really? How 'bout that?" Smiley Burnett sat down at the little supernumerary's desk and cocked his feet up lazily. "Who was she?" he asked with a mouthful of bologna.

"How the fuck should I know! You think I know every whore in Fujioka?" He lit a cigarette and studied Smiley. "And don't chew so fucking loud, goddamit. You'll wake up the guard."

"Now what the hell?"

"Nothing," Dallas said, "go ahead and eat; eat all the sandwiches if you like. Anyone back there wake up?" he asked, his sudden rage gone, jerking his head toward the sleeping quarters.

"Nothing would wake them bastards," Smiley grinned. "Bunch a fart sack hounds."

"And you ain't?"

"Sure. Next to the Marine Corps, I love sleep."

Dallas leaned back in his chair, stared thoughtfully at his logbook for a moment, then looked back up at Smiley. "You love the Marine Corps, hunh?"

"Haw."

"I guess you love niggers, too," Dallas jeered. "I bet you love just about everything, eh Smiley?" He took a savage drag on his cigarette. "You feel sorry for that Jo-san out there? That went off her nut?"

Smiley analyzed the question with his sandwich. "Yeah, I guess so."

"That's what I figured," Dallas said. "You love everyone in the world; and feel sorry for them. You feel so sorry for people, whyn't you run up to Middle Camp and fight with the niggers yestiday? Or maybe you rather go out and carry the flag for the gooks?"

"Just because I feel sorry for them," Smiley said, "don't mean I have to like them." He finished off his sandwich, got up and walked back over to the cardboard box and got another sandwich, went back to his little desk and sat down, all the while watched by Dallas.

"Well, I don't," he said when Smiley had sat down. "I don't feel sorry for no-fucking-body, see? I ain't a twentieth-century man." He glared at Smiley, the rage working in him again, boiling, not caring to hold it down. "I hate niggers, Jews, Catholics, Protestants and queers. I just soon kill 'em all. I'm unnormal, see? I'm prejudiced. I hate all the downtrodden races of humanity and don't suffer for them a bit. You suffer like hell, Smiley, but you're from Ohio."

Smiley's freckled face reddened. "Now that ain't true, necessarily."

"As long's you're feeling so sad over the human condition," Dallas said, "why the hell don't you feel sorry for yourself? No one else feels sorry for you. No one at all feels sorry for the gentiles or the poor white trash—or the Arabs, take the Arabs. Who feels sorry for the Arabs?" he grinned, watching Smiley stop chewing.

"What'd say?" Smiley demanded. "I don't give a shit about any of that. Whyn't you get off my back?"

"You know who I feel sorry for? I feel sorry for me. I'm an offspring of the Trail of Tears quite a few generations back. I feel sorry as hell for me. I could cry over me," he said mawkishly. "Only I wouldn't cry and I don't ask anyone to feel sorry for me and I sure as hell don't feel sorry for anyone else. You phony sonofabitch," he said bitterly, "go ahead and feel sorry for all the world, while you get stabbed in the back. You fucking fool." He stood up from his desk, glaring down at Smiley who gaped back, walked

312

over to him and jerked the sandwich out of his hand as Smiley recoiled.

Dallas took a large bite and handed it back and grinned. "Lousy sandwiches, ain't they?" he said, turned and walked back to his desk. "Now goddamit quit making so much noise. You're my supernumerary and you do as I say. Just be quiet. I don't want the guard woke. How come you're always preaching, Smiley?" he said woodenly. Smiley started to say something, but Dallas waved him quiet. "You tell anyone what I said tonight, I'll have Jesus Queecho bust your neck, hear? Now shut up and leave me alone."

Dallas watched a thin grin spread Smiley's freckles around a bit. An ungenuine grin, not even a grin at all, more like a smirk, he thought. Smiley never smiled, he thought curiously, swiveling around in his chair.

It had been a long time since he'd even thought about the Trail of Tears, the old inherited story from his people; half of his people, he corrected, but nevertheless, his inheritance. The only fucking one he had. But it was a good one. He remembered how he had been told of Andy Jackson, who all the Cherokees thought was their friend, their blood brother, whom they all trusted and who knifed them in the back. The bastard. And then John Ross who tried to make white people out of all of them. A great inheritance that—all of it.

That was about all he remembered from the stories his people had passed down to him. That and what they endured on the Trail of Tears: starving, humiliated, driven and harried into the Cookson Hills in Oklahoma where once again everything was taken from them. Yes sir, a great inheritance. And he hadn't felt sorry for any one of them then, when he heard the stories, and he didn't feel sorry for them now. Maybe Smiley there would feel sorry for the Cherokees too?

And the inheritance led to what? He asked himself staring at the box of sandwiches in the breathing silence of the guard office. The inheritance led to nothing, he answered himself. It was hard to concentrate on any of that at all. It had happened so long ago.

Yet it seemed that there were only four things, four events in his life that were important to him. And none of them were inherited. They were all self-made. Partly anyway.

The first factual event that was still as bright in his memory as the morning's guard mount was when his old man cut his braids off. He was in the first grade, just started school. All his classmates made fun of him because he wore braids. He fought them all, he remembered, and beat most of them, and when he got home his old man pulled out his pocket knife, stuck his head between his legs and cut the braids off. That was the first one.

The second was when he enlisted at sixteen. He had enlisted straight out of the county jail where he was serving six months for bootlegging, running liquor in from Arkansas. The marine recruiting sergeant had offered him the way out from jail: enlist. It was only afterwards, when he was on his way to San Diego, that he found out the juvenile judge had split the five bucks the recruiting sergeant got for a new man: two and a half bucks apiece for one warm quarter Indian body. And they got most of them out of the jails. Between the judge and the recruiting sergeant, he thought, they probably made thirty bucks a month. That was the second important event, he decided.

And the third came in Hawaii on Hotel Street where he beat a flip to death. He had come walking down toward the end of Hotel Street, him and a Scotch-Irishman named Lewis, when the flip cat gang advanced on them and one pulled a knife. He had knocked the knife out of the flip's hand, held him against the wall of the Hula Whorehouse and beat him till his eyes and ears and nose and face were unrecognizable while Lewis tried to pull him off. None of the other flip cats tried to help their buddy. The Marine Corps gave him a carton of cigarettes and a transfer, and apologized to the authorities in Honolulu but said it was justifiable because the flip had pulled a knife. No, he won't come back to Wahoo any more. That went along with the transfer. If the Crotch ever stationed a large outfit in Hawaii again, he sure as hell wouldn't be there.

No, you won't go back to Wahoo any more. And that was the third important event in his life.

The fourth event came in Korea, when he went over with the Brigade, and that time it came at Frozen Chosen. It was strange he didn't think of the Pusan Perimeter or even the Inchon Landing as important. Just the Frozen Chosen, because it was up there that he had found out exactly what he was, and there was no retreating. It was still as fresh in his memory as his first piece of ass, only he had been hot with his first piece of ass; up to the Chosen he had been cold, a snow-chilled cold with all the C-rations frozen, except for an occasional small fire that failed in thawing them without burning their hands . . .

. . . Sometimes the troops were not aware that they were walking, sometimes they stumbled, but kept moving on down south to Hamhung, fighting all the way, carrying the dead and the wounded and everything that could be carried, destroying that which could not be carried, all the while those bugles blowing up with the cold night wind of the Chinese coming down from the other side, coming in hordes and never-decreasing numbers, and you asked yourself where everyone was where is the Army, where are our flanks, why are we so suddenly all alone out here?

Why hadn't anyone listened to us when we said the Chinese were in the war? We were the first ones to catch them, knew they were in it, why hadn't anyone believed it? Did they want us killed? No one listened. No one ever listened—and the motherfucking Army, someone said, where the hell are they?

Dallas huddled with his squad below a ridge, a fine point so that when he stuck his head up he could look over the ridge and see the other ridges to the north for perhaps five thousand yards growing hazy and dark with snow now at sunset, and there had been no sun all day. And down on the road below him winding through the valley was the tail end of the Outfit going to Hamhung. He leaned against the frozen earth watching it move out, thinking they would hold this position as long as they could, then bug out and rejoin the Outfit again farther south if they could make it without getting killed. He watched it disappear behind the last curve, the feet of dead men sticking out from under the canvas tops of the trucks; then he turned back to the squad and looked at their faces in the trench that was not a trench at all because you simply could not dig in this cold. All faces of strangers, men he did not know—what company were they actually from? what were they?—cooks, clerks, truck drivers, could be anything; anyone who could fight was being used now and there were so damn few of them. The only similarity in their faces at all was that dumb frozen apathy, all of them living only from hand to rifle, instinct.

But now to sleep, he thought, just for a while. It was his turn to sleep now that another man who had joined them that morning was on watch. Just to try and sleep for a little while, if it wasn't so cold. Then he would get up and massage his feet, keep his blood running, and tomorrow, hellyea, man, tomorrow, they would get back to the Outfit. How far were they from Hamhung? No one knew. No one knew a damn thing.

Sleep came in a fit, all dreams, hazy and clear, about everything, with a shadow of death in all of the dreams, an Indian chant, was this the Trail of Tears? Was Chosen the Trail of Tears? a voice kept repeating through his sleep. Was this what was meant by that? No difference at all. Far off he heard a bugle, then another, then more, hundreds of them. It was bad, now that he dreamed of them too. Then he realized that he was awake.

He jerked his head around quick and looked through the darkness down the trench to his squad. They hadn't heard anything. No one moved. He sat up, holding his rifle, and crawled on his knees down by the men as they slept on, while the bugle screamed in challenge from the north. Where the fuck was that new man?

He found him at the end, asleep, sleeping peacefully, a sort of smile on his face. The bugles were getting closer.

"You motherfucker," Dallas muttered in a hoarse voice, surprised at the sound. "I'll kill you."

The man did not wake up.

Dallas turned and hustled back along the squad, seven men, waking them, most of them coming to anyway with the sound of bugles. What is it? Again! Yeah. Get up. Come on. Get up. I thought they's another squad in front of us. Nah, we're the point. We got some people on our flanks. Come on. They'll be here any minute.

When he'd finished waking them all, they looked over the ridge but could see nothing, just hear the cry of the bugles like a baby's tears. Then the flares went up, light. Then the firing started, disorganized. So much fire in front of them, everything in front of them. Them with three rifles, two BAR's, two machine guns, every one was an ammo humper.

I'll kill him, Dallas thought, I'll kill him. Everyone started firing. Get in a good volley before we bug out, give a hell of a lot, then let's move. The man, the sentry for them, was now fully awake, jumping around nervously.

"You went to sleep," Dallas said.

"Ahhhhhh!" the man half cried, half groaned, half yelled. "No, man: I'm tired. Where they at?"

"In front of you," Dallas said, pulling his .45 out of his canvas overcoat. "Right here."

The man looked at him for just a second, startled, then Dallas pulled the trigger and the man heaved forward, rolling down the hill for five yards and coming to a stop.

Let's go! Move goddamit! Down the ridge! Don't stay on the road, skirt it! They're coming up behind us! Nem' mind. Just move!

Night was their friend, night comforted them, it came to their rescue and led them along by their tired grimy hands, and then night left them, ruthlessly, and the day came and they could see the Outfit and way over the tops of the last ridges they could see the winter ocean and Hamhung . . .

. . . Dallas turned back in his chair and picked up his pencil again, pulling the logbook in front of him as Smiley Burnett's head bobbed sleepily across from him.

He logged in the incident about Kayo-san being picked up by the Security Police and the slight melee at the main gate. Then he closed the logbook and slid it away from him. He wondered who they'd get to replace her at the Blue Moon?

Well, to hell with it. But there were only those four events that he remembered so clearly. All of them, he knew, were the reasons for his volunteering for Japan a second time, for taking this backassward stand he took. Yet it was always someone like that Bohane who came out with the medals, big shit, and believed it.

At four o'clock in the morning, when the four-to-eight had been posted by Corporal Kindred of the third squad, Dallas went back into the sleeping quarters and lay down on his bunk as the relieved watch began filing in, cursing tiredly, taking off their wet clothes and climbing into their bunks.

He watched Giff make his way over, walking sluggishly, smoking a cigarette.

"Dallas?" he called. "Goddamit, where are you? Can't see a fucking thing in this dark."

"If you take another step," Dallas said, "you'll step on my balls."

Giff laughed and sat down, an urgency in his action. "Know what I seen tonight?" He leaned his rifle against the wall and slipped out of his raincoat.

317

"Sure," Dallas said, thinking *Here it comes*, remembering the fifty bucks he'd lost on the Popcorn bet and remembering too how she'd looked lying on the *tatami* the other morning when he woke Giff up. "I know. Kayo-san flipped and went running down the street bare-ass naked. And they hauled her off to jail."

"Oh," Giff said. "You seen it, hunh? Well, you'll have to start living from hand to prick again."

"When that day comes," Dallas said with a grin, "I'll be dead."

"We'll all be dead." Giff finished undressing and slipped under his GI blanket on the bunk across from Dallas. "Know what? In four hours walking that fence post I took 33,648 steps. You wouldn't believe it, would you?"

"Killer," Dallas said, "I'd believe anything you said. If you say it's so, it's so."

"How about knocking off the shit?" someone said from the obscurity of one of the bunks.

"The only shit I'll knock off is you," Giff said, "if you open your mouth again. One of the privileges of being a rear rank private," he grinned at Dallas. "I can dust off anyone I want."

"But you can't punch a corporal," Dallas told him. "I'd run you up for hittin' an NCO."

"Try me," Giff said. "You'll be picking your ass up with both hands."

"I'm so scared now I can't go to sleep."

"Quit shaking in your boots. I wouldn't hurt you."

"Thanks, buddy," Dallas said. "Now I feel one hundred per-fucking-cent better."

19.

They came off guard at eight-thirty that morning under a sodden October sky, weapons rusted, uniforms wrinkled, and all of them feeling miserably wet and cold, marching in a shambling semblance of order back to Hog Company barracks to prepare for late chow, then to clean their rifles and gear for the next day's guard.

Moving into the dry warmth of the squadbay, yelling and chiding like a platoon of men gone wild, they tossed their rifles on their bunks and lit up dry cigarettes. They were still sitting around loafing waiting for chow when King Solomon swished into the squadbay and said very succinctly that Emil Kizer, Captain Emil Kizer, wanted to see Stack Renshaw immediately.

Stack shrugged, ain't done no wrong his face said, and walked out with Solomon.

He was not back by the time Giff and Dallas went to chow with the rest of the platoon, but when they came back, bellies filled with watery scrambled eggs and dry old toast, Stack was sitting on his bunk crying disconsolately with furious indignation.

"What the hell's the matter?" Giff tossed his mess gear on his bunk. "Your best dog die?"

"I've been fucked," Stack said, his voice congested. "Framed! They got me by the balls!"

Cinamo Dallas climbed up on his bunk, lay on his belly and stared down at Stack. "How so?"

"I've got to get married!"

"Hunh?" Giff said, sitting down. A small crowd had started to gather around Stack as the troops came back from chow. "Get married? Aw, man; come on now. What's the matter?"

"Goddamit," Stack cried. "I just tole you. I have to get married. I got to go Stateside and get married. To a girl I don't know."

Gradually Giff managed to coax the story from the outraged Stack. It appeared that Stack had enjoyed a short affair, just a couple of hours, with a girl in Oceanside, California, just before the Divvy left for Japan. It also appeared, Stack fumed, that the girl was pregnant! He cursed himself savagely for ever having given her his real name. So she had told the Red Cross about it; the Red Cross had contacted the Crotch and nailed him. And now they had orders to send him back on emergency leave to get married! What was he going to do?

"Well"—Giff paused—"Jesus, I dunno, Stack. You could go over the hill, I guess."

"Oh sure," Stack nodded, "that's dandy advice. Go over the hill. You're really helpful."

"How you know it's your kid?" Dallas asked quietly from his bunk.

"I don't! How could I? Oh shit, they got me!"

"Maybe when you get back there you can prove it ain't yours, Stack," Giff said helpfully. "Get a blood test on it, you know what I mean?"

"In California I don't stand a chance. That's rich—prove I ain't the father. Hah! They'd have me on a rape charge."

"It might not be so bad," Dallas said cheerfully. "Look at it this way. You get married then get a divorce, and you still get a couple weeks' leave in the States."

"It's damn easy," Stack said, "for you to talk about it. Ain't you gettin' married. It's me! And I don't even know who she is or what she's like!" He stared at their faces for sympathy.

"I think Dallas got the best idea," Giff said. "Marry her and then get divorced. You might have a good time in the States."

"I don't wanna go Stateside!" Stack protested. "I wanna stay here." He banged his fist on the iron of the bunk. "And I don't wanna get married to nobody at all. Oh shit! They'll take all my money, all of it. Even if I get divorce."

"Take it anyway," Dallas suggested. "I was you that's what I'd do; marry her and get a divorce. Hell with the money."

"When you got to go, Stack?" Giff asked.

"Right now. In couple a hours. They're going to fly me back."

"You got enough shekels?" Giff had never seen the bulbous-nosed Hoosier so upset; it was like looking at a different person.

Furiously, Stack pulled his pockets out clean. "Broke. Fat ass broke! But you know what?" he said bitterly. "The Red Cross going to pay my way. Ain't that helpful? You know what happens then? They take all my paydays with interest. I'm broke for the rest of my life."

"We get in this war coming up," Giff said, "you'll get an extra forty-five bucks a month; that'll help some." There was a chorus of agreeing grunts from the peanut gallery around them.

"Yeah," Stack said, disgruntled. "But we ain't in it yet. What if we get in it while I'm gone?"

Giff looked at Stack, then at Dallas, then at the gallery

who were all shaking their heads solemnly. He shrugged. "Can't you get the Kizer to help you out?"

"He's the one sent me!" Stack said. "Him and that bastard, that no-good syphilitic bastard Top Condrum. They say I got to do it on 'count of honor. Give a black name to the Crotch if I didn't! Oh, that miserable bastardly Top Condrum."

"He's here to he'p you," Dallas said with a grin.

"Fuck you," Stack said. No one laughed.

"I can give you a couple bucks, Stack," Giff offered. "So you won't have to borrow so much from the Red Cross. They'll cheat you."

"You ain't just a turd-birdin'," Dallas said. "Them bastards made us pay two-bits for coffee and doughnuts Christmas in Korea. The Red Cross," he snorted disgustedly. "Wouldn't wipe my ass on 'em."

Stack stood up wearily and sighed. "Well, I've had it. That's all. I got to start packing. Married," he said far off. "But married!"

Giff and Dallas helped Stack pack, gave him ten bucks apiece which Stack said was a waste of money; he'd only stay drunk on it all of the time—but married!—he couldn't stomach it. The rest of the platoon, even the Negro faction, chipped in some loose change, the race war momentarily forgotten under this new tragedy that was closer to home and therefore deserved precedent.

Tears streaming down his face, cursing the fates bitterly, giving his word he would be back before they went to war, he left the barracks with his seabag on his shoulder to go Stateside and get married.

Somehow Giff could not help but feel that that was merely one of those fragments of the grenade. It had obviously gone off and the first bits of shrapnel were beginning to hit. And for it to happen to Stack of all people!

Old Poke Turner would probably get a kick out it, he thought suddenly, when he got out of the brig and heard all about it. Poke and Guppy Talagua both would be getting out in a couple days. But they didn't seem real any more. They had ceased to exist the moment they had left. Like Stack just now. Almost like in combat—it wasn't hard to believe they were dead.

It rained the rest of the day and night and on into the next day and night, unceasing, challenging; and the second platoon went grumbling back on guard duty.

Wednesday night at twelve o'clock after Dallas had posted him, Giff bulled his way along the path by the fence under the torrent of rain, wondering how he would kill this four hours. It was turning into a great life. No sense counting steps again; he had that down tight. Maybe he could count minutes? See how long it took him to walk down to the motor pool and back to the guardhouse? A sweet-tasting life. He wondered if the old crew in Korea was having just as much fun.

He stopped halfway down the path and just for the hell of it, stood in the rain getting soaked, looking out at the town across from him. It was dark and dismal. For the last three nights he had not seen it lively. Only dark. Dim outlines against a rainy black sky.

Yet somewhere behind those dark faces small lights burned in cozy rooms, and almond-eyed girls lay naked on *tatamis* with jack-knifed thighs and swollen breasts. And he was here inside the fence that was built to keep people in.

Was he going bamboo?

No, he wasn't going bamboo. He knew what he had to do. He had pulled the pin on that hand grenade himself. And it was exploding. He wasn't going out just for a piece of ass. He was going out for himself. To get rid of himself. He had tried it before, and the Silver Star had always come back into the picture, forcing him out and back into himself. Maybe this time, if he went all the way, the Silver Star couldn't help him.

He found a small hole down by the motor pool and crawled through, breathing the free wet rainy air of the Outside. He wouldn't go down to the Blue Moon. No, hit Skivvie Lane, head down to old Rotten Crotch Mary's, pick up a bottle or two of Akadama. If he was lucky, and she wasn't shacked up tonight, he might even get a short time off Cherry-san, the thin girl old Half-Slick Willy had brought in for him during the false monsoon. She was a hot one, a regular fireball who'd play the game just the way you wanted.

Staggering back along the road an hour and a half later, Giff lifted his face to the rain and howled at it drunkenly, a full bottle of Akadama in his hand and two empties in his belly. Got to keep quiet, he admonished himself. Play it cool like in the motor pool. Heh heh, but at ol' Cherry-san was one wild one. Yup. He raised his face up again nearing the hole in the fence, his helmet-liner falling to the ground, and howled like a coyote at the black watery night.

"Halt! Who goes there!" a challenging voice came from the other side of the fence. Giff heard some footsteps behind the voice come sloshing through the mud. A hazy outline stopped just inside the fence facing him. Giff saw the rifle in his hand.

"Better not shoot," he said thickly. "I got a rifle too. I'll shoot back."

"Who the hell is it?" The voice came through again.

Through the bleariness Giff recognized the voice that time: Pfc. Simmons, a rifleman in Corporal Walsh's squad. "Jesse James, you sonfabitch. And I'm gonna rob the South Campo bank."

"Bohane?" Simmons questioned. "That you, Bohane?"

Giff chuckled and walked on over to the fence. "Fooled you, did I? Bet you thought I was Jesse James, hunh?"

"What're you doing off post, man?" Simmons said fatuously. "What if the OD comes around?"

"Offer him a drink. You want a drink?"

"No," Simmons shook his head. "You better get in here though."

"I'll get in there," Giff said slyly. "Don't you think I won't. Where's at ol' hole I came through?" He staggered down along the fence, hunting for his hole. It was around there somewhere couldn't go anywhere. Ahah! there she be.

He bowed his head and crawled on through, snagging his raincoat and tearing it, helmet-liner forgotten in the street, rain washing down over his head. He walked triumphantly back up to Simmons. "You want nuther rifle?"

"Ah, come on now, Bohane. You should ought to go back on post. Maybe go up the guardhouse see'f Dallas'll replace you."

"I'm irreplaceable," Giff countered thickly, staring through the rain at Simmons. "Ain't nobody gonna replace Bohane. You dumb sonfabitch of a Phildelphia Easterner."

"Ah horseshit," Simmons said. "I don't care what you do. Only you better not let the OD catch you."

"Motherfuck the OD. Motherfuck a whole bunch of OD's. Fuck the sar'nt of the guard, too. Fuck 'em all, the long the short and the tall, and especially motherfuck you, Simmons, you old fuddy-duddy duck." He laughed up-

323

roariously, took a drink of his Akadama wine with a rain chaser running down his chin. "Know what?"

"No. What?"

"I'm goin' back the barrix an' sleep. I don't have to guard this fence. It don't need guardin'. You see anythin' round here needs guardin'?" he demanded.

"You."

"You fuckin'-A whoopee John!" Giff said. "But I'm capable of guarding myself. And I don't need a rifle. See? I ain't got a rifle. Tossed it away somewhere. I quit. I quit before they fire me."

"You'll go to jail."

"Can't go to jail," Giff informed him. "I quit. If I quit they can't send me to jail." He turned and walked down the road toward the barracks, drinking from the bottle. Then he stopped and looked back through the wall of rain.

"Simmons!"

"What? Simmons' voice carried faintly down from the fence.

"You better quit too," Giff said with a deep thick conviction in his voice. "Better quit before that fuckin' grenade goes off. Blow us all up. That ol' grenade get us all."

There was no reply from up by the fence.

To hell with it then, Giff thought. He walked on leaving Simmons, his rifle and helmet-liner behind him. Nobody listens, hell with them. Old boy was right when he said a prophet was without honor in his own camp. Damn rights. Ain't none of them going to listen. Ain't none of them can see the grenade. The blind bastards.

He wagged his head at the rain; a guy could drown out here; thing to do was get to barrix and sleep.

Goddam but this road was muddy. Well, how about walking on the boardwalk. Too late for that; already at the barrix.

Indecisively, he stood in the center of the street between H Company's Barracks and the Officer BOQ, while the rain pounded down around him.

A light burned in the head in the middle of the barracks. Fine. That was good. He'd just traipse on in there, finish his wine and go to bed.

He walked stealthily around the barracks to the side door so as not to disturb the people in the squadbays. Good people. All of them real good people. Fine folks. Stout fellows!

324

He opened the side door and stepped in out of the rain and walked into the head where the firewatch, a short thick Italian named Tasnaddi, sat leaning against the deep sink.

"Hello, wop!"

Tasnaddi's swarthy face broke into a sneering grin. "Thought you were on guard."

"I quit," Giff said unequivocally. "There wasn't one fuckin' thing to guard, see? So I quit. Want a drink?"

"Sure," Tasnaddi said. "But keep your voice down. Don't want the staff up here."

"Motherfuck the staff." Giff handed him the bottle and leaned against the row of washbasins grinning at him. "You silly Eye-talian shithead," he said. "What the hell you doin' on firewatch. Watchin' fires?"

"Earning my keep," Tasnaddi said.

"What'f you get run up?" Giff said, taking the bottle back. "For drinking on post. What'f I get real chicken shit and run you up, put you on report?"

Tasnaddi laughed awkwardly.

Giff straightened up from the washbasins. "You know any songs in Eye-tie?"

"No."

"Didn't think you did," Giff said. "I know some songs in Irish and I ain't full Irish. And you don't know any songs in Eye-tie—and you're a full blood guinee." He took another drink and wiped the back of his mouth. "I know some songs in Eye-tie. Know the one about Columbus? *Ohhh, there once was a Dago from old Eyetalie who roamed in every street and pissed in every alley.* And you don't know any Eye-tie songs. You don't show me much, dago."

"Better take it easy, Bohane," Tasnaddi said.

Giff nodded vaguely. "Sure, I'll take it easy." He motioned at the squat Italian with his finger. "Come here. I want to show you something."

With awkward apprehension Tasnaddi stepped in closer and Giff let one go from down around his knees, hitting Tasnaddi full on the jaw sending him spiraling back crazily, booming off against the deep sink and falling to the floor.

"Take it easy, hunh!" Giff sneered at the fallen figure. "I'll show you how easy I'll take it, by God."

Savagely he turned on the mirrors over the washbasins. They glimmered his reflection back at him. He grasped one with his hands and pulled it free, nuts and bolts and plaster

325

clattering on the floor, raised it above his head and threw it against the commodes, the mirror crashing in a loud explosion.

Tasnaddi was getting to his feet but Giff did not see him. Searching desperately, he walked over to the row of commodes and began tearing the wooden butt-supporters off, bellowing like a wounded fear-crazed animal. Show them, by God! The Bastards! All them!

Then the arms grabbed him from behind, pinioning him. Instinctively, he swiveled his hip and slapped his hand back in a judo chop hitting Tasnaddi's balls. The thick Italian screamed, released his grip, and Giff, his hip still extended on an angle, reached around with his other hand and pulled the firewatch over, flipping him on his back. Tasnaddi yelled as he skidded across the broken glass on his ass.

"Sneak up on me, will you!" Giff bawled. Got to get out of here fast! he told himself. Go down Bamboo Alley or someplace. Get away from enemies. No man's land. But as he turned to the door he saw swimming bodies of men in skivvie drawers staring at him curiously.

"Good people!" he shouted, and ran for them, diving into the midst of them, his fists flailing wildly.

Immediately he was aware of fists and feet pummeling him (some heathen sonfabitch had his arms pinned again) —and voices, not making sense, loud soft incoherent boomed all around him. Then he seemed to sink way down into the cement of the head floor and more cement was poured over him until there was only smothering darkness.

He woke quickly and started to rise but could not move his arms. Where the hell was he? What the hell they have him in?

The guardhouse. He knew the single wood-paneled cell of the guardhouse. But why the strait jacket?

Struggling, he began to wiggle out of it. Those bastards sure did a lousy job. Damn, he was sore.

A face bobbed up at the little square screen window in the solid door. Giff glared back at it.

"Sarjint of the Guard!" the face's voice hollered excitedly. "Sarjint of the Guard! He's gettin' out the strait jacket!"

Let him yell, Giff thought. I'll bust his neck for fair soon's

326

I get out of this, he told himself, just as the thick door opened and Sergeant Jesus Queecho moved in.

Giff did not have time to duck, to even think, or grin or anything. Queecho's hand shot out in a judo chop at the throat and Giff went toppling backwards and down and out, lying motionless on the floor.

When he woke again he did not know what time it was. It was only very dark in the cell and the air was cool around the damp floor. His head pounded behind his eyes and he was no longer in the strait jacket. It was still raining heavily outside and the water ran past the single high barred window like a lazy waterfall, black with the night.

Panic and fright fired through him in sharp bursts. He felt completely cognizant and very clear-minded, except for the incessant throbbing. Then it rushed back on him, the night with its warped images and leering faces, all coming so fast following on the heels of everything: going through the fence, Rotten Crotch Mary and Cherry-san, the Akadama, Simmons, Tasnaddi, the strait jacket, Jesus Queecho.

He stood up and stepped over to the solid door and peeked out on an angle through the small screened window. Mute voices came to him from the guard office past the sleeping quarters where men huddled in blankets sleeping unperturbed.

He felt like screaming—feeling suddenly very alone, unhuman with none of his own race around him—just wanting to get someone back here to talk, to prove he could talk, to laugh and joke.

After a moment he turned back to the darkness of the damp cell, skittishly weak. The floor was very cold and he moved his hands around hunting for the strait jacket. Finding it, he pulled it over him for warmth.

This was it: the *coup de grâce*. They probably got so many charges on me I look like a pincushion. Well, he had always known he would do it. Cinch it up tight.

Funny, wasn't it, that he had known it? And so long ago too, and even then he did not want to stop it, did not want to interfere. It was so funny he almost felt like vomiting. It only happened after you were gut-wounded by an exploded grenade.

Wrapping the night around him like a protective shroud, hoping to stave off that first gray of morning that would bring all the answers he did not want to hear—yet had to hear! Wanted to talk with someone, joke about it, and at the same time wanted to be alone and hold off the devastation of the day.

Sleepily, he curled in the strait jacket. He hoped they would not waste any time in court-martialing him. That was what was bad: the waiting.

In how many places had he waited in the dusk of experience with his lonely body floating free, head on the chopper's block, waiting for the double-edged ax blade to come hurtling down?

20.

He waited till the first dirty streaks of morning imprisoned the watery sky outside the high barred window. Waiting was to him like a Jo-san who opens her thighs to fate, knowing only the more fickle will fate become; like a man listening to the hand-clapping song of the primeval death chant that does not help circumvent the long dark night of the soul. And no voices, no physical presence, could suspend the waiting for him, because he no longer knew what it was he waited for at all.

It was an interminable time and even when the day came the waiting moved on with him.

Not since Christ made corporal had they rushed a man to jail so fast, Giff pondered heavily after noon chow of that same day of waiting, as he headed north to the Middle Camp brig in the back seat of the jeep. It had taken all of that morning to arrange his confinement papers, and he had not yet been court-martialed.

Sitting in the back of the jeep holding his old bulkily packed laundry bag on his knees, he stared straight ahead between the two men sitting in front at the dirty afternoon, rain-streaked under a dismal black sky.

The driver, a Pfc from South Camp motor pool with a hook nose and beady eyes, had kept up a chattering questionnaire ever since they'd pulled out of the rear gate. But

Giff did not listen or deign to answer, only grunted non-committally and glanced at the back of the other man, his chaser, Corporal Cinamo Dallas. Dallas was not animated to talk either; in fact he appeared consummately bored with it all.

Giff felt a dark reluctance in him for what he'd find in the brig. Also, mingled with it, an intense curiosity. Through slop chute and barracks talk where duty stations, brigs, and legends were exchanged over cans of beer, he knew it would not be a picnic. Yet he felt, obscurely, that he had set the table under the pines and spilled the sugar for the ants.

Somehow he had known it would come like this: him in the back seat of a jeep riding up to the brig with an unknown and unpredetermined amount of time before him. A month? Two months? How long? And he hadn't even been court-martialed yet!

Gradually, as the rain sliced past the windshield of the jeep and Giff listened to the incessant chatter of the driver, it made itself felt upon him, the cycle of events that had led up to it . . .

. . . At eight o'clock that morning, while he waited unconsolably in the South Camp guardhouse, they'd come for him—Hugh Thorton and Koko Hobbs—and taken him under a sort of jovial rancorous arrest back to the company barracks. Thorton, especially, was jovial. Hobbs was more or less filling in time.

"Out of the hills of South Korea comes Red-eye Bohane," Thorton jeered as they escorted him out of the guard office. "Bohane rides again!"

Giff tried to mask all of it with a silent smirk and his characteristic cockiness. He remained sheepishly silent all the way to the company office where a pleased Top Condrum waited for him.

"I'm here to he'p you," Top Landrum said, his dead eyes cold, the red-veined nose under the feathery brows flaring. "You better give your soul to God, because your ass belongs to me."

Giff did not answer, did not feel like answering, but kept trying to mask his face with the indifference. He walked over and sat down by Quiller Carpenter, who offered him a cigarette with a grin and said, "What'd you think of them onions, champ?"

Grinning back and smoking a little nervously, Giff

watched Thorton and Koko Hobbs fill their coffee cups at the staff coffee mess by King Solomon's desk as they waited for the Kizer.

When Emil Kizer strode massively into the office five minutes later, it was furiously obvious that he knew all about it. The large bulletheaded man did not speak to Giff, did not bother to return his lame "good morning, sir." He called Thorton and Hobbs and Top Landrum into his office and slammed the door vehemently.

"Man, you had a fuckin' ball last night," Quiller Carpenter grinned, red-eyed and frazzled-looking from his own night on the town.

Giff studied him over his cigarette. "Yeah, and I'm about to pay for it now. How many charges they got on me?"

"Enough to make the Kizer go back to the BOQ and have three stiff shots of whiskey," Quiller said amiably. "I don't need to tell you he's pissed off. Highly."

"You sure don't," Giff said. "Looks like I'm going to jail same day two my buddies get out."

Quiller swiveled around in his chair and checked his TO board on the wall. "Yep. That's right. Turner and Talagua gettin' out this morning. That's all right then." He turned back and grinned. "Long's we keep sendin' a man from the company up there we get quite a showing. Got to have representatives."

A few minutes later the Kizer's door opened and the four men came out: Thorton grinning without humor; Top Landrum dead-faced; Koko Hobbs immaculate and handsome; and Emil Kizer florid with unconcealed anger.

Slapping his swagger stick against his thigh, he stormed out of the office, this time glancing furiously down at Giff, almost stopping, then fuming out, banging the window-door shut behind him.

"Okay," Top Landrum said happily. "You're going to jail, boy. Let's get these papers signed."

Giff walked over and signed the papers quietly.

"We'll hold him over at the barracks till you get a chaser," Thorton said, curling his mustache. "He won't be going anywhere till afternoon. It'll take him that long to check his rifle and gear in."

Flanked by Thorton and Hobbs he walked to the barracks where he was met with the open-faced admiration of notoriety that is accorded those who have stepped outside the marine-made laws.

330

Cockily, he tossed grins back at the men, swaggering a little as he walked down the aisle between the bunks to the second platoon squadbay.

"On back to the staff quarters," Thorton said. "You too, Hobbs." He led the way down through the third platoon squadbay on the other side of the head, where Giff was met again with the conquering hero's return. It made him feel good, knowing none of them held anything against him. Except perhaps Tasnaddi.

Excluding Itchie, the houseboy, the staff quarters were devoid of personality. They walked back to the poker table while Giff looked around curiously at this place he'd never been in, feeling like a whore in church and shaking like one too. But that was the wine, he told himself.

"How long you think you'll get?" Thorton said, straddling a chair by the table.

"Depends on the court I get; I get a Summary," Giff said, "be thirty days I'll get. That's all they can give me."

"A Summary!" Koko Hobbs curled his lips, not really a sneer, or scorn. "You'll be lucky you don't get a General. And if they was anything higher than that you'd win the pot."

Giff shrugged, still standing.

"Don't get your hopes up," Thorton said, inspecting his fingernails. "Itchie! Get on over the PX and buy me some doughnuts."

The small Japanee houseboy slipped into his raincoat and shambled out of the quarters.

"Okay, here," Thorton said. "Sit down." He kicked a chair back with his foot and Giff sat down watching him cautiously. "I don't have to tell you that you've just about managed to fuck up my platoon royally."

"According to how you look at it." Giff looked up at Koko Hobbs and then back to Thorton.

"The way I look at it," Thorton said measuredly, "is that you've done just that. But I expected it. I knew you would. Now, I'm going to give you a chance to redeem yourself."

"I don't care to redeem a motherfucking thing," Giff countered. "I'll take what I got coming."

"I wish I was tough," Thorton said lazily. "Well anyway, I'll tell you what you're facing. With what's on your record since you been in Japan you'll get the load: six six and a kick—a Bad Conduct Discharge or a Dishonorable. BCD if you're lucky and get a Special court. The way things are wired right now, you'll probably be getting a General. You didn't make any friends in the higher echelons."

Giff licked his lips probingly and lit a cigarette. "I still got my ace in the hole," he said. "They ain't about to give me a kick. I won't get drummed out."

"No," Koko Hobbs said. "They won't use a drum on you. More'n likely be a firin' squad."

"You got one chance," Thorton said, and Giff was surprised to find benevolence in the mustachioed man's eyes. "You play it like I say and you won't have any trouble."

Giff laughed. "What do I got to do? Become a chaplain?"

"Take a psycho," Thorton said levelly. "Play nuts and you'll ace out of it."

Again Giff laughed. "That's one big chance, ain't it? You want me to take a psycho and where will it leave me? On the Outside, a nut who couldn't get a job even being sane."

"Okay," Thorton stood up. "It's your ass. I'm only telling you how to keep from getting a kick. Otherwise you've had it."

"How do you know I'm gettin' a kick?" Giff asked, standing too, and facing him. "I ain't even been awarded a court yet."

"I'm not wasting my time," Thorton said. "I wouldn't shit you. You don't believe me, okay. Do what you want. But do me one favor. When you get it don't blame anyone but yourself. And remember one other thing: I ain't helping you any by giving you this advice, see? I'm only looking out for myself. Either way—the psycho or the kick—you'll be outa the company and out of my platoon." He twisted his mustache deftly with both hands. "I haven't lost anything."

"Then don't bother yourself about it," Giff said stolidly. "I don't care to have people worrying over me. When people worry over you they only cause you trouble. I always figured it's a backhanded way of worrying over themselves."

"Well, well," Thorton said. "A philosopher. A barracks room philosopher. Okay, let's get on up front. The sooner I get you out of here the sooner I can reshape my platoon."

"The sooner Hobbs can do it, you mean," Giff corrected. He had just about had a bellyful of the sonfabitching dogooder. But Thorton only grinned broadly, calm and contained, and the three walked on out.

It did not come as a surprise to Giff when Thorton put Dallas on as his chaser. In a way he had half expected it, that he would do it—either through some untellable joke or some twisted sense of justice, but Giff was not unpleased with it—and he and Cinamo Dallas stood looking at each other in the second platoon squadbay, both grinning tightly.

It was a look of accepted understanding as they watched each other for those few fleeting seconds. Cinamo Dallas, pistol on hip, tall with his deceptively cruel face looking harsh. Giff, lean rawboned and hungry-looking in dirty dungarees, the prisoner, thinking it had been an odd series of events, weird decisions, that had finally, irrevocably, led them both here. And he knew too that it embarrassed both of them when they did not speak.

By the time he'd checked in all his gear (Dallas perpetually behind him walking with his ass-slung-low confident walk, pistol slapping on his hip, a feeling Giff would soon be so familiar with: a man with a weapon on his back), it was noon chow. Giff was not hungry but he decided to force himself to eat anyway. Hell, he might be on cake and wine tonight . . .

. . . Now moving up the muddy road, the jeep's tires slipping occasionally and the driver ceasing his talk to straighten them out, Giff felt the same apprehension of the unknown he'd had on the ship when he first came to Japan. How long ago was that? Four months . . . four months; Jesus God! he thought, it had seemed so much longer, like half a lifetime.

The jeep turned sharply at the Middle Camp crossroads, and Dallas swiveled around in his bucket seat. "We're in the homestretch. Better take a last smoke."

"Don't much feel like it," Giff lied, and continued to stare out the watery windshield.

Up ahead through the rain were the first clumps of small trees that was Middle Camp and he stared hard at them. The long low outlines of green barracks were just like the ones at South Camp, except there were more of them. But then Middle Camp was the Regimental Headquarters, he remembered. He wondered where the brig was as the camp loomed larger through the wet vista of the windshield.

"How long you think you'll be here?" the hook-nosed driver asked anxiously, with a half turn of his head.

"I dunno," Giff muttered. He reached up and tapped Dallas on the shoulder. "Do me a favor?"

333

"Sure."

"You see Popcorn next time you're out, tell her I won't be around for a while."

"Sure, okay," Dallas grinned. "I'll keep her company."

"You do that," Giff grinned back, not caring, feeling as though it was all over anyway, actually knowing it was, now that this new life skidded before him. Then, in a strange way that he could not put his finger on, he felt that by going to the brig, becoming a prisoner or anything else that might happen to him—getting kicked out or anything—the being locked up would free him from stepping all the way into that other side of the life he hated and had come so close to. Then the thought was gone, replaced by the tension which washed back over him.

The jeep slid to a stop at the main gate of Middle Camp.

"Where you goin'?" the MP sentry at the booth stuck his white-helmeted head out into the rain.

"Brig," the driver shot back, throwing his jeep in gear. "Got a man for the brig."

The MP waved them on and the jeep growled through the mud down the main street of Middle Camp, Giff studying it all, jittery. A triangular-shaped park spread out from the long regimental office with small elm trees on it planted like the rifle squad on line along the curbs. Middle Camp was a lot nicer than South Camp, he decided. But then the Colonel lived here, didn't he?

He wished it was still morning. Or even last night. He wished he was in bed. He wished a lot of things just then, as the jeep pulled to a stop, turned left off the main street and down a shallow dip to a small rectangular barracks with a white porch and finally stopping dead, killing the motor, in front of the white porch. The sign hanging from the eaves of the porch read REGIMENTAL BRIG, MIDDLE CAMP FUJI, HONSHU, JAPAN—and was crested with the red and gold colors of the Division insignia.

Giff could not see in the single window of the door and he noticed all the windows in the barracks had been boarded up. Then he felt a wave of relaxation move over him. Maybe this was it, finally, at last, the end of the line. Well, only one way to find out.

"We can't sit here all fuckin' day," he said with sudden alacrity. "Let's go in and see what my new home looks like."

334

21.

Dallas opened the canvas door of the jeep and climbed out. Giff followed, carrying his laundry bag, and stepped in under the white porch. A face peered out through the window of the door and he stared back. By the doorknob was a button; PUSH THIS BUZZER a sign said under it. Aware of Dallas behind him, Giff pushed the buzzer. The face moved inside and the door opened.

"Get in here!" the voice, belonging to a piebald Negro, ordered saltily, and Giff started walking in.

"You don't walk in here, lad!" The Negro shoved Giff, clouting him so that he half fell across the cement floor inside; and in the time Giff was falling he swept it all in with his eyes. On his left were two drinking fountains, then a door through which he spotted some urinals; on the right were two Marine Corps desks flanking a chainmesh door that was part of a larger chainmesh enclosure with double bunks, about fifteen deep on each side, bare naked and lifeless; the two men at the desk he saw were looking at him amusedly as he stumbled across the floor but he did not get a good look at their faces. All of this he saw in the short few falling steps it took him to reach the other wall across from the door.

He turned back around, not knowing what to do, still holding his laundry bag just as the piebald Negro stepped up beside him.

"Nose and toes against the wall, lad." The Negro shoved him against the wall, smashing his nose against it, and Giff straightened to attention. He felt his cap being lifted from his head and slapped across his neck several stinging times.

"You take your cover off when you come in here, lad," the Negro said from behind him.

"This the one from South Camp?" came a low mellow voice from one of the desks.

335

"That's right," Giff heard Dallas say. "I'm supposed to pick up two men and take them back."

"Yair," the low mellow voice said again. "They's in the head. Corporal Fishback, get those two men out the head so this here chaser can take 'em home."

Against the wall, face flush with the board planks, Giff heard a chair creak at one of the desks and the heavy tread of a large man lumber into the head, pause, come out again followed by a pair of other footsteps and Giff turned his head—stupidly, he knew it was, but he couldn't help himself—to see Poke Turner and Guppy Talagua, both clutching laundry bags, looking hard-bitten and hunch-shouldered as they moved out of the head. There was no sign of recognition on their faces at all. They did not even look the same, he thought, as his head was smashed back against the wall again and he wondered painfully, eyes watering, why his nose hadn't broken.

"That be it, then," the mellow voice said. "You're free to go, Chaser."

"Okay," Dallas said, and Giff heard footsteps double-time out of the brig onto the porch. The door closed quickly, the sound of rain suddenly stopping.

"What's your name, lad?" the Negro asked Giff from close behind him this time.

"Private Bohane," Giff answered the wall as something hit the back of his head, slamming him into the wall again.

"Your name Five, lad," the Negro said softly. "And you call everyone in here 'sir.' Understand?" He pushed the palm of his hand against Giff's head five times for emphasis, and Giff's head bounced off the wall five times in answer.

"Yes, sir!" Giff said.

"Five," the Negro said, "you one those white boys like to start race war?"

"No, sir!" Giff said, wishing now he'd had something to do with it.

"Turn around, Five," the low mellow voice said.

Giff executed an about face and stared straight ahead.

"Get over here, Five," the voice commanded again and Giff ran over to the desk, the one against the wall by the door, seeing a very small man with a flat imperceptible face, immaculately dressed in greens. Then he felt his legs go out from under him and he was on the floor.

336

"You have trouble with your legs?" the man behind the desk said. "Get up here!"

Scrambling to his feet, Giff stood at attention in front of the desk. The man must be the Duty Warden, he thought quickly, and the man at the other desk, whom he hadn't seen too well but was the one who walked heavily, was the Duty Turnkey. The piebald Negro must be just a guard. The man in front of him, the small man, was a buck sergeant.

Slowly and methodically, the Duty Warden pulled out a slip of paper and a pencil. "What's your height?"

"Five foot ten, sir."

"Five foot ten what? Carrots?"

"Five foot ten inches, sir," Giff said. Something boomed into his kidney and he felt bile rising in his throat.

"You see the word 'sir,'" the Negro's voice addressed him from behind. "You use the word 'sir' before and after each thing you say, lad. Understand?"

"Sir, yes, sir," Giff said.

"No, you silly shit," the Duty Warden said. "Not on 'yes, sir' and 'no, sir.' Just on sentences."

The Duty Warden went down the line filling out the questionnaire, while Giff answered each one loudly, remembering to use *sir*, standing at a rigid attention. He was nervously aware of the two men behind him, feeling they would be on his back any minute; aware too of the empty chainmesh compound, figuring the prisoners were all out at work and wishing they were back. He knew it wasn't good, being alone like this. No, sir! he told the Duty Warden, he did not wish to have any mail or to write any letters (they were all opened and read coming and going, the Duty Warden told him; Giff did not know who would write him anyway, what the hell), and that finished it up. The Duty Warden took his wallet and all his personal gear and put them in an envelope and laid it on his desk. Scrupulously, Giff had left most of his money in his seabag locked up at the supply shed, back home.

"You ever been in the brig before?" the Duty Warden asked, leaning back in his chair.

"No, sir," Giff said.

"Take him in the head," the Duty Warden said tiredly. "Fix him up. I'm sick of lookin' at him." He nodded his small ferret head. "When you're through, bring him back."

337

"Get in the head, Five," the Negro said curtly, and Giff spun on his heel and made for the door. Then automatically, like remembering something from another world, Giff stopped at the wide red line in front of the door.

"You better have stopped," the Negro said. "Now get on in there!" He stepped up and shoved Giff across the doorway past the urinals. "Over there against the wall by the washbasins."

Giff stood at attention against the wall across from the washbasins. The piebald Negro walked slowly up to him, followed by a large barrel-chested bristling crew-cut man with a chalky round face.

"Strip your clothes, Five," said the large white man, a corporal—the man Giff had decided was the Duty Turnkey —and walked heftily over to the three commodes, bent down and came out with a No. 10 can while Giff began undressing quickly, seeing both of them move in front of him without looking.

The Negro leaned against the washbasins, folded his arms and faced Giff. "Don't be so careful with them clothes, lad. Kick 'em over in the corner. They be lots worse by the time you get out."

Giff, standing naked, totally exposed, shoved his clothes down the wall to the corner. Then he stood up at attention, facing them.

"You think he's got the crud, Butch?" the Negro said to the white Duty Turnkey.

Butch, the corporal, the Duty Turnkey, held the No. 10 can lightly in his hand and stared hard at Giff. "Yeah; he's got the crud all right," he said, and threw the contents of the can over Giff.

He had seen it coming but he did not duck and barely had time to bat his eyes before the white powder hit him in the face, some of it catching him in the mouth. He recognized the smell and taste of DDT. The powder hit him again in the loins, and still he stood at attention staring straight ahead without really looking at anything, his mind tightly closed in a huge fist of impotent hatred. The rest of the powder Butch poured on his head, shaking the can clean.

"Okay, Five," Butch the Turnkey said in a basso voice. "Rub it good all over you." He leaned up against the basins next to the piebald Negro.

"Don't start beatin' your meat, lad," the Negro said blandly. "We don't allow that in here."

"Aww," Butch said, "he couldn't beat his meat. He ain't got enough to beat."

The Negro laughed, watching Giff spread the powder sickly sweet-smelling all over his body. He was aware of the laughter and the talk with his throat closed up now an flecks of black anger burning behind his eyes. Roll with the blows, he told himself, roll with the blows.

"You satisfy many women with that dorque?" the Negro asked in an unctuous voice. "Or you got to use your motherfucking hand all the time? Don't look like you got enough to do much good with anything."

The powder thoroughly rubbed over him, Giff stood back at attention and stared blindly ahead. He saw the Negro move for him, without actually seeing it at all, and felt the first dig under his ribs. He grunted and hunched forward slightly.

"I ask you a question you answer me, lad." The Negro backed off a little. "Now we try it again. You satisfy many women with that dorque?"

"Yes, sir," Giff said in a funny strange voice. He felt like he hadn't spoken in years.

"Haw!" Butch, the Duty Turnkey, stepped in hands on hips, his moon face just a few inches from Giff. "Who you tryin' to shit, Five? You're about the poorest specimen of a man I ever seen, bar none." He spat with each word into Giff's face, then grabbed him by the throat and pushed him back against the wall.

"I'll tell you something, Five," he said in a foggy basso. "You might think you're a tough brig rat, but you ain't. And you came to the wrong place if you think you're tough." He slammed Giff's head against the wall, stepped back and brought his knee up in Giff's balls. Giff screamed, choked it off with tight lips, bent double and fell to his knees.

"On your feet, Five," Butch said.

Slowly, locking his knees, Giff stood up again. His balls hurt like a hot fire, and he felt something pull in his belly.

"You know who I am, Five?" Butch moved in closer to his face.

"No, sir," Giff said in less than a whisper.

"What?" Butch cocked his head. "I can't hear you, Five."

"No, sir," Giff said hoarsely.

Butch hit him twice in the belly. Giff's shoulder folded in but he remained standing.

"You gettin' your hands dirty, Butch," the piebald Negro said and stepped up beside him. "You don't want to dirty your hands on him."

Butch took five as his relief moved in.

"What the matter with you, lad?" the Negro said. "You let a man hit you like that and you don't even know who he is?"

"No, sir."

The Negro punched Giff in the breastbone with a short right. He felt the wind go out of him while a dizziness floated behind his eyes. Before he focused again, the Negro kneed him in the balls. Giff bit his lip as he fell. The Negro brought his foot up and kicked it down on the back of his head. Giff bounced on the cement floor. Somewhere he heard footsteps retreating from the head. They were Butch's, he recognized faintly, congratulating himself on his consciousness.

As he got back to his feet, a little wobbly, Butch came back in with a thin sheaf of papers stapled together. He handed them to Giff with a grin.

"Those are your brig orders," he said blandly in his deep voice. "They're the only thing you carry with you in here outside your handkerchief." Then, while Giff was looking at them, Butch hit Giff alongside the head with his open hand. He wobbled again and straightened up, but dropped his orders on the floor.

"Pick 'em up, lad," the Negro said.

Starting to bend, his head went light and he moved his foot forward to regain his balance. His bare foot landed on the spit-shined toe of Butch's dress shoe.

"You ignert bastard!" Butch exploded, shoving him back with both hands. "Stay off my hocks!"

"Yes, sir," Giff said. Roll with the blows, roll with the blows. Roll with their party. Sickly he wondered how long it would last. Don't think, he told himself sternly, don't hurt. He did not see the next one coming. A closed fist that hit him on the cheek spinning him around, and this time he fell. Three or four sharp jabs of shoe toes dug into his ribs. Butch's or the nigger's? Grudgingly, a part of his mind admired their professional diligence, knowing how he would get nothing broken. Later perhaps. But nothing now. Funny

340

the way the cement floor heaved and tossed beneath him like the deck of a ship: tremors of the earth in an explosion.

"On your feet." A voice swam through the thick swelling of his head.

Doggedly, involuntarily, he regained his balance and stood up. There was suddenly no more pain in his head. He was as wooden as Hank Williams' cigar store Indian—and was his face red?

"What's your second brig order, Five?" Butch said through his thick meaty lips. They were almost as thick and liverish as the nigger's, Giff thought. Or maybe it was his eyes. But then both their eyes seemed to have that strange glazed look that comes with backward sex, he thought, hearing his voice say, "Sir, I don't know, sir."

The Negro came forward and pulled his nightstick from its sheath. "What all this 'I' shit, lad," he said blandly. "You ain't no I. You's number Five. You know what Five is?"

"Sir, Five is me, sir." Giff thought it was logical to say that.

The Negro jabbed the nightstick deep into Giff's belly.

"I don't think he'll ever learn," Butch said.

"He a sad sack of shit, ummm *hmmm*," the Negro said.

"You're only a number now, Five," Butch said.

Giff stifled a laugh at the comicality of it, the real hamminess of it all. He just wanted to laugh and laugh and roll with the blows.

"I think we have to show him what we mean, Butch," the piebald Negro said.

They began working him over in earnest. Giff remained standing as long as he could. They did not work on his face much, but continued peppering him with sharp stiff punches from the V-split in his rib cage to his knees. Sometimes with the nightstick, sometimes with their fists, sometimes with their knees, until the hot gall pain gushed up behind his eyes and he fell on his face smacking the cement hard.

Cold water stung his face. Shaking his head dumbly, feeling the slice of water on his eyelids, his mouth and nose, he came around.

He was under the shower, naked, in the head. What the hell was he doing here sitting with his back to the wall under a shower, hunh? The water stopped and the DDT powder was a sort of paste on his body.

"Get back over there and get your clothes on, lad," the piebald Negro said placidly.

,Giff peered through his wet lashes. Sure. Now he remembered. Well, where was Butch? Feeling a tinge of pride
spark lightly within him, he got to his feet and stepped out
of the shower past the Negro, and double-timed over to
the wall. His balls ached excruciatingly when he moved.

He dressed wet in the same dungarees he'd come in with.
The same ones he'd worn last night on guard.

"Button all your buttons, lad." The Negro walked lazily
over to Giff. "I don't want to see one unbuttoned. Or you
an' me will take a little trip back to Segregation and have
a party."

Giff stood at attention. It helped his loins to stand at
attention, he noticed. That was odd.

"The Duty Warden wants to see you now," the Negro
said oilily. "You better not fuck up with him, lad. You won't
like it." Turning his back on Giff he started to walk away.
Giff waited a moment, started double-timing after him. The
Negro stopped, spun around and hit Giff in the belly with
his fist.

Giff's knees weakened and starting to fall, he caught
himself and stood back up at attention.

The Negro shook his head deprecatingly. "You got a lot
to learn, lad. You don't go anyway till you called. Like a
dog, lad. I'll whistle when I want you." Walking blithely out
of the head he left Giff standing at attention.

From where he stood by the deep sink inside the head
Giff could see through the door, giving him a rectangular
view of part of the prisoners' compound, the Duty Turnkey's desk and a narrow aisle by the left wall separating
the boarded-up windows from the chainmesh compound.
He wondered momentarily where the corridor led to, probably to the black hole. A jolting pain echoed redly through
him. Don't think. Roll with the blows: a dogged unrealistic
refrain now tinged with futility.

Outside, the rain shuttled past the boarded windows. He
guessed it was about two o'clock in the afternoon. He
couldn't have been here more than an hour.

"Get out here, Five," the Duty Warden's mellow voice
sounded resonant and clear.

Giff double-timed up to the head door and right on
through without thought of stopping on the red line. And
that was as far as he got—just outside the door.

Butch, the Duty Turnkey, grabbed him by the collar of

342

his neck-buttoned dungaree jacket and slammed him against the wall between the two drinking fountains.

The Duty Warden stood up from his desk. He was really very small, ferret-headed, sharp-featured with red close-cropped hair. "How long is it goin' to take you to learn about red lines?" he said.

"Sir, not long, sir," Giff said, facing the entire brig with his back against the wall.

The Duty Warden snorted disdainfully. "Throw him his laundry bag, Butch."

Butch picked up the laundry bag and tossed it at him. Giff caught it, setting it beside him.

"Dump it all on the floor." The Duty Warden eased one of his buttocks up on his desk.

Giff dumped the contents on the floor, shook the bag a few times to make sure it was empty and dropped it too. Maybe that was all they were going to give him, he thought hopefully. Just that first runaround in the head, no black hole. Hell, that wasn't bad at all. Take that with a grain of salt. Then the stony hard-bitten looks on Poke's and Guppy's faces flashed in his mind.

The Duty Warden picked up pencil and clipboard and began calling off items of clothing and personal gear: razor, cigarettes, soap; and each time he called them off Giff held the items up and the Duty Warden took a check of them and wrote the number down.

The Duty Warden, the Duty Turnkey, and the piebald Negro each took a pack of Giff's cigarettes and tucked them neatly in their socks.

The clothing inventory finished, he stuffed everything back in the laundry bag excluding his personal gear, which Butch took and placed in a pigeonhole along the wall next to the head. The pigeonhole was in a large cabinet secured on the wall with forty other pigeonholes.

"All right, Five," the Duty Warden said. "Take your gear back to the storeroom and stack it in your shelf."

Giff stood there dumbly. The "storeroom" was as foreign to him as South Camp right now.

"You're sure an ignert shit, Five," Butch said. "Ain't he an ignert shit?" he sneered and sat down at the Duty Turnkey's desk.

"The storeroom," the Duty Warden explained in his mellow voice, "is down that hall by the wire; all the way to the end. Now get your ass back there!"

Giff took off at double-time, his loins biting sharply with each lift and fall of foot, and he moved out as though there might be some safety back at the storeroom. Moving past Butch's desk, the moonfaced man stuck out his foot and Giff went flying through the air still clutching his laundry bag and smacked his shoulder hard against the wall. Then he was up again and running down the hall between the chainmesh of the compound and the boarded-up windows of the wood wall, hearing the laughter erupt behind him.

The hall opened up into a small square to the right at the end of the compound, then another short hall cut to the left to a solid door. On the left of the shorter hall were three red-doored Segregation Cells, black holes; on the right directly across from them was the storeroom. Up from the storeroom was one office labeled BRIG WARDEN on the door.

Giff double-timed up to the door of the storeroom and stopped carefully on the wide red line at the door. "Sir, Five wishes to cross the red line, sir," he said heavily.

Inside, an immaculate Pfc in greens sat perched on an orange crate slapping a nightstick in his hand. All along the walls were large square boxes with dungarees and skivvies and socks and towels packed neatly in them. Across from the Pfc, sitting on the floor shining shoes, was a child-size Latin-looking man with regulation glasses behind which shifted two beady eyes. Apparently he was a trusty.

"Cross," the Pfc said after an affected hesitation. "And look," he added, slapping his palm. "That ain't the way you say it. It goes like this: 'Sir, Prisoner Number Five requests permission to cross the red line, sir!' You got that?"

"Yes, sir," Giff said, standing at attention just inside the door. He was simultaneously aware of the other prisoner's eyes moving all over him like a hose, yet it was almost as if he wasn't even there. "Sir," he said, "where does Prisoner Number Five put his gear, sir?"

"Five, hunh?" the Pfc said, scratching his chin with his club. "Well, you put it in that box there that's marked *five*. How long you in for?"

"Don't know, sir," Giff said, untying his laundry bag and pulling his gear out. "Prisoner Number Five hasn't been court-martialed yet, sir."

The Pfc guard nodded with a sort of grin and went back to slapping his hand, and Giff was vastly relieved. He turned to, packing his gear in the large boxy square with his back to the Pfc and did not hear the man leave his orange crate and come up behind him.

Something smashed against the large muscle between his neck and shoulder and he felt his right arm go numb. Then another smash and his left arm went numb. Instinctively, he stood up and spun around. The Pfc jabbed him in the chest with the point of the club knocking him back against the shelf of boxes. Off to the side the shoeshine trusty laughed happily.

"You're pretty goddam salty, ain't you?" the Pfc said. He carried the same accent Poke Turner did, Giff noticed as the guard grabbed him by the jacket front, half pulling him back out through the door, and slammed him into one of the Segregation Cells. Giff fell backwards into the narrow confining semidarkness, and lay looking up at the Pfc. Roll with the blows, he remembered, roll with the blows. If you strike back, you've had it.

"Git up, Five," the Pfc said disdainfully. Giff rose and faced him at attention. The Pfc set his jaw and began working out on his belly as if he were a heavy bag in the YMCA gym.

Giff tightened his already bruised stomach muscles and took the punches for a few short rending minutes. Then his muscles capitulated and he caught the brunt of the blows and the air swooshed out of his lungs, his knees buckled, his mind went nauseous black, and he fell heavily like a sack of spuds.

The Pfc stood over him for a moment, then walked out of the Segregation Cell and back into the storeroom.

"Get back in here, Five," he called after a moment.

Pulling himself from the floor, feeling sick and bilious, Giff moved out to the red line at the door. "Sir, Prisoner Number Five requests permission to cross the red line, sir."

"Cross," the Pfc said. "Get in here and stow that gear." He went back to slapping his nightstick.

Once again, Giff turned to packing his clothes neatly and carefully in the large square with shaking hands. The other prisoner, the trusty, snuffled again behind him.

"You from South Camp, Five?" the Pfc demanded.

"Yes sir."

"They's a lot of bad asses at South Camp, ain't they?"

Giff spun around and stood at attention just as the Pfc started to rise from his orange crate again.

"That's much better, Five," he drawled. "You stand at attention when you're talking to a guard here."

"Yes, sir," Giff said.

The Pfc looked at him for a minute thoughtfully, then went back to his orange crate. "If you're finished," he said, "get back up front. You're makin' me sick just looking at you."

Giff double-timed in two-steps up to the door, stopped on the red line and requested permission to cross. He heard the Pfc step up behind him softly, then he was catapulted across the hall, fell against the Segregation Cell Door, gathered his feet and started running back up the corridor to the front of the brig. He rounded the end of the compound by the Duty Turnkey's desk without being tripped this time and halted at attention in front of the Duty Warden, who sat inertly at his desk.

"Sir, Prisoner Number Five reporting as ordered, sir," he said loudly, surprisingly discovering that as long as he was busy, moving around, the pain of the initial beating did not ache so much. Yet, like a dog, he wanted to crawl off somewhere and inspect his wounds.

The Duty Warden sprawled out in his chair and looked up disgustedly at Giff. "*Who* ordered you up here?" he said mellowly.

Giff tried to answer. He couldn't. He didn't know. He felt like the man who was caught in his own lie and could not think of another one fast enough to cover it.

"Get over between the scuttlebutts," the Duty Warden said, leaning forward over his desk.

Giff pivoted and ran over between the scuttlebutts, the two drinking fountains, and stood with his back to the wall.

"For bein' with us two hours, you don't know shit," the Duty Warden said. Butch and the piebald Negro looked on anxiously.

"How long you been with the Divvy?" he continued.

"Since I left Ko-rea, sir," Giff said.

The Duty Warden shook his head mournfully. "What's this 'I' shit again? You ain't ever going to learn, are you?"

Giff knew it was coming then, starting all over. He did not expect to be anything but clobbered and it surprised him when no one advanced. Casually, the Duty Warden started him doing exercises, calisthenics, by the number.

He started out with side straddle hops, counting loudly, and then still louder when the Duty Warden said he

346

couldn't hear, till Giff was almost screaming the one-two! The movement of his arms and legs opened up the pain in tiny sluices running through him, but the flowing of the blood eased and counteracted a great deal of the pain, and he knew that in the morning would be the worst pain. If he made it till then.

An hour later, under the approving looks of Butch and the piebald Negro, the Duty Warden stopped Giff on his side straddle hops. Giff's counting voice had ebbed to a foggy whisper, and his eyes spun dizzily in his head. The moment he stopped he felt the great tiredness seep into him and his muscles refused to work with his mind. He stood at attention and waited, his throat parched, sandpaperish, saliva gone replaced by hot paste.

The Duty Warden regarded him with professional interest and then ordered him to do deep-knee bends. Giff's legs would not function at first, then they did, strictly by will power. He knew, somewhere far off, if he couldn't do them it would be worse. The deep-knee bends with a rocker went on for thirty minutes. All the time he counted wildly, hoarsely.

After the deep-knee bends, the Duty Warden combined forces with Butch and the piebald Negro and they had Giff perform push-ups, sit-ups, double-timing (which he did all the time anyway, no one walked any more it seemed) until his eyeballs rolled dangerously in his head; his breath was gasping, and all or most of the liquid he'd consumed in the past week was being released from his body. His dungarees, that had partially dried after the wetness of the shower so long ago, were now vinegary-smelling, drenched with sweat, and the salty fluid ran burningly into his eyes. He kept the calisthenics up.

Two hours later he was still at the exercises, his nerves quivering as if he were afflicted with St. Vitus's dance, when the buzzer on the door swam distantly through his weak counting of push-ups. Three pairs of hands grabbed him and ran him over to the wall on the other side of the Duty Turnkey's desk, slamming him against it. He was too tired to fall down.

"You hit that wall when the buzzer sounds, Five," Butch hissed behind him. "You sonofabitch."

Lurking behind the drunk man's fog of exhaustion, Giff felt a penetrating sliver of admiration for himself work through. They were pissed off at him. He had pissed them off! Because he hadn't passed out. Not yet. God, he was tired. He wasn't sore any more. But to have a drink of water. Cold spring water. Or a Coke! A Coke to fill some of this dryness that swirled in him like the night desert wind. No beer. Strange he didn't want a beer.

The buzzer stopped behind him and the door opened. Footsteps beat a silent shuffle behind him coming in groups of fours, running on back down the hall by the wire and the boarded-up windows of the wall. Finally the footsteps stopped running and the door closed. Voices rose in the front of the brig by the Duty Warden's desk: "Goddam this rain. Can't chase prisoners for shit in this rain." "So what's your bitch? You got liberty tonight, ain't you?" "Knock it off," the Duty Warden's voice came mellowly through. "Get those prisoners shook down. I got a new man needs attendin' to."

Giff listened to it all, blood pumping adrenaline into his head, and from the corner of his eye he watched the men along the wire begin undressing, stripping all the way down. Then they picked up each article of clothing and shook it out to show they did not have knives or cannons in their socks and skivvies. They dressed again and ran back to the front of the brig and stopped on the red line of the chainmesh door in front of the compound. The first man requested permission to cross, was denied by the Duty Warden and pushed out of the way. And Butch and the piebald Negro walked into the compound and tipped over all the bunks and stamped across the sheets and blankets, all of it sounding like shrapnel in slow motion moving through glass and clapboard and tin.

The Duty Warden came up behind Giff, leaned close to his ear. "Get your brig orders out and read 'em," he said.

Giff did. It was the first chance he'd had to read them. There were three pages, mimeographed, all signed by Colonel Klepteris. He skimmed over them swiftly, figuring on reading them later. Then he decided to read them: it might alleviate some of the burning thirst in his body and divorce all that was going on around him; his eyes held to the printed words:

Having been confined in the Camp Brig for reasons which have been explained to you, you are considered to be a marine who has certain rights and responsibilities; however, you have been deprived of your

freedom temporarily. During the period of your confinement you will comply with the orders and instructions set forth herein:

Then the three-page orders went on listing certain rules
under DO's and DON'TS. *You Will use your assigned bunk
only* topped the list, followed by other equally monumental
orders and then *You Will Not* section: *Hide any object
either outside or inside the brig; under any circumstances
have knives, firearms, ammunition, or any type of weapons
in your possession; if confined in a cell, have any articles
except religious reading material, and authorized bedding.* Through all of it Giff read without reading, the thirst
coming back into him threatening his shaky limbs, and the
only thing he could see on the orders was a tall icy glass
of water.

22.

He did not get any water. Not even when they were all
marched to chow an hour and a half later. During that
time his throat was thirst-swollen, a condition enhanced by
two trips to the head (each trip more ingenious than the
first one he'd had so long ago in the afternoon) with Butch
and the piebald Negro. And then he was cast into the
chainmesh compound and assigned a bunk while the other
prisoners were busily repairing their broken bunks and
stacking them up again. Giff's was the third bunk from the
front and he slept on the bottom.

The sheets and blankets felt like strange alien artifacts
that a race, long dead now, had held in its hands. He
managed to get his bunk made, stretched taut, and no one
helped him. Through the swimming-under-water hazy focus
of his eyes he saw the other prisoners, all of them silently
stony-faced, alert, tight-lipped, hard-bitten, scarred, moving
around their bunks like so many noiseless machines, emotionless and involuntary. Yet mingled was the determined

dogged resolution of indomitability that Giff had seen on Poke's and Guppy's faces, and also on most of the men he had known in Korea—thoroughly ingrained in these faces, an indelible hardness, so that he did not feel alone at all, but suddenly somewhat confident and secure with familiarity around him. And when chow call went, he slipped into his brig-issued field jacket and buttoned all the buttons carefully and fell out moving by the numbers (he was fifth in line) out the chainmesh door of the compound across the front of the brig to the back door.

The back door, located between the Duty Turnkey's desk and the cabinet of pigeonholes, opened out into an outside compound surrounded by barbed wire, fifty feet long perhaps and twenty feet wide. And they ran out into the black evening of rain and formed a column of twos inside the wire.

Outside the wire, on the cinder ash between the brig and the large metal Quonset hut that was the First Battalion Mess Hall, four chasers stood with riot guns loaded and locked, cradled loosely in their arms, as Butch unlocked the huge padlock on the double swinging gate and the Duty Warden came up behind him wearing his .45 pistol. Then they were all marched over to the mess hall through the rain: ass hole to belly button at a half step.

Two pairs of chasers were standing on each side of the column in the fifty yards between the mess hall and the brig, and the Duty Warden stood by the mess hall door, holster flap open, hand resting on the butt of his pistol.

Giff, moving ass hole to belly button (if one man started a break the chaser would cut two down with one shot), thought of water or milk or even coffee in the mess hall.

Shuffling at the half-step march, they moved inside the mess hall, removed their caps slapping them down across their thighs loudly, and then walked up the side of the mess hall to the steam tables laden with food where they took bowls, trays and mess gear.

The cooks and messmen, sweating at the steam tables, doled out the food in equal portions and Giff did not take all the variety. He was really not too hungry. Only thirsty.

Then, following his instinct, he moved behind the other two prisoners in front of him. Through the parched fog he decided they must be Prisoners Three and Four. One of them was a slim Mexican, the other a short, broad-faced Negro. They walked to the rear of the mess hall to the excluded cluster of small four-man tables where the chasers and Duty Warden stood at pre-appointed positions, and there they stood at attention behind chairs at one of the small tables.

The prisoner behind Giff joined them. He must be Prisoner Number Six, Giff thought, his mouth thick, eyes flicking sharply around the table for water.

When all the prisoners had gotten back to their mess section the Duty Warden ordered them all to sit, and they sat, sitting at attention. The Duty Warden then ordered them to eat, and they began eating. There was no water on Giff's table. Only a steaming pitcher of coffee. It was better than nothing.

He poured his soup bowl full with coffee and began eating, scrupulously silent. Amid the jaw muscles chewing, mouths full with broccoli and pork chops and gravy and bread, he let his eyes dart out momentarily at the three men he sat with. They ate wolfishly, quiet. The coffee did not alleviate his thirst.

"They give you your party?" the prisoner who had been behind Giff said. Giff heard him but he did not raise his head or move his eyes. The voice had been almost imperceptible coming through the food.

Giff took a bite of broccoli. "Yeah."

"The Great Unwashed and Uncle Tom are damn good at that," the man said. Glancing out of the corner of his eye cautiously, Giff studied him, then looked right back down at his plate. The man was thin and lank with a badly broken nose that had never been set, crooked over a malevolently thin mouth. Back in the brig when he'd been making his bunk Giff hadn't got a real good look at any of them; probably the prisoner slept somewhere close to him, on the bottom bunk next to his if his number was Six.

"They work you over pretty good, looks like," the prisoner went on through his pork chops. "You didn't give in?"

"No," Giff said thickly, relieved at this chance to talk, picking it up fast: talking through the food through the chewing mouthfuls that the chasers and the Duty Warden could not discern. "But I felt like it," he added sourly.

"Who don't?" the broad-faced Negro said. "Especially with Uncle Tom. He always after this young ass." He put some sugar in his coffee. "I wouldn't budge either—the sonofabitch."

The broken-nosed man with the tight mouth wiped his

351

pork chop gravy clean with a piece of bread. "When we get back, do what I do you want a smoke."

"I'd rather have water," Giff said suddenly, carefully, and wished he hadn't said it.

"Well, you won't get any, hoss," the other said. "But you'll be over it in a few days."

"I'll take the smoke then," Giff said. The talk gave him a muscle-tautening confidence. He felt better than he had all day. He wasn't very hungry now so he quit eating.

"Eat it all," the malevolent-looking prisoner said. "You don't eat it all you'll catch hell."

"Thanks," Giff said, and forced the rest of it down his throat. He swilled the coffee after it. It only augmented his thirst.

"Let's speed it up," the Duty Warden said impatiently from the doorway. "You've already used up your five minutes."

The prisoners continued eating steadily. Under the tin on tin of mess gear and the loud forced chewings, Giff felt that conspiratorial talk was going on at all the tables, pleasing him immensely.

"Stack 'em," the Duty Warden said.

Giff waited. He watched the other men slick up their trays with bread crusts and pass them around to him. He didn't know what to do.

"Just stack 'em in front of you, hoss," the friendly prisoner said. All around the mess hall the prisoners passed their trays to one man sitting at attention staring blank-faced ahead.

"All right," the Duty Warden said. "When you get up I don't want to hear a sound. No chairs scraping the deck, nothing. When I say that, I mean it. Ain't none of you want to have a party tonight, do you?"

He walked forward from the door and motioned two of the chasers to go on outside. A creeping quiet entered the mess hall. Far up front by the steam tables the cooks and messmen watched the scene curiously as if this were the first time they had seen it.

"Stand up," the Duty Warden ordered.

In a body they stood up with animal stealth, carefully eased their chairs back under the tables and stood at attention behind them.

"Over against the wall!" the Duty Warden bawled.

They moved quickly against the wall. Giff followed the

Negro, again aware of his stranger-friend behind him. They formed a single line ass hole to belly button on the wall. Giff did not get a count but he guessed here must be about twenty-five or thirty prisoners. He had thought there would be more.

"Break it off, Four," the Duty Warden said. Four, the Negro in front of Giff, took off at double-time and the man behind Giff nudged him slightly and Giff followed.

Formed in two ranks, with two chasers behind them in the mess hall and two outside, the Duty Warden marched them back out into the rain.

The double-swinging high gate was open and they moved into the outside barbed-wire compound, shoulders hunched up slightly under the rain. The Duty Warden disappeared inside and two chasers stood on the other side of the fence giving them mark-time march. Then the Duty Warden came out again, pistol-less.

"Smokers on the bulkhead in numerical order." He leaned against the door frame of the brig.

"Follow the nigger," the man behind Giff said.

Giff moved closely behind the short Negro in front of him to the door, a sort of queue behind him.

"Do like the nigger does," the man behind him said.

Giff watched the Negro stand at rigid attention just outside the door, his eyes almost on the kinky curls of hair under his dungaree cap. Through the beam of light in the open door, he watched from an angle as the Duty Warden opened the cabinet with the pigeonholes.

"Get in here!" he bawled.

The Negro stepped in under the doorway, snatched his cap off and popped it wetly on his thighs. "Sir! Prisoner Number Four, sir!"

The Duty Warden tossed him a cigarette. The white tube went high in the air and the Negro caught it deftly. He did an about face and double-timed back out into the compound down to the other end by the paint lockers.

Giff stepped up to the door. He mustered all his strength to combat the hoarseness. "Sir! Prisoner Number Five, sir!"

The Duty Warden tossed one of Giff's cigarettes in the air and Giff reached out for it. The Duty Warden watched him grab it with narrowed eyes. Then Giff followed the Negro to the back.

When the smokers had all gotten their cigarettes (one man didn't catch his and was taken immediately to the head), they stood at attention in a column of twos. About eighteen men. Giff cupped his cigarette in his hand to keep the rain off it. It was an abortive attempt.

"Get in here against the wire!" Butch's voice boomed from the doorway, and Giff heard the feet of nonsmokers running into the brig, each crossing through the door with a loud smack of their dungaree caps.

Standing under the rain he wondered how long they'd be there? There were no matches. No lights. His cigarette was getting damp. One end was already wet.

"Five!" the Duty Warden sang out. Giff turned and double-timed to the door.

"Sir, Prisoner Number Five reporting as ordered, sir!" he said.

"Is it wet outside, Five?" the Duty Warden said pleasantly.

"Yes, sir," Giff said.

"It's too wet to smoke, ain't it?"

"No, sir."

"Callin' me a liar, Five?"

Giff felt the rain moisten his lips. "No, sir."

The Duty Warden reached out and grabbed Giff by his field jacket and pulled him up under the door arch. "I don't like to be called a liar, Five. You should know better than to call me a liar. Now get out there and collect all those cigarettes."

"Yes, sir." Giff spun around and ran back to the smoking formation. He moved down the two rows of men taking their cigarettes in his hands. An electric vibration of hatred charged from the bodies as he took them. Then he ran back to the Duty Warden holding them all in his hands, standing at attention.

"Eat 'em," the Duty Warden said.

Giff did not move.

"Eat 'em," the Duty Warden said again. Behind him, the laughing round face of Butch moved into view. "I won't tell you again, Five."

Giff shoved the cigarettes into his mouth and began chewing. He coughed, choked, fell to his knees, and spewed out the cigarettes with the pork chops and gravy and bread and coffee, all of it curdling and steaming under the rain.

"Smokers in here on the wire!" the Duty Warden or-

354

dered. "That means you too, Five." He stepped up and kicked Giff in the shoulder. Giff fell backwards, stood up groggily and joined the formation running into the brig.

He moved through the doorway, slapping his cap on his thigh, not knowing what to do, and started running down the hall by the wire behind the Negro. Under the sudden shift of moods the great dehydrating thirst left him momentarily. Along the chainmesh of the outside of the compound, and in the hall between the compound and the boarded-up windows, prisoners stood at attention nose and toes against the wire. Giff fell in beside one in a rather large space. There were already several prisoners in the compound by their bunks, dressing. The chasers, the Duty Turnkey and the piebald Negro were frisking the men on the wire.

Momentarily at a loss, Giff stood fully dressed, leaning on the wire.

Something hit him hard in the kidneys. He did nothing. The something hit him again. He stared through the chainmesh at the boarded-up windows of the compound. He was hit again. He felt the sickness slither through his belly.

"Well, what the matter with you, lad?" a voice sounded behind him.

"Nothing, sir," Giff said. He was hit again, a sharp pinpointed pain.

"He a new man," the dapper piebald Negro said mildly from on down the wire where he was frisking a prisoner.

"Yeah?" the voice behind Giff said. "You don't know too much, do you, new man?"

"No, sir," Giff said.

"Anyone ever tell you how to take a frisk?" The voice came closer behind Giff's ear. "You're wastin' my time, lad."

"I take him," Uncle Tom said from down the wire. "Soon I get this one frisked. I want that one, Al."

Giff heard the man, Al, retreat from behind him. Then he heard Uncle Tom's blithe footsteps coming up. He saw the prisoners already frisked moving into the compound clutching their clothes against their bellies. Then they shed the rest of their clothes down to their skivvies and lined up on the red line inside the compound. He watched them, fascinated, wondering what they were getting ready to do. The man with the badly broken nose was the first one on the red line—his stranger-friend who had no great love for

355

the Great Unwashed and Uncle Tom. He heard the footsteps stop behind him. Roughly he was jerked around, and he stared over Uncle Tom's shoulder.

"I don't know what I going to do with you, lad," he said calmly. "You don't read your brig orders. You don't do what you told." He stepped back and leaned against the wall. "Take off your field jacket."

Giff unbuttoned it, took it off, and held it in front of him.

"Hold it up this way"—Uncle Tom moved his arms out in front of him—"so I can search it, lad."

Giff did while Uncle Tom slipped his hands through the pockets slowly. Then he jerked it away from Giff and flung it on the floor. "Now you know what to do, lad?"

"No, sir," Giff said.

Uncle Tom pursed his lips. "Unbutton your dungaree jacket and trousers and get your brig orders and handkerchiefs out of your pocket and face the wire."

Giff unbuttoned his trousers and jacket and faced the wire standing nose and toes at attention, keeping his ass hole tight so his trousers would not fall. The heavy end of the nightstick punched him in the kidneys.

"You feel that, lad?" Uncle Tom said blandly.

"Yes, sir." Giff tasted bile in his throat.

"When you get hit like that," Uncle Tom explained smoothly, "you spread-eagle on the wire. You know how to do that, lad?"

"Yes, sir." Giff watched the prisoners in the compound form on the red line, ass hole to belly button, stonily silent. He was hit again and it felt like it was a rapier slashing fire all the way through him. He tautened himself and spread-eagled on the wire, throwing his feet back and out, and his muddy boondockers hit Uncle Tom's finely creased pants. Uncle Tom brought the nightstick down on Giff's shoulder muscle. Giff fell to the cement. He got back up.

"Send him on in the compound, Harris," the Duty Warden said from his desk. "Don't waste no time on him now. You got tomorrow and quite a while yet, Harris."

"Pick up your clothes and get in the compound," Uncle Tom said behind Giff.

Grabbing his clothes, Giff ran around the chainmesh past the Duty Turnkey's desk and stopped short on the red line going into the compound facing the single file of one face and thirty bodies inside. The man with the badly broken nose stared out at him, unrecognizing.

"Sir, Prisoner Number Five requests permission to cross the red line, sir," he tried to yell.

Butch, the Duty Turnkey, the Great Unwashed, got up heavily from his desk and unlocked the chainmesh door. The next thing Giff knew he was being propelled forward uncontrollably off balance, almost flying through the air. He hit his stranger-friend at the knees and the single file of men fell backwards on the chain reaction, all sprawling on the floor.

"Back on the red line!" the Duty Warden snapped. "What the hell all you shitheads doin' on the floor? You got showers to take."

Giff shucked his clothes by his bunk and fell in at the rear of the line.

"Red lines are neutral while the showers are going," the Duty Warden said. "Take off."

The prisoners moved out in a line running, clad in skivvies and boondockers, clumping heavy-footed, back around the corner past the Duty Turnkey's desk down the hall by the wire to the storeroom. They moved in and out picking up a clean set of skivvies, socks and soap. Giff followed them doing exactly as they did. He was the last man.

When they got their fresh gear they moved on up to the front of the brig and formed a line by the pigeonhole cabinet. There they were issued toothbrush, toothpaste and razor. After drawing that gear from the Great Unwashed, they filed into the head.

In the head, its atmosphere totally changed from what it had been that afternoon when he was alone, Giff undressed quickly, watching out of the corner of his eye, then walked over to the shower.

"Four men in the shower." Uncle Tom put his nightstick up, slapping Giff across the chest. Giff waited standing at attention by the deep sink. Men were shaving at the basins and some were taking craps on the three commodes. Uncle Tom peeled off four squares of toilet paper to each man who crapped. He gave them two minutes. The men shaving had three minutes; the showers were one minute. One man took four minutes shaving and Uncle Tom raised twin welts across the back of his thighs with his night-stick. Another man asked for four more squares of toilet paper. Butch, the Great Unwashed, banged his head back against the wall behind the commode.

The tension abated somewhat, leveled off during the

showers. When each man finished showering and shaving and shitting he turned his gear back in to the Great Unwashed, who stood bulkily in front of the pigeonhole cabinet. Then they ran on back to the storeroom and put their dirty clothes in their laundry bags and returned to the compound.

During his shower, Giff tried to get some of the shower water in his mouth but Uncle Tom watched him carefully. Nor did he have a chance to drink when he shaved and brushed his teeth. The ubiquitous piebald Negro watched him closely.

When all the prisoners were assembled back in the compound, freshly dressed, standing in front of their bunks at parade rest, reading their orders, the Duty Warden and the Duty Turnkey walked in.

They nosed around each man like a pair of bird dogs ganging a crippled cock, inspecting the bunks. Most of them they tore up again, dropping the bedding on the floor and walking over it, dirtying it. They would stop in front of each man, who would immediately snap to attention, and ask him something. The man would always answer wrong and suffer some stiff jabs in the belly, loins and thighs. No one yelled. No one protested. No one breathed hard, except Giff who was totally dehydrated.

Then they had the prisoners doing calisthenics for two hours, all counting loudly in unison, until finally at 2100, which was taps in the brig, they held muster. Starting with Prisoner Number Three (the One and Two ranks were empty), who shouted: "Sir! Prisoner Number Three, sir!" the men yelled their numbers out right on down the line to Prisoner Number Twenty-eight, who was the last man and who also slept across the aisle from Giff.

The counting done, the Duty Warden ordered them into their bunks. Then he ordered them to sleep. Somewhere a light switch snapped and the compound was bathed in darkness. From up front, dangling between the Duty Warden's and the Duty Turnkey's desks, a lurid night light burned on.

Giff lay sweatily under the sheet and blanket of his bunk as the night quiet moved through the compound. His lips felt thick and hot, and he could not swallow. Feverish dreams of cold water danced in front of his eyes. The thirst came back to him full force now since he'd quit moving around. The pain in his body was numb. On his back he stared at the springs of the bunk above him. He wondered how he had gotten off tonight; they hadn't come for him, worked him over like the afternoon. He had expected they would. How many days would he be here? Or how many weeks and months? He tried to think of an answer. It wouldn't come. He hadn't even been court-martialed yet. But he *had* made it through the first day, he thought proudly.

"Hey, hoss," the voice of the stranger-friend came through the darkness. "You sleep?"

Giff turned slowly on his pillow, seeing the dim outline of the broken nose and tight lips. Under the lips, clenched in his hand, the man held a Rosary and he spoke over it. "No," Giff answered wanly. "I ain't asleep."

"My name's Swannie," the man said. "What's yours?"

"Bohane."

"From where?"

"South Camp."

Swannie nodded. "Okay, now look; we can talk for about ten minutes is all. By that time they'll be gettin' wise. We can get away with it cause of this," he grinned, looking at the Rosary beads. "Feller was here when I made the brig two months ago donated it to me. Pretty neat trick, hunh?"

"Yeah," Giff croaked. "That's all right. What're you in for?"

"Aw," Swannie said disgustedly in a low voice, "I hit a nigger over the head with a habachi pot. Out in Skosh Town—during the race war. Hear about it?"

"Yeah," Giff said weakly. "When can I get some water? I'm about dead. Ain't had anything to drink all day."

Swannie fingered the beads curiously. "Well, hoss, it'll be about five days. That's what it usually is. Now you'll get liquid, and maybe some water too, but you won't get over your dehydration till four five days."

"Great," Giff said, looking at the next few days in his mind. "Thanks for helpin' me out at chow."

"Was nothing," Swannie said. "You wanna watch what I do; or else Speedy Gonzales," Swannie jerked his head up toward the bunk above him. "That's the little greaser. The nigger, Williams, sleeps above you—he's in on account of the race war too, hit a guy with a belt buckle, then took a knife to him. We'll probably catch our workin' parties together, us four. You ever been brigged before?"

"No"—Giff shook his head on the pillow—"this my first hitch. You made it before though, hunh?"

"Sure," Swannie said expansively. "Pulled fifteen days here in August. I'm an old hand," he grinned, fingering his misshapen nose.

"Where we work?" Giff asked, sinking into an aching fatigue.

Swannie mumbled something incoherent over his beads. "Mostly on the rock pile." He grinned sourly. "I figure I got to mumble something over the beads ever now and then for play-actin'."

"I guess so," Giff grinned back, feeling a little better with the other personality from *his* own race and understanding to talk with. "When you get out?"

"I made six months," Swannie said not unhappily. "Be out in March. I don't lose any more good time. I lost so much now it don't make much difference though."

"What's the Duty Warden's name?" Giff asked, casting a sharp glance up to the front of the brig at the empty desk.

"That one?" Swannie said. "That's Little Bill. The one comes on at noon tomorrow we call Big Bill. Me and Big Bill don't see eye to eye. They're both a couple of royal ass holes. Only difference is Big Bill laughs when he stomps your ass. Little Bill don't."

"That's quite a distinction," Giff said wearily, the ache increasing under the pulsing throb behind his eyes. "I thought I was goin' to lose my balls this aft'noon—or my head."

"They work you over good," Swannie agreed. "Most the troops come in here can't take it that way the first day. Man, you pissed them off. You don't know how you pissed them off. I wouldn't want to be in your shoes tomorrow when Big Bill comes on. If they can't whip you, it pisses them off. You notice how they get that glazed look in their eyes when they're workin' on you?"

"Yeah" Giff bobbed his head. "Like they's just about to get their rocks off."

"The sons a bitches." Swannie shook his head over his beads.

"Who's the big guy that always works with the nigger?" Giff asked.

"The Great Unwashed," Swannie grinned. "Named him that myself back in August—God, but he stinks! His true life name is Butch Fishback. The spotted nigger I called Uncle

360

Tom and personally I think he's queer but I ain't sure," he said wonderingly, suspicious. "Williams says he is. Williams ought to know. He's black too."

"Yeah," Giff whispered.

"On Sundays," Swannie said, laying out the method, "you can sit down if you go to church. It's the only time you can sit, the only chance you get to sit. Don't matter what service you go to, you get to sit for an hour. Almost everybody goes. You get ideas though; like the beads here."

"You got to request it?" Giff heard his sleepy, hoarse voice ask.

"Yeah; you request it on Saturday night. That's all there is to it." Then, "That's all the time we got tonight, hoss," Swannie said. "I given you the scoop, that's all I can do. You're alone in this, like everyone else. You can watch me, see how I do things—unless I fuck up. You don't want to fuck up so soon. Wait a week or so before you start workin' on 'em." He grinned an acidly tart, malevolent grin. "Other than that, you're alone."

"I know it," Giff said, realizing it for the first time, the truth of it penetrating his soreness.

"Then that's her," Swannie said. "Tune in tomorrow night for old Swannie's talking show, free a charge."

Giff nodded his head on the pillow and watched Swannie hold his Rosary up, kiss it once, and place it under his pillow. He wished he could have brought HoTi with him. But then someone would have taken it. It would be safe with his seabag in the company.

Yeah, the company. So many miles and days away, he thought with wry condescension through the obscuring fog of tiredness and pain.

The thirst swelled back up in him and he fought it off, lying motionless, inert in his bunk as the apartness rolled over him like a fleet of belching grumbling troop trucks. Through the rising dust and rancid exhaust he felt he was losing something, rescinding that something that had dogged him now for so long, and locked in the chainmesh compound, his balls swollen from the beating, his breath coming hard through his tight chest, the drought in his body dull and heavy, shackled and sealed off in the corner of nowhere, he began to feel a sleepy freedom that somewhere far off glimmered at him.

23.

At four-thirty in the morning Giff awoke with a galvanized bucket screaming past his head. It hit the man next to him in the ear and the man fell out of his bunk. The lights glared on in the compound and all the prisoners piled hurriedly out of their bunks.

Giff pulled himself out from under the blanket and the pain shot through his body, all the bruised stiffness molded by the sleep, crippling him.

He was only halfway out when Little Bill and the Great Unwashed came storming through the compound kicking over the bunks of the men who did not get up when the lights were snapped on, and Giff's was the first to fall.

He felt the jar of feet on steel as the bunk toppled, braced himself as it fell, glad he was on the bottom. Williams, the broad-faced Negro who slept above him, hit the deck and bounced.

Giff pulled out of it, pain like an old friend beating inside his chest, and helped set the bunk up again. He moved quickly, divorcing himself from the pain by force of will, and began dressing. It took him five minutes to dress and make his bunk and he fell in with the other prisoners on the red line for morning wash-up. The clock outside the compound by the Duty Warden's desk said 0435.

Mornings, he soon found out, were still another completely different phase of this new life. There was none of the pummeling of night and day, but a sort of hurried, harried, work-goading drive.

The prisoners double-timed into the head, brushed their teeth, washed, and returned to the compound where they did exercises until 0500, chow time.

The thirst moved back over Giff, lashing him, and the pain poked holes through his skin when he moved. He had tried to get some water in the head when he washed his face but the piebald shadow, Uncle Tom, had hovered over him like a dry wind.

During the exercises, the new flow of blood helped to carry some of the clotted ache away, and except for the thirst he felt measurably better when, at 0500, they fell out for chow, running into the outside compound and forming a column of twos. It was still very dark but the rain had stopped falling and a shrouding fog had rolled in during the night.

Breakfast went silently in the massive metal Quonset hut. Not even Swannie offered any conversation. The prisoners ate their mush, toast, coffee and shit-on-the-shingle, maintaining their stony-faced, withdrawn woodenness as the chasers stood with riot guns behind their tables.

When they got back from chow Giff was put on the early-morning detail along with Swannie, Williams, and Speedy Gonzales; just like Swannie had told him, the four worked together. And again smokeless, they were chased over to the regimental office by a neat smooth-faced Pfc chaser in starched dungarees.

Giff, who had not been able to grasp the routine completely but had watched Swannie, doing as he did, did not know the early-morning detail. He simply fell in, following Williams when his number was called, the breakfast threatening to leave him, knees shaky, and marched over to the regimental office.

The early-morning detail comprised of cleaning out the regimental office, Colonel Klepteris' office, and the long hallway in front of the lesser offices. They drew brooms, swabs and rags from the Regimental Police Sergeant's shed behind the office and, carrying them at right shoulder arms, moved with the chaser, who stood cradling his shotgun loaded and locked, into the office where their fate was decreed.

Under the yawning flickering lights in the great hall, Williams and Gonzales swept as Giff and Swannie followed them with the swabs. The chaser walked backwards, facing their backs, as they worked mechanically.

Each time they needed fresh water for the swabs, the chaser would line them all up and march them into the Colonel's head where they rinsed them out.

Standing with his swab over the deep sink as the cold water flowed out of the large faucet, Giff felt a sneaking salvation seep into his mind. Carefully, as he held his swab under, he let the cuff of his field jacket soak up some of the water. When he was through rinsing his swab they walked on out. During the rest of the swabbing of the hallway he would, quite naturally, run the cuff of his field jacket across his mouth and suck some of the water out. He congratulated himself on his improvisation.

When they finished they were chased back to the brig, drew eight-pound handleless sledgehammers and were taken to the rock pile.

The rock pile was located on the south side of the Middle Camp, set in a shallow of cinder ash, a box canyon that stopped at the same high wall of barbed wire that encompassed the camp. Beyond the wire, stretching on in a rolling flat, were muddy brown rice paddies and small clumps of naked trees rising in an autumn rust all the way to the black jagged upthrust of the giant Fossa Magna range.

Rocks of all sizes and shapes lay in bunched groups, like coal slag brought down by an unknown truck driver from an unknown world, who would make no return trip.

Prisoners squatting gook-style on their hams (four prisoners to a pile) held their handleless eight-pound sledgehammers like armed grenades and pounded a feverish staccato on the rocks that never broke. They weren't meant to.

Behind them, the chasers stood shifting their weight, fastidiously neat in pressed dungarees and white web belts, cradling their riot guns. Occasionally, the thumbing of gun hammers would snap in bored impatience. From time to time, if no one was looking, the chasers would break regulations and sneak a hurried smoke. But their eyes never strayed from the prisoners working in groups of four on the inexorably unbreaking rocks in wooden deadpan silence.

Giff squatted with the three other prisoners of his group: Swannie, Williams and Speedy Gonzales. Clutching the sledge tightly till his knuckles showed white, Giff began pounding a rock with steady rise and fall of hand, the weighted sledge bouncing back up with each smack, leaving only small dents in the rocks as evidence that he was trying to break it.

This too was interminable work, and the old waiting was

back on him like a predatory cat digging its claws into his back. Yet the waiting on the rock pile was better than being back in the brig. Back there, where they would get worked over all day, the waiting was longer. Still, they had the nights and mornings and the noontimes to work them over; making up for the loss of time then, he decided heatedly. Let them. He could take it. He already had, hadn't he? Grimly, he smashed at the rock.

By eight o'clock the murky fog lifted and a bleak November sun raked across the land, the paddies, the hills, the camp. There was a cool crispness in the air that promised no more rain for a while and the sky was a startling blue. Long thin shadows moved through the fence and touched the sweating prisoners pounding rocks. Their acrid bodies burning, stifling under their buttoned dungarees, working on, meaninglessly, fruitlessly. No longer mercenaries.

The weather held good for the next five days. During this time Giff gradually and gratefully threw off the cloak of dehydration and his body mended and healed and was no longer stiff and sore in the morning when the madman's reveille was tossed through the chainmesh of the prisoner's compound.

He became an integrated part of the prisoners in the brig, carrying on a solid unbreakable core of hardness that was even more unbreakable than the rocks on the rock pile.

Of course, this infuriated Little Bill Claggle, the Duty Warden on Giff's first day, and Big Bill Higgins, the other Duty Warden whom he met the second day.

Big Bill was a potbellied, gross-looking S/Sgt with glinting eyes, who laughed and guffawed when he pounded a prisoner senseless, beating his head on the cement floor. He did not use the silent methods of Little Bill.

Still, the core could not be broken. It was as if in the strength of their silence alone, the prisoners formed a wedge of dogged resistance that lighted the fires of frustration in the guards' eyes.

Through the choppy conversations while eating, through his own acts of endurance, Giff was accepted into the sweaty fold of the prisoners' fraternity, but only after they were all positive (through a chained man's instinct) that he was not a *pogue,* or a *lamer,* but was, in fact, and always had been, one of them.

365

To Giff the most pace-breaking times of all were the taps talks with Swannie, who sneeringly pulled out his concatenation of little black beads each night after Lights Out.

"You ain't heard about your court yet?" Swannie asked him over his Rosary on the fourth night in the darkness of the compound.

"No." Giff leaned casually on his side. "Not a fuckin' word. I'm beginning to wonder if I ever will."

Outside the compound, the night light dangling above the Duty Warden's desk burned on.

"Jesus Christ and little apples," Swannie prayed over his Rosary with great reverance. "Man, you'll hear about it soon enough. What you think you'll get?"

Giff studied the malevolent-faced Swannie. "I thought it'd be maybe two three months. I shouldn't get no more than that. I still got my medal, you know what I mean?" He had told Swannie about the Silver Star; it hadn't made a heavy impression on the broken-nosed man but the word got around to the other prisoners and that more than anything else, Giff thought, was the reason for his acceptance. What would happen when Little Bill and Big Bill discovered it he did not know.

"Yeah," Swannie told him. "You still got that pulling for you. But I wouldn't put too much faith in it. Not when they want a part of your ass."

"Hell," Giff said under his blanket, "they already got a part of that. Anyway, we get in this coming war we'll all be free."

"Free!" Swannie whispered indignantly. "Haw! That's a hot one, hoss. We ain't never been free in our lives. I'm livin' proof," he grinned lopsidedly, his broken nose protruding.

"It's better to be fighting than in here," Giff offered. "This ain't no different than peacetime, except maybe more horseshit."

"Okay," Swannie nodded, "I'll go along with that, hoss. But we better catch one pretty skosh. We don't, they won't be a Crotch." He fingered his beads thoughtfully.

"I just wish I knew when I'd get my court," Giff said.

"Dear John, that's all she wrote." Swannie kissed his Rosary. "Ain't that a hot trick?" he said proudly, sneered at the chainmesh and slipped all the way under his blanket.

Giff lay listening to the breathing in the compound for a moment. Up front the wall clock bonged nine-thirty. He

366

was muscle-quivering tired from the rock pile and the old thirst was gone with his body growing more lean and hard. He had a fresh scar on his jaw, pink and tender, the mark of the Midnight Special.

A blissful sleep began rolling over him like surf on sand and he sank back into his mattress. He wondered just how long it would be before he did get his court-martial, how long he'd have to . . .

The waiting, like an old Achilles' heel, wormed its way through the tiredness and his eyes opened quickly. He was back to that again: the waiting, trying to think of some way to combat it, some tangible way of meeting it and fighting it and finally destroying it. With the blur of combative thoughts rousing his vitality and his emotions, coupled with the work of the day beaten down, hammered inside, he fell fitfully asleep.

Actually, the weapon against the waiting came in a strange way. And had he performed some conscious act it would never have happened. That, he knew later. And somehow, it not only destroyed the waiting but also gave him the thing he had been looking for.

Of all places it came on the rock pile.

He would squat with his handleless sledgehammer pounding on the rock under the cool November sun, hot and pungently sweaty under his buttoned sooty dungarees, with the unorganized rhythm of hammers on rock all around him, beginning to withdraw into himself, folding himself up tight, all the time staring at the dents in the rocks and never looking at the chasers or out through the fence at the view he had tired of.

While the presence of the other prisoners made themselves felt in his blood— Blood, he thought, like imagination was fire in the veins. A man never thought with his brain at all, he thought with his blood.

It was a song of blood, dripping red from the prisoners around him and all the other prisoners from so long ago Giff did not know, had never known, existed. A song hammered out on rocks with eight-pound sledges in a repudiated identity . . .

. . . The sweaty song of the Mesopotamian who hauled the giant stones with which to build the pyramids for the Pharaohs, his shoulder rope-burned from the hauling, a straggly beard on his coarse face sunburned to the bone, the rumble of rock on logs thick in his ears, chanting a curse as he worked to erect an edifice, still singing in spite of knowing he would never see the last stone laid . . .

. . . The guttural song of the savagely fighting bony-faced Hun whom Caesar had conquered and enslaved, then offered a chance to fight with the Legions to be rewarded with cattle, horses and goats and slaves of his own; and so he crossed the Alps for the wealth on the horizon picking up his battle scars, never to get the spoils because he died in Gaul . . .

. . . The oar-slapping song of a grizzled galley slave, forty years shackled to his oars in a steady inexorable forward and backward movement, never going anywhere, never seeing the port where the ship stopped, bellowing like an animal when he was tossed his bread and water, at last a part of the sea in burlap wrapping . . .

. . . The savage chant of the African blackman picked up by the British and chained to the hull of a rotting ship in filth and disease, to be sold on the market block to the wealthy American plantation owners, but still singing his incantation embracing the pain of the sizzling-hot branding iron . . .

. . . The swampy fetid cricket-filled night song of the leg-ironed man on the Georgia chain gang, linked at night to all the other prisoners in a tight-packed, sweaty barracks serving a six-month hitch, finally released penniless and picked up again for vagrancy, rechained and beaten, a narrow-eyed, alert life with the baying of dogs behind him . . .

. . . The bullish stubborn song of the left-handed Irishman, meaty-shouldered, who pulled a turning plow in hell, stuck in the black pit of a cell while the waters from an inflowing river rose high around him, not crying out, lying there waiting as the drowning waters filled the pit, a song of silence . . .

It was the savage song of the rock pile that lost Giff his identity, kept him moving clear and farther away outside himself in a steady monotonous beat that was lost in the shuffle of the song of the cores.

So it was the blood that came to his rescue, fighting the existence of time, the waiting.

And each day he looked forward to the rock pile where he forgot himself and each day he strengthened the hard core of the untouchableness. And gradually the waiting abated and died, replaced by something inscrutably inherent that he had never seen before, never recognized. But now he could see it in his reflection, see the decline and fall of himself.

It was as if the very cells in his body had undergone a transformation—his thinking cells, his acting cells, all his cells. The new cells, to which he had not entirely become accustomed, grew and produced and reproduced, feeding him with vitality, and he clung on hard to the growth with both fists because he knew he could never go back the other way.

He was not court-martialed until the sixteenth of December. One man came to see him in those nine weeks: First Lieutenant Brickett, the Regimental Legal Officer, a balding mustang with a thin mustache and gray eyes who informed him he had been awarded a Special court-martial *in absentia*. Lt. Brickett made it evident that Giff was damn lucky he didn't get a General court. And how did he wish to plead?

"Guilty, sir," Giff said. They were sitting in the Brig Warden's office with the door closed. It was the first time he had sat down since he'd been in the brig, except for one hour each Sunday at church.

"That's your best bet," Lt. Brickett said sagely. "If you pleaded 'not guilty' you wouldn't stand a whore's chance of making it." He smiled, a little condescending.

"There's no sense in pleadin' 'not guilty,' sir."

"Not with the charges and witnesses against you," Lt. Brickett said amiably. He leafed through his Manila folder, bringing out a small slip of mimeographed paper, and slid it over to Giff. "You should sign Article 31," he said judiciously, "before you say any more. Do you understand Article 31?"

"Yes, sir," Giff said, taking the slip and scanning it. Article 31 was the military counterpart of the 5th Amendment to the Constitution of the United States. A bitter knowing grin curled his mouth as he read: he didn't have to say anything at all, just refuse to answer on grounds it might intend to incriminate and defame him. He signed it and handed it back to Lt. Brickett.

"Ordinarily," Lt. Brickett confided, "I wouldn't ever take a case for defense myself. I'm the Legal Officer. But," he shrugged, "no one else wanted it."

"You don't have to defend me, sir," Giff said stonily. "I'm pleadin' guilty. I don't need a defense counsel."

369

"Well, you need a representative in court," Lt. Brickett said. "By the way, in checking your record I find you have a Silver Star." He looked at Giff questioningly.

Giff stared back at him. "Yes, sir."

"Are you going to utilize that in court? On your extenuation of mitigation?"

"No, sir."

Lt. Brickett nodded his head. "It's a dandy weapon to use," he said. "Though I suppose the court will take that into consideration. But," he emphasized, "your record since you re-enlisted and came to Japan is not what one would call exemplary."

"I guess it isn't, sir."

"How about your record before you shipped?"

"It's nullified, sir," Giff said, respectfully cool. "It always is when a man re-enlists. You know that, sir."

"Of course," Lt. Brickett said with a flicker of a grin. "But it's *still* on file in Washington. Anyway, the court never takes previous convictions into consideration."

"No, sir," Giff said. "Of course they don't."

Lt. Brickett studied him for a moment, took the signed Article 31, put it back in his Manila folder and stood up. Giff followed him, standing at attention.

"I think it's wise you pleaded guilty," Lt. Brickett said. "After all, you are guilty. Damn guilty in fact. And by pleading guilty you'll save the court a lot of trouble."

"Yes, sir," Giff said.

"I hope you've learned a lesson," Brickett said. "The brig is where we make marines. By the way, how have you been treated?"

"Fine, sir," Giff said. "Fine. No complaints."

"Good," Lt. Brickett said cheerfully. "It's a well-run brig and its aim is discipline. Discipline is what counts."

"Yes, sir."

"Your court is set for the sixteenth of December," Lt. Brickett informed him, walking to the door, the skin of his ears reddening a little. "I'll see you then. If you have any questions, tell the Duty Warden and I'll come back." He looked back at Giff but his eyes wandered aimlessly around the office. "And you're certain you'll plead guilty?" he asked the wastepaper basket.

"Yes, sir," Giff said.

"Good," Lt. Brickett said and shrugged again. "It

wouldn't make any difference anyway, actually. You'll be found guilty."

"Yes, sir," Giff said.

Lt. Brickett paused at the door, looked at the knob thoughtfully, nodded his head as if in some kind of agreement with himself, and walked out leaving the door open. Giff reported to the Great Unwashed and was chased back to the rock pile.

Two men from South Camp, chasers, came for him on the fifteenth of December. They had been drafted by the Third Battalion sergeant Major to escort Giff to his court-martial.

Shamefaced, because they were taking one of their own kind (they were not MP's or guards of brigs, but field marines), they waited outside the door of the brig on the little white porch, blowing steam in the biting cold morning.

Giff collected his personal gear from the Great Unwashed, who jabbed him hard in the kidneys with his night-stick: "For luck, Five," he told him, shoving him out the door. Then he was outside in the wintry air, climbed into the back of the weapons carrier with the two chasers behind him as the truck lurched and bounced grumbling back along the road to South Camp.

Giff smoked five cigarettes on the way down and did not speak to either of the chasers although they peppered him with questions about the brig. All the way down to South Camp, the whole ten miles, he rolled it over in his mind, straightening it out. He knew what he was going to do coldly and implacably and objectively. It formulated in his mind until the weapons carrier ground to a stop in front of Horrible Hog Company's office at South Camp.

Horrible Hog Company was gone. They were in the field, up to the Jig area for cold-weather training on a two weeks-bivouac. Only Top Landrum and the two company clerks, Police Sergeant Oscar Zorn, and a few shirkers were left in the company. Giff was glad. He did not want to see any of his old buddies.

Apologetically, the two chasers (Giff did not know what company they were from) escorted him to the H Company supply shed where he drew his seabag, took out a set of wrinkled greens and turned them into the company office to be pressed for his court-martial. He did not take his ribbons or medals out of the seabag.

371

Top Landrum, in his insidious baleful way, wanted to know if there was anything he could do for Giff. After all, that was what he was there for. Giff told him no thanks there was nothing he could do to help.

Then he was marched over to the South Camp guardhouse and confined there to wait for his court-martial. The guardhouse cell had not changed at all since he'd been in it the last time. Except there was no strait jacket in it now and there were two bunks.

He lay on the bunk all day, forcing his mind away from himself. Once, during the long shadows of the cold afternoon, the street noises of Fujioka pierced through the high barred window, and he fought and suppressed an urge to climb to the window and look out at the town, winning that bout too.

In the morning, December the 16th, two different chasers (they were both shamefaced too) chased him back over to Hog Company's barracks where he dressed in his freshly pressed greens after he'd showered and shaved and cleaned his fingernails. Clean, immaculate, with his face more spare and squarely cut now, he moved ahead of the chasers to the South Camp chapel under a heavy low-floating gray overcast.

The chapel, other than being used for Sunday church services, was used for all courts-martial and combat films. It was directly across the road from the battalion office. The officers of the court-martial board were waiting for him when he arrived.

His court-martial did not last over five minutes. Giff, without one ribbon on him, sat beside Lt. Brickett. No Silver Star, no combat ribbons, no battle stars. He pleaded guilty to all charges. On a plea of guilty there was no need for witnesses.

The senior court-martial board member, Major Luten, a beefy cigar-chewing VMI graduate, wanted to know, after the board had heard his plea, if Giff liked the Marine Corps.

"I stand on Article 31, sir."

Major Luten leaned forward, glanced at his colleagues who glanced back at him, and looked back at Giff, nonplused. "Do you want a Bad Conduct Discharge?"

Again Giff stood on Article 31.

Major Luten asked him if he was proud of his Silver Star and why wasn't he wearing it?

"Sir, I stand on Article 31."

Chewing his cigar, infuriated, Major Luten glanced once again at the other members of the court-martial board, who had suddenly found something abstract to occupy their eyes. Second Lieutenant Burrows, the junior member of the board on his first court-martial, had become interested in the lines of an eraser. Major Luten cleared his congested throat, chomped down on his cigar and looked from Giff to the Regimental Legal Officer, Lt. Brickett. No one responded. Major Luten then excused Giff quickly.

Giff waited outside with the two apologetic chasers, smoking in the gloomy morning. A minute later he was called back in by the court-martial clerk, Pfc. Keene. Giff walked back in, his two chasers behind him, and stood at attention in front of the court-martial board.

"Do you wish to make an extenuation of mitigation?" Major Luten asked, his face florid.

"I stand on Article 31, sir."

Major Luten promptly and irritably excused Giff from the chapel again.

Giff did not have time to smoke a cigarette this time. He had been outside for less than a minute, watching the charcoal-colored clouds rolling across the sky, when Pfc. Keene stuck his head out the door and told him they were ready again.

This time Lt. Brickett faced the court-martial board with Giff.

Without preamble, Major Luten informed Giff that it was the order of the court-martial board that he be sentenced to six months' confinement at hard labor, the place of confinement to be the Regimental Brig, Middle Camp brig, Middle Camp Fuji, Honshu, Japan; that he would lose all pay and allowances for like period applying from the date of sentence; and that he, Private Gifford Cael Bohane 1444004 USMC, would receive a Bad Conduct Discharge at the termination of his sentence.

Giff thanked Lt. Brickett for his defense and legal advice and was marched over to the battalion office, where he signed the necessary papers for his confinement. Then he was escorted back to Horrible Hog Company's barracks where he packed all his gear, everything he owned, under the baleful stare of Top Landrum. Neither of them spoke. And he was taken back to the Middle Camp brig to start his sentence.

He was welcomed back into the brig with a prolonged party in the head. The Great Unwashed and Uncle Tom did the honors under the judicious eye of Little Bill Claggle. Little Bill also relieved Giff of the three hundred dollars in script he had in his seabag. Little Bill did not get HoTi. HoTi was safely secured in the seabag in the storeroom as an unwanted item. None of the guard personnel saw any value in it. After the party Giff was chased out to the rock pile. It had started to snow.

That night after taps, with heavy thick clusters of snow-flakes falling lazily outside the boarded-up windows of the brig, the first real snow of winter, Swannie pulled out his old Rosary and began mumbling in the secluded darkness. "They give you the load," he said with an almost imperceptible shake of his head. "You shoulda taken advantage of your medal, hoss."

"What medal?" Giff said, feeling the freshly battered skin taut on his rawboned face. "They give me what they wanted. I tole you before, they had it laid out. I wasn't begging for anything."

"They's still a chance they'll remit the kick," Swannie said encouragingly. "They usually do if they's going to be a war."

"If there's a war," Giff agreed, staring at the springs of Williams' bunk above him.

"They's been a lot of talk about one," Swannie said, his satanic, hook-nosed face graven. "Before too long now, they say."

"There was talk of one four months ago, too."

"Well, don't lose hope, hoss," Swannie said. "They's always the chance."

"Fuck it," Giff said.

"Okay, hoss," Swannie said. "Merry Christmas."

Giff lay sleepless on his bunk staring at the six months. Six months. And then a BCD, and a free ticket to the States without privileges of a citizen.

A deep bitterly cold knot twisted in his belly as he looked at it lying naked in front of him. Maybe Gunny Thorton was right after all, the mustachioed sonfabitch. Maybe he should have taken a psycho. Like Swannie said, they's still a chance, hoss. Remember that, he told himself. But even if there was a chance, he thought sleepily, he wouldn't take it if he had to go back to the other life, the way of living he had come to the brig to stamp out in the

374

first place. He knew he was right and he would not trade it for anything, BCD or no.

Wrapping the consolation of what he felt was his score in the court-martial—the passiveness—around him with the scratchiness of the wool GI blanket, he shut his eyes hard in the coldness of the brig.

24.

All that Hugh Thorton learned of Bohane's court-martial was gleaned from Quiller Carpenter, Hog Company's clerk. And what Quiller told Hugh only helped add another coal to the fire of steadily increasing misconceptions which plagued him. He felt in some way that he was amassing a fortune of deftly handled blunders. And what Quiller told him, multiplied with all the other mistakes, actually horrified him. In fact it was so devastating to his confidence that the only way he could partially assuage it was to get loop-legged, savagely cursing drunk; which he had already done up at the Jig area during the winter training when he had witnessed another event on the shattering roster of *Hugh Thorton's Wrongness*. The getting drunk, he knew, would not alleviate all of it, but it would take him away from it for a while.

Of course, neither Hugh nor the rest of the company had any way of finding out about the court-martial until they returned from the field. Hugh returned one day early in charge of the vanguard to prepare the barracks for the rest of the company which would arrive the next day, the twenty-second of December. And when he arrived, hunkering in the front seat of a mud-splattered weapons carrier while the growling fan-driven heat rolled over him, he was already irritably hungover. South Camp and the security of the barracks for once did not look cheerful after two weeks in the field.

The night before, up at the Jig area on the slopes of Mount Fuji in knee-deep numb-cold snow, he had gotten

375

heavily tingled on two dozen bottles of sick bay brandy (it was carried by the Navy corpsmen for frozen casualties). That binge, in preparation for the one he was facing, was purely in defense.

He could not recall if it was exactly when Bohane was first confined in the Middle Camp brig or shortly after that, but things began to go to hell in a rocking chair.

In all honesty he had to admit that he had kept an open mind to all of it—to his life and the lives around him, to everything. Or at least he had tried.

But he had been outguessed, just as he had not expected, on just about everything; and one salient boner which still made him shiver when he thought of it: Gunnery Sergeant Leroy Finch had sobered up.

Actually quit drinking.

Hugh cursed himself for losing that opening in his game. He who had wired the deck was suddenly wiring himself into a pat losing hand.

Who in the hell said you couldn't beat the dealer?

It had all started somewhere around the time when Blood-and-Guts Bohane was first caught going over the hill. He knew now he should have done something then, stepped in and taken an adroit hand in it, but he had merely looked on humorously, as if it was a field marine's privilege to go over the hill when he felt like it. It had not seemed to him then that Bohane was an inveterate poacher of regulations. But (damn him!) he was undoubtedly a neat-handed law-breaker if there ever was one. Why couldn't the sonofabitch have been subtle like Koko Hobbs or that last of the Mohicans, Cinamo Dallas, and never get caught?

Then, later, when the bastard went over the hill from the field—*from the field!*—leaving all his gear up there and was promptly busted, Hugh thought perhaps the bust would straighten him out.

But obviously it hadn't.

Because only a short while later the bastard was over the hill again.

While on guard.

Deserting his post.

Now it would be permissible, even humorous, if Bohane had been in someone else's platoon, Hugh admitted. But he wasn't. So quite naturally the head rollers felt that he,

Hugh, was not doing his job—not if he had an inveterate fuckup in his platoon and could do nothing about him.

It would be nice, Hugh thought, if he could just march up to the battalion office and tell the colonel that it was not *his* fault Bohane was like that. According to the Pythagorean system that Hugh had worked on Bohane, there was nothing he could do to stop it. But he would look damn silly explaining metempsychosis to the colonel: so silly he would be marking time with Bohane in the Middle Camp brig. There did not seem to be any consolation anywhere.

And it wasn't just Bohane, Hugh ground his teeth, it was the whole platoon. There was Stack Renshaw, the blocky German Hoosier, who had come back from the States after thirty days: married, and totally changed. The Red Cross had put a lien on his paydays to get what was legally its —the money it had taken him to get Stateside, to buy a wedding ring (Stack proudly told everyone he paid $65 for it), get married, no honeymoon, get divorced, and stay drunk the rest of the thirty days. Then, when he arrived at South Camp, a tracer from the States followed him enumerating Stack's sloppy appearance in uniform, which fit him precisely when he rolled into the barracks still drunk, cursing his homeland and all the untouchable miseries of life that had forced him into this degrading position —Hugh was, once again, held to blame. Another one of his men had caused a scene that was unbecoming and definitely uncongratulatory to the Crotch.

What in the hell had they expected him to do with Stack Renshaw?

Why, straighten him out, of course.

But he could not.

Stack no longer took pains to look sharp and poised as he had back there when they were stationed at Camp Pendleton, Hugh thought, or even those first few weeks they were in Japan. Until that bunch from Korea arrived, Hugh's mind narrowed coldly: *Bohane* in a word. And the mothering misery of it all was that he, Hugh Thorton, had been going to put Stack Renshaw up for corporal. He could not very well do that now. Hell! He couldn't put anyone up for rank in the platoon now.

Then Poke Turner and Guppy Talagua, whom he had been free of when they were sweating out their thirty days at the Middle Camp brig, were released. And they were changed, too. Everybody was changed.

Poke Turner was no longer his eloquent happy-go-lucky I'll-go-over-the-hill-if-you-do sort of rear rank private. He was withdrawn and silent. The same applied to Guppy Talagua. They still mingled with the same denizens of Fujioka at the Bar New Blue Moon, but in the barracks they were uninterested. No, uninterested was entirely too weak a word. They were apathetic.

And Dallas, in whom Hugh had always had faith as a sort of molder, was still one somewhat, but he had changed too. Dallas still hung out with Poke and Stack and all the rest of the platoon (damn near) down at the Blue Moon, but back in the barracks he was Corporal Dallas, first squad leader, second only to Jesus Queecho, the right guide who had replaced—go ahead, speak of the devil—Giff Bohane. It was the first time in seven years that Dallas had been an NCO.

So, out of the whole company, winnowed down to one individual, the only one Hugh could count on was Jack Koko Hobbs, who was still immaculate, handsome, calm and cool and ran the platoon—Hugh's platoon—as platoon sergeant.

Up until the cold weather training at Jig area though, Hugh felt he had managed to scoop together the fragments of his crumbling empire and started to putting it all back together, getting it wired again; and he was at that point congratulating himself on his astute recovery, when Gunny Leroy Finch suddenly changed tactics on him.

If anything, Hugh did not want Finch to get so drunk or fouled up he would lose his position as company gunnery sergeant. Because if he did that, then Hugh would be the only man to take his place. And he did not want that. On the other hand, he did not want Finch to completely sober up so he was cognizant of what was happening in the company because he would interfere with Hugh, who wished to work it all from the sidelines. But that was exactly what had happened—Finch had finally sobered up.

And Hugh kicked himself in the ass because he had been wrong about Finch just as he had been wrong about damn near everything: about Bohane, the platoon, the company. He who had prided himself on his remarkably perceptive judgment of people, he who had congratulated himself on his appraisal of them, he who was never amiss on a live warm body, was suddenly disastrously all wrong.

During the two weeks at Jig area in the cold weather training, Gunny Finch had displayed sober tendencies of leadership and an uncanny knowledge of weapons that had been previously unnoticed.

When · he had, and suddenly without any warning, sobered up, he left Hugh Thorton holding his bleak scrotum with both hands. Thinking back over it, Hugh thought it was like a little kid getting caught masturbating, with practically the same idiotic consequences, because there had been a misconstrued value of importance placed on it.

Finch took over explicitly and Hugh did not, as he had before, run the company himself.

It was strange watching Finch come out of it like he did. The gaunt, cadaverous T/Sgt sobered up the first day going up on the forced march and remained sober, although he shook perceptibly the whole time. In fact he took charge, leaving Hugh nothing to do since Koko Hobbs was running the platoon. It was this which made Hugh turn inside himself again and take a long searching look: a prospector's examination.

So he had come up with fool's gold.

It wasn't confusion—he would have been glad if only he were confused. Funny thing though was that he never got confused, he thought—just all torn up inside and peeled into little shreds. Confusion he could have handled. Maybe he would have been better off if he'd been confused. It was simply the cold staring knowledge that he was WRONG.

And he knew he couldn't take it much longer without an outlet. He had bribed Doc Forbes, just the night before, into giving him his two dozen two-ounce bottles of sick bay brandy and had taken them to his squad tent up in the thick cold snow (the staff and the officers occupied squad tents as a sort of headquarters), under a low-hanging gray late afternoon—itself a dismal premonition—and huddled himself in his sleeping bag on the hay, like a goddam camel, and began drinking. The rest of the staff were out with their platoons, as was their job, he thought miserably; and Gunny Finch was out supervising the digging of another slit trench since the first one they'd built began to stink horribly with the accumulation of Hog Company's excrement.

He lay with the heavy sleeping bag wrapped around him, the two cardboard boxes of brandy nestled under his arm, and drank, feeling excruciatingly sorry for himself, suffering with exquisite pain the foibles of his life. He knew he would not make it through one more day up there in that damnable snow, even though they were permitted to build huge roaring wood fires; knew that he was going back to barracks in the morning with the vanguard, in charge; and knew that he, Hugh Thorton, could not stand another night or day surrounded by the hands he had dealt so neatly and lost his shekels on.

The brandy warmed and soothed him, and at first he lost his misery and became slightly happy, lying there alone pleasantly tingled. But the more he drank, the more bitter and incensed and dissatisfied he became, so he sat up belligerently, legs crossed, and stared at the flap of the tent. If anyone was going to come in he would certainly kick them to hell out, even if he did not gain any lifelong friendships.

The staff, when they sauntered in one by one, took his savage insults silently, paying him little if no attention, listening to his ranting and raving, occasionally giving him that what-the-hell? look, until he finally passed out with the bitterly uncontrolled anger still boiling.

Earlier in the morning, feeling flagrantly abused and suspecting that Doc Forbes had cut the brandy with sick bay alcohol, shakily hungover, he escorted the vanguard of Horrible Hog Company back to the barracks to pave the way for the glorious return of the company the next day. It was just three days from Christmas. And that was when he found out about Bohane's court-martial. To Hugh, on top of everything else, it was like walking into a whorehouse the first day after being circumcised.

The sight of the barracks and the snowy clumps of South Camp did not move him with nostalgia when the weapons carrier chugged in through the main gate. The acute memory of the two weeks in the field and all that happened before left him at a new low.

He dismounted from the weapons carrier when it pulled up in the company mustering area, lugging his heavy pack and sleeping bag, all muddy and stained, his dungarees wrinkled and soiled, a two-day beard on his face, his handlebar mustache drooping, and stood shakily on the cinder ash as his detail clamored out of the rear of the truck.

In the gnarl and confusion of the happy-faced vanguard, ten men in all, only one from the second platoon, Hugh gave them orders on what to do. Most of it was simply: field day the barracks, bring in oil for the stoves, survey all the lines, sheets, in the company, and, he sneered, check out the Christmas tree from Special Services and set it in front of the company office.

Finished with the instructions, Hugh lugged his gear over to the stairs leading up to the window-door of the company office, dropped it all in the snow, and climbed the steps.

Pfc. Quiller Carpentèr, the company clerk, sat hunched over a huge steaming canteen cup of black coffee, his morning's work scattered in front of him. Across from him, on the other side of the office, King Solomon, Unit Diary Clerk, Corporal, sat engaged with his unit diary cards. Top Condrum was not there and Hugh found himself wishing, fleetingly, that he had stayed in the field as he stepped down inside.

"Hello, Gunny," Quiller Carpenter greeted, his red eyes matching Thorton's. "Merry fuckin' Christmas and welcome back to the confines of Hawg Company." He leaned back in his chair.

"Many happy returns to you, too," Hugh said, trying to unsnaggle his handlebar mustache. "Where's your boss?" he asked dully and walked over to the staff coffee mess.

"The top sarjint," Quiller said, "is over to battalion talkin' with the sar'nt major. About some legal shit. I ain't sure. You back to stay?"

"Yeah." Hugh poured a cup of coffee. He felt he should have grumbled or growled or at least grunted something inarticulate. "I suppose everything's ready for the holiday festivities."

"Sure 'nuff is," Quiller said cheerfully. "All ready to hit the beach for four days and man, I am going to have a ball." He straightened up suddenly in his chair and snapped his fingers. "Goddamit, whoa! I almost forgot then to tell you. Your ex-right guide got his court."

Hugh lowered his cup from his mouth. "He did? What'd he get? Couple months?"

"Haw!" Quiller chortled. "Couple months my ass. He caught the load. Six six and a kick."

Hugh walked over and sat down by Quiller's desk, facing him. "Who defended him?"

"No one," Quiller answered blithely. "No one atall. At least he wouldn't let anyone defend him. He pleaded guilty."

"All right," Hugh said, suddenly interested. There was the chance, the slim chance, that he might have been right on this one, might save a grain of his vanity. "That's what I figured he'd plead. He didn't have much more of a choice. What all'd he tell the court? In his extenuation of mitigation?"

"Well, now, that's the good part," Quiller said musingly. "He didn't even give one. No, sir. Old Bohane—he's a good old sonofabitch, you know it?—Well, he didn't say a word. Not through the whole court."

"He didn't defend himself? Ask for clemency? Stand on his Silver Star? Nothing like that?"

"Nope," Quiller said proudly. "That sonofabitch shot it right back at them. He stood on Article 31 the whole time. He wouldn't answer none a their questions or nothing. And never once asked for a fucking thing. I know. I was there watching."

"You were there?" Hugh said, nodding his head. "He didn't say anything, and so they give him a load, slipped it in him?"

Quiller sipped his coffee with a grin. "They sure did, Gunny. I thought maybe he'd say something about the Star but he didn't. You know," he probed thoughtfully, "he's changed somehow. He don't look the same. Course, they worked him over up the brig. But that ain't it. He just don't look the same, that's all. I 'member drinkin' with him down the Blue Moon and I'm telling you he ain't the same man."

So the house is broke, Hugh thought gloomily, staring back at Quiller. "I guess he would be," he said for no reason at all. "If he's getting a kick he would be. Well, that finishes that. Was it approved?"

"Oh, they'll approve it all right," Quiller grinned. "Man, old Major Luten was pissed off like a man who's paid his shekel and can't get a hard-on. He couldn't crack ol' Bohané at all. The sonofabitch jist stood there and kept saying, 'I stand on Article 31, sir'—just like that. He's a good old sonofabitch." Quiller smiled proudly. "Ain't he?"

Hugh stood up, his coffee untouched, and stepped up to the window-door. "The company'll be back tomorrow,"

382

he shot back over his shoulder as he left. "Tell Top Condrum that when he comes in; and tell him the vanguard is back."

He hefted his gear on his shoulder, looking like a cowboy with his saddle and no horse, and trudged wearily across the purple cinder ash to the staff quarters, his beetling brow wavering, his black handlebar mustache drooping, forlorn.

Itchie, the thirteen-year-young Japanee houseboy, sat in the spotless staff quarters pressing uniforms on his locker box. He glanced up happily as Hugh came in.

"*Ohio,* Thoton-san," he beamed. "You all finish with field, *ne?*"

Hugh did not look at him. He walked over to his bunk, dropped his gear on the floor and collapsed on the soft bunk. Yes, naturally Bohane got a BCD as he had predicted. But he hadn't believed it. But that wasn't what hurt. What hurt was the fact that he hadn't used his Silver Star as a weapon. He would have placed money on Bohane doing that. He had lost that bet with himself.

"You *toxon* tired, *ne?*" Itchie called out gleefully from the locker box, his acquisitive face blank. "But havo good time Chlistmas?"

Thorton remained staring at the ceiling, at a nail in the plaster board. "Itchie," he said slowly, "Itchie, you can go home. You don't have to work today. Just go on home and come back in the morning. The other staff'll be here. You'll have plenty to do then. Just go on home." He heard Itchie scramble to his feet and his quiet noise of putting the pressing gear away. Then the footsteps came over to the bunk.

"You have tobacco *jodi?*" Itchie asked. "Itchie's all out of smokes."

"In the locker," Hugh said quietly. He reached into his pocket and pulled forth an old key and held it out. "There's two cartons in the locker. Take them both."

"*Arrigato!*" Itchie said thankfully. He got the two solid cartons and handed the key back. "I give one to my old man for Chlistmas."

"You do that, Itchie. Give one to your sister, too. The one you're going to fix me up with."

"*Hai.*" Itchie stuffed the cigarettes down the front of the jacket. "When you come stay Itchie's house? Havo dinner?"

"I might come very soon. And I might stay the rest of my life. The idea of having my own rice paddy and watching it grow entices me. I think I would like to meet your sister since she is such a nice conservative country girl. Now get the fuck out and leave me alone."

Itchie quickly shuffled out the door, and Hugh lay there on his bunk, eyelids heavy, watching the ceiling diminish. It wouldn't be such a bad idea, maybe. Maybe that's what he should have done a long time ago. When he was a prisoner of war. Bought a rice paddy. Jesus, but that was a long time ago. When he was a POW—and here.

Of all things, to come back *here* to the same spot. Could that, in some intangible, ephemeral way have anything at all to do with the last six months? All the time they'd been in Japan? Was it his own turning up here again that in some obscure way sent everything going to hell?

No, definitely not. If he started thinking like that he would only be making a hero out of himself. That was all. If he could take the blame for all of it, it would mitigate some of the pain of his being wrong when he thought he was right.

Apparently, he was always and invariably wrong.

Then if he was wrong about Bohane, and Finch, and all the fucking rest of them, why couldn't he be wrong about himself, too? Or Chebe-san? In fact, when he held it up to the light and looked through all its chemical solutions, he was sure he was wrong about everything.

There wasn't any of it had anything to do with him coming back here. None at all. But if he was so smart, why couldn't he figure it out? He was suddenly getting too close to his own prize story of "Slim the Cannibal Turned Grasshopper Eater." It was not only disconcerting as hell but actually threatened to jump out and devour him.

Well, so Bohane got a BCD. Now, how about that? Wonder what will ever happen to him? Hah! Wonder what will ever happen to me? Go ahead, he told himself, feel sorry for yourself. Feel good and sorry, and why shouldn't you?

To hell with Hugh Thorton.

The egotistical bastard.

He felt suddenly as if he had nothing to touch. Nothing that belonged to him. What if Finch remained sober from now on? Oh Jesus Christ on a machine-gun cart!

There was, however, one consolation: Chebe-san—petite,

384

lithe, supple, the only one he had been able to count on since he'd come back to this place. By God, she was in his corner.

Thinking of her he began thinking simultaneously of Christmas, four days off. With his pay, and with what he could goad from Koko, he could forget the company and spend it all with Chebe-san. Maybe he should even buy her a present?

Then, lying there in his sweaty nervous shaky hangover, he began thinking of the company again: all of Horrible Hog Company. There was only one thing to do with a hangover like this one.

He got up, wobbling, fished around in the bottom of his wall locker and produced a full quart of V.O., uncapped it and lay back down holding it in his two large hands like a baby with a milk bottle. It tasted raw on top of last night's brandy and he nipped at it cautiously.

Only two days till Christmas Eve. Well, he might as well start his celebrating early. Just to show he was not an old Scrooge and could get in the swing of things, be one of the boys. It wasn't that he enjoyed Christmas any more than any other time of the year. It was just another day, or rather this year, another four days off where no one would harrass him.

The V.O., instead of soothing him, partially saving him, as he had lied himself into believing it would, only brought on the depression. Heavy buffets of V.O. fumes brought it all back in technicolor pictures and the only thought that roamed freely through his mind was that he had been wrong all along. Totally and subjectively wrong. About people and himself and things. He felt if he didn't see Chebe-san he would be more fucked up than Hogan's goat.

But he would not see her till Christmas Eve.

Between now and then, he told himself, he would prepare for it with his V.O., because he meant to be jolly and *toujours gai* for Chebe-san.

A sneering deprecating smile reached up from his mouth, and his mustache followed it shaggily. Holding the bottle loosely on his chest in both hands he studied his special nail in the ceiling. The ceiling and the nail, neither one, told him anything; extolled none of his merits. Ceilings were always like that, he thought. Not friends at all.

Well, to hell with ceilings and nails! No matter what, he would have a fine Christmas. Gradually, he passed out.

25.

Horrible Hog Company came gratefully out of the field the next day, the twenty-third of December. Muddy, weapons rusted, unshaven, disheveled, unbathed, looking as if they had just come off of five years on line, or ten years of fighting in the north against the enemies of their country, they straggled onto the company mustering area and stood in formation at attention listening to the Kizer compliment them on their field work. He told them he would rather go into combat with this company he now held than any other company he'd been in; and men, he added proudly, that's been a damn lot, almost thirty years of it.

The troops stood staring out at the purple cinder ash, black now under the snow-filled racking clouds that blotted out the hills and valleys; Mount Fuji herself was gone, indistinguishable. And through their bearded dirty faces and apparently cynical, contemptuous eyes, gleamed the prospect of four days off with their pockets loaded with shekels. Four days. And if they ran out, their cynical eyes said, they still had their watches to hock, didn't they?

So they stood and listened to the Kizer make his speech with all of them getting a little impatient, wanting to get inside and clean up their gear and weapons so they would not have to worry about it on their four days which, to them, was like a leave: no harassment, no police sergeant's details. And they each prayed silently to their various clouded forms of gods that if there was a war please to hold it off until *after* Christmas— Okay?

Hugh Thorton stood in the staff quarters watching all of it through the window by his bunk, not wanting at all to go out and join it. The staff would be back in a minute and he would have to sit around and listen to all of them gibber about nothing. Especially Finch! Perhaps the dead sonofabitch would, as he hoped, get back on the bottle again over the holidays.

386

Hung over again, but clean and shaven, his mustache impeccably curled and glistening from the cosmoline, he stared out the window at the formation. He had to take it one more night. Then, by God, tomorrow night he'd advance on Fujioka and Chebe-san with both barrels primed.

Christmas Eve rolled around with a thickly falling blanket of fluffy solid white snow covering the black cinder ash. Black spirals of oil smoke rose steadily from the chimneys of the barracks in the early afternoon with the men of Horrible Hog Company inside, prepared, even before liberty call at 1630, all feeling no pain, happily and beligerently drunk in their respective squadbays.

Outside the company office stood a Christmas tree, naked, with hardly any boughs, red and blue and green and amber lights dull against the gray-brown of branches. Still the men were proud of their tree because the Christmas spirit, whatever it was in barracks, ignited each man with the same febrile flame, making them all proud of anything and everything. And at 1630 they converged with howls on the company office, shoulders hunched against the thick downpour of snow, to draw their liberty cards.

The Staff of Horrible Hog Company had started their celebration early too. As was protocol, each staff bought a bottle for each of the other staff: it was their way of giving. Hugh Thorton had given Gunnery Sergeant Leroy Finch two bottles. He had almost given him three bottles, but he decided that it would have been too obvious.

After the giving, Hugh did not intend to stay around the staff quarters sitting at the poker table, drunk, and talking about how it was on Christmas in '37 at Shanghai, China. He dressed hurriedly, his back to the table in his prize pale blue Hong Kong tailored suit, half listening to the bellow of raucous conversation.

Dressed, he sauntered over to the table, took a healthy invigorating drink from Koko Hobbs' bottle. Koko, who had given him fifty bucks, did not look up but was engrossed in the vagaries of old duty stations, and Hugh turned to leave. No one said anything to him.

All the way walking out of the camp, head bowed under the falling snow, feet packing it on the white streets, he thought of Chebe-san. He remembered her in detail. Each small indenture and joint and ball socket movement of her body, her throaty whiskey voice and sincere laugh and black inscrutable eyes. Then, when he got to the main gate and looked out at the bright lights of the town, he did not want to go see her. Not just then.

He walked on through the gate and stood under the snow in the main street of Fujioka. It was already dark, only five o'clock in the afternoon, and it would not be light until almost eight o'clock the next morning: Christmas morning.

Fujioka lay spread out like a great soft woman, arms open to embrace and comfort the naked desperate lives that wandered aimlessly through her many sliding doors. From up the street "Silent Night" whispered through the snow clashing with "Honky-Tonk Woman." All around were the mottled and unorganized stone age noises of voices and laughs and guffaws and splintering glass, laughter and scorn, pain and luxury, and the bars gleamed with as many different lights as were on Horrible Hog Company's Christmas tree.

Mistletoe and holly boughs hung in the windows of the bars, and on Hock at Henry's hockshop a cardboard Santa Claus and his reindeer flew skyward.

Hugh looked up the street at the stucco of the U.S. Bar, the shafts of light plowing through its windows showing yellow squares of fat snow, falling and falling. Two MP's in white gear, whiter even than the snow, tall and heavy, their nightsticks brushing their hips, walked silently by and turned up toward the black hole of Bamboo Alley.

Hugh stood for another minute, indecisive, then he turned up toward Bamboo Alley himself, following the rapidly disappearing footsteps of the MP's, feeling the snow lick at his face and mustache. It had been a long time since he'd been down Bamboo Alley. The last time was with Chebe-san when they had gone down to the Arizona Restaurant to eat.

Bamboo Alley was just as deserted as Main Street, but the bars were packed and the doors all closed. He stopped in the cul-de-sac and glanced through the windows of the Bar New Blue Moon where most of the men in his platoon clutched Jo-sans in evening finery drinking and laughing. He saw Cinamo Dallas and Stack Renshaw with about half a dozen girls around a table, all involved in several facets of partiness. Dallas was apparently with the Jo-san with the pony tail, Hugh thought, who was pouring his beer.

388

Hugh shrugged, and turned down off Bamboo Alley to Skivvie Lane. If he walked long enough it would take him out on the main street again.

Rotten Crotch Mary's was halfway down Skivvie Lane set between two now dry rice paddies: a crude clapboard bar with one sliding door and one window and no porch light, no sign, no pretense. Without pausing, Hugh slid the door open and walked in.

The solid warmth of the potbellied coal stove hit him, flushing his face after the damp cold. Rotten Crotch Mary's, which was not really Rotten Crotch Mary's at all but was officially the Madein Bar—spelled that way, Hugh thought, either through some sign painter's erring American or some marine's lampoonery. The Made-in Bar, then, he thought, was not doing a booming Christmas business. Five Jo-sans, besides Rotten Crotch Mary, sat playing Casino at one of the tables and Rotten Crotch Mary herself stood leaning behind the bar. The Jo-sans looked up as he entered and smiled. He smiled back and sat down at the bar.

"Gin and cider," he said, curling his wet mustache, watching Rotten Crotch Mary prepare his drink with a lazy smile. "Business, him no good tonight?" he asked.

"Ahh," Mary said with professional complaint. "Him pick up late on, you betcha. You maybe stay all night, *ne?*" She looked at him propositioningly, and set his drink in front of him.

"Hell, no; I got duty tomorrow," Hugh lied. "Here, set the bottle on the bar. And that bottle of cider too." He nodded at the two bottles behind her. She set them on the bar, lit a cigarette for him and cleaned off the bar with a rag.

"You want maybe hear Chlistmas music?" she asked politely. "Play some good *Baykoko* Chlistmas music?"

"Sure. Whatever you want," Hugh grinned, hearing the soft murmuring of the Jo-sans at the table behind him over their games of Casino. The Madein Bar, he thought, was the only bar in Fujioka that did not allow their women to wear Japanee clothes—no kimonos or even slit skirts. American clothes all the time. Rotten Crotch Mary, being White Russian and feeling noble, probably did not allow it.

He sat there listening to "God Rest Ye Merry Gentlemen," "Away in a Manger," and some others he did not know the names of, and proceeded to work his way

389

through the bottle of gin while the overwhelming depression, the black despondency of the past month, flowed out of him. Hell, it was Christmas! And there was no reason why Hugh Thorton should not enjoy himself on Christmas.

Maybe that was the trouble, he thought, squinting hard at the bottle of gin in front of him. Maybe he was all the time thinking of Hugh Thorton enjoying himself. Well, why shouldn't he? Who else, he asked himself and the bottle in silent unison, who else would want to enjoy him?

Chebe-san Ito, of course, the bottle and he answered silently.

Yep, that was right. He ought to go down there and see her. She might be worrying about him. She had a tendency to worry about him, he thought. She even worried about him when there was no reason. That is, since they had gone to Numazu so long ago. She was truly a fine good girl and she deserved something nice for Christmas.

A present?

Feeling full of excessive good will, Hugh mused over a present for her; something nice—and inexpensive—but nice, that she would like to have. Clothes maybe? Jewelry? Shit, it had been so long since he bought anyone anything he didn't have the foggiest notion what he should get.

He was still thinking hard about it (on his second bottle of gin) when the door slid open and Tex, the old Japanee man with the fiddle and cowboy outfit, came walking in, his goose cocking its long neck behind him. Tex, his one blank gray dead eye catching no glints from the light, his other narrowed almost shut eye as if in a perpetual wink, looked vaguely around the bar. He held his fiddle in his hand, his other hand fingering the pistolless cap gun holster.

Sitting at the bar, Hugh stared at the goose. Then he grinned up at Tex. "Hello, Tex. Come on over and play me something."

Tex walked spasmodically over to the bar, the goose in tow.

"How about a Christmas song, Tex?" Hugh pulled out a hundred-yen bill and placed it in front of him. "You know 'Silent Night'?"

Tex grunted, the only vocal communication he had ever had with anyone, Hugh knew; a grunt for both assent and dissent, started stamping his foot and began playing "Deep in the Heart of Texas."

390

Hugh listened, let him finish, and took another drink as Mary watched from behind the bar with a curious grin.

"That was fine, Tex," Hugh said. "I like you. How about playing 'Deep in the Heart of Texas'?"

"Unnh." Tex stamped his foot for rhythm and started in with the Marines Hymn.

While the hawk of the violin screeched out through the bar with the old Japanee man lost in the intricacies of his expression, Hugh contemplated the hissing goose at his side with a gin-hazy fascination. Each time Tex brought his fiddle to his chin the goose bowed its own long neck and flapped its wings. And when the long-necked goose began stamping on the wooden floor with one of its web feet, accompanying Tex on the Marine Hymn, Hugh almost fell off the stool.

As the last phrase screaked out, Hugh lay a five-hundred-yen bill on the bar, watching the goose cease its stomping, flutter its wings and hiss. Tex picked the money up, bowed, and stared like a one-eyed parrot at Hugh.

"That's quite a bird you got there, Tex," Hugh said, looking at the goose. "Want to sell it?"

Tex started to raise his fiddle to his chin. Hugh stopped him. "No," he said. "No music. Do you want to sell the bird?"

Tex grinned at him.

"The goose," Hugh said in Japanee, thinking what a fine present for Chebe-san! "Do you want to sell the goose?"

Grinning, Tex nodded and looked fondly down at his goose.

"I want to buy it," Hugh said. He reached down and patted its fat sides as the goose craned its long neck around and pecked Hugh hard on the hand. "Hey god-dammit!" he howled, jerking back and kissing his hand. The Jo-sans twittered behind him.

Tex applied some rosin to his bow.

"I want to buy him." Hugh inspected his hand tenderly. "The sonofabitch."

Tex looked dumbly at him.

"Okay," Hugh said, keeping one eye on the goose. He pulled out his wallet, lay three thousand yen on the bar, pointed to the money and then to the bird. "Changee changee, ne?"

Tex grunted, slipping the rosin back into his cap gun holster.

Cautiously, Hugh reached down for the goose and grabbed him by the neck, holding it grimly in one hand. The goose flapped its wings, beating Hugh savagely on his arms. Amid the flurry of feathers and indignant hisses and loud squawks, he managed to pinion the wings to the goose's sides.

"Naw, I ain't going to hurt him," Hugh said. "I want to buy him." Again he pointed to the money and bobbed his head at the goose, which tried desperately to snap off his nose.

Tex nodded and bowed. He picked up the money and pocketed it. Then he picked up his fiddle and walked dreamily over to the door, his round gray eye dull against the lights of the bar.

The goose, which Hugh now held firmly in his arms, began bawling and flexing its muscles as Tex slipped out of the door.

"Hold on, goddamit!" Hugh chastised his gift. Chebe-san ought to be damned happy to get this, he thought. Behind the bar, Rotten Crotch Mary began laughing raucously.

"I'll see you later, Mary," he said, rising off the stool, holding the goose's head and keeping the large wings folded down while the goose kept up an incessant chatter of protest.

Hugh walked over to the door, slid it open with the help of a slim smiling Jo-san, and stepped out into the snow, then closed the door behind him.

"All right now, goddam you," he admonished the huge white bird. "You just keep quiet and don't go snapping at me." He grinned at the frenetic goose protesting wildly as he started up Skivvie Lane.

The snow lay like a white carpet on the thin path of Skivvie Lane, footprintless, guiding him. He would not have any trouble following it. But he was glad there was no water in the rice paddies; he'd freeze if he fell in. The gin began boiling in him with the outside cold and he hoped he would sober up by the time he got to the U.S. Bar. He didn't want to be drunk when he saw Chebe-san.

He had gone only about thirty yards when he heard the heavy footsteps come tramping through the snow behind him, preceded by the guttural incoherent inarticulate grunting of Tex. He looked over his shoulder and saw the tall skinny man dogtrotting up toward him.

"Now, I bought this goose fair and square!" Hugh yelled

392

out, starting to run up the path, casting his eyes over his shoulder while the goose struggled determinedly at the sound of Tex's voice. "I bought this goose from you, Tex!" Hugh howled, picking up speed and holding the goose tightly.

Skivvie Lane sloped up and away from him and he saw the light where it opened onto Main Street by Hock at Henry's. If he could make it there, he'd be all right.

A fiddle came whizzing by his ear through the falling snow and the goose, getting one wing free, began beating Hugh as he ran, now lifting his legs high in the snow hearing Tex grumble behind him as he tried to grab the flailing wing again and, doing so, lost his hold on the goose's neck.

The goose lashed out with its long neck and clamped onto Hugh's ribs, tearing the pale blue Hong Kong tailored suit.

"Eee-you!" Hugh cried, losing his balance, and went snowballing into Skivvie Lane, still clutching the goose by one web foot. The goose turned on him again and snapped at his hand, catching a finger. Hugh doubled up his fist and hooked a left across at the goose's beak. The goose reeled back, relinquishing its hold on his finger, as Tex came running up.

Hugh skidded to his feet, slipping and spinning around as Tex scooped up his wobbling goose and began running back down Skivvie Lane, stopping only long enough to retrieve his fiddle. Then he and the goose disappeared in the snow.

Hugh stood there watching, wiping the snow from his suit and feeling the bite on his ribs burn like fire. His finger looked blue and red and swollen. Miserably, he watched Chebe-san's Christmas present being spirited away in wet silence.

Goddam that Tex! That old Indian giver. Paid good money for a goose and then the heathen sonofabitch wants it back. Hell, he might have been killed by that fiddle.

Holding his injured hand, tucking his elbow against his ribs, he walked up Skivvie Lane. A man couldn't tell about birds. That was one tough goose. First time he'd ever fought a goose. Tex took the money, didn't he? What had he thought he wanted with that old goose?

The gin led him to the end of Skivvie Lane and out onto Main Street. He paused, catching his breath, and walked on up to the U.S. Bar.

Still clutching his mangled finger tenderly, Hugh bent over and peeked in the window. The U.S. Bar had gone all out for Christmas this year: the Jo-sans were dressed in long flowing evening dresses. Some of them even had flower corsages pinned on them right above their breasts. He saw Chebe-san sitting at the bar talking with a M/Sgt whom he did not know. Koko Hobbs and Pappy Dreek were both sitting at a booth. And off in a corner was D'Agastino. Probably the whole goddam staff from Hog Company was there.

Straightening up, he walked around behind the bar and slipped in through the back door. He slipped quietly out of his shoes, using his good hand, and tiptoed to Chebe-san's room. He set his shoes down just outside the door, then walked to the corridor that led to the bar.

Mama-san Tokudo was shuttling back and forth with ice from the bar to the kitchen. When she came back he caught her, surprising her, and he told her to send Chebe-san back to see him. He would be in her room. But not to tell anyone else he was here. He kissed her on the forehead and patted her butt as she walked stoop-shouldered back into the bar.

He walked back to Chebe-san's room and peeled his coat and shirt to inspect the damage. Beak marks, about an inch and a half long, followed down to his last rib. They were red and blue and black, but the skin had not been lacerated like his finger. He did not want to look at his finger. He dragged himself up to Chebe-san's tiny mirror in the sparse cold room and looked at his face. His mustache was drooping and his hair was rumpled and glinting wet. His deep-set eyes under the beetling brow were red and inflamed. He held his finger up in front of him and looked at it in the mirror.

Dejected, he pulled out the *tatami* mat and sat down. It wasn't fair. Not fair at all. What he had envisioned, a quiet but storm-tossed weekend with Chebe-san, a holiday, had started off just like everything else. Like the camp, the company, Finch—and now this! Couldn't even buy a goose without getting all fucked up. Then he heard the footsteps patter delicately in the hall, stop, and the door slide open.

"It isn't fair," Hugh said to Chebe-san.

She was wearing a white off-the-shoulder evening dress; her small breasts, enhanced by falsies, rose and fell steadily like twin firm mounds of face-smothering softness.

She looked down at him with a distant tender regard.

"It isn't fair, Chebe-san," he repeated. "Everything gone to hell. Ain't no-thing right any more. I'm a whipped man!" He shifted his eyes from her breasts to her face for approval. "Merry Christmas."

"You are a drunk man," Chebe-san said warmly in her throaty whiskey voice, stepping all the way in the room and sliding the door shut behind her. "You haven't been out to see me in more than three weeks."

"I've had so fucking much trouble," Hugh lamented. "You don't know what it's like. Always being wrong! You just don't know. Look at this!" He held his mangled finger up in the air as if it were some sort of alien human appendage.

"Oh, Hugh-san," she sighed, seeing the finger, her face breaking into an emotional concern. She started to kneel down to him and reached out for his finger.

"Retribution," he grinned, and pulled the finger away from her, slipped his good arm around her waist and pulled her down to him.

"You'll ruin my dress," she protested.

"Your dress? Look at my trousers! All covered with blood!"

"Shhh." She put her finger to his lips. "You were in a fight, *ne?*"

"No, no, no. Yes, yes! I was in a fight," he said decisively. "With a goose. With a damn goose."

Chebe-san looked at him, puzzled, and drew back a little.

"No, goddamit," he said. "I'm serious's all billy hell. I bought a goose for you, for Christmas, a present." He shifted his eyes to her breasts. "I was gonna give it to you to cook for Christmas dinner. Oh, that mean goddam bird." He pulled her to him and began rocking her tenderly as if she were a small doll.

"There, there, Hugh-san," she cooed. "You'll be all right. Chebe-san doesn't need a goose for Christmas. It's all right."

"But you don't understand! I wanted to get you something. I wanted to buy you something. I don't know why I picked a goose. Honest, I don't. I should have got something else. You wouldn't want a goose."

"It's all right," she appeased. "I would have liked the goose— It's awfully cold in here— Is that what happened to your finger? The goose? Where?" She pulled away from him again looking penetratingly into his eyes, which did not penetrate back but had a difficult time focusing. "Where did you find a goose?"

"I had no business buying it in the first place," Hugh chastised himself. "I conned him into it was what I did. It was his goose, the only friend he had and I conned him into it. Took advantage of his slow weak mind."

"Tex? It was Tex's goose?"

"Yeah." Hugh made a wry face. "Old Tex's goose." He picked up his lacerated finger and held it in front of her. "Look what that feathery sonofabitch did!"

Chebe-san started to smile, grinned, and then began giggling and finally, laughing almost uncontrollably, smothered her face in her hands.

"It sure enough is funny, all right," Hugh said bitterly. "I get injured. Look! I'm wounded! Look at my finger!"

She took hold of his hand and kissed the finger lightly. "I'll get something to fix it up with."

Hugh watched her slip lithely out of the room, looked up at the window and saw fat snow flakes falling thickly. He waited silently until she came back, carrying a small blue box with iodine and gauze and unguents and all medical supplies for superficial injuries, and knelt down beside him, crossing her legs carefully under her dress.

"You're so good," Hugh said, admiring her. "You're kind and decent and I think I love you. Yes," he said, bobbing his head, "I think I love you. I do. I love you."

"You do," she said with a half grin.

Mama-san shuffled into the room with a steaming can of water, grinning with mockery, set the pan down and shuffled out.

"Hold still," Chebe-san admonished him gently, holding his hand and pushing it toward the steaming pan.

"But that's hot."

"It's good for you."

Reluctantly, Hugh let her guide his swollen finger into the near boiling water. He gritted his teeth as the water seared into the open flesh. It started the blood flowing again, cleansing it, and all the time Chebe-san held his finger she rubbed his forehead soothingly with her other hand.

When his finger had soaked for about five minutes she pulled it out of the water, took some dry gauze and wiped it clean of all the dirt and bits of flesh. The swelling had gone down appreciably, and like a dutiful nurse who had a favorite patient she applied some pungent-smelling grease to it, a dull black salve, and Hugh watched the operation feeling his romantic nature he had thought he had lost so long ago bubbling up in him like an erupting volcano, and his eyes glazed a little. After the grease she wrapped some loose gauze around the finger and taped it comfortably so the bandage would stay; then she set the pan and blue box aside off the *tatami*.

"And your side," she smiled. "How is your side? Is it all right?"

"It hurts something bad," Hugh said, looking down to inspect it. The skin along his last rib was heavily bruised, pinched, but it was not a gash like his finger and was not really painful at all.

Chebe-san ran her finger over the bruise and Hugh winced and pulled her to him again. "Don't worry about that," he said. "It's all right now. You fixed me up fine."

"You be all right now, *ne?*" She held his head in her hands with a strange expression on her face.

"Oh, I'm fine," he said. "Tiptop shape. Merry Christmas." He kissed her on the mouth and pulled his head back. "You don't have to go out there again, do you? I mean, how about staying back with me the rest of the night?"

"It's Christmas Eve, Hugh-san," she said with the same weird far-off expression that puzzled him. "All the Jo-sans have to be up front on Christmas Eve."

"Well, you don't," Hugh said. "You're going to spend the night with me anyway, ain't you? You don't have another date, do you? You knew I'd be out, didn't you?"

"*Hai,* I knew."

"You know," he said carefully, "I've really missed you. More than I thought I would. More than I ever did before." He started to move closer to her, wrapping his arm around her, his bandaged finger dangling impotently off to the side.

"*Hai,* and I missed you too," Chebe-san said with a faint grin. "But business is business." She pulled away and dropped her hands from his face.

"Ahhh," he evaded. "Business is business! Well, goddam Chebe-san! I'm business. I want you. Now. And all the rest of the weekend. All the holidays."

"No good over the holidays, Hugh-san," she said.

"Chebe-san sick sick now. No good." Embarrassed, she turned from him and slipped out the door, paused and turned back to him.

"You maybe catchie someone else," she said, wiping her hand across her forehead. "Chebe-san no good when sick." She lapsed into her pidgin American with a look of total and unredeemable guilt on her small face. She slid the door shut and walked down the hall.

Hugh sat cross-legged in an unpleasant, exquisitely painful stupefaction. So still another life carried still another wrong conclusion off into the snowy dismal winter night. That was great. It meant, if he could count it as a consolation, that he was hitting the target in the black with every shot. Before, when he had been right—or thought he had—he hit the black too, all the time. Now, when he was wrong, he was hitting the black too. There did not seem to be a middle of the path for people like Hugh Thorton.

Goddam it all to hell, anyway.

So Chebe-san was sick. Carrying the occupational hazard of her trade. Trade? No, art, profession, from which, once a month the *curse* or *plague*, whatever it was, he thought dismally, impeded her from making her living. There ought to be some sort of labor union that doled out compensation for those days of the month, like unemployment checks, so they would not starve or get old and worn out. But that was foolish. They could no more get off the merry-go-round than he could. They were no more twenty-year women than he was a twenty-year man—he saw himself in his mind's eye standing right up there alongside all the whores in the world in the night's snowy twilight.

And he Hugh Thorton, who was not ignorant, dumb, or slow on the uptake, who, in fact, saw the world stretching out in front of him—drunk or sober—knew definitely what was going to happen and where, just as all whores did. Probably because he was one himself actually, a whore of some kind, who made his living prostituting his talents, and not for money—no whore ever got rich.

Subsequently becoming a menace to society because he did not admire any governments but went against them, simply because it was in him to do it and he didn't know why; just did it that was all. A lower element of the unrespectables, the world's undesirables, whom all the self-

398

righteous people including the NAACP and the NSCPA and the WCTU and the Admen all eschewed and shunned and pummeled down, hated more implacably, and were simultaneously more afraid of because they feared these recalcitrants who did not believe in inertia more than they feared the Communists or the Atom bomb and could not control them at all. There was no AEC for the thoughts of mind, no people's club like the Rotary or the Chamber of Commerce to bridle and suppress the ones like him—whores of a sort, sisters and brothers under the skin. . . .

Hugh's lantern-jawed determined chin bobbed on his chest and he blinked his eyes open. Must have dozed off. Goddam that gin was potent, sneaked right up and kicked a man in the ass, it did. Ought to have another drink.

Flexing his muscles in a long stretch, he looked around the room, still sitting cross-legged, his back ramrod straight. Snow still fell in fluffy eddies outside the window and a chill stole into the room. It was only eight o'clock. His mouth was dry and his head ached slightly. But there was gin outside in the bar and it was Christmas Eve!

He stood up and inspected his bandaged finger, which miraculously did not hurt at all now; the black acrid grease had been a fine soother. Chebe-san Chebe-san Chebe-san, the hands of a healer. He got a firm grip on himself and slipped out of the room. He found Mama-san in the kitchen sweatily chopping up some ice for the drinks.

From the bar came the happy jolly festivities of the holiday season, laughter and guffaws, and he paused for a moment listening to it, then stepped up to Mama-san and had her get a fresh quart of gin and took it back to the little cold room at the end of the hall without looking into the bar to see if Chebe-san was there.

Back in the room, sitting cross-legged again facing the wall, he drank thirstily, warming himself. Merry Christmas. If he got too cold he could pull out the wool quilt and wrap up in that. But the gin fought the cold well enough for now. The only thing to do was to get drunk and pass out. He would not even hang up a stocking in hopes that Saint Nick would soon be there. He would wake up on Christmas morning and maybe, hopefully, some of the depression and despondency would be gone. Getting a tight hold on himself and more of a tight grip on the bottle, he swilled his way through it and passed out in a logged, lumbering, thick-lipped drunkenness, and his mustache tickled his nose vaguely before he went black.

He did not know how long he'd been asleep, or even if he had been *really* asleep or simply suspended, but a jarring crash brought him around.

Outside, filtering through the still falling snow, was the sound of fist hitting skull and the muffled shouts and cries of a payday melee, and he sat listening to it, immobile. It was coming from behind the bar. Between the U.S. Bar and the Diamond Bar.

"Oh you sonfabitch!" the words came like a haunt through the night followed by a body-slamming smash against the ground and a heavy grunt. Then Hugh was on his feet, barefoot, impelled into action, and rushed out of the room and down the hall, sliding the back door open and stepping out into the ankle-deep numbing snow.

Dark shadows of all shapes moved like phantoms against the white of the snow in a twenty-yard radius between the U.S. Bar and the Diamond Bar. Little splotches of red blood darkened the snow in spots. A flurry of fists and feet kicked out from the phantoms, and men grunted and swung back amid the epithets of combat.

Hugh stood just outside the doorway, holding his bandaged arm up, naked to the waist, still drunk and trying to focus his eyes, when a body hit hard on the side of the head yelped and came rolling through the snow and stopped fitfully at his feet. The body belonged to Poke Turner.

"What the hell's going on?" Hugh stuck his good arm out and lifted Poke to his feet. "What's the fight about?"

Poke Turner shook his head vigorously, clearing himself, and looked up at Hugh, narrowed-eyed, cynical and derisive. "Them fuckin' Tankers," he said through a swollen mouth. "They got wise with Dallas up the Diamond Bar. We was makin' our Christmas rounds." He grinned crookedly and looked back at the fight that still raged on. "Hope no MP's come in, the pricks."

"Goddamit, Poke!" a voice called out in exasperation. "Get your ass over here and lend a hand!"

Hugh squinted out through the falling snow at the whirling shadows, listening to the sound of bone-crunching fists. Someone howled in pain.

400

"You all right, Turner?" Hugh said, mustering up a small corner of sobriety that was in him.

"Yeah. I'll be all right in a minute." He stood watching it with Hugh, shaking his head.

"So how'd Dallas start it?"

"Some fuckin' Tanker was mouthing off," Poke said, rubbing his bruised knuckles. "And Dallas tole him, 'You wouldn't make a pimple on my ass.'"

"Oh," Hugh said. "How many of them are there?"

"Shit, I dunno. I got to get back give them a hand. I'll see you, Gunny."

"Aw hell." Hugh curled his mustache. "I'll go with you. You punks might need some help."

Hugh followed Poke out to the battleground, wading cold-footed through the snow as Poke broke into a run and slammed into a Tanker who had Stack Renshaw by the throat—or at least it looked like Stack Renshaw to Hugh, who was already looking around for a target and still holding his bandaged finger high in the air.

Something hit him from behind and he fell to his knees in the snow, but rolled instinctively as a foot whizzed past his face. On his back he kicked up hard, straightening his foot, and heard a man howl and fall back helpless.

The Jo-sans from the Diamond Bar began filing out, standing under the short eaves chattering excitedly in their Christmas finery and watching the battle royal with worried and apprehensive looks, fearing that possibly the fight would start back in a body into the bar.

Looking around him, one man out of the way, Hugh felt the bellicosity of not letting himself go wild for so long suddenly wind up through him in a savage growl.

Through the snow-pelted darkness it looked like Cinamo Dallas was lying on his back with a man sitting on top of him hammering away with both fists. Another Tanker apparently was standing guard over them.

Hugh moved up in a crouch, holding his injured finger gingerly high, his sudden manifestation from nowhere startling the man standing guard, just long enough for Hugh to lunge forward with all his weight behind him, hitting the man just under his ear. The man went ass over teakettle into the small drainage ditch in front of the Diamond Bar. The Jo-sans raised an impartial octave in their excitement.

Hugh turned back to the beaten form of Dallas, who was still under the Tanker, grappling; then the tall quarter Cherokee reached up with both arms and clamped them hard around the Tanker's neck, pulling his head down on his mouth.

Hugh watched him twist his head savagely like a dog shaking a dead pheasant. The Tanker yelled in a long bellowing animal cry, jerking his head up. And as he did, there was the ripping sound of tearing skin and the sharp gnash of teeth.

The Tanker clamped his hands to his forehead where blood pumped out in heavy gushes over his left eye.

Dallas got up quickly, spitting eyebrow and skin and blood from his mouth and stepped up to the Tanker, then kicked him expertly in the chest.

Shrill blasts of whistles broke through the night and the sound of heavy boots came lumbering through the snow. From the blast of whistles Hugh figured they were as far down as Hock at Henry's and that gave him enough time to sort things out.

Looking around him, he saw Dallas breathing heavily, his savagely high-boned face very swollen and square. Poke and Stack dragged themselves to their feet beside them.

The MP whistles had stopped what would have been a nifty celebration, Hugh thought, watching the Tankers gather themselves up and take off back into the Diamond Bar, already having their yen in hand for bribery.

Hugh turned back to Dallas. "What the hell happened to your jaw?"

Dallas looked at him without recognition.

"Is it broke?" Hugh persisted.

Dallas did not say anything.

"Goddamit," Hugh said irritably, "say something. If you can talk, it ain't broke. Those MP's are getting closer."

"Let's get on back to the Blue Moon," Dallas said.

"Thanks for the help, Gunny," Poke said. His nose was leveled off across his face and his eyes were blackening.

"Don't mention it," Hugh said, the drunkenness coming back into him with the outflow of adrenaline. "Just get your asses outa here before the MP's come. I don't want to see the rest of my platoon in jail, goddamit."

He watched the blocky indomitable trio move quietly down behind the Diamond Bar to the paddy dyke that

402

would take them down to the creek. The crowds were getting back in the bars and the music started up again. No one had come out of the U.S. Bar. Hugh guessed they hadn't heard it up there.

The cold snow felt like cactus needles on his bare feet and he dog-trotted back to the rear door of the U.S. Bar and slipped in just as the two MP's came charging up the alleyway, their feet packing the snow.

Grinning slyly, Hugh slid the door shut and trudged down the hall to his room. It was a quarter to eleven.

Inside the room he sat down wearily on the *tatami*, shivering, and picked up his bottle of gin. There were still three drinks left in it and he took all of them, one right after the other, fast, and lit a cigarette. His teeth rattled like an old freight train. Even with all the sleep he'd had, he was still loop-legged—and freezing!

Those whoremongering sons of bitches in his platoon were really something. They couldn't stand prosperity, that was all. If there wasn't any action they simply made some. And every goddam one of them would fight at the drop of a hat. Jesus Christ! it hit him through the icy half-drunkenness; it wasn't just his platoon, it was all of Horrible Hog Company.

The gin gone, he crawled over to the corner of the room, pulled the huge thick quilt around him, hunkered under it and rolled up in a ball, waiting for warmth.

There was nothing quite like being cold, freezing windy cold, and wet, as he was from the snow outside. It was like the raw cold of Korea up at the Reservoir, or that one bad winter when he was a POW back in '43. It was the kind of cold, drunk or sober, you had to lie down with, but if you had a thick quilt you could get warm under it while the cold moved over you, and you were not about to stick your head out and taste it. Of course, it always helped if there was a girl.

In the gradually growing warmth of the quilt, smothered by the darkness, still shivering spasmodically, he heard the doors being closed and locked up front in the bar and the duets of footsteps, unstable, moving off to the various rooms, and he lay alone under the quilt, his feet still pinching cold, his hair and back wet from the snow, half drunk, wide-awake, without a woman. Well, he temporized sagely, he was not truly without a woman. This was Chebe-san's room and she would have to come back here, wouldn't she? If it was her room? But she had the great sickness. Shit fire.

From down the hall in one of the rooms came the muffled sound of laughter, a faint giggle in the pillow. A bottle being set heavily on the wooden floor echoed through the bar. In a minute he would sneak back out to the bar and get another bottle. But he didn't want to go up front too soon. He didn't want to be seen. He wondered where the hell Chebe-san was?

A few minutes later he heard the familiar patter of her footsteps moving lightly down the hall; the door slid open and he felt her presence there in the room. He snuggled around under the quilt and peeped out through a fold with one badly bloodshot eye. The dangling light burned his eye and he watched her breath come slowly, with a smile on her face causing steam in the cold room.

"You slept a long time," Chebe-san said, looking at his one eye.

"I guess I did," he said in a foggy voice. "Is it Christmas yet?"

"Almost."

Hugh shifted a little, bobbing his head out from under the quilt, clutching it tightly around his neck. "How about bringing in a habachi pot? It's colder than my Granny's crotch in here."

"We'll go somewhere else," she said and walked over to him. "How is your finger? It hurts no more, *ne?*"

"Not a bit. Go somewhere else where? No, you fixed it up real fine. How's business tonight, good?"

"*Toxon.*" She nodded. "There was trouble out back. A fight I think. The MP's came in and asked some questions."

"No shit?" Hugh said. "Well, a fight ain't rare around here."

"Why don't you go somewhere else and stay?" she said bluntly, apparently not chilled at all by the cold in the room.

"Go somewhere else and stay!" He straightened up a bit. "Don't you want me to stay here?"

"You can't do anything." Chebe-san looked down at her small feet. "You can have no fun; no push-push."

"Hell, that's all right," Hugh lied. "I don't care. I just wanted to celebrate Christmas with you."

She reached her hand for his and he took it, looking up

at her in wonderment. She tugged at him a little, and still puzzled, he stood up.

"I have something to show you," she said distantly.

"Where we going? What's wrong with this. It's your room, ain't it?"

Guilt flushed through Chebe-san's face, and she averted her eyes. "No." She shook her head. "Chebe-san's room is in back. This is workroom."

"Well, now, what the hell?" Hugh said. Was this still *another* barb in the flesh of his back? My God! If he kept discovering things like this about people he'd probably have a nervous breakdown. Then, yielding, it all left him, the old pressure of the backwash of wrongness. "Okay. Let's go. But I want to pick up a bottle first, doll." He wrapped his arm around her waist, feeling a little cold in the naked room.

They walked down the hall to the corridor that opened out into the bar. She broke away from him, dipped behind the darkened bar top and came back with a full quart of V.O., Stateside.

"This what you like, *ne?*" she grinned. "Presento; Merry Christmas."

"Ah," Hugh said, taking it. "Chebe-san, you're a real doll."

"Come on," she said, still distant, and they walked on past the kitchen down to a part of the bar that Hugh had never been in before, to the last door.

"This is Chebe-san's room." She opened the door and snapped on the light.

Hugh stood, clutching the bottle, staring into the room, his drooping mustache wagging as if he were going to sneeze. He took all of it in with a brief gaze: the large Stateside bed, the lace-curtained windows, the soft mellow glow of the night light by the bed and the fluffy frilled vanity, the sofa chair in the corner; the room was almost three times as large as the one they had just left.

"*This* is your room?" Hugh said, turning back to her.

"*Hai,*" she said, embarrassed. "I have wanted to show it to you before. I was afraid if you saw it you would not want to come back, ever."

Hugh followed Chebe-san in and shut the door. It did not slide, it shut, Stateside-type. Then he leaned back against it and watched her walk over to her closet and pull out two kimonos, Japanee style.

405

"You better put one on," she told him.

"It's not that cold," he said, walking over to the sofa and sitting down with a limber satisfaction. Then he uncapped the quart bottle. "So how you rate all this?"

Silently with her back to him, Chebe-san slipped out of her white evening dress. It had only a short zipper on the back and she brought her hand around easily and unzipped it. She was wearing only her panties and bra with the falsies under it. She shucked them and slipped into her kimono, and Hugh glared at the slight bulge of the cloth belt around her loins. And it was Christmas Eve!

"So, how do you rate all this?" he asked her again, and took a drink of the smooth whiskey. "Black market?"

Dressed in her kimono, his draped over her arm, she walked to the bed and climbed up onto it, tucking her knees under her chin and clasping her hands around her legs over the kimono. She looked down at Hugh's kimono lying beside her. "Because I have the money," she said carefully, biting her lip, not looking up. "I run all of this."

Hugh looked up at her bowed head. "You run all what, Chebe-san?"

"The bar, the U.S. Bar. I own it. I am Mama-san, Hugh. And I own too the Pachinko Parlor in Bamboo Alley."

For a moment, long enough to take a drink, Hugh felt his face register surprise, a short breeze of indignation; then it was gone, a rumbling bellow gurgling up from his belly to his throat and he erupted with loud guffaws. "Oh Jesus!" he gasped, rolling forward in the sofa chair. "Oh my Christ!" He continued laughing, his stomach beginning to hurt and tie up from the convulsions. "It figures!" He set the bottle on the floor and rubbed his hands vigorously over his face laughing hard through them.

"Stop it!" Chebe-san said, exasperated. "Don't laugh! Stop it!"

It suddenly seemed to Hugh that some weird unearthly two-headed alien should stick his head in the door and tell him he was not Hugh Thorton, not a T/Sgt in the Marine Corps, but a carrot or a head of cauliflower. Tears of mock humor running down his face, he slid off the chair and rolled on the floor laughing hysterically.

"Stop it!" Chebe-san screamed, fear and anxiety and guilt flashing across her face. "Don't laugh. Please don't laugh!"

Gradually the throes ebbed, trickled off into a weak

giggle, and he sat back on the sofa and rubbed his eyes with both fists, his bandaged finger sticking up awkwardly. He picked up the bottle again and set it between his legs.

"You mean," he gasped. "You mean you own the bar and everything. You're not a business woman?"

"I lied to you," she confessed, "about all of it. But, Hugh-san," she said, "a woman needs something more than this." She waved her arm wearily toward the bar.

Hugh was caught up short again by the occasional flashes of Westernism that leaped out of her. He could never quite get used to the fact that she was Japanee. Sometimes she was, and sometimes she wasn't.

"It's more than the push-push," she went on. "A woman needs to be needed in more than just push-push." She looked at him seriously, her head bending over her knees, tears glistening in her dark somber eyes.

"You don't have to convince me of that. I know that. You don't think I come around here just for that alone, do you?"

"I no know."

"Well, I don't." And he didn't really, did he? No, by God, he did not. If it was just push-push he could get that anywhere. "So don't go thinking that," he told her. "But why the hell didn't you tell me about this before? I wouldn't have cared."

"I was afraid to." Chebe-san came forward on the bed and touched his bare arm with her hand. "I didn't want to lose what I had with you."

"You still have it," he said. "You know that. Hell, I don't care you told me or not." He took a drink of whiskey. "I love you."

"You see, what I told you that time in Numazu about myself wasn't true. I was fooling *myself*. But I have to hang on to it," she said. "I have to hang on to that. If I don't, nothing else makes sense."

"Nothing makes sense anyhow. And I'm not mad about it." He studied her impassively. "I don't hate you." He leaned forward and kissed her knee under the kimono.

"Oh, Hugh-san." She put her hand on the back of his head. "You don't know what it is like. Day to day. No goal. No place to go. And what happens when you leave, when all of you leave?" She retrieved a portion of her Oriental passivity and strength. "I will not become large and fat in the belly and work in a rice paddy. Never."

"I don't blame you," Hugh said softly, his head lolling on the bed, his buttocks on the sofa. "You got to make hay while the sun shines."

She lifted his head in her hands and they sat looking at each other. And what he read in her eyes—or what he thought he read—was that here, with this woman, even with this totally surprising development of her ownership, she had not in any sense lost any of that honesty that he had first seen in her. The first thing that had attracted him to her so long ago, the bit of himself he had seen in her. And what he read was that she was thinking the same thing, and his knowing they both knew that it was only ephemeral and if they did not claw at each other and hem each other in, if they could live without the ego vanity pride shotgun bursting conflicts of emotions—if they could live untouchable and not let the other affect the other—then they could go right on without either of them destroying themselves.

Yet now they were allowing themselves to touch the other, and that was what was bad. That was where the trouble came in.

"No, Chebe-san," he said finally. "I'm not mad with you. And remember what you said in Numazu? If you're honest then there is no love, not really. So don't feel bad about lying to me. That was what you were supposed to do. Or you wouldn't have done it."

She began crying then, her old façade completely broken down, exposing herself, and it embarrassed Hugh. She rolled over on her face, heaving and crying, and Hugh picked up his V.O. and prepared to go back to the cold room and get drunk. It always happened this way, he thought. Make a vow not to become involved and there he was: involved.

He stopped at the door and looked back at her, taking a drink. Then it hit him that she was not crying because she had lied to him at all. She was crying because she had had to tell him that she had lied. And that, exposing herself that way, had touched something within her that contained a great deal of pride. With a start he realized it was analogous to his bandaged finger. He looked at his finger, then at Chebe-san, and took another drink.

After a bit she quit crying and lifted her head up toward the chair where he had been sitting. When she saw it was empty she whirled around on the bed, startled, then smiled when she saw him standing at the door with a confused look on his face.

"You must think I'm a fool," she said, wiping her eyes dry with her hands.

"Hell no," he said. "I don't think you're a fool at all." He capped the bottle. "Look," he said. "Listen. I'll cut a choge on down to your other room," he grinned, "and we'll get together on New Year's or sometime. Okay?"

She scrambled off the bed and walked quickly up to him, her small curved hips swaying under her kimono, pressed against him on the door, wrapped her arms around his back and lay her head on his bare chest. "You don't have to go, Hugh-san." She kissed him just above his belly button.

Hugh felt a little something thrill up through him. "I don't?" he said, still holding the bottle. "Do you want me to stay? Even the way you are?"

"If you want; then it is all right."

"You ain't doing it because you feel sorry for me?"

"No."

"Or because you think I'm mad? Or because you lied to me?"

"Of course not." She nipped at his skin with her teeth.

"Okay." It was her small nibbling bites more than anything else that made him want to stay. Hell, he might as well. He loved her, didn't he? Well . . . sure he did! And even if she did want to sleep with him because she felt a ridiculous guilt over something, so what?

"Okay, doll," he said softly and kissed her on top of her head. "Okay, doll." He reached behind him and snapped off the wall light and only the small night light by her bed gleamed, casting soft glints around the room. He hoisted her in his arms, feeling very much the romantic devil (oh, when I was a corpril I was a divil of a man, eh?) and carried her over to her Stateside bed and laid her tenderly on it. Then he set his bottle on the night stand and lay on his side beside her.

She moved into him, her small rounded body molded into his large frame, and he caressed her over her kimono muttering weird meaningless hanging phrases, groaning at times, catching his breath at others until finally, his loins heatedly threatening to burst on him, he slipped her out of

409

her kimono, dropped his trousers off and kicked them on the floor and untied the little cloth belt around her thighs and hips.

The many times before when they had lain talking came back to him but he knew if he spoke now he would ruin it. So he lay silently expended, his belly moist on hers, with this, the most different of all, and trying to understand it, knowing he never would. He felt a great distance away from her, almost locked up inside himself, and he knew it would never be like that one time again: like that time in Numazu.

While he slept, cuddled with Chebe-san, the dream came visiting, visiting nerve-rackingly in the snow-clouded night: it was a wild, totally unrelated dream where he Hugh Thorton was an old bitch dog giving birth to pups, and he was having a bad go of it. He knew, through nature's instinct, that he was carrying thirteen pups but he had only twelve paps and therefore there was going to be one of the pups shit out of luck. Wildly, not without fright, he gave birth to the pups, all thirteen, and it was quite a task, but he could not recognize their faces. They were not exactly dog faces, no long noses and pointed ears, and they were not exactly human faces either. And the thirteenth one, the last one to come creeping into life from the tunnel of darkness, bore no resemblance to any of the others at all! The last pup was wearing winter greens, a T/Sgt with a bushy mustache, but he was uncovered, no cap, and Hugh chastised him for not wearing his cap out of doors as was the regulation. But the pup paid no heed to this that had given it birth, merely wagged its tail (the tail wagged it, actually) and walked off jauntily on his hind legs, and Hugh tried to stop it but he was too busy shuttling the rest of the pups together for chow. He kept calling after it and the pup kept retreating, moving away, losing contact; and the dream stopped inconclusively, insensately, foolishly.

The night light threw soft yellow up at the lace-curtained window against the falling snow, the flakes large and pointed, and falling straight, piling up on the sill; and Hugh did not wake up when Chebe-san slipped out of the bed later on, almost morning, and got the present from the closet in her room.

It was almost noon when he woke on Christmas. He was alone under the bedspread, warm and fully awake, rested

410

but a little jittery from the booze he had consumed. Then he remembered the dream with a frightening start. My God, was he going mad? he wondered, crouching down under the bedspread again. What kind of dream was that? Him giving birth to pups! And that last one. Ah yes, the last one. He'd better keep quiet about it, not tell anyone —they'd think he was crazy. Yet there was something about the dream that bugged him. Something he felt was important, analogous. He could not help but wonder irritably what it was.

Mulling it over in the warmness of the bed he could not come up with a solid answer. So he lay there acclimating himself to the day. The snow had stopped falling and was already beginning to meet under a bright December Japanee sun. Larded squares of yellow fell through the window, broken only by the four-wood-cross of windowpanes.

There was music drifting in from the bar, fighting with the talk and laughter, all a holiday noise, coming to him in waves. Lifting himself on his elbow, being careful with his bandaged finger, he leaned forward on the bed. Then he saw the present.

It was lying on the night stand wrapped with beautiful red paper and tied with a white satiny bow. He stared at it, confused for a moment. Then he picked it up and read the small card tied to the bow.

To my number-one skivvie honcho, was written in an artistic feminine hand.

A deep well of tenderness opened up in him weighted with a strange love and he untied it slowly, wondering what was in it and thinking it was the first Christmas present he had had since the thirties. One hell of a long time ago.

Inside, wrapped in tissue paper, was a small box with a series of ornate designs on it. Hefting it, Hugh saw that it was made of metal, not gold though, he decided; maybe copper? Perhaps three inches long and an inch and a half wide and beautifully engraved. On the lid was an old Samurai Warrior geared for combat with Mount Fuji behind him. Then, a little in the background and off to one side, was a Japanee woman with her head bowed slightly. It was truly a beautiful box, somewhat like a snuff box. He opened the lid and peered inside.

The long rubber object stared back at him, its red and

yellow and green tentacles folded up listlessly; the same French Tickler he had slipped into Pappy Dreek's pocket last summer.

"Chebe-san!" he yelled suddenly, unconsciously, unable to choke it off. Outside, the din of conversation ebbed, there was a lull, then it picked up again. He heard footsteps coming down the hall. He lay in the bed staring at the small box.

"Whatsa matta you, *dio?*" Chebe-san came into the room. She was wearing her daytime clothes: skirt and sweater. The evening dress would go back on that night, Christmas night. "Your finger hurt again?"

"Chebe-san," Hugh looked up at her, holding the box in his lap. "You got me a present for Christmas. You didn't have to do that."

She smiled warmly, slyly, and sat down on the bed. "You didn't have to buy me a goose either."

"Jesus, I ought to get you something." Hugh shook his head. Then he grinned broadly, pulling the long rubber out of the box. "But what's this for?"

"A joke, Hugh-san," she said with a short giggle. "Just for a joke. You like the presento, *ne?*"

"Oh, yeah!" Hugh sat up and studied the engraved pictures on the lid. "Did you have this engraved or was it like that when you bought it?"

"Oh, no; it is a very old box. It is maybe four five hundred years old."

"Yeah?"

"There is a story on the picture," she explained. "The engraver always paints a story but there is no one who knows what the story is except himself. One can only guess." She shrugged. "But you like, *ne?*"

"*Toxon,*" Hugh said, wondering what it was for but not wanting to ask. He'd find out from Itchie maybe, later on. He set the box down and reached out his good arm. "Come here, doll. Come over to me."

Smiling, she bent down and kissed him on both of his eyes. "You feel *toxon* better today?"

"Hell of a lot better than yesterday. Merry Christmas," he said happily. "Old Santa Claus bring you anything last night?"

"The Jo-sans give each other gifts," she said, running her hand through his hair.

412

"But you're in charge of the Jo-sans," Hugh grinned. "You probably get the best presentos of all. The *honcho* usually does."

"Chebe-san catchee some nifty presentos," she said coquettishly. "But don't you tell anyone," she cautioned him, placing her finger against his lips.

"Tell anyone what? That you got presents?"

"Oh, no. That I run the bar. No one knows this but the Jo-sans. They will not tell," she said with that inscrutable Oriental mysticism. "Chebe-san does not want anyone else to know about it. Or this room either."

"Well, sure not," Hugh complied. "All right. Hell, I don't care. In fact, I like it better that way. Yes, I think I do. Adds the element of mystery," he grinned devilishly. "Makes for more drama. No, doll, I won't tell a soul, not even my aged mother." He winked at her and started to get out of bed.

"You come out to the bar now, *ne?*" She straightened her skirt.

"Like this!" Hugh stuck his finger in the air and cast a withering glance at his blood-stained trousers in the corner. "Hell no! I'm going to take that kimono and slip on back to the other—your other—room. And just for kicks, on account of it being Christmas, I'll have some noodles for breakfast and some toast. Okay?" There was nothing in the world, Hugh thought abruptly, quite as good as Japanee toast. Or noodles. Especially after a rousing mind-shattering, body-devastating, losing-himself sortie.

Slim, extremely short, with that graceful but enticing pendulation of her hips, Chebe-san walked over to the door. "Okay, skivvie *honcho,* me fixee noodles. Down in other room."

"Wait a minute." Hugh swung his legs down from the bed. "Who's all out there? From Hog Company?"

Chebe-san stared thoughtfully at the ceiling. "There is the sahjint Hobbs, and the gunny Finch. And the Italian man. Why?"

"Koko, hunh?" Hugh ran his good hand over his mustache. It felt like rock wool. "Tell Hobbs to come on back to the little room. I want to see him. Tell him it's important. But wait till I get back there." He stood up and snatched the kimono off the sofa chair and slipped into it. He walked over and kissed Chebe-san lightly on her cheek,

413

slapped her firm soft buttocks and scooted her out of the room, wondering why it was that every woman he saw he wanted to slap her buttocks?

The corridor was empty. With a wary eye Hugh slippered down the cold wooden floor, on past the opening into the bar where Chebe-san turned off, and then on back to the little room.

When he got inside the dreariness of it hit him like a solid blow to the stomach. It was still miserably cold but the kimono helped some. His jacket to his pale blue Hong Kong tailored suit lay crumpled on the floor, brown dried blood adorning it. He turned from it and sat down, resting his back against the wall.

Five minutes later Koko Hobbs came in, inquisitively, his woman-trapping handsomeness fresh and alert after Christmas Eve, and Hugh wondered how he did it.

"What the hell happened to you, sultan?" Koko asked coolly. He was in full greens, a Marine Corps poster picture. "You have a run in with some gay divorcée's mother-in-law?"

Hugh grinned. "My name is Hugh Thorton and I'm women's answer to the butter-and-egg man. Actually I'm a gamekeeper and I was bit by a woodland creature who didn't get the word."

"Yeah?" Koko said, amused. "What is the word?"

"Bird," Hugh said. "The word is bird; Old Crow; let's get a fifth."

"Already got one," Koko said, leaning against the door-jamb. "I didn't know you were out here last night. Must have come in late, hunh?"

"Not late enough," Hugh said. "How about doing me a favor, buddy?"

"How much will it cost me?"

"You mercenary bastard. Cost you about thirty minutes and a little leg work. I want you to hit out for the barracks and pick me up some clothes."

Koko reached down and pulled a pack of cigarettes out of his sock, flipped one in his mouth and tossed the pack down to Hugh. "What the hell happened to your clothes," he grinned. "Someone steal them? Or you forget to wear any when you come out last night?"

"That ain't important," Hugh said evasively. "You'll do it?"

414

"Sure," Koko shrugged. "What'd you want? Uniform or civvies?"

Hugh sneered, merely sneered, his mustache waggling like a pile of brush blowing in the wind.

"Okay," Koko said. "I'll bring your civvies."

"And some cosmoline for this little baby." Hugh rubbed his cookie duster affectionately.

"You hear about our babes in arms?" Koko asked casually. "Seems like a few of our potential leaders had a fracas last night with some Tankers."

"No shit!" Hugh said. "Do tell." He shook his head and regarded his cigarette. "Well, they're always fighting Tankers. They get locked up?"

"Nope. But they got banged up pretty good. They look real sharp this morning."

"Long's they don't get locked up they'll be all right. We got enough men in the brig as it is."

"We only got one."

"And *that* one's enough. It's a small wonder he didn't march the whole fucking platoon up there with him, just for company."

"Well, you won't have to worry about him any more."

"Thank God for little favors and combat pay."

"You think they'll make his BCD stick?" Koko said casually, uninterested, but Hugh caught the inflection—the tone of a man betting on a dark horse with his last dime.

"I hope to shit in your mess gear," Hugh said. "They got him where they want him and they ain't about to turn him loose again. What would you do, Koko," he said tentatively, "if you had a sheep-killing dog and you were the only one who knew it?"

Koko hooked his thumbs into the small loops of his battle jacket. "I guess I'd take it over the hill and shoot it."

"No, you wouldn't either, Koko," Hugh informed him. "You'd train it to kill the sheep you didn't like."

"That don't tell me nothing."

"I didn't aim for it to."

"All right, mister sonofabitch." Koko straightened up. "I'll get your civvies and cosmoline. You want me to bring out your toothbrush too?"

Laughing contentedly, Hugh watched the dapper S/Sgt walk on out, hearing his footsteps echo down the hall. If it wasn't for Koko he'd really be up shit creek. And sitting there, smoking his first cigarette of the day (Koko's cigarette) he really felt good, magnificently fine, imperiously happy. It was only Friday—Christmas! And he would not have to be back to the rigors of the company until Monday.

Then the Christmas Eve's memory came drifting back to him, the complete fiasco of it, although it hadn't seemed like that at the time. Up at the Jig area during the winter training, and even when he got back to barracks and found out about Bohane's court-martial, he still quite naturally assumed that Chebe-san was his partial salvation, that he could count on her. Then last night, after all that other she had told him about her running the bar— What an ass he had been!

The accumulation of those wrong conclusions, piling up steadily as if he was digging a gigantic hole and throwing dirt out in neat stacks until there was no daylight left, had finally, inexorably, reduced him to a state of utter humiliation.

They could call him wrong-way Thorton, but that wasn't too original; or maybe dipped-in-shit Thorton, which was more apropos; or perhaps rice-paddy-daddy Thorton, which had more romance to it, a tinge of the dramatic.

Yet out of the humiliation and the self-castigation there was nothing quite like self-castigation he discovered, it was even better than self-praise. All his life he had noticed that people would rather sit, drunk or sober, and tell you they were the lowest thing on earth, that they had always been wrong, and that their lives had always been full of mistakes. And he knew why this was, too. By thoroughly deprecating one's self was brought on the pity and some other warm body coming closer to touching you, being a part of you. The only trouble was, if they all continued castigating themselves there would be nothing of value left. But he always had an ace in the hole when people began singing their miseries to him. He would simply deadpan his face and say: *"If I had my life to live over, I'd live it over a saloon."*

Warmly, he embraced the fact that he, Hugh Thorton, knew as little or less than the average ignoramus. And for the first time in his life he began to understand what *"The evil thereof"* actually meant.

The old sufficient-unto-the-day-is-the-evil-thereof came back to him, rushing in a body, with more confidence than

416

ever before. He was not sure what had caused it. And he wondered how long it would last. How long he'd be able to think like that. Being honest with himself, which hurt immensely, he figured it would last about five more minutes. But the thing to do was not to think about it. After all, he wouldn't have to mess with the company again till Monday and that was a long way off. Maybe by that time he would have his old deck of cards working again.

26.

A sweet blowing wind under an azure December sky, crisp and chilling, met Hugh on Monday morning after the Christmas weekend as the company fell out for troop and stomp all decked out in field jackets, gloves and blowing steam—quite a sorry kettle of marine stew.

Under the clean-shaven faces of the company (no one had been locked up over the four days, it was remarkable, everyone commented on it) lurked the healing bruises and scars and swellings, all the toll of the holidays. Cinamo Dallas, Corporal Cinamo Dallas, Hugh's first squad leader, still sported a lumpy jaw; and Poke Turner, with his black eyes, looked like a ring-tailed raccoon, although he had lost none of the cynical eloquence he had carted away with him from the brig. Stack Renshaw, recently married and divorced, had a nice gash along his eye, and the remainder of the platoon appeared as if it had been involved in a huge tag team match and lost. Surpassing all this was Hugh Thorton's still battered, chewed on, pecked, bandaged finger, and all the company stared wonderingly at it albeit no one approached him with a why.

The knowledge that he was not alone in his injuries did not make him feel any better as he inspected his platoon —a rather difficult task because his finger kept getting in the way when he snatched a rifle.

Like a break in the dam, the water having poured out in heady gushes, then temporarily stopped over the holidays, now back with the sandbags giving way, all that Hugh had resolved over Christmas he had suddenly repudiated. Or else something within him repudiated it for him. He felt no closer to the universe—save the answer that he had before.

And that was the way it went for the rest of the week and even on after New Year's. Gunnery Sergeant Leroy Finch remained remarkably sober and began to show an interest in the company, something which gave Hugh a hackle-rising, implacable scorn because now there was no way he could stick his fingers into the still warm pie, sitting in the window to cool, that was Horrible Hog Company.

Consequently, on the New Year's weekend, harried and driven like a runaway slave with the air-snapping crack of whips behind him, he bundled himself up with Chebe-san and took her hopping across the ice on a rousing celebration up to the Fuji New Grand Hotel, high on the slopes of Mount Fuji.

Surrounded by the sky-reaching green pines—the sturdily built hotel that was the outcome of the MacArthur White-God influence for servicemen, a special services recreation hotel that the Red Cross had not been able to get its hands on—Hugh relaxed and made up his mind to enjoy himself.

Rallying the New Year in, the year 1954, Hugh looked forward to it with gusto, even though it still carried an unfamiliar-sounding number. A fine year. Things should be different. He decided to start it off with an open mind, another decision made on the spur of the moment while he was away from the company and alienated from it.

1954, he mused, lying on the Stateside bed in the Fuji Grand Hotel while the probing January sun raised dust motes in the freshened clear air, and the sound of splashing water drifted from the bathroom as Chebe-san showered. Oh yes, 1954. A year of change! And progress. And what, oh leader of men, must be the change? There was the certainty, if he lived that long, that he would be thirty-one this year. Thirty-one! Now, how about that? Couldn't beat the dealer any way you looked at it.

1954, though, meant a good deal more than that to him, he reflected. According to his estimates, it was the year that his life had waited for, had been circling for a long time. And it was finally coming into focus. He felt it was the consummation of everything he had done previously, and everything he had ever been trained for. And he had thought of it a tremendous bit, since way back before the Korean War. The whole cycle of war that had started long before that, which he had titled *Hugh Thorton's Forty Years' War*. Hugh Thorton was the sole possessor, manufacturer, and instigator of *Hugh Thorton's Forty Years' War*. And he had had to wait until the year of our Lord 1954 before it could be put into practical theory. That, he decided, was why he had to go through all those miserable days in 1953 and preceding that. So he would be ready in 1954. If it worked, which he was sure it would, it would be more than adequate compensation for his travail.

The promising thought of 1954 suddenly reinvigorated his confidence and sent Horrible Hog Company cowering back into a dark corner.

By utilizing the concept of the Forty Years' War, which he had spent so much time figuring on, it meant that 1954 would be the end—or beginning!—of a new cycle of wars. Hah! A never-ending progression of crackling rifle fire. And with the world suffering from the hangover of peacetime (hell, no one made any dough, no world bank, no insurance companies, no politicians or chiefs of staff; and more important: no $45 extra a month combat pay), this lewd hangover would have to be brought to a screeching halt. That was all there was to it. And there were any number of places to start it, he thought craftily, listening to the shower running, thinking fleetingly of Chebe-san, whom he had tried not to think too much of at all. She was just too damn fathomless, too inscrutable; and who was to say Kipling was right? *Did the twain ever meet?* Nonetheless, she was in there showering not ten feet away, and in his mind he could see her clearly.

According to his mental maps and charts and figures and calculations, he had just naturally assumed—hell no, not assumed!—iron-clad formidably deduced, or seduced, from his mind—that 1954 was *the* year that would start all of it.

He had first captured the idea in his mind during the Korean war when he was a buck sergeant up at the Reservoir. Oh, the cold creeping crud and dead stiff bodies of the Reservoir and the frozen food and the equally frozen apathy, the Stalingrad of Syngman Rhee. That was when he started thinking about it. In essence, it was so simply and outlandishly plain that he wondered why no one else had thought of it. And damned if he was going to disclose any of his findings either.

Korea, according to his calculations, was more or less a springboard for the Big War which would follow. A sort of Spanish Civil War set amid the organized confusion of the Far East. And at the same time, simultaneously, the war in Indochina was raging. And Formosa which the Madam and the Generalissimo still held (a so involved collaboration with the world no one could quite figure it out). Those three, Korea, Indochina, and Formosa, were the lead-offs to Asia, a three-pincer movement to knock out China and then to force Russia to relinquish its hold on Asia. Russia would have no choice then, since her bare bottom would be displayed to the heathen decadent capitalist states, or going still farther, Hugh decided, listening to Chebe-san hum some Japanee myth song in the shower, and curling his mustache cunningly, it could and might go farther: right on into Russia.

With the build-up in Western Europe they could move in on Russia from the west with their Armies while they—my marines, Hugh thought—would move right on up through Asia. Merely another idealism of the war-to-end-all-wars. It was only too obviously clear that that was what they meant to do. If, he thought wryly, they could all get their heads together and make some decisions. And think of all the people it would please!

The Forty Years' War explained, according to Hugh's foresight of which he was immensely proud, why the Korean war was stopped when it was. They just weren't ready in all the places. But they were getting ready now, he was sure. Everyone, it seemed, was going to liberate everyone else. Everyone was going to be freed. The Communists were going to free the enslaved democracies and the democracies were going to liberate the enslaved Communists and everyone then would make front page. Hell, it would make Hitler look like a poor man's John Brown.

That was what it sifted down to in Hugh's mind. It had all started in 1914 and if it was going to last forty years it would have to come in this year 1954. Just another link of the Forty Years' War. And this would be the last one, the last war: the war to end all wars. It had just taken forty years to get it going. From Flander's Field to Frozen Chosen, a couple of lifetimes almost.

420

And think of the religious converts!

And that was where the happiness came in, Hugh thought, enjoying the early-morning January coldness outside his window while he lay warm on the bed. The happiness evolved from his being right once again. He felt much better. It was, in fact, becoming hard to remember when he'd been wrong.

Feeling vastly pleased with this secret knowledge, he relaxed back into the thick mattress, happy enough to wait, and the prickling skin-pinching knowledge that he would not be so optimistic when he went back to Horrible Hog Company on Monday to start the year 1954 rolled back over him gloomily.

The only thing to do was not to think about it until he got back.

And that was exactly what he did when Chebe-san came out of the shower still dripping, a little wet, in a terry-cloth kimono.

"Let me dry off first," she said coyly, seeing the twist of his mustache.

"Dry off in bed," he said. "Happy New Year, doll. Welcome to 1954. And if you're really a good girl, I just might take you on another vacation come Easter." He tossed the covers back.

"And if you are a good boy," she said right back, her small face lighting up, "Chebe-san might take you out to dinner tonight."

"Now that's real white of you," he said, pulling her down to him. "But let's not think about that now. Let's not think about 1954 or any of that now. It's not important."

"*Hai*," she agreed. "Nothing is important at all now. And no matter what happens, it will not be important, will it, Hugh-san? Like we speak before, last summer almost: no matter what happens it will not be important."

Hugh lost all those other thoughts then, feeling them leave him in the same sharp burst and velocity as a rifle shot. "Don't worry about that. You worry too much. Way too much." But he could not elude the feeling that she was holding out on him. That she had something important she should have told him and didn't.

Afterwards, lying there half drowsily, he decided he had probably been seeing too much of her lately. That must be what it was. It wasn't good like that. Living so close together, it made for bad blood. If he was going to keep his wits, which he meant to, he had better remember his own story about Slim, the man who wouldn't eat his wife. And if anything came—the war, a dose of clap, a Care package, himself, anything—the way he felt right now, he didn't give a big rat's ass at all. He was ready for it. Let it come!

But he did not feel that way when he got back with the company that first week in January. Apparently, all the snow of the season had come and gone those few short days of Christmas, and only the first feeble clinches of an early spring Japanee sun moved across the clean blue sky. Mount Fuji shouted whitely with a fresh dazzling cone of snow starting less than halfway up and biting into the sky.

The men of Horrible Hog Company, taking advantage of the weather, started their field training again, running across the frozen ground in the nippy air.

Somehow, Hugh observed, the company had changed over the holidays. There was none of the exuberance of preparing to go to war that there had been in '53—now a lost year, meaningless. The men had grown more bitter, if that was possible, Hugh thought as he spent more and more time with his platoon in the field.

Gunnery Sergeant Leroy Finch still remained sober, and this bothered Hugh too. He wondered what it would take to put Finch back on his bottle. With the first quivering knees of spring opening slightly ashamed, Hugh caught the hint in the air—something intangible—and he was suddenly quite sure, even that first week in January, that his calculations were right.

The proof came a week later. On January the 12th, 1954.

It came in the *Pacific Stars & Stripes*. The cursing recalcitrants of Hog Company sat on the commodes taking their morning craps and reading all about John Foster Dulles' speech on "massive retaliation" against the Communists or powers thereof. That was the trigger, the detonation, that gave all the men of South Camp, a bona fide solid impetus to keep their chins above water—an unrumor, a fact substantiated by the leaders of their civilization that gave rise to all their hopes and spirits.

Besides, they argued heatedly over their towering stacks of slop chute beer cans, they were already getting a little tired of this place, weren't they? It was time for new horizons, new lands, new peoples to conquer, and especially and most important, they all agreed, the chance of new women.

Leroy Finch, T/Sgt with two hash marks, was the most pleased of all.

When the "massive retaliation" speech came through, Gunny Finch, the hollow-cheeked T/Sgt had scrambled back to his bottle and lapsed into his former self-pitying drunken existence, and for this Hugh thanked whatever hooting providence had seen fit to come to his aid. Hugh was riding loose in the saddle once more.

And he had adherents. Captain Emil Kizer began laying plans of his own for the coming war, which now, he told his staff at their daily meetings, was imminent.

It was just shortly after that, after the speech, that a shipment of brand-new flak jackets came into the supply sheds of the companies, to be placed on the top furthermost shelves in their cardboard boxes waiting to be issued. Old weapons, and those with malfunctions, were turned into the armory for survey and rejuvenation. A phenomenon none of them had ever witnessed before.

A subtle change moved across the camp, coming all the way from CMC in Washington down to the rearest, rankless privates; it was in the air like the sun, an entity, something to be counted on, a sure bet, and all of it had to do with what Hugh Thorton, who was still wrapped up in congratulating himself, had figured. He could not recall a period in his life when he had been so pleased, with the openhanded chance to work things out the way he wanted —behind the action. Hugh did not have to lead anything. Hell, he didn't even want to lead anything, did not want to be a leader, never had—just wanted to watch all of it from a distance, being able to run those things without showing his face. He was just about the happiest man alive.

Buttressing the instincts and formulae he had worked out so long ago was Chebe-san. Obviously she knew all of it, and more than she was telling, too. But she nevertheless corroborated all of his hunches and beliefs and agreed solemnly that the war was coming before long now. (He had spent one entire night explaining his Forty Years' War and she had been impressed.) Of course she was still inscrutable and devious with her answers, but she joked about bundling up her bar and moving with him when they left, a sort of camp follower.

It was almost the end of January when Koko Hobbs launched *his* formulated ideas to Hugh Thorton about a member of the company who all this time has been a jailed man.

"Well, I ain't going to bat for him," Hugh protested, hunched over a can of beer at the poker table in the staff quarters. Most of the staff were out with their platoons. Koko Hobbs had turned the second platoon over to Jesus Queecho so he could come in and talk with Hugh. "No, sir," Hugh said adamantly, "he caused me nothing but trouble when he was with us before. Far as I'm concerned he can rot up there in that Middle Camp brig."

"But he'll be an asset to our platoon. Especially in the war. Hell, we can keep him bridled till then. He won't cause that much trouble in the platoon."

"No, of course he won't," Hugh sneered and finished his can of beer. "Look, Koko, I think it's damn nice of you to be playing the good Samaritan, but you just about over-stepped your limits on this one. Bohane asked for a BCD and he got it. No man in his right mind would pull what he did at his court-martial. That wasn't even half-ass sense! He purely asked for it!"

"Maybe so," Koko temporized. "But I still think we ought to try and do something to get him out of that. As short-handed and understrength as we are we'll need every man we can get."

"I'll agree on that." Hugh nodded. "Every *man* that is. But not every psycho like Bohane. He'd have the platoon killed even before we started fighting. Either by deciding it'd be better to do it his way or maybe to hell with all of it and talking them into getting drunk with him."

"You sound as if you're almost scared of him." Koko stared at Hugh. It was the second time since Hugh had known him that Koko had made an open comment of insult, and he sat looking at him passively.

"I tole you before he got his court-martial," Hugh went on, "that he'd get a BCD. I was right. He got it. I also offered him a way out. He didn't take it. No, buddy"— Hugh twisted his handlebar mustache—"I ain't scared of him. But I ain't sticking my neck out either. I ain't inter-fering. A man who plays the game the way Bohane does don't need any help."

"That's a rare philosophy. Tell me something, Hugh," Koko said calmly. "What would happen to you if I was gone and Jesus Queecho was gone and, say, Corporal Dallas was gone? What would you do then?"

Time seemed to hang in suspension, and the two looked at each other seriously, Hugh wondering with a blank face what Koko had on his mind. Then he laughed raucously. "I'd do what I always do, Koko. I'd find replacements."

"Okay then. It's your platoon. Run it the way you want. But I still think you're making a mistake."

"Everyone thinks that at some time or another," Hugh said confidently. "Everyone thinks I'm making mistakes. But the funny thing is, I'm usually right." He glanced up at Koko, his eyes dark under the beetling brow.

"Then you can't be taught." Koko shrugged, turned on his heel and walked out of the staff quarters and into the biting cool January morning.

"Eat the apple and fuck the Corps in '54!" Hugh called cheerfully after him.

27.

Giff Bohane, up in the Middle Camp brig, had no taste for apples, let alone carnal association with the Marine Corps. He felt he had lost his virginity to the Crotch long ago (or vice versa). And with both of them no longer possessing the sanctified maidenhead, they had no right to insist on casual petting.

He knew with the streetwalker's acumen that he had brought it all on himself (or vice versa). He was not sorry. He had not been raped, or raped them, or lasciviously molested.

Somehow, on looking back at it since he'd arrived in Japan so long ago, he felt he had sprawled on his back (or they had) without fixing a price: each doing it for free out of good will and *esprit de corps*. So, like the ancient hackneyed myth of the good whore, the kindhearted whore, the whore with a heart of gold, he had resigned himself to his fate since his court-martial on the sixteenth of December, 1953. His BCD, he reflected, was very much like an incurable case of VD. And as yet no one had discovered a miraculous cure for it. Except perhaps the rock pile.

Of course he had no illusions of being released or having the BCD remitted. And in a way it was a relief. In the sentence handed down by his superiors it left no opening, no two ways about it. Simple. Mathematical. A cold clear fact. He would serve his six months, collect his BCD, and be drummed out—undoubtedly in the States.

The only way he could look at it now (since he was in no position to barter) was that it was inevitable, a foregone conclusion and there was no sense fighting it. It had come his way, the way he wanted it. He knew he had been right in what he had done at his court-martial, probably the only right thing he had ever done in his life. And he hung on to it grimly. It wasn't much to hang on to, but it was something. Like a sinking raft in the middle of the Pacific.

Then there was the possibility of a remittance which plagued and confused him and caused a hot conflict within him. Swannie, the cynical broken-nosed optimist, still incessantly hammered away that he was confident Giff would get his BCD remitted. But Giff did not put too much faith in it. He had learned, since he had been confined in the Middle Camp brig, to expect the worst and hope for the best. That way it was a compromise without challenge, and he was quite sure he would not be disappointed.

The finest feeling to come out of the court-martial was that he was no longer a "new" prisoner. He was hardened: hardened on the rock pile; hardened in the head; hardened under the calisthenics; hardened from the core of his being to the outermost reaches of himself; and sometimes too, in the womanless brig, he was hardened by hand. But that was not too much relief, except for the visual part and the memories.

He had learned the protocol of the brig, learned it well during the time of his confinement before his court, and he knew how to mold with the other prisoners to form the hard wall of resistance. This perplexed the guards and Duty Wardens (Little Bill and Big Bill) and Giff's old friends: the Great Unwashed and his Negro companion Uncle Tom. They, the brig personnel, had just naturally assumed that a man awarded a BCD would break under the circumstances or at least try for a Section Eight. It had developed into a game.

In the three weeks following his court-martial Giff was even surprised at himself. He no longer thought the way he had before, moved ate slept drank or breathed the way he had before. Sometimes he would startle himself when he caught himself in a mirror during the evening showers while he was shaving. It was as if there had been two of him before where now there was only the one. And he felt he had made the break, the change-over to something entirely new. But he wasn't sure just exactly what it was.

Over the holidays he had been put to the test and he had won. He could not help but think that the old Bohane would not have won. But then, of course, there was hardly any resemblance. He even felt, fatuously, like thanking the brig personnel for this. Even when he hated their guts. It was the holidays, though, that had proved to him that he had been right—and at that time he was a man who needed proof.

Little Bill Claggle, S/Sgt, very small, ferret-headed with close-cropped red hair, had the duty over Christmas. This did not stop him from relishing the festivities. He came on duty noon of Christmas Eve just as the prisoners were preparing to march stonily back to the rock pile after noon chow.

Standing beside his desk at the front of the brig, gazing through the chainmesh of the compound as the prisoners hustled into their field jackets, he informed them in his well-modulated deep voice that he was going to throw a party for the prisoners! A Christmas party! And, he added with a sly grin, everyone was invited.

Now this type of party, as Giff knew from the ones they'd had Thanksgiving, was entirely different than an individual party. An individual party, like the ones they had performed on him, were never quite as bad as the parties where "everyone was invited." On those occasions there seemed to emanate from the brig itself a sort of contagious fury to rip and tear and maim. In a way it was like watching a fight, he had reflected: the large crowd looms around two gladiators and their very fighting itself throws out waves of contact making the crowd, the spectators, want to fight too. And of course they always did.

The prisoners had double-timed across the cinder ash

427

under the thickly falling snow at 1630 on Christmas Eve
—the chasers, their riot guns loaded and cocked, close behind them—coming in little groups of four back from the
rock pile to the brig.

The preliminary of the party started immediately with
calisthenics in the compound, the warm-up supervised
casually by the guards who casually punched several men,
warming up themselves. But the party did not catch its full
stride until after chow and by then all the prisoners knew
it was going to be a doozy.

Giff sat in the mess hall at the small four-man table with
Swannie, Williams, and Speedy Gonzales, the taciturn
Mexican, eating dinner. Sitting at attention, feet planted
firmly on the floor, they spoke softly through their huge
bites of food.

"If it's anythin' like Thanksgiving," Speedy Gonzales
said through his Salisbury steak, "they're not going to
catch this kid. I had it after that. I won't take any more."

"You'll take all they got," Giff told him, his lean rawboned face working exaggeratedly on his bread. "And you
know it. There ain't a fucking thing you can do about it."

"Just because you got a BCD," Speedy pointed out,
"don't mean all the rest of us have to put up with it."

"Knock it off," Williams the Negro said. "That sonfa-
bitchin' black bastard Uncle Tom is watching us."

They ate in silence for a while, aware of the scrutiny of
the guards and Little Bill Claggle on their backs and faces
and hands and feet.

"Don't you worry none about my BCD." Giff chomped
hard on his cauliflower. "That's me concerned with that
and no one else. I got six months to put up with and if I
can take it, *you* sure as hell can."

"Maybe I don't want to," Speedy said, his eyes flashing
darkly. "Maybe I'm sick of it."

"Not sick like them new men," Swannie said. "They still
don't know if they's comin' or goin'. Ain't that right, hoss?"
he directed his voice at Giff.

"Yeah," Giff answered wryly. "They'll get initiated tonight."

"That's so. But I'll tell you somethin', hoss. I agree with
Speedy. I wouldn't blame no one for gettin' tired a this
place. Ain't any of us quite that high we can make
a decision for someone else."

Giff knew this was true. He also knew that misery loves

428

company. He was misery, and company was just around the corner. But he had no right to bring any of them along with him. It was his ride. "Yeah," he said. "You're right, Swannie. I guess I sort of figured everyone should have gone with me."

"Well, I ain't," Speedy said stolidly. "I ain't goin' with anybody. I'm takin' my cards like they fall."

Williams sort of sneered over his coffee. "We all take our cards like they fall. Alone."

But when chow was over and they were marched back to the brig, ass hole to belly button, not receiving any smokes and frisked before taking showers, they all of them knew no one was taking this ride alone.

Little Bill Claggle rushed them through their showers and shaves and shits quickly. Then, when they were all standing at Parade Rest in front of their bunks, like twin rows of crack troopers, reading their brig orders, Little Bill leaned back in his chair at his desk with an elaborate twinkling explosiveness in his eyes.

"Is everyone ready for the party?" he asked in his deep voice. Across from him at the Duty Turnkey's desk, the Great Unwashed sat smiling happily, his chalky face unreceptive.

"I said," Little Bill repeated, "is everyone ready for the party?"

The prisoners in the compound snapped their heels together in one loud answer. "Yes, sir!" they shouted in unison.

"Well, well," Little Bill said. "Everyone *is* ready; now isn't that fine. Five!" he barked. "Get up here!"

Giff broke away from his position of attention and double-timed up to the little red feet painted inside the compound on the cement floor beside the Duty Warden's desk and stared through the chainmesh at Little Bill Claggle.

"Five," Little Bill said casually, "I heered you was talkin' at chow tonight? Is that true?"

"No, sir."

"Callin' me a liar, Five?" Little Bill said. "It seems all the time you callin' me a liar. You think I'm a liar, Five?"

"No, sir."

"You think whoever tole me was lying?"

"Yes, sir," Giff said foolishly, but he could not stop it before it was out.

"Hear that, Butch?" Little Bill said cheerfully. "Five's callin' *you* a liar." He swiveled back to Giff. "You think the Duty Turnkey's a liar, Five?"

"No, sir," Giff said, his mind working quickly; if they had him they had him good, nabbed by the balls. Even if they had to make up something to punish him for. Well, if he was going to get something it wouldn't be for nothing. "No, sir," he said seriously. "Prisoner Number Five does not think the *Dirty Tunekey* is a liar, sir."

"What was that?" the Great Unwashed demanded. "What did you call me?"

"The Dirty Tunekey, sir," Giff said. "Oh, no, sir," he corrected himself lamely, "I mean the Duty Turnkey, sir."

The Great Unwashed pulled out his ring of keys and opened the chainmesh door. "Get in the head, Five," he said. "The red lines are neutral."

Giff moved out on the double-time, through the door of the compound, across the front of the brig and into the head and stood at attention by the urinals, nose and toes against the wall. Then he heard the commencement of calisthenics going on in the compound, all the loud voices drowning out the other sounds. They really got to make some noise, he thought wanly, to drown out this beating if he screamed.

Then his head smashed into the wall and the party started. The Great Unwashed and Uncle Tom worked him over with professional methodicalness. They came fast; it was Christmas Eve and there were other prisoners to deal with. Giff was not alone. Although it kept his mind working out and away from him, letting them pummel him down to the cold cement floor till he was almost unconscious, then tossing him into the shower reviving him, then pummeling him again.

The Great Unwashed kept up a single haunting question through it all: "Who am I, Five?"

When Giff could answer, when his mouth was moist enough to answer, he told him without rhyme or reason: "Sir, you are the Dirty Tunekey, sir." Until finally, his voice hoarse, his throat raw from the repetitive phrase, he could no longer speak.

Vaguely, he felt he was being lifted under his arms—there was no pain, the pain had stopped so long ago, oh, so long ago, he was only numb—and the arms carrying him, his feet dragging on the floor out of the head and

430

along the chainmesh of the compound all the way back to Segregation. Dimly he heard the incessant shouting of the other prisoners.

He was shoved face forward and thought he bounced on the cement floor. He felt his dungarees being ripped off him, then his skivvies and shoes and socks, and naked felt himself being picked up again and heaved down in the first Segregation Cell.

Perhaps an hour later, he did not know what time it was (but it wasn't taps yet, he knew), a light burned through the rectangular eyepiece on the steel door.

He rolled himself around on the cement floor, inspecting himself to see if anything was broken. It wasn't. But his ribs burned icily, and his lip was split. He giggled a little. Maybe he'd get out of here with a hare lip?

Through the deafening buzz in his head he heard the commotion still going on in the brig. He wondered how many of them were still standing and thinking they should have braces for prisoners' legs so their knees would not buckle.

But actually, he thought, they didn't need braces when the cement was so soft and yielding. They could just lay all the prisoners down on the soft cement, let them sink into it and then walk over them. The wet cold cement floor of the cell was so warm and cuddly and soft and pliant like a woman's breasts and he felt his face sink into her breasts as she asked him who hath suckled mine sweet breasts while the paddy-daddy snowflakes fall frolicking outside?

Oh, he was very lucky, he told her, he was the only prisoner in the brig to have a woman, she did not know how lucky he was, but please do not tell anybody or they'll take you away from me and your breasts are so soft but you can see I am no good for one of my balls is turning black and I think I have lost one of them— Don't cry little boy, she said, don't cry— But I'm not crying, those are not my tears, those are bloodless beads of sweat and they will keep the bed warm, so don't you cry little girl, don't you cry—Goddamit! I'll buy you fucking violets! DON'T CRY! No, now I'm sorry, please don't cry, you're so soft, just let me lie here. . . . No, don't go away, don't leave, I'll share my cake and wine with you three times a day, don't go away, don't go away crying I don't want to see you cry you're so pretty don't go away. . . .

He seemed to drift in and out of a small creek, floating face down, yet he knew he was on his back washing into small pools and eddies where trout swam leisurely, sometimes coming out of it, sometimes sinking; then he was washed out of it into a large harbor on the beach where the sun did not shine and the footsteps of people were muffled by unending wind and he was sitting leaning against the wall and the bones of his ass ached and he gradually became cognizant.

The pain had set back in with the blinding darkness and the breathing silence of the brig outside. He eased down on his back and tried to control his breathing so it would not hurt his chest. He would fog up, then come clear, and fog up again in a deep painful sleep.

They kept him in the Segregation Cell for three days: all of Christmas, the Saturday following and all of Sunday. Naked, he lay on the floor replenishing the strength of his body. They brought him bread and water three times a day. Usually it was the Great Unwashed who brought it back to him: a pitcher of mess hall water, six slices of bread and some salt.

Giff ate all of it silently in the darkness, slowly and carefully, and kept a wadded piece of bread in his mouth to chew on all the time. And lay on his back the rest of the time waiting and healing, and the soreness began to abate.

At taps on Sunday night when they came for him, they did not beat him. The Great Unwashed and Uncle Tom half carried, half pushed him back into the chainmesh compound where the lights were already turned out. They had taken a set of dungarees from his square in the storeroom and tossed them by his bunk.

Wobbling, he crawled into his bunk, wondering why they hadn't partied him again. He turned on his side and looked across at Swannie's bunk, but the broken-nosed, malevolent prisoner was already asleep. Giff did not think he would have been able to talk anyway.

He slept, dreaming of himself being used as a battering ram by a multitude of hands, and when he woke, falling out of his bunk Monday morning, it was to go back on the rock pile, the Christmas party a thing of the past.

True to Speedy Gonzales' statement of his "being sick of it," he had proved it on Christmas day, Giff found out

432

at breakfast. They had taken the wiry Mexican back to the Segregation Cell down from Giff's afternoon chow that day and broken his leg. It was not a hard thing to do with two men working on him and Giff wondered in awe at the remarkable fact that old Speedy had not passed out. He had been taken over to Charley Med and confined in the brig section there. Giff did not find out why they had done this to Speedy until that night, Monday night, when, with the day's work pumping blood back through him, Giff talked to Swannie, who had survived the party without showing any signs of being hurt.

"You back on your feed tonight, hoss?" Swannie asked amiably over his black beads. "I thought for a while you were going to check out on us."

"I'll be all right," Giff said. "As long's I keep moving around, keep the blood going, I'll be all right."

"Well, you won't have to worry about that," Swannie said with a satanic grin. "Little Bill'll keep your blood circulatin'."

Giff grinned tightly, his eyes moving around the bunk above him where Williams slept and then over to Speedy's bunk which now was empty, a barren mattress. "How'd they bust his leg?" he asked. "How'd they bust old Speedy's leg?"

Swannie looked at Giff curiously, then he fingered through his beads. "They took him back to Segregation and folded him back on it. A real clean break."

"Why'd they do it for?"

"'Cause he doubled up his fist at Uncle Tom; he was askin' for it all along. Just like you did the other night. I figure he'd helped them some on it. Maybe fall back on it, you know what I mean?"

"He's a goddam fool," Giff said in a hushed voice. "Anyone do that is a goddam fool."

"So are you, hoss," Swannie said without malice.

By New Year's, Giff was back to normal. The buzzing had ceased in his ears and his bruises had turned black, then yellow, then red, and finally mellowed in with his skin. There were only four days in that week to work on the rock pile and that, more than anything else, helped Giff to come back into himself.

Big Bill,. on New Year's, threw a party for them too. And a new man, a pudgy fat-faced clerk from North

Camp, brought in on a fifteen-day hitch, decided right off he "couldn't" do the things the other prisoners did. He was an insult to the men like Giff and Swannie and the Negro Williams, and they all resented him with a black rancor because when he, the new man, made a mistake all of them suffered. But the new man slit his wrists on New Year's Day night when the guards in the head weren't looking during shower time and they barely got tourniquets on him before he bled to death. They moved him in at Charley Med with Speedy Gonzales and he never came back.

Giff moved through the New Year's holidays without catching the brunt of any one special attack. He could not help but think that word had gone out that he belonged to Little Bill Claggle and the Great Unwashed and Uncle Tom so he was to be saved for them. But then he decided it was just simply that Big Bill had his own nemesis in the brig and he wasn't it.

After the holidays, Giff slipped back into the old routine of the brig. Beatings decreased somewhat, and he was on the rock pile again six days a week. He had served almost one month of his six-month sentence and he had been in the brig almost four months. It had become slightly boring, except for the parties, and he did everything by rote. He did not feel a part of anything: not the Marine Corps, the brig, the country, or himself.

Once during that time the monotony was broken up by the arrival of a new prisoner. A well-built, powerful-looking man with a face that flashed with good humor was brought into the brig for two days. He was a buck sergeant from North Camp, the brig grapevine found out, who had severed the head of a Mama-san in a bar up there and tossed her head out the window. Then he had turned himself in. He had given no excuse or reason for what he had done, but had come laughing into the brig. He was a special case and none of the brig personnel worked him over—explicitly a hands-off case. The buck sergeant had been sentenced to hang at the Big Eight Stockade in Tokyo. He did not seem to mind. He thought it was funny.

It was also found out, through the brig grapevine, that the buck sergeant had served three different stretches in the Korean war: a total of almost three years.

Giff had wanted to talk with the man, but since he was

434

kept in segregation all the time, the two days, he did not even see him at chow. He only saw him when he was brought in, laughing, and when he was taken out, laughing.

When the middle of January rolled around and the talk, coming from all quarters, moving through the air in loud truth, slipped into the prisoners' lives at the Middle Camp brig, Giff was not prepared for it.

The talk was of the coming war and how everyone, all the companies, were gearing for it. It was much more impressive than the cheap free scuttlebutt back there right after Korea. Giff was never quite sure if it was because he was locked up that he didn't believe it or if it was the change in him that did not believe it. It seemed unreal. He never really knew which it was. But Swannie, who had told Giff that a war would save his BCD, was inordinately pleased.

"And I just ain't whistlin' Dixie, hoss," he told Giff the third week of January over his Rosary. "You just wait. You'll get that kick remitted. I know."

"Well, I ain't heard nothing about it at all," Giff said in the dark of the compound. He shook his head slowly on his pillow. "If I do it'll surprise the hell out of me."

"Well," Swannie shrugged, "maybe I won't be around to see it. But I still bet you do, hoss," he grinned. "I get sprung in two months. Man! Will I be one happy bastard!"

"Don't blame you," Giff said ruefully. "But you'll probably fuck up again and land back here before you get out."

"Jesus Mary Mother of God," Swannie mocked. "When that day comes, I'll just think up a nice way to check my way out. No sir, buddy, I get out I'm stayin' out. They ain't too happy with three-time losers around here."

"If I'm going to get it remitted, I hope you're around to see it. Just so you can collect your bet."

Two months later when Swannie was released (he tossed a departing phrase to Giff the night before which did not make anything more pleasant for him: "I'll drink some beers for you tonight, hoss"), Giff had heard nothing about his BCD and in fact was not expecting to hear anything.

Without the taps talks Giff felt a loneliness creep into his bones. And he would lie awake, as he had for the past month, for a half hour after taps figuring it all out, mulling it over. The talk of war was still going on: all the prisoners talked about it at chow with their mouths full of greasy food, and still there was no obvious change in the brig.

Swannie, released in March, gradually faded into non-existence and Giff still hammered away on the rock pile. Swannie had become just as alien as Dallas or Poke or any of the company, and even Popcorn—none of whom he thought about any more.

March too brought the first tints of green to the hills and rice paddies, and hints of leaves showed on the trees. The days grew longer and warmer and in the afternoon, their bellies laden with food, the prisoners would return to the rock pile without field jackets.

The second week in March, the supernumerary from the brig, a roly-poly beaming Pfc, came out to the rock pile in the almost hot spring afternoon and took Giff back to the brig. Giff did not ask, as was regulation, what it was for.

Lt. Brickett, the graying mustang officer who had defended him back in December, the Regimental Legal Officer, was waiting for him in the Brig Warden's office back by the storeroom. For the second time since he had been in the brig, Giff sat down.

"Good news!" Lt. Brickett said cheerfully, without preamble. "You're a pretty lucky man, Bohane." He grinned across the desk at Giff.

"Yes, sir?" Giff questioned.

Lt. Brickett pulled out the court-martial record from his Manila folder, still grinning, and set it in front of Giff. "You've had your BCD remitted," he said bluntly.

"I did, sir?" Giff felt something gnaw in him. "Well, that's fine, sir. Who had it remitted?"

"What difference does that make?" Lt. Brickett shrugged and tossed his hands in the air. "The important thing is you'll not be getting your kick. Bet you didn't expect that after your court?"

"No, sir, I sure didn't," Giff said, thinking fleetingly of Swannie.

"Well, I can truthfully say," Lt. Brickett said truthfully, "I didn't expect it either. Not after the way you acted during your court. You wouldn't give me any chance to defend you."

"That was the way we talked it over, sir," Giff said. "I said I was going to plead that way."

436

Lt. Brickett ran his finger along his thin military nose. "I don't think I need to tell you that if you hadn't invoked Article 31 all the time you would never have gotten the BCD in the first place. But as it turned out it didn't matter."

"What does that do with my time and fines?" Giff asked. "Will any of that be dropped?"

"The fines, yes," Lt. Brickett said authoritatively. "But the time is not suspended at all. You still get the six months, all of that. But your fine is only good for three months."

"Then I'll get released in June, sir?"

"No sooner, no later." Lt. Brickett grinned, his triumphant grin. "And let me give you some sturdy advice," he said paternally. "If you get another court-martial, don't for God's sake stand on Article 31. That pisses them off. Play the game like they do.

"I'll remember that, sir," Giff said. "Thank you, sir."

"Don't thank me"—Lt. Brickett waved him off—"I didn't do anything." He ducked his head back to his Manila folder, picked it up and stood up.

"Will I get a copy of my court?" Giff asked, rising to attention.

Lt. Brickett nodded. "You'll have yours sent down from Regiment. And that's that then." He started for the door, stopped, and turned back. "You still have no complaints about the brig?" he asked, with wonder showing behind his eyes.

"No, sir," Giff said flatly. "None at all."

Lt. Brickett nodded without expression. He opened the door and walked out.

Back on the rock pile that same afternoon, hunkering gook-style under a warming March sun, dazzling in a clear blue sky, Giff was vaguely aware of an ambivalent tugging at his emotions. By all standards he should have been elated, he thought, lavishly so. But he wasn't at all.

It was weird, he thought, that he had no sense of joy or thanks because he had gotten the Bad Conduct Discharge remitted. Half of him was sort of happy about it; half of him instinctively rebelled. Somewhere along the shreds and loose ends of his life he knew that it had all lost its importance. There was simply no value placed on any of those things he had once thought valuable.

Even the war, which was still a persistent topic of conversation, did not then have any importance. Except of course that eventually it would snare him, pulling him up by the boot straps; but he was not pushed for it or into it. Nothing, he felt, could touch him now.

28.

When Hugh Thorton read about Bohane's remittance (it was tacked to the company bulletin board outside the company office), he was not even mildly surprised. He had expected it. With a war looming precariously on the horizon, the Marine Corps would not kick a man out. Not when they needed him to fight. And no matter how much of a troublemaker Bohane appeared to be, Hugh knew through past experience that he was the kind of man the Crotch counted on.

It did not injure his ego in the slightest. He had prophesied that Bohane would get a BCD. He had. And he had also known that if there was a war, Bohane would get it remitted. He congratulated himself on his own astuteness about human character.

Having finally assuaged the acute trauma of 1953, back in the saddle now, riding loose with his old healed-up confidence, he was finally (as he was always supposed to be, he decided) totally prepared for all the vagaries in this or any other life. He thought he had dealt his hand—a winner of course, with remarkable control. The old dealers control was right back with him: reinforced.

Horrible Hog Company, however, upon discovering that one of its number had been snatched from the fickle finger of justice, his head removed from the neck slot of the guillotine, *was* surprised. With all that Bohane had done, had instigated in the company, the men did not quite understand how he could have gotten off. But they were nonetheless pleased with it. Any demise other than death was, to them, without much honor. And they were all so enrapt with the prospect of coming action that anything, at that time, seemed pleasant, natural, and a pat hand.

438

Even the Kizer, Hugh noticed, was ebullient about it: bubbling with a tinkling happiness because one of his men, one of his special men, Bohane, had actually outwitted the long-reaching arm of the UCMJ. (He had confided in Hugh, since Hugh was Bohane's platoon leader, that he felt certain Bohane was actually a fine marine. "Anyone with a Silver Star had to be, didn't he?" he had said, rubbing his fingers over his own Navy Cross, and he for one was damn glad Bohane got it remitted; he felt it had taught him a lesson, "eh Gunny?") The Kizer much preferred the *Rocks and Shoals* for the form of military government. He had never been able to understand why they had changed that and adopted something fatuous like the UCMJ.

The news of Bohane's remittance was only hot for a couple of days; then it was lost and dropped, completely forgotten like yesterday's short arm inspection.

Hugh Thorton, Hugh Thorton thought, was a very, very busy man. Not counting his overseeing of the second platoon, which he worked with in the field now almost every day, he had the company to contend with. With the sure-fire war hanging in the belly of the Far East he wanted *his* platoon to be ready for it. Most of the members of the platoon were already combat hardened as was most of the company. And he had worked his platoon from January to March, when Bohane got his BCD remitted, into a well-honed weapon. He was excessively pleased with himself.

Gunny Leroy Finch was drunk almost all the time again. Babbling incoherently about his losing his life as he was sure he would in this next war, drunk, he would repeat his old autobiography over and over: "I been shot at too much." This, of course, was fine and dandy with Hugh. The more Finch drank the easier it was for Hugh to step around the company checking up on things. He began working at it with a zealous excitement, enjoying it more than anything he'd ever done in his life.

Oddly enough, he was getting to the point where he actually enjoyed leadership. Although he was not actually in essence a leader—of anything. Gunny Finch was the company gunnery sergeant, Hugh was not; Koko Hobbs was the platoon sergeant, Hugh was the platoon leader, yet he did not run the platoon; Emil Kizer ran the company (in a way, a very strange way, he decided) and Hugh did not run the company. Still, in a way, he did. He, Hugh

Thorton, did run all those things. He had Gunner Ham Haley on his side. Ham Haley helped him with every turn. Perhaps the old beer-bellied mustang saw something in Hugh that he had missed.

It was, in Hugh's definition, a working of his old theory that he saw in people only those things he saw in himself. And his best qualities, his favorite qualities, were coming into view all around him.

Feeling extravagantly happy, dealing his cards again during the brief cold weather of January to March, rounding up and molding the company, he felt that the situation and terrain had been attacked, conquered and secured. With very little mopping up.

All of the dealing had, he thought, left him with an inescapable desire to put himself in as the leader in fact as well as deed. He wanted to be Horrible Hog Company's gunnery sergeant. When the war came he wanted a seat from which he could control it. After so much time as an operator, a behind-the-curtain cue caller for troops, Hugh Thorton wanted to be a leader. Something he had never been in his life. Not even with the rank of T/Sgt.

Feverishly, with the burning thrust working inside him, he began working his mind around it, formulating it. It would really not be much trouble at all, to deep six Gunny Finch. A man like that would only hamstring the company in combat anyway, and undoubtedly get several men killed.

He would probably though, he thought, need a little help, a backer behind the dealer's slot. The backer would quite naturally have to be Koko Hobbs, just about the only one he could confide in. With Koko in his corner he was quite certain it could be done. And very soon.

He approached Koko with his plan that night, March 10th, feeling energetic, goaded, seeing all of it blooming out in front of him. Since it was entirely a military-business deal Hugh did not want to discuss it in town, and when he told Koko it was Hugh's night to howl at the Staff Club and *he* was buying, Koko protested that he wanted to go on liberty—not to some damn old Staff Club with a shitpot full of twenty-year men—and get drunk. Hugh mustered up his pained charm (his point being that he was buying, implying, he thought, a change of heart) and Koko grumblingly agreed—but only for a couple drinks goddamit.

In the midnight blue of the clear night at nine o'clock

440

Hugh walked with Koko over to the Staff Club past the EM slop chute, maintaining a chattering accolade of good will.

"Well, at least," Koko said coolly, "you ain't nickel-and-diming me to death for a change."

"A complete change of ethics," Hugh said, his mustache twitching in excitement. "It's time for a change."

Koko looked askance at him, his dapper face calm and unexcitable. "I'll back you on that," he said. "But if you don't quit jumping around you're like to piss your pants."

Laughing heartily, Hugh opened the door for him and they walked on into the pale dim light of the Staff Club and sat at the bar where the young Japanee bartender, Johnny-O, hustled up to wait on them.

"Business him not so good tonight." Hugh grinned at Johnny-O with a quick glance around the club where sparse groups of staff sat drinking boisterously with the blare from the jukebox.

"Him no good all time close to payday," Johnny-O grinned back. "Panther piss or havo beer?"

Koko snorted. "Panther piss for me." He reached back for his wallet.

"No, no." Hugh stopped him. "On me tonight, I said."

"Just habit," Koko said.

"One bottle Lucky Tiger Beer and a double shot of panther piss," Hugh told Johnny-O, who scooted away to fill the order.

"So who's been supporting you?" Koko asked, watching Hugh lay five bucks on the bar. "The United Nations?"

"Koko, I'm through taking shekels off you for nothing. I decided to spend my own money. I don't think I've been fair."

Koko coughed wrackingly, his face congesting. He pulled his handkerchief out and blew his nose. Then he looked at the mirror over the bar, at Johnny-O mixing his drink, at the staff sitting at the tables and lit a cigarette cautiously. "Who you want me to kill?" he asked.

"Aw shit, Koko," Hugh said, "I'm serious. I mean it."

Johnny-O came back with the drinks, set them on the bar, made change and leaned down on the bar. "No havo liberty tonight?"

"Yas, we got liberty," Koko said. He took a drink. "Jesus Christ! Johnny-O, what you put in this crap?"

"Panther piss," Johnny-O grinned.

"It's V.O.," Hugh said. "It's what I drink all the time."

"It's panther piss," Koko said. "Why'nt you drink something good? Like Southern Comfort?"

"I'm a Yankee," Hugh said.

"Yankee go home," Johnny-O laughed.

"Git the fuck outa here!" Hugh said irritably. "We got something to talk about."

"Me come back when you ready for more drink," Johnny-O said solicitously and moved on down the bar to take an order from a puffy-faced M/Sgt.

"So what's so important?" Koko asked casually.

"I'm going to take over the company," Hugh said bluntly.

"I'm moving into the White House," Koko said. "Soon's I sell Mexico to Russia."

"I'm serious." Hugh curled his mustache. "I'm getting rid of Finch. If I have to put him on report. Anything. I'm taking over as gunnery sergeant."

Koko whooped. The staff at the other tables looked over at him.

"What's so fucking funny?" Hugh demanded.

"Nothing," Koko said with a grin. "I just wonderin' why you took all this time to do it? You coulda done it in the States."

"Wasn't time," Hugh confided. "With this war coming up, I want to be where I can run things, see?"

"It's a noble idea."

Hugh watched him silently for a moment, timing it. "I'm putting you up for T/Sgt when I do. You've wasted enough time as a S/Sgt. How you like to be a T/Sgt?"

"Sounds all right," Koko agreed. "I like the idea of having some rank."

"The way I see it is that the company will go to hell if Finch is running things. He can't be depended on."

"No, he sure can't."

"But you can," Hugh said. "That's why I want you for a backer. I'll make you T/Sgt. With you behind me, with a higher rank like that, we can wheel and deal." He looked at Koko expectantly, thinking no one would turn down a deal like that, feeling himself running over with anticipation.

Koko bobbed his head, pursed his lips and took a lazy drink. "I'm for it. You doing all this because of this war coming?"

442

"Sure. It's time. I been waiting for it."

"It's a cinch to get Finch outa there. That won't be any trouble. How about Top Condrum?"

"That sonofabitch?" Hugh said indignantly. "He can't see any farther than his charge sheets. No sweat there."

"No strain no pain, hunh?" Koko finished off his drink. "How much I have to pay you for the rank?"

"Oh, now, Koko," Hugh said unctuously. "You don't have to pay anything. I told you, I've had a change of heart. It's your dough, you earned it. Hell, I didn't do anything for it."

"True," Koko said.

"But," Hugh shrugged, "I think maybe you ought to get out of the black market for a while. Lay low. Since the war's coming it might not be safe."

"Your beer's gettin' cold." Koko nodded toward the untouched quart.

Hugh took a cooling drink. "Seriously, if I was you I'd play it a little closer to my vest." Hugh studied Koko's face for a sign of assent, thinking he had it wrapped up now, all set. Good old Koko. He'd always be able to count on him. "If the CID ever got close to you, war or no, you'd be in jail. And you've been getting away with it for a long time."

"That's right," Koko said uncomfortably.

"And if there's a war and you got killed, all that money wouldn't do you any good anyway," Hugh bored.

"That's an occupational hazard."

"Then you'll go for the idea of getting Finch out of the way?"

"Yeah, sure," Koko said. "I said I would. If you run the company it'll be better all the way around."

"I think so," Hugh said. "Ready for another drink?"

"Since you're buyin'."

Hugh motioned for Johnny-O and the little Japanee replenished their drinks.

"There, you see?" Hugh said. "This was important enough to skip one night's liberty, wasn't it?"

"Un-hunh," Koko said. "But since I've missed it, how about getting me special liberty tomorrow?"

"Anything you say," Hugh said magnanimously. "I'll still stand on that advice about the black market though. Maybe it's time you pulled out of it?" He didn't want anything to happen to Koko now, now when he had it all wired. And he wouldn't mind the time he spent protecting him, either. It was for the cause, he thought, for Hugh Thorton's cause.

"You know," Koko said, "I've seriously been considerin' that. Quitting it all together. Yep, I think I will."

"Good," Hugh said. "I think it's your best bet."

They stayed at the Staff Club till it closed at ten-thirty, Hugh buying the drinks, which did not bother him (if he was pinched or pressed he could get some from Chebesan), talking over the deal, making plans and discussing ideas, and Hugh was slightly surprised that Koko was such an avid proponent of the scheme. He congratulated himself, for perhaps the ten millionth time, on his shrewd summing up of people. On the way back from the Staff Club, mellowly drunk, Hugh stopped at the company office and informed the Duty NCO that S/Sgt Jack Koko Hobbs would be on special liberty all of tomorrow and if there was any dissent from the Top to come see him personally by God and he'd take care of it. Then he went drunk to bed. The dawn of spring had impressed him mightily and he was at peace with the world—almost.

The next day, S/Sgt Jack Koko Hobbs left South Camp early in the morning, just after morning inspection, dressed in tailored greens, immaculate, handsome and cool. He was feeling the first warmth of deceptive spring himself and was tolerably happy.

He caught a taxicab outside the main gate and rode up to Gotemba, whistling pleasantly, thoroughly relaxed and decisive. A relaxation he had not felt for quite a while. He did not even think of the war that was coming, or South Camp, or *Gunny* Thorton and his promise of promotion.

He paid the cab driver in Gotemba and walked through the morning's bartering activity up to the Gotemba Japanee Bank of World Commerce, greeted the tellers graciously with his more-than-dapper woman-loving smile. He drew all his money out, explaining to the teller that his company was now in need of it—the company fund which served as a fund for the poor marines who needed to draw from it for cash sales and other commodities. He told the teller that he would be back with more of Hog Company's funds

444

later on when the inflation stopped, tossing him a joke, and took the money in 1000 yen bills and walked out, the bulky envelopes feeling excessively light under his arm. And he was sure it had been just about time because the teller had carried a certain restrained chill with him. My, he thought, how beautiful this warm March day is.

He caught another cab, a long haul for which the cabbie was grateful, down to Yokosuka. There he rented a locker at the Fleet PX and locked his envelopes up. Then he went to Harry Fong & Sons Tailors and had three suits measured for him with express orders to have them ready in a week.

The rest of the afternoon he spent at the Four Winds Japanee night club where all the class hung out, the officers and civilians with *toxon okane*.

He caught a train back to Fujioka late that evening, stopped briefly at the U.S. Bar, and went back to the barracks, happily describing to the other staff members the fine one-day holiday he had spent in Numazu.

When he'd finished changing clothes he started a game of five-card stud going and invited Thorton to play too, something he was never wont to do, and he was vastly pleased when Hugh Thorton grinned devilishly, his mustache dipping, and sat down.

Magnanimously, Koko slid the cards over to Hugh. "Want to deal, Gunny?" he said coolly. "After all, you've got dealer's control."

Amid the grumbling castigation at the cards as the staff increasingly lost and Hugh Thorton increasingly won, Koko thought he had never ever in his entire life felt so happy about losing and it was nice, after all, for Thorton to win. Hell, he needed it.

29.

With the first quick awakening of spring in late March, the monsoon came back with a hidden fury. But not the long-lived incessant drowning rains of the fall monsoon. The new storm stole quietly into the late afternoons and rained during the black nights, mixed with inexplicable fog. Then, in the first gun-metal gray glints of morning, the rain would abate. Huge racking black clouds scudded across the Fossa Magna Range and headed on out to sea, retreating from the morning's brilliant sunshine. Lush green showed everywhere around South Camp: in the hills in the valleys in the rolling flats. And the days were crisply warm with that quick breath-snatching aura of a freshened year.

Then the monsoon gathered itself, not coming every night but perhaps three times a week and never violating the days. Training was speeded up and orders came down from CMC to Division to Regiment to Battalion to Company to Platoon to Squads to Fire Teams and even to Searching Parties. Orders that placed the emphasis on guerrilla tactics, hit-and-run methods of operation. Kill and bug out. Everyone knew what it was for.

Maybe Luke would jump off again in Korea but they, the 3rd Divvy, would not go there. They would go to a country where guerrilla fighting was predominant. The popular belief that that country was Indochina reigned supreme in the rumor-riddled air of the slop chute.

Hugh Thorton had, during the first three months of 1954, been seeing less and less of Chebe-san Ito. He felt that was better. By seeing less of her he enjoyed her much more when he saw her. It was a highly efficacious decision, as it turned out.

Chebe-san, since he did not spend so much time with her any more, opened up to him with a tender self-exposing understanding. This, in its own way, helped Hugh with the working of the company. Too, it was slightly devastating when he saw her for the first time in two weeks on March the 18th.

He had just finished giving Pappy Dreek's armory the once-over on the finally returned, rejuvenated weapons that day. It had taken all afternoon, checking them out, seeing that there were no more malfunctions in them. And oddly enough there weren't any. But it had been tedious, unrelenting, almost boring work (actually Finch's job) and Hugh was more than glad when he was finished with it.

He had showered early, while the rest of the company was still in the field, donned his debonair beige Hong Kong tailored suit with a new red Aloha shirt.

446

Feeling very smooth and refreshed under a dying March sun still casting warm long rays and black thick shadows, he walked to town.

Dogs barking, people chattering, stoop-backed shufflers, wood fires burning, all the smell of Fujioka hit him and he felt an imperious elation walking up the dirt rock road to the U.S. Bar.

No one was there this early. The floor had just been dampened to hold the dust down for the evening's traffic. He bellowed happily for Chebe-san and sat on a bar stool surrounded by the familiar.

She came out, running a brush through her short hair, dressed in jeans and shirt, smiling girlishly.

"Long time no see, Sah-jint," she said in her whiskey voice and walked languidly up to him.

Hugh felt something thicken within him. "Yeah, I'll buy that, doll." He looked her up and down with his deep eyes, curling his well-trained handlebar mustache. "I just pulled in from the last roundup, and my horse needs watering."

"Ah so," she grinned coyly, still running the brush through her hair. "You maybe want Chebe-san short time, *ne?*" She broke into pidgin American. "Push pull, makee love."

"Well, now," Hugh appraised, "I just worked my way up the street. Fourteen bars, if you know what I mean. And I'll have to wait a spell before another one," he grinned at her.

Delicate, a small slim doll, she walked over to him, put her arms around his waist and hugged him. Then raised her head up and kissed him. He kissed her back, not hard.

"I've missed you, Hugh-san," she said sincerely. "I don't like for you to stay away so long."

"You wouldn't like it if I stayed around all the time either," he said, feeling her in his arms. "You'd get tired of me fast. I know. It's always like that. You wouldn't want me around all the time."

"But you're here now. And Chebe-san catchee you now."

"Sure," he grinned. "I can even pay for it. How about that?"

Chebe-san essayed a slap at his face, then pouted. "You no havo pay, whatsa matta you, *dio?*"

"Bamboo. I've gone bamboo."

"Hai. I can believe that." She slipped out of his arms and walked behind the bar, took a quart of Asahi beer out of the cooler, opened it with a loud resonant pop and set it foaming and sweating in front of him. "On the house," she said, running the brush back through her hair again.

"You going to work tonight?" he asked in his best carefree voice, guzzling a long pull of the beer. "Or you going to be free to run off to the bushes with me?" Some of the beer foam had caught on the bottom of his mustache, glistening.

She toyed with the comb in her hair. "You are pretty *toxon* happy, *ne?"*

"Goddam rights." Hugh took another drink of the refreshing cold beer. "Everything's fine. Why?"

She shrugged almost disconsolately, surprising Hugh the way she never failed to surprise him with her sudden transformation from Japanee to American—especially when she was holding back on something that was important. "I thought maybe something was wrong in the company."

"Now why the hell would anything go wrong in the company?" He turned from her and looked out the open door of the bar. Flies had started probing around the dusty twilight. There was something here, he told himself with a hackle-rising instinct, that he was not getting. He had lost the gist of it. It wasn't that she was cold or distant. He turn back to her. "Why?" he repeated. "Why should something go wrong in the company?" When she was like this, he thought, it was as hard to get a steady flow of answers from her as it was to get a kind word from Top Condrum.

"Oh," she said vaguely, "I thought maybe there had been some trouble that was all. Maybe somebody go to Monkey House."

"Christ no," Hugh said just as vaguely. "They're letting everyone out. To go fight the war."

"I still don't think there will be one." She looked up at him intently. "Before, I did. Now, I'm not sure."

"That's wishful thinking. It'll come all right. Remember what I told you about the Forty Years' War. So what's all this got to do with the company?"

"I just thought of it," she said. "It's not important," she grinned, not a convincing grin, not even a grin at all ac-

448

tually: a covering-up grin, Hugh thought. "Want another beer, Hugh-san?"

"Sure," Hugh handed the empty bottle to her. "Well, *do* you have to work tonight or can you run off with me?"

Her back to him, she pulled a fresh beer out of the cooler. "No, I can go," she said simply, and turned around, a fresh smile touching her face. "I'll get dressed. Where we go?"

"I thought maybe Go-Town, see a Japanee movie," Hugh said on the spur of the moment, without reason. "I haven't seen a Japanee movie in a long time."

So they went to the Japanee movie at Go-Town. And afterwards they shacked up at the Hotel Saito. Hotel Saito was a Japanee hotel, replete with all the customs. Please to takee off shoes, they were informed politely as they stepped up out of the delicately ornate stone foyer into the lobby and Hugh paid for the room. Chebe-san stood very much like an American, distant, eyes roaming, untouchable. And she had been acting funny all night, strange sort of, Hugh thought but he could not put his finger on it.

After the transaction for the lodging, he gave her the bill (already paid for) and went back out to get a bottle, wishing he had picked up a quart at the Staff Club or at the U.S. Bar before going on liberty.

When he returned to the room, sober but still confused over Chebe-san's actions, she was sitting on the floor, legs crossed, still dressed in her tailored soft brown suit, expressionless.

"Madam Butterfly," he chortled, walking across the small room, sitting down and leaning his back against the wall. "Now, what's with you, doll? You going bamboo too? Like all the rest of us?"

"Can I have a drink?" she asked politely, surprising Hugh. Now what the hell was this. She never drank anything before—nothing at all.

"Sure," he said and passed the bottle to her.

Taking a deep breath, Chebe-san hefted the bottle and swallowed, then grimaced, frowned, looked about to cry, gasped, and patted her chest over her small breasts (she was not wearing falsies tonight). *"Eee-yadimo!"*

"Like it?" Hugh leaned forward, studying her with a puzzled eye, a squinting half curl in his lips hidden by his mustache. One spear of his mustache shot up like a stalk of sugar cane.

"Hot! *Etai!*" she said, swallowed heavily, tried to burp, swallowed heavily again. Hugh took the bottle back and drank out of it himself. Well, well, he kept thinking, well, well.

He took three good swallows of the rich V.O. and her hand was out for it again. Grudgingly, he handed it to her. They both sat across from each other over the empty floor on the rug.

After three more head-swagging drinks, the burps, the pats on the chest, and the half-Japanee, half-pidgin American exclamations, her eyes, slanted as they were, slanted even more so. "You drink that all time?" she asked throatily.

"Unless they make something better," Hugh said, wondering. "You like it?"

"*Toxon!*" She reached for the bottle again.

"Unh-hunh," he said, and held his hand up. "Not yet, doll. Not till we find something out." He grinned at her, curling his mustache.

"Ah so, Hugh-san," she muttered. "You bad man. Shame on you." She stuck out one finger and ran the other across it.

"That perhaps is quite true," he admitted. "But I been worried about something. I'm a heavy worrier. A worry wart is what they term people like me. I been worried since I came on liberty tonight. And Chebe-san, what I been worrying about you haven't told me. Yet."

"Nothing to worry about," she said gaily. "Nothing at all. Why worry, *dio?*"

"Let's have it, doll," he said, still holding the bottle away from her. "You were talking about trouble in the company. Something about maybe somebody was going to the Monkey House. What did you mean?" He watched her eyes fluctuate, then waver considerably then focus again. He still couldn't get over her drinking like that. Hell! She never drank. He took a drink himself, still watching her over the bottle.

Quite suddenly she began crying. It wasn't the hard belly-grinding chest-heaving sobs of a man, the convulsive explosive deep-rumbling man's cry of rage or frustration; and it wasn't the tinkling, just plain tears cry of the woman —the tears welling up in the eyes without noise and spilling down over the cheeks that always surprised Hugh. It was not like either of them. It was like a dry-eyed cry, not shoulder shaking, not stomach convulsing, but a sort of almost imperceptible cringed-up face, a weary sad expression, and it aroused instinctively with a depth of protection that, while embarrassing him, also awakened a feeling of acute perception within him. It took all he had to keep from going over and putting his arms around her.

Finally, about five minutes later, Hugh still watching her, she stopped whatever it was she had been doing and looked him full in the eye. "It's all gone, isn't it?"

Hugh did not say anything. He was still trying to pull himself out of this round black pit he had fallen into and his arms were very weary.

"It is no more," she lamented. "All is gone, for good. Forever."

"What is all gone?"

"This."

"Well," Hugh said. *This?* It didn't tell him a damn thing. "You mean because of the war? I told you long ago it would be that way. But that ain't it at all, is it?" he said, wondering what had happened to his presence of mind. Why did he have to be so dumb all the time? "Now goddamit, Chebe-san, you're irritating me. What do you mean about the company?"

Scooting around, putting her leg that had been on top under and the one that had been under on top, she contracted herself into a regal dignity. "Jack Koko Hobbs."

Hugh looked at her blank-faced. *Jack Koko Hobbs.* Jack Koko Hobbs! Had that handsome lady-propositioning bastard been sleeping with her? Has she been stepping out on him? Sleeping with the second best friend he, Hugh Thorton, had? Jealousy of a nature he had not thought he was capable of flooded up in him, overflowing hotly. That sonofabitch. That motherless bastard.

Still looking at her, she remaining speechless, he thought Well what the hell? She ain't no property of Hugh Thorton. She runs a bar, she is a business woman, there for the taking with the right price. So what? It was almost funny if you looked at it that way. It wasn't the first time he'd been ditched, dumped on a used condum garbage dump.

Then it got him, and he cursed his dumbness once again with a savage self-loving hatred. What an ass he was! Of

451

course she wasn't sleeping with Koko!— Koko: the company: the Monkey House: he finally got it. That was what she meant by trouble. They were wise to Koko. They had gotten onto his black market scheme. They were watching him.

A deep knife-in-hand resentment for his own assininity, his own bitter reasonless no-grounds-for jealousy, smothered him blackly. He was really a rotten bastard. To have ever thought that. That showed him just how much he trusted himself. To think that about Chebe-san, who had given him more than any person he had ever known. Disgust for himself filled him. And a loving, almost unbearable pain of never seeing Chebe-san again ripped and snarled at him.

"They know about Koko in the black market?" he said chokingly. "The CID? The Japanee police?"

"*Hai*. They know. And they will get him. They are waiting for him to make another transaction with Henry."

"But they don't have anything on him yet?" Hugh demanded, still feeling the warm love for her. "And they can't do anything till they catch him in the act."

"But it will hurt you when they do," Chebe-san explained. "When they get him it will hurt you in the company."

"That is the understatement of Fujioka," Hugh said sorrowfully. But then maybe it wouldn't hurt him, he thought with swift exulation. That was maybe the key to what he'd been trying for. A way to take over the company like he wanted. One way or the other they'd nab Koko. And he'd be busting rocks in Sugamo Prison and living on fish heads and rice. But with Koko gone there would be no recourse but to get rid of Finch fast, get him out of the way. And that in itself would be simple enough. He just wouldn't watch over Finch, and the emaciated T/Sgt would get himself busted and then he'd be the only one to run the company. There were no other T/Sgt's around. Ah, he calculated, ah, it was remarkably simple. He knew how to handle it.

He focused his thoughts back on Chebe-san. "So that's why you didn't tell me, because you were afraid it would hurt me?" He looked at her, and looking, seeing her again, all the rest vanished as if a huge rubber eraser had swabbed his mind clean, and he wanted hungrily to hold

452

her. What a doll, he thought, what a doll. And what a lousy sonofabitch he was.

"Yes," she said, "that is why." Her eyes opened wider and her face set warmly. "You are not angry with Chebe-san?"

"No."

"What will happen to you with Koko gone?"

"Jail probably." He frowned, wondering why he never understood her thinking; he never would.

"But it will not hurt you?"

"Nothing will." Hugh felt very much the man with the jawbone of an ass—his ass. "No, it's all right."

Grinning genuinely now, she took another drink, running through the charted spasms again. "I don't want you hurt," she said. "Ever. I love you, Hugh-san. Love. Love. Love. It is a good word, *ne?*"

"Hardly," Hugh said. "It's a shitty word. It means nothing. It means nothing but nothing. The least of everything and the most of nothing. That's what it means."

"You no love Chebe-san?"

"That all depends where we are," he said. "And I think I love you now." He pulled on the bottle, enjoying its burning in his throat. She was getting quite drunk, he thought. Better have her lay off the stuff for awhile.

But she didn't lay off at all. She kept drinking and who was he to refuse her? Hell, it was his party. He ordered himself to keep a clear head. He had to see Koko as soon as he could.

He never did get to take her to bed. He tried though. But she was too far gone, so he accepted his fate with a wry-happy half-assumed philosophy and watched her. And she was really getting stoned. About seven or eight sheets to the wind under full sail. Then she got the giggles. Giggling, with her woman's throaty whiskey voice, her small body shaking happily, *she* even tried to make love to him. But she could not navigate, neither celestial nor dead reckoning, yet kept repeating her love for him in a sweet singsong way that tickled Hugh. He wasn't a bit mad at her getting drunk. She deserved it, he thought magnanimously, watching her turn playfully away. Just as she was starting to get out of her suit, fingering for the zipper, she went out cold, in a loose rag doll heap, a blissful half grin dancing across her slack mouth.

Hugh slowly bundled her up, straightened her suit, and carried her, his arm around her waist supporting her, out of the hotel.

Gotemba was shot with bright neons and horn honks and people scrambling about: Japanee, Korean and American, soldiers and marines. Hugh stood in front of the hotel looking up and down the street, finally spotted a cab and called it up to him.

He had to hold Chebe-san in the back seat to keep her from falling. The cab driver giggled he-he-he all the way back to Fujioka and pulled in bouncingly just as the bars closed at eleven o'clock.

Scrupulously, he carted her through the rear door to her fine room with the lace curtains while the worried Jo-sans huddled around and chattered excitedly. He told them she was all right, just drunk, and tossed in a wry grin.

He undressed her while the girls watched protectively, slipped her in bed and pulled the blankets up around her neck, the faint flickering smile still playing on her face.

When he shut the lights off and walked back into the corridor the Jo-sans looked disdainfully at him.

"She's all right," he said again. "Just a little drunk. Don't have to worry about her. Tell her I'll be out to see her tomorrow. Be good, girls," he said suavely, walked out the back door and into the black March night.

He walked quickly down the deserted street, in through the main gate, and half ran to the barracks.

The terse snoring grumbles of the staff met him when he burst into the staff quarters, trying to be quiet, and looking all around at the bunks. Koko's bunk, across from his own, was empty. He walked slowly, breathing hard, over to it.

Koko's wall locker was open and empty. So was his foot locker, except for Marine Corps gear.

Hugh walked back to his own bunk and sat down wearily. It had been a hell of a night. He lit a cigarette and in the flare of the match saw the envelope pinned to his pillow. He reached over and pulled it loose. Then he opened it and read it, using the match for light. It was written in Koko's own handwriting:

Old buddy:
    When I was fourteen I went to California, saw the Pacific Ocean, turned around and went back home

to East St. Louis. I guess I never got over that.

(Gung Ho) Koko Hobbs

The match had burned down and Hugh dropped it. Then he folded the letter up and put it in his wall locker.

That sonofabitch!

No good bastard!

To do that to me! he thought indignantly, just when he was getting everything set up. But he couldn't help but grin. That sonofabitch Koko . . . he was probably a long way away by now. But he couldn't have left until after taps, until it was dark, not and left that letter on his pillow. I'll be go to hell, he thought. If that don't beat all.

Old Koko had got the last good punch. Now how about that? He had simply fled in the dark of night, leaving him holding the platoon and his dignity in a sievelike sack. He must have known about the CID—or maybe he hadn't. Maybe he had just had it figured that way for a long time. Somehow Hugh could not help but think that if he hadn't talked with Koko the other night the sonofabitch wouldn't have taken off.

Well, maybe the company thought he'd be back, but Hugh knew different. Koko would never be back. Not with the dough he had.

It didn't really make any difference. Koko was gone for sure now, one way or the other. He was out of the company. And he was no longer Hugh's platoon sergeant. So, the only recourse then was to start figuring again.

If Koko had left, say, a month ago, he would have been more indignant. Now he was happy over it. Things were falling into the right notches across from the dealer's chair. He didn't need Koko at all. And now, he realized suddenly, he didn't need Finch either. He had put that off too long; two weeks too long.

Koko Hobbs, he thought, old Koko. "That sonofabitch," he said at the darkness.

The staff snuffled, choked and sputtered a few times, then went back into a groggy sleep.

"He's still a sonofabitch," Hugh told the sleeping staff. But answer came there none.

Hugh looked over at Finch's bunk. He slept dressed, as usual. Well, in the morning he would see about that. He went to sleep figuring.

The next morning after a sausage and egg and toast

455

breakfast (Finch was still passed out in his bunk) Hugh returned to the staff quarters, whistling cheerfully in the early-morning darkness, twisting his immaculate mustache, his mind made up.

Horrible Hog Company's gunnery sergeant was still passed out when he got back to the staff quarters. He lay in his greens under his drab blanket, snoring fitfully —gaunt, cadaverous, scared.

Hugh did not waste any time. He merely checked Finch to see that he was still asleep and then walked sedately over to the Officers' BOQ, just across the street from Hog Company's office.

Several of the officers, mostly lieutenants, were already up and moving around from their private rooms preparing for the day, and Hugh said a dutiful good morning to them and did not bother to knock on Ham Haley's door, but went right on in and snapped on the light.

Marine Gunner Ham Haley lay snoring on his back, his large protruding beer belly heaving and falling with each harsh breath, his flat, broad face peaceful.

"Hey, hard charger," Hugh said ebulliently, "your belly button's showing." He sat down leisurely in the old frame chair by Haley's bunk. The gunner did not move. Hugh reached over and grabbed a hold of his large foot under the blanket and squeezed hard.

Snorting painfully, turning, choking and grumbling, Ham Haley lurched up, his eyes blinking, mouth working silently.

"Morning, sir," Hugh grinned.

Ham Haley coughed and cleared his throat and rubbed his eyes. Then he rubbed his large beer belly, all seventeen years' accumulation of it, scratching himself all over. Then he was awake and his watery eyes open. "Well," he said groggily. "Are you my latest illusion? Or you just come around waking officers up all the time?"

"It's my job." Hugh kept grinning. "I like to wake officers up. They haven't got anybody else to do it."

"That's noble as hell. Don't you know this is officers quarters? Out of bounds to EM's." He sat up full in his bunk, reached behind him for his cigarettes and lit one.

"Oh, is this officers quarters?" Hugh said, feigning surprise. "Now who would have guessed that. I mean with you here. I didn't know you were an officer, Mister Haley."

"You going to sit there all morning as the star attraction?" Ham Haley said flatly. "If you are, pull that bottle outa my trunk and have a drink."

"This early?"

"You got something against drinking in the morning?"

"Well, it's against regulations."

"Since when regulations bother you?" Ham Haley snorted.

"Since I decided I was going to be gunnery sergeant," Hugh said nonchalantly.

Ham Haley studied him through his cigarette smoke for a moment. "Now I'm sure you better get the bottle out."

Fumbling around in the old trunk, a vestige of the days in the International Settlement in Shanghai way back before Big Two, Hugh produced a quart of Jim Beam, half full, uncapped it and in deference passed it to Ham Haley.

The marine gunner seized the bottle in a huge hand and took a wake-up drink. "Ah," he said, "for the croup; it's bad in the morning." He passed it back to Hugh.

Hugh took a drink, lit a cigarette and held the bottle by its slim neck.

"Now that I'm alive again," Ham Haley said, "what was that you said about making gunnery sergeant?"

"I want Finch busted and I want to take his place."

"Okay," Ham Haley said. "I'm for that. I told you that a long time ago. But why now?"

"A lot of reasons. One: *I* want it. Two—" He nodded his head to the large map of Indochina on Ham Haley's wall. "Three: Sarjint Hobbs deserted last night."

Ham Haley scratched his gray beard, looked out his window at the darkness and studied the bottle in Hugh's hand. "He's smart. I hope they don't catch him."

"They won't," Hugh said, thoughtfully admiring the grizzled man. Ham Haley had been an enlisted man too long before he became a warrant officer.

"You think you can handle it now?" he said to Hugh, dismissing the other. "What about your platoon? Who'll run that?"

"It's simple. Jesus Queecho can handle it. It wouldn't be the first time a buck sarjint ran a platoon. And with the TO so understrength now, it'll fit all right."

"Got it all figured out, have you? What about Finch. After he gets busted?"

"A transfer," Hugh suggested. "Up to Ordnance maybe.

Somewhere out of the company. You won't have any trouble with the Kizer, will you?"

"Ha," Ham Haley snorted. "The only trouble I have with the Kizer is over Top Condrum. That bastard would be the only stopgap in it. But he can be handled all right." He reached over for the bottle. "My croup's getting worse," he grinned. "Well, it'll take maybe a couple of weeks.

Hugh shook his head. "This morning, Gunner."

"Jesus Christ!" Ham Haley exploded. "You don't give a man time to get out of bed. Okay, what we going to use to bust Finch with?

"It's already made to order," Hugh said. "Dereliction of duty. If I put him on report they wouldn't even listen to me. That's why you got to do it. The Kizer'll listen to what you've got to say. Tell him you been watching Finch for quite a while. Tell him Finch is drunk all the time and not handling his job. The Kizer'll agree with you. He'll even tell you he knows all about it and had it in mind all the time. And Top Condrum won't get in your way."

"This morning . . ." Ham Haley mused. "Okay, I'll handle it. But don't you pop up around the company office. I'll let you know all about it."

"You won't have to send out a searching party for me." Hugh stood up and walked over to the door.

"It's a good thing the rank and file run the Marine Corps," Ham Haley said behind him with wry humor.

"It's a good thing there are some officers like you to work with."

"I'm no officer," Ham Haley said laconically. "Anyway, like I said, I'd a done this for you a long time ago."

"It wouldn't have worked then," Hugh said, and opened the door. "It'll work now, all right. See you later."

Walking back across the street to the barracks as the first pale of March dawn touched in the east with the faint glow of red, Hugh felt inordinately pleased. It had worked out fine and it was going to be a jim-dandy day, he thought. Now all he had to do was wait. He passed several stragglers from the company walking back from morning chow, their mess gear clattering, and he did not return their greetings when he passed. He was too involved with his own scheme.

He waited till almost nine o'clock. He had taken his platoon, following the morning inspection, behind the barracks for close order drill, troop and stomp.

458

The platoon, as the company, all knew of Koko Hobbs' disappearance. Hugh had not told them anything at all. But they knew. It showed on their faces: sly, sympathetic, proud, Hugh thought, and even a little superior because Koko had been *their* platoon sergeant.

Leaning up against the old gnarled Japanee elm (the same one Bohane and Dallas and Poke and Stack had drunk under, their first night in the company), leaning there, his arms folded, Hugh gave his platoon a repeated to the rear march and watched their indignant faces happily.

It was obvious they missed Koko Hobbs. Not because they enjoyed his company, but simply because Hobbs was not crazy. And any man who would lean against a tree giving a repetition of to the rear march was crazy. Hugh thought it was exceedingly funny.

At nine o'clock, King Solomon walked up to where Hugh stood in the slant sun rays leaning against the tree, still drilling, and informed him he was wanted in the company office. Hugh nodded and turned the platoon over to Jesus Queecho, the right guide, and walked back around the barracks up to the window-door of the company office.

Inside, Leroy Finch sat dejectedly in a chair by the coffee mess in greens, his sunken red eyes dead in his gaunt hollow-cheeked face. Corporal Solomon sat back down at his desk, oblivious to what was happening. Pfc. Quiller Carpenter sat grinning at his desk, his hangover perpetually omnipresent, warming in the office. Top Condrum, at his desk, shot Hugh a withering glance under his feathery eyebrows as he stepped down into the office.

"Somebody over here want to see me, Top?" he asked, taking his dungaree cap off and tucking it under his belt.

"Captain Kizer," Top Landrum said. "You can go on in."

Hugh walked past Finch, looking down as he did. The spectral gray ashen face of Horrible Hog Company's gunnery sergeant looked up. Hugh said nothing. He walked on in to the Kizer's office. Ham Haley was sitting across from the desk.

"Good morning, skipper," Hugh said to the Kizer.

"Ah yes, Gunny Thorton," the Kizer boomed, his Prussian energy as bright as the morning's sun. "Sit down, sit down."

Hugh pulled up a chair beside Ham Haley and sat, quietly.

"Like some coffee, Gunny?" Emil Kizer said. "How about a cup?"

"Well, no thanks, skipper. I'll have to be getting back to my platoon pretty soon."

"That's what I like to hear!" Kizer blasted. "A man who understands his position. Who knows what his job is. In a military organization—or for that matter any organization —a leader has to be single-minded. I like that in my NCO's." Then his face moved into a graven stolidness. "But there seems to be a little trouble in the company at present." He turned his massive jaw and peered out the window. Hugh heard Ham Haley snort softly and squirm in his chair.

"You mean about Sarjint Hobbs' desertion?" Hugh questioned.

"Who said Hobbs deserted?" Kizer demanded, swinging around. "That is a presumption. He hasn't been proved a deserter yet. He has only been logged AWOL for today. He'll probably be back."

"No, sir, that's right," Hugh agreed. "He hasn't proved a deserter yet."

"For my dough," Kizer said, "I think he'll show up in a week or two. He's too good a man and far too much of a marine to desert."

"Oh, yes, sir, I'll go along with that," Hugh said, and drew his face down blank.

"But that isn't his immediate problem is it, Mister Haley?" Emil Kizer directed his booming voice to the heavy-bellied warrant officer.

Ham Haley closed his face up seriously. "No, it's far more serious. And what happened last night, or even the night before, has no meaning any more. A battle over with is a battle forgotten."

"I'm making changes in the company," Kizer blasted out. "No need to beat around the bush. I'm busting Sarjint Finch and having him transferred."

"Finch?" Hugh said. "Why Finch?"

"Oh, come now, Gunny." Kizer waved him off with a small tight grin. "You don't have to protect him any. I know what he's done. In fact, I've known for quite some time that he's been, shall we say, dropping the ball?"

Hugh forced himself to display an awkward embarrassment. "That's true, sir."

460

"And I'm placing you in as company gunnery sergeant." Kizer looked across the desk unflinchingly. An aura of authority lay heavy in the room.

"Me, sir!" Hugh said, trying to sound surprised and complimented at the same time.

Ham Haley growled, pulled his handkerchief out and blew his nose. "You're the only man for the job, Thorton," he said, wiping his handerchief under his nose. "You're the only T/Sgt in the company. Don't you think you can handle it?"

"Oh, I can do well enough, *Mister* Haley."

"That's what I wanted to see you about," Kizer broke in peremptorily, nodding his head. "You've nothing but fine marks on your record book. A fine leader, if I do say so myself. And I don't think you should have a bit of trouble handling the company. None at all."

"No, sir," Hugh said. "I won't have any trouble."

Emil Kizer's eyes lit up, his old fire-fight ravaged eyes glinting. "We'll need a tight organization when we go to combat," he said levelly, but loud. "And that's what I—and Mister Haley here—are going to build within the company. I'm quite sure that in this war we'll have to rely on company strength alone. I fear the good old days are over with."

"You don't think they'll use the bomb, do you, sir?" Hugh asked.

"No," Kizer bellowed. "They won't use the bomb. But where we are going (and I don't want this conversation to leave this office) it will be mostly jungle fighting, guerrilla tactics. That's what we've been training for. And it will be for the main a company-run organization. Quite different," he grinned expansively, "but somewhat like the old Nicaraguan campaigns, eh?"

Hugh shook his head in dramatic wonderment. "Well, of course, sir, I won't let a word of this get out. You can count on that."

Emil Kizer lifted his weighted swagger stick off his desk and began pounding his hand with it. "That's all, *Gunny*" —he smiled with the word—"it's your company now—and *mine*," he added quickly. "Spend the next few days getting everything set up, get the feel of things."

"Aye, aye, sir." Hugh stood up and walked out into the typewriter clacking of the company office where Leroy

461

Finch still sat dejected, an unbelieving look on his face. Hugh passed him and went up the short stairs and out into the warm morning sunshine.

He paused on the cinder ash and lit a cigarette, the blue smoke swirling lazily about his head, feeling as if he had won the last pot of the night. The richest man in town. It was strange too, he thought, how in just a matter of days—hours actually—he had been pushed to a position of leadership, something he had entirely eschewed in the past. Yet it was not strange. It felt natural in a sense. He heard the window-door open behind him.

"Well, it's your company now, *Gunny*," Ham Haley snorted.

"Sure enough is, *Mister* Haley," Hugh said with a faint grin, his black handlebar mustache flapping a little. "Is there anything I can do for you, sir?"

"Only one thing, Gunny," he said. "If you get a wild hair up your ass let me know about it, too. Someone should." He winked and walked away, his spindly legs under his huge belly carrying him lightly, leaning forward.

There were no wild hairs attached at all, to any part of him, Hugh thought watching Haley walk off. Maybe he was a wild hair himself. But if he was, the wildness had just started and, he thought, it was about to spread.

Throughout the rest of March and stretching into April, all the way up to the last week, there was no further sign of war. But the company, Horrible Hog Company, did not have time to suffer over it. With their new gunnery sergeant, T/Sgt Hugh Thorton, running their already lean asses off leaner, they did not have time to think about it. They trained, hard and fast and every day.

And a sweeping change transformed the company. Instead of being lax and slack, they were moving into a pinpointed weapon of precision. Of course the training previous to the new Gunny Sergeant had been rigorous, but it was not with the same intensity that Thorton indoctrinated. With Thorton the company began improvising. He tossed the rule book away and tossed in, instead, a new set of rules: Hugh Thorton's rules.

It became a chant around the camp that there was the Right way, the Marine Corps way, and Gunny Thorton's way, and Horrible Hog Company was being run Gunny Thorton's way.

In the field, running over the now green knee-high

brush, down ruts and hills and through the pine forest, sweating fiercely, Hugh taught the men some pointers that very few of them knew. And they listened avidly. His lectures were not soporific and boring like Lt. Van Preter's or Fischer's, the two company officers. He taught them hand-to-hand combat that was excluded from the books. He taught them how to take communication wire and strap ten-penny nails around their hand grenades for added destruction, how to take gas or oil or kerosene and tape a Willy Peter (white phosphorus) to the can for a hand-to-hand Napalm Bomb. He taught them how to flush out snipers in the pine forest like ferreting out a sly bear, the use of a garrote became SOP for each man in the company. Most of the field training, under Hugh's supervision, consisted of practicing ambushes and raids. It was a field training that the troops looked forward to, and which thoroughly surprised everyone from Colonel Dantes, the battalion CO, on down to Lt. Van Preter, who could not understand it at all.

The company did not suffer. Even with the time-consuming field, it had its compensation. It was Hugh Thorton (through Ham Haley and the Kizer) who had the liberty hours lengthened till seven o'clock in the morning. And the company thanked him gratefully for it in silent respect.

Still, there was no new sign of war.

Then, on April 20th, they got their first sure-fire news. It was on the front page of the *Pacific Stars & Stripes*: the U.S. Air Force began flying French paratroopers into Indochina as the Vietminh pressed closer on Dien Bien Phu, the siege in the saucer. It was reported too that the U.S. Air Force was sending personnel, on civilian orders, into Indochina for partisan work and the troops wondered if they were getting paid extra for it?

Spirits reached a new high (in the men, in the bottles, and in town) and the troops of South Camp talked it all the time in an excited undertone of activity. At the slop chute a new song sprang up, a parody of a Stateside song that was becoming popular: *Indo, Indo, that's where we're going to go e o . . .*

Courts-martial reached a new low. Very few were handed out by the battalion any longer. The word was out: save personnel. And those who suffered Office Hours from company commanders got off easy.

Even on May Day (the Communists' national holiday)

there was not the expectant fervor among the troops of perhaps being able to take a shot at some slopeheads when the Communists from Numazu staged their little rally in Fujioka just outside the camp. Liberty, of course, was restricted that day and the guard was doubled on the fence. Three Japanee citizens of Fujioka were killed, two Jo-sans and one papa-san, ostensibly in an act of reprisal for associating with Americans. The troops, however, shrugged it off in the slop chute and barracks with a philosophical who-wanted-to-waste-any-energy-on-a-pissyass-Communists'-rally-when-they-could-save-it-for-Indochina?

Indochina was now a definite prediction for the burning ground they would inherit. They were sure they would not go to Korea again. The First Division was there; they could handle Luke if he jumped off. It was simply that there was not, they all decided, any place else to go.

Then, on May 7th, it was obvious that it would not be long. Dien Bien Phu fell to the Communists, and everyone was making speeches about it, the final humiliating defeat in Indochina, in the Far East. Yet a few days after that men wondered why they still hadn't moved out?

There was no answer, so they waited; and trained.

May passed hotly. The sun was back in its late spring orbit searing the mauve cinder ash of the camp and the days were long and sweatily uncomfortable. The human feces rising from the rice paddies clung in the air like rifle smoke and the men hung around the slop chute in khakis again, sitting on the picnic tables in back, or sat in the barracks looking out the windows as the long shadows moved across the purple ground.

On into June they waited, each day bringing closer something tangible to believe in about the coming war, each day moving with an impetus to sleep and meet the next day—each day merely a way of passing time till the word came down. But the training did not decrease with the waiting. If anything, it increased—and the tight-lipped cockiness, the swaggering bluster, and the knowing grin were frozen on each man's face.

30.

The first week in June, Hugh Thorton, his senses keyed to a sharp peak, *his* company honed down to a sliver of Damascus steel (all good things coming to Hugh who waits), took three days' special liberty and planned them all for Chebe-san—a final tryst, he thought, before his theory materialized.

He had seen her, naturally, as often as he could during the hectic meshing of himself into the job of company gunnery sergeant. And when he made it she was very pleased and congratulated him. She was always there, he thought, hovering in the background like a panacea for his own frustrations.

With her Hugh could lose himself, detach himself dispassionately from the company. They did not argue over trivial matters. (This, Hugh decided, was because he didn't spend as much time with her as he had in the past.) But somehow, Chebe-san had changed too.

At first when Hugh told her about his theory of the coming war, the big one all the way through China and Russia, she had disagreed with him. Not stubbornly of course. A more or less civilized disagreement, if there was such a thing.

Chebe-san, according to the *word* she received on the business women's grapevine, did not believe there would be a war. The grapevine had come down to her with a simple message that it was not time yet—not the *right* time for another war. That it would only be a trumpet of war, not the real thing.

Hugh would have none of this. And finally, after many loving hours of talking it over, hashing it around, he had convinced her he was right. After all, he was an American, wasn't he, a damn smart one too—perhaps a little *baka*, he told her, grinning—but he did not miss the call on this one.

So on the first week of June, when Hugh took his three days off to take Chebe-san on a vacation (they had been almost everywhere within his limited radius of Camp Fuji), he was feeling really supremely good. And he did not care to go anywhere at all. He was content to stay in the U.S. Bar, in his home base of operations.

He had checked out, wearing his dark blue Hong Kong tailored suit (one that hadn't yet been ruined) in the late evening when the shifting purple still clung in the western sky throwing the looming silhouette of Mount Fuji high among the first stars of the night sky. In the early summer twilight a blue cloudy haze, like smoke in the far-off mountains, moved lazily around the town.

He did not even bother to stop at the Staff Club for a short one but headed right into town, and worked his way up the street.

Passing a knot of marines standing on the cement bridge, he saw old Tex and his goose, both waddling, on the other side of the street. Neither Tex nor his goose looked at Hugh, and he glared at them for a moment, his mustache twitching, and walked on up to the U.S. Bar and in the back door.

He no longer used the front door. He always entered by the rear door and passed the word by Mama-san, or whoever was handy, to tell Chebe-san that he was there. Then he'd go back to the little room with the lace curtains on the window and flop on the Stateside bed, wrapping himself in the arms of momentary security.

As if she had known he was coming, sensed it in the air, she was waiting in her beautifully decorated room, sitting on the Stateside bed in her most expensive kimono, blue and pink and white. Bright and slanted-eyed and bushy-tailed, she smiled up at him, a warm smile full of promise, yet veiling something too.

"Ain't going to dress up tonight?" he grinned, closing the door behind him, the ten days since he'd seen her vanishing quickly. He walked over and kissed her on the forehead, holding her face in his hands. Then he sat down in the sofa, opened the small door to the liquor cabinet she had thoughtfully put in the room, and produced a quart of V.O.

"No, Hugh-san, not tonight," she answered in faultless American.

466

"Well, that's all right with me," Hugh said airily, taking a drink. "I got three days off and nothing to do. But I'm content to stay here the whole three days." He offered her the bottle with a mischievous grin on his face and Chebe-san grimaced and turned her head. "So," he said still grinning, "I figure I'd come to town and see how my favorite butterfly is getting along."

"Butterfly!" Chebe-san said indignantly. She scooted around on the bed, tucking her legs under her. "Me no butterfly."

"Me ain't got no Yo-yo either," Hugh said, thinking she was sure getting odd lately. But what the hell? He'd have to put up with her vagaries, he thought magnanimously. People put up with his own, didn't they?

"Three days, *ne?*" Chebe-san said in her throaty whiskey voice. "And you are going to spend them all with Chebe-san?"

Hugh nodded behind the bottle, shifted his mouth, his mustache spears rising. "Yeah," he said. "But you don't look none too happy about it."

"No, Hugh-san," she said, her eyes regarding him. "I'm *toxon* happy about it. If you had not come out, I was going to send in for you. I have been wanting to see you for a long time."

"I'd a got out sooner," Hugh said, "but I been busy as hell. Putting the company back together." He put the bottle back in the cabinet, his taste and thirst suddenly gone. There was something wrong about all this, he reasoned. She was just a little too strange. Sure, she had been like this before, or close to it, but never quite this locked up in herself. "Why?" he asked, suddenly cold. "Was there something you wanted to see me about?"

"*Hai.* It is not really of any importance except for me. You would not really be interested."

"Now that's not true," Hugh said, a chill that was not from the open window creeping into the room. "Anything that concerns you concerns me just as much. You know that."

"No." She shook her head, her face adamant. "You remember almost a year ago in Numazu?"

"I'll never forget that one. Why? What about it?"

"And the story you told me of the man who would not eat his wife?"

467

"Yeah; all that."

"That is what it is with me. I too am like the man. The man in your story."

"Okay." Hugh leaned forward in the sofa and rested his arms on his thighs. "What is it? What are you going to do? I don't like to play games," he said, suddenly angry. "You got something to say, say it."

"I'm moving out," she said. "I have already sold the bar and the Pachinko Parlor. I am taking the money and leaving."

"Why?" he heard himself ask in a small voice.

"It is like you say." Chebe-san's voice raised a little, her words coming faster, running out. "There is a war coming. All marines will leave South Camp and there will be no more business. You will go to the war. Chebe-san cannot stay here. There is nothing left for me here." Then she slowed down, her voice dropping to its naturally lower tone, and looked at him.

"Well," he said softly, a little wanly. "Well."

"After all," she told him. "I am a business woman. It takes money to run a business. And people. And there will not be any people left here."

"Where will you go?" Hugh asked, trying desperately to set his face in the same stolid stony cast as hers and failing. "Down to Tokyo? Yokohama?"

"I am not sure. It is hard to tell yet. Perhaps down to Sasebo or Kobe."

"Well. That's probably a damn good idea. I mean you'll be protecting your interests and everything. And that's what you have to do. If you're a business woman."

"But you are mad about it."

"Oh, hell no," Hugh said angrily. "Me mad? Naw. I expected it. I mean it had to come. It's your life and job. I got mine too. Samey same."

A happy laugh shrieked through the bar, moving into the room along with the people sound of music and the popping of beer bottles.

"I did not want you to be mad," she said. "Because there is no reason for it. We talk that time in Numazu about love. You remember?"

"Sure. I always talk about love when I get half tight. Love is a good thing to talk about when you're drunk. So what about it?" He could feel his eyes clouding up with a heavy film of dull anger. The anger poured inward on him viciously.

"And we talked about love and honesty," she went on, watching him. "No one who is completely honest can fall in love, Hugh-san."

"Great philosophy. Only I don't know any people who are completely honest. Never have."

"No; and that is not what I mean," Chebe-san said evenly, unemotional. "I mean that any person who falls in love is not being honest with himself."

"Shades of Buddha," Hugh smirked, the flaring anger working deeper in him, thinking he was not in the right pew. Chebe-san was acting just now as she had that first day in Numazu. And when she was like that she didn't talk sense, he decided swiftly. But then, no gook ever talked sense at all. Not any of them he knew at any rate. He raised his head and peered through his anger at her. Then he grinned, a sour acrid bitter grin, the grin he thought he had lost when he was released from the POW camp in '45, right here, the same grin he had carried for those five years.

"Okay, doll," he said. "Ain't no sense making an issue out of it, is there? It's cut and dried. I figure you got to do what's best for you. Ain't no one else can tell you what to do."

"It is something I have been thinking about for almost three months," she explained. "Since you first started to talk of the war. It is true and it makes sense. So I must leave before it comes—or I will never get my money out of it."

"Well, who the hell's going to buy it?" Hugh demanded, reaching into the cabinet for the bottle, looking disdainfully at it, putting it back. He needed a drink like he needed two left feet. "If—and there will be—the war, who'll buy a bar that won't do any good? Christ! This town'll die without marines."

"There are still some who do not think there will be a war. They are taking the chance that there won't be any war. And that the marines will stay here."

"It's their ass," he said, his mustache drawn tight. "So when are you leaving?" he said, trying to sound casual.

"Next week. I've already packed everything I am going to take with me. There is nothing to do now but wait."

"Sure. Well, that's that. Hell, I kinda figured you'd pull out," he lied. "And personally I think you're smart. Get out now and start a bar somewhere else or something. You made enough money to take you quite a ways."

Then, for the first time since Hugh had entered the room, Chebe-san's facial countenance fell: no longer adamant and unyielding, no longer inscrutable Oriental. She smiled a little timidly, then her eyes grew glistening moist, and watching her, Hugh felt something choke up in a knot inside him.

"And you are not mad?" she asked. "You are not upset by it."

"Course not. Why would I be upset? Like I said: I think it's the smart thing for you to do."

"I will miss you, Hugh-san," she said warmly. "I will miss you very much."

"You'll get over it," Hugh said angrily. "It's only a short phase of your life."

"*Hai*," she nodded, "I will get over it. But now you have three days," she smiled suddenly cheerful. "You can havo Chebe-san for three days."

"Naw," Hugh said, his eyes feeling red hot. "I don't think so, doll. I don't think it's wise. Besides, I might not have three days. The war comes, I'll be gone in a matter of hours." He tried to look nonchalant, hating himself bitterly for saying that, wanting to take her to bed, to love her, something inside him protesting—and he wondered what it was? Vanity? Pride? Conceit? All of it rolled together. The something made him desist from taking her to bed. The something making him feel foolish like an ass. But he could not stop it.

He stood up and stretched, a long arm-reaching stretch, relaxing the tension, then he walked over to the door. Chebe-san's eyes followed him.

"You do not wish to spend the three days with me?" she asked from the bed.

He had his hand on the doorknob and stood looking back at her, the stiff grin enhanced by his somber mustache. "I guess not, doll. I might get out to see you once before you leave," he lied, wanting to leave, to run out. It was almost beyond physical and emotional endurance, standing there in the room with her. He had really, truly loved her.

"I would like for you to stay."

470

"I couldn't do it."

Languidly, she straightened up on the bed, her face fathomless. "Then perhaps I will see you again?"

"Could be. Anyway it's been a nice ride."

A faint smile touched her mouth. *"Hai.* It has been that. *Synada,* Hugh-san."

"Synada," Hugh said, opened the door, slipped out and shut it quietly behind him.

For a moment after he'd left, Chebe-san sat on the bed looking at the closed door. She was suddenly very tired and overwrought. It was unnatural for her to be like this. It set her ill at ease. She had had to do it, what she had told him. It was the best way. And he needed something else beside her. She suddenly felt that he had never needed her.

From the noises of the bar it sounded as if they were doing a good business tonight. *Hai!* that was good. It was Friday night, before the weekend, and everyone had money. It would be a profitable weekend. Her last, she thought.

She stood up and walked over to her closet, her hips swaying slowly. There she brought out a neat trim little summer dress, colorful, one she had always liked. It was the same one she had worn to Numazu last year.

She unwrapped her kimono from herself and hung it up in the closet. Then she slipped into her panties, nylons, and brassière (after affixing the falsies) and pulled on the dress. She brushed her short hair and applied some lipstick, just enough, checking it in the mirror over her vanity.

Completely dressed and ready for work, she opened the door and walked out into the hall.

"Partying is such sweet sorrow," she said in her deep charming voice, moving up the corridor to the bar to join the never-ending three-o'clock-in-the-morning party.

Hugh Thorton, when he left the U.S. Bar, was for a moment indecisive. A part of him wanted to go back, to rush into the bar and stay with her for the three days. Why had he been such a shithead? So he walked on down the corridor to the back door, opened it, and slipped out into the warm pleasant June night.

Smoking lazily, standing just outside on the path that led up to the Florida Bar, where he'd stood so many times in the past when he felt good, he wondered about Chebe-san, about her, about himself, and mostly about what a strange unmodified self-fooling life he had always led.

Then he moved off down the path to the main street and turned right, suddenly decided to go down Bamboo Alley—maybe hit the Blue Moon and see what was left of his old platoon which Jesus Queecho now ran.

People moved up and down the street: marines in cheap civvies, some in tropical worsteds, their pisscutters cocked rakishly low on their foreheads, drunk sober pissed off and happy, searching and testing—always testing and testing and testing, Hugh thought.

It had been truly fine with Chebe-san, he thought. He'd never known a woman like that in his life. And he would undoubtedly never meet another one like her. With a sudden flash he knew he had, for the first time in his life, actually loved. Actually been in love. Or whatever it was.

There was no taut wire pulling inside him now, no remorse, no mawkish strands of a hooked-up love affair. That was why it was so good. That was why he had been able to love her. There was no demanding on either side. He knew he would never quite find another one like her.

She had been right and he had been right, and the war had been right. He suddenly felt that he was at the end of a long climb uphill and when he got there he only saw another long hill rising up in front of him.

The darkness of Bamboo Alley closed in on him and he moved light-footed down it, trapped by the warm darkness, feeling as if he were walking on Bouncing Betsy mines all the way down to the Blue Moon.

Pausing outside, lighting another cigarette, he looked through the broken lines of the swinging saloon doors at the life and the people and movements inside. Strains of a tired hillbilly song clattered with the sound of bottles and talk and laughter, the whole of it a sound of meaninglessness.

He moved up on the stoop and pushed through the door as the eyes converged on him with hostility.

In the back, surrounding a table, sat the unholy four: Dallas, Turner, Renshaw and Guppy Talagua. They all nodded at him, then went back to their drinking.

Jesus Queecho was sitting at the bar and Hugh walked up to him indifferently, pulled a stool out and sat down.

"Out slumming, Gunny?"

Thorton snorted pleasantly, the old shoot-them-down-with-one-burst feeling back with him; he was not lonely, alone, or disgusted or even sad. He was beyond all that. "Nope. I'm just out checking on my company. Somebody has to," he said, and ordered a quart of Asahi from the one-legged Jo-san behind the bar, the one he'd seen Dallas with on Christmas Eve. "How's everything coming in the platoon?"

"As fucked up as ever," Jesus Queecho told him, his black eyes darting around the bar, coming to rest on the four in the back. "No trouble. No one causes me any trouble."

"I didn't figure you'd have any trouble. Except for a few brig rats."

"Them?" Jesus Queecho jerked his head back. "They don't cause me the least trouble, Gunny. In fact, they the only ones I can get to do something right."

"The classic tale of criminals."

"Yeah," Jesus Queecho said leisurely. "And one's coming out next week. Wednesday. An old friend of yours."

"I know." Hugh nodded, thinking when he finished his beer he'd hit some other bars, check some new women out, get the feel of something new. "But you won't have any trouble with Bohane. Six months up there will straighten him out. Straighten anyone out."

Jesus Queecho looked over at Poke Turner and Guppy Talagua and Cinamo Dallas sitting at the back table. "I ain't seen it fail yet," he said flatly, and turned back to his beer.

31.

On the morning that Giff Bohane was released from the Middle Camp brig he was as jittery as a dog-pecker gnat around cats. When the other prisoners double-timed out of the compound after calisthenics to work on the rock pile, he stayed behind as ordered.

Standing in front of his bunk at parade rest he reread his brig orders and felt deeply—if obscurely—separated, watching the other men file on out, sensing he should be going with them out to the rock pile. He could not yet accept the fact that he was getting out.

So he stood there in the torn and patched dungarees that smelled like vinegar and watched them scramble out without him.

In the eight months he had been confined he had seen a lot of men come and go. Men who had been there before him like Swannie and Williams, and men who had come in after him. Prisoners who had been sentenced anywhere from fifteen to twenty days to thirty days and two and three months. He had seen them shuttle in and shuttle out and he had never known most of their names. Yet he felt a closeness that no names or numbers would ever disqualify.

Watching the prisoners clatter out silently, stony-faced, their heads bowed in a portrait of hunching up hard against those elements which they could not fight, Giff felt a great sense of loss. Then the door banged shut, the chainmesh door on the chainmesh compound, and Giff for the first time in those eight months stood alone in the compound. A chilly aura of silence swept through the brig.

Up front, Duty Warden Little Bill Claggle perched sleepily on his desk watching some flies buzz around the drinking fountains. The Great Unwashed, the Duty Turnkey, was engrossed in the profundity of a Donald Duck comic book. The only sound, other than their labored breathing, was the *tick-tick-ticking* of the clock on the wall.

Giff read his brig orders, thoroughly memorized by now, without reading them, his eyes catching the flat slats of June sunlight through the boarded windows of the brig. He wondered what time his chaser would come. Probably before nine, he hoped. They would have to send him back to dress before long, and in his mind he saw his greens hanging in the storeroom—pressed, chevronless, and ribbonless.

The clock up front on the wall chimed eight o'clock.

He thought of the rock pile, the parties, the faces he had seen flow in and out. It was no different than combat. Or the Crotch he guessed. People came and people went. Right now he could not even remember what Dallas or Turner or any of them looked like. He could not even remember what the Kizer looked like.

474

The Great Unwashed grunted soddenly, his puffy jowls working in heavy sweat, and rose from his desk in his spotless tropicals. Giff heard the movement and tensed himself instinctively.

"Wanna get him dressed?" the Great Unwashed said in a low droning voice.

"Five?" Little Bill said. "Yeah. Send him back to the storeroom. Harris'll take care of him."

"Five!" the Great Unwashed hollered and Giff double-timed up to the chainmesh door, stopping on the red line. The Great Unwashed unlocked the door and jerked an abject thumb back toward the storeroom and Giff took off on a run around the chainmesh down the corridor to the storeroom, where his old buddy, Uncle Tom, sat loafing, surrounded by the forty large squares filled with prisoners' clothes.

Giff stopped at the red line going into the storeroom. "Sir, Prisoner Number Five requests permission to cross the red line, sir!"

"Cross," Uncle Tom said, bored.

Giff moved in and turned to getting his gear silently, his black-fringed blue eyes casting out solid glints. He pulled his seabag down from the top of the squares, unsnapped the carrying strap and pulled out his dress shoes that he had thoughtfully placed on top to keep them from getting scuffed. His uniform hung off to the side, still pressed neatly and Giff pulled it down seeing the emptiness of it: no chevrons, ribbons, or emblems.

"Gettin' sprung today, Five?" Uncle Tom said behind him.

"Yes, sir," Giff said, dressing. The greens felt foreign and unsure on him, and they were a little loose around his waist where he had knocked off several cans of beer. He snapped the carrying strap back on the seabag and tied his shoes.

"Is you pissed off, Five?" Uncle Tom asked blithely.

Giff, without moving a muscle, his face set, his back to Uncle Tom, neither turned around nor snapped to attention. "I stay pissed off, sir," he said, and waited for the nightstick to come down on that big muscle between his neck and shoulder. He did not hear Uncle Tom move up behind him or the whistle of the stick as it sliced air, but the wood on skin shot fire up into his head. He did not turn around.

"You all finished, Five?" Uncle Tom asked in a twisted voice.

Giff turned around then, standing at attention. "Yes, sir. All finished."

"I'll tell you somethin', Five," he said, his piebald face growing darker. "You ever come back here again, mother-fucker, and I fix you with a few broken bones you not forget. Remember that."

Giff did not reply. He looked woodenly at Uncle Tom. Uncle Tom jammed the blunt round head of the nightstick into his belly and Giff winced, bending slightly. Uncle Tom stepped back. Giff reached down and hefted his seabag onto his shoulder and walked up to the red line. He requested permission to cross. The permission came in a size ten dress shoe in the small of his back, slamming him across the hall against the Segregation Cells.

Giff rebalanced his seabag on his shoulder and ran back up the corridor to the front of the brig without pausing or looking back.

The chilly dusty environs of the brig met him at the front with the Great Unwashed and Little Bill. He went through the same rigamarole of unpacking his seabag and dumping it all on the floor as he had eight months ago with his laundry bag. Little Bill took the inventory and the Great Unwashed unlocked the cabinet with the pigeon-holes and brought out Giff's personal gear. When it was all completed Giff was ordered to stand nose and toes against the far wall with his seabag beside him.

Shortly after the clock chimed nine-thirty, an hour and a half later, the buzzer on the door jangled and Giff felt the first wave of freedom breathe over him, his nose and toes still against the wall.

The Great Unwashed walked heavily over to the door and unsnapped the lock and Giff heard their muted conversation and then the clearing of a .45.

The door closed again and Little Bill spoke to the stranger, the outsider who had come to chase Giff. Then the door opened again and the chaser went out. There was the metallic clack of the slide of the .45 going home. The door did not close again, and Giff waited.

"If you ever come back here again, Five," Little Bill said, "you'll think this time was a picnic. I promise. Now get to hell out!" he yelled.

Giff spun around, hoisting his seabag to his shoulder in

one motion, and started double-timing to the door where the Great Unwashed stood, and as Giff crossed the front of the brig the chalky-faced man actually turned his head and began studying something in the wall. Little Bill was working his hands together on his desk.

Then he was outside, stepping off the porch, the bright June morning sunshine smacking him with heat, warm and clean. He stopped, seeing the chaser in dungarees standing behind the idling weapons carrier that was belching and rumbling. Then he heard the door shut behind him.

In the time it took a man to blink, Giff looked at the chaser thinking how strange the man looked to him, a man of his own cut and material from South Camp, yet a man who had not been in Giff's metamorphosis of the brig, and for an instant Giff saw the rock pile in his mind and the handleless eight-pound sledges chipping away fruitlessly at the rocks, and the malevolent broken-nosed face of Swannie mumbling over his beads, and the jaw-chewing muscles of the men in the mess hall talking through their food, and the shouts and animal stifled cries of the men getting parties, and the pummeling nightsticks on his body were fresh and reinvigorated, and the swollen parchness of his mouth going through dehydration, all of it running in an endless reel in front of his eyes. Then he grinned at the chaser.

The chaser grinned back, a mixture of apprehension and curiosity on his face, his hand slapping his holster. Giff walked up and tossed his seabag into the back of the weapons carrier, then climbed in behind it, still grinning. The chaser followed.

On the ten miles back Giff did not speak to the chaser. When they rolled up in front of the battalion office Giff tossed his seabag down on the road and climbed after it, the chaser behind him.

"The old man want to see me?" Giff asked, moving his head around at South Camp. Half a dozen platoons were moving through troop and stomp on the parade field, dark spots of sweat under the arms of their dungaree jackets. Clouds of dust rose from their tramping feet and the hoarse orders of the platoon sergeants echoed off the barracks.

"Yeah," the chaser said in a wan voice. "That's where I'm supposed to take you."

"Let's go," Giff said and propped the seabag up on his

shoulder, casting one glance at the camp chapel across the street where he had been court-martialed, then walked down the narrow cement sidewalk to the battalion office.

Inside, the chaser disappeared and Giff stood at ease by the empty bench where the battalion runners whiled away their time. The clacking of typewriters did not cease, and the morning was filled with business. Then the Sergeant Major motioned for him to come over and Giff left his seabag leaning on the bench and walked over to the Sergeant Major's desk. The Sergeant Major quickly escorted him into Colonel Dantes' office.

Colonel Dantes sat behind his oak desk in the spare office, flanked by an American flag and a Marine Corps flag, smiling benignly. Giff stopped at attention in front of his desk.

"Do you think you've learned your lesson, Bohane?"

"Yes, sir."

"I don't want to see you in any more trouble," Dantes said. "That's all."

Giff marched out of the office, through the industry of the battalion clerks, picked up his seabag and stepped out the rear door of the office.

Outside, he set his seabag against the building and adjusted his pisscutter with a seagoing dip. Then he looked up the narrow alley-street toward Pearl Harbor Road that led to Horrible Hog Company's barracks, rutted and dusty in the late morning sun where troops walked by lethargically, troops who were a part of him, or had been. And the camp was not the same either, not a part of him nor was he a part of it, and where once before he had thought of himself as a part of it, a part of the whole without which it couldn't have existed, he could see it all now, that it had all gone on without him, not needing him. And *it* moved down the road in the swirls of dust and the smack of rifle stocks as forty pairs of hands grabbed them in unison to a swift present arms that would never again be a part of him.

It was like seeing for the first time in his life a sudden solid revelation, intangible and unique, that spoke to him through the heavy hot air saying that no matter how many lives one body moved through, the body did not affect those lives at all. No life was actually affected because no life could ultimately be touched, moved, or even destroyed by another life.

It was that single individual untouchableness that in the end had caused him pain and suffering and happiness and sadness and even destroying him if it saw fit. Through pain there was the learning, through the suffering there was the evolution, through the conflicts of himself there was the illumination, and with all of them, endowed with them, there were no forces alive that could break through the perimeter and touch him.

Wherefore art thou, Bohane? the revelation asked him. Yea, though you walk through the valley of the shadow of Bamboo Alley it is not for naught.

He hoisted his seabag and started walking down the alley-street to the barracks. Once or twice he looked around and was surprised to find that there was no riot gun behind him.

Someone waved to him from the company boiler room as he passed, but he did not wave back. He hadn't recognized the man. Rounding the corner of the barracks he walked up the cement stoop and stepped in the double doors.

It hit him like a volley of mortar shells bursting around him: the old inveterate life, the ingredients of his past living, when he saw the men sitting around on their bunks chattering, dealing cards, the clatter of dice resounding off the baseboard in the head. And the furious preparations for liberty voiced themselves in the low-ceilinged squadbays—and he knew it was payday, the old familiar holiday atmosphere of marines with shekels in their cheap civilian trouser pockets. But he was not a part of it.

Several of the men spoke to him with open friendliness, others nodded with sedate reserve, as he walked through the squadbay to his old bunk.

He did not see Cinamo Dallas or Stack or Poke or any of his ex-associates. He sat down on his old bare bunk, the mattress stained from many people sitting on it to keep their own bunks stretched tight.

Lazily activated, the platoon moved over to where he sat on the bunk and began talking with him awkwardly at first, then openly interested.

They all wanted to know about the brig although it was obvious they already knew a lot about it (perhaps not the

Middle Camp brig but some they had done some time in elsewhere). Giff did not elaborate on the brig. There was no way for him to express it. He merely nodded yes and shook his head no to the questions. Then he asked them about the company.

Koko Hobbs' desertion did not astound him; Thorton's promotion to gunnery sergeant was simply accepted; and Finch's transfer to Ordnance was not even important. The center, the meat of the conversation, wheeled right around to the coming $45 extra a month combat pay that everyone felt was not far off. That was the thing that was important and yet so natural that if an alien man had suddenly been told that these men were going to war he would have gone away a disbeliever.

Gradually though, they broke away, moving on back to their gambling and liberty preparation, and Giff sat smoking, wondering what to do with himself.

He had just finished his cigarette, still undecided, when Cinamo Dallas came walking in from the head. The blockily built, bulbous-nosed Stack Renshaw was right behind him. They walked up to Giff grinning broadly.

"Howdy, Corporal," Giff said, without standing, without offering to shake hands. "Hear you been going up in the world."

"Hellyea." Dallas appraised Giff briefly. "You don't look hurt none."

"And he ain't," Stack grinned. "They ain't invented a weapon yet to puncture his hide."

"How's the old married man?" Giff asked and watched Stack's face weave into a sneer-frown.

"How long you been out?" Dallas asked casually, sitting down.

Giff inspected another cigarette before he lit it. "About an hour. I just got in the barracks. What you been doing? Gamblin'?"

"Shootin' dice in the head, cousin." Dallas tossed his hand out in imitation and patted a bulge in his pocket. "Got to make some shekel for liberty."

"Yeah?" Giff said. "To hell with liberty tonight. Which one of you got a jug in your locker?"

"Just happen to have one," Dallas said loosely. He got up and walked over to his wall locker, opened it, and pulled out a fifth of gin, tossing it to Giff.

"Jesus Christ!" Giff said. "Won't you ever learn? It's against the law to have liquor in the barracks."

"That ain't liquor," Dallas said. "That's horsepiss, gook style." He walked back over and sat down by Giff. "Ain't you in kind of a big hurry to get some liberty?"

"No more'n usual," Giff said, opening the bottle. "Why?"

"Thought maybe you wanted to get down and see your girl."

"What girl?"

"Popcorn."

"Hell," Giff said and took a drink and frowned. "She ain't my girl."

"That's good, cousin," Dallas said. "Cause I been fuckin' her."

Stack coughed awkwardly.

"Well," Giff paused with his second drink, "if you live with cripples you learn to limp."

Dallas' deep V brow quivered a little, his eyes went black, then he grinned sheepishly, the first time Giff had ever seen any sign of embarrassment on his face, and he laughed loudly. "Don't hog all that gin."

"Play it cool," Stack warned. "That sonofabitch Top Condrum comes through here we'll all go to jail."

The three of them sat drinking out of the bottle suddenly immersed in conversation, the thin ice broken, and Giff thought it was patently like an Irish wake. Their conversation was only interrupted by sudden guffaws and laughter and sly digs by each of them. Then Stack went up the squadbay, weaving slightly, and brought Pfc. Dahl down from the first platoon. Pfc. Dahl was the only man in the barracks who had a phonograph and records and Stack thought it would be great if they had some music, a little shitkicking music he told them. Giff agreed, pleasantly relaxed.

So they sat drinking and talking and listening to the shitkicking music (mostly Hank Williams of course—and some Patti Page) and when the first bottle was gone, Stack promptly drew another one from his locker. The rest of the platoon drifted over from time to time, hanging around soliciting a short drink, then dashing back to their gambling. Even men from the other platoons came over and surprising to Giff old Half-Slick Willy Woechowski came over from machine guns and shook Giff's hand lugu-

481

briously, but left when he found they were drinking on duty. And finally Poke Turner came walking in, his narrow cunning face twisted with a lopsided grin, dungarees sooty, and Giff found out that it was Poke who had waved to him from the boiler room. Poke was on boiler room duty. Even Guppy Talagua came in with a rousing welcome and immediately wanted a drink. A few of the NCO's around the barracks walked by with stolid nods and terse hellos. Jesus Queecho walked through once (he now slept in the staff quarters because he was the platoon sergeant) and appraised Giff in his usual cold voice.

Surprisingly enough, none of the staff came snooping through the squadbay although there was a good deal of noise reverberating from locker to locker. This token of luck was attributed to it being payday and the staff was probably getting drunk too, or already out on liberty (though it was still morning) and still no one had come for Giff. He wondered if he had been forgotten by the company somehow, taken off the rolls. He didn't have a rifle or web gear or even a squad yet and he wondered if, should the war come now, he might have to steal a rifle?

Another thing that puzzled him, sitting there drinking talking listening, was that the gin had not hit him. The brig had dehydrated him, carted away the excess baggage of booze, and the cells and complicated tubes and gauges inside his body had equalized the effect of alcohol. It simply did not affect him the same.

At eleven o'clock, still sober but warm and unlaxed in the late June morning barracks, the sun's shadows across the cinder ash outside narrowing and shortening for its apex, Giff debated whether to steel himself and march on the company office or wait until he was called, and just then, in the middle of his debate, Pfc. Quiller Carpenter came booming through the front door of the barracks grinning, hungover as usual, and advanced on Giff's coterie around Dallas' bunk.

"Hello, pogue." Giff offered the clerk the bottle. "How's the old remington raider this morning?"

"Badly in need of a drink." Quiller took a long pull and nodded at the cluster of men. "And runnin' my young ass off on errands. Like for you, Bohane." He handed the bottle back. "The Kizer wants to see you over the office."

482

"All right." Giff stood up and stretched. "I'm on my way. Come on, Quiller, you old pencil pusher."

The two of them walked down the narrow aisle between bunks to the front door and on outside into the hot sunlight. Still dressed in greens, the sweat broke out on Giff's face as they crossed the mustering area.

"Ain't you got any tropicals or khakis?" Quiller asked helpfully.

"In my seabag," Giff said, wishing now he had taken them out when he first got back.

Top Condrum was not in the office. King Solomon was working at his desk. Giff felt foreign, suddenly freakish, in this that was his company's office.

"The Kizer already here?" he asked. "In his office?"

Quiller nodded and walked over to the Kizer's door. "I think he wants to see you right now, too." He knocked a couple of times, opened the door and stuck his head in and said something Giff did not catch, then pulled his head back out and nodded for Giff to go in.

Tucking his pisscutter under his belt, Giff walked in blank-faced, stopping at attention in front of the massive captain. "Private Gifford Bohane reporting as ordered, sir," he said quickly, unfaltering.

"At ease, Private!" Kizer exploded. "Glad to have you back aboard. Thought for a while you weren't going to be with us long." He grinned up at Giff.

"Yes, sir."

"It's all right," Kizer qualified. "You've made your mistake, or mistakes, and you've had your punishment. I'm not the kind of man that would hold your conviction against you. As far as I'm concerned you come to my company clean. Without a blemish on your record book. Understand?"

"Yes, sir."

"You simply had a bad go of it your first few months with us," Kizer went on. "But that's to be expected. I've had trouble in my career, too. Hah! Wouldn't believe that, would you?"

"No, sir."

Emil Kizer nodded his Prussian head gravely. "Spent some brig time once in China— No, by God! It wasn't China either—was Cuba I think— No, the Canal Zone. Sure! The Canal Zone. Thirty days. Course, the Marine Corps was different then." He toyed with his swagger stick. "The old Corps, you know?"

"Yes, sir," Giff said.

"Just between you and me," Kizer explained, "with this war coming up there will be a lot of rank floating around to be snatched up. I don't think you'll have to worry about catching some of it." He swiveled around and looked concertedly out the window. "Keep your nose clean and you'll make it. Good luck," he said sternly. "That's all."

Giff snapped to attention again, about-faced, and strode smartly from the office. Quiller Carpenter was grudgingly at work. King Solomon was sweating over his unit diary cards. Neither of them looked up as he walked out.

Back in the barracks, Giff did not continue drinking although the rest of them, taking advantage of an excuse for a party, had cumshawed two more bottles.

He unpacked his seabag, squaring his wall locker away neatly. Then he showered and donned a fresh clean set of starched dungarees. After the lazy hour and a half of rest after noon chow he drew his rifle, bedding and web gear. Then there was nothing to do but wait until liberty call at 1630.

At 1630 he borrowed ten dollars and a pair of cheap civilian slacks from Dallas and prepared to go on liberty. Dallas figured they would all go down to the Blue Moon. Giff said he might be down later, but that he did not want to go down so early.

He took the ten dollars and walked alone over to the slop chute where he had three beers with Half-Slick Willy, who could bend cans over his nose just as adroitly as ever. Then he walked on out into Fujioka in the early evening.

In the lapsed eight months, the town had not changed at all. It looked identical to Giff, even down to the last rock in the dirty streets and the shabby paint on the bars, and the women with their unchanged faces calling from the doorways. He did not feel that he had missed anything of importance in those eight months. He would not have traded those eight months for anything. It meant more to him than anything he had ever done in his life. And he could not explain it.

He did not go down to the Bar New Blue Moon later, nor did the desire ever to go back enter his mind. The Blue Moon was, to him, a part of his life that was finished—that had no more meaning—and he could see no reason for taking that life up again. Not after spending so much time and energy refuting it.

That first night on liberty in eight months, he hit a few of the bars in Fujioka, then walked down the railroad tracks to South Fujioka and spent the night in the Grass Hut Bar. He had never been in the Grass Hut before, and even for a payday it was not doing a heavy business. He shacked up with a stocky, well-built Jo-san and woke on his own at 0430 in the morning, dressed and returned to South Camp without a hangover.

Dallas and Poke and the rest of the denizens of the Blue Moon and Bamboo Alley wanted to know where the hell he spent the night? They had a party planned for him for Chrissakes. Giff said he had gotten drunk and passed out and they did not question him about it any longer.

The training in the field did not decrease during the rest of June. Giff was out in the field every day running with the second platoon. Jesus Queecho had assigned him rifleman in the 3rd Fire Team 3rd Squad. Giff did not even mind the field, the sweat, or the dirt and he was amazed at Gunny Thorton's zealous handling of the company. He had never thought before that Thorton was much of a field marine. Apparently, Thorton knew more than he ever let on. Giff found himself admiring the mustachioed sonfabitch, grudgingly.

His life moved on that way into July, not pushing, not yielding, not forcing anything. He did his field work and was never called down during the inspections. At night, when he had liberty, he would go out by himself and hit some of the bars for a few beers. He did not drink Akadama wine or gin, only beer. If he felt like shacking up he would find a different Jo-san each night. Sometimes he would not shack up at all, but merely catch a short time.

Twice he went down Skivvie Lane to Rotten Crotch Mary's and talked with Cherry-san, the wild-eyed Jo-san whom Half-Slick Willy had fixed him up with during last year's monsoon. He never did shack with her, but simply talked and once spent two hours trying to beat her at casino and failed shamefacedly. (Cherry-san had not propositioned him, nor had she mentioned that business fact of his shacking up with her.) And when he stopped in at Rotten Crotch Mary's, on those two occasions, she stopped whatever it was she was doing and talked with him—and played casino. The first time she asked him where he had been for so long. He told her the Monkey House. She did not ask him anything else.

It was the most easygoing period of his life, the simplest routined phase he had ever known. And he did not become involved in anything outside of himself. He did not get into fights, or even drunk. And he pulled his liberty by himself. Sometimes, he would run into members of the company and talk guardedly with them over a beer. He did not pull liberty with his old buddy Dallas, and scrupulously, Dallas did not accost him after that first night when he had not gone down to the Blue Moon.

It was enough to wait. And that was all he was doing. Waiting for the war.

32.

Everyone had been galvanized for war for so long, ever since the Korean cease-fire when rumors were their hottest (during the first few months after that, and then early in 1954 when the fuses were lit all over the world: the stepped-up training schedule, the U.S. Air Force helping the French in Indochina, the fall of Dien Bien Phu—all of it culminating, snowballing so that war was a foregone conclusion). They had not only been galvanized for it, but were expecting it, *spoiling* for it in such a deceptively calm and natural way that when it did come, it did not come as a surprise. And yet it did.

At four o'clock in the morning, July 15th, while the troops of Horrible Hog Company were breathing steadily in that last true hour of sleep before reveille, the best hour of sleep, not tossing, unfitful, the Duty NCO, Corporal Geiler, a thick-necked, red-faced man, burst into the barracks and snapped the lights on, hustling around and waking the NCO's.

"What the hell is it?" someone asked in a voice hoarse from excessive drinking.

486

"Jesus Christ!" another complained, "it's only four o'clock!"

"I got to quit drinking," another man decided sleepily, incoherent.

"Don't never ask me to ship over," one said bitterly.

"Don't never come for me you got a war; take a reg'-ment to get me back."

"Go on back the office, Geiler," a disgruntled squad leader from the first platoon rallied. "You drunk on duty or something?"

All through the barracks men were rising from the warmth of their bunks, the sudden glare of naked lights burning their sleep-puffed eyes. Outside it was still heavily dark, and the slight chill of the early July morning made them pull their blankets up closer around their necks. Their faces showed genuine puzzlement but all of them began piling out of their bunks instinctively: the ingrained professional soldier's unwanted, but always there, compliance with authority.

"Get dressed and fall out for muster in fifteen minutes," Geiler said laconically. "Gunny Thorton's holdin' muster. That's all I know. But the Kizer's in his fuckin' office," he added, as if he were talking to himself.

The troops dressed hurriedly and scurried out, tucking in their jackets, lighting cigarettes to catch those first few drags before throwing them away for muster, chattering in nervous loud voices, and formed ranks on the ash mustering area, their feet scuffing the ground impatiently.

Gunny Hugh Thorton had been in a dead sleep when Corporal Geiler slipped into the staff quarters and pummeled him awake at four o'clock.

"What the fuck," he said, rubbing his hands over his face. "All right, goddamit; I'm awake. What—who is it?"

"You got to get up," Geiler said in an apologetic tone. "The Kizer's in his office, higher than a kite, wants to see you."

"Drunk?"

"No, just high," Geiler said. "He's actin' like the shit hit the fan."

"Okay," Hugh said, sitting up, looking around the staff quarters. "What about the rest of the staff?"

"He only wanted to see you."

"Tell him I'll be over in a minute." He got it now. He

had been expecting it any day. But it was odd that it should come like this, so natural. He had almost expected to hear a bugle calling somewhere, or a brass band sounding off. A tremor of satisfaction leaped through him, and he felt as if he had just beaten the house at their own game, without cutting the cards. "Yeah," he said, "tell the Kizer I'll be right over."

Geiler nodded and walked out, his face puzzled.

When Hugh had dressed and washed his face and curled his mustache, he walked quickly over to the company office, its lights burning with a frenzy in the early morning. Geiler was not inside. The door of the Kizer's office was open and he could see the massive man rummaging through his desk, a .45 hanging heavy on his hip.

"Good morning, sir," he said, stepping into the office.

"By God it is at that!" Kizer shouted. "A great morning, Gunny." He kept on leafing through his papers. "Got the word an hour ago. Moving out. Field transport packs. Everything. Moving out."

"Yes, sir," Hugh said, forcing the excitement in him to drift down to a small current of self-reliance. "What's it all about?"

"We'll be outa here in a few hours," Kizer said, stacking all his papers on the corner of his desk. "Won't come back neither. No sir, by God. Moving out."

"What about it?" Hugh said again.

The Kizer looked up for the first time, his face beaming, his eyes lit up, guttering like candles, and as if he had just suddenly become aware of another human presence in his office. "Ah yes, Gunny Thorton. The company officers are getting fixed up over the BOQ. They'll be over in a minute. What I want you to do—"

"Pardon me sir," Hugh said, lighting a cigarette. "But what is this all about?" He had to play the game right, according to the rules, give the Kizer the lead.

"What is it all about?" Kizer yelled. "Why man, we're going to war! War, boy! We're going to start earning our keep, makin' our paydays count! War!"

"Yes, sir," Hugh grinned. "This is official then?"

"Goddam yes it's official," Kizer said, patting his .45. "I got the word direct from Colonel Dantes. He got it direct from Colonel Klepteris. And the Old Man got it direct from Division. This is it. Oh, this is the one."

488

"Everything's set up?" Hugh said. "Transportation and all that? All ready to go?"

"Everything. I sent Geiler up for coffee. When he gets back send him over the barracks and wake the troops. Oh, will they be glad to hear this! Then you hold muster, I'll give you the instructions. But you already know what to do, eh?" He winked at Hugh. "Then get the rest of the staff up. Get 'em up now. We can't waste any time."

"Yes, sir," Hugh said. "I'll take care of it. Be right the fuck back." He turned and left the office, feeling the excitement surging back, cutting it off cautiously, and walked over to the staff quarters. Everyone was still asleep, snoring.

Hugh flipped the lights on. "All right, motherfuckers," he said happily, "leggo your cocks and grab your socks. Come on. Get your asses up."

"It's only still night!" D'Agastino protested.

"I had a bottle round here somewhere," Gross mumbled, dragging his arm along his bunk.

"She was only a butcher's daughter," Wasluski said not fully awake, "but oh how she could beat your meat."

"There'll be some meat beating before long," Hugh said. "In the field, Indochina. We're going to war."

As one body, the staff sat up in their bunks wide awake and looked at him, their faces dry and frozen. Then the frozenness left, and grins spread over them.

"That's right," Hugh nodded, "we're going to war."

"Whyn't you say so?" Gross said, leaping from his bunk.

"I'm going out to hold muster," Hugh said. "When you get dressed, pack up field transport packs. Then get over to your platoons, square them away. You've all been through this before. I don't need to give you any directions." Hugh walked out of the squadbay and back over to the company office and prepared for muster. A salty sonofabitch like himself could roll a pack in ten minutes.

Now he stood in front of Horrible Hog Company smoking, pacing a few steps one way, then another, twisting the pointed spears of his mustache happily, collecting his bet from himself. His Forty Years' War! You couldn't beat the dealer.

When the company had formed, the last straggler shuffling into ranks, Hugh took muster and quite naturally (he hadn't bothered to check the liberty log), there were almost ten per cent of the men still on liberty. Well, that was no problem. He was just about to give them instructions when the Kizer, Captain Emil Kizer, strode from his office to the front of the company and stood at attention, his pistol on one hip, holding his swagger stick on the other, a ponderous shadow against the barracks wall.

"I have something to say, Gunny."

Hugh glanced at his watch. A hush descended over the troops. He backed off to the side, watching the Kizer with curious intent.

"Men," Kizer said in a clear voice that exuded strength and command, "men, we have gathered here this morning to put an end to an intolerable peace. This suffering that we have endured since the end of Korea is at last coming to an end. We are going to war."

A murmur rippled through the troops like a huge swell at sea, then faded out.

"Yes," Kizer said, "all that we have endured is not now going to be wasted. True, we have all of us been bitter during this past year, and that bitterness has caused us heavy distress. It has probably destroyed some of us to an extent. But now we are going to be redeemed. This that we are going to do now, this going to war, is why we are all here. Why each of us in our small way enlisted, the most important of whatever other various reasons we had at the time."

Oh Jesus, Hugh thought, but he was vaguely touched.

"If it were up to me," Kizer said, "I would never have made you men carry this cross of the past year. If I had the power I would have seen that this war came sooner; that our peacetime, or whatever it is, was run entirely different.

"Now there will be a good many of us who won't make it back from this one. That is a fact. For some of us it will be better to die—this time. For others, it will be simply another notch on your stocks."

Another murmur rippled through the company.

"I have always had faith in this company," Kizer went on. "I believe it is the finest company in the division. None will touch it in combat. It is with pride and humility that I have had the luck to lead this company. And perhaps if I don't get a chance to lead it all the way, if something

490

should happen to me, I want you all to know that this company is me. I am this company. It will always be like that. So roll your packs and pick up your fucking rifles— We're going to war!"

A roaring cheer went up from the troops as the Kizer walked back toward the company office, staunch, massive, the picture of a Caesar.

Hugh Thorton, watching him go, felt something pang inside him, like a packet of gas; then his confidence asserted itself again.

"All right, knock off the bullshit!"

The troops quieted down, twitching nervously, murmuring.

"Chow goes in fifteen minutes," he said, peering through the moonless darkness at the company. "When chow's over get your asses right back here and pack up full field transport packs. Then pack your seabags. You'll get the tags to mark 'em."

Quiet muffled murmuring rolled through the company, the sharp expectancy of giving birth to an overdue and belabored child of time.

"Knock it off!" Thorton said emphatically. "I'll assign p'toon sarjints from each p'toon to make a goddam muster of all men still on liberty. Then send a man from each platoon out to bring 'em back. But make sure you send a man who's ready to go. You can go in dungarees. But bring them all back! If you have to tear down the bars to do it." He started walking up and back, his voice loud and clear in the morning air. "But most of you know where the men hang out. Now," he went on didactically, "when you get your packs made up fall out and make formation and you got to be in ranks by five-thirty. That's all. I want the right guides up here."

When he had the right guides assembled, Hugh gave them instructions on the time schedule: when to check out weapons from the armory, flak jackets from supply, and everything else that he could think of that was halfway important.

There was, all through the now lighted barracks of South Camp, oppressive nervousness of another transition, a transition of men and sparse equipment.

Giff Bohane was picked as the man from the second platoon to head to Fujioka and check on the six men who were absent from muster. He himself had gotten very drunk the night before but had managed to steer his way back to the barracks after a short time at the Silver Star Bar, as he had been doing since his release from the brig. He had known this was coming and it had not surprised him this morning when he had wakened with the rest of the company and fallen out. Although his head was ballooning with blood and his mouth was so dry it merely begged for water, the hangover took second place to this that was coming.

He rolled his field transport pack five minutes after they were dismissed from ranks, breaking a record that he himself had set previously for pack rolling, then turned to helping Dallas with his. Dallas was still a little drunk along with Poke and Stack. They had been down to the Blue Moon last night and had only come in one hour before the surprise reveille. They had brought a bottle in with them and were all now sharing it. All around the barracks, in each of the squadbays, more bottles were brought out and very few men went to chow.

"I wants to thank you," Dallas said. "I never could roll that fucking pack this morning. Not the way I feel war or no."

"Nothing to it," Giff said, over the hubbub of the squadbay. "How about another drink?"

Dallas passed him the bottle.

"Save some for me," Poke said, tying up his pack.

"I got another bottle in my locker," Stack said.

"Maybe we'll get a chance to buy some more," Poke said. "Hot damn! We goin' to need a lot for this war."

"You don't think they make likker in Indochina?" Giff said. "Hell man, they make it everywhere."

"Indochina," Dallas said. "That's a glorious fucking idea."

"Man, you are drunk," Giff said.

"Gonna get drunker, too," Dallas said.

"All gonna get drunk," Poke said.

"I'll bet the Kizer's drunk," Stack said. "With that speech he made, he'll have to be drunk."

They all turned on him, anger in their faces.

"I mean," he said, "take a drunk man to make such a pretty speech."

They all turned back to their work: clearing out their wall lockers, rolling packs, throwing things away. Giff kept

492

nothing except the barest comforts and necessities. He tossed out all his little odds and ends that did not make sense, saved his cunt pictures that he had paid five bucks for long ago, and everyone else was doing the same thing. The GI can was quickly filled with a heap of love letters, trinkets, souvenirs.

Hugh Thorton came walking through, checking on the company's progress, and stopped short when he saw the long line in front of the GI can. "What the hell you throwing away?" he asked Giff.

"A sore ass hole."

"A what?"

"An old corn plaster."

"Oh."

Giff looked up then, moved out of the way as more men advanced on the GI can, and found himself looking into Thorton's eyes. For a moment they stared at each other's blank face, neither flinching, then they grinned simultaneously, tight natural-forced grins. Then they both turned away from each other and went about their business.

Giff surveyed his wall locker which was empty, his sea-bag which was pathetically sagging, and his pack which was bursting, listening to the sounds in the squadbay, feeling his hangover go away, and the first sparkles of drunkenness coming back. He sat down on his bunk and looked around.

In the face of each man there was registered all the unfulfilled wishes of a life that could never be fulfilled, and all of it covered up with that tight grin of drunkenness, each lying to the other as they packed and filled the GI can with their unfulfilled mementos. Some of the men were trying to sell their civvies, what little they had of them, others selling or bartering for a drink, which they got free gratis anyway. It was all of it like a family reunion, but Giff felt, strangely enough, that he was outside. That was when Jesus Queecho came into the squadbay and informed him he was to go to town and collect the fragments of the platoon.

It was the first and only time that Giff had come through any main gate anywhere without having to show a liberty card. The gate was swung wide open and men were dog-trotting in from all over the town in the darkness that was now beginning to lighten with the first hints of deceptive dawn. All the lights in the bars were on and a great clamor was rising from the sea of people that ran up from Bamboo Alley and Skivvie Lane and Main Street.

He had no trouble finding the six men, for he ran into them just as he was going down Bamboo Alley. They had already gotten the word, they told him, and what about that? Wasn't that something? Man, they was getting their cotton-picking asses back to pack. Were they all ready to leave? No, Giff said, not for a while yet. He grinned. One of those hurry up and wait things, you know what I mean?

He told them to go on back and tell Jesus Queecho that he would be right in, but that he was making a last-minute check for men. They said they would. Then he walked down to the Heart Bar and bought three bottles of gin, tucked them under his field jacket and listened to the excited chatter of the Jo-sans who were all up now and confused.

"Yeah, it's a war all right," he said. "Be leavin' this morning."

"You come back, *ne?*"

"Well now I don't know," Giff said to all of the Jo-sans. "Maybe come back for R 'n R. But if I was you, I'd pack up my gear and come along for the ride." He winked at them. "We'll be needing you."

They began chattering again, fright and suspicion in their faces, for they too now had lost an unfulfilled life, and something stirred in Giff's bowels, as he left, thinking what all this would look like without the town there, his town. He brushed the thought from his mind. He walked fast back to the main gate and into South Camp.

Two six-by transport trucks were being loaded down by Hog Company's armory and supply shed. The four men working, wiping sweat from their faces, swearing, were stacking ammunition on the trucks. Giff stopped and passed one of his bottles around for which they all thanked him with extravagance. Then he walked into the barracks to wait for word to fall out, to drink with the platoon, which was now ready for war, primed and loaded, packed and killing time.

The first breaking pink of dawn filled the eastern horizon as the companies began falling out, prodded and scooted by NCO's who did not need to prod and scoot but who were merely doing their jobs, all laden with combat gear, each of them taking one last look inside the

494

barracks, wondering if they would ever see them again, thinking they had lost nothing really.

Six men from the company were staying behind, a sort of peacetime mopping up to get the administration in order, and then they would join up later. Five of them were terribly disgruntled and even cried at this shameful duty of staying behind. The sixth man, Oscar Zorn, Hog Company's police sergeant, thought it was great.

Horrible Hog Company, drunk but not staggering, walking proudly, backs ramrod straight, Emil Kizer stepping out at the head of the column chest out, shoulders back, chin high, moved heavily up to the South Camp parade field and formed battalion ranks there.

Five minutes later, just as the first clear red ball of sun swept over, they marched in a battalion body out of the main gate and up through the town as the women lined the streets waving at them, chattering, exchanging quips with the men as they passed.

They turned left at the railroad tracks and marched down to the South Fujioka railroad station. Trains were already puffing and steaming and they boarded quickly, settled down on the uncomfortable wood seats, and in three hours they were in Yokohama. There they marched through the busy streets, surrounded once again by Jo-sans who lined the sides of the wide thoroughfares, to the docks to board the ships.

All along the docks, the APA's were loading swiftly: men, guns, ammunition, the works, all a part of the trade. And they loaded in record-breaking time. By noon, the ships were steaming out to sea.

Gambling broke out immediately on ship—fast, hard, reckless burning gambling—and money changed hands quick. It was no surprise for a man to bet a hundred bucks on the throw of the dice or play twenty bucks on blackjack. The usual customary poker—draw, stud, and seven card—was not played. It took too long, too much time, and blackjack and dice reigned.

Also, there were many fights on the ship. Tempers had drawn taut the three days on the ocean before they finally dropped anchor offshore somewhere (none of the troops knew if it was Indochina or not, but they were quite sure it was)—at any moment a man was apt to lash out viciously even if insulted with good nature.

495

They dropped anchor in the South China Sea early in the morning on July the 18th in a large bay where the water lapped but never boiled, and in the hazy distance all of them could see the gray and green and black and brown ruggedness of the land. And they all knew it was Indochina then, yet no word had been passed.

That afternoon in Horrible Hog Company's hold, Giff listened to the booming voice of the Kizer, who now had the scoop: that *was* Indochina they saw in the distance. Emil Kizer informed them that they would embark in the morning and to all intents and purposes there did not appear to be any opposing forces. Each man would be adequately furnished with ammunition. They would run through boat drill in the later afternoon, and, he added with a blasting voice, grinning broadly, by this time tomorrow they would be back in war!

That night few slept. But it was not because of nervousness. There was still the gambling going on: money had changed so many hands in the past three days that no one was sure whose money it had been to begin with and who had been the big losers and the big winners; even yen, which was defunct in Indochina, was gambled with, for there were some diehards who still expected to get R 'n R in Japan. But no one listened to them, because Hong Kong was much closer and it was far better than Japan, they had heard.

Men sat on their bunks cleaning their weapons, sharpening their bayonets to a razor's edge (against regulation in peacetime), and others talked and talked and told jokes and laughed, a little impatiently, having to wait until morning. All were thoroughly agreed that they could have gone in during the afternoon just as well as morning.

At two o'clock in the morning of July 19th, reveille went with the shrill blast of the bosun's mate's whistle and most of the troops were already awake and on their feet, dressed and ready. Chow went hurriedly (they were supposed to get steak and eggs—they got mush and hash). Then swiftly back to their compartments donning their combat gear, sweating profusely in the cramped quarters, waiting to receive word to fall out and fall in with their boat teams.

But the word never came.

Captain Emil Kizer strolled massively into Horrible Hog Company's compartment, his face hangdog, his Prussian countenance defeated, tears of frustration and impotence glistening in his eyes, Gunny Hugh Thorton walking expressionless behind him.

Emil Kizer stopped in the middle of the compartment and the men huddled around him anxiously, puzzled. He took a deep breath, let it out slowly and studied their faces.

"It's all over with," he said in a choked voice.

"They reached an agreement last night. They've signed an armistice. There ain't no war."

Then, without another word, too choked up to talk, he turned and walked out.

"You can all go back to bed," Hugh Thorton said in the dead silence, his voice flat and cold. "We'll be in Japan by Friday." He curled his immaculate shiny mustache thoughtfully, turned, and followed the Kizer.

If someone had triggered a flame thrower in the compartment it would not have seared the men half as much, filling their lungs with heat, choking their breaths, cutting out vocal chords. A dark pendulous silence fell on them and through the open hatch on the main deck they could all hear the water lapping on the ship's hull.

When the initial shock abated and the trauma collapsed, the men began moving around again. They grinned sheepishly and talked in shaded low tones while in their eyes glinted their outraged rebellion.

By noon of the same day the convoy was underway cutting a trail back to Japan, and in those few hours from the time the Kizer informed them of the fiasco, and the finality of it had sunk in, the troops were back in their old restless groove.

Cards, dice and money reared up their fevered heads and the gambling went right on as though nothing out of the ordinary had happened. But it was not the cold and hot heedless gambling that had flourished on the way over. Dice and blackjack took a hindseat to regular poker and the playing became professional and mathematical.

The last night on the ship before they docked in Yokohama, Giff stood by himself on the rail watching the phosphorus in the water sparkle against the black, holding the God of Good Fortune in his hands. In his pocket he had almost three hundred dollars, gambling wins, more than he had lost on the way over, and he felt excessively pleased over his luck as he rubbed HoTi's belly.

Looking at HoTi, he seemed to look backward at himself, and that time almost a year ago when he had first come to Japan, and all that had happened in between—Japan, Fujioka, Bamboo Alley, the brig, all the wild midnight carousing—was now a dimming memory in the past to him. It didn't exist. And Korea. Korea was so far behind it seemed to emanate from a different life.

And the life that loomed up in front of him remained uncharted.

In the head off the compartment where the staff slept, Hugh Thorton sat on the wooden slats over the rushing water, not taking a crap. His face was flushed from the liquor he had black-marketed off one of the sailors and his mustache was growing wildly disheveled, glistening black with sweat. In his hand he held a battered deck of cards and slowly, methodically, he peeled one card off at a time, ripped it in two and dropped it in the slushing water very carefully, until the last one slewed away. Then he stood up wobbling and staggered back into the compartment to hunt for his bunk.

33.

One month after the abortive war, Hugh Thorton stood leaning against the file cabinet behind Quiller Carpenter's desk in the company office, drinking coffee leisurely, staring out the window at Horrible Hog Company moving through its torpid ritual of morning inspection.

His handlebar mustache shinily black, spears sharp and pointing skyward, Hugh watched the company: the platoon sergeants inspecting each man and his rifle, moving down the rank and file smartly. He wondered half cynically at the changes that had come just in that short month, since the Indochina washout—abortion.

Under the already high early-morning August sun, the heat was penetrating the office and the barracks, and the

498

mustering area outside glinted with dust now in dog days. There would be a mugginess in the air till the monsoon season started fresh again in September. And the nights would not be cool, but moist and crisp and most of the troops would be in the slop chute or out in town, drinking cold beer as the sweltering heat shadows crossed their faces.

He took a sip of his coffee, his deep-set eyes under his beetling brow inquisitive, probing, ferreting out the faces in the company, standing evenly spaced in their platoons outside. He knew most of them. In fact, in a sense, he knew all of them. But there were new faces now, too. Young faces, punk faces, faces of noncombatants. Civilian recalcitrants and juvenile delinquents, he thought with a wry twist in his mind. And he Hugh Thorton was supposed to be in charge of these men.

In a way it was almost like when he had first come in, the first time: back in '40. Only he did not think he looked quite as addled and dumfounded as those new men out there, now filling ranks with the old cynical mercenaries who had constituted the company before Indo—(he thought a little self-effacingly)—china.

The new draft, the first replacement draft from the States, had come in only two weeks after they had returned from Indo . . . hell with it . . . china. Kids really, he thought, watching them. With no more than four or five months in the service—in the Crotch! And they were as different from the older men, the derisive combatants, as his new shackjob was from Chebe-san.

Off to his right, Quiller Carpenter punched his typewriter savagely, his eyes red—hungover as usual—doing the morning's work on the new men's record books. Morning work to Quiller Carpenter was like a Catholic priest eating beefsteak on Friday.

Yet it wasn't only the new draft that had changed the company Hugh analyzed. More than anything, he guessed it was the war that didn't come. *His* war. *Hugh Thorton's Forty Years' War.*

And what had happened to it?

Well, he told himself, there were probably a good many answers. The way he had planned it was that the precipitation of the third World War, when all the *free* nations would band together to fight and destroy all the oppressed nations, would start with Indo—(the pain of being

499

wrong)—china: then Korea and China and the Slavic and Baltic States on in to Russia herself. And he was quite certain that the big shots (don't forget to dot the "i") had it planned that way, exactly. But something had happened. Someone had dropped the ball. And it was anyone's guess who that someone was.

He heard the Kizer cough in his office, the door closed. Emil Kizer now spent more and more time locked in his office, Hugh reflected. It seemed that since the abortion the Kizer had lost some of his zeal and robustness. Oh sure, he still had the old booming voice and bulletheaded Prussian dignity, but there was something in the old man that was defeated. Hugh was quite sure that it was the unassailable fact that Indo—(Chebe-san had been right) —china was the old man's last chance for a war. He was getting pretty old and the next war (Hah! there he was: planning it again) would come too late for the Kizer.

Ham Haley, the company Executive Officer, had informed Hugh that the Kizer was drinking a little more lately, more than he ever had before (Ham Haley was certain of this because he was spending all *his* time drinking *with* the Kizer), and did nothing but talk about the old days all the time. Well, the Kizer would probably be around, outlast all the rest of them. Even himself.

"Shit!" Quiller Carpenter scowled. "Ain't had nothing but mistakes since I started this morning." Furiously, he erased the mistake on his Form 115. "That new bunch has fucked me up more than Hogan's goat."

"Why don't you quit clerking and go back to being a field marine?" Hugh goaded.

"With those punks in the company now?"

Hugh turned back to his coffee, grinning at Quiller, then looked over the steam of the cup out at the company: the long faded green line, he thought cynically again, immaculate in their dungarees and leggins, rifle barrels shining under the morning slant sun rays. Yeah, and then there was the new draft.

Hugh had been a very busy thirty-one-year-old—(young damn it!)—gunnery sergeant since the new draft arrived. He had had to mold them into an integral part of the old company and he thanked the mischievous fortunes that were for not sending him any NCO's with this bunch. The thought of placing noncombatants over men who had

500

formed the company to begin with would have been too absurd.

Well, how would Koko Hobbs have handled it? the new men? That was something to think about. But Koko Hobbs, Hugh thought, had never handled anything but himself. And as far as anyone knew, Koko Hobbs was still handling himself. It was hard saying where he was. Or where he would turn up. If ever. Grudgingly, Hugh hoped the son-ofabitch would make it—wherever he was going. Even though that had been a rotten thing to do to him, Hugh Thorton.

The inspection was moving rapidly; after that there would be troop and stomp. At the most, Hugh had thirty minutes left before he fell out with the Kizer and took the company to the field. They had still been training hard, even after the blunder of Indo—(the cease-fire)—china. And it looked as though it was not going to stop. But he did not enjoy it any more the way he had before when he was sure of his Forty Years' War.

Thinking of the Forty Years' War, his infallible plans for it, he thought simultaneously of Chebe-san. She had been right. When she said there was not going to be a war she had been right, unmistakably right, right on down the line. But he had been so sure, so positively certain of it, so cocky and vain at his own rightness, that he had convinced her there would be one, too!

Consequently, she had absconded with her loot to some other place: another camp town? The cities? Maybe even a respectable place? Like a restaurant? But he didn't think so. He didn't actually know what to think. He could merely speculate.

It was not important any more, one way or the other. Not since he had his new shackjob.

Of course, his new shackjob was entirely different from Chebe-san—but just as loveable, he amended. Her name, according to Itchie the houseboy who was her brother, "Spring Forever," but Hugh did not place too much belief in names like that.

He had, when they got back from Indochina, taken Itchie up on that belated dinner invitation, and with gratifying results. He had three sisters to choose from, all country girls, and he had taken the one in the middle: Spring Forever, who was overjoyed, he thought, at his choice. And he had been spending a lot of time at Itchie's on weekends and liberty nights.

The family, Itchie's family, had taken him in like a lost member. Probably, he thought suspiciously, because he always brought cigarettes and luxuries down to them. And once, by God, he had even worked in the rice paddy with Itchie's old man. That was something he had never thought he would do. But it helped relationships with Spring Forever, whom he was growing very fond of and who could speak very little American. Still, it was a promising romance and who could say where it would lead?

The Kizer coughed once more in his office. There was the sound of a bottle being pulled from his drawer.

Outside, the platoon broke up, dismissed, their troop and stomp completed, and straggled into the barracks to prepare for the field and Hugh watched them, not really feeling like going to the field today. But it was his job. Then he saw Corporal Cinamo Dallas come walking up to the company office, ass dipped, arms swinging, his face cold and relaxed.

At least, Hugh thought watching him, he had done something for that man. A man like Dallas with eight (or was it nine?) years' service, twice Korean vet, should be an NCO. Dallas was a good leader, he thought, a damn fine leader.

The window-door slid open and Dallas climbed down into the office.

"Mornin', Gunny," he said pleasantly, his face set. He reached his hand out, clenched, laid it by Thorton's coffee cup, unclenched it to display two corporal chevrons, red and green. "You can have them back, Gunny," he said in his thick Oklahoma drawl.

"What?" Hugh said, puzzled. "Have them back? Have what back?"

"The fucking rank," Dallas said. "The stripes, the chevrons. I don't want 'em any more. I'm takin' an automatic bust." He turned and walked out.

Hugh stood staring at the chevrons, aware of Quiller Carpenter's typewriter ceasing its fury—replaced by a sardonic happy snicker, and felt that he was suddenly knee-deep in quicksand. Not Dallas! his mind exploded defiantly. Not Dallas! Yet the mute evidence lay on the file cabinet beside his coffee.

Hugh laughed in howling belly guffaws, heedless, hys-

terical. If that didn't beat everything. My God! You couldn't beat the dealer no matter what.

Finishing his coffee, he walked across the office, watching the men as they began straggling back out of the barracks with field marching packs, already sweating under the weight in the August dog day's sun. He lit a cigarette, studying them, wondering what it all totaled up to. For him. For him personally.

A prisoner of war in this place during Big Two, and then to come back and wade through his cycle, a cycle that was not a little more than a year. And what did it all mean? To him: personally? Maybe he would never know. Then, with a start, he remembered that night so long ago when he had gone on liberty to look up that Jo-san that Koko had told him about, Chebe-san, and how Koko had almost insisted that he take her. And how now both of them were gone. A bleak futility stirred uneasily within him.

Did a spiral staircase ever know where it was spiraling to? Or did it only spiral to latch on to that part of it that it had been divested from? Was that why a dog chased its tail? To contact itself?

He left the office, walking down the short stairs, moving lightly across the cinder ash to the staff quarters to strap on his .45 and take Horrible Hog Company to the field. After the heat and sweat of the field they would all be wanting their beer tonight. He felt like Danny Deever, except he wasn't going to be hung.

Well, he had less than two years left to do on this hitch: his last, unless he shipped over again. If he shipped again, he was a twenty-year man for sure, no getting out of that. If he didn't ship, well . . .

Anyway, it was something to think about.

34.

On the first Saturday in September, Giff Bohane sallied forth with the last fifty dollars of his gambling wins from the Indochina cruise. He had decided to invest it in lots and houses: Rotten Crotch Mary's whorehouse and lots of her whiskey.

It was the last chance he would have to throw an all-out bust before Horrible Hog Company departed on a three weeks' Field Exercise, and he meant to take advantage of it.

Since the Indochina war had not panned out, there was not any waiting left to do. And he who had been the expert waiter in that month before they had left for Indochina, alone, reticent, even aloof, suddenly found himself thrown back into the old breed. His aloneness, since he had been released from the brig, had suddenly stopped when the war hadn't come off. It was a sort of going downward with the aloneness, then a gradual coming back in with the group, a rising from the ashes in the wind of something new; and in this wind he did not feel he had to brace himself against its force.

The advent of new faces in the company had something to do with it, he thought. The new faces, which were to him a bloodless-faced group, blank-eyed, uncomprehending and appeared to view everything with intolerable awe, were all in another world, inexperienced, and he could not recognize them as anything he had ever lived with.

The new men knew about the Silver Star of course and almost all of his record, including the brig stretch, and regarded him with a reserved but prideful deference which he thought was foolish. Perhaps he should have received their adulation and played the role, but somehow his old dramatic Irish wildness had been lost in the past year. He no longer gave a damn what people knew about him, or what they thought of him. And as for the Silver Star he

504

never even thought of it any longer. There was, in effect, he thought, nothing there really to think about. It was all right if the new men, and even some of the old breed, believed in his legend, but he would not.

That legend had been lost on the rock pile a long time ago when he had come so close to believing in it himself. No matter what he had done personally, no matter what forced him to do it, whatever it was . . . he was free.

When they had come back from Indochina in August, almost one year since he had first arrived in Japan, Giff had looked back on it with a wry appraisal. Remembering that first night in the company when he and Dallas and Poke and Stack had sat under the old elm and talked about the company and especially about Lew Diamond, he thought he could understand how it had all begun then. How he had felt that first apprehension of becoming a Lew Diamond, a nameless legend who was actually no legend at all, but a pawn for the legend makers. That, he thought, was when he first started to rebel.

Now he felt the rebellion was finished.

Sometimes, though, he could feel it coming on again, a different form of rebellion against something else. He saw he would have to watch it. He also saw that it was going to be a constant battle.

He had played the perfect marine all through August. He was never late for roll call, always spit and polished up, never giving any backtalk, and simply doing his job. But that was all. He did not put out anything else: only his job.

Also, during August, he had pulled most of his liberty down in Skivvie Lane at Rotten Crotch Mary's. He usually shacked up with Cherry-san, but if she was not available he would take one of the other five girls. He had entertained the idea of catching Mary herself but she was Half-Slick Willy's steady, and he was usually down there when Giff was.

He did not pull any liberty with Dallas, Corporal Cinamo Dallas. It was not because he had anything against Dallas, it was simply that Dallas pulled all his liberty at the Blue Moon and Giff shied away from there. The Bar New Blue Moon, he felt, was a part of his old life. Poke Turner and Stack Renshaw did not much care to pull liberty anywhere else but the Blue Moon, because as

Poke said, it was the only bar in town that he could exist on with jawbone. Of course he drank with all of them at the slop chute, but it was not the slop chute drinking of a year ago. Dallas had closed up somehow, and there were not the facets in any of them any more that had welded them together before. Giff thought this too could be attributed to the new men coming into the company.

Then Dallas took his automatic bust, without giving a reason. Giff did not attempt to coax a reason from him. He knew it was useless. Rankless, Dallas, to all outward appearances, was still the truculent Dallas.

On that Saturday morning, the first weekend in September, the first and last liberty weekend for Hog Company before they went to the field for three weeks, Giff received liberty at eight o'clock. He had caught the firewatch for the night before, Friday night, while the rest of the company howled out on liberty for the three days. He and three other men from Horrible Hog Company. The other two men were Half-Slick Willy Woechowski and Private Flin Gorsuch. They had all decided to go to town together, since they were all agreed on going to Rotten Crotch Mary's. Flin Gorsuch said he was doing it purely in defense because none of the new men ever deigned to go down there.

Giff showered and shaved and dressed in a clean set of tropical worsteds, chevronless, ribbonless, in the almost deserted squadbay, and without breakfast walked jubilantly to town with Gorsuch and Half-Slick Willy.

That Saturday marked the last dying throes of dog days—the frog belching, cricket chirping, rice paddy shit-smelling, thick air muggy and heavy (that only cold beer could cool)—and they had all started to sweat before they got to the main gate, stains sullying their armpits.

Through the languid dust rising from the baked main street of Fujioka, which still groaned sleepily after its Friday night party, they walked past Hock at Henry's and down Skivvie Lane on the narrow paddy dyke up to Rotten Crotch Mary's.

Mary herself was busy throwing water on the wood floor to hold the dust down when they walked in, her eyes still hinting of sleep, dressed in her nighttime kimono, and when she saw them her eyes awakened considerably.

"Willy!" she beamed happily. "Me no think you catchee liberty."

506

"By God I didn't think I'd catch it myself for a while," Half-Slick Willy grinned broadly, his square face laboring with sweat. He walked ponderously over to her and hugged her.

"How about some cold dudes, Mary?" Giff sidled up to a stool and plopped down. "After that hot walk in from camp I'm about to die of thirst."

"You ain't shittin'." Flin Gorsuch snatched off his piss-cutter and flopped it on the bar and ran his fingers through his blond hair. "Where's all the women, Mary? Shacked up?"

"Ahh." Mary shrugged diffidently, let go of Willy and walked behind the bar. "Business no good last night. No one stay. All Jo-sans sleep."

"Well, get them to hell up," Gorsuch said. "We'll be going out the field for damn near a month—and I'm gonna stock up for it. Startin' now."

"You want a piece of ass this early in the morning?" Giff asked.

"Does a bear shit in the woods?" Gorsuch said.

"Three beer-o," Mary smiled, setting the thick quarts on the bar. "You want Jo-sans now, *ne?*"

"Guess so," Giff grinned. "Go tell Cherry-san to get her money-making ass out here. Gorsuch here just convinced me I been leadin' a wrong life."

"Not wrong, buddy," Gorsuch said, "just turned around."

"Man oh man," Willy said, "ain't no beer tastes as good as in the morning." He hefted the quart up, held his head back, and the beer flowed out of the bottle down his throat without a pause.

"Jesus Christ, Willy!" Giff slapped his wallet on the bar. "You won't last till noon drinkin' like that."

"If I don't, I'll kiss your ass on the parade field at high noon and give you thirty minutes to draw a crowd."

"If that's a promise, I'll pay for your beer till noon," Gorsuch said blandly. "Just to see it."

"You want more beer-o you catch Willy," Mary said generously. "Me go back get Jo-sans." She walked from behind the bar and disappeared down the hall to the back rooms.

"Ain't she a fine woman?" Half-Slick Willy looked proudly after her. "Do anything in the world for you."

"Do anything for you, not us," Giff corrected. He finished off his own beer and loosened his tie. "It's going to be another hot one."

"'At's the only thing I got against fuckin' in hot weather," Gorsuch said thoughtfully, "my belly all the time gets a rash."

"The creeping crud," Willy guffawed, walking behind the bar to get more beer.

They drank three more beers apiece waiting for the Jo-sans to come out, talking over the vagaries of Hog Company since the new draft came in, a never-decreasing-in-popularity topic. They all enjoyed basking in their old-breed glory.

Giff felt the old ingrained to-hell-with-it-all attitude swimming up through him with the beer. The liberty days and nights in Fujioka, the never-ending cycle of experience that each of them, he suddenly knew, searched for, and never found. But it was through the looking that they found something else. It was through his own looking that he had found it, something ineffable that he would carry with him for a long time. And tomorrow was as remote as the first quart of beer he had drunk.

He stepped down off the stool and stood leaning back against the bar, hatless, tieless now, sweating and cooling off with the beer and looking out the door at the murky waters of the rice paddies with their green shoots swaying in the hot unfreshened wind.

"You people are slow as hell with them beers," Willy said disparagingly, opening fresh quarts. "I thought you were drinkers."

"Nah, sir," Giff said, "ain't drinkers atall; lovers. Me and Gorsuch are lovers."

"You *toxon* butterfly," Cherry-san said walking in from the back room in a tight-fitting summer dress. "You no lover, Giff-san. You all time changee changee."

"Hello, hot one," Giff grinned at her as she stepped behind the bar and pushed Willy out. Willy walked glumly around to the front, pained at having lost his job.

"You stay all weekend with Cherry-san," she said, her eyes glinting playfully.

"If I do," Giff said, "I'll never make it to the field come Monday."

"But it's a good way to go," Gorsuch said, eying Cherry-san himself. "Can't think of a better way to go."

508

"Then I guess I'll stay," Giff grinned. "If you promise not to wear me out."

Cherry-san laughed. "Me no wear you out, kiddo, you the one wear me out."

"A real lover, ain't you?" Gorsuch smirked. "Well, goddamit, where's all the rest the girls?"

"They come out, more skosh," Cherry-san said. "No one say anything about a party this morning."

"There's going to be a party all right!" a voice boomed thickly from the doorway, and they all turned their heads to see Cinamo Dallas, Private Cinamo Dallas, weaving in the doorway, a large gash under his right eye. "I want to have a goddam party," he said heavily. "Hi, old buddy," he said to Giff.

"Out slummin'?" Giff said. "What the hell happened to your face? I thought your headquarters was at the Blue Moon?"

"Fuck my face," Dallas sneered.

"Watch your language," Cherry-san said, and poured beer into Giff's glass.

"Gettin' high class?" Dallas said drunkenly to Giff.

"What happened to your face?" Giff ignored the remark.

"Don't say it again," Cherry-san stopped him as he opened his mouth.

Dallas grinned wickedly, helped himself to some of Gorsuch's beer and handed it back. "My face," he said, "is the outcome of a private's fight for his peacetime rights. That's what happened to it."

"Who with?" Half-Slick Willy said.

"I couldn't take it no more," Dallas said sitting down beside Giff at the bar. "I just couldn't take it."

"I think he needs a transfusion," Gorsuch said.

"I think he's sufferin' from a trauma," Giff grinned.

"To hell with you sons a bitches," Dallas said in a low voice, watching Cherry-san cautiously. "I was sitting up the Blue Moon drinking, see? Been there all night with Poke and Stack, all of us shacked up. And those goddam punks come in, about a dozen of 'em. I just couldn't take it. They infiltratin' everywhere. So I tore into them, cleaned house."

"Somebody use a bottle on you?" Giff asked.

"I dunno." Dallas ran his hand gingerly over his cheek where the gash was. "Look, goddamit, I got a pocketful of shekel. Let's close this old bar up and have a *real*

party. If we lock the door those new punks can't get in."
He staggered over to the door and closed it loudly. It was
the first time Giff had ever seen Dallas stagger.

"You wouldn't have to close it," Giff said indifferently.
"No one in his right mind would be caught dead down
here."

"You sonofabitch," Cherry-san said.

"Except you and me, honey." Giff winked at her.

Rotten Crotch Mary came walking out with three Jo-sans
in tow, saw the door closed and looked inquiringly at Half-
Slick Willy.

"We're going to have a party," he pacified. "Dallas'
goin' to pay for all of it."

"Not for me," Cherry-san said.

Dallas bowed sweepingly, pulled a handful of yen out
of his pocket and handed it to Mary. "All yours, every bit
of it. If you don't let no one else in."

"Hokay," Mary agreed. "Other boy-sans pay too, *ne?*"

"Boy-san!" Giff wailed, with a smile. "If Dallas is buying
I'll pay," he paused, "for Cherry-san."

"Come on, boy-san," Cherry-san grinned. "Me make you
man-san."

"I'll make you sore-san," Giff said walking past the bar.

"All right, women," Dallas suggested, "just gather round
here at this table. You can fight over me."

"Marine *joto-ni,*" Cherry-san said, moving up to meet
Giff at the door to the back.

"Goddam rights," Giff said. "No fucking good. Never
will be either."

"Hey, goddamit," Gorsuch said. "Wait for me! I get a
woman and come on back with you."

"I don't need an audience," Giff grinned. "Come on,
Cherry-san," he said mellowly, "let's see 'f we can make
babies. Don't let none of that beer get hot," he called
back over his shoulder.

"Which one of you wants me?" Dallas asked the other
three Jo-sans.

"Don't be so particular," Gorsuch jeered. "Hi baby," he
said to a short plump Jo-san.

"I'll help you with the beer, Mary," Half-Slick Willy said
heavily. "Then we'll go on back, okay?"

The Jo-sans had started laughing and playing around
with Dallas and Gorsuch, as the tall quarter Cherokee

510

stacked his money on the table in front of him.

"Marine *joto-ni*," Cherry-san said to Giff as they moved away from the bar. "No hucking good."

"Don't worry about it," Giff said, "you've still got me."

In Gratitude

The author, for the writing of this book, expresses his deeply felt thanks to Lowney T. Handy—for her firm belief in my work and her remarkable creative understanding and editorial advice. To Peter Israel, of G. P. Putnam's Sons, for his assistance and encouragement in editing. And to Harry E. Handy for his mutual backing and support while working on his own book.

J.P.